BY ALYCIA CHRISTINE

SYLVAN CYCLE
Skinshifter

SYLVAN PRELUDE
The Dryad's Sacrifice

TEMPEST MAIDEN
Thorn and Thistle

SHORT FICTION COLLECTIONS
Musings

SHORT FICTION
"The Cleaning"
"Hero's Moment"
"Paper Castles"
"The Twirling Ballerina"
"When the Medium Shatters"

Find out more at AlyciaChristine.com.

SKINSHIFTER

BOOK ONE OF THE SYLVAN CYCLE SERIES

SKINSHIFTER

BOOK ONE OF THE SYLVAN CYCLE SERIES

ALYCIA CHRISTINE

Purple Thorn Press
www.purplethornpress.com

Skinshifter copyright © 2015 by Alycia Christine
Dreamdrifter excerpt copyright © 2015 by Alycia Christine
"Map of the Sylvan Continent, End of Third Age" copyright © 2016 by Alycia Christine
The Dryad's Sacrifice excerpt copyright © 2015 by Alycia Christine
Cover and interior illustration copyright © 2015 by Purple Thorn Press
Cover design by Alycia Christine
Interior illustration design by Alycia Christine
Book design by Alycia Christine
Set in Palatino Linotype

This book contains excerpts from the novella *The Dryad's Sacrifice* and from the forthcoming book *Dreamdrifter* by Alycia Christine. These excerpts have been set for this edition only and may not reflect the final content of the forthcoming editions.

Purple Thorn Press books may be purchased for educational, business, or for sales and promotional use. Please contact Purple Thorn Press for more information.

Purple Thorn Press logo designed by Alycia Christine.
First Purple Thorn Press trade paperback edition published 2015. Printed in the United States of America by CreateSpace.

www.alyciachristine.com

www.purplethornpress.com

ISBN 978-1-941588-28-4

For Dad, whose love of books is so contagious. Thank you for your gentle guidance and your gallant encouragement.

CONTENTS

Castle
Fort
Fortified City
Village
Ruins
Capital

Northern Continent

Cael

Aribem Channel

Peix Isles

Protegir   Blindar   Tombamar   Aquest   Portasol

Summersted   Klorevind

Kaylere   Nordparet   Nord Road

Joiariure   Feral Plains

River Dole
                    Pautat   Migparet
        Bonasal   Beskytter

Tyglere Isles
                    Tyglesea   Great Guard
River Tyglesea   Wall & Road

                Bosc Road   Sudparet
            Mana   Kings'

                        Boscgrens   Crown
Astratahtbrilla   Portarbre

River Arbre   Magehous   Sylvan
Kingport   Forest

Sylvan   Brehton
Continent   M...
                                        Maan   S...
            Mage Road   Zola
Zeeford   Ferienton
                                  Croswudi   Vihous Road
        Vihous   Sylvan
                                              Boundarie Road
            Seaward   Sylvan
            Leas   Dreem
                        Lochmille   Ge...
Jorn   Zoet   N...
                                      Boomstad
River Zoet
                    Bards   Etheal
Westylere   Mersc   Glade
Sea   Drumden   Gap Passage

                Leas   Hamos   Barak   Marsh Passage
River Ehud   Edelsteen
                                  Uitgraven
            Suuthe   Hag's   Kel
            Marshes   Nest   Ten Fang
                    Orclag   Jhalag   Marshes   Merrow
        Wisp   Shamgar
River Naya   Lake Azuralle   Naiad Passage

PREFACE

A SPECIAL THANK YOU TO READERS

When I first published *Skinshifter* in September 2015, I held no immediate plans to issue an updated edition of the book. By their reviews, I knew that readers were delighted with the story. Even so, a few people requested specific changes: a stronger beginning, a full world map, and a more comprehensive character glossary. I accepted the wonderful challenge to fulfill these requests because I knew that rewrites would add more depth to *Skinshifter* and provide convenient access to all of the book's extra features.

I reworked the pacing of the first five chapters. In doing so, a rejuvenated tension weaves its sharp undercurrent throughout the rest of the story. This mounting tension led me to add a few extended scenes throughout the rest of the book to intensify the characters' motivations. I considered contracting out the map's creation, but instead I wanted to make it myself as a labor of love. Using my drawing, photography, and graphic art skills, I designed something that felt and looked like a map that Katja and her packmates would use on their numerous journeys together. In addition, the updated Character Glossary should add to the story. All of these changes culminated in the new edition you hold in your hand.

I poured many hours into these projects and it was your encouragement as well as your passion for this story and its characters that has kept me going when the daylight ebbed into twilight, and then flowed inexorably into a new day's dawn. Now, we come to the end of all of the work and I am elated. I am excited that the project is finished, but, more than that, I am overjoyed because I get to share with you the fruits of this endeavor.

Like any artist, I enjoy accolades and high-ranking reviews, but I desire more than anything else to know that your experience with *Skinshifter* is as enjoyable as possible. You all are the reason I write. So once again, I must thank all of my amazing readers for the reviews and critiques—positive and negative. Your attention to detail and willingness to share your opinions have helped me to make a dynamic story even stronger.

This is only the beginning of the excitement for this story, its characters, and all of us that follow them. I hope my writing entertains and encourages you on the first read, and continues to enthrall and inspire you on the twenty-fifth.

May we each rewrite our world for the better!

Alycia

SKINSHIFTER

BOOK ONE OF THE SYLVAN CYCLE SERIES

PROLOGUE

The Sphinx wondered if her death was imminent the moment the half-breed's uncanny magical signature roused her from a centuries-old sleep. The mage's abilities spoke of fireforger power steeped in the oldest of Sylvan bloodlines, but he also bore a Víchí's pointed teeth and ears. Even the fireforger's guttering yellow flame sprang from a hand adorned with the blackest of claws.

"How can a fireforger mage, even a weak one, harbor the corruption of the vampires within his blood?" she asked him. "Fireforgers are immune to the Asheken deadwalkers' Bites of Turning."

He watched her for a moment, anger warring against sorrow in his icy blue eyes. "I intend to find the one who is responsible for my family's brokenness, so that I may ask. Now let me pass."

The ancient magic compelled the Sphinx to obey all fireforgers' requests no matter what her own wishes were. With great uneasiness, the stone-skinned being lowered her massive body into the chasm that separated the continents. She crouched with her head level to the cliff on which the young mage stood and opened her great maw to allow him passage through the protective enchantments.

After he had walked across the width of her flinty tongue and onto the Northern Continent, the Sphinx noted the long gash winding down the half-breed's left arm from shoulder to wrist. The wound looked weeks old, but it still bled. The half-breed winced and shrugged the injured arm further into its sling as he walked along the road just beyond the Sphinx's Gape toward the Thornblood Sands encircling Blaecthull.

She puzzled about him long after his disappearance among the red dunes.

* * *

A fortnight passed before the Sphinx saw the half-breed again—this time with a healed but jagged scar adorning his left arm. The blood-spawn returned leading a company of three hundred deadwalkers including several scores of zombies, a squad of ghouls, and two platoons of dullahan. When she refused passage to both the deadwalkers and the half-breed, they drew their weapons against her. The iron blades were of little consequence, but the half-breed's own sunsilver swords proved far more deadly. She howled in fury as the burning blades cut hissing gashes through her hardened hide and pulled her head away from the road to expose the deep gorge that travelers faced without her presence.

The force of her voice slammed the deadwalkers onto their faces, yet the half-breed still stood his ground. Dark, leathery pinions unfolded out of his back as the fireforger traitor launched himself onto the winds. The huge Sphinx pumped her own feathery wings hard to meet him. Together they wheeled and dodged each other's attacks—performing a deadly aerial dance that only one could hope to win.

The Sphinx's fangs and claws slashed only air while the hybrid's fiery swords found their way through her stony skin again and again—driving her back toward the perch where she had kept her watch between the continents. When she finally collapsed to the sea-washed ground from the toll of her wounds, what remained of the Sphinx's once towering body now looked like the cracked cliffs around her. Her huge head drooped in shame as she felt her life seep away. Tears brimmed in the old guardian's eyes as she felt the protective enchantments dissolve. The fiendish troops marched across her exposed back onto the Southern Continent and on to war. With her failure, who now could protect the Sylvans from the murderous Asheken hordes?

Through the agony of her wounds, the Sphinx managed

to raise herself into a reverent crouch and whispered the death prayer of Aribem: "Creator, I commit my soul to you in this, the end of my bodily existence. Pass what strength is left in my soul through my bones and on to others so that the pure may yet be saved from evil. Lo aideem."

With her last word, the Sphinx felt energy radiate beyond her body and into the canyon around her. Her body shook in rhythm with the resulting quake and caused the last third of the deadwalker company to fall from the cliff to the jagged rocks below. A final howl escaped her broken maw as the last wave of power erupted from her soul and caused her body to collapse onto the fallen undead—crushing and burning them beneath her.

* * *

The griffin king Canuche roared awake with the Sphinx's death cry. The ancient guardian's magic had finally shattered the slumber enchantment over the old king's soul and his stone-carved body sat motionless no longer. He smiled at his newfound freedom. Although he could not move his stone body from the foundation where it stood, the king could dreamdrift along the night winds once again. In his mind's eye, Canuche saw the Sphinx's dying memory of the Asheken invasion and knew he must warn the Sylvan mage leaders before all was lost.

The dreamdrifter's first attempt to penetrate the guarded minds of the Ring of Sorcerers or any other mage on the Isle of Summons failed. The griffin king tried again to communicate his thoughts and again failed. After the seventh attempt, he grudgingly acknowledged that the distance between his stone-walled prison and the Isle of Summons was too great to cross. Disgruntled, the old king settled for brushing the minds of those mages nearest him with his own.

The Sphinx's scream echoed through the dreams of many Sylvan sleepers, but only two others had jolted awake besides the griffin. Curious, he watched these two on the fringes of their respective minds until the dawn sun brought its reassuring light to their eyes. Both mages' minds registered a depth of magic the old king had rarely seen in his existence. These two mages might prove quite valuable in the upcoming war against the Asheken deadwalkers—if they survived long enough to be properly trained.

The griffin wove a dreamdrifter's Spell of Calling into the two young mages' minds and prayed that it would be strong enough to penetrate their thoughts. If he could draw them to him quickly enough, they might yet escape the deadwalkers' wrath.

"Creator, keep them!" Canuche whispered, even as his mind's eye glimpsed the deadwalkers' malignant darkness descending toward one of the nearest Sylvan villages. Without the Sphinx to protect them, the Feliconas Clan werecats had no way of thwarting the evil that would soon fall upon them.

I

FROM METAMORPHOSIS TO MASSACRE

The dewy grass whipped wet against Katja's hind flanks as she loped along the edge of the meadow. She sniffed the morning air. It was cool with the promise of rain and carried a faint stench like that of a sea-drenched corpse. Katja sneezed and then growled in the general direction of north. There was little hint of prey in the wind, hardly even a ground squirrel. That was an irritation. Katja needed to bring a large animal — perhaps a young buck — back to the den. She wanted to stalk and kill quickly before the storms came. The rain certainly would not spoil the meat, but being the proper werecat that she was, Katja hated being wet. After all, it could take hours to lick all of the tangles out of her golden fur after a good soaking, and that was such tedious work.

The werecat adjusted her leather loincloth around the base of her long prehensile tail and focused again on the task at paw. She slipped toward the stream at the other side of the meadow hoping to find larger prey drinking from its cool waters. Dropping onto all four paws, she slunk low along the tree line and peered through the tangled trailers of a vine-cloaked shrub — her round, tuft-tipped ears twitching at every sound.

Ah, success! A fat ram was drinking on the bank less than five body-lengths from her. Katja crept around the shrub and scaled the thick trunk of an ancient oak. She uncoiled a sinew rope from around her waist and, after fastening one end of the rope to a sturdy branch, she looped the other end deftly around the ram's curled horns. The ram bucked, but to no avail. The rope defied the erdeling beast's every escape effort.

Katja jumped down from the tree, landed softly on her back paws, and slowly circled the vulnerable ram from just outside of the slack of the rope. With an enraged bleat, the erdeling beast rushed her. Katja sidestepped its charge in time to attack as the rope snapped its head back. When the stunned beast fell against the ground, she rushed it. The werecat deftly broke its neck with her clawed forepaws before the ram had time to recuperate from the whiplash. She deftly sliced its jugular with one large, clawed forepaw and let the beast's blood drain into the leaves.

Smiling in satisfaction at the clean kill, she climbed into the tree to retrieve the rope and then wrapped its length around the ram's legs to make it easier to carry. She realized upon inspection that the rope was badly strained in one spot—too strained to hunt with again. She would have to make a new one, but that should not take long if one of her brothers could help with the project. Katja wished they were here now to help carry the ram back to the den, but tensions against the western werewolf clan were high now and so her brothers were on watch rounds. Although Katja was well within the safety of her clan's territory, the fact that she must hunt alone today bothered her more now than it had before she sniffed the uncanny stench. She had felt uneasy ever since the ground tremors had shaken her awake a few nights ago and this unnatural smell now made her apprehension even worse. The Feliconas Clan member warily eyed the north again before hefting the ram across her shoulders and bounding toward the safety of home.

* * *

"You are late," Keepha snarled as Katja entered the den.

"It took time to track, kill, and carry home my quarry," Katja shrugged. "If you want to whine, do so when I come home empty-pawed."

Katja's older sister narrowed her chestnut-colored eyes and growled in retort as she sniffed the carcass. "Well, at least the rain washed the fur clean."

"Jierira, please don't remind me," Katja growled irritably.

She set the ram down on the large, flat eating stone that jutted from the cave wall opposite the entrance and shook out her soggy fur. The action sent water droplets flying in every direction.

"Katja!" Keepha lunged at her youngest sibling. "Get out of the eating hole before I twist your ears off!"

Katja dodged with ease. "Fine, I'll go dry off somewhere else."

"Sniff out your brothers and bring them back with you to eat."

"Very well. Please leave me some of the ram's stronger tendons. I need to make a new rope."

"Rippezahne to you and your silly ropes. Did the last one snap on you?"

"No, it held." Katja tossed the rope to Keepha. "It's too strained to be of much use on another hunt though."

"Good, I'll use it to tie down the carcass for our eat instead. Now, go hunt down your brothers!"

Without a reply, Katja sprang out of her birth den in search of Kayten and Kumos. Since the brothers were still on their watch-rounds, Katja had to sniff around for a time before she located either sibling's scent. That only added to her irritation because her nose was beginning to lose some of its usual sensitivity thanks to the retched full moon. To add to her growing discomfort, her fur had begun to dry into a myriad of little coiled knots. Katja growled about not moving fast enough to avoid the afternoon shower.

She found both of her brothers doing more wrestling than watching. They were grappling at one of their favorite lookouts—a high ridge sliced out of the northern side of the mountain. She crouched and watched them a moment and then pounced into their fray.

"Katja, don't do that! It's rude to jump in on us when we're in the middle of a match!" Kayten panted.

"Angry that I startled you, sibbe?"

"We knew you were there the whole time. Didn't we, Kumos?"

"Of course we did." Kumos looked dubiously at his younger brother.

Katja's lion-like face formed a look of contrived innocence.

"What? You don't prefer it when I approach on the leeward side of the wind? After all, what fun is slinking when my prey can smell me coming?"

Kayten grunted and changed the subject. "Did you catch some food?"

"I did. Keepha sent me to find you two. She wants all of us to come eat." Katja surveyed the forest below them and froze. Perhaps it was some trick of the late day's light, but she swore she saw a smoky haze drifting toward them from the northern horizon.

"Kumos, what is that?" She pointed a claw toward the haze.

"I'm unsure. We've seen it moving in the valley all day. Perhaps some beings are burning brush at the edge of the forest again."

"A fire with smoke that blows against the wind?"

"They probably have a fireforger mage with them."

"Even fireforgers don't have the power necessary to fight nature's laws like that; only members of the Ring of Sorcerers can perform such miracles."

"Several mages then?" Kayten shrugged. "By their behavior, they aren't a werewolf raiding party, so it doesn't affect us. Why brood about it?"

"Have the clan scouts come back from our northern border yet?"

Kumos shook his head. "Not that I've been told. Why?"

She frowned "It's just that I smelled something odd earlier today—the foul stench of something dead, but not. It was coming from the north."

"Dead, but not? Lytzsibba, that makes no sense."

Katja watched the smoke as it drifted lazily south in their direction and tried to articulate the nameless dread that she felt. "I know, but…"

"Do you smell it now?"

Katja slowly shook her head. With the sway of the full moon already dulling her senses, she couldn't smell much of anything now, but she dared not tell Kumos that. Her siblings could never know what she was or what she became on nights like tonight. It was too dangerous for them and for her.

Kumos placed a paw on her shoulders. "If it troubles you

so much, I'll alert the village elders about the smoke on our way back to the den. Agreed?"

Katja nodded in relief.

"Come, let's go!" Kayten grumbled. "I'm hungry enough to eat a basilisk."

"I'm for that!" Kumos exclaimed. "I'll race you both to the den!"

With that, he sprinted down the mountainside with the other two in close pursuit.

* * *

The evening's eat left the four Escari siblings all content and lethargic. Gradually, each slipped off to the comfort of his or her separate den hole to think or sleep. When Katja reached her own hole, she tied a thick hide across the round entrance for privacy and then gathered what supplies she would need for the night. She slipped through a secret tunnel she had dug in the back of her den hole, and slunk across the ancient forest toward her hideaway.

The sun had almost set when she crawled inside and covered the entrance with a flat, lichen-encrusted stone. Unlike the sprawling stone den she shared with her siblings, this muddy hideaway was small and plain—its one entrance mostly concealed by thick brambles. The one room was dimly lit by an iridescent green moss that grew through a cleft between the west wall and ceiling. Its aroma masked the werecat's changing scent. Through the crack above the moss, Katja watched as the last rays of hope dwindled into twilight.

As dusk turned to darkness and the full moon's light finally won the heavens, Katja transformed. The feline's physical journey to humanity was slow and excruciating. She lay on a pile of furs and did her best to endure the skinshift that so segregated her from others of her kin. Her beautiful fur, which was always the first to go, came out tuft by tuft, moment by moment, until all but the hair on the crown and back of her head was strewn across the cave floor. Her skin itched in a thousand places simultaneously, but she could never adequately scratch to relieve it because her clawed paws, which never altered until the end of her skinshift cycle, were of little use in such delicate work. Only after she had watched her golden fur slough off—leaving her shamefully exposed—did Katja's eyes, round-tipped conical ears, and flat nose each lose most of their sensitivity. The sudden loss of sensation felt like being thrust into murky water.

When she finally did adjust to the vagueness of human senses, the worst of the metamorphosis occurred. Her fangs pushed themselves up into the gums of her maw so that only the mere tips were visible. Then the other teeth in her mouth flattened out to resemble those of a human. She spit blood several times to clean her palate and the taste left her gagging. Her ears flattened into the skin at the top of her head so that she could not swivel them to listen, and then a new, more-wrinkled set emerged on the sides of her face near her neck. Her claws, which were naturally retractable, drew back into her digits and a layer of skin covered the openings from which they usually sprang. The bones and skin in her forepaws felt eerily like liquid as her stubby, clawed digits elongated into nail-tipped fingers. Strangely, the change in her forepaws was not as uncomfortable as the rest of the transformation; however, if Katja ever tried to flex her claws while in human form, the claws would cut through flesh and nail with their reemergence.

The metamorphosis was not perfect. Katja kept her prehensile tail—although it was hairless now—and her hind limbs and hind paws also never changed their contour. Her thumbs also did not change; they were opposable and constantly clawed in either state. Although her nose became more bulbous, most of her facial structure had never really changed. Nor did the color of her unusual eyes, which were always emerald green with golden rings encircling the round pupils.

The full moon sat in the center of the sky when Katja finally finished her skinshift. She curled up on the fur pallet and draped an extra hide over her suddenly chilled body. It might have been her overwhelming exhaustion, but she felt more defenseless than usual tonight. She knew she could still outrun most other living beings, even if she could not fight them in this frail human form. Yet even that knowledge was small comfort now.

Her former uneasiness had now grown into full-fledged

terror, but of what? This fear was unnatural and raw. She felt a strong urge to sink into the rock behind her lest evil eyes somehow find her hiding hole. She searched the shadowy forest with every modicum of her maimed senses. She witnessed the world grow silent around her. The full moon's light was snuffed out as if it were no more than a candle flame. The world around her faded into utter darkness, and Katja remembered the horror of this blackness. She had seen its presence in corporeal form the day her parents had died...

*

That horrible memory had been made on a warm morning with the fields' flowers barely in bloom. Katja should have been with her parents because it was to be her first fishing lesson. The young catling, however, had forgotten her fishing spear and had to rush back to the den to retrieve it. The rocks fell as she was running back along the mountain path to meet her parents at their favorite fishing spot. She remembered seeing huge boulders of granite smash down the path several hundred body-lengths ahead of her.

Instinctively, she scrambled up a huge tree and edged her way along its limbs away from the mountainside, leaving her spear to be demolished by the stones rolling underneath her. Thankfully, the tree was situated on a rise beside the dirt road, which curved so that the boulders rolled down the slope away from it. When the rocks' riot had finally finished, she felt a foul presence slinking up the road toward her tree. She huddled against the rough bark and sniffed the wind. A horrible reek burned her nostrils and nauseated her to the point of fainting. Just before she lost consciousness, she saw a decrepit shadow creep to where her broken spear lay. It seemed to sniff the spear; it then raised its hooded head to look at the tree where she huddled. The putrid stench of the creature threatened to overpower her senses as it drew near her.

Distant shouts startled her. Katja looked to see her clan's village elders loping along the path toward her. The misshapen creature gave a gurgling hiss and fled into the forest beyond the path, barely escaping discovery. Strong paws pulled the catling out of the branches and cradled her protectively, then. She gazed into the face of Kumos and knew by his eyes that something was terribly wrong.

"Thank the Creator you're safe!"

"Where is Mother?"

Kumos shook his head, his eyes glistening. "I'm so sorry, Katja. Our parents couldn't escape the rocks…they…they are dead."

Katja's stomach lurched. She tried to speak, but retched instead. Her heart and her head hurt so much. The world spun—its colors swirling into dizzying blackness, and then she had known nothing…

*

In the gloom of this unnatural night, Katja again smelled the stench she had smelled this morning and finally recognized it as the same shadowy scent of her youth. It was now strong enough for even her human nose to single out. Fear overpowered her as she realized that the shadowy being who had tried to kill her with the rockslide that had taken the lives of her parents was hunting her again tonight.

If it hunts me now that means…the village! If it finds the village, it will kill my family and clansmen trying to find me!

Katja kicked at the rock guarding the cave's opening in desperation. *I have to get out!* She managed to roll the stone aside and scrambled through the entrance—badly scratching her face in the brambles. *The den! I have to get to the den!* She had to warn her siblings; she had to protect them. She knew now that their parents had died because of her. She could not let her siblings suffer the same fate!

Katja stumbled out into the open darkness and tried to find her way through the thick mountain forest. She could not see or smell all that well, but she could hear—partially. She listened as hackle-raising screeches and roars pierced the night. Her clansmen were dying. They were being slaughtered in their own sleeping furs! She struggled toward the sounds of those shrieks, then stumbled and fell.

She lifted her head and sniffed, smelling the horrid stench of death. It was coming closer. She felt so weak. She rose onto her hands and knees and tried to crawl away from that stench. In her blindness, she fell again. Then, she felt a rush of wind and felt powerful forepaws lock around her head. She tried to scream, but couldn't. She fought the stranglehold around her head. Then something hard slammed into the base of her skull. The ground felt soft as her head sank against it and she knew no more.

* * *

"Katja, wake up! Please wake up!"

Katja warily opened her eyes and then squeezed them shut again as the painful light of day flooded into her vision. She struggled to lift her face from the furs on which she lay and winced.

"Don't overdo it; you're in pretty poor shape."

"Kayten?" She twisted her throbbing head to look at her sibbe. He was sitting on his haunches, looking down at her with bloodshot amber eyes. Katja pushed herself into a stiff sitting position and then crawled into her brother's arms. "Kayten, I had the most horrible nightmare..."

Katja was seldom in the habit of succumbing to such passionate outbursts because she, like most Feliconians, considered excessive emotionality a sign of weakness. This dream, however, had unnerved her beyond all rational decorum. Indeed Kayten would have normally pulled back from such an emotional display, but instead he cradled her close against his tawny chest.

When Katja pulled away to look at her brother, he held her paws gently in his own. It was then that she noticed that his furry forearms and chest were scratched and smeared with dirt and dried blood. She stared into his amber eyes and judged fear and sorrow to rule them. She then gazed at her own body. It was its usual feline shape, but it was peppered in cuts. Her shortened fur would need another two days to grow back to its normal length. Katja slowly raised a paw and felt the base of her head, hissing at the sharp pain that issued from the light touch.

Katja's breath caught sharply in her throat, "Kayten, it wasn't—"

"Real? Oh, yes, it was quite real."

Her brother's haunted eyes stared behind where she sat. Katja slowly turned to look behind her. What met her eyes smote her soul. Behind the two werecats lay the ransacked ruin of their village. The central meeting den had been leveled down to its stone foundation. The various dens dug into the sides of the hills were cloaked in red gore. Mangled bodies were strewn everywhere.

Katja saw kits and catlings she knew and loved lying in blank-eyed death beside their parents atop the crimson ground. Katja gaped at the carcasses of friends and mentors. The young and innocent had been annihilated along with the aged and wise. She shrieked when she saw her father's oldest friend. He had died at the entrance of his now-ruined den while fighting to protect his family—a pike still clutched in his paw. Behind the werecat's butchered body lay the mauled remains of his wife and daughter. Their eviscerated bodies already writhed with maggots.

Katja jerked her head around and shut her eyes against the horror, a soft moan escaping her maw.

"Did anyone else survive?" she asked in the barest whisper.

"No, we are the last living of our family and our clan." Tears streamed silently from Kayten's amber eyes.

For the first time in her life, Katja let loose the tears bulwarked inside of her since their parents' deaths. Her powerful shoulders heaved as she shrieked a wild screech that shook the mountain. Then she bowed her head to the ground and moaned in utter anguish. Kayten pulled her to him and rocked her gently as she sobbed into his fur. Together they sat amidst the carnage and wept for their clan and their family.

* * *

Burning the dead took Kayten and Katja several days. The whole process was agonizing work. Flies hovered in clouds above the corpses. The stench of death was so sickening that the Escari siblings had to tie cloths over their noses just to breathe. Because the village body count numbered close to two hundred, Kayten decided to move the dead Feliconians to the central amphitheater—the only place large enough to hold all of their kin. Once all of the corpses were laid along the amphitheater's dugout steps in their final resting poses, Katja and Kayten covered each body with cloth or hide, anointed it with herb oil, and set it aflame.

While moving and preparing the bodies, the siblings had noticed that every werecat had been maimed so that they had suffered intensely before death. The siblings thought this, at first, to be the work of some vengeful werewolves, but after looking closely at the cuts, they discovered that the slices were angled in the wrong way to be cut by werewolf claws. Instead the whole village had been mauled by far more dreadful creatures.

Village elders were among the worst of the mauled victims. These members were always lacerated in the same gruesome way: the abdomen slit open and the same portion of gut missing. Katja had heard of this horror before. According to the clan's historical archive, deadwalkers and dark mages would sometimes eat the entrails and brains of their victims in a magic rite used to gain the wisdom of their enemies.

From the claw cuts on the victims' abdomens and the shape and size of the paw prints left in the soil, Katja thought the attackers must be human. Yet these humans had long, curved claws on their back paws. The resulting print looked wholly unnatural and it caused Katja to suspect that deadwalkers might indeed be involved in the massacre. Katja's mind protested the thought that such monsters were once again hunting on Sylvan soil, but what else could it be? Not even werewolves would commit this kind of desecration!

Keepha and Kumos were the last to receive burial rites and, since they were close family, Kayten and Katja decided to bury them separate from those laid to rest in the stone-carved amphitheater.

As the siblings anointed their bodies, Katja remembered something. "Kayten, we need to bury our brother and sister with our parents."

"Katja, we cannot defile our parents' grave with the scent of their children's murder! Our parents died in peace. Our siblings died in war. You know that the oldest Sylvan Code forbids the mixing of the scent of murder with the scent of nature."

"I know what the Code states and I follow it. We cannot defile Sylvan soil with a new grave to rest a murder when the old grave rests murder already."

"Katja, what are you saying? You know that our parents

were killed by a rockslide. Rockslides are not of murder; they are of nature."

"Do you smell this nauseating scent on our clansmen's bodies?"

Kayten slowly nodded.

"I have smelled this scent before."

In a hushed tone, Katja told Kayten about her memories of their parents' deaths and of the shadowy monster. When she finished, Kayten sat quietly. Finally, he said, "Katja, I think I may have unwittingly saved our lives."

"How's that?"

"What is the last event that you remember on the night of the massacre?"

Katja closed her eyes. "I remember crawling toward the shrieks of the dying. I kept thinking that I had to protect all of you. I knew I was what the monsters wanted and that they would kill until they found me. I remember crawling, then I remember forearms wrapped around my neck choking me and that horrible stench slinking toward me...then nothing."

"Those were my forearms."

"What!"

"I found the tunnel you dug out of your sleeping hole on the night of the massacre. I didn't bother telling the others about it; I just followed your scent as far as I could. I wanted to make sure you were safe." Kayten looked into the distance with troubled eyes before speaking again. "I was deep in the forest when darkness overtook the moon. I hid in fear of something I could not explain and felt evil pass by. Then, I heard the screeches from our village. I rushed toward the shrieks when I smelled a human female—at least, I thought she was human. I thought that she must be somehow connected with the attack so I decided to capture and question her. I then sniffed one of the monsters approaching and once more felt the fear I could not name.

"I needed to hide, so I knocked the human senseless and carried her to a tiny cave hideaway I found. The cave had your supplies in it, as well as blood-covered tufts of your fur. It looked like the human had tortured you, but the scent was too muddled to recognize.

"I covered every crack I could find, lest that rancid

creature discover us inside the cave. There I waited until the next morning just after sunup to see if the world was right again. I tied up the human and searched the forest outside the cave. Then I saw the village…"

Katja's shudder mirrored Kayten's.

"I…I went back to the cave intent on making that human regret her involvement, but instead of the human I found you. I finally understood then that you and the human were one and the same, which explains why you are always mysteriously absent during the full phase of the moon." He gazed at her in sadness. "Katja, just how long were you hoping to keep these little transformations a secret?"

Katja sat with her eyes downcast in naked shame. "For as long as I could. I couldn't bear for any of you to think that I was a turncoat."

Much to Katja's surprise, Kayten gently pulled Katja's head up so that she looked into his kind eyes. "How long have you been able to do this, lytzsibba?"

"I've experienced full moon changes since I had roughly twelve winters of life," she said.

"So you've been able to skinshift for almost six winters now?"

"Yes."

"Strange that none of us ever noticed you slip away before."

"I've done my best to hide my changes, though it's been difficult because I become a little more *human*" — she spat the word — "with each cycle."

"If certain elders knew what I can do, they would have banished me from the clan. Our family was broken enough, and I thought that if I could just hide my abilities long enough, we would come to know no more pain. I could not bear to be forced from my only home and family, but now it seems I have no choice."

"How so?"

"Our clansmen's murderers must have been looking for me. I don't know why, but I feel that they hunted me for the same reason our clansmen would drive me away—because I'm a changeling."

"Katja Kevrosa Escari, do not ever use that word! You

are my sister, not some vile traitor. Besides, you being a skinshifter mage should not make a difference with a pack of murderers. Even if the beings that killed our clan were deadwalkers—Creator, keep us—I think it would take more than an untrained skinshifter to spark their interest."

"Kayten, deadwalkers do not attack clans of the Sylvan Order on a whim—"

"I was using deadwalkers as an example! How can you even say that deadwalkers could ever roam Sylvan soil? They can't go south into the Southern Continent except through the Sphinx's Gape—which is closed to all except fireforgers. You know that, as well as I."

"Yes, I know, but you have to admit there is something unusual about our clansmen's lacerations, and you yourself agreed that the smell is unnatural."

"Yes, but trolls give off similar odors," Kayten remarked and sighed. "Either way, though, you and I are not safe here. We need to finish the ritual burning of our kin and leave as quickly as possible. We can seek refuge and peace with our cousin clan across the mountains; they should be able to protect us well against the assault of anything dangerous."

"But not against deadwalkers," Katja muttered. She turned back to Kayten. "We shall see. First, let us finish the ceremony for our siblings and lay our parents to rest beside them."

"Agreed."

* * *

Katja rose before the sun the next morning with the vile odor of the burning amphitheater hanging heavy in her nostrils. She watched the flickering flames that she and Kayten had set to consume their kin a long moment. With tears in her eyes, Katja scribbled a message into the dust beside Kayten's sleeping figure, which translated: "Do not follow me. Seek our cousin clan."

She then quickly gathered her supplies and slipped silently away from her home and her brother. The sun found her pouncing from rock to rock along the stream that ran near the village. She decided to follow the stream westward until it emptied its fill into Kings' Lake in Crown Canyon. She stayed

in the stream as much as she could to throw her brother—
and anything else that tried to hunt her—off of her scent. Her
sibbe had always tried to protect her, but now it was her turn
to protect him. If the full moon once again betrayed Katja,
any Sylvan beings that discovered her secret would also
punish Kayten for knowingly bringing a skinshifter into their
territory.

Katja refused to be thrust behind thick walls or be
guarded fearfully by others night and day. That was not how
a werecat—a Feliconian—should live. That was not how she
could live. She was going to find a way to live her life fully
and not fearfully.

She wanted peace and solitude and time to cope with the
burden of a survivor's grief. Without really knowing why,
she felt that the abandoned territory of Crown Canyon might
grant her that freedom. With these thoughts, Katja bounded
her way into the pale new dawn.

II

RACING THE MIST

Katja sat crouched upon a sun-dappled rock surveying the forest around her while licking excess flesh from her claws and spitting fresh feathers out of her fangs. This was the sixth scrawny bird she had devoured during the morning eat, yet she was still hungry. Where was a plump doe when she needed one?

She had traveled southwest along the stream that fed into Crown Canyon and Kings' Lake for three days now and she was growing impatient with herself for taking so long to get there. Of course, it was hard for her to run quickly across the hilly terrain, especially when she had to cover her tracks so carefully. She no longer worried about being discovered and coerced into custody by her overprotective brother. Now she had much worse troubles to fear—her clansmen's murderers were hunting her.

She had first caught their scent and felt their hostile presence tracking her two days ago while she was weaving along a forest path near the river. She still had no knowledge of how many enemies where tracking her, nor could she clearly see or hear them. She knew they were there because she felt their pestilent presence grow in her mind with each passing day and, despite her best efforts, she could not seem to throw them off her scent. She felt their presence mostly at night, but every so often she also caught their scent during daylight. The smell of musty decay overlapped with hints of water and salt had nearly overpowered her twice already on this journey.

Knowing ill intent was set against her by a nameless enemy sent Katja's already fragile mind down some dangerous treks of thought. She could not fight what she could not see, so she knew that the refuge of Crown Canyon was her only hope for survival. According to the Feliconas Clan tales, the canyon's Ring Spells kept all beings but the pure of heart from entering the ancient stronghold. For the sake of anyone else hunted by this evil, she hoped her clansmen had been right. For her own sake, she also hoped that she would somehow prove worthy enough to pass the spells' purity test.

Katja stood up cautiously and spit the remainder of the fuzzy feathers from between her fangs. She then hoisted her buckskin rucksack onto her back and began bounding from boulder to boulder downstream with the river once again. She tried to stay off the grassy bank lest broken leaf stems reveal her presence to trained eyes. The trek along the shallows was grueling work, but she welcomed the near constant splash of cold water on her furry toes because it helped keep her alert.

The werecat had not been able to sleep solidly since the Feliconas Clan Massacre. She had slept better with Kayten near her, but now that she was alone, she could not avoid meeting her clansmen's mangled bodies in the darkness of every dream. Out of desperation, Katja resorted to quick naps to avoid prolonged confrontations with her nightmares.

The dearth of sleep in combination with constant exertion and an inadequate food supply had heavily drained her energy. But there was no help for that now—not until she reached safety. She guessed that she needed no longer than a day or two to reach the canyon. Her strength should hold for that long—she hoped.

As she bounded across the boulders and fallen trees that wove a dry path above the swirling waters, Katja looked longingly at the arm-length trout swimming in the deeper pools beneath her. She wished more than anything now that she had let Kumos teach her how to properly spearfish. She had refused to learn in the seasons since their parents' deaths.

She turned her eyes toward the horizon and tried to ignore the hungry protest of her stomach. Katja judged that the day's light was already one-fifth spent, so she decided to push her pace harder in anticipation of reaching the Crown Canyon foothills sometime after noon on the morrow.

* * *

At its zenith, the sun found Katja overlooking the stream from her perch upon a limestone outcropping roughly a standard spruce-length high. She had caught two fat hares during her forage around the base of the craggy hill. Their flesh was succulent and she ate every edible morsel with relish as she surveyed the landscape below her. The river curved just over the edge of the horizon to the southwest. She sniffed the wind, noting the high humidity and strong fragrances of water-loving plants filling the breeze.

Had she misjudged the distance to the canyon lake? The scents seemed to indicate such. Katja's hope sparked anew. She might be within the sanctity of the Crown Canyon before dark if she ran hard. She swallowed the last bite of meat from the second hare and quickly trimmed the animals' hides. She wrapped the furs around the rabbits' skulls so that she could use their brains to help tan the skins later. There was no sense in wasting perfectly good furs when she could so easily tie them to her rucksack for future use.

As she secured the hides and sack together with a length of sinew, the werecat sensed something sinister behind her and swiftly surveyed the spine of the hill toward the forest from whence she had come. A small, shadowy tendril of mist floated upwind along the gaps of the trees. Katja froze. The shifting wind was heavy with scents of rotting flesh, mold, and sea salt. She could feel the nameless fear emanate from the tendril as it slunk through the underbrush—hugging the shadows of the now-silent forest floor as it moved. She had been right; her clansmen's murderers were indeed hunting her.

Caution was pointless with the shadow so close. She sprinted as fast as she dared down the steep slope and rushed along the riverbank toward the southwest. The food and her fear fueled her limbs. She could hear the acceleration of the mountain stream's current; its tremendous speed seemed to match her own quickening heartbeat.

She felt her throat tighten and her tongue swell from lack

of water, but she dared not stop to drink. Frightened birds fluttered from their perches and flew past her to escape the misty shadow stalking ever closer. Their speed made her suddenly wish for wings. Even at her fasted pace, she knew the shadow would overtake her, but what else could she do? The tendril's smell was rapidly growing into a nauseating stench. Katja felt her body weaken and the world swim before her from the lack of air coupled with the creature's scent.

Swimming? Katja looked toward the river. It was moving fast—faster than she. The flowing water was deep with few boulders, so swimming might work. The werecat had rarely practiced the skill because she hated being wet, but swimming seemed the only plausible escape.

Katja saw a fallen tree leaning far over the river ahead of her. It looked to be the best diving place available, so she ran with all remaining strength toward that dead tree even as the mist enveloped the world around her.

She reached the fallen trunk and clawed her way to its end. Then the darkness descended on her in full and she sensed nothing—not the water rushing beneath her, or the rough bark of the pine between her claws. Then the black of the world transformed into a landscape of grays which contrasted entirely with the forest that had surrounded her before the inkiness had engulfed her vision.

Instead of looking deep brown, the pine log she perched upon now appeared as white as bleached bone. The gray grass swirled in ghostly rhythm with a thousand silent eddies of wind in which Katja's nose found no scents. The sky had dimmed from bright blue to deepest black and the water swirling beneath her carried the only color in the landscape: a deep bloody red.

Katja sat frozen in a half-perch on the end of the dead log, staring down its bleached length into the vile black eyes of her main hunter.

"Well, Little Katja, it has been a long time since I have seen you. I must say, you've grown into quite a comely female." The ghoul's voice was sickeningly pleasant, while its dead black eyes betrayed malicious hunger.

"Who are you, deadwalker?" Katja growled.

"I am called Curqak by my master. Mark the name well,

for it will be the last you know while you are yet Unturned."

The deadwalker's hollow eyes threatened to engulf Katja's soul and she had to look away. Once she did, Katja recognized the scents of other deadwalkers and forced herself to search the shadows for enemies. Although she could see none, her eyes narrowed as one particular smell overpowered the others. Finally she understood the mixed scents of salty mist and fetid death that she had smelled in her village and while on the run.

"Tell me, Curqak, how did you manage to coerce a brolaghan into shielding you from the sun, and on land no less? Very impressive." Katja watched the ghoul's face soften with sudden surprise before hardening with hatred again. "Yes, I know his scent; I smell your allies' rotten stench, too. We both know full well that deadwalkers are not allowed on Sylvan soil, so how did you ever get through the Sphinx's Gape?"

"Well now, aren't you a clever *changeling*," the ghoul said the name slowly with a mirthless smirk lighting his sallow face. "The brolaghan has Turned into a revenant, so he is loyal to me. Don't waste your breath trying to persuade him to free you from his illusions. And don't irritate me with some other desperate escape attempt. My underlings completely encircle you, so either come to me without a quarrel or join your dead clansmen. Make your choice."

This ghoul knew she was a skinshifter? That meant that he must have tracked her purposely. If this were true, then her fears were correct—Katja was indeed responsible for her clansmen's deaths. The ghoul had hunted her, and now he would either kill her or Turn her into a deadwalker like him— or worse. She looked around her in desperation. Escape was impossible while the revenant monster shrouded reality and controlled the water beneath her.

"And what are you going to do with me?" Katja's eyes narrowed and her crouched stance stiffened into a defensive position. She needed to distract the ghoul for as long as possible while she searched for a way out of this disaster. Perhaps, if she could run at the ghoul she would have enough momentum to slice his throat. Nothing could completely destroy him except fireforger's flame or a sunsilver blade, but she might be able throw him off balance and confuse his slow-witted counterparts long enough to break through their ranks. She recalled from her archive readings that deadwalker slaves were none-too-smart, so as long as there was not another ghoul—or worse a Víchí—slinking around the vicinity, she might have a chance. Even with such a chance, she still was not sure how to escape the revenant.

Curqak noticed her stance shift. "Now, now, no mischief. I have had a difficult enough time tracking you this far and I'll not lose any more days to your stubbornness. My master is not patient when he wants fresh blood and a changeling makes a fine meal," he cackled.

The werecat hissed. "And who do you call master, fiend?"

"Enough stalling! Come now or you'll bleed slowly just like your brother!"

The ghoul's smile was full of fang as he tossed a shred of leather toward her. She stared at it as it landed with a thump on the rough bark in front of her. It was covered in dried blood. She recognized the tooling as her brother's own handiwork from the rucksack he had carried the last day she'd seen him. The blood smelled of him, too.

"No...Kayten!" Katja felt her mind's defenses collapse at Curqak's answering cackle. She gazed at him with renewed hatred. This monster had tortured her brother, likely preventing his soul from seeking the Dyvesé Realm upon death. She had tried to protect Kayten and had failed because of the claws of this worthless Asheken!

Something dangerous stirred inside of the Feliconian. Her sight blurred. Then a molten power surged through Katja's soul and found shape through her voice.

Curqak was stalking closer now. "You have lived on borrowed time long enough—"

The roar of rage that thundered from the werecat's throat cracked the false black sky. The ghoul howled in pain as if he had been stabbed with a smoldering hock. The other deadwalkers, some of whom had boldly moved toward the riverbank during the last of Curqak's harangue, now cowered and covered their black-tipped ears. Even the revenant gave a windy shriek and lost its hold on the illusion. The revenant's blanketing mist shredded and sunlight flowed back into the world. The deadwalkers all bolted into the underbrush, covering their blistering skin.

Before her enemies had time to recover, Katja took a deep breath and plunged into the swirling waters rushing past her log. She did not know if ghouls or sklaaven could swim, but she would rather find out later than perish on a dead tree now.

I am sorry, My Clansmen, for my part in your death, but I swear I will find a way to bring justice to our enemies. Katja cast the thought out as her body hit the cool water and prayed that the Creator would give her strength enough to avenge her loved ones soon.

She sank deep under the water and let the current sweep her away from her hunters. She dared not surface for breath until she was much further downstream, so she sustained herself by taking small gulps of air from the empty water bladder that she had in her rucksack. After swimming and drifting a while, Katja found an outcropping of stone perched just above the water and swam under it to catch her breath. She filled the bladder with air again and dove into the full current once more.

The second time she surfaced for air, Katja swam under an arm-sized lily pad growing in a shallow pond just off the main river channel. The werecat poked her nose out from underneath the lily pad to check her surroundings and sensed the faintest smell of dead flesh. She knew from clan stories that most deadwalkers feared moving water, so she expected them to stay on the riverbank searching for her paw prints when she left the river. This kept her relatively safe while underwater, but it also posed a problem in her escape. Katja knew she would have to hide in the stream much longer and hope that the revenant was too injured to come after her. Either way, the odds were set hard against her leaving the river before nightfall.

As Katja swam in the current and drew breath from the bladder, she stealthily wound her way around boulders and sandbanks. Although Katja's roar had shredded the deadwalkers' protective revenant shadow, she knew from the scents drifting across the water that they had regrouped and were hunting her once more. The werecat knew she would no longer be safe once night's darkness descended — whether she was in water or on land.

To make matters worse, the river's current was accelerating, and that meant that she was getting much closer to the river's waterfall that fed into Kings' Lake. If she didn't leave the river now, Katja would drown.

The werecat swam desperately, trying to maneuver out of the swiftest pull from the current. The swirling waters slammed her against a boulder—adorning her side with a deep bruise—as she groped her way toward the left bank of the river. Finally she managed to make her way to where a grove of trees clung to a small, water-swept sandbar. Katja caught hold of two low-lying limbs as they skimmed the frothy water and used them to pull herself onto a sturdier third branch.

Sore and shaking, she climbed the branch to the tree's crown. As she nestled between the forking branches, she caught her heaving breath and ate the last of the dried meat from her sopping buckskin sack while searching the gathering gloom with wary eyes.

She watched the sun set slowly—its lingering light giving a bloody hue to the underbellies of plump purple clouds. In the opposite sky, ebony and indigo hues ruled Katja's eyes, punctuated by the pale piercing of night's first star. Somewhere in the distance, she heard a dove's mournful call upon the soft breeze. Its plaintive cry echoed her mood. As far as she had come, Katja still could not see the canyon and she had little time left.

Shadows already stretched across the ground and the wind was winding in cool whispers through the tangled trees surrounding the river. Katja traced the long shadows with her eyes and then turned to look at the northern length of the river. There, she felt rather than saw the canyon wall that was the barrier to her haven. She smelled water chafe against stone and lush green growth and heard the rushing flow of swirling water suddenly cascade into a long-forgotten chasm.

As she recognized these sensations, it seemed as if a painted veil were suddenly ripped away from her sight to reveal that the forest a spruce-score from her position was nothing more than an artful illusion. What she now saw was not endless forest but the majesty of the ancients' Crown

Canyon. The rough-hewn granite towered above her, a gray colossus of jagged stone walls. Its height breached the clouds as if it wished to touch all the stars in the heavens.

Katja shuddered back from that immensity and squinted at the river. It swept down into the canyon mouth after straining through a series of rapids and then dropped sharply to fill the lake below with its frothy contents.

"Creator, give me strength!" Katja whispered to the night.

She ate the last morsel of meat and then carefully rose onto all four paws. She swayed, feeling the heavy ache of weariness grip her bones and muddy her wits. The charnel reek of her enemies wafted past her nose, then, and she was moving.

She crawled along a stout branch that twisted across another tree's bough and then hauled herself onto that bough. She followed the bough to the tree's crown and then hopped onto another neighboring limb. She bounded from limb to limb and tree to tree, following the tangled pattern of living wood toward the steep cliff walls. She dared not touch the ground again, lest one of Curqak's allies sniff out her scent trail and catch her. Even so, the water dripping off of her fur and her rucksack onto the leaves far below made her sick with worry.

Roughly half of a spruce-length away from the cliff's base, Katja discovered an odd break in the entangled trees. At closer inspection, she noticed that any branch growing near the break curled away from a certain spot as if flinching away from an invisible barrier. That barrier seemed to completely encircle the entire canyon, rising up between the grass blades and penetrating high into the dark dome of the night sky.

"Ring Spell," she whispered.

Katja crawled the length of a limb close to the barrier and cautiously reached out one clawed forepaw. Her paw touched something seemingly solid and she felt an immediate shock of pain pour through her arm to the elbow. It felt as if her entire forearm had just grazed hot iron. She jerked her paw back with a surprised screech and immediately covered her maw with her paw. A quick search showed no enemies near her, but she knew that they had likely heard her startled cry. If the Ring Spells protecting the canyon would not allow her entry now, her last hope was of survival was gone!

"Please grant me refuge!" she whispered.

The werecat looked back at her arm. Instead of looking burned, her furry forearm was actually healed of all its cuts and bruises. She frowned and then gazed at the place her paw had touched. The print of her paw was outlined in rainbow hues swirling through midair. She watched the shimmering outline grow larger. Then the circle broke as if it was an iridescent bubble and a circular opening formed in the barrier large enough for her to walk through. What had existed as the center of the gap now streamed toward Katja as an iridescent walkway floating high above the ground.

Katja hesitated a moment. What if she fell? She was three body-lengths above the ground and this pathway smelled highly irregular. On the other paw, the deadwalkers would soon find her if she stayed here. So she must either step across this threshold of faith or stay here to fight and die alone.

A hackle-raising groan came from somewhere behind her and its sound sealed her decision. Katja's hind paw touched the surface of the pathway and found it to be soft but resilient. She felt the same spasm of pain as she watched her paw sink into the walkway as if into fast-sand. Quickly she stepped onto the path with her other hind paw to try to steady the first. The pain subsided as she looked down at her body. All of her wounds were gone! Not only did the Ring Spells shielding the canyon repair her entire body, they seemed to test and purify her very soul. She felt a strange peace as the multihued path hardened under her paws and allowed her to walk on what would otherwise be mere air. She moved quickly across the gap and onto the outstretched limb of a tree hugging the base of the canyon wall on the other side.

Katja turned to see the walkway dissolve back into the iridescent opening and fill the breach in the barrier. An audible pop signaled the barrier's invincibility once more. It closed not a moment too soon. A moment later, a deadly shadow crawled up the tree she had just vacated on the other side of the Ring Spells.

The deadwalker shifted its head from side to side, snuffling the air. The little werecat sat frozen in fear. Could he see her? She should be in perfect view from its perch in the tree. But as Katja watched its thoughtless eyes shift in their decrepit sockets, she realized that they seemed to slide off the barrier to look toward the forest on either side.

Katja watched the monster that was once a living being, noting differences in its body structure from those of the ghoul Curqak. While both deadwalkers had roughly the same reeking, dead-white skin, Curqak's bulged tightly over powerful muscles. This deadwalker's skin looked more like a tattered cloak covering bare bones and oozing organs. Its eyes were milky with barely a trace of rounded black pupil, while Curqak's eyes boasted no white at all. Katja had seen dangerous intelligence steeped in those black eyes, while she saw none in this hunchback's. This deadwalker seemed to possess neither wit nor will, and, as it shifted its body, Katja saw in horror that it possessed only misery. The monster's back was covered with deep claw-marks, whiplashes, and bites.

The brute finally gave up its hunt and slowly clambered out of the tree to drop heavily onto the ground several body-lengths below it. Katja cringed at its awkward landing; the same jump would have earned her several broken bones. The deadwalker, however, seemed to feel no pain as it loped easily away in the direction of the river.

"Sklaaf," she whispered the Felis word for slave.

This was no ordinary sklaaf either. It was a sklaaf der seele—a soul-slave, or zombie as humans called them. So the clan archive's stories were true; the deadwalkers did enslave their own depraved kind.

Katja shuddered and turned to gaze toward the cliff's base. The sheer granite walls seemed to allow nothing but the river to enter the canyon realm. She slunk over the tree branches drawing ever nearer to the area where the swirling water met the windswept wall.

She scaled a tall tree near the now-rocky banks of the river and noticed a partially-concealed outcropping of rock jutting out and up from the main cliff. Time and nature had worn superb footholds in the upper portion of the outcropping so that it resembled a steep staircase beginning about nine body-lengths above the ground. The staircase was hidden so well by the jutting rock on its outermost wall that Katja would have never seen it had she gazed upon it from ground level.

A semi-flattened stone platform had formed to one side of the stairway about two body-lengths below the branch where Katja perched. She took hold of a springy limb and jumped down onto the platform using the limb's resistance to slow her decent.

The last of the sun's golden rays were lost inside the pocket of the world as Katja began her ascent of the stairs. The now-moonlit pathway wound around the cliff and then severely twisted to encircle the cliff face above the rushing river. After another sharp turn, the trail led onward through a low stone archway carved from the side of the canyon's wall and began a slow decent toward Kings' Lake in Crown Canyon's heart.

Katja trudged wincing down the escarpment. What cuts and bruises had healed during her entry through the protective barrier had now reappeared during the slick-stoned descent into the inner canyon. Her eyelids had grown heavy and even her ears drooped in exhaustion.

The werecat stumbled along the path until she saw a small ledge jutting away from it. The ledge widened into a stone shelf where a nest woven from sticks, vines, and feather down lay tucked away from the wind under a canopy of rock. The nest was twice the size of Katja's torso. Katja stiffened. She sniffed the thin air and listened for any sign of the nest's makers or other occupants. She heard no cries save the wind's whispered whistling as it wound around the cliff. She smelled only stale scents of long-left harpies and decided to risk a closer investigation.

After sniffing every corner of the ledge and discovering no scented sign of anything living, Katja crept over to the nest and sank into its woven warmth. She curled into a furry ball, wrapped her now-dry hare pelts around her chest, and fell asleep in the next moment.

Far below the little werecat, the lake's waves lapped gently on the dark sands of the shore. The night was brilliant with sacred constellations and the gibbous moon. The canyon itself was alive with the chatter of night creatures and the subtle hum of power from its protective Ring Spells.

For the first time since her clansmen's deaths, Katja slept in peace. She dreamed of summer hunts and bountiful harvests and smelled the sweet scents of myriad flowers. Her mind's eye watched small pixies flit from flower to flower on early-morning errands of petal and pollen gathering. The world, then, seemed warm and wonderful.

Then, upon the soft breezes of the canyon, the Feliconian heard a strong voice whisper tales of old kingdoms crumbled and of faraway threats drawing near and of faint hope flaring anew. Katja slept on in the womb of the rock as a long-forgotten griffin king wove his tales inside her mind. She listened until the sun once again brought morning light to her eyes and she awoke with no memory of Canuche's plea during her dreams.

III

A VISITOR IN EXILE

The sun's warm rays shot through the craggy crown and found its target in Katja's sleepy eyes. She had slept soundly for the first time since the night of the massacre, but now the morning glare forced her to leave her dreams and once again face the stark reality of her situation. She was safe, but she was alone. Katja squinted down at the lake and wrinkled her nose. Among other things, she needed more food, fresh drinking water, a safer shelter, and a bath.

With a fang-revealing yawn, she stretched her body against the nest's interwoven twigs. Sleep had helped alleviate some soreness, but she still winced as she stowed her things in her still-damp rucksack. After a meager meal of dove, the werecat picked her way down the ridge toward the canyon's heart. The long trail down gave her time to consider her circumstances and decide what action to pursue.

Katja had to climb down the inner canyon wall before she could dress her wounds, because the only source of clean water inside the canyon was Kings' Lake. Although it took considerable time for her to descend, the journey proved fairly easy compared to the steep ascent along the outside path. The numerous pawholds and resting places along the inner wall suggested that the descending pathway had actually been manually cut from a more dangerous sheer cliff. She became even more suspicious of its unnatural origins when her descent led her close to the southwest waterfall that fed Kings' Lake.

Just above and behind the water's final plunge, Katja had spied the remnants of a land-bridge that had once spanned the gulf in the mountain wall cut through by the river. Katja had no way to judge its age from her present distance, but her mind smoldered with curiosity. From the way it was constructed, Katja guessed that its makers were dwarves—the original settlers of this place.

The werecat abandoned her hope for a better look when a misplaced paw sent rocks skittering down the narrow ridge to the beach far below. She would, however, keep watch for any sign of other beings. Centuries had passed after the Dwarven Plague had destroyed the dwarves living in this part of the world, so Katja had to assume that other brave souls would seek Crown Canyon's relative safety should the deadwalker attacks spread. With her brother gone, the werecat could rely on no one but herself for safety. The Ring Spells were designed mainly to keep ghouls, zombies, and other deadwalkers out of the canyon, but not other Sylvans like Katja. Therefore any other "purified" exiles living within the canyon would likely still be hostile to her, especially if they were trolls or werewolves. Yet here, she reminded herself, a skinshifter mage would be far less likely to endanger anyone else in hiding and that thought brought her some comfort.

Concerning more practical matters, she had one large problem—the canyon's most abundant prey lived underwater. Katja's escape from Curqak and his deadwalker underlings had proved that she was barely adequate as a swimmer. She had lived through the experience only because she had been able to drift with the stream's current rather than fight against it.

Being a poor swimmer and fisher meant she would have to scavenge on land much more often. This could pose a problem in the coming winter. However, she would deal with that concern after she found a defendable shelter; and finding such a shelter could wait until after she washed and dressed her wounds.

The werecat bathed in a shallow lake inlet semi-protected from the wind by a wall of boulders. She scrubbed herself with soapwort, donned her loincloth, and dressed her wounds with a paste made from some nearby daisy plants. After she had finished bandaging herself, Katja began hunting for shelter, hoping to find food along the way. She managed to kill a small goat and devoured its meat greedily as she searched the cliffs' sides.

By the sun's zenith, Katja had still found no suitable den. What she did find, however, was far more significant: a fresh trail of paw prints along the western side of the canyon valley. Katja was not alone.

The trail itself contained two sets of prints: one belonging to a four-pawed creature, the other belonging to a creature that walked upright like Katja. The paw prints, or more correctly hoof prints, had the round shape and dusty scent of horses' hooves; however, these prints were nearly four times the size of normal horse hooves. The other prints were tiny in comparison and so light that they barely bruised the marsh grass. The prints smelled like tanned cow hide, but were shaped like those of a human.

"It must wear leather coverings on its feet," Katja murmured.

Why was a human in Crown Canyon? Most humans preferred to live in the coastal kingdoms and settlements far to the west of Katja's home. The closest horse-riding humans were the humans of the western coastal kingdom of Tyglesea, who never ventured beyond their own kingdom's borders for fear of the wilder magic existing among members of the rest of the Sylvan Orders. A citizen of Vihous was more common this close to the western edge of the Nyghe sol Dyvesé mountain range, but in either case, the human had to be in some sort of desperate situation to ride this far from home without the company of others of its race. Perhaps it was a fellow exile or maybe a scout for a larger group.

Very rarely had Katja seen humans unless they were members of guided groups come to trade supplies with her clan's elders. She had not seen horses since she was a kit. Her curiosity stirred so strongly that she almost abandoned her hunt for a den. Finally, she decided to search the north side of the canyon for a shelter. This was where the prints seemed to lead, and Katja had every intention of keeping a close watch on this oddity.

When the sky held a quarter of her blue veil between the

sun and the western line of the world, Katja finally found a suitable den. It was a place where time and rain had cut a grotto into the shadow of the larger mountains just northeast of the lake.

After digging out the excess silt, Katja wormed her way through the narrow mouth for a closer investigation. The cavern was three standard body-lengths deep with a ceiling that loomed two body-lengths tall at the deepest part of the cave. The entrance was a tight squeeze to be certain, but Katja was small enough to enter and exit it easily enough. She could also stand upright in most of the space, which was a nice improvement on her den hole at home.

Home...the very thought of it made her eyes ache with bitter tears. If only she had done more to warn everyone. Katja knew that the smoke she had seen with her brothers had meant danger, but when the clan elders ignored Kumos's report, she had stayed silent. Why had she stayed silent? Why had she not voiced her uneasiness?

"Because I, like everyone else, never expected deadwalkers to freely roam on Sylvan soil ever again," she hissed. "I did not recognize their scent until it was too late. If only I hadn't skinshifted, I could have done something, I could have saved someone..." Then she remembered Curqak's grotesque smile as he tossed Kayten's shredded rucksack to her.

She shook her head as she pulled the scrap of tooled leather from her rucksack. "It would not have mattered anyway. I'm no fireforger. I am one cursed being against hundreds of monsters. I would have died too and then no one would have honored the dead. My humanness distracted Kayten long enough to save him, only for him to die when I abandoned him. It's my fault, all my fault for being what I am." Katja held her tear-streaked face in her sandy paws and shook as the memories of her loved ones and their murderers churned in her mind, her sorrow and anger threatening to drown her.

* * *

Katja gulped down water to both quench her thirst and temporarily drown her hunger. She would need food soon if she was to keep herself strong.

"It seems I'll forever be dominated by hunger," she muttered.

She sniffed again at the human's tracks, marking their freshness. She had hunted the human and horse since well before daybreak and her entire body was stiff from this latest mistreatment. Besides the one night in the nest, she still could not sink into anything deeper than a short nap because of her nightmares. Perhaps she would be able to rest better after she knew the human's purpose. At least staying curious kept her mind from drifting into the abyss of grief caused by the Asheken murderers.

Asheken, commonly called deadwalkers, had not roamed Sylvan soil since the Second War of Ages over three hundred years ago. To find them on the Southern Continent again was unthinkable. Katja felt her heart flutter and tried to swallow her panic. The Second War of Ages had begun with a Sylvan invasion of the cursed Northern Continent to destroy all Asheken and open the Northern Continent to Sylvan expansion. When the attempted purge had failed, Sylvans were mercilessly slaughtered or Turned into deadwalkers themselves. If the deadwalkers had not been betrayed by one of their own, all Sylvans would have surely been destroyed under the corruption of the deadwalkers' Víchí masters.

How was it that in both wars the actions of one being had changed the outcome? Blessed Aribem had ensured Sylvan victory in the First War of Ages when he called fire from beyond the physical Erde Realm to imbue the first Sylvans with the magic of fireforging. During the second war, the Víchí elder Calais had found redemption through a fireforger's flame and again became the mage Caleb. Caleb then helped the Sylvan mages and the ethereal Pyrekin to trap the Asheken hordes north of the Sphinx's Gape. Myriads of Sylvans had died. Even the Pyrekin races, who were basically eternal, had vanished back across the First Veil into the Wraith Realm. Now not even a dragon remained.

Katja shook her head and looked around her at one of the last surviving strongholds from the Second War of Ages. Crown Canyon was one of the few places left unclaimed by any particular Sylvan race out of respect of the long-dead dwarven mages whose spells still resided within and around it.

Katja sniffed the human's tracks again. By their freshness, the human and horse couldn't be far from her crouched position. Katja cautiously crept toward the rocks that broke the eastern lakeshore into a jagged cluster of intermingled sandbars and shallow pools. She peered around a large boulder and spied a canvas tent tucked away under the shadow of a narrow granite outcropping. A small campfire stood a few paces from the tent with an array of metal containers strewn in the sand around it. Two forked, wooden branches stood erect on either side of the fire pit with a straight branch running between them half of a body-length above the flames. The straight branch had been sharpened to a point on both ends; and, as Katja pondered the reason for this strange contraption, the answer presented itself with a small gasp.

Katja jerked her head in the direction of the noise and discovered a human youth's dark-blue eyes staring warily into her own. The lanky, auburn-haired female was sitting cross-legged atop a slightly submerged boulder four body-lengths away from Katja's crouched position. Katja cursed herself for not checking the direction of the breeze. This human had been downwind of her and Katja had had no chance of smelling her before she herself was discovered.

The two steadily regarded one another. While Katja had seen humans before, she doubted that the startled human had ever seen one of Katja's kin. As the wind shifted, the werecat discovered why. The human's clothing smelled of flowery perfumes and sea salt. Her chest-cover was the sort worn by a human male. Its deep-blue material was expertly woven and richly embroidered with the silver symbols of a sea bird flying with wings fully outstretched over a crossed double-bladed sword and axe. Katja's ears twitched. This garb was not of Vihous and neither was the pale-skinned human wearing it.

In her slightly shaking hand, the human held a whippy branch with a thin string tied to one end. The string trailed off into the water far beyond the human's boulder. As she scanned the three large, finned bodies splashing in the shallow pool near the human's feet, Katja realized that the human was using the branch and string instead of a spear to catch fish—and faring well, too. What an ingenious way to catch food without getting wet!

The human followed Katja's eyes to the fish.

"Un bon dia per a vostè, meva senyora. ¿Vols un peix?"

Katja's eyes swiveled back to the human's and judged cautious kindness in their depths.

The human paused and added, "¡Mai he vist un de la seva classe! ¿D'on vens? ¿Com es diu a si mateix? ¿Si més no menja peix?"

Katja finally realized this human's origins. The crest on her chest was from Tyglesea and the salty perfume of her clothes gave further proof of her kinship with that west-coast kingdom. Her dialect was one of formality and education. She must be someone of high status among her kin to have these sorts of manners. Why was she here?

The human looked imploringly at Katja and repeated the formal greeting.

"Sorry, sorry! Yes, I understand. I not take you hard-earned labor, but thank for the hospitality." Katja spoke awkwardly, while stretching out her right paw with its pad up and bowing in formal salute. She had not spoken Tygyré since her days as a catling and her pronunciation proved raspy by comparison to this highborn's smooth diction. Both females winced slightly at Katja's accent, but the human smiled courteously and copied Katja's show of respect.

"Are you more comfortable with a language other than my own?" the human asked in Tygyré.

"I speak Felis and Shrŷde regularly."

"I speak Shrŷde fairly fluently. Shall we try that instead?"

"Yes, please," Katja agreed earnestly.

"Very well then," she said in the trading language adopted from the faeryken. "My name is Lauraisha. I am, as you might have realized, a stranger in these parts."

"I am Katja Kevrosa Escari, born of the Feliconas Clan of the Sylvan Order of werecats," Katja said, matching the human's formal politeness. "May I ask what family and clan of the Tyglesean Human Order you represent?"

Her face fell as she replied, "I am of the House of Astrat'a."

Katja felt her heart quicken in a mixture of fear, shock, and curiosity as she sank to her knees before the human. Small wonder that this human spoke like a highborn. Astrat'a was the house from which Queen Manasa claimed her bloodline—therefore this human was of the highest noble birth outside actual Tyglesean royalty.

"Forgive my impertinence, Your Excellency!" Katja bowed her head in honor of the young noble and cursed herself for her impudent thoughts of stealing a fish. To Katja's astonishment, however, the princess gave a shocked cry and implored the werecat to stand.

"Please, please do not bow to me! I act as no one's superior, nor would I ask to be treated as such—and certainly not by someone so extraordinary!"

Katja regained her stance and, not knowing what to say, simply watched the human for a cue of how to proceed. Lauraisha apparently sensed her dismay and turned to pull hard upon the fishing stick in her hand. Katja heard several splashes as the noble stood and laboriously towed the string out of the water using a spool attached to the fishing stick. Katja watched as a fish writhed desperately against the line Lauraisha was winding. She finally caught hold of the perch, untangled the string and hook imbedded in the finned beast's mouth, and wrapped it and the three others in a net.

"Well, I'd say that this plus the others should make a fine meal as well as left-overs for the two of us. I hope you like redfins." Lauraisha added while tying the leftover string around her fishing stick.

Katja hesitated a moment as the human tossed the wriggling net onto her back. Did she really trust this human? No, but a highborn's eat invitation was not to be refused no matter how strange the circumstances. Katja reluctantly picked up the fishing stick and followed the human toward the camp.

The whinny of a horse greeted Katja's ears as she and the human approached. Its fearful snort caused Katja to halt.

"Forgive me, but I dare go no farther, Your Excellency."

The noble stopped and frowned at her. "Call me Lauraisha. And why not?

Katja bowed her head slightly in apology and explained that horses had an inherent fear of her kin. "Going near the horse would risk harm to it and to me if it becomes violent in its attempt to flee from me."

"Oh, is that all!" the human laughed and then whistled thrice to the huge horse, which answered in a calmer whinny. "I strongly suggest that you do not get too close to him then— unless I'm with you, of course. He's rather flighty, even by horse-standards, but he shouldn't do anything daft while I'm nearby." Lauraisha smiled at her companion before continuing toward the camp's fire pit. She set the fish down beside a flat stone near the pit and pulled a knife from her belt. Slowly, she began cutting open one fish and peeling the flesh from its bones.

"What are you doing?" Katja asked in shock.

"Cleaning the fish, of course. I cannot properly cook them without stripping out the organs."

"Cook?"

"Well, of course I cook my fish. I certainly wouldn't eat them raw and whole."

Katja stared at the giggling youth. Instead of eating a fish whole, she intended to burn it? What was wrong with her?

"Tell me that you at least save the fish eggs and brain."

"Whatever for?"

"Flavor! If you're going to burn perfectly good meat, at least add some spice to it!"

"Oh, that is what these are for." Lauraisha drew several small tins out of a rucksack and handing one to Katja.

The werecat sniffed its contents before cocking her head at the human.

"Rosemary," she answered cheerfully before pointing each of the other pouches and naming them in turn: thyme, sea salt, black pepper, sage, oregano, ginger, sassafras, and sugar. "My older brother Saldis is absolutely fascinated with the arts of cooking and healing. These herbs and spices are from his own supply."

"How kind of him to share them with you."

"Indeed," she replied and continued to prepare the fish for burning.

"If you don't mind, I'd prefer that you didn't discard your scraps and let me have them instead."

"What will you do with them?" the human asked in genuine curiosity.

"Eat them."

"Eat them? Well wouldn't you rather have the filets of meat instead?"

"Perhaps, but you plan to burn that. Werecats do not eat burnt meat, or cooked meat…as you call it."

"Werecats don't cook their food? That is just strange."

"Perhaps, but we consider your 'cooking' strange."

Lauraisha laughed. "What an interesting dilemma! Well, then you must eat your fish your way and I shall have mine my way."

"Fair enough, but I think my way is faster." Katja retrieved Lauraisha's scraps and another whole fish that the human offered and began devouring them.

"Perhaps, but mine still tastes better." The human wrinkled her nose.

The females both laughed and then talked of various racial customs while the human used a lidded metal box to "bake" the first fish's filets and the pole-contraption set over the fire to "grill" the other two. Each redfin was almost as long as Katja's arm so the task of eating them was quite a challenge. Katja managed to consume all of the scraps plus her whole fish (except the bones, of course), but vowed not to eat again for at least two full days. The human fared far less well—having only consumed a fourth of the filets before leaning back in sweet defeat.

The midmorning eat gave way to a comfortable afternoon interlude in which the two conversed about various subjects, but most often about their different lifestyles. On the whole, Katja found the discussion quite freeing and relaxing. In Lauraisha, Katja found an avid communicator—willing to share and listen to experiences with equal enthusiasm. Lauraisha seemed kind and sincere in her intentions. The human also had an intriguing talent for picking up threads of conversational interest with her companion and edging away from those topics that might agitate the werecat.

Katja learned about Lauraisha's family and about life in Tyglesean society. Lauraisha also talked about her passion for cooking and what herbs she had found useful in curing common ailments like cuts or coughs. Katja found it odd that a young female of noble birth would know such arbitrary things when most Tyglesean nobles would likely spend their time creating art or reciting prose and poetry. Lauraisha seemed quite unusual for a noble, but as Katja discovered more about the human's family she began to understand why.

Like Katja, Lauraisha was the youngest in her family. She was barely fifteen winters of age and had spent much of her childhood learning boyhood games since her mother often left her in her four brothers' care. Lauraisha had mainly learned her impressive hunting and fishing skills from the second-born brother Tryntin and the fourth-born brother, Sandor. From Saldis, the third-born brother, Lauraisha learned her love of cooking and some knowledge of healing. She understood love, compassion, and horsemanship from her eldest brother, Ashomocos, but knew nothing other than spiteful contempt from her only sister, Kyla.

Katja had the impression that Lauraisha lived somehow apart from the rest of her family, but whether the separation was physical or simply mental Katja could not guess. Katja also noticed that Lauraisha would not speak frankly about either father or mother. As for Katja's own family, the werecat gave enough details to satisfy her companion's curiosity, but otherwise sheltered the precious memories of her kin within herself.

As gilded sunlight began to fade into violet dusk, Katja politely took her leave of Lauraisha and traveled north under the waning light. Her sleep that night was fitful despite the relative joy she felt at meeting the human.

The werecat believed Lauraisha benign; however, Katja was troubled by the fact that the noble had avoided answering her questions regarding her presence in the canyon. She was quite sure that the human's flight from her home country was somehow due to her family, but Katja had no idea what they could have possibly done to estrange such a seemingly kind person.

As she curled upon the sweet rushes of her new bed, Katja found herself with more questions and answers about her strange new neighbor.

Why would one of noble blood flee from the comforts of home and hearth when the outside world was so much crueler? Living like royalty with servants bobbing around her ankles must be far better than having to catch and eat her own food, no matter what the human might say to the contrary. Katja had no reason to stay in the place of her childhood since there was nothing left but the ashes of the dead to keep her company. Lauraisha, however, had left behind at least seven family members, most of whom she dearly loved.

Why would a Tyglesean flee so far outside the borders of her own country and then exile herself in a place so steeped in ancient magic? Tygleseans, for the most part, hated magic. Ever since King Kaylor began his bloody rule, Tygleseans had tried to expel all magic and mages from within their borders. And yet one of their kin acted as if she had been drawn to the magic of the Ring Spells protecting Crown Canyon. It made no sense.

Katja stared into the indigo night beyond her new den's maw and frowned as a new question formed in her mind. Could Lauraisha be a mage? The werecat promised herself that she would watch the human to find the truth of the matter. Only then did she finally closed her weary eyes and let sleep overtake her…

*

Katja felt bright blades of green grass whipping wet past her furry flanks as she sprinted through their midst. The sun overhead was bright with warmth emanating through the thin clouds encircling its edge. She sniffed the rich air. It was alive with scents of salty sea, sand, grass, birds, fresh fruits, and seedling sap. She looked over the escarpment toward the sea. There was a storm closing fast over its boiling waters. The wind howled and shrieked as it bore bulging black clouds weeping angrily within its clutches. She ran for cover under a tree and flinched back as a bolt of white fire singed a barrier at her feet. The tree was struck to pieces by the lightning's blow and her only other choice was to dive for cover in an abandoned badger burrow.

She lunged toward its safely just as the sky's white wrath attacked again and found herself in a small cave with intricate symbols carved in a circle around its walls. As she watched, the symbols began to glow with the same fire that she had stepped through upon her entrance to Crown Canyon. The symbols lifted themselves off the stone walls and began to spin in the air around her, growing brighter and moving faster until they formed a solid ring with her as their center.

Suddenly the ground beneath her shook and an altar sprouted under her paws. A smooth green emerald blossomed in its center. She picked up the stone and held it close as the altar melted back into the floor and a voice called in the shadows before her.

"This is your future."

She saw herself reflected in the stone's silky surface, not as she was, but with a human's head attached to her werecat body, a segmented black tail curving up from her backside, and a terrible fury haunting her glowing green eyes. The image faded away to be replaced with the likeness of a powerfully-built werewolf with azure-emerald eyes, standing fully erect on his back paws, with a huge double-bladed war axe covered in ancient runes held ready in his furry forepaws.

Next she knelt in a dark castle corridor with grand buttresses looming over her. A red carpet marked a path to a closed door. At her touch, the door creaked open to reveal a red carpeted room beyond with a full-length mirror standing in its ancient iron frame. Someone was inside the room with the mirror, but the doorframe blocked the being from her view.

"This is her past," called the voice.

For a moment the mirror reflect only blackness, and then it seemed to be a window. Through its surface she spied a midnight storm breaking over a castle by the sea. She felt herself being sucked into the scene as a bolt of lightning struck a section of the castle's battlements. Two horses bearing cloaked riders galloped wildly through the castle's war-torn gates and out onto the castle clearing toward the sanctuary of the forest far in front of them.

Arrows arced from the unscathed section of battlements and rained down upon the racing fugitives. Three arrows struck one rider—a valet wearing the old royal Tyglesean coat of arms—and sent him tumbling to his death as the other rider wailed in anguish. The survivor's hood snapped back in a gust of wind and Katja spied a human female who resembled Lauraisha in all features save nose shape, hair color, and eye hue.

"Arlis!" the human screamed as she escaped with both horses into the sheltering edge of trees.

"Time grows short!" the dream-voice called. "Come quickly before all is lost…"

*

Katja gasped awake. She wiped cold sweat from her brow and sensed the human across the lake do the same. Together they stared unseeing at their surroundings as the last remnant of dream faded from their shared vision. Their minds' magical bond lasted only a moment after consciousness, and then it was as insubstantial as the mournful wind wailing just outside the werecat's new den.

IV

RUNES AND RUINS

K atja, we really need to reach a compromise about this," Lauraisha said.

"There is no compromise, Lauraisha! If you want to go exploring, then go exploring. I'm not going with you though, so don't beg."

"I wasn't begging—"

"Yes, you were, and I'm not going!" Katja roared.

The unlikely pair had been together for over a week now—sharing stories, food, laughter, and dreams. Each night since their first meeting, Katja and Lauraisha's dreams had played host to the same voice begging aid—a voice which grew in desperation with each passing night.

At first, Katja had suspected that the Dreams of Calling had somehow come from Lauraisha herself. The young human certainly had an uncanny ability to sense the tone of Katja's thoughts and feelings. Katja could almost smell the dreamdrifter magic within Lauraisha, especially when they discussed the subsequent dreams they shared.

Lauraisha, however, had sworn to Katja that the mental Calling was not coming from her. Instead the human was certain that the voice belonged to someone else residing in the canyon. The naïve Tyglesean, of course, wanted to immediately investigate its source. Katja, on the other paw, was not quite so eager to trudge all over the canyon in search of an ethereal voice that could just as easily issue from a foe as it could from a friend. And this divergence of opinion was finally getting full voice through the current argument.

Katja had expected Lauraisha to storm off as soon as the werecat had roared at her. Instead, though, the human just watched her. "It isn't like you to retreat from a good challenge, so why are you so uneasy?"

"Nothing," the werecat said as she tried to smooth her bristling neck and tail fur.

"Katja, I know when you're troubled about something."

The werecat flicked her ears and glowered at the human. Lauraisha crossed her arms on her chest and waited.

"Jierira, very well, then." The werecat finally gave in. "Before I found sanctuary inside this canyon, I had monsters hunting me. I would prefer to not go looking for whatever voice is calling us and find my enemies waiting for me instead."

"What enemies?"

"Asheken hordes."

"Deadwalkers! You can't be serious! Are they in the canyon?"

Katja was slack-jawed. "You know what they are?"

"Of course! I've heard a few stories of zombies killing and eating Sylvans during the First and Second Age Wars. After meeting you, I've put more stock in those tales than most of my countrymen."

"What do you mean, 'after meeting me'?"

"Most of my countrymen don't believe werecats exist. My brothers would laugh at me if I told them about you. But since you do exist, then perhaps the wars really happened and zombies and vampires and imps and all those other races of deadwalkers exist as well."

"You know, you're rather smart for a Tyglesean." Katja grinned.

"Thank you so much," Lauraisha said derisively before returning the smile. "Now, are the deadwalkers inside the canyon?"

"If they were, they would have found us both long before now. I think the Ring Spells left from the First War of Ages still shield the canyon from deadwalker infiltration."

"I hope that you're correct or we'll both be in a pit of trouble. This may be all-the-more reason to search the canyon for this voice. After all, if the deadwalkers know you're here and find a way past the spells, it will only be a matter of time before they find and destroy us. On the other hand, they could just wait for us to come out of the canyon. Why are they pursuing you?"

"I'm not certain, but they want me very much. They killed off my entire clan while hunting me—"

Katja shut her mouth on her betraying words, but it was too late. She cursed herself silently when she saw Lauraisha's face blanch in horror.

"The dead faces in my dreams...those were your clansmen?" she whispered her words through trembling lips.

"You knew?"

"I have shared those and the dreams of the voice with you since I met you. Oh, Katja, I am so sorry. No wonder you seem so lonely." Lauraisha uttered those words and stepped forward with her arms ready to embrace the werecat.

"Don't touch me! Don't you realize what I am? Cursed! All of those I have ever loved have died because of me and now you will die too if they find you near me! It's hopeless!"

Katja withered to the ground and understood nothing but the anguished sobs leaking from her jowls. Lauraisha's small hands wrapped around her shaking shoulders and held the werecat until her tears subsided. When they finally did, Lauraisha loosened her grip and sighed.

"We make quite the pair. You have nothing to go home to and I have no safe home in which to stay." She began rocking on her heels and chewing her lower lip thoughtfully. "Quite the pair indeed..."

"I'm sorry I brought you into this," Katja said after she had regained some of her composure. "It was never my intention to cause you any harm. It seems that I'm cursed no matter what I do." The werecat spat in bitter self-contempt.

"My father wishes me dead, so I would be in danger whether you had met me or not. Stop blaming yourself."

Katja blinked in shock and horror at the human. "What?"

Lauraisha sighed and then explained that on the day of her birth a priest had told her father to be wary of his youngest child, because she was prophesied to one day destroy his power. From that day on, her father blamed Lauraisha for making her mother barren with her birth and swore that his youngest child would have no part in the family heritage.

To protect her from her father's further wrath, Lauraisha's mother extracted a promise from her father not to harm her. She then sent the child into exile in the unused parts of the old castle of Summersted. Lauraisha's older brothers were charged with her care and tutelage, while priests and monks oversaw the finer points of her education.

"Summersted!" Katja stared at Lauraisha with renewed awe.

"Ah, you know the name I see. You may as well know, then. Not only do I have aristocratic blood flowing through my veins, but I actually bleed maroon."

Maroon, Katja knew, was the color of royalty. This meant that Lauraisha was the youngest daughter born to King Kaylor Ryhnus and Queen Manasa Astrat'a of Tyglesea.

"Oh, stop that!" Lauraisha said when Katja began to bow to her with both palms raised to show her complete fealty.

"Now, if it's possible, I feel even worse about pulling you into danger."

"Will you please be quiet! I told you before that it doesn't matter in the slightest if you are with me or not. I'm still hunted by my father's own guards."

"But you just said that King Kaylor swore to your mother, Queen Manasa, not to harm you."

"Yes, but Kaylor is never very good at keeping his promises, not even to my mother." Lauraisha's expression could have frozen a field of flowers. "I narrowly escaped an assassination attempt before fleeing the country. If it hadn't been for Tyron's speed and intelligence, I would not have made it this far. When the horse was born, Father thought that Tyron would be worthless because of his cross-breeding and yet he has proven superior to most other horses at every opportunity."

Katja turned her gaze to the eighteen-hands-tall stallion with newfound respect. The huge beast might be finicky toward the werecat, but he was certainly gentle with his rider.

Katja turned back to Lauraisha. "It seems that we really are in the same pit, aren't we?"

"Indeed. I'd say this is all the more reason to find the

voice. If we are both being chased, then maybe he can help us out of this dreadful mess. Let's go exploring, please?"

"Have you seen the humans Kaylor sent after you hunting in the canyon?"

"No. They probably are having the same sort of trouble with the magic shields as your Asheken are."

"I doubt it. Deadwalkers are wicked by nature. However, your human hunters may not be malevolent themselves even though they are obeying a tyrant's orders. If that is the case, they will be able to move through the Ring Spells just as you and I did."

"If so, why aren't they here then?"

"Probably because they met the deadwalkers first."

Lauraisha and Katja both grimaced at the thought.

"Look, as dangerous as it is to search for him, the source of this voice may be our only hope of escape from either set of hunters," Lauraisha said. "I am going to find him no matter what you decide. Even so, I think it's far safer for both of us if we seek him together."

The werecat growled at her in frustration. She hated the risk that this posed. And yet, as much danger as she had already added to Lauraisha's life, Katja knew she could not justify abandoning the human now.

"Very well, I will go with you," Katja said, hoping that her decision to protect her newest ally would tip the human's scales of destiny in favor of life. So far, no one else had proved that fortunate.

* * *

"Gorgeous!" Lauraisha exclaimed, pointing to the mists retreating from their earlier perches in the crags' shadows.

Katja nodded her agreement. She could see for a league from atop the knoll where she and the human were standing. Together the midday light and breeze caressed the face of Kings' Lake and kissed the waters with a myriad of sparkles that danced in honor of the sun. The clear, warm day had made for fine fishing and might yet provide decent hunting too.

Even Tyron pawed the ground and nickered in seeming appreciation of their newest adventure. Katja watched the sorrel stallion with amusement. The huge horse really was an odd beast—the result of an accidental siring between a draft horse and Lauraisha's father's prized racing mare Marissa. Tyron had inherited his sire's large size coupled with his dam's short head, swift legs, and finicky personality. When the horse caught Katja inspecting him, he flattened his ears and bared his teeth in warning.

Katja's answering grin was wicked. "He's so much fun to annoy!"

Lauraisha grimaced. "I wish you two would learn to like each other. It's maddening to have to stand guard between you all day."

"It won't be as much fun once he realizes that I have no intention of eating him."

The human shook her head and sighed dramatically before she and Katja carefully ascended the narrow slope above the knoll. The pair climbed a lower outcropping to the southeast of the canyon, surveying the scene of sun-dappled water and wondered what to do next. Ever since their morning argument, Katja had quietly followed Lauraisha's leading toward Crown Canyon's eastern wall without knowing what exactly the human was hunting. The growing emptiness of the werecat's stomach had all but undermined her remaining patience when Lauraisha's searching expression turned triumphant.

"There!" she said, pointing to an outcropping slightly northeast of their position. "That's where we need to go."

"Are you sure?" growled the werecat.

"Absolutely! It will be a slight deviation in our present course, but it's important nonetheless."

"Deviation?"

"Yes, yes, yes, of course," the human said impatiently as if her statement cleared all questions or doubts away from her companion's mind.

Katja flicked her ears and snorted in annoyance. It was so irritating when Lauraisha refused to explain herself.

Lauraisha turned to the werecat. "Shall we go?"

Katja rolled her eyes and worked her way down the hillside behind the slow human. They turned northeast and followed a faint pathway through the craggy comb toward

Lauraisha's goal. Lauraisha then turned sharply southeast once they neared her original goal and skirted around the granite spires' edge until she reached the base where the spires met to form a single face of rock that fed into the rest of a mountain.

She began rummaging around the ground. "I know it's here somewhere…"

But Katja was not looking at the ground near Lauraisha's feet. Instead she was staring at a place two body-lengths above their heads.

"Lauraisha, come stand beside me."

The human did as the werecat instructed and suddenly shared Katja's smile.

"When in doubt—"

"—always look up!" the human completed while grinning.

Katja had discovered a perfectly round hole not much taller than a ten-winter-old catling, which had been cut through the side of the granite wall. Runes were carved around its edge—weather-worn yet still legible.

"How do we get up there?" Lauraisha asked in frustration.

Katja studied the cliff around the hole and finally spied a slight outcropping that—like her original pathway into the canyon—had been fashioned into crude stairs. The steps began just out of their reach.

"Climb on my back. I think I can jump us both up there as long as you don't throw me off balance."

The human nodded and clambered onto the werecat's back. Taking a deep breath, Katja jumped and managed to land solidly on the fourth step. The two made their way to the hole and stopped at its entrance to study the runes.

"I've seen these runes before," said Katja. She traced their strokes with a paw. "They were mingled in my dreams the first night after I met you."

"What do they say?"

"I don't know, but I know they are important."

"I've never seen their like."

"Judging by the detail of the carvings, they must be an ancient form of Drän."

"What's Drän?"

"It's the language used by the dwarves. Since it, Felis,

and Jakkle have similar linguistic roots, you'd think I would be able to understand some of these characters, but I have no idea about any of this." Katja paused while she traced the runes again. "I guess the only way to find out what they mean is to explore the tunnel."

"This will be a tight squeeze. Are you sure this is wise?"

"Says the one who was desperate to explore in the first place." Katja smirked. "No, of course it isn't wise, but it is necessary. These runes are somehow important and I need to discover why."

"Very well, after you then."

Katja was suddenly grateful for her small size as she wormed her way through the hole into the tunnel beyond. She could hear Lauraisha crawling behind her and called over her shoulder for the human to keep her lytzahn dagger ready in case they ran into rock that required chipping away. *Or,* she thought with revulsion, *in case we meet a hostile creature.*

After three body-lengths of crawling, the tunnel thankfully opened up into a dim chamber large enough for them to stand. Lauraisha was apparently just as happy about this as Katja because she immediately slumped against a wall and sighed upon pulling herself out of the tunnel.

"Where are you? Katja?"

"What do you mean where am I? You're looking straight at me."

"I am? Oh. I can't see a cursed thing."

"Jierira, wonderful," Katja snorted. "I forgot humans were so blind."

"Be nice! It's bad enough not to be able to see my own hand in front of my face without being harassed about it."

"Wait a moment," Katja said while searching the walls and floor for something to burn. Nestled in one corner, she discovered a rusted iron ring cradling a crude torch.

"Lauraisha, I need your flint and steel."

The human took both from her belt purse and held them out before her. Katja took them, struck an igniting spark, and lifted the flaming torch off the wall before giving the fire starters back to the smiling female.

"Thank you!"

"Gladly. Shall we continue?"

Lauraisha nodded and followed her down a larger passageway that wound left out of the main chamber. They walked hunched-over throughout its length past three more openings to smaller chambers until Katja found a second large chamber with a rightward tunnel branch. Her claws scraped along the wall as she led Lauraisha down the passage and eventually into a chamber with a floor covered in black sand.

Katja stopped at the chamber's mouth and waited for Lauraisha to catch up.

"Why the black powder?" the human asked.

"I don't know." Katja sniffed the cool tangy air. "This doesn't smell right."

She bent low to sniff the sand. As she did so, a burning ember fell from the torch onto the sand. They watched a tongue of flame bloom from the contact and then kindle a good-sized blaze in the sand.

This time Lauraisha breathed deeply. "It is black powder mixed with crumbled peat moss to make it burn steadily. We need to get out of here before we take in too much foul air. Come quickly!"

But Katja wasn't moving. Her eyes had spied something that had been hidden in the shadows before the conflagration had fully sparked. On the opposite side of the chamber, a round, paw-sized stone lay on an altar that had been carved out of the left sidewall. Instinctively, the werecat knew that that blue-gray stone had to be rescued before she left the catacombs.

"I have to get to that stone."

"Have you taken leave of your sanity? That fire will surely scorch you if you try to cross."

"I know, but I have to retrieve that stone nonetheless."

Instead of arguing further, Lauraisha pointed to the left wall and told Katja to use the paw holds she found there. Katja hesitated, and then launched herself onto the first shelf she could see. Her back paw almost slipped and she had to take a moment to balance herself before jumping to the next jut of stone.

She reached the carved altar after three more short jumps, one of which almost caused a burn because her watering eyes had misjudged the distance. By now, the room was clouded with sooty smoke and carried a stench horrible enough to make her gag.

"Hurry or we'll suffocate!" Lauraisha shouted over the crackling conflagration.

Katja grabbed the leather pouch on which the dark-hued stone sat and then, on impulse, bowed toward it until she had brushed her forehead against its smooth, warm surface in silent salute.

The moment her head met the stone, a wide ray of multi-hued light shot from the altar to connect with the entrance. It looked similar to the one that had brought her through the Ring Spells bordering Crown Canyon. She immediately jumped into it and ran its length toward a very wide-eye Lauraisha just as the fire found a concentrated amount of powder and caused blue flame to explode from floor to ceiling.

"Run! Run!"

They sprinted hunchbacked toward the first chamber guided by Katja's previous claw marks along the walls. They found the chamber they had discovered second and stopped within its cool depths to clear their burning lungs and let Katja string the stone's leather pouch across her shoulders.

They were about to continue onto the tunnel that led toward the first chamber when Katja heard a scraping hiss come from within its depths. The werecat stopped dead in her tracks and hissed a warning to Lauraisha. A huge serpent was slithering steadily toward them through the tunnel, just beyond the torch's circle of light.

When she turned to find an escape down one of the other five tunnels connected to the chamber, Katja realized by sound and smell that a basel snake now occupied every tunnel save the one they had just exited. They were trapped!

"Lauraisha, stay away from the tunnels and be on your guard!"

"What's coming?"

Before Katja could answer, the triangular head of the first basel slipped into view. Its head was the size of her chest. Lauraisha screamed as it struck. Katja feinted left out of the path of its attack and swept unsheathed claws at the snake's right opalescent eye. The creature hissed in pain as Katja's middle claw found its mark. She pulled her paw free and blocked the snake's clumsy lunge with her opposite forearm—dancing away from the greenish-gray head.

She spied the shadows of the second and third snakes out of the corner of her eye. They had reached the tunnel entrances simultaneously. She lunged under the first basel on its blind side just as it reared its head, and she struck at its neck glands with both paws. She felt jarring pain as her paws struck bone and staggered under the snake's weight as it began to convulse. She laboriously pinned the twitching body against the wall with a small boulder and then jumped back into the fray.

"Lauraisha, they're most vulnerable if you strike at the spine just behind their heads!"

The human had drawn her forearm-length dagger and stood waiting in a loose stance for one of the two snakes to lunge out of the tunnels. Katja grabbed the torch from Lauraisha's hand, lit the wall sconce behind her, and then threw the torch at the nearest basel. It hit the monster full in the face. The serpent ducked its head, leaving the human open to strike at the base of its skull. Lauraisha drove her knife through the bone—the resulting crack was nauseating.

Two serpents now lay dead, but the other two had entered the cave. Katja had engaged the third, but Lauraisha stood vulnerable to the fourth because her knife was still lodged solidly in the second snake's skull. Katja realized with horror that the human had no weapon, but the werecat could do nothing to help her while she was still fighting this serpent.

Katja heard Lauraisha scream just as the werecat sidestepped a ferocious lunge-and-snap. She swiped at the snake's scaly head—leaving faint gashes along its length—and rolled to her left while trying to see what had happened to her companion. A chill crawled the length of Katja's spine. Lauraisha was nowhere in sight and the fourth basel had now turned its full attention to Katja.

"Lauraisha!"

The serpents' malevolent hisses were all that answered her.

As the smaller third snake lunged at Katja, she again feinted left and jabbed defensively, all while trying to edge closer to Lauraisha's last-known position near the dead second snake. Lauraisha was gone! As Katja looked around in shock, the fourth snake took the opportunity to slip toward Katja's right and corner her near the place of Lauraisha's last stand. Katja realized at that moment that there was an opening in the floor just large enough for the human to fit through. Lauraisha must have fallen down it when the fourth snake had gone after her. The snake was too large to follow her down the hole, so it had focused on a closer meal: Katja.

The werecat snarled in defiance as the third snake slithered alongside the fourth to trap her. Then, in a display of dominance, the fourth basel struck at the smaller serpent when it came too close. The hierarchical dispute between the two allowed Katja enough time to wrench the human's blade from the dead snake's head and drop down the hole after her companion. Her last thought as she descended into utter darkness was a prayer to the Creator to let them survive whatever came next.

V

A DEAD KING RISEN?

K atja slid down the smooth darkness of a tunnel for what seemed an eternity, clutching Lauraisha's dagger in one paw and cradling the warm, round stone in the other. She saw no light until she felt the floor of the stone ramp widen underneath her. The ramp melded gracefully into a smooth floor and the werecat's descent finally slowed to a stop.

She stared in awe at the expansive cavern looming over two spruce-lengths high above her head. The cavern's ceiling boasted glowing stars spinning in a perfect model of the night sky. She saw the noble phoenix illuminated to the west, the mighty dragon to the east, the first fireforger Aribem with the great northern star — the Seer's Jewel — in his scepter, and the gallant hippopyre marking the south. These star-etched kings stood in their nightly courts ready to do battle for the sky's protection.

The starry guardians of these kings also stood in protection over the night: the salamander and pyrefay to the northeast, the manticore and sphinx to the northwest, the gorgon and chimera to the southwest, and the hippocampus and nymph to the southeast. A hazy constellation stood in the center of these kings and guardians. The uncanny figure loomed over all the heavens — all stars bowing humbly before it. Katja's clan's astronomers often called it the symbol of the Creator since it stood central to these other creations. Katja stared at it in wonder. It had a more defined shape in this model instead of the misty uncertainty it showed when seen in the actual night sky. The figure reminded her simultaneously of an eye, a mouth, and wind.

The dizzy werecat looked away from the scene and surveyed the chamber. Incandescent blue light drew her attention and she stared toward what must be the center of the room. A flaming azure orb bobbed above a pedestal as if it were a lure on a fishing string resting in a pond. *How odd.*

"Lauraisha, where are you?"

"Behind you."

Katja turned around to see the princess sitting near her by another ramp exit on the cavern floor.

"Are you hurt?"

"I caught my ankle on something sharp on my way down. It's really sore, but I think I can manage to walk on it with a little care. Are you well?"

"Well enough. Glad to be rid of those snakes, too. It was a good fight though," the werecat grinned at the human through the cavern's gloom. "Oh, I almost forgot…your lytzahn, Your Highness."

Katja handed Lauraisha the dagger with a flourish and then helped her to her feet. The human slowly drew herself up off the floor and, with dagger drawn, began cautiously creeping toward the azure light while silently motioning for Katja to follow.

The faint light illuminated Lauraisha's face enough for Katja to note her strangely hungry expression. Instinctively, Katja held the large stone in its sack a moment before shifting it to swing on her back. Only then did she follow Lauraisha toward the uncanny light.

As the females came closer, Katja realized that the light orb was indeed suspended above a carved stone altar similar to the one upon which the werecat had found her mysterious stone. Sapphire and ivory hues swirled and chased within the sphere's depths, giving light enough to see the detail of the four stone shrines surrounding the altar. Each shrine was intricately carved in the shape of the constellation king above it. All were situated on a circular dais that measured half of a spruce-length in diameter.

The werecat yanked the Tyglesean back just as she was about to step onto the dais with her hand outstretched.

"Are you daft!"

"What?"

"You don't know where we are or why this is here and yet you immediately want to touch it! Terrible things can happen when you meddle with magic!"

"After your act in the black powder room, you're cautioning me?"

"That was different. I just knew that I had to protect that stone."

"And I just know that I have to touch that sphere."

"That sphere is a floating fireball! It will sear your hand off!"

"No, it won't because the voice in our dreams—"

Lauraisha was interrupted by a vengeful hiss. The third basel from their previous fight burst through the tunnel Katja had just exited and skidded toward them. Its girth caught Katja full in the stomach and knocked her, dazed, into a statue. Its fangs then found Lauraisha's shoulder while her dagger simultaneously found its throat. Lauraisha screamed in agony and fell under the snake's convulsing weight. Despite her best tugs, the human could not remove the snake's broken fang from her bleeding abrasion.

Once her mind was clear and her lungs were full, Katja crawled to the other female and heaved the scaly carcass off of her. She then dragged Lauraisha further into the sphere's burning light so that she could see well enough to tie a tourniquet, dig out the fang, and lance the wound.

"Bite on this and brace yourself," she handed the human a wood chip that lay on the stone floor near them and, after Lauraisha's grimaced nod, began delving into the wound with a claw.

The fang fragment was deep enough to scrape the bone and proved grueling for both of them to dig out. By the time Katja had finished the task, her flattened ears were ringing with the human's semi-muffled screams. The snake's venom had already spread through Lauraisha's body enough to paralyze her right side and Katja realized with horror that the poison was already too deep to simply extract. It was spreading unchecked through the human's body, rapidly destroying flesh and function, and Katja was helpless to stop it.

She looked into Lauraisha's already fading eyes, her own brimming with tears.

"Lauraisha? Lauraisha!" the Feliconian shook her only companion. "Stay with me!"

"Kat…"

"Not another death. Not on my paws. Don't leave me! Lauraisha, don't go!"

The human mumbled something through the left side of her whitening lips.

"What do I do? How can I save you?"

"Touch…"

"Touch? Touch what?"

"Fire…" The human panted the slurred words.

Katja looked at the female lying in her arms. What choice did she have? Lauraisha's heart would soon be stilled by the venom. Katja may as well grant her friend's last request even if she thought it asinine. The werecat lifted the human in her arms and stretched the human's right hand toward the glowing azure sphere.

"Creator, help us!" the werecat cried, and thrust the human's hand into the sphere.

As Lauraisha's fingers touched the flames, the jolt of the contact shot through her body and slammed into Katja. The force sent Katja tumbling back into a statue upon the stone dais yet again. She hunched and groaned over her broken right forelimb for a moment. Then she felt the pain melt away just as it had when she had crossed the Ring Spells' barrier into Crown Canyon. The bones within her mended themselves within mere moments. She stared at her right forearm in awe and then looked for Lauraisha. Lauraisha was not lying on the dais as she should have been. Instead the human had been lifted into the air above the altar with the blue sphere floating directly above her upturned face—her unconscious countenance eerily lit by its swirling fire. As Katja watched, the sphere broke open and ribbons of flame arced around the human's rigid body—touching the altar under her suspended feet as Lauraisha began to rotate above it.

"Lauraisha!" Katja screamed.

The human's arms never left her sides as she spun among

the swirling blazes. The flames shot and spiraled around her body until at last they all struck her simultaneously. Katja screeched and turned her eyes from the resulting explosion of light.

As the flash dimmed, Katja heard a voice intone in the darkness: "Princess Lauraisha, Katja Escari, I honor you!"

Sudden flames kindled in the braziers hanging from stone buttresses jutting from the ceiling and from atop stone basins along the cavern walls. The dais beneath Katja's paws quaked and rumbled as the solid stone pillar forming its foundation pushed out of the floor. The dais finally halted its movement halfway between the sandy floor and the stony ceiling, with Katja at eye level with the visage of a colossal monument that had been previously concealed in the darkness.

Katja licked her lips in apprehension. This statue was the effigy of a great griffin carved from amber, granite, and alabaster. It loomed over the room—its agate eyes piercing through Katja's soul as if the griffin were *alive*. It had the gold-feathered head, yellow talons, and chestnut-colored chest of a golden eagle and the muscular lower body and mane of a rare white lion. Huge wings formed a canopy of stone feathers behind its back. The griffin carving sat perched on a bejeweled stone throne with its left talon gripping the throne arm and its tuft-ended tail regally draped around its lower body.

Katja realized as she gazed upon it that the statue must be the stone counterpart of the dead King Canuche, the most powerful of any griffin in Sylvan history. Breathless, Katja bowed to the statue and then hurried to where Lauraisha lay on the altar. She checked the human's breathing. She was alive, but unresponsive, and the werecat wondered how long it would be before she must bury another being she had come to care about.

"Take heart! She will not die."

Katja whirled to stare at the effigy. Had its amber eyes just twitched? The rumbling of the room began anew as the carving shook, and then shimmered. Rock moved like flesh and then the creature shifted its head to look first at Lauraisha, and then at the bowing werecat. "This simply will not do, for I must speak with both of you."

Katja felt a surge of energy pass through the air between

the statue and the human and felt her heart quicken as Lauraisha finally stirred.

"Awaken, Princess. We have much to discuss."

Katja looked up toward the effigy and realized that it was talking with the same authoritative voice as the one in her dreams. How could this be? King Canuche had died centuries ago during the Second War of Ages. How could a stone statue have the ability to speak with the authority of a long-dead king?

"Please don't fear me, Feliconian. I have called you here to give you aid and to seek yours in return."

"Why were you so urgent in your messages, My Sir? I could barely hear my own thoughts over your dream-voice." Lauraisha had propped herself up on one arm. She looked healthy but dazed.

"Lauraisha! Are you all right? Are you hurt?"

"She should recover well. Dragon fire has immense healing properties."

"Is that supposed to comfort me?" The human was trembling. "I feel as though I could burst into flames again at any moment!"

The werecat was aghast. "Please, Lauraisha, don't raise your voice to one so honored as His Majesty, King Canuche."

With a grating sound, the monument shifted its head to scrutinize her. "So you recognize me even in this façade? I am truly honored, Katja." The king shifted its lithic gaze and focused again on Lauraisha, its eyes passive. Lauraisha stood paralyzed—with fear splotching her face. "Thank you for being so persistent in your quest to find me, Your Royal Highness."

Tears came to Katja's eyes as the griffin bowed low on his throne toward Lauraisha and then to the werecat. A king as great as Canuche should never bow to someone like her. "Why do you do this, Your Majesty?" she asked.

"Because of all that you have already lost and all that I still must ask of you, it is only proper that I show such respect, Katja. I am truly sorry that the quest of finding me nearly cost you and Lauraisha your lives—and, worse, the lives and freedom of those you love. I tried to warn you both of the dangers you faced, but after three centuries of slumber

I was not strong enough to weave more than a simple Spell of Calling into your dreams. Still you are here and Unturned, and I take some joy in that."

"What is it that you wish of us, Your Majesty?" Lauraisha asked formally.

The king sighed. "What I must ask you will test your courage. I must ask you to leave Crown Canyon."

The werecat was stunned. "But where else would we go, My Sir? This place offers us what little protection we have!"

"I know, but I need you to seek out the twelve members of the Ring of Sorcerers who are presently convened on the Isle of Summons."

Katja gasped. "That island is on the leeward side of the Nyghe sol Dyvesé mountain range! It's over six hundred leagues southeast of this canyon!"

Canuche sighed. "Please understand that I do not make this request lightly. I have sought the minds of many beings since the Sphinx's death cry first woke me, but there are no others as able or willing as the two of you. No one that I trust to survive such a perilous journey."

Katja stared at him. "The Sphinx is *dead*?"

He nodded.

The werecat licked her lips in nervousness. *With the Sphinx gone and no one else to protect the continent, he asks us to do this? He's mad!*

"But what protection would we have on the road?" Lauraisha asked. "Even now this place is besieged by my father's troops to the west and Katja's clan's murderers to the east!"

The griffin looked sharply at the werecat. "How many of your clan survived the deadwalkers?"

"Only my brother Kayten and I survived to anoint the bodies of our kin," answered the werecat.

"But you did burn them too, didn't you?"

"Of course, My Sir! I would never dishonor them! Their bodies were purified with oil and fire as tradition dictates."

"That is good, lest your clansmen become deadwalkers themselves." The werecat and human trembled at Canuche's remark. "Where is your brother now?"

"Destroyed, according to the ghoul Curqak," Katja said

before explaining the horrific events that had befallen her and her clan. As she finished she noticed Lauraisha stifle a sniffle beside her and could have sworn that she had also glimpsed a tear rolling down the griffin's stone cheek.

"I knew parts of what had occurred through your dreams, but not all. Words fail to describe my sorrow for your loss," the griffin king said. He once again bowed his head. "You mentioned a ghoul by name."

She nodded. "He called himself Curqak, My Sir. The name is familiar to me, but I cannot think why."

The griffin nodded, the corners of its powerful beak straightening into a grim line. "You likely heard his name while studying your clan's histories about the Second War of Ages, young one. Curqak is a particularly clever deadwalker. Beware."

"Who is Curqak's master, Your Majesty?"

The griffin hesitated and then sighed. "He once belonged to Lord Calais, but now he answers to the eldest of Víchí elders, the First Turned."

Katja felt the blood drain from her face. "Luther?"

The king nodded. "The very same. It is possible that Curqak's orders regarding your clan came from a different source. He also could be partially driven by his own desires."

Katja gulped. "Is it even possible for a deiner der seele to have any agenda apart from that of his soul's master?"

Canuche nodded. "So long as it doesn't contradict the soul-servant's master's agenda, yes."

Lauraisha moved to grip the suddenly stiff werecat's shoulder. "Oh, Katja, what are you going to do?"

"Fight them and repay their actions toward my family if I can."

"Then I will help you," the human murmured.

"As shall I, if you'll indulge me."

"No! Neither of you can help me! I cannot allow anyone else to come to harm because of their association with me."

"Alone you will surely fail!"

"He speaks the truth, Katja. You will need help, which I freely give."

"And both of you will require the assistance of others if you are to succeed."

"No!" Katja's ears went flat with her snarl. "You, Lauraisha, you almost died in my arms moments ago! I don't know by what miracle you were just healed—"

"Pyrekin panacea and mage fire," Canuche interjected.

"—but I'll not allow another to die in my stead! Not now! Not ever again!"

"That is not your decision, werecat, and I'm coming with you whether you 'allow' it or not!"

Katja stared at Lauraisha in awe. She had never seen the human angry before nor did she really believe that the human had been capable of real rage. Katja hid a sudden smile at the other's resolve.

"What!"

"Nothing," the werecat said and turned back to Canuche. "How is it, Your Majesty, that you came to be here of all places…and alive?"

"Ah," the king grimaced. "That is a truly dark tale. I, or more correctly my soul, has dwelled in this ancient dwarven fortress since the first battle of the Second War of Ages."

"Why did the dwarves abandon this place?"

"That is a story for another time and place. Perhaps Katja can enlighten you on that particular catastrophe while the two of you are traveling together."

Katja was suddenly alert. "My apologies, My Sir, but neither one of us have agreed to your proposed journey."

"That is true, you have not. I do believe, however, that you both might be more willing to entertain my proposal once you listen to my story." Canuche closed his eyes and bowed his shuddering head. After a moment, the griffin king spoke:

"Of all hymns for heroes brave,
These keens pierce to the quick.
A ballad for free and slave,
None better can proclaim.

"Thus I sing of griffins gone
Whose bones lay pale and thick
Upon the Eppon Vale's lawn
Where justice has no fame.

"There stood the griffins' great might
Against the walking dead.
They stood strong for three suns' sight
Until the fourth day's drain.

"As dusk fell upon their wings,
Each griffin's wild war bray
Shattered all amidst their king
Of Víchí claim or name.

"Yet their czar lay cold and dead;
Lost was their regal chain.
While griffins wept on his head
Their sobs stung heaven's main.

"O weeping wails did persist
Past the break of dim day.
A storm amassed in vale's mist
To tame the Asheken aim.

"Thunder boomed and lightning burned,
While wind did swirl and sway.
The firestorm thus born now churned
Upon the bloody fray.

"Flames did flare upon the mist
To strike all in their midst
Whipping through each last resist
Thwarting all but pyrefay.

"Replacement troops stood silent
While tears flowed abundant
At the sight so abhorrent
Shown by cruelest sun ray.

"There the brave lay black and burned;
No live griffin remnant.
Mage fire consumed all those Turned
And squelched the loudest bray.

"Cry evermore for those lost
Upon that blackened day,
But sing longer of the cost
Allayed by dauntless play."

Canuche bowed his head and Katja and Lauraisha both copied his motion in honor of the righteous dead. It had been a long time since Katja had listened to "The Griffins' Bray" and she felt all the more moved because of the identity of its singer. The ballad spoke of the Second and Fourth Kirni Griffin War Wings' last stand against the deadwalkers during the Second War of Ages and the catastrophe that resulted from their fireforger mages' use of the rites of Crawhmongue.

"The legends tell of your death amidst the Eppon Gue Battle. How then did you escape, Your Majesty?" the werecat asked in awe.

"Escape?" Canuche laughed bitterly. "I did not escape; I was betrayed!"

Katja and Lauraisha frowned.

"I was deceived by a mage who, while professing himself to be an ally, lured me to this doomed bondage and betrayed us all! Perhaps I should explain the whole of the story for our Tyglesean princess?"

Lauraisha emphatically nodded.

"Very well. The Battle of Eppon Gue took place in what was then called Eppon Valley, which is but a few leagues from this canyon. The griffins under my command were defending several villages within the vale from deadwalkers. Fresh warriors and supplies had been delayed by a rock slide on the mountain valley's only entry road. Instead of retreating through the air and leaving the valley's village refugees vulnerable to Asheken corruption, we held our position against the onslaught for three days and nights in the air and on the ground."

Canuche explained that while the battle raged, he and his rider Ella were attacked by several deadwalkers while trying to save one of their allies—a Feliconian skinshifter. The werecat ally then betrayed and attacked them—causing both griffin and rider to crash into a stony embankment. Canuche's rider managed to escape, but the griffin king was not as fortunate.

Canuche was mortally wounded in the fall and could do nothing to defend himself when the deadwalkers attacked again. A vampire performed one of the Bites of Turning on him, separating Canuche's soul from his body and killing him. Instead of being Turned into a deadwalker; however, Canuche's soul was sucked into the vampire's bloodstone for safekeeping.

The vampire then took wing to deliver the stone to Luther himself. However, she was attacked by one of the griffin warriors as she flew out of the valley and dropped the stone while the griffin pursued her through the sky.

Canuche sighed. "The stone shattered when it hit the rocks above this place, releasing my soul. I knew then that if I did not find a suitable body to contain my being and a way to purify my soul, that I would never gain entry to the Wraith Realms. Instead I would waft through our world in the Erde Realm as a poltergeist, Tainted by the deadwalkers' evil. Rather than cursing all who came near me, I chose exile in this dwarven effigy. It was fortuitous that the dwarves were so skilled at capturing one's likeness in both stone and magic. When I found this place, the Ring Spells of Crown Canyon helped to purify me and this carving provided my soul with a temporary body to house it. It is most ironic, however, that what was meant as a gift in my honor has now become my prison.

"I watched through dreams and visions as the Crawhmongue firestorm swept through the ranks of deadwalkers and then screamed as its backdraft hit my own warriors, including my own beloved lifemate." Another tear rolled down Canuche's stone cheek. "That valley is called Eppon Gue Vale now, and it is fitting that such a place would be shunned as a site of eternal mourning and death.

"I have wept many times as my dreams showed my once brave race's descent into leaderless chaos after the war. Now, griffins are strewn along the southeastern portion of the Nyghe sol Dyvesé range, and the glory and honor of our former kingdoms are all but lost in bickering bitterness and clan wars. And I can do nothing! I can do nothing to mend the splintering of my race; nor can I join the ranks of my forefathers in the Halls of the Divine, because I cannot leave this statue's confines without the aid of powerful mages." The griffin's head drooped.

"Why are mages essential?" Lauraisha asked.

She must be well, thought Katja. *She's asking questions about everything again.*

"Only a wraithwalker's and fireforger's combined power would be enough to set my soul free from this place."

Now Katja was curious. "Why both? Wouldn't the fireforger be enough?"

"No, a wraithwalker is needed to help the fireforger call a Pyrekin to help guide my soul from the Erde Realm through the First Veil into the Wraith Realm and beyond. Because of the unique curse upon my being, I do not trust a fireforger alone to free my soul."

Katja nodded in understanding while Lauraisha continued to look perplexed.

"Are you all right, Lauraisha?" Katja asked.

"I feel perfectly well, but I'm a bit confused by all of this."

"I'll explain His Majesty's discussion later," Katja gave her a wraith of a smile and turned once more to Canuche. "What do you require of us, Your Majesty?"

"I *ask* you to deliver a message to the Ring of Sorcerers who oversee the Council of Mages on the Isle of Summons. You must tell them of the Asheken deadwalker invasion and of the subsequent doom that awaits all Sylvans should the Ring and the Council fail to act in defense of this continent and all of its races. I ask this favor and another, that you would return one day and help free me from bondage.

"Since I can neither leave this place nor influence those far beyond its borders, I cannot offer you much protection against the dangers that lurk along your path outside this hallowed canyon. However, I can offer you wise counsel should you deem to accept it while you are here.

"If you do these tasks for me, you must do so by the peace of your own conscience. I am the ruler of a nation no longer, nor do I rule you, therefore I cannot command you. I can only ask as one Sylvan to another. Would you do this for me please?"

Katja and Lauraisha gazed at one another. Katja could see the human's face reflecting the fear lurking in her own mind. "Is there no one else? As much as I long to see my clan avenged, I know I am not ready to accomplish that task. There must be others who are better equipped to undertake this journey."

"There are a few who might prove gifted or courageous enough," the king said while watching Katja with a measure of calculation she did not understand. "But great deeds are not accomplished by the able; they are accomplished by the willing."

Katja bent her head in concentration. If they stayed here in the canyon, they would be safe enough from the deadwalkers; however, they still might have to deal with Lauraisha's father's soldiers. That would by dangerous enough. If they left the canyon, they might manage to evade Kaylor's troops, but still have to deal with the far more dangerous threat of deadwalkers. On the other paw, if they did nothing, other Sylvans would die and be Turned. Could her conscience even *let* her hide while deadwalkers massacred even more Sylvans?

The faces of her brothers and sister came to Katja's mind then, and she shook her head. *No, if I have the chance to stop them and stem the slaughter, then I must take it.*

Katja looked up at her friend now sitting demurely on the altar before her with the firelight casting deep shadows across her weary face. The harsh scene was profound. Lauraisha had almost sacrificed her life while following this griffin's summons. How much more hardship would she face if she and Katja agreed to this griffin's request? How much danger would Lauraisha face if she followed Katja into the world beyond this canyon? There was the possibility of an existence far worse than death if the human and the werecat were ever trapped by the claws of the deadwalkers. And that, it seemed, was exactly where they were going.

The werecat looked at her friend and noticed a small smile tugging at the corner of the human's mouth. *She's agreeing to this? Why?*

Katja turned to Canuche. "May I persuade you to allow me a moment to confer privately with Her Highness, Your Majesty?"

The stone griffin bowed his head. "Of course."

Lauraisha slid off the altar and bent close to Katja. "Well, what are your thoughts?"

"The whole situation is frustrating!" the werecat growled. "I don't like this one bit."

Lauraisha waited expectantly.

"Jierira, very well then," Katja said by way of acquiescence and proceeded to explain her conflicting thoughts to the other female. Her final remark about feeling trapped between Canuche's plea, the deadwalkers outside the canyon, and the threat of Kaylor's soldiers' invasion caused Lauraisha to nod her head in agreement. Katja continued, "As it is, I still see no reason to entangle you in this disaster. I will probably start out for the Isle of Summons soon and see how far I can get. Hopefully, I can draw both the deadwalkers and the soldiers away from here so that you can have some peace."

"You are not leaving me behind, Katja! We are stronger together and I will be hunted whether I go or stay just as you will." The human's blue eyes had turned flinty with her resolve.

The werecat snarled. "The last thing I need is to add your blood to the count already soaking my paws. I very nearly lost you just now!"

"That was not your fault, nor were your family members' deaths!"

The werecat snorted derisively. "So you say."

"So I do! What of it? Don't try to punish yourself by taking up this task alone."

"Lauraisha, you have a chance at peace here—"

"No, Katja, I had a chance to rest here. Just as you did... but we both know that neither one of us will find true peace until our transgressors are brought to justice. Let me help you seek revenge against the deadwalkers. Then you can help me combat my father's lunacy and restore my kingdom to balance."

"How?"

"How indeed?" Canuche interrupted.

Katja gave the griffin a narrow-eyed glare out of the corner of her eye, feeling resentful at being so deftly manipulated.

"I can aid you both. Individually, you each are strong— far stronger than you know. Only together, however, will you have strength enough to possibly complete the challenge.

That being said, I am not so naïve as to believe in the power of just two. This is why I will send you by a road that will lead you swiftly to the Zolaramie Tribe of the Dryad Order where you will find additional aid…if, that is, your minds are of one accord concerning the upcoming quest. Do both of you consent to this journey without any reservation?"

Katja looked at Lauraisha who nodded her consent and then turned back to the statue. "We do."

"I thank you, noble Katja and gentle Lauraisha. May you both find solace on the roads you travel," Canuche intoned formally, bowing his great stone head toward them once again.

VI
A TROLL'S HOSPITALITY

K atja watched the cool mist swirl around her paws as she and Lauraisha followed the water of the underground stream through the middle of the stony gloom. Occasionally the werecat's soft voice would echo in the clammy silence to check their direction. However, she usually preferred to keep quiet and contemplate all that Canuche had shared inside the relative sanctity of her own mind.

Once Canuche had gained their promises of aid, he had slipped both of them into a Sharing Sleep where he could more easily dispense information to them. It had been an incredible and uncanny experience having her own mind's dreams linked with those of Canuche and Lauraisha. They had relived much of the Eppon Gue Battle together so that Canuche could teach them some of the deadwalkers' fighting strategies. He had then explained all he could about the journey ahead through various shared visions. What should have taken days to communicate was conveyed in mere hours.

Katja's head was still throbbing from the resulting overload of information cast into her mind. She winced as a particular memory pushed past the other jumbled ideas and lodged itself firmly in the forefront of her thoughts.

"Lauraisha, where is that weapons trove supposed to be?"

"According to *her*, it should be in one of the next two tunnels on our right side."

"Which one, though?"

The human was clearly agitated when she turned to the

werecat. "How should I know?"

"Well, you *are* the one who has the Guide's home swinging from around your neck."

Lauraisha shuddered and looked away.

The Guide, as Canuche had called her, had apparently unnerved Lauraisha as much as she had Katja. Of course, the werecat could not blame the human for being intimidated at the sight of a very contrary pyrefay suddenly exploding from the necklace around her neck. Even Katja, who was fairly used to the antics of all sorts of beings, had not been prepared for that!

Canuche had awakened the two of them from the Sharing Sleep and was explaining the last details of Katja's and Lauraisha's upcoming journey when Lauraisha had uttered a surprised cry. She then jerked a necklace out from under her tunic and stared at it. The necklace held a deep-blue stone pendant that had begun glowing with the same fire as the orb Lauraisha had touched to purge herself from the snake's petrifying venom. The stone pulsed with a brilliant white light and released a brilliant blue flame that blazed across the cavern before settling on the altar in front of them.

Katja stared, awestruck, when the floating flame changed shape into a female pyrefay no longer than the werecat's forearm and far more beautiful than any creature she had ever seen. Large almond eyes were set in an oval face sporting a small upturned nose and full, pouty lips. The creature's azure hair cascaded in flaming ringlets down her back between her blazing dragonfly-like wings. Her graceful figure was covered by a flaming robe that lovingly hugged every curve of her beautiful blue body.

The pyrefay, or firesprite in common Shrŷde, was of course not a sprite or any sort of fairy at all. She was in fact one of the Pyrekin beings that usually lived in the ethereal Wraith Realm, which was separated by the First Veil from Katja's own Erde Realm of physical existence.

The firesprite shared her fiery power with legendary creatures like phoenixes, salamanders, unicorns, and dragons. She was their equal in every aspect except her diminutive size. What Damya lacked in stature, however, was certainly offset by her explosive temperament. Not a moment after she had finished her transformation on the altar, did the little creature begin darting around the enormous room ranting at one being or another about her absolute annoyance at having been summoned so late. The sight of any Pyrekin was raw on the nerves, especially when the one in question could change color patterns to express her flitting mood as she scolded every creature in range of her harping diatribe.

Katja shuddered and finally pushed her thoughts away from her uncanny memory of the Guide and toward the present problem. The werecat dropped to all four paws and began sniffing at the ground and the cave walls. After a few moments she turned her gaze back to the human.

"Nothing. Not even a hint of metal to guide us."

Lauraisha sighed heavily. "Well, I suppose there is no help for it. She'll have to be called."

"Who? *Her?*" Katja's eyes went wide.

Lauraisha nodded before resolutely pulling the stone amulet from beneath her tunic and staring at it intensely.

"Damya, we need you."

The stone's hard surface seemed to liquefy before a brilliant flame swirled out of its opalescent core, revealing Damya, the Guide.

"Now what do you want?" The Pyrekin crossed her tiny arms.

"We are looking for the tunnel offshoot containing the weapons that Canuche told us about, and we're lost."

"Oh, is that all? Well, it is fortunate that you called me then. There's a trulle who prides himself on hording that collection. We'll have to swindle quite a bargain out of him if you're to leave his dwelling with any of those priceless pieces."

"Trulle?" Lauraisha looked at Katja's startled face in puzzlement.

The werecat grimaced. "She's using the archaic Shrŷde pronunciation for the word 'troll.'"

Katja watched Lauraisha's face blanch and she put a comforting paw on the human's trembling shoulder.

"Will he harm us?" the agitated human asked their peevish companion.

"No, not if we're polite. Although I've heard rumors that this one has a fondness for eating beings' toes," she replied while floating toward the first of the two right side tunnels.

As they headed down the tunnel after the little blue being, Katja noticed her friend's face turning a nauseous shade of green.

"My sentiments exactly," growled the older female, her own nose wrinkling at the stench coming from the tunnel. They traversed several spruce-lengths worth of winding, smelly tunnel before coming upon the first signs of habitation. The tunnel, which had narrowed to allow only one being to pass at a time, finally opened up enough to allow two to walk abreast. The air smelled fresher here, yet Katja still snorted at the stench of decaying flesh.

"We must be getting closer. Do you have anything to bargain with?" Katja asked the human in a low whisper.

Lauraisha shook her head, her eyes darting wildly from wall to wall.

Katja could not blame her fear. Trolls were renowned for their often vicious temperaments and cruel senses of humor. Most trolls lived largely solitary lives, mating and raising offspring only when necessary. Usually trolls stayed in underground dwellings and only hunted at night due to their extraordinarily sensitive eyesight. Unless provoked, they habitually ignored most beings, unless they were merchants or mineworkers.

It was strange that this particular troll would choose these originally dwarven settlements in which to make his home. Dwarves and trolls hated one another and constantly fought over precious underground resources. Dwarves usually mined precious mineral deposits and traded them with different races for various new goods. The more social dwarves often carved large networks of cities under the mountains, while trolls tended to store up their excavated treasure and hoard it for themselves. Katja had heard clan stories in which impetuous dwarven youths would sometimes seek out and attack trolls for their hoarded goods as a rite of passage among their kin. The conquests almost always ended badly for the dwarves.

If this troll was old, he must be very clever indeed to have survived the dwarves' era of power in these parts. Either that or he had moved in after the last clans' exodus and began amassing his treasure trove off of the dwarves' leavings, which was more likely.

"Why did the dwarf clans leave Crown Canyon?" Lauraisha asked, evidently reading Katja's thoughts.

The werecat shuddered. "Don't do that! It's highly unnerving when you pick thoughts out of my mind!"

The human blushed. "Sorry, it's just that I haven't been able to completely break our mental connection since Canuche woke us from the Sharing Sleep."

"And I don't think you will, either," Katja grunted. "Canuche knew you had largely latent dreamdrifting abilities. My guess is that he put us into that sleep more to unleash your abilities than to actually provide us directions—"

"And to awaken me," their firesprite guide called from up ahead.

Katja bowed her head toward the creature in agreement before continuing, "The griffin is no fool, after all. He knew that we would need all the help we could find."

"Which is also why he sent us down here," Lauraisha concluded glumly, looking at the widening passage. "Should we even be talking? Perhaps it would be better to move more stealthily."

Katja flattening the ears that crowned her head to show her adamant dissent. "The last action you want to pursue is the surprise of a troll. Trust me."

"He should be somewhere further up there," Damya said pointing toward to the left passage in the upcoming tunnel split. "Come along you two. Hurry!"

Katja and Lauraisha followed silently, their eyes watchful. Katja could also feel Lauraisha's mind attempting to probe the area for another being's mind. *Awake indeed*, she thought to herself. She felt herself pulled along by Lauraisha's thoughts until they hit upon a solid blank wall in the fabric of space.

"He's shielding himself," Lauraisha muttered.

"Did you expect him not to?"

"I don't know what I expected; I've never attempted this before," Lauraisha replied to the werecat.

"You two, stop playing around with the magic! You'll startle him to death!" Damya turned scarlet in her ire.

"Sorry, My Madam!" They replied simultaneously. Then Katja felt Lauraisha jerk her thoughts back into her own mind.

Damya flashed golden-orange in annoyance before flicking back to pale blue and singing a ballad of camaraderie in archaic Shrŷde to the yet-unseen troll. The three walked along the passage for two more spruce-lengths in this manner until the tunnel opened into a circular chamber roughly three spruce-lengths deep and two spruce-lengths high. Its length was interrupted by at least four other tunnel entrances, the last of which was situated next to a high-walled hovel. The dwelling's structure spanned three levels and was constructed from flat stone slabs held together with a sturdy clay compound.

"Impressive," Katja commented, admiring the structure's masonry.

"Thank ye," boomed a gravel-worn voice from somewhere in the cavern. "Now what be yer intent here?"

Damya spoke before either of the other females dared. "We seek your advice, My Sir."

"Ye seek me treasures, too."

"True," Damya replied. "Canuche said that you had the best weapons against deadwalkers on this side of the Nyghe sol Dyvesé."

"Did he now? Be that yer purpose, then?"

"Indeed it is, My Sir."

"Well now, what do ye bring me for a trade?"

"May we discuss that in more hospitable circumstances?"

"That ye can…ifin there be no tricks ye plan te pay me. Me tinks two mages and a Pyrekeen travelin' agether means a somot serious purpose. Will ye give yer word o' honor that ye mean me no harm?"

"We do," they all replied.

"Well, then." The troll stepped out from the shadows of the farthest tunnel entrance. He was a strong creature who carried himself well in spite of his hunched back. His skin was similar to that of the basels in its dull hue, but bore no scales as their gray-green flesh did. Instead his skin was gnarled like the trunk of a windswept tree and his face was weathered like sandstone. He stood roughly one-and-one-half body-lengths tall and saw the world from his elevated position with two large brown eyes that squinted myopically around a bulbous snout. Ears protruded like leathery bat wings off of the sides of his head. The troll's ears and flat head were topped with gray fur as fine as the wisps from a spider's web. He was old indeed! "Come sit ye bones by the fire. We'll talk trades a spell. Me name's Durhrigg."

"Thank you, Durhrigg," Damya replied while Katja and Lauraisha both formally bowed.

The troll grunted and then hobbled over to stoke the flames of the fire pit in the center of the room. He brought a large iron pot from inside the house and arranged it on a flat stone in the pit. The kettle, as Lauraisha called it, contained water and a sweet-scented black root that Katja recognized. The sweetwood root bubbled with the water to produce a pungent broth that the troll ladled into bowls for the others to drink and then garnished each with sliced mushroom.

"Reckon this stuff ain't fit fer yer consumption, My Ma'am," Durhrigg said to Damya. "But mayhaps ye'd prefer to feed on me flames a bit?"

"Thank you. You are most kind," Damya replied with a smile and began bobbing in and out of the fire, licking her lips as she flitted through each flame.

While the troll was busy preparing their drinks, Katja took her chance to observe the rest of their surroundings. Durhrigg's home was littered with the debris of bones, dried furs, and—to Katja's revulsion—necklaces boasting the teeth of dwarves and fangs of basels. The fangs looked ancient and Katja wondered at their large size. She stared at the fire, realizing that it was fed not by wood but by peat and animal dung. She thought that extremely efficient given that dung-fueled fires always seemed to cook food more evenly.

After they all had sipped the strange brew awhile, Katja got to the point of the meeting.

"We have a long journey for something specific, My Sir," she told Durhrigg. "We need good weapons that can help defend us against whatever enemies we face."

The troll whistled low. "That'll cost ye a bright-sized bit."

"We don't have money or jewels to trade with you—"

"We have only this," Damya interjected pointing to the ash and sand beneath her floating feet.

"This be a jeer," the troll growled.

"Wait a moment, Kind Sir," Damya said in a businesslike

tone.

The firesprite pulled a golden line of flame from the fire and heated it until it was as pale blue as she. Damya then cast it into the ash and sand beneath her in a fashion that resembled the uncoiling of a rope. When the fire touched the ground, it melted the soil into a series of glowing loops. She pulled the fired substance into the air and molded it with her hands and breath to create a series of different-sized orbs and loops. The result was a breathtaking sculpture of multihued glass balls wound around one another on a spiraled glass wire. When it was finished Damya set the sculpture on a rock just inside the fire's flames to slowly cool so that the new glass would not shatter.

The troll whistled low once again. "Ye have no mean bit o' talent, Wee Ma'am. But 'tis not fair for you to trade the work of your hands for the profit of theirs." He jerked a clawed thumb at Katja and Lauraisha.

"Does a mother not provide for her child?"

"True 'nough, but ye are no mother to these two."

"True, but I am their guide and their protector for as long as they need me. That is the way of a mother."

"Ye bear the responsibility for these two?"

"I do."

The troll scratched his wrinkled head. "All righ', yer word be good 'nough fer me. Well, come ye three to me stores, then. Mind ye don't touch anythin' though, or me fangs'll find yer fingers faster than lightnin'."

They set their drinks aside and the three followed the troll around the outside of his house toward the back, where the composite wall met solid granite. Where the two walls merged, a fissure ran from the ground to a point just above Katja's knee. Durhrigg stopped before it and pulled a large uncut sapphire from a pouch in his animal-hide waist-wrap. He took the sapphire and placed it into a hole just to the right of the crevice and stood back as the crack widened circularly to reveal a stone door. The troll then stooped to stroke the gem with one stubby finger and the door swung inward.

With Durhrigg leading the way and Damya lighting the way, the small party entered the tunnel beyond the door and descended its steep length into the chamber below it. The tunnel spread beneath them into a wide gallery carved from obsidian—the facets of its cut walls reflecting their bodies with elongated angles in Damya's radiance.

This galley led into a larger obsidian-walled chamber filled with everything one could describe as precious. The floor was covered with mounds of gold coins and tarnished silver objects reaching precariously to its one-half spruce-length ceiling.

The werecat purred with satisfaction.

"Pretty, ain't it?" Durhrigg grinned with pride. "Took most of me life to amass it so far. O'course the dwarves helped a bit."

"Helped?" Lauraisha asked, bewildered.

"Aye, they left mos' o' this behind when they vacated the premises."

"Why would they do such a thing?" Lauraisha was incredulous.

"Well, it be hard ta carry all this stuff when ye be sick an' dying. Ye see, little human, the dwarves left these mountains an' fled east when the deadwalkers' curse fell upon 'em and made 'em all ill with plague. 'Course that was all just before the Second Age War. I moved in shortly after that—knowin' that the curse couldn't hurt me—and went to work. Been collecting ever since."

Lauraisha stared aghast at the troll who was busy digging through one of the piles and whistling to himself merrily.

"What kind of a troll is so happy to be parting with his treasure?" Katja whispered to Damya.

"Durhrigg is unusual for a trulle—"

"I'll say!" Lauraisha interrupted.

"He's not nearly as testy as most of the members of his race tend to be. However, he does expect to drive a hard bargain; we'll find out his terms once he finds the items he wants." The firesprite sighed. "I don't expect to be of much use when we leave this place."

"Whyever not?" the human asked.

"According to Canuche, Durhrigg has a soft heart for rare artwork. Therefore he'll probably expect me to create lots of glass sculptures for him in exchange for his goods and using that much magic will make me extremely weary."

She looked solemnly at Katja and Lauraisha. "You two will need to be supremely cautious as you leave the canyon. Since it will likely take me several days to completely recover from my creative work here, I will not be able to adequately protect you against attack."

They both nodded before turning back to watch the troll's antics.

"What is artwork?" Katja whispered to her friend.

Lauraisha looked aghast. "You don't know?"

The werecat shook her head.

"Art is essentially anything produced for—how do you say—aesthetic appeal only. Art has no practical uses other than to be beautiful and delightful to the beholder. It is creativity in its purest form."

"That's ridiculous!" Katja said before being promptly hushed by both Lauraisha's and Damya's glares.

Her voice dropped to a whispered hiss. "Well, it is!"

"Perhaps," supplied Damya, "but he apparently would disagree and that attitude is certainly useful to us."

Katja snorted in disgruntlement. She'd done creative projects like sculpting clay plates and bowls before, but those pieces always served a function. She couldn't imagine simply creating something just because she thought it looked pretty. That was a waste of time.

She flicked her ears before turning to watch the troll, who was busy yanking a ornate candelabrum out of his way before diving back into the contents of the third pile in his quest for a half-buried sword. Once the smelly fellow was finished rummaging, he bound all of the contents together in a loosely-woven fishing net and hoisted that upon his hunched back.

"Let's go back to the warm fire an' speak a bit more," Durhrigg said, gesturing them toward the doorway once more.

After they all had come back up the passageway, the troll set his bundle down with a metallic clink and warmed his paws near the fire. "Ifin' ye wish to trade, then ye'd best not mention where ye picked up these goods exactly. Don't wish to lose me head o'er this stuff after all."

"Your secrets are safe with us," Damya replied while Katja and Lauraisha adamantly nodded their consent.

"Good then. Thank ye kindly!" He opened the net and began to arrange the items for all three females to see. There were several swords of varying lengths and types as well as a variety of daggers and knives. There were also unstrung bows, arrows, fighting staffs, whips, spears, pikes, and other curious weapons for which Katja knew no common name.

"Ye'll be needing weapons surely, but me thinks ye'll have use of some o' the other as well," he said, pointing to the rest of the contents in the net. This included drinking cups and bowls, leather bags, tools, small sacks filled with precious gems, and various gold and silver objects.

Katja, Lauraisha, and Damya all stared wide-eyed at the menagerie. Even this small hoard would be worth a king's ransom.

"Choose," the troll encouraged. "Take what you need and keep in mind that the jewels be good for tradin' later on."

"My sir—"

"Durhrigg," the troll corrected.

"Durhrigg," Katja amended herself, "we cannot hope to trade adequately for any of this."

"Do ye think me foolish enough to think meself in need of more things? Trade with me the glass yer guide made and be on yer way."

"That's it?"

"Well, hmm, ifin' it means that much for ye to trade more then give up yer present dagger, human, an' that'll make things even."

Lauraisha bowed her head at his request and removed the holstered dagger from her belt before presenting it to the troll. He took it solemnly and then said, "choose" while examining her blade. Lauraisha began picking up and putting down several swords and daggers—testing their weight and sharpness. After she chose a rapier with a blade engraved in mages' runes and a twin set of daggers, Katja chose her own pieces.

Although the remaining swords were beautifully crafted, she did not like the feel of a langzahn in her paws. Instead she chose a weapon more suited to the fighting style of her kin—a white staff roughly half of her own body's length. As she held it, the staff's surface seemed to warm to her touch and she felt the stone in the pouch beside her quiver.

Durhrigg looked at her wistfully. "It seems ye found me bone staff."

"Bone? From what?"

The troll shook his prune-like head. "Don't know. 'Tis a grand mystery. One thing is for certain, though: this piece was meant for you. Guard it well."

Katja nodded before claiming two throwing knives for herself and looking toward Lauraisha who eyed the pieces speculatively once more.

The human chose and then Katja chose until they each had what they wished from the menagerie. The items they did not take went back into Durhrigg's piles of amassed treasure.

Durhrigg sat politely throughout the process, but Katja saw him wince whenever she or Lauraisha chose more valuable items. Though he tried to hide his mood, the troll's eyes belied his conflicting emotions. It must be a great sacrifice for him to give up even these few prizes that he had guarded so jealously. Why was he doing it? It certainly could not be for either Katja or Lauraisha. He must be doing this out an enormous respect or fear of Damya. Looking again at the glowing being, Katja certainly understood why.

"Well, ifin that be all, then ye best be on yer way."

"Hold a moment, Durhrigg. I wish to examine the females' chosen items."

Durhrigg looked none too happy at Damya's command, but he bowed his consent and Damya began to touch each and every selected piece. Though Katja had no idea what the firesprite was looking for specifically, she guessed that the creature must be checking the items' quality.

After Damya was finished scrutinizing the weapons specifically, she looked at the troll. "Durhrigg, this will not do. There is barely enough sunsilver in most of these weapons to harm a imp, much less a vampire."

"But surely they'll not be dealin' wit' anythin' worse than zombies!" When Damya's grim expression did not change, he blinked in surprise. "Do ye even think them capable o' wielding such blades?"

"They have no choice," she replied darkly.

Katja's posture straightened in surprise. Sunsilver was

only forged by the most talented fireforger mages. Because it was the deadwalkers' only bane besides fire, Sylvans regarded it as priceless. A palm stone's weight of pure sunsilver could, in fact, buy an area of good land twice the size of the Feliconas Village. How could Damya so flippantly request weapons forged with it? More than that, how could she expect Durhrigg to even own such weapons?

Durhrigg only nodded and scooped up those weapons Damya had criticized, including Lauraisha's rapier and Katja's throwing knives. He wobbled away to add them back into his hoard. After a time, the sullen troll slumped back under the weight of a pair of finely crafted ebony cases.

"Ye drive a cruel accord, Firesprite. You should expect to pay tenfold the original price fer these."

"As is proper, Durhrigg. As is proper."

The troll grunted while carefully laying the cases before him and removed their contents with a belabored expression. One box revealed a magnificently carved ebony bow with a quiver of sunsilver arrows and eight spearheads, while the other held two lightweight sabers, a matching pair of daggers, another pair of throwing knives, and a curious golden vial the length of Katja's forepaw. He then explained that Katja and Lauraisha must each carry a knife and dagger. Lauraisha was given one of the swords and told to protect the other until she felt it right to give it to another member of their party. Katja was instructed to also guard the vial and use its contents only at the time of her or another's greatest need.

"Canuche said that ye'd be traveling to the Dryads' Glen. So if they offer ye help, ye must give them these in return." He pointed to the bow and arrows. "The bow once belonged to a dryad, an' so it's right to return that to her kin. The Queen Mother'll know what te do wit' 'em."

Durhrigg then turned to the sunsilver-spun spearheads. "These must be worn around yer necks at all times fer protection against yer enemies. Any other Sylvans to join in yer quest should also wear one," he said, while finding the chains that attached to each spearhead. "Katja, yer must keep three—one fer yer neck and two for the bone staff. Ye'll find that the spearheads will meld into each staff end when ye touch 'em together. Use them only in times of great need."

Durhrigg then bowed low to Damya. "These are the best of me stores, Honored Firesprite. Do they please ye?"

Damya bowed her head toward him, smiling. "You have done well, Durhrigg. We are deeply grateful." She paused, gathering her breath. "And now for your reward."

She clapped once and the thunderous sound shook waves through the sand about their paws. A gust of wind from nowhere swept a fourth of the sand and ash into the air, swirling it up against the ceiling. Damya laced the swirling mass with her own azure flame and with minerals gleaned from the cavern walls. The three Sylvans stared in awe as the firesprite wove the silt into an intricate knot of shapes and held a blanketing layer of golden flame around it for slow cooling. The result was a magnificent starburst pattern set into the stone of the ceiling—its glistening layers casting prism colors along the walls of the cavern.

"Oh, Me Ma'am! 'Tis a splendid creation!" Durhrigg clapped his paws and bowed gleefully toward the darkened firesprite.

"You are most welcome, Noble Durhrigg. It is my pleasure to return such generosity," she panted.

Katja saw the firesprite's glow beginning to wane and knew they must leave before Durhrigg demanded anything else taxing of her.

"We add our most sincere gratitude, Durhrigg, for all you have shared. Now we must depart and make ready for the long journey. May we meet you in the paths of friendship once more," she intoned formally and then bowed with both paws upturned as Lauraisha added a blessing of her own.

"Soon," the troll agreed while returning their smiling bows, and then handed them a torch lit from his fire before escorting them to one of the tunnels. "Follow the tunnel always te the left 'til ye find the river again. Follow it until it leads ye te daylight once more. Honor be with ye both; may yer souls all find peace along yer journey!"

The two youths bowed precariously under the new weight of their gifts and thanked him again. Then the three females turned away from the varied-hued light of Durhrigg's cavern and stepped into the gaping darkness of the tunnel beyond. The werecat led the way, carrying their net full of treasure while the human followed—holding the torch with the exhausted pyrefay cradled in the depths of its flames as steady as she could. Katja couldn't help but ponder why they had been given such incredible gifts, nor could she fathom why she of all Sylvans had been launched on this dangerous quest in the first place.

"This all reeks of prophecy," she muttered before giving a nose-scrunching laugh at the absurdity of the statement.

The werecat turned left along the tunnel route and moved further into the unknown, with the light-bearing human keeping good pace just behind her.

VII
FRIENDS AND FIENDS

"Tunnels. Why is it always our fate to travel through tunnels?" Lauraisha complained.

Katja looked back at her human and horse companions, her ears twitching in annoyance. "How else do you suggest we escape both the deadwalkers and your overzealous hunters?"

The three females had managed to find their way back to Lauraisha's camp from Durhrigg's home in time to see the waxing moon set on that strange second day. The next hours of both night and day had been devoted to sleep. The following four were then dedicated to preparing food, cleaning, and packing for their journey.

Katja, Lauraisha, Tyron, and the slumbering Damya left when the sun greeted sky on the seventh day after their encounter with Canuche. Canuche had warned them not to leave the canyon in the same area that either Katja or Lauraisha entered because either the soldiers or the deadwalkers would surely find them if they dared to try. Instead they traveled cautiously toward the southwest portion of the canyon. The company crossed the river waterfall by way of a second dwarven bridge hidden just behind its plunge. They then skirted inside the canyon's southern edge until they found the cavern passages that Canuche had assured them would guide them safely under the southern canyon ridge and beyond.

The tunnel network wound through the ground for a few leagues before resurfacing into the forest beyond the canyon. In olden days, the dwarves had used the passages to network a mercantile route with the main dryad clans. Katja almost felt like she and her companions were repeating history, and mentioned this to Lauraisha.

"Dwarves and dryads traded? Really?"

Katja swiveled her ears and cocked her head to one side. "You didn't know that?"

The human shook her head.

"What exactly did your elders teach you about Sylvan history in your kit years?"

"Not much," Lauraisha shrugged.

"Apparently. Do you at least understand what the First and Second War of Ages were about?"

"Of course, but please do not expect any other Tyglesean to know such information."

Katja flicked her ears again and growled. "Why are Tygleseans so ignorant of basic history?"

"Easy there!"

"Sorry, but why?"

Lauraisha sighed. "Are you sure you really wish to know?"

The werecat snorted in exasperation.

"Fine, then. It's a matter of national pride."

Katja's eyes narrowed. "This has to do with your father's usurpation of the throne, doesn't it?" Katja dodged a low hanging tropfstein stalactite and then looked back expectantly at the human, who had stopped in mid-stride Lauraisha's face blanched and the lost look in her eyes suddenly made the werecat wish that she had not mentioned Tyglesea's revolution so casually.

"What do you know about that?"

"Not much." She shrugged with honesty. "Only that Kaylor's 'emancipation' of the country was a bloodbath. Many a good mage died in that revolution, including every member of the rightful royal family."

The Tyglesean nodded, her eyes fixated on the empty space in front of her.

"Lauraisha, are you well?"

"This is my father's legacy...to destroy every mage in his grasp."

"Ah, so that is why you fled."

The human nodded again. "My mother said that she sensed something different in me when I was born, but I had no unusual abilities to speak of as a child, so we all thought I would be safe from my father's wrath. But when I became a woman that all changed."

She gazed at Katja with haunted eyes. "In my twelfth winter, I began to *dream*. At first I dreamed of my brothers and sister, but then I began to share their dreams. I knew their favorite memories; I knew their eeriest nightmares..." Her voice faded into the hollow silence of the tunnel.

"One night I shared a particularly bad dream with my mother. It was a dream about Father's revolution and his killing of the royal family...it was horrible." Lauraisha shuddered and fought to control her breathing before she continued. "Mother sensed me fighting in the nightmare's grasp along with her, so she questioned me the next day. After it became clear that something unusual had occurred, she and I secretly sought her priest's advice. Father Arcos surmised from our story that I was a dreamdrifter mage and advised Mother that I would likely be put to death if Kaylor discovered my talents. Mother hatched a plan with my brothers to help me escape the country. I was smuggled out of Tyglesea in the care of Father Arcos who then guided me toward Crown Canyon."

"Why didn't the priest come with you?"

"He did." Lauraisha sadly held up the stone amulet that was Damya's usual resting place. "He gave this to me before Tyron and I fled into the woods and told me to guard it with my life. The soldiers caught him moments later; they accused him of being a warlock and shackled him on the spot. He must be dead now."

Katja bowed her head. "So we both have lives to atone for then."

Lauraisha nodded and lowered her eyes.

"Why is the king so set against mages?"

"It is part of his *power*." Lauraisha spat the last word with disgust. "Tygleseans view anything connected to magic with distrust and contempt. They blame magic for the near-downfall of Tyglesea's economy during the years following the Second War of Ages.

"My mother told me that Kaylor gained his power on the

promise that he would purge Tyglesea of its magic and rid the masses of evil mages who spied on the humans in their midst. In the spirit of this purge, my father slaughtered and scattered all opponents through his witch hunts during the Warlock Wars. Anyone who dared oppose him was proclaimed a witch or warlock and promptly burned at the stake or drowned in the sea."

Katja nodded. She remembered the clan stories of the Tyglesean massacres. It was those stories that had made her wary of Tygleseans and humans in general. Tygleseans had once lived in harmony with the rest of the Sylvan Orders, but Kaylor's rule had changed all that. Now, no Sylvan other than a human would dare journey into the kingdom for fear of death. Kaylor had closed the main trade routes, which then expanded the widespread poverty already choking the country.

To compensate for the economic losses, the king had increased the witch hunts to keep the masses turned against mage scapegoats. Eventually he set thousands of Tygleseans to work building fishing boats and warships. The resulting ship-building industry boom coupled with a decreased population finally helped to stabilize the nation. Meanwhile Kaylor began fortifying the country and building several series of stone walls to "protect" the country from outsiders and to centralize his power.

He was the only king in Sylvan history who would not submit to the authority of the Council of Mages or the Ring of Sorcerers. Katja had no idea why the Ring of Sorcerers had done nothing to prosecute him for such insolence. He was too dangerously self-absorbed and unpredictable to keep careful watch against deadwalkers on the Northwest Sylvan borders.

Lauraisha's sniffle broke Katja's concentration. "If ever Kaylor discovered that a mage lived in his own house among his own family members, he would most likely slaughter every heir he had and possibly even my mother."

"It is rumored that Kaylor slaughtered the entire royal family himself before he took the throne."

"I cannot be sure whether he did it directly, but it wouldn't surprise me. They were certainly slaughtered at his orders— all but the youngest daughter."

Katja's ears pricked forward in curiosity. "What happened to the youngest daughter?"

Lauraisha shook her head. "I don't know. Most people believe that she was killed along with the rest of the family, but Mother believes that the girl had escaped the castle. She never would tell me why she thought that, though. I can only wonder what has become of the lost princess."

"Well, she certainly would not go back to Tyglesea after that massacre, not if she hoped to live."

Lauraisha nodded, absently stroking Tyron's neck as the stallion stood beside her and nickered at Katja. "How much further?"

"It shouldn't be more than half a day's walk before we see sky again."

"Good."

"Agreed. Toss me some more of the dried fish, will you?"

"Katja! This is your third helping already this morning!"

The werecat looked around the dark depths of the stone chamber illuminated by Lauraisha's torch. "How do you know it's morning?"

"Because I awoke only a short while ago and whenever I'm up, it's morning," Lauraisha retorted. "No more food for you or you will eat us completely out of our stores!"

Katja shrugged and turned to lead the grouchy human and finicky horse farther along the underground passage. It did indeed take the remaining portion of the "morning" before Katja and her companions reached the tunnel's end. They followed its steep curve upward until its length suddenly ended in a stone wall.

"Now what do we do?" the human cried, her voice a mixture of exasperation and panic. "Should we call Damya?"

"No. Let her sleep; she has yet to regain her strength," Katja replied, briefly glancing at the place where she knew the stone amulet and its sleeping occupant lay beneath Lauraisha's blue livery tunic. The werecat turned back to the rock wall in front of her. "Keep hold of your horse a few moments and let me feel around. There has to be some way to open the wall."

Lauraisha stamped her foot, but fell silent.

Katja's paws roamed the stone's smooth surface surveying every irregularity in its rugged façade. Finally her right paw closed around a raised disk set in the center of the wall. As she pushed against it, the werecat heard stone grind against stone and a long, thin crack appeared along the left side. The gap widened to reveal a sun-dappled world of lush grass and tall trees.

Katja peered cautiously out through the door and breathed in the forest scents before she motioned for Lauraisha and Tyron to follow her. As the waning sun greeted their eyes in full, the werecat smelled danger on the wind once more.

The Feliconian froze; then she shoved Lauraisha and Tyron back inside the tunnel. Crouching at its entrance, she listened. The forest was full of birdsong and insects' rhyme, yet something seemed very wrong.

Katja waited, her breath coming slowly so it would not dissipate the weak scent wafting near her nostrils. It was a mixture of horse and human sweat that had none of Tyron and Lauraisha's familiar characteristics. There was also a scent of cowhide and rust mingled in the fresh breeze.

Katja gestured for the human and horse to stay hidden before bounding into a nearby gully and crawling stealthily downwind of the scent. The sweaty scent's sources were a group of twenty-five human males whose camp was twenty spruce-lengths northeast from the tunnel entrance. Their campsite looked set for the night and Katja reported this to her human friend when she returned to the tunnel entrance.

"Did you see any specific colors or symbols on their clothing?"

Katja nodded. "They bear the arms of Summersted Castle though the hue of their tunics isn't the same as yours; it's more of a pine-needle green rather than a sapphire blue."

Lauraisha's worried look brightened considerably at this news. "That's the Fifth Falcon detachment from the Summersted garrison! Commander Escos is in charge of it! Tell me, did you see a male with reddish-brown hair and very broad shoulders with them? He has a scar above his right eye and a full beard closely cropped at the chin."

After the human explained the notion of a beard, Katja replied, "There was a human fitting that description, only the 'beard' as you call it was very bushy."

"I imagine it would be after spending such time away

from any real civilization."

Katja cocked an eyebrow at the last comment and then sniffed the wind once more to make certain that there were no unannounced humans near them. The scent had kept its faintness so she was reasonably satisfied that no one had followed her.

"That must be Escos!" exclaimed Lauraisha in excitement. "He will be able to help us! We need to talk to him! Maybe if we could lure him away from the other men, we could—"

"Go after a single being in that large den of humans? Are you insane! What happens if he's loyal to your father? What if one or more of his underlings is? What happens if they follow him and find out where we are? I'm a good fighter, but I do not savor the thought of sparring against twenty-five fully-armed warriors."

"You worry too much."

Katja flicked her ears. "And you not enough."

"Escos has always been loyal to Mother, so he would never harm us. He'll be able to give me news of home and deliver messages back to my mother and brothers. Please, Katja, this is important!"

"This has death engraved on it." Katja stared steadily at the other female.

"Please, Katja, I have to know if my family is safe!"

Katja looked into the princess's eyes and beheld an anxiousness that mirrored what she had felt during her village's destruction. How could she possibly deny Lauraisha knowledge of her family's well-being? The werecat sighed with sudden weight as she bulwarked her emotions and uttered words she knew were necessary but hated anyway.

"Lauraisha," she snarled. "The issue at paw is not whether your family is safe, but whether you yourself are safe. Your family risked their lives to give you freedom; do not throw that away! How do you think they would feel if they discovered that you risked your safety now after all of their care?"

"How can you act this way when you yourself know the burden of losing family?" the human complained.

Katja now flattened her ears and hissed, "Don't be foolish; you know this is the right action to take."

Katja saw the tears welling up in the other's eyes and turned away to keep her own in check. What a terrible decision they must make, but what an important one.

"I am sorry," Lauraisha said quietly. "I just want to know of my family."

So do I, Katja thought before speaking aloud once again. "You will not regret this."

"Oh, but I know I will," the fifteen-winter-old human whispered.

* * *

The werecat, human, and horse spent the rest of the waning daylight slinking through the forest beyond the tunnel. They followed animal paths instead of the wider trade trails and slinked as silently as possible to evade the Tyglesean warriors. Progress was dismally slow because of the mountain foothills' winding terrain.

The odd company finally stopped when the sun's last rays seeped slowly below the world, and night once again settled itself overhead. They lit no fire for fear that its light would reveal their presence to unfriendly eyes and ate the dried food from Crown Canyon in uncomfortable silence.

Lauraisha spoke rarely and stayed huddled near her horse. After the eat, she curled herself into a tight ball to sleep and left the werecat to take first watch alone with her thoughts. Although she was slightly put off at the human for ignoring her, Katja couldn't really blame her for being angry. Katja was sure Lauraisha's icy demeanor would eventually thaw and they would soon be back to genial conversation. For now though, she'd rather the human be irate and safe than in a good mood while in danger.

Katja gazed around the small thicket clearing that held their campsite. The scene was picturesque under the bright gibbous moon—a world full of soft browns and greens with a touch of silvery luminescence from the moon rays. Katja perked her ears as she sat in her watch tree. A gentle breeze rattled the leaves and that, mixed with cricket song, added a touch of peaceful harmony to the night's dreamy essence.

Then Tyron's uneasy whinny nudged Katja out of her revelry enough to note the change in the forest scents carried upon the breeze. The werecat quietly climbed higher in the tree, searching for a better view and sniffing point. The tang of unwashed skin filled her nostrils while the smell of leather and metal grew stronger.

Tyron whinnied again—this time in true alarm. Katja's eyes swiveled in his direction and caught movement behind the thick shroud of leaves to the left of where the horse was standing. The shadows suddenly took on solidity as two large Tygleseans stepped from the leaves and approached the horse with ropes held ready. Two more warriors followed their cohorts into the clearing with drawn swords ready.

Katja hissed softly while carefully checked her surroundings—squinting to see every detail in the bright moonlight. No other humans seemed to be in scent range of the camp nor did these humans seem aware of the werecat's existence.

The warriors moved toward the horse, whose now frantic neighs finally awakened the sleeping Lauraisha. Her startled movements distracted the Tygleseans so that they took no notice of the werecat crouched high in the tree above them.

With her claws unsheathed, Katja readied herself to pounce on the nearest of the four. Then Lauraisha freed Tyron's lead rope and set him loose on their would-be captors. The horse charged too fast for the Tygleseans' ropes to be of any use. He reared and his vengeful hooves left two males flat on the ground and a third reeling. The last was left wide open for Katja's own attack. Lauraisha screamed as Katja slammed him to the ground.

"No! Don't harm him!"

Katja stared at her in confusion and then looked at the being under her paws. After a moment, she realized that the terrified, scruffy-faced human staring up at her was none other than Escos himself. She heard the pounding of running feet and growled. She jerked the commander to his feet, spun him so that his back was to her, and wrapped her naked claws around his neck.

"Back off or he dies!" She snarled at the new wave of warriors now swarming the camp.

"Lauraisha, translate for me!" She yelled before dragging Escos bodily to where the princess and her flat-eared horse were cornered.

The female translated her words in a shrill voice and the ten fresh warriors backed to the edges of the clearing, dragging the wounded with them. Still growling, Katja pulled the large man into a tighter headlock and backed close to Lauraisha.

"You wouldn't really harm him, would you?" Lauraisha whispered in Shrŷde.

"I will if he tries to harm us," she retorted flatly.

"Call your warriors off, Commander!" Katja hissed in Escos's ear. "Have them lay down their weapons and back away from the camp!"

After Lauraisha's translation, he did so and the other retreated from view, though Katja knew from the shifting wind that they had not gone far. After making the commander swear that he would neither fight her nor try to run, the werecat released him from the headlock.

"See here, what is this all about?" Escos demanded in broken Shrŷde.

"You tell us, Commander. After all it is you hunting us, not us hunting you," Katja snarled.

"Us?" Escos looked in surprise from the werecat to his princess.

"Yes, Escos, us." Lauraisha's reply was in Shrŷde, probably for the werecat's benefit. "This werecat has proven herself a valiant protector and loyal companion to me these past few weeks. I doubt neither her courage, nor her resolve. Do not test her. Now, if you please, tell me why you have tracked us."

After another sidelong glance at the werecat, Escos replied, "It is my charge that I should bring you back unharmed to His Majesty for your protection."

"My protection?" Lauraisha laughed bitterly. "What a cruel jest! If anything, I'm far more secure here than I am in his clutches."

"You actually prefer the company of *that*?" he said in Tygyré—nodding his head at Katja.

She snarled and thumped her tail on the ground in warning. "You are pushing my patience, human," she hissed ominously in broken Tygyré.

Escos recoiled away from her in surprise before regaining

control over his nerves. "Who are you to threaten me?"

Her eyes narrowed. "I am a werecat of the Feliconas Clan, the kit of Kevros and Devra Escari. I speak with the strength of my clan and my race. Any other queries before I ask my own?"

Escos slowly shook his head.

Before Katja could even ask the first question, however, she felt pain shoot through the back of her skull. She fell hard to the root-entangled ground beneath her. Dimly she heard Lauraisha scream her name. The soldiers closed in around her as Katja fought to stay awake. Two of them were binding her heavy limbs when the darkness finally draped her eyes. Her last thought was the realization that the wind had shifted, and so she hadn't smelled the ambush behind her.

* * *

Katja awoke in the dusk's gathering gloom. She was alone—caged inside thick wood slats strapped with iron which sat inside a low-walled supply cart. She gently touched the knot on the back of her head and hissed as the contact sent shards of pain racing through her tender skull.

"Katja?" Lauraisha's voice issued from the crate next to her.

"I'm here," she groaned.

"Are you okay?"

"Mai pixies furz auf ihre köpfe!" she growled in Felis.

"Pixies fart on what?"

"Never mind," Katja snapped and scooted her back against the rough crate, trying to stretch her legs out within the cramped space. With little success, she turned to the right and squinted through the slats at the human imprisoned in the cage beside hers. "Where are we? How long have I been out?"

"We're in the Tyglesean soldiers' camp and you've been mostly unconscious since last night. Escos decided we would be 'safer' if we were locked up."

Katja snorted derisively. "Yes, well, safer to him, maybe—"

Sounds of soft footsteps drawing near interrupted her.

"Ah, I see you are awake. Lathin really concerned me when he knocked you over the head. I was afraid he had cracked your skull."

"You'll probably wish he had by the time I get finished with you!" Katja snarled back.

"Please understand that my intention is not to harm you—either of you—but I must complete my mission and see the princess safely back to her king."

"Your king, Commander Escos, not mine," Lauraisha retorted acidly.

"I'm sorry, My Madam. I do not pretend to know what folly set you upon this perilous path, but Tyglesea is where you truly belong…"

"Escos, I will die if I go back! You know as well as I the dangers Kaylor's ill-favored are met with there! My life and that of Katja's will be forfeit! Please, Escos, trust me and serve me as you always have. Free me! Do not send us to our death!"

Lauraisha's begging gave way to sobs. Whether theatrical or not, the werecat could not guess, but they seemed to move him. Escos's voice changed to one of immense pain. "I'm sorry, My Precious Madam; I…I have my orders and I cannot escape…them."

He turned and fled from their cages. Katja could swear that she saw tears streaking his cheeks. She sat in shadowed silence for a while before turning to the princess once again.

"Does he know exactly what you are?"

Lauraisha shook her head. "I don't think so, and I don't think it wise to tell him either. Enough talk of that sort. How do we get out of here?"

Katja began kicking at the wooden slats, testing weaknesses before she answered. The slats felt unnaturally sturdy, even if they were made of oak as their faint smell suggested. The werecat cocked her head and flicked her tail in both confusion and frustration.

"I don't know." She shook her head in the darkness.

"Katja, I cannot go back!"

"I know."

Neither one spoke for a time as dark thoughts overwhelmed them. To calm her frayed nerves and throbbing head, Katja concentrated on breathing and listening to the night sounds; she tried to glean as much information from the world beyond her cage as possible. She watched the last sun rays fall beneath land and plunge the world into the pitch hue of night, only to be replaced by star glitter and the purist moon glow. With each passing moment, she felt a growing hunger for moonlight. She longed to feel its cool light play across her vision and brighten a world far too dark with trouble and toil. She saw it finally rise in full beauty, pouring its bountiful rays into her cage.

Then Katja realized suddenly that the moon was changing her.

Once again she felt her body twist into the unfamiliar shape of humanity—her forepaws into hands, her fangs and claws retracting and dulling, her jaw realigning and adjusting with the melding features of her face, her senses numbing, her fur falling out, and her back paws finally flattening into human feet. She had once again kept her now-hairless tail, but her body, besides that, looked perfectly human. The metamorphosis had occurred with far less pain then she had ever known before. Though it was still highly uncomfortable, it was somehow simultaneously healing. Her head no longer ached as much as it had before the skinshift.

Katja touched her soft skin glowing in the dappled moonlight and noticed tiny bumps prickling its surface. She hadn't realized how chilled she was by the night's unusually cool air now that she was half-naked with no way to cover herself. She searched the crate for her rucksack and found nothing. All of her belongings were missing, save the loincloth she was wearing.

"Lauraisha, I need a cloth or hide, something or I'll freeze!"

"You're actually cold with all that fur?"

"Um, I'm lacking fur at the moment," she said awkwardly.

The human gawked at her through her cage's slats. "Are you well—wait, you're...you're human!"

Katja put her face in her hands and closed her eyes against the sudden tiredness she felt. "It's the moon."

She then looked over to see Lauraisha staring incredulously at her. "You're a changeling?"

"Please don't use that word!"

"Sorry, I don't mean to give offense, but isn't that what you are?" Lauraisha began to rip her blue livery tunic.

"Yes, I am a skinshifter mage, but I'm not evil as many

would suggest!"

"Well, of course you're not! But how did this happen? You turning into a human, I mean. Do you do it because you are a werecat?" Lauraisha asked as she began stuffing the torn strip of the tunic through the slats. Katja pulled the fabric through and began wrapping it around her chilled chest.

"Not precisely. A skinshifter can be a werecat or a werewolf, but not all werecats or werewolves are skinshifters. The ability to actually shift skins is very rare. I've never known another in my clan to be able to skinshift from a werecat into a human or even into a full lion, which is good since the trait is despised by those who know its history." Katja then explained her personal history and how her ability related to her clan members' deaths.

"Is your mage ability the reason the deadwalkers are hunting you?"

"Kayten seemed to think so."

"That basically puts us in the same pit then, doesn't it?" Lauraisha rocked back and forth against the crate wall in thought. "Well, on the lighter side of broods, you'd be able to hide your true identity quite well in Tyglesea."

"Lauraisha, this change isn't permanent nor is it undergone by my own will. Tonight I will stay human as long as the moon arcs the night sky. Tomorrow I will be a werecat once again, albeit with shorter fur than usual."

"I see. I wish you could do it whenever you wished; that would be far more useful."

"Useful? I don't see what is very useful about it. I feel like I'm blind, deaf, and numb in this form. You humans are horribly lacking in decently developed senses!"

"I wouldn't know," Lauraisha replied. "I can't change races and compare the two."

"Sorry," mumbled the new human upon hearing the edge in her friend's voice.

"This does complicate things, because I was hoping that you would be strong enough to break open our crates. However, since you are now as weak as I, we'll have to use another plan. We also need to find shoes for you and—"

A shrill shriek cut her off mid-sentence. Its chilly cacophony resonated in their bones and traced terror up their spines. Katja pressed her eyes closed in silent supplication.

"What was that?" Lauraisha's voice was cowed to a whisper.

"They've found us," Katja answered with grim resentment.

"Who?"

"Deadwalkers."

"What do we do?"

"Die, I'm certain," a cold voice replied.

VIII

ESCAPE TO THE GLEN

The females both jerked their heads to the left side of their cages and stared at the approaching figure. It was tall and lean, but firmly muscled. This was no deadwalker, but a Tyglesean warrior dressed in the Fifth Falcon colors.

He sneered at Katja when he drew near the crates. "So, you *are* a changeling. My, my, Princess, what scandalous company you keep. I'm curious if the fiend will be worth more to the deadwalkers or to Kaylor. I guess we'll find out."

"Lathin, let us out of here this instant!" Lauraisha commanded.

"Oh, no, Princess, I don't think I will. You're far more valuable to me alive, at least for the moment. I'll be promoted if I bring you back safely to His Majesty. I think I'd infinitely prefer that to being burned alive for aiding a pair of witches."

"We are not witches!" hissed Katja.

"Hmph," he spat and began to wrap ropes over the crates, securing them to the wagon. He then strapped wide-eyed horses in front of the cart and jumped up into the driver's seat.

"Now, don't you two yell or I'll be forced to come slit your throats and, as I said, I would prefer you alive—"

A sudden wet gasp interrupted his last word, and then Escos appeared to their left with a blood-stained dagger.

"What are you doing!"

"Obeying your command, Your Highness," he said while wrenching the blade against the nails sealing their crates.

"The camp is in chaos; deadwalkers are killing my men

left and right. You must flee if you are to survive." He opened their crates and looked around warily. "Princess, your steed is hobbled outside my tent; take him and an extra horse and flee."

"Why should we trust you after you imprisoned us?" Katja's voice dripped with ire.

The Tyglesean stared, stunned, at the sight of Katja in human form.

"You're a—"

"Skinshifter mage. Yes, Commander, I know what she is," Lauraisha said tersely as she folded her arms across her chest.

Escos bowed and murmured, "Your Highness truly keeps interesting company!"

"Why should we trust you?" the former feline repeated.

"That is your choice, isn't it, My Madam? But, either way, I must defend my men." Escos bowed and plunged into the brush beside the cart. They glanced at one another and then sprinted after him, keeping as silent as they could. The journey to Escos's tent, though short, proved arduous for the suddenly tender-footed Katja. By the time they untied Tyron and loaded their supplies into his saddlebags, Katja's feet were bleeding so much that she had to bandage them.

Though the commander's tent's location was removed from the rest of the camp, they could still hear horrific screams echo across the clearing as if the fight between the humans and the deadwalkers were right outside the tent flap.

"Go! Go! Quickly! Take my horse and flee!" Escos said.

"What happens to you?" Lauraisha asked.

Escos's face was resolute. "I cannot leave my warriors."

"But they have no chance against deadwalkers!"

Escos grimly nodded before he charged into the foray beyond.

"Esc—"

Katja's hand clamped down on the princess's lips. "Not now, mourn him later!"

The females clothed themselves in additional garments, grabbed their gear from inside the tent, climbed atop Tyron and Escos's own piebald charger, and raced out of the tent's shadow into the moonlight. The scene that met their eyes was horribly similar to the Feliconas Clan Massacre. Bloody bodies littered the ground, their scarlet flow bathing the vegetation. Those humans still living fought desperately beside their comrades' fallen bodies against zombies numb to all pain but their insatiable hunger for live flesh.

"Fire! Fire! Use the fire!" Escos cried. He charged the deadwalkers, swinging flaming torches with each fist. Two of his blows landed and flames leapt across the animated bodies, consuming them. Other men raced to grab burning branches from their cook fires to flail at the assaulting minions.

Lauraisha and Katja plunged their horses directly into the middle of the battle, leaving a trail of flailing deadwalkers in their wake as they rode to freedom. Katja desperately gripped the piebald horse's sides with her legs and the holding straps with her hands while Lauraisha guided the galloping beast behind Tyron with a tether rope.

As they charged past the camp's horses' picket line, Lauraisha's saber snapped the rope and sent horses galloping in all directions. The resulting melee allowed the Tyglesean soldiers to set fire to those zombies knocked down by the panicked mounts. Under cover of the horses' distraction, they plunged their mounts into the welcoming green beyond the camp clearing.

"Lauraisha, head southeast!"

"Why?"

"That's the direction of the dryads' home. Push the horses! It won't take long before the deadwalkers catch our scent. With my back paws bleeding like this, it won't be hard to find us, either."

Even though Katja had bound her shredded feet while inside the tent, she knew the rags were now too sodden to contain her blood. She saw it drip from her covered toes onto the forest floor with each jolting impact of the horses' hooves. She hissed at the pain and clung to the piebald's neck as they pushed further into the woods along the remains of a long-forgotten trade trail.

Katja ached as she bent low over the piebald's back. Riding taxed her in a way she had never before known. Each contact of the horse's hooves with the ground jarred her body and sent pain flicking across her raw thighs and hands as they rubbed against the saddle and riding straps. Lauraisha pushed the horses on mercilessly despite her friend's growing discomfort. Katja groaned, her stomach becoming more and more unsettled despite having almost nothing in it.

"How much farther?" Lauraisha called.

"To the end of this trail," she replied.

"Which is?"

"Don't know."

"You are no help whatsoever!" the true human called back in exasperation.

Katja groaned again and kept her head bent to one side of the galloping horse—prepared to retch on the run if need be. "Creator, why is my freedom always so temporary?" she muttered miserably to the wind.

"Are you well?"

"It doesn't matter; just keep going!" Katja emptied what little was left in her gut onto the leaves beside the trail and cursed herself for giving even more evidence of her presence to their enemies.

Minutes later she cursed herself again as shrill cries of triumph met their ears. Lauraisha muttered something horribly unbefitting her proper upbringing and pressed the horses faster.

"How much farther, Katja?"

"Just go!"

Katja began seeing crimson streaks glimmer in the hollows between trees as the females' steeds pounded down the dryads' trading trail. She could smell the acrid stench of walking death growing more potent with each hoof beat of their horses. The skinshifter was suddenly grateful that her stomach was utterly spent as her nausea grew again.

The road ahead split toward the southwest and the east. Katja saw gray shapes congregating on the eastern fork and realized that the zombies were trying to turn them away from the dryads' stronghold.

"Lauraisha, take the eastern fork!"

"But—"

"They're trying to drive us away from safety!" she yelled over the thunderous steps of their straining mounts. "If they won't move, trample them!"

It was a dangerous decision. Any of the zombies could

grab the horses' reins and steer them awry or swing off a tree branch and land behind one of the females on horseback. What was most likely, however, was that the deadwalkers wouldn't move at all from the roadway. They would wait until the last instant and then crouch with pikes, spears, or swords and present death by impaling to the horses and their riders. But what choice did they have?

The resolute pair charged toward the wall of dead flesh and steel with their own weapons ready. As the deadwalkers crouched, ready to skewer the stallions, a voice from nowhere sang a single piercing note of such beauty and power it brought tears to Katja's eyes. Then a light of purest white flashed forth from Lauraisha's sapphire amulet and Damya appeared before the horses in all her minute blue brilliance.

A clap of the firesprite's hands produced an arc of multihued light under the horses' hooves and Katja and Lauraisha found themselves and their horses galloping over the astonished deadwalkers before plunging back upon the road. The arc of light then cascaded around the screaming deadwalkers like flaming rain. Those who escaped immediate destruction now tore at their own scorched flesh in agony.

"Nyekel jeung tahan eta!" Curqak's venomous voice screeched in the soul-slave language Qak over the deadwalkers' clamors as the horses pounded ever closer to the twin pillars marking the Glen's border gate. The other deadwalkers concealed within the forest surrounding the trail boiled out of the screen of trees in a last desperate attempt to stop the fugitives.

Zombies closed in as they raced over the final spruce-length's span to the Glens' gateway columns. Damya, meanwhile, faded back into Lauraisha's stone amulet, her remaining energy clearly already spent.

The deadwalkers prevailed even with flailing horse hooves, Damya's remnants of fiery rain, and the females' deft weapon work. Katja and Lauraisha fought in panic as dead flesh hemmed in around them, cutting off their escape. The gateway was less than two body-lengths away. Katja longed for those columns like a being lost in the desert longs for water. She could see her oasis and yet could not get near it. Her screech of frustration and rage and terror shook the trees.

"That won't save you this time, Changeling!" Curqak cackled in glee. "You are mine!"

The Asheken reached toward her, threatening to pull her off the horse when a storm of arrows rained down upon them. Not one of the bolts strayed near the females or their steeds, yet all the deadwalkers around them were marked by a feathery shaft at least once.

"Come, humans!" a female voice called.

Katja and Lauraisha saw several sets of pale-green hands level reloaded bows out of the thicket beyond the stone pillars even as the deadwalkers scrambled for shelter. Katja sensed the magic woven within each arrow and, as they struck their targets, she saw vines burst from their shafts to encase the struggling deadwalkers in growing green life.

"No! Hold them! Tahan eta! I will not be denied my prey twice—" Curqak bellowed, until a bolt struck him full in the throat, cutting off his airway with the sharpness of its arrowhead and the noose of its spelled vines. The ghoul fell back gasping, his clawed fingers clutching at his bloody throat. His underlings' actions turned into muddled chaos without his orders. As some deadwalkers hid from the arrows behind tree trunks, the trees' boughs suddenly gained independent movement and flayed the decrepit invaders with century-thickened wood. After seeing the loss of their leader and witnessing the trees' sudden attacks on their undead brethren, other sklaaven either ran in circles moaning in confusion or continued the desperate assault until they too were struck down by arrows or branches.

Lauraisha took advantage of the pandemonium to push past the remaining hordes and leap the stallions across the gateway pillars and into the sanctity of the Glen beyond. Green vines as thick as ten-winter-old oaks erupted from the ground behind them, effectively bulwarking the Glen's Gateway against invasion. Once inside the Glen's perimeter, Katja realized that the moving trees and tall grass running parallel to the Gateway actually formed a woven net whose paw-length barbs and thorns proved a lethal barrier against unwelcome guests. Never was she more grateful that Lauraisha and she had not strayed any closer to that vine wall.

The armed dryads slowly stalked toward them from the

sheltering trees. Seeing their grim faces, Lauraisha decided to dismount and encouraged Katja to do the same so that they both would appear less threatening. The moment her raw feet touched the soil, however, Katja fell to the ground with a screech.

Lauraisha was instantly kneeling by her side even as a beautiful, scarlet-haired dryad stood before them with her battle sickle leveled at Katja's throat.

"State your names and you purpose here or you too shall share the deadwalkers' fate," she said.

Katja gulped back her pain and terror in the face of this new threat as Lauraisha spoke, "I am Lauraisha of Tyglesea. This is Katja Escari of the Feliconas Clan. We are weary travelers, raw from our ordeal with the Asheken deadwalkers. Please let us stay in your glade of peace. We wish harm to none, but have been sent here to beg the wise ear of your Queen Mother. Would you please present us to her?"

"You are not fit for her sight in these retched rags. However, I will convey your wishes to her. For now, though, you are our captives until such a time as she seeks to convene with you." The dryad raised her sickle slightly, before adding, "If ever."

The other dryads flanked the two wary companions, motioned them to remount, and then led them along the ascending moonlit trail toward the heart of Mount Sol'ece, the dryads' home. The party passed under the shade of a single line of tall cotton trees before moving on through a vineyard. The lone mountain of Sol'ece was sectioned into three terraced rings—each one winding higher than the next around the low mountain. As they moved across the expanse of tilled and viny land and arrived at a tree line marking the end of the vineyard, Katja realized that they were about to ascend the first of the three stone terraces—the First Tier of Ascension.

From somewhere in her catling tutelage, Katja recalled the dryads' three Tiers of Ascension served the dual purposes of added protection against unwelcome guests and a pilgrimage of sorts for devotees of the dryad Queen Mother. The werecat suddenly wondered if she and Lauraisha would be left at this wall to earn their place as 'pilgrims.'

As if in answer to Katja's silent musings, the scarlet-haired leader turned toward her and spoke, "Know that you must prove yourself pure of heart before we take either of you further into our home or ever grant you audience with our Queen Mother. Therefore, as a test of your perception, you must find and open the entrance of the First Tier of Ascension without our aid."

The two humans nodded and moved their steeds forward to examine the lichen-covered wall.

"Katja, I cannot see a blazing thing in this light," Lauraisha muttered softly.

"Nor can I, sadly enough. But I doubt it would matter in this case."

"Why?"

"My guess is that this door cannot be revealed by sight alone. The door is probably hidden by magic, so we must *feel* the door rather than see it."

Lauraisha frowned at her in the darkness. "I do believe your sanity is slipping."

Katja winced at the pain in her feet and her head before she shrugged at the princess. "At this point I rather doubt I had it in the first place."

The skinshifter turned once again to stare myopically at the wall. She shut her eyes so that her dim vision wouldn't distract her and lifted a tender hand to the rough stone. She had always carried an acute sense of magic's presence and now she used that sense—somehow strengthened in this human form—to probe the wall for something hidden. She felt Lauraisha's mental link grow strong for the first time since they had left Crown Canyon and, after a moment's hesitation, welcomed it into her own mind.

Katja felt the impression of a question not her own form in her mind. *For what, precisely, are we searching?*

I'm unsure. Just dream, drifter, and I am certain you will see it—whatever it is. She cast her thought back toward the princess; then she awkwardly nudged the piebald to walk forward along the stone wall. She kept her eyes shut and her hand outstretched and mentally felt Lauraisha do the same.

The terrace's first impression was that of a constant ring of discouragement—unyielding, unrelenting, and impregnable. Then the impression slowly changed and Katja understood the stone's constant siege by its environment. Her fingers felt a thousand different chinks where rainstorms had washed weaknesses from the wall's surface and piled them as fine sand beneath the horses' feet. Though it might take centuries, placid patient water would eventually win this duel of creation. Her hands traced the paths water had worn through the rock until her fingertips stopped with a jolt on a curve unfamiliar…

This isn't water worn.

It was Lauraisha's thought echoing in Katja's own mind. Katja opened her eyes and saw Lauraisha sitting on Tyron less than a body-length away. Katja watched Lauraisha's fingers trace a long double curve carved into the wall even as her own traced the same arc. It was smooth—like the stone had melted quickly rather than been worn away by several seasons' passing.

The two humans watched each other silently—their connection unchanging.

We've found the entrance.

Yes, but that is not enough. We still have to open it.

How?

Katja shook her head and then peered, puzzled, at the stone tier. It seemed so solid, like the dwarven tunnel door she had opened once before. So similar, in fact, that she swore she could make out old dwarvish runes inlaid upon its surface. They were barely visible in night's shadow, but there nonetheless.

What are dwarven runes doing in the middle of dryad territory? Lauraisha asked.

Who knows. This would indicate that the two races did far more than just trade occasionally.

"Well?"

Katja and Lauraisha both whipped their heads toward the speaker's direction and realized the scarlet-haired dryad leader was standing behind them.

"We have found the entrance and feel the dwarven runes protecting it."

The dryad looked from the stone to the skinshifter and suddenly laughed. "You think those are dwarven? Look again!"

Katja traced the runes with her eyes. The square form was clearly evident; but, as she looked once more, Katja saw a different script just under the initial runes. These were not boxy like dwarven runes. Instead their contour curved smoothly with a single round point placed above each slinky stroke. The form was foreign yet she felt it should be somehow familiar.

Lauraisha moved her horse closer and she and Katja both stared at the beautiful language embedded in the rock. Without knowing why, they reached out to touch the script— both tracing the center set of delicate strokes with their fingers. The carving warmed under their touch, then glowed with light like the flame of a candle. Sounds of grating stones greeted their ears as the stone before them tipped forward slightly to reveal cracks where none had previously existed; it then fell back to reveal a passageway ascending around the terrace trees' roots.

The remaining dryads had joined them and tittered to one another with wonder over the humans' accomplishment as they began to guide the strangers toward the heart of their home.

Lauraisha looked at Katja in bewilderment. *What act did we perform that is so phenomenal? We did nothing more than touch a symbol!*

I'm not sure, but I am certain we'll discover the significance of this soon enough.

Lauraisha nodded and Katja felt the human's mind once again draw away from her own awareness. The resulting void of mental contact felt like a frigid echo where a warm presence should have been. Somehow Katja felt lonely despite being the center of attention. She also became once again acutely aware of her throbbing feet as everyone marched onto the slab of rock that acted as a ramp between the tilled earth of the vineyard and the root-entangled soil of the First Tier. The roots overhead were thankfully high enough to admit the skinshifter while still riding the sixteen-paw-high piebald. Lauraisha, however, had to dismount and lead the giant Tyron during most of their journey.

The party members walked on around the breadths of enormous trees whose roots entangled thickly enough around the trail to seem more like the walls of a dwarf cave tunnel than a tree-lined passageway. Every few steps Katja caught a glimpse of moonlight cascading through a gap in the roots to light their way, but found no other illumination besides. Dryads had excellent vision, after all, and had no need to risk a burning torch near their precious vegetation.

Katja observed the dryads as they passed in and out of shadow. Their size and features made them seem almost human despite their aspen-leaf-shaped ears, root-like toes, and pale-green skin. Most had long hair cloaking the tops of their heads, which cascaded in vine-like waves of scarlet, corn silk, moss, or bark hues down their graceful backs. They all were incredibly tall by Katja's standards—most stood at least a body-length tall plus a fifth—and were very thin despite being firmly muscled.

The dryads' clothing was among the best camouflage the werecat had ever seen. They bound their bodies with earth-toned and green linen strips which hugged every curve. Over that, they wore wooden armor and leaf-net drapes over their chests, hips and legs. Some wore helmets formed of the same dense, lacquered wood as their armor while others preferred to don leaf-nets to hide the colors of their hair. All carried weapons ranging from glaives to spears to chain whips or sickles. Each also carried a strung bow and a quiver of arrows. Together, the twenty females formed a very formidable sight and Katja felt oddly at home among such warriors.

The dryads' home held an ethereal quality that reminded the skinshifter of a vision from a waking dream. The root tunnels slowly gave way to an open path winding slowly around the tree-cloaked mountain. The misty, moon-dappled forest beyond was alive with night creatures' songs—adding a sweet lullaby to the night. Huge trees towered above a fern-and-vine strewn forest floor. Green life grew out of time and place in this glen. Oak, orange, apricot, ash, aspen, maple, hickory, poplar, pine, palm, spruce, redwood, walnut, and other trees all mingled together in impossible harmony. Here and there bark-walled huts nestled between gnarled tree roots that had branched aboveground. Other trees boasted staircases made from odd-shaped boughs spiraling round the trees' trunks to their crowns. Occasionally, an old oak or redwood would even have a door carved into its stalwart façade. Curious balls of glowing lichen hung from every inhabited tree's branches like lit Aribemasse ornaments.

As they climbed further up the mountain, Katja and Lauraisha began to see larger grass-covered gaps between trees and water-filled hollows where glowing pixies buzzed between leaves, and toadstool folk clans of gnomes and brownies all poked their tiny heads out of the foliage to watch the party pass. Soot-covered leprechauns merrily greeted the company from their miniature forges near sandy pond banks before turning back to their metal crafting or cobbling. The fall of their tiny hammers added a tinkling percussion to the pixies' flute-like voices.

"Wait here," the scarlet-haired dryad commanded before sprinting off with two others around a screen of trees toward the left.

They returned after a time and led the rest of the party around the trees to a surprisingly flat grassy meadow flanked on the left by a shallow cattail-ringed pond, and on the remaining three sides by towering trees. Katja realized they had prepared a tree-den near the shallow pond for Lauraisha's and her use. It was a large gum tree so full of gnarled branches that the boughs had twisted together to form a solid wooden room above the tree's trunk. Katja saw no breech of bark save a slit just large enough for the humans to crawl though. Whether this peculiar structure was naturally grown or artificially encouraged, Katja had no idea. Either way, it was a strange sight.

After the humans had picketed their grateful horses on the lush green, Lauraisha and one of the dryads helped Katja limp to an area blanketed by soft moss beside the pond. Under the light of a pair of lichen spheres, the scarlet-haired leader then bent to unwrap the bandages from the skinshifter's ragged appendages. Katja gritted her teeth and snarled as the fabric pulled out of the lacerations.

The leader winced. "As deep as the wounds are, it will take some weeks for this to heal completely. I'm afraid you won't be able to have full use of your feet until then. I'm amazed that you haven't fainted yet from blood loss."

The Feliconian grimaced. "I can tolerate much pain if the

need is great enough."

"So I see."

She called over two of the dryads and instructed them to gather dittany root, lion's paw, garlic, aloe vera, lemon verbena, and daisies, as well as some plants that Katja did not know. While they hurried off to complete their task, the dryad went to the base of the tree-den to retrieve fresh linen cloth, which she tore into strips and lay on the loam beside Katja. She wet a piece in the cool clear pond water and began gently washing debris out of the gashes. Lauraisha, all the while, knelt beside Katja and the dryad, watching the process with fascination.

"Do you use garlic to fight any infection?" she asked.

"Yes, as well as daisies and spore nettle to help draw out any remaining toxins and numb the pain," the dryad responded as she began to mix some of the ingredients just handed to her by the two now-panting dryads.

She made swift work of crushing the leaves together between two flat grinding stones before amassing them in a provided wooden bowl and adding water to create a poultice. "You've knowledge of plants. That is odd for a human."

"One of my brothers is adept at the cooking and healing arts. Much of what I know I learned from him."

"I see."

"May I be so bold as to inquire your name and rank among the Glen Folk?"

"You may. I am Zahra Zahlathrazel and I am well known among my kind for my skillfulness as a warrior and my kinship to our Queen Mother, Zahlathra," she replied while applying the poultice and binding Katja's feet.

Katja meanwhile felt a tingling sensation overwhelm her body. She looked wildly at the sky and saw no moon. It must have already set!

"Not so tight!" Katja reached toward Zahra as she tied the bandage. Her body convulsed, throwing her back against the moss as she felt the transformation take her. She screamed as her fangs and claws pushed through the melding skin of her mouth and hands.

She heard startled shouts as Lauraisha and Zahra both jumped clear and the dryads circled her with weapons drawn.

"No! No! Leave her be!" Lauraisha cried. "She can't help it."

"A skinshifter," Zahra murmured in awe. She motioned sharply to the others. The dryads all gave the werecat a wide birth, but kept their weapons at the ready. Katja lay writhing on the ground in their midst, crying in pain and humiliation. Her skin itched and prickled as the golden fur regrew. Her hands and feet felt like liquid fire as the bones flowed back into their usual form. Her jaw realigned while the soles of her four paws toughened—causing tremendous pain as the back paws' calloused pads grew around her open wounds. Her normal senses flooded back to her, leaving her mind overwhelmed as the last changes to her face took place. When it was finished, Katja lay face-down whimpering upon the ground—her breath coming in uneven gasps between her sobs.

"Katja?" Lauraisha's tentative voice was filled with apprehension.

Katja didn't answer, but concentrated on trying to control her tears and breathing.

"Katja?"

The werecat clenched her fangs and clamped her eyes shut as the last aches of her body slowly faded. She tried to push herself up and only managed to lift her head. She stared at Lauraisha long enough to say, "I'm all right," before she felt her head hit the ground and the world go black.

IX

TRAILS AND TRIALS

K atja fought the sleep, drifting in and out of consciousness while voices on all sides raged around her.

"How did you come to be a companion with a *changeling*, human?" interrogated a stranger's voice.

"My name is Lauraisha *Astrat'a* of Tyglesea and I will answer to that title alone—"

"Astrat'a as in of the royal house?" Zahra sounded stunned.

"Of course..."

Zahra spoke again, "My apologies, Your Highness, we will certainly bring your entreaties before the Queen Mother as is only proper. However, you must understand that we cannot allow you or the skinshifter to wander without chaperones in our homeland—"

"Oh, certainly!" Lauraisha replied coolly. "A matter of security for us, I'm sure. All I ask is that you ensure a safe place of rest and healing for the two of us."

"Tyglesean princess, hah! She is a pawn of her father's, sent to spy on us! It's small wonder that she would shelter the changeling—!"

"Qenethala! How dare you show such discourtesy toward a royal or a mage!" Zahra screeched in rage. A loud slap echoed in the damp air.

"My apologies, esteemed Zahra, I mean no disrespect... but are not skinshifters often used as spies by our northern enemies?"

"Too true!" another dryad added.

Lauraisha spoke firmly, "Katja is no spy! I can assure you of that. She is a most trustworthy companion. In point of fact, she has saved my life twice on our journey thus far. I could do no less than repay the same debt should the opportunity present itself."

"Do not worry about your companion, My Madam; she will be as welcome here as any other Sylvan and I will personally see to her care."

"Thank you, kind Zahra..."

* * *

"Let us check her wounds and see their progress."

"I beg your pardon, Zahra, but what good would it do? It's only been half a day since you first wrapped them," Lauraisha asked.

"Indeed, but we should add more medicine..."

"The wounds are gone!"

"So they are," Zahra replied. "I wondered if her skinshifting abilities might help her heal. It seems I was correct."

"I never would have imagined such a thing," the Tyglesean exclaimed.

"I certainly did not expect a complete recovery this soon; this skinshifter is truly powerful. I question that her technique is not more refined though. The more powerful skinshifters tend to display great control of their bodily transformations... far better than she did last night. Has she had any formal training?"

"In truth, I do not know. I doubt that she would really trust anyone to formally teach her. I think she despises the ability, and little wonder since others seem to judge her so harshly by it."

"She would probably do well to learn nonetheless; it would at least lessen her pain."

"Is there one among your kin who could teach her such things?"

"Of mine, no. Dryads usually do not inherit such abilities..."

* * *

"She cannot stay here, Zahra!"

"Calm yourself, Qenethala. She is a guest until such time as Zahlathra meets with her."

"She reeks of burned bones and the dead! I know you smell it! She and the human brought those deadwalker fiends to our very gate! They got past the First Tier so easily…a feat surely accomplished by dark witchery! They must be expelled before they find a way to bring the other fiends in as well!" the dryad screeched in panic.

"Silence, Qenethala! Our Queen Mother will decide their fate. Until then they are my charges. Would you dare defy me?" There was no mistaking the ominous edge in Zahra's voice.

"No, Elder Sister, no of course not," the dryad said, her voice quaking.

"Then stop raising a panic and let them alone…"

* * *

Katja finally woke and peered blearily around her. She could see the late summer light peeking through the entry crack between the gum tree's branches and realized she was nestled inside the old tree's uncanny limb room. Her body lay on a paw-width thick pallet woven of aromatic grasses stuffed with seedless cotton and feather down and covered by linen sheets. It was the most comfortable cushion she had ever laid on and, consequently, she refused to move until the sounds of a large splash and laughter finally overwhelmed her curiosity. The werecat regretfully left her bed, crawled the three body-lengths to the wide slit entrance, and poked her head into the dazzling afternoon light.

"It's about time! I thought you were going to sleep all week!"

"How long was I out?"

"Today is the second da—"

"Lauraisha?"

"Yes?"

"Why are you bare-skinned?"

Lauraisha was indeed naked and wading up to her shoulders in the pond waters.

"Well, I can't very well take a proper bath while clothed!"

the peals of the human's laughter emanated like silver bells upon the breeze.

"You purposely submerge yourself bare in cold water… for fun?"

"Oh, come now, Katja, do not tell me that you have no knowledge of swimming."

"Of course I do! I just hate doing it," Katja retorted, her ears and cheeks burning. She averted her eyes and began carefully climbing down the tree—testing a paw on the rough bark before confidently planting it on the ground less than a body-length below her. Lauraisha, meanwhile, stepped dripping out of the pond to grab a cotton-woven cloth from the branch of a young oak tree nearby. She dried herself off and then began wringing the moisture from her hair. The late sun turned her usually subdued locks into ringlets of scarlet fire.

"Per myn ehre! Your hair looks almost at brilliant as Zahra's!"

"It does, doesn't it?" She finished cleaning the water out of her ears and then dressed in a long linen smock with green overdress and hip sash that the dryads had evidently provided. "It has seemed redder of late, probably because I've lived under the sun more than usual."

"So where are Zahra and the other dryads?"

"I was told that they would be along soon. I cannot believe that your wounds have healed so quickly!"

Katja's ears drooped as she remembered that particularly agonizing experience. "I thought that the pain of skinshifting had lessened for good. Apparently, I was wrong."

"How so?"

"Turning into a human was always difficult; turning back was always easier. Yet when I changed into a human this last time, it was almost effortless while turning back was excruciating."

"Why?"

"How would I know?" Katja retorted, her ears flicking.

"Fine, but don't twitch your ears so much! You've a right to be irritated. Just refrain from thrusting your annoyance on me, please."

Katja bobbed her head in apology before surveying the

golden wood around her. Even the late afternoon's light could not dispel the dreamy quality of the landscape. Gossamer-winged pixies in flowing rainbow-hued garments fluttered past the two larger females and darted glittering, across the meadow. Occasionally, one would swoop close enough to scold the pair with an incomprehensible chitter before flitting away once again.

Katja grinned. *What timid beings pixies are.*

Lauraisha giggled at her silent comment.

Still smiling, the werecat followed the flight of one across the meadow where Tyron and the piebald grazed until an approaching figure caught her eye. The lone dryad's bearing was purposefully proper yet she still moved with all the ethereal grace of her kind. Although Katja could not discern the dryad's features with her face cast in contrasting shadow, the Feliconian recognized her from her half-made memories of the past two days.

The twenty-winter-old dryad wore a shimmering green cloak pushed back from her shoulders while a circlet of gold-dipped olive branches encircled her brow and her semi-braided red ringlets. Under her flowing green cloak, she wore a soft white organdy gown gathered upon her left shoulder by a leaf-shaped jade clasp. The cloth cascaded from the clip like a misty waterfall flowing across her slender body before pooling on the grass behind her. She bore a pair of ornate silver-sheathed sickles upon the golden belt slung across her hips as well as a pair of sunsilver throwing knives tucked under the calf-length thongs of her dark-brown sandals.

As green as most other dryads' skin seemed, hers was somehow richer without being darker—like the lichen globes growing on the old oak trees. Her eyes were almond shaped and reminded Katja of the rich brown soil flowing under her own paws. Those eyes held quiet power behind them. Indeed, her every breath somehow made the world around her more verdant and all plants seemed to bend lovingly toward her.

"It is time," Princess Zahra Zahlathrazel told the pair. "Please make yourselves ready to attend our Queen Mother."

"Yes, Your Highness." Katja formally bowed before disappearing into the gum tree to change her garments. She splashed water upon her face from a basin made from a branch hollow and then shed her buckskin loincloth in favor of the dryads' provided clothing. She arranged her smock, overdress and hip sash carefully before climbing out of the tree to stand once again before the dryad.

"Bring your weapons, please."

Katja and Lauraisha exchanged bewildered looks before obliging the dryad's request. Katja also retrieved Durhrigg's ebony box of bow and arrows meant for the Queen Mother—carrying it across her back by its leather strap. Once Zahra was satisfied with their overall appearance, she led the way across the meadow.

The three ascended Sol'ece Mountain—passing under alternating root tunnels and tree canopies until they came upon a set of steep stairs formed from soil packed between broad roots. As they ascended the staircase, Katja observed the world around them change from the myriad variety of plants of all climates to only those usually suited for the foothills surrounding the Nyghe sol Dyvesé Mountains. Tall aspen, oak, hickory, and other such trees became far more prevalent while orange, olive, orchid and other tropical and semi-tropical plants receded in number.

The staircase led up a stone wall marking their passage from the First to the Second Tier of Ascension. Their remaining journey required scaling a series of close-knit limbs passing from trees growing out of the wall's apex. The limbs stretched across a sheer gorge spanning roughly four body-lengths wide and one spruce-length deep to embed in a forested slope on the far side. Lauraisha was shaking uncontrollably and Katja fared little better by the time the three had crossed the treacherous barrier between the Second and Third Tier.

Zahra turned to the pair when they both stopped to regain their composure, "We must hurry if we are to arrive punctually before the Queen Mother. She does not tolerate tardiness."

"A moment more, please!" panted Katja, who had placed a paw protectively on Lauraisha's shoulder as the human fought for breath.

"I...am all right."

"You can barely stand!" Katja protested while still feeling echoes of Lauraisha's terror in her own mind.

"I don't...relish great heights, but I will be fine. Let us continue." The human smiled weakly before shrugging off the werecat's paw and stepping resolutely after the dryad who was once again scaling the slope ahead.

Katja flicked her ears before continuing uphill after the human. Without the aid of stairs, the three had to climb up the slope using exposed roots. All were panting by the time they had crested the last hill.

"Pilgrimage, indeed," Katja muttered softly.

"How much further?" Lauraisha asked.

"There." The dryad pointed to a break in the thicket of gnarled trees in a valley just west of their position atop the bald hill. She smiled. "You are truly fortunate; few outlanders have the opportunity to see the actual place from which our home derives its name."

Katja stared in awe at the true Dryads' Glen, a place where legendary kings had been crowned and where great mages were still blessed. She and Lauraisha followed meekly as Zahra led the pair along a tree-choked path toward the dell. As they drew near, a pair of dryads in green-tinged armor barred their passage with crossed glaives until a herald formally announced their presence. A second pair of guards then escorted them into the clearing where the setting sun in combination with a myriad of hanging incandescent lichen globes lit the grassy glade. Some fifty dryads sat in the crowns of trees encircling the area—their elevated observation positions giving Katja the sense that she had walked into a dug-out amphitheater rather than a clearing.

Zahlathra, the dryad Queen Mother, stood waiting for them on the branch twisting down from her throne, which was actually grown out of the towering oak on which it perched. The dryad stood on the limb of the sacred Millennial Oak dressed in a long-sleeved robe of golden linen covered by a sleeveless green organdy overdress adorned with red embroidery and two silk sashes: a maroon one indicating her royal rank and a pale green one signifying her proficiency as a sproutsinger mage adept. The monarch's right hand gripped an emerald-encrusted maple staff while a heavy gold and silver chain was wrapped around the palm and fingers of her left. A tiara fashioned from sunsilver and diamonds graced her vine-like auburn curls, which freely tumbled down her back to her hips. She had a broad face with deep green eyes and dark green lips. Her skin was as green as Zahra's, although it held a slight brown undertone indicative of the dryad's immense age. The vast beauty and power held beneath that lined façade amazed Katja. It was little wonder all dryads regardless of clan ties called her "Mother."

"Navega a luz," Zahlathra said to Zahra by way of formal greeting, then repeated the same to Lauraisha.

"And who is the Tyglesean princess's escort?" she asked Lauraisha.

"This is Katja Escari of the Feliconas Clan of werecats, My Madam," the human said with a formal bow, which Katja mimicked when she was acknowledged.

"Navega a luz, Katja. And why do you and Her Royal Highness seek my protection and counsel?"

Katja glanced around at the assembled Glen Council before answering, "We are being hunted by deadwalkers, My Madam. The old mage keep of Crown Canyon is no longer impregnable and we knew of nowhere else to go…"

Murmurs immediately simmered among the assembly, but swiftly died as Zahlathra's staff butt struck her throne tree. "Silence, please! Katja, kindly continue your story."

At the Queen Mother's encouragement, Katja recounted the tale of her village's destruction, her first encounter with Lauraisha, and their journey together thus far. She purposely left out key details about their time spent in Crown Canyon. Somehow she felt that revealing Canuche's circumstances and Damya's or Durhrigg's existence to the general assembly would not be prudent at present. After she had given her account, Zahlathra also heard Lauraisha's account of the matter, which emulated Katja's omissions.

The human's story gave Katja more insight about the princess's family and the circumstances surrounding their reign in Tyglesea. The Feliconian knew a good token of King Kaylor's bloody putsch to the throne and the resulting tyranny of his absolute monarchy, but she was unfamiliar with Tyglesea's current politics.

She was surprised to discover Lauraisha's family politics excluded the marrying off of daughters once they came of age at fifteen winters, which had been typical in historical Tyglesean and Vihous human societies. Instead Lauraisha's elder sister, Kyla, would be kept within the family household long enough to earn a full education before Kaylor arranged her marriage to a suitable aristocrat when she reached twenty-one winters of age.

Kaylor's discovery of a prophecy supposedly linking Lauraisha to his future demise set in motion the events that led the princess to escape to Crown Canyon. Upon the cancellation of her societal debut, Lauraisha and her siblings became suspicious of Kaylor's motives. Lauraisha's ever-resourceful elder brother Saldis stumbled onto the truth and warned his sister about the first of two attempted assassinations. Her mother and brothers then helped smuggle her out of Summersted Castle and out of the country in the company of Father Arcos, the family priest to the House of Astrat'a.

In addition to Kaylor, Lauraisha had made several enemies within the Tyglesean aristocracy as well as several allies. Chiefly counted among her enemies was Evita, Kaylor's personal suasor—a Tyglesean term used for the king's chief adviser in domestic affairs. Queen Manasa had suspected Evita of ordering her daughter's assassination to gain further favor with the king, but had no way to prove it. Rather than risk the life of her daughter to find out, Manasa had begged Father Arcos to help Lauraisha escape.

Despite having lived through such an ordeal, the Tyglesean princess spoke of the past with a calm detachment that Katja marveled. The gawky human, who sometimes seemed far more catling than full-grown, now showed enormous regal poise in the face of a harrowing barrage of questions.

"Truly maroon blood runs deep," Katja murmured before being interrupted by her own round of interrogation. Zahlathra and several council members took turns asking about her clan's massacre, her various deadwalker encounters, and her statements regarding the sklaaven's motives. By the time Zahlathra called for the council's adjournment, the werecat's ears were twitching uncontrollably thanks to one dryad's remark about her "imagined tale of woe."

"Easy, Katja," Lauraisha whispered, her hand on the

trembling werecat's shoulder.

"The day has waned and we still have much to discuss. I call a close to the Glen Council's session for the present. Tomorrow evening at sun's end, we will recommence discussions. You are all free to go until then. May the grace of our Creator go with you."

"And also with you," the council members simultaneously answered her. Then they made their way out of the clearing.

Katja and Lauraisha stood watching the others depart, not knowing what to do. Then Zahlathra motioned Zahra to approach her. After a whispered conversation with their dryad guide, the Queen Mother bowed to the visitors and left the clearing with her escorts.

"What now?" Katja murmured when Zahra returned to the pair.

"Just follow me."

Zahra led them further up the mountain to an old oak tree whose lowest limbs had arced down to the ground on one side. True to dryad design, the boughs touching the soft forest loam were so well interwoven that they formed a solid arched room. There, under the soft light of a score of hanging lichen orbs, the Queen Mother greeted them.

"Come and sup with me; I feel we have much more to discuss," Zahlathra said before disappearing under the tree's arched entrance.

Zahra and Lauraisha both followed her, but Katja stopped short at the archway. Something smelled wrong in this place of plants. She smelt masculine musk mixed with the scent of warm fur. She smelled *wolf!*

Katja immediately crouched into a ready stance and snarled as she saw the two werewolves sitting at the far side of the tree den. The youngest of the two immediately responded in kind, his ears perked and his eyes wary.

"Peace, werecat!" the Queen Mother said. "Know that you will be safe as long as you wish to remain in my care. Come, sit, and show no further insult to my guests."

It was not a request. The werecat grudgingly did as she was instructed, but did not move her gaze from the werewolves. When she sat beside Lauraisha, the Tyglesean gave her a quizzical look.

"I'll explain later," she muttered.

Lauraisha's head-bob was barely perceptible.

"I should introduce you since you are now all aware of one another." Zahlathra looked pointedly at Katja before continuing, "Princess Lauraisha Astrat'a of Tyglesea, Katja Escari of the Feliconas Clan, may I present Chief Fenris Bardrick and his son Felan of the Geirgerd Clan of werewolves."

Katja's ears perked. The Geirgerd Clan chief carried himself as one distinguished among his peers, which made perfect sense given the fact that the Geirgerd Clan was the most powerful of all werewolf clans. Fenris was an older male who was predominately black-furred with the light-gray markings of age flecking the fur around his muzzle and golden-green eyes. He was surprisingly short for a werewolf, reaching barely above a body-length and a fifth tall. Even though he looked well over fifty winters old, the elder's stocky frame was still well muscled. He wore a loincloth similarly fashioned to Katja's, but decorated with elaborate orange-painted embossing. Fenris also wore a plain leather jerkin and axe-sling across his muscular chest. The rune-etched axe he bore upon his back was massive compared to any weapon Katja's kin ever carried and she flinched involuntarily when she saw it.

Felan was larger both in height and build than his sire. The twenty-winter-old towered a head and shoulder above Fenris. His fur was mostly black like his father's, yet he bore pure white along his maw and around his uncanny blue-green eyes. Gray ears crowned his dark head and streaks of gray and white fur also raced down his neck to pool upon his massively-muscled chest and stomach. He wore only a dark leather loincloth around his waist that—while not as elegant as his father's—was also tooled with intricate Jakkle markings.

Katja glanced at the werewolf script in contempt and then gazed at it again in surprise. Her eyes widened as she interpreted: *Brave in battle…Skilled with war axe and crossbow…*

A Gab Cloth! Felan was here as a would-be suitor to one of the dryads! Zahlathra must truly trust the pair of them if she was willing to allow such an arrangement. After all, Dryads customarily married few beings besides elves.

Zahlathra's words interrupted the werecat's thoughts.

"As you have heard tonight, Fenris, terrible fiends come to us on the heels of these females."

"Indeed, My Madam, indeed." Fenris nodded.

"I believe there is more of the story that these two wish to explain. However, before we come to that point of the discussion, I should wish to know why you hold that box so protectively, Katja?"

The werecat had almost forgotten about Durhrigg's gift, even though she had guarded it jealously in the clearing. Now at long last she knew circumstances were fit to explain it.

"It is a gift to you, My Madam, from the troll Durhrigg whom we met in Crown Canyon. He bids thee honor," she said, bowing formally before offering the ebony case.

Zahlathra knelt and cautiously opened it. She then gasped as she saw what it contained. "A troll *gave* this to you?"

"Yes, My Madam," Lauraisha answered her. "He traded many items to us before we left the canyon, but he said to give this only to you…"

For a moment, the Queen Mother was silent as she ran her fingers along the bow's upper limb. Love and sadness warred across her expression as she stroked the ancient wood. "At long last, Ella's bow has come home to her family…" she whispered.

Zahra frowned. "Mother, are you certain?"

The Queen Mother nodded. "Princess, you must have ransomed half your kingdom for this weapon alone!"

"No, Madam, he traded it gladly to Damya in exchange for sculpted glass."

"Damya?"

In answer to Zahlathra's question, Damya wafted out of Lauraisha's stone pendant and bowed to the Queen Mother. "Forgive me, Zahlathra, but my time is short; travel within the Erde Realm of existence taxes me greatly and I have already given up much strength to guard these two females along their journey thus far."

"A Pyrekin awake! How can this be? Are the Keystones unlocked then, My Madam?" Zahlathra was suddenly very alert, as were Zahra, Fenris, and Felan.

"The Keystones still slumber in their hidden places. They must wake soon; however, their whereabouts should not be your concern yet. It is far more important that these two be delivered safely to the Isle of Summons first. If they fail in their mission there, all of the Sylvan Orders will surely perish."

"You mean that all Sylvans will be saved by this pair of pups?" Fenris scoffed and Katja bristled at his statement.

"No, but these two and those who accompany them will be the harbingers for the final salvation of all Sylvans from the Asheken and their allies. As of now, our most powerful mages sit in their chambers blind to the soul marauders who tread ever closer toward them on their own lands.

"Queen Mother, you should know that King Canuche is alive. Princess Lauraisha reawakened his soul as it slumbered in the dwarves' abandoned mine halls at Crown Canyon. It is he who prompted them to seek your guidance and his faithful servant Durhrigg who sends you these tokens. You and Fenris must send Katja and Zahra to the General Mage Council with aid. You both know they are no match for deadwalkers alone. I have not the strength to aid them while the rest of my kin still sleep."

"But the dryads routed the deadwalkers on the night of these two females' first appearance. I had heard that it was a grand victory, too. Do you mean to say that more deadwalkers will come?" the werewolf chief asked.

Damya nodded. "The Sphinx is dead and her maw stands open. For the moment, several deadwalker scouting squads are all that defile Sylvan soil, but Sylvans cannot avoid a full invasion of the Asheken forces for long. The dryad victory here is also short-lived. Several deadwalkers escaped the fire crews dispatched to slay the dismembered zombies after the Battle at Sol'ece Gate. The ghoul Curqak is already hunting again."

"Curqak is *here*! Creator, keep us!" Zahlathra said. "What would you have us do, then, My Madam?"

"Send Zahra and Felan with Princess Lauraisha and Katja as a proper guard."

"*What!*" Fenris roared. "You would have me send my own son against the fangs of damnation just to protect two wayward females?"

Katja's ears went flat. She snarled even as Damya faced him coolly. "It is no more than I am asking of Zahlathra. Katja's and Lauraisha's chances of success improve dramatically with others added to their number. Who are you to judge a Pyrekin's word?"

Fenris shrank away from her as if singed.

Then Zahlathra spoke slowly, her eyes glazed as if remembering something learned long ago, "The Seer, the Arbitrator, the Sower, the Guardian, the Pariah, the Discerner, and the Renewed…The Sphinx lies dead, the greatest griffin king of all has reawakened, and a troll sends me one of the dryads' most heralded Second War of Ages weapons as a *gift*. Is it time, then, for one last fellowship to unite against the Taint of evil?"

Damya nodded.

Comprehension dawned on the old dryad's face. "The Sower…I understand," she said, smiling sadly.

Fenris's eyes bulged. "Zahlathra, you cannot agree with this lunacy!"

"'Tis not lunacy, but prophecy we are dealing with now, Fenris. Surely you know the destinies that stir in this, the Third Age of Existence?"

Fenris nodded. "I do, but surely *that* prophecy cannot apply now?"

"Why not?" Zahlathra asked. "It is heralded by a Pyrekin."

Fenris stared at Zahlathra and Damya for a long moment before finally bowing his head in grudging affirmation.

The darkening firesprite bobbed her own thanks in midair before turning to Zahra and Felan. "Do each of you willingly consent to aid Katja and Lauraisha?"

Felan and Zahra both bowed to her. However, Felan's ears flicked and his lips parted in a wraith of a snarl as he did so.

"Good. All is prepared, then. Forgive me, I must rest now." Damya inclined her head toward each being before fading into Lauraisha's stone once again.

Silence pervaded the tree den after her withdrawal.

At last, Zahlathra spoke. "Zahra, since you are to go with the princess and her escort, you must take Mother's sacred bow and the sunsilver arrows for protection. I also wish you to carry sunsilver sickles."

Zahra bowed and received the weapons reverently.

"Thank you, Mother."

Zahlathra sighed. "There is much to be done. For now though, Katja, Lauraisha, please tell us of your meeting with King Canuche."

The werecat and human recounted the full events of Crown Canyon. As they finished, the Queen Mother nodded with tears in her eyes. "Truly King Canuche favors you both! Someday I must meet this troll!"

"I am sure Durhrigg would be honored, My Madam," Lauraisha replied.

"Not as honored as I. Durhrigg saved my mother's life long before I was even born and then restored Ella's bow into my family's keeping!" Zahlathra sighed again and passed a hand over her watery eyes. "Let us adjourn for the evening, the hour is late and I believe sleep would be most beneficial to all."

The bright moon descended as they all formally bowed and bid farewell to one another. Katja's mind reeled with exhausted confusion as Zahra led her and Lauraisha back over the gorge, down the mountain, and finally to their gum-tree home.

Katja had left the meeting with more questions than she had carried upon her earlier arrival. How did Zahlathra know of Damya and Durhrigg? Why would Damya send a dryad and, more importantly, a werewolf to protect them? How could Zahlathra give up her daughter and Fenris his son to such a journey as perilous as the one to the Isle of Summons? What did the Queen Mother expect in return for helping them? And why did she reference prophesy?

The werecat felt the human brush her mind with an impression of a thousand questions perched upon her silent lips.

"Not tonight...my skull might split open if I think anymore," she murmured quietly.

An impression of pure alarm met her thoughts.

"Not literally!" she retorted aloud.

Her outburst caused Zahra to stop, turn and stare at her quizzically. Katja's cheeks and ears burned with embarrassment and she stayed silent in mind and maw for the rest of their journey.

Once they finally returned to the gum tree, Katja and Lauraisha bid Zahra good night and gratefully surrendered to the comfort of their beds and the promise of sleep.

X

WAKING DREAMS

Sinister nightmares once again besieged the werecat's mind, destroying any possibility of a restful slumber. Katja dreamt that the werewolf Felan went into a maddened rage and slew everyone around him with Fenris's great battle axe. As she looked upon the pallid faces of the dead, she swore that some of her own clansmen were among them.

She then dreamt a dream originating in Crown Canyon. She watched the young human aristocrat ride away from the burning royal palace of Summersted with archer's arrows arcing dangerously close to her body. Katja winced at the human's anguished cry when the soldier's arrows struck her valet and screamed alongside the Tyglesean as his lifeless body toppled off the horse and hit the ground.

"Arlis!"

Her outcry roused her and she briefly woke to witness the night's peaceful sounds before her vision clouded with dreams once more. She whimpered at the image of a male sphinx and a female manticore, both of whom were standing in the midst of a corpse-strewn battlefield with dark blood still dripping from their claws. The red sun rising behind them illuminated the dismembered carcasses and cast the victors' faces in sinister shadow.

The slumbering werecat's vision then faded to another scene. This time she was standing in a large cut-stone corridor with a lush red rug covering the polished marble floor. She began to walk down the hallway, feeling increasingly uneasy.

The scent of ancient evil pervaded the structure and every so often Katja had to stop and scrutinize her surroundings lest some fiend catch her unaware.

She suddenly felt Lauraisha's mind brush her own and knew that she had been drawn into one of the human's original dreams. The princess appeared beside her and covered her own mouth with her fingers to signal silence. Katja nodded her head in agreement and together they moved toward an ornate sunsilver door that stood at the end of the corridor.

As they approached the gigantic door, Katja realized with simultaneous relief and horror that they would not have to open it, for it already stood ajar. Whispers seeped past its crack to tickle their ears as they warily drew near.

Lauraisha's face contorted with consternation as she peered through the paw-width span into the red-carpeted room beyond. Katja followed her gaze and a chill ran through the werecat's spine. She saw something standing, cowled, with its back to them while it faced the only other object in the room: a full-length mirror with an age-blackened frame and a reflection as deep red as dried blood…

*

Morning light pulled Katja and Lauraisha's minds back to the world of wakefulness before they could discern anything in the mirror's crimson surface.

This might be for the best, Katja thought as she shook herself out of her tangle of covers and slowly opened her tired eyes to see the sun's first shafts pierce past night's indigo veil outside the tree. She stretched and yawned before sitting up and looking over at the human.

"I take it you are just as pleased to be awake as I am?" she said while trying to rub the chilled sweat out of her fur.

Lauraisha shuddered in response.

"What was that about?"

"I have not a wraith of a clue. It was certainly pertinent, although I know not why."

Katja frowned. "Why so formal in your language?"

The human shrugged. "I was raised with eloquence; I may as well practice proper language—at least upon occasion."

"That is the second time I have had that dream!" the

werecat hissed.

"Correction. It is the second time *we* have had that dream." Lauraisha shivered. "Only this time it was more detailed."

Katja grimaced. "I'm not sure I want to have it in more detail; I certainly have no desire to discover what lies under that cloak and cowl!"

Lauraisha said nothing, but stared at the landscape beyond the tree slit.

"It's the second time I've dreamt of Felan as well," Katja said, and shuddered.

"Really? When was the other?"

"When we were in Crown Canyon, I saw a vision of him standing tall and holding his father's axe. Just now, I watched as he used that axe to slaughter those of my dead kin ill-fated enough to stand near him." Katja closed her eyes against the memory and shuddered again.

"You don't trust either Felan or Fenris, do you?"

"I have no reason to…they're werewolves."

Lauraisha cocked her head to one side in apparent imitation of one of Katja's own expressions. "Odd. You hold such staunch prejudices against others despite being the victim of prejudice yourself."

"Per myn ehre, you certainly give your opinions freely!" Katja snapped.

"And you of all beings cannot criticize me for doing so. Besides, I trust you far more than most, so I give my opinion easily with you because I know you will value it."

Katja flicked her ears even though she knew Lauraisha spoke the truth. "You must understand that my clan has had many treacherous dealings with werewolves. There have been numerous clan wars between our races over land and livelihood.

"It is not uncommon for werewolves to capture and ransom my kin in exchange for hunting grounds, trade route access, and other resources. Some roving werewolf packs have even been known to steal werecat females, rape them, and then return them to us pregnant for no other reason than to disgrace us. Such would-be mothers often kill themselves to avoid the shame of birthing a half-breed; those that don't often die during birth-giving or are sent with their young to scrape out a separate existence from the clan."

"That's horrible!" the outraged human gasped.

Katja nodded, remembering the time when her eldest brother had rescued her from such a fate. She had been hunting and Kumos had found her just as she had come across a wild werewolf pack. They were hunting on Feliconian lands and an irate Katja had planned to give them a bloody lesson of werecat law before her sibling tackled her and pulled her with muffled maw to the safety of an oak grove. Katja shook her head, remembering Kumos and Keepha's roars later that night. What did she—a mere twelve-winter-old catling—think she was going to do alone against four fully grown male werewolves?

Lauraisha's words dammed her stream of memories. "Why would you shun the half-breeds and their mothers? The mothers did nothing wrong nor did the babies!"

"True, but half-breeds have no place in either werecat or werewolf society. If they even survive their birth and kit years, felwolves have no way of functioning normally because of their physical deformities."

"What deformities?"

Katja shrugged. "They look like neither cat nor wolf, but a vulgar combination of the two—much like the canis packs of ancient times," she said, before pausing. "Those who look more cat than wolf can operate on the fringes of our society, but those are very few indeed."

"That's horrible! To treat someone differently just because of their outward appearance…it is just cruel. It's wrong!"

Katja cocked her head to one side and arched an eyebrow in bemusement. "You—a maroon-blooded Tyglesean—are belittling the role of one's race and appearance in a social setting? Tygleseans have never allowed anyone to dwell in their country other than human without mage talents."

"Yes, as is plainly noted by my presence here instead of in my own *country*," Lauraisha spat the last word. "I certainly do not judge you because you are different than me, so why should others?"

"Yes, you most certainly do! You see that I am a werecat and assume I can do things you cannot. You would have never expected me to be strong enough to break out of Escos's wooden crate had I been human and more-or-less remarked such to me when you saw that I had changed into one."

"Yes, well that was dif—"

"No, in point of fact, it's not. You expect me as a werecat to be stronger than you. I expect you as a human to be more cunning and crafty than me. It is simply a matter of racial strengths. Felwolves, for example, are never as strong as werewolves nor are they as agile as werecats. That fact, along with the indecency with which they were conceived, does not endear them to either race. The Feliconian way of life is full of freedom, but that freedom isn't gained without great cost. To survive life in the mountains, you must be tough and have a clear understanding of the Erde Realm around you. Otherwise you will die. It is simply the way of things."

Lauraisha was adamant. "But to force someone to leave their home because they are different is immoral. You and I both know this. We are both victims of other's prejudices because of our mage abilities. If the Creator had a problem with our mage abilities, He would not have deemed us to have them in the first place."

Katja snorted. "Oh, yes? And that great argument certainly explains why Luther, his Víchí covens, and their soul servants and slaves attack our lands and Turn our Sylvan brethren into monsters through tainted magic while the Creator does nothing! Obviously, their cause really must be righteous or He would lift His holy paw against them! Hah!

"Do not assume anything about the Creator except what is written by Aribem and the prophets! You do not know what the Creator allows—for good or ill—to advance His divine plan upon this world."

Lauraisha's eyebrows knitted together high on her forehead in a look of incredulousness and exasperation. "Do you honestly think that you are evil?"

"I have the potential for great evil, yes, but also for great good. As do we all. I try always to walk on the side of virtue, but I don't always succeed. In short, I am flawed. I honestly believe that one's measure of evil is defined by one's flaws and I have a great many—not the least of which is skinshifting. My skinshifting ability has cost my family and my clan their lives, so I deem that it must be a great evil both to them and to me.

"I am not alone in my assessment either. Others fear skinshifters because of the six skinshifter traitors lead by Fritjof who spied for Luther's mate Naraka during the Second War of Ages. I'm no conscious traitor, but I share in that horrendous lineage of disgrace nonetheless simply by being what I am."

Lauraisha shook her head in sadness and turned her back to the werecat. Katja meanwhile lay back on her bed and stared at the top of the tree-den without really noticing it while the human searched for her daytime clothes. "If you're a dreamdrifter as Canuche believes, why am I the one dreaming the visions?"

"Probably for the same reason Sandrie and I dreamed together when I was at Summersted Castle." Lauraisha's voice was muffled as she pulled her chemise over her head. "Some beings that I deeply trust often seem to share my dreams."

"Why do you trust me so much then?"

Lauraisha stopped straightening her garment and frowned at the werecat. "You've saved my life—twice! What more reason do I need?"

Katja turned to look at the human again. "Once. The second attempt with Escos's soldiers failed so it doesn't count. Besides, if you hadn't pushed the horses so hard, I'd have been killed or Turned into a nemean deadwalker the night of our escape to the Glen. So you've saved my life once as well. If we're keeping score, then it is even and we owe each other nothing."

"That is the way true friendships should be anyway: even."

Katja's lip twitched in a half-smile and then she changed the subject. "Do you and your brother share dreams now?"

Lauraisha shook her head before running a comb through her hair. "Not since I arrived at Crown Canyon and shared those first dreams with you, which were sent by Canuche. I think distance affects the abilities."

"Do you dream of me, then?" Katja asked, sitting up.

Lauraisha nodded solemnly. "I dreamed just last night of the massacre of your clan."

Katja was stunned. "You've seen it?"

The human nodded with sudden tears in her eyes. "Many times. Why do you think that I—a Tyglesean who has never encountered a deadwalker before—quaked when you first mentioned them? I had already seen them and their destruction through your eyes."

"You know, then…" Katja whispered, while remembering the screams.

"Oh, please don't think on it now!" The human swayed as if ready to faint. "Our bond still lingers and I can feel the terror…"

Katja jerked her mind away from the memory, startled. "I'm sorry! Did Canuche strengthen our mental link?"

Lauraisha leaned against the wood wall to steady herself. "I think you did, actually. I was the only other being you had seen after your clan was destroyed. I was a fugitive just as you were and so you felt comfortable in my presence. You were so lonely and so was I. We needed each other, so we bonded quickly.

"When you discovered from Canuche that the deadwalkers were moving and that your presence could be a danger to me, you tried to protect me. You tried to leave without me just as you left Kayten—yes, Katja, I've dreamed about that, too—but, my stubbornness along with Canuche's insistence proved too much for you to fight. Thus, you're stuck with me." Lauraisha's mouth held a wraith of a smile and her eyes were full of kindness.

"Don't you dare pity me!" the werecat snarled.

"If I pitied you, I'd also have to pity myself for my situation. Pity won't keep either of us strong, will it?"

"No, probably not," Katja relented, before scratching an ear. "Do you think they have food for us yet?"

Lauraisha frowned and peered out of the slit. "There is something set up in the usual spot."

"Good, I'm starving!" Katja said, kicking the woven cotton blankets off her back paws and straightening out her loincloth. She splashed water on her face from the branch hollow, dashed down the tree, and called back to the human, "Hurry! Come eat!"

"It's not going to run away, you know!" Lauraisha called back while stepping carefully down from the slit so that her skirts didn't get caught on the rough bark.

"In my experience, it often does!" Katja laughed. "Come!"

* * *

The two companions stretched leisurely across the grass, reveling in the warm shade of the gum tree and the fullness of their bellies. The noon eat had consisted of all manner of exotic vegetation and meats amassed from the Glen's bounty. Katja was extremely grateful for the nourishment especially since she knew the frequency of such splendid meals would wane dramatically once she and the others departed the dryads' homeland.

With the fast approach of season's change, that departure must come soon. If they tarried here too long, they would risk being trapped on the westward side of the Nyghe sol Dyvesé by the early autumn snowstorms that often threatened the pass at Reithrgar. It would take more than a month of travel to reach Reithrgar and so Katja was antsy to begin.

Zahra had come to see them earlier to convey Zahlathra's thoughts concerning the impending journey and to speak privately with Katja. The werecat closed her eyes, remembering the earlier conversation.

*

"Katja, I am concerned about your show of hostility toward Felan; I don't want your disdain toward him to be a burden on our group."

The werecat had crossed her arms. "I will be courteous to him so long as he proves respectable, but I've known far too many werewolves who were brigands, thieves, and ravagers to trust him."

"Really? I have not held such immoral acquaintances. Felan is a good male and I sincerely hope you recognize that soon."

Katja's eyes narrowed and her ears flattened back in warning as she snarled. "Zahra, I am no fool nor, despite the popular theory, am I—in any form—a villain. Do not deem me as either! I will work with him, but do not expect me to blindly befriend him. He has proven nothing to me of his motives or his abilities. The fact that Zahlathra obviously trusts him enough to approve him as a dryad suitor is of strong repute; however, it is only one such commendation. I, however, have the validation of a Pyrekin to confirm *my* honor."

Zahra's lips thinned and her eyes narrowed. "My apologies, it was highly inappropriate of me to imply any wrongdoing on your part *at this time*; I simply wish to make certain neither of you will pose a danger to the other or to anyone else due to personal biases. We need unity, not division, within our group if we are to survive this mission. Upon your honor, you will show him courtesy?"

"Per myn ehre, I will! Provided that he shows the same such respect toward me and all others." She had said.

*

Katja squinted up at the sunlight filtering through the leaves with her own promise to the dryad still ringing in her ears. Could she really trust her life to this Felan? The foul fact that he was a werewolf—not to mention one of the larger ones she'd seen—coupled with her dream of his murderous rampage had set the werecat ill at ease. Katja was at least grateful that Felan's particular clan had never caused problems for her clansmen, but that was probably because their territorial range existed so far to the south of her own clan's borders. Still, Zahlathra vouched for him, as did Zahra. Out of respect for both of them, she couldn't be openly antagonistic toward him. However, she would watch the werewolf very closely to see if his actions actually could prove him worthy of their praise.

A change in scent roused the werecat from her thoughts and the horses' startled neighs seemed to confirm what she smelled. Katja sat up and looked around, her ears perked.

"What is it?" Lauraisha asked without moving.

"Werewolf," Katja replied quietly, seeing Felan approach.

Lauraisha opened her eyes and sat up while Katja peered at the approaching male. His gait was slow and he walked upwind of their location so that Katja could smell his scent long before she could see him. Clearly, he had no wish to startle them. The werecat and human stood when he drew near and bowed with one-hand salutes toward him.

Felan returned their gestures deeply. "My Madams."

"My Sir," they replied in unison and then waited expectantly.

Felan looked at Katja. "I wish to speak privately with you, My Madam, if I may."

Katja frowned and looked over at Lauraisha uncertainly.

I'll stay close, Lauraisha promised through their minds' link. *Call me if you need my aid.*

The werecat nodded ever so slightly before giving her consent to the werewolf's request. Cautiously, she followed Felan to an aspen copse two spruce-lengths away from the gum tree.

"I am sorry to intrude on your solace," Felan said, turning toward her, "But I must discuss a matter of some importance with you."

Katja bowed her head to show her consent and Felan continued, "You were introduced as the sole survivor of the Feliconas Clan and a member of the Escari family line. I assume that would make you the daughter of Dev'lynn and Kevro'lyn Escari. Is that correct?"

Katja's eyes widened in surprise at his use of the mage adept and master rank moniker of "lyn". Her mother Devra had been a harmhealer of menial skill while her father Kevros had acted as the village seer. Because of their magic, both were long-lived—having never sired kits until they were both over three hundred winters in age. How could this werewolf know her parents were mages when their status as such was a closely-guarded clan secret? For that matter, why would he assume that they were adepts or better of their respective crafts? Frowning, she nodded. "I am the daughter of Devra and Kevros; none in my clan would ever call them by mage adept names, though."

Felan watched her silently for a moment and his expression seemed oddly hopeful.

"What?" she blurted, feeling increasingly uncomfortable.

Felan shook himself slightly. "Forgive me. You're lineage boasts great power—especially in light of your parents' efforts against the deadwalkers during the Second War of Ages."

"That war was an epoch ago, so you and I are both far too young to know of such deeds directly, My Sir. Besides, their involvement is mere rumor—nothing more."

"Perhaps. Forgive my abundant curiosity. I was simply interested in the nature of my future packmates. Every Sylvan will certainly know Lauraisha's history since it deals so directly with the aftermath of Kaylor's usurpation during the Tyglesean Uprisings and subsequent Warlock Wars; however, few will guess yours."

Katja flicked her ears. "And what about my history is of concern to you?"

"I'm not exactly sure how to explain my thoughts on the matter." He watched her a long moment before continuing. "I just…I cannot imagine the pain that you have suffered from the loss of your family. My father always spoke of your father with the utmost respect."

Fenris knew Kevros? Katja had expected many things from this potential enemy, but sympathetic genealogical discussions were not one of them. This werewolf must want something from her and was therefore trying to ingratiate himself toward her. That made her even more wary of him. "How could your father have possibly known mine? Our clan has never had dealings with yours."

"No, no, not in direct trade, certainly, but, you see, my great grandfather Fenraz had told my grandfather several stories of the Second War of Ages, which he then told to me. Fenraz had met your father and your mother during one of the war campaigns. My great grandfather said your father was 'the bravest werecat I ever saw, certainly worth ten of any others of his kind.'"

Katja hissed. "This is the important matter you wish to discuss? You come here under the pretense of offering me your condolences for the loss of my family only to mock and belittle my race? How dare you!"

Felan's maw fell open. "No, no, I meant no offense. Fenraz's words were meant as the utmost praise! Surely you can see that—"

"Do me the favor of not thinking me so dimwitted that I will believe your 'praise' is anything other than a thinly veiled insult! Just like a deceitful werewolf to demean someone in the midst of her grief and then try to recant his remarks!"

Felan growled low in his throat. "Take care what you say. Members of my clan weren't the ones who betrayed the rest of the Sylvan Orders during the grimmest days of the war."

Katja stared at him, stunned. The remark might as well have been a full-clawed strike to the face. "You dare to mention Fritjof and the undying shame of the Feliconas Clan at a time like this? What kind of male are you?"

"I—" Felan started and then stopped. She watched the sudden anger leave his eyes. "I'm sorry. I was just trying to explain my great grandfather's statement." She saw affected sorrow gather in the werewolf's eyes, but it was too late. The damage had already been done.

Katja's icy expression could have frozen a Pyrekin. "Zahra sent you here, didn't she?"

Felan's face gained a guarded expression. "She suggested that you and I should learn more about each other. Discuss certain similarities—"

Katja's ears went flat. "The only similarity I see is that we both have a bossy mutual acquaintance who likes to belittle those less regal than herself and who doesn't mind using her allies to accomplish her schemes. You may tell Her Royal Highness that I will not abide her manipulation nor will I endure your insults. When either of you care to be genuinely hospitable to me, I will return the favor. Until that time, don't you dare speak to me!"

Katja barely inclined her head toward the werewolf before leaving the werewolf to stare after her as she stamped away hissing.

*　*　*

"What happened?" Lauraisha asked when Katja returned to the gum tree.

"I do *not* wish to discuss it!" Katja snapped.

"Very well." Lauraisha frowned while she watched the werecat. "You should find an improved composure quickly though; we've been ordered to appear again before the Glen Council…now."

Katja hissed her ire, but then curtly nodded.

The council meeting was more of a formality than a truly functional session. The Glen Council had agreed with Zahlathra prior to Katja's and her new allies' arrival that the four should indeed journey to the Isle of Summons with all due haste. Consequently the four companions arrived in time to listen to what amounted to several hours' worth of farewells.

Several dryads as well as many other faeryken leaders gave their individual blessings and advice to Katja and her fellows about their upcoming journey. Many, including the leprechauns' King Myph'lyn and the browries' arch-seer Taug'lynn, also offered prayers of guidance and protection to the Creator on the party's behalf.

Such prayers were both a welcome comfort and a slight annoyance to Katja. While she was devout in her belief of a sincere prayer's benefits, the werecat had little patience for embellished speeches and had to stifle several yawns through some of the longer harangues.

To help herself pass the time, Katja began reading the expressions of the assembled beings and soon she discovered that she wasn't the only one examining others. Much to her displeasure, the werecat caught Felan glancing several times in her direction. Try as he might to catch her eye, she ignored his entreating gaze. She was in no mood to ease his disposition. Let him sulk! Neither he nor Zahra had any right or cause whatsoever to insult her or her kin!

* * *

It took Katja and her new companions the better part of a week to prepare for their journey. To avoid raising enemy suspicions, the companions planned to depart with the dryads' regular trade caravan bound for the Geirgerd Clan's territory. The two parties would then split paths when the trade route forked just inside of werewolf territory. The caravan was always well-guarded, so any extra security would be easily dismissed; however, Zahlathra was still quite concerned that Tyron and the piebald might be recognized by deadwalker spies. Zahra's idea to stain their coats seemed the perfect solution until Katja and Lauraisha actually performed the task.

Tyron trotted over easily to her when Lauraisha called him, but the piebald stayed where he was—his nose snuffling the air apprehensively. When Katja moved forward to coax him close, he backed away in panic. She tried again a second and a third time to no avail.

"It's no use; he won't let me near him."

"He must be afraid of werecats," Zahra said.

"That's of no aid to me!" the disgruntled werecat called back.

She stared sullenly at the flat-eared horse. *Now what am I supposed to do?*

Without warning, the horse charged her, his teeth bared. Before the werecat could even react, however, Tyron charged between them. She watched dumbfounded as the huge stallion reared and kicked the piebald. Then Felan was there—lunging forward to yank her to a safer distance.

The piebald meanwhile tried to turn in mid-stride to retreat, but Tyron dropped again to all fours and raced after him. The huge horse vengefully bit the piebald's rump before evading a panicked kick and crowding the smaller horse on one side. Tyron's teeth clamped down near the other's withers as the sorrel pushed his bulk further against his opponent and forced him to change course. The piebald screamed as blood streamed down his back before finally submitting to Tyron's dominion.

"War training indeed," Katja muttered, as they all watched the two horses finally trot back toward them.

She turned to Lauraisha. "Since when did your riding-beast decide to like me?"

Lauraisha shook her head, her face a mask of bewilderment.

Katja turned back to the sorrel and bowed deeply toward him. "Thank you," she whispered and glimpsed Felan also bow to the horse in appreciation.

The huge horse whinnied and affectionately nuzzled her outstretched paw before curiously snuffling Felan. The werewolf slowly held a paw open for the horse to nudge. Tyron snuffled him and then gave a satisfied snort before trotting back to Lauraisha.

Katja frowned as she watched him go. She had just received aid from two of the least likely sources and that confused her. She noticed Felan watching her in the corner of her vision and turned to curtly nod her thanks for his assistance. Felan returned the gesture deeply before turning his attention to the piebald.

The piebald stood shaky-legged with his head down, the blood oozing from his neck. It was difficult to tell who he feared more now—the weres or the other horse. Zahra took pity on him and cautiously approached with bandages, salve, rags and black dye. The piebald quietly withstood her attention while watching Tyron receive his own dye treatment from Lauraisha.

"I doubt this will hide him, since he is so large," Lauraisha said to Zahlathra once Tyron's coat gleamed black.

She nodded. "His size is a problem, but I think we will be able to draw less attention to it by letting him pull one of the larger carts."

"You are turning him into a draft horse?"

"Well, considering his impressive girth, I think he would do well as one, don't you?"

Lauraisha looked at the horse speculatively and agreed. "The cart should be teamed by tall dryads as well."

"Agreed."

"How many spruce-scores do we travel under guard?" Katja asked the Queen Mother.

"Spruce-score?" Lauraisha looked puzzled.

"A spruce-score is the standard measurement that most Sylvans use to interpret distance; it's the equivalent of twenty spruce-lengths," Katja explained.

"One league is the exact equivalent of 158.4 spruce-lengths or 7.92 spruce-scores," Zahra clarified for the still-bewildered human.

"Oh! So a spruce-length is the equivalent of one hundred Tyglesean feet or twenty Feliconian body-lengths?"

The dryad nodded.

The human smiled in full comprehension. "So basically Tyron can trot almost eight spruce-scores in an hour."

Katja nodded, grinning.

"It will take you at least a fortnight to reach the route's branch," Zahlathra continued. "After you take your leave of the caravan, you must travel Reithrgar Road southeast for a month and a half before you reach the pass."

"Creator, keep us if there's an early storm," Felan murmured.

"A snowstorm will be the least of your worries once

you leave the caravan's protection and pursue the Pass at Reithrgar."

Zahlathra's words sparked a memory—one that was neither Katja's nor Lauraisha's, yet they both shared it in that moment...

*

The horrific sight of battered caravan carts had blazed into view. Mangled corpses of elves and humans and centaurs littered the ground around the splintered wagons. Katja's and Lauraisha's vision floated above the wreckage along with the savage mountain winds and then dropped to the ground in the midst of the putrid carnage. As they surveyed the obvious work of deadwalkers, their eyes discovered a fresh trail of scarlet where a human female had managed to drag herself into a ditch half-hidden by a thorn bush. Katja and Lauraisha saw the terror on her blood-smeared face as they came closer.

The Víchí whose memory the human and werecat now shared folded his black membrane wings behind his back and then watched the dying female for a moment.

"Well, fireforger? Can you yet destroy me?" the vampire asked mockingly in Shrŷde.

A single flame whispered into view in her palm before it guttered and died. The vampire hissed in triumph as he stalked slowly toward her.

"Creator, help me!" she had gasped, before the females' vision faded back to that of reality...

*

Katja and Lauraisha both found themselves on their paws and knees gasping for breath.

"What happened?" Felan asked, startled.

"Lauraisha has...visions..." Katja said slowly, blinking back tears of utter terror. "I sometimes share them."

"Lauraisha, will you both be well again?" Zahlathra asked.

"Yes...eventually," the human panted.

"In all my seasons upon this world, I have never met a dreamdrifter who dreamed even when awake," Zahlathra said as she and Zahra helped Katja stand while Felan pulled

Lauraisha upright again.

"Where did *that* came from?" the werecat asked the human.

Lauraisha shook her head and then clutched it in both hands, moaning. Her ashen face was covered in sweat. "That was one of the worst I've had."

"Agreed," Katja said grimly. "I guess that answers the question about our chances of safety on this journey."

Lauraisha looked up frowning. "That was a vision from the past, not the future. The female was a human; the male…"

"A vampire."

Lauraisha frowned again. "It felt like the dream we have shared in the castle hallway with the door and the mirror—"

"Jierira! Don't remind me!"

"Are you certain that the two of you are well?" Zahlathra asked, walking over to them.

"Yes, My Madam, we are always quick to recover from these sorts of dreams," Katja said as Lauraisha slowly nodded in agreement.

"Well, if you're certain." Zahlathra hesitated. "I can make the necessary arrangements to have the caravan leave on the morrow…*if* you feel you can be ready to travel by then."

Katja and Lauraisha smiled and bowed their heads to show their consent, even though both secretly loathed the decision.

XI

THE PARTING OF PATHS

On the day of the journey, Zahlathra came to inspect the caravan once all travelers were ready to depart. She suggested to Zahra and Katja that the party move during daylight and take up defensible positions at night so that they would be less likely to encounter a nocturnal ambush. Free daytime movement was almost certain because deadwalkers, especially the weak zombies, were vulnerable to the sun and would avoid its light whenever possible.

"Traveling in daylight won't make a difference if they keep a revenant with them," Katja growled. "It will just block the sun for them as it did when they attacked my clan!"

"You said that you banished it when they attacked you on your way to Crown Canyon."

"I believe I did. Brolaghans hate the sound of a werecat's screech; I guess their Turned counterparts do, too…"

Zahlathra nodded her agreement. "Revenants are also infamous for being one of the few kinds of deadwalkers to hold a strong affinity for running water. However, they will reside in the murk of swamps and the depths of large lakes when necessary. They also hold a great fear of consecrated symbols, so perhaps Durhrigg's spearheads will indeed help you."

"Let us hope so," the werecat replied as she presented Durhrigg's spearheads to Felan and Zahra.

"Do the spearheads serve any other purpose?" Zahra asked.

"None that I know of besides added protection, if even that," Katja replied dubiously.

"Possibly one of the mage charmchanters on the Isle of Summons can discern their true purpose," Felan added.

Katja shrugged. "Perhaps."

"In any event, you should only pass near small ponds and streams on your trek deep into the mountains; hopefully that will give you some security against both revenants and their protected deadwalkers. By my decree, the home trees of all dryads are open to you and your allies should you need our protection again."

Katja bowed and sincerely thanked Zahlathra for her hospitality and aid before politely taking her leave. She left the Queen Mother and her daughter together and climbed into the back of a nearby canvas-covered wagon to crouch down beside Lauraisha.

"I fear it's time we run the gauntlet," the Tyglesean muttered darkly.

Katja smirked when she received the human's mental image of a scrawny squire running between two lines of glove-wielding knights intent on striking him. She then lost her grin as she looked past the canvas covering into the shadowy forest beyond the protection of the gate. She prayed to the Creator for the caravan's safe passage, all the while remembering the vision of another caravan with its shattered wagons and mauled carcasses.

* * *

Much to all caravan members' relief, ten days passed along the trail without incident. Even so, both dryad and werewolf scouts were constantly surrounding the caravan as it entered the Geirgerd Clan's territory. Katja was less than overjoyed about the whole situation and spent much of her time avoiding the matter's discussion with anyone except Lauraisha.

"Buoy up, Katja! At least we're safe from the deadwalkers for the moment," the human told her as they sat near a campfire after the sixth evening's eat.

"And what consolation is that when we must tread through the heart of werewolf territory in order to avoid the

Víchís' slaves!" The werecat sniffed sullenly.

"Quiet or someone will hear you!"

Too late, thought Katja as she heard the crumple of a leaf behind them. She and the human turned to see Felan standing in semi-shadow just beyond their campfire's circle of flickering light.

Lauraisha bowed to the werewolf and quickly took her leave. The werecat watched the human's retreating form with panic before facing the werewolf again. She noted how the shadows played across his body and embellished his already well-defined muscles. Katja remembered the strength of those muscles when Felan had snatched her away from the feuding horses and expected the werewolf could probably take down a charging bull with his bare paws if he wished. She licked her lips. Even with all her skill and agility, she stood no chance against him.

"So you still do not trust us."

"Felan," she said carefully. "It takes a great deal of effort for any being to gain my trust and you are no exception."

"I see."

He watched her solemnly and Katja suddenly felt the need to clarify her statement. "Please, do not misunderstand me. I hold you in high respect, especially since you kept me from harm when Tyron and the piebald were fighting. But I don't yet know if you or any other werewolf could possibly be a good..." Katja searched for the right word and found it ironic that the werewolf tongue of Jakkle held a better fitting word-translation than any of her own, "...a good *packmate* to me."

The werewolf pointed out that whether they wished it or not they would be packmates for probably close to a season's time.

"And I do not loathe that fact, Felan. It's just that I have had bad relations with your kind in the past."

"My kind..." Felan whispered. The werewolf bowed his head once, whether in agreement or disappointment Katja did not know, and changed the subject. "So you escaped a ghoul and a horde of zombies by roaring at them and then swimming down a river?"

Katja nodded.

"That's it?"

She blinked and cocked her head in confusion.

"There's nothing besides that?"

"No, why?"

"I just find it odd that they didn't come in the water after you."

"I suppose they would have if the current hadn't been so strong; I barely escaped it myself and the only reason I did was because I could suck extra air through an empty water bladder. They fanned out along the water's edge looking for me once evening approached. One of the sklaaf almost caught me, too."

Felan looked off into the distance, his eyes troubled.

"What?" Katja asked.

"It just seems too easy."

"Easy? You think being the sole survivor of my clan is easy?"

"That is not what I meant! Do not take offense!" Felan stepped forward. "I just mean that they seem to specifically target you. I question why the Víchí would want you so badly and why they would spend such great effort tracking you only to misjudge your abilities twice." Felan's eyes narrowed. "Zahra told me of your second escape."

Katja looked at him, careful to conceal any emotions. "And what did she tell you?"

"That you and Lauraisha rode into their territory with the deadwalkers literally clawing at your heels. She told me that she even had to call the trees for aid in order to free you."

The werecat was suddenly alert. "Zahra was the one who called the trees? I didn't know that she is a hag."

Felan's eyes darkened and his voice took a defensive edge as he spoke. "The term is a sproutsinger, I believe. Not a *hag*."

Katja winced as she remembered her proper etiquette too late. "My apologies, I'm accustomed to the use of slang words for certain kinds of mages."

The werewolf frowned. "Your kinsmen must have thought none too highly of mages, then."

"On the contrary, my clan often produced highly skilled mages…some more honorable than others, but that is a story for another time. I must remember to thank Zahra for her sproutsinging. She and Lauraisha and Damya were responsible for my second escape, of course. I was too busy trying not to get bucked off that infernal horse." Katja's ears twitched.

Felan bowed his head and the werecat thought she saw a flicker of a smile on his maw.

"May I ask a personal question?"

He nodded his consent.

"What was your real purpose in coming here? You must have had a reason to come to Lauraisha's and my part of camp tonight other than recounting stories. What was it?"

"Actually, I came to give you this." Felan took a small wrapped package from the leather pouch at his hip and deposited a silver signet crest and chain in her waiting paw. "I believe it belongs to you now. I had tried to give it to you before we left the Glen, but you walked off before I had the opportunity."

Katja flushed slightly at his allusion to their previous fight and turned her eyes to the sunsilver amulet. It had her clan's crest wrought in exquisite detail upon its face, accented by a light green peridot gemstone set in its center.

She looked at the werewolf, awestruck. "Where did you find this?"

Felan smiled gently and sadly. "My father has had it in his possession for a number of winters. I believe it belonged to your father once. It was lost during a trade meeting between our clans long ago in the time when our territories were much closer together. Two pups found it while they were grubbing for fishing bait one day and brought it to him. He always kept it with him as a tribute to your parents. He thought that you as their surviving heir would be its rightful bearer."

Katja stared at the signet amulet in her paws. She remembered seeing it as a catling. It had always hung around her father's neck on its sunsilver chain until that fateful trip. By all rights, Kumos should be the one to keep it now, not her. If Kumos died before having kits of his own, then Keepha would inherit their parents' treasures. If Keepha died, then Kayten should have them. Katja was the youngest and therefore never destined to inherit anything of her parents' besides their love. The werecat began to shake uncontrollably with fury, with sorrow, with guilt.

"It should have been me, not them," she whispered, turning the amulet over in her paws.

Felan's eyes darted toward hers in alarm. "Are you quite well?"

"I'm sorry, Felan, but I need to be alone now. Thank you for giving this to me and please give my deepest thanks to your father as well."

Felan's ears drooped and his face filled with consternation. "Are you sure you'll be all right?"

"Please," the little werecat whispered sadly, "just go."

The werewolf bowed his head and retreated out of the campfire light. Katja's gaze followed his trek out of the hollow and then turned her eyes back to the amulet.

"It should have been me to die that night..." she murmured again, thinking of her clansmen's deaths as she clutched the crest over her beating heart. She felt the languid trickle of a single tear slide through her cheek fur. "Oh, Creator, why wasn't it me?"

* * *

Lauraisha was livid when she returned to their campfire. "What in the name of vile Víchí fangs did you say to that poor male?" she thundered. "I have never seen his head hang so low!"

Katja said nothing, but instead showed the human the crest.

Lauraisha looked from the crest to the werecat and back again. "What is it?"

"It was my father's...Felan gave it to me tonight."

"Katja, Felan just did you a great service by bringing you something of your parents and you spurned him as if he'd slighted you! You must stop pushing others away! We're here to help, not hurt you!" Lauraisha's mental nudge prompted Katja to cross her arms and send the human a mental image of a stone wall.

"Katja, you have to talk to me at some point! You might as well do so now."

The werecat said nothing.

"Does this have something to do with the massacre?"

The Feliconian's ears drooped.

"Katja! You need to stop blaming yourself for your clan members' deaths. It was not your fault!"

She stiffened and flicked her ears. "Simple for you to say! You didn't have to anoint and burn their corpses after hiding in a cave like a coward!"

"I've watched your memories in my dreams, Katja. I know what happened. You did what you could to help them…"

"But it wasn't enough!" she snapped, suddenly standing up. "Nothing I ever do is enough to protect those I love! I should have died that night instead of them. Instead of death, however, I'm rewarded for my crimes with my father's only surviving possession—another reminder of my weakness, my failure!"

"Katja, you can't—"

"Leave me be!" the werecat roared and threw her father's sunsilver medallion into the ashes at Lauraisha's feet. The Feliconian was moving before the other could speak again. Her paws carried her into the woods beyond the firelight faster than she could blink and in the next instant she had scaled a tree and sat perched among its high branches, watching the forest below her while Lauraisha's calls echoed in the distance.

"You know it's not wise to wander alone at night."

Katja almost fell off her limb in surprise at Zahra's voice. The dryad was sitting on a bough just above her on the opposite side of the thick tree trunk. "Why didn't I smell you?"

Zahra's brow arched under a sap-based paint that matched the tree's reddish-brown bark perfectly. "What would you smell besides more plants?"

"Good point."

Katja scanned the forest below her before speaking again. "Any sign of our enemies?"

"No, my guess is that our last little encounter shook them up fairly well."

"You know that you didn't destroy very many of them. They won't die unless fire or sunsilver is blazed through their guts."

"I'm quite aware of that, which is why I repeatedly order campfires built despite the fact that I and my kin despise the things. If the Asheken are here—and I'm sure they are—they know exactly where we are, but they also know that we have fire ready for them. They'll likely be far more cautious pursuing you than they were previously now that they know you have allies."

Katja looked up at the dryad. "Felan told me that you were the one who called the trees to our aid. You have my deepest gratitude."

Zahra smiled. "Told you, did he? I had not expected that. He must think you trustworthy."

Katja grunted. "Does he know what I am?"

"He may have guessed the truth, but I certainly have not told him. I surmised that you would wish to do that yourself when the right moment came."

"The right moment?"

"Well, we split from the caravan within four days' time. After that the four of us will only have each other for companionship and protection. We must trust each other if we are to survive."

"And will he trust me once he discovers that I'm a skinshifter?"

Zahra shifted her position slightly so that she could scan northwest of their position. "I believe he has already formed his opinion of you…as have I. You have a good soul, Katja Escari. I have no doubt that you will be a good packmate to us all."

"Even though I'm the reason you are now hunted?"

"The deadwalkers would come for all of us sooner or later. You just happened to be their first chosen prey."

Katja bowed her head. "I should have been their only chosen prey. I alone should have been devoured, not my family. Not my clan. They didn't deserve their fate."

"Few do. You survived for a purpose, Katja. Perhaps because you were the strongest or perhaps because you are destined for a life spent in revenge. Don't regret surviving the massacre; that guilt will rob you of your strength."

Katja hung her head. "Could you live with yourself… knowing that you were the reason your family…your entire clan and race were dead?"

"And what proof is there that you were the direct cause of

that? Did you slay your own kinsmen with you own paws?"

"No, but I might as well have—"

"Don't forget whose claws ripped life from the bodies of those you loved. If you could have stopped the massacre, I have no doubt you would have. Don't be foolish enough to think another's crimes stain your own paws. As the sole survivor, you alone have record of your loved ones' deaths and you alone must ensure that justice be brought to their murderers. Don't waste precious time flirting with self-doubt or pity. There is very little luxury left for that."

Katja grudgingly bowed her head in agreement. "I suppose I should apologize to Lauraisha now. I snapped at her moments ago."

"That you should and soon. Lauraisha might sulk if you leave her feelings injured too long."

Katja's smile was rueful. "I owe you an apology too, Zahra, for misjudging you. I thought you manipulative and bossy. Yet here you sit giving me some of the wisest counsel I've known."

The dryad laughed. "Only because I give myself the same advice every evening!"

Katja bowed and spoke her thanks to Zahra. "Find me when you need relief from your guard duties tonight."

"Thank you, but it's already arranged. However, I'll remember your promise at a later date," the dryad said, smiling.

Katja smiled back and turned to climb down the tree. She froze when she glimpsed a large creature flying fast across the inky sky under the quarter moon. Her eyes darted back toward it, but it was already gone. It was most likely a harpy swooping below the trees for her next meal, but Katja peered nervously around her again anyway. She crept down the tree and slunk back to camp, all the while peering behind her and sniffing the breeze incessantly. She halted when she heard a hiss, but relaxed a little once she smelled a king snake's scent.

Oh, how she hated sundown now. Even though she saw very well on all but a moonless night and even though she knew there were at least five sentries between her and the rest of the forest, the darkness now held far too many fears for her tastes. Only when the light of the campfire bathed her sight again did the Feliconian find relief from her anxiety.

* * *

The caravan members broke camp early the next morning and used dawn's light to help guide and protect their southeastern trek toward the mountains. The sun's welcome rays warmed the party members as they followed the path onward. Yet, despite the morning's balminess, the werecat felt quite chill.

Her attempted apology to Lauraisha the night before had brought nothing more than a curt head-nod from the princess. Katja then spent the remainder of her waking moments listening to the human's grouchy mutterings that the werewolf needed an apology far more than she.

After two more days of such treatment, Katja finally surrendered her pride and dutifully hunted down Felan. He accepted her apology with surprising graciousness and seemed to understand the werecat's motives.

"You have little over which to apologize, Katja Escari. I would have probably acted the same in my grief. I know you will need time to cope with the deaths of those you love and I swear to you that I will do whatever I can to help you."

Katja nodded in stunned silence. When she finally looked up to meet the werewolf's eyes, the gentleness in his expression shook her to the roots of her soul. For a moment, she saw Kumos mirrored in his expression.

"Thank you," she managed to whisper and then had to turn away to keep her composure. Felan bowed and suggested they both find the others and hunt down something to eat.

* * *

The next day oversaw the caravan members' parting of paths. Many of the members exchanged affectionate farewells; however, Fenris and Felan were not among those. The father and son's parting was bittersweet at best. Fenris tried for a final time to guide his son to proper reasoning and Felan endured his father's arguments against his accompanying the females with annoyed impatience.

When it became clear to him that his eldest son would not convert to his own views, Fenris finally sighed. Before the old werewolf left for his village, he firmly clasped Felan's shoulders with his paws in blessing and then passed the great battle axe in its sheath to his son.

"May it guard you as well as it has all those it has served before you. Remember your family and honor your clan, Felan."

"Father..." Felan said with awe and frustration flitting through his voice. But Fenris had already turned, his shoulders stooped slightly as if they now bore the burden of something far heavier than the axe.

Felan stayed silent for the remainder of that day and the day after. And although he and Katja could easily keep a running pace even with Tyron and the piebald, the group kept a slower cadence at the werewolf's lead than Katja had expected. After two more days, Felan led the pack off of the main road and onto a less-traveled trail that snaked southeast among the tall foothills.

"My hope is that this shorter route will hasten our progress and throw any enemies off our scent for the moment," he had explained.

Despite the increasingly mountainous terrain, Felan's plan seemed to work. The pack covered an average of eighty spruce-scores per day, or basically ten leagues by Lauraisha's reckoning. Their rapid progress was aided by the path's relative straightness and also by their resoluteness to stop only when absolutely necessary to rest and replenish themselves and the horses during daylight. The group members had somehow synced their natural rhythms after a week or so together and this added enormous proficiency to their daily travel routine.

Tyron and the piebald made little trouble for Katja or the others even though they often bickered with each other. In fact, the piebald had remained quite meek toward the werecat ever since his first fight with the sorrel stallion and Zahra's subsequent riding of him. This proved to be some reassurance for the skinshifter since she often ran close to him on the narrower trails.

The days passed easily enough over the first few weeks, but the nights always made everyone uneasy. Since Katja and Felan spent most of the daylight scouting and running, they left much of the nighttime sentry duty to Lauraisha and Zahra who could easily dose in their saddles by day to help make up the lost sleep. Although the arrangement worked fairly well, Katja still fretted about the fact that the two beings with the worst night-vision had the main night-watch responsibilities.

The werecat's nerves were helped only by the fact that she and Felan could cover the pack's tracks so well and by the fact that Zahra could sproutsing a fairly safe hiding place for all of them each night. As long as the group could find a small glen in which to camp, Zahra could encourage the foliage to cover any evidence of their hiding place. Some nights, they allowed themselves cook fires—mainly for Lauraisha's sake, since she could not eat raw meat aside from certain types of fish—but most nights they went without fire and hoped that any nearby deadwalkers would continue to overlook their presence.

Damya appeared occasionally to check their safety, give them guidance, or tell them current news from elsewhere in their Erde Realm and from her own Wraith Realm. She told them that their names and the names of several long-slumbering deadwalkers were now sometimes spoken in tandem by some of the more unscrupulous in Damya's realm. This fact deeply worried the firesprite even though she tried to conceal her flickering emotions. It was a comfort to know that a Pyrekin was scouting for them in her own realm of existence, but Katja often wished that the firesprite knew more about why their names were mentioned among the Pyrekin and in their enemies' conversations.

The only true peace Katja received throughout the entire journey came in her few chances of dreamless sleep. Yet as the pack moved ever closer toward Reithrgar Pass, increasingly dangerous dreams assaulted the werecat's slumber. She and Lauraisha shared dreams more frequently with each passing spruce-score whether they were asleep simultaneously or not.

The dream of the door to the red-rugged castle chamber was the pair's most recurrent dream, but it never finished playing out before one or both of them broke its hold with wakefulness. Not until the party camped in the very shadow of the Nyghe sol Dyvesé Mountain Range did the nightmare reveal its full conclusion…

*

Once again Katja and Lauraisha were floating through a dim stone hallway past several old metallic doors, all shut against the air, until they reached the last door, heavier than the others and held slightly ajar. Light streamed through the crack and, after some hesitation, the females peeked into the richly red-carpeted room. The room was again empty except for a lone figure staring into a full-length mirror. The figure was again cowled in black, but as the human and werecat watched, it lifted a gloved hand and pulled back the hood hiding its face.

A gasp escaped Lauraisha's lips as they both stared at the male's pale profile. He was almost elfish in his features, yet he possessed a strong chin and an aquiline nose, which added a roguish quality to his handsome face. He untied the cloak and let it fall in a careless heap about his boot-shod feet without taking his brilliant blue eyes away from the age-stained mirror. The act exposed waist-length black tresses cascading freely down bare shoulders and a leather-jerkin-covered chest. He was powerfully muscled, and even though he was a paw-width shorter than Felan, Katja sensed that he could probably match the werewolf in speed and strength.

The warrior leaned toward the mirror while holding his quarterstaff like a shield across his chest and stared intently at his reflection. Katja and Lauraisha followed his gaze and spied his likeness staring back at him. As they watched, however, his reflection slowly changed into a sallow-skinned image, which retained most but not all of his features. The creature in the mirror had a deep, purple scar that ran the length of his left arm and still wore his black cloak draped over his right shoulder. The most shocking difference between the two, however, was their eyes. While the warrior's blue eyes betrayed a soul smote with anguish, the reflection's blue eyes burned with terrible ire. His expression held insatiable hunger and hatred so vile that Katja had to turn away from the sight. She moved her attention to the cloakless male and beheld conflicting tremors of rage and grief wreak havoc across his face.

As the werecat and human watched, the figure in the

mirror began to laugh—a cold, cruel sound that exposed the fully developed fangs of a vampire. The fiend's laughter filled Katja's being with revulsion so powerful that it made her want to retch. As the creature's laughter continued, it intensified and the creature's face morphed from that of a half-elf into the most horrible creature Katja had ever seen—a full Víchí with glowing red eyes, yellow fangs, corpse-white skin, and black-clawed fingers. The mirror emitted a sullen red glow around his body, making him seem even more terrifying, and Katja swore that she could smell the putrid stench of pure evil smoking off of the mirror's surface.

The laughter turned into a triumphant shriek of insanity, but was cut off abruptly as the burning end of the cloakless warrior's metallic staff smashed through the mirror. Glowing red shards exploded outward from the staff, lodging in the stone walls, high ceiling, and floor of the room. The unhurt male was bowed in exhaustion over the rubble of the mirror. His panting breath rattled dry in his throat and his eyes were shut tight against the world as he whispered, "Brother, how could you?"

XII
SHIFTING PERSPECTIVES

Katja and Lauraisha sat up with simultaneous gasps.
"Not again!" the werecat panted. She sat on her sweat-soaked sleeping furs, unwilling to lie down again.

Lauraisha held her head in her shaking hands. "S-sorry about this. I had no idea how bad it would become."

"I'm not blaming you."

"What happened?" Zahra said, looking over from her perch high on the bough of a nearby tree.

"Dreams," Katja and Lauraisha said together.

"Again? That's the third time this wee—"

"We know!" Katja snapped. She watched the Tyglesean princess's shaking frame. After a moment she spoke again to the dryad, "We dreamt about the male and the mirror again."

Lauraisha nodded. "I saw his face this time...I watched him destroy that thing in the mirror..." She shuddered. After a moment, Lauraisha added, "He's a very handsome human."

"He's not human," Katja half-growled. "The features are too beautiful, the skin too fair."

"Well, what else could he be then?"

"Víchí." Katja said it darkly, anxiously watching the human who had become so dear to her.

"A vampire! But he doesn't seem evil at all, just mournful."

"Wouldn't you be mournful if your soul was tarnished beyond repair?"

"I suppose." Lauraisha looked at the werecat dubiously.

"If you two are quite finished gossiping, would you

mind helping me pack up the camp? It's time to start moving again," Zahra said.

She jumped down from the tree and began rummaging through her supplies. Katja and Lauraisha gave twin grunts of annoyance and began organizing their own belongings.

"Where's Felan?" the werecat asked the redhead.

"He's off gathering herbs and breakfast; he should return soon."

"I hope so," muttered the skinshifter. She rubbed her empty belly and peered above the trees. She couldn't help but notice that the sky's expanse was cloaked in a predawn veil of rich, deep blue. Her mother had called the color "cobalt", and it was both Devra's and Katja's favorite hue. She sighed at the memory and turned again to her few possessions. As she shook out her sleeping furs, something smooth and hard rolled over her left back paw. Suppressing the urge to curse vehemently, the wincing werecat bent to retrieve the offending object. She held up the round stone from Crown Canyon and looked at it critically in the dim light.

"Lauraisha, do you remember the stone being this size when I found it?"

"It looks the same to me. Why do you ask?"

"For some reason, it just seems larger to me."

"You must be imagining things," she said through a yawn before turning back to her packing.

Katja looked back at the stone she had rescued from the burning room at Crown Canyon. It did indeed seem bigger. She swore that its width-span had enlarged by about a claw-length although it felt no heavier despite the size increase. It also had darkened in hue from its original blue-gray to almost black. Katja squinted at it, wondering if the size and color were simply a trick of her own sleep-deprived mind. She shrugged after a moment and stowed the stone in its own sack before continuing her activities.

The pack left soon after their hasty morning eat of dried meat, tubers, seeds, and berries. As was customary, Felan ran at the front of the pack, followed by Lauraisha riding on Tyron and then Zahra on the piebald while Katja loped behind the group. Katja preferred this arrangement even though she despised having dust perpetually kicked in her face because it allowed her to work more easily with Zahra when covering the pack's tracks.

The group members and horses would often trot single-file to hide their paw prints and Katja could then use her tail to drag a broad tree limb across their tracks as she ran. Although the branch would leave its own impressions while sweeping across their imprints, its path was far harder to discern than their paw prints among the forest undergrowth.

Zahra also helped shield the group from unwanted hunting by using her sproutsinging abilities to encourage the healing of any plants that they trampled upon in passing. On occasion, she might also persuade a dying limb to fall across the road behind the party to block further passage along the route by large or mounted hunters. Zahra and Katja's contributions made the path look long unused by travelers. They worked so well together that even Felan—the most experienced tracker in the pack—often complimented their efforts.

The companions stopped briefly to rest and eat at midday and then continued along the pathway. This largely unused southern trail allowed them to avoid other Sylvans in an effort to keep their movements as secret as possible, but that would become increasingly difficult as they neared Reithrgar Pass.

Because Sylvans had experienced an unusually harsh spring and summer, Katja was certain that the subsequent fall and winter would be severe as well. Fall's leaf-death had already begun in the upper reaches of the Southern Continent and that left the pack little time before the seasonal change found them as well. If the pass at Reithrgar became blocked by fall's early snows, the packmates could be trapped between the cold mountains and their undead predators with little chance of help from the Sylvan warriors garrisoned on the leeward side of the snow.

Besides worrying about the fast-approaching winter weather, Katja had spent the last week disconcerted over the moon's waxing progress. It had been three full moons since Katja's village's moonlit massacre. The fourth would come tonight and that weighed far more heavily on Katja's mind than anything else at the moment. She had managed to discretely endure one moonlit skinshift while on the trail with the pack and she hoped to weather another without Felan knowing of her ability. Despite Zahra's past reassurances that the werewolf would not rebuke her, Katja had not told him of her abilities because she felt she could not risk the loss of one of her few allies. Despite her best efforts, she'd grown to respect and even halfway trust the werewolf and that fact alone was a dangerous enough compromise of her good judgment. Kayten had been the only family member to know Katja's secret and he had taken it to his grave. Would those who knew the skinshifter's secret soon share his fate?

In the evening, the packmates made camp at the site of an ancient-looking stone ruin that had once been a shadowshaper mage's home. The werecat was amazed that the illusion spells still functioned even though the place itself had long been abandoned. Katja had been the only one to sense the wards guarding the place. She took great pride in that fact and playfully teased Felan about his being such a great tracker even though he missed the clues suggesting the wards.

"You laugh at me for not noticing the absence in smell and feeling? Oh, come now! Who can smell an absence of smell!" he growled, but Katja saw the corners of his maw twitch with the exertion of holding back a laugh. She grinned at him before helping with eating preparations.

Since they had the luxury to build a large cooking fire while safe inside the wards of the mage's old domain, Felan and Katja took full advantage of the area. Both of them hunted wild game within the borders to help replenish the companions' meat supplies and then helped Lauraisha salt and smoke the buck and four hares that the hunters had brought back.

The mood around the fire that evening was considerably jovial—a stark contrast from the usual tension. The packmates all laughed and joked with each other over the evening eat and even Katja was cheerful this full-moon night. Later in the evening, Katja offered to take the first watch. Lauraisha and Zahra knew her reasons for this and readily agreed as did Felan, after his initial surprise.

As everyone else went to sleep, Katja crept a safe distance from the camp to an outbuilding with a fallen-in roof. She waited out her moonlit metamorphosis within the relative privacy of its walls and bit on a piece of wood to keep from screaming during the more excruciating changes.

Once the transformation was complete, Katja wrapped a blanket around her nauseated form and began crawling on sore hands and knees along the shadows toward the nearby flowing fountain. The blanket's hem was covered with twigs and grass burs by the time she was able to rinse the blood from her lips, teeth, hands, and feet in the cool water. Katja drank deeply and then huddled against the cold stone with the rough wool prickling her bare skin. She stared miserably at her human reflection in the fountain's rippling pool.

So this is what she looked like now. It had been a long time since she'd looked at her reflection while in human form. Even in the soft light, with her poor sense of sight, she could see that time had added even more femininity to her temporary skin. She was completely human with this transformation, lacking even her tufted ears and thumb claws. No fur could now hide her body's curved hips, full breasts and firm stomach. Her back paws, which had almost always kept their werecat form, finally looked like normal, flat human feet. Even her tail was gone in the full moon's light. Tonight human femininity and weakness were the same.

"What am I?" Katja hid her head in shame.

The crackle of a leaf snapped Katja's head up. She jerked her head toward the noise and, at seeing a tall werewolf's figure, Katja shrank back into the fountain's shadow and pulled the blanket close around her.

"Lauraisha?"

"Felan, leave me please! I wish to be alone," she hissed.

"Katja? What are you doing wrapped in a blanket? Are you well? Why does it smell like human in this place and why is your voice cracking…" Felan stared at her in shock. "Katja?"

Katja hugged her knees and hid her face in shame. "Please just leave me be," she whispered while trying to hold back the tears.

Felan stood still as a statue under the dark cover of the trees.

"You're a skinshifter." His voice seemed strangely joyful given the graveness of the situation.

"Not a word to anyone outside the pack! Please, please,

I beg you!" Katja's tears stung her swollen face as the cold breeze swirled around her.

"Why didn't you tell me?" Felan now seemed genuinely upset.

Katja could not find the courage to answer him swiftly. Finally she spoke. "I was afraid if you knew what I really am that I'd lose your trust. I have enough difficulty finding and keeping trust with others. I've lost so many I care for; I could not bear to lose another packmate. But, now it doesn't matter anymore, does it? For now you see me for what I truly am…a changeling, a monster."

"You? A monster? Never!" the werewolf said, then paused, seeming to decide something. Finally he spoke again, "Katja, I need to show you something. Will you look at me… please?"

Katja heard conflicting emotions overflowing in Felan's gentle voice: joy, sadness, worry and hope. Cautiously, she lifted her eyes…and witnessed a miracle.

Felan had moved into the moonlight and let it fully bathe his bulked body. Then the werewolf transformed. He shivered, and then completely shed his silky black and gray fur. His long claws and sharp fangs all melted into nails and flattened teeth while his now-hairless tail shrank beneath his loincloth in a matter of moments. His skinshift seemed to be more a melding of his skin and bones from his solid werewolf form into a more fluid transitional state and then into the final solid form of a dark-haired human male with pale skin close to the color of Katja's own. The human who still wore Felan's clothing walked toward Katja, his blue-green eyes straining to catch hers.

"How…" she started and then broke off.

"You are not the only one with gifts," he said, his voice filled with a strange mixture of emotions.

In the dim light, Katja saw the male before her smile. It was a gentle smile, like every smile Felan had ever given her. She stared in awe. Even as a human, he was handsome. Fur no longer hid the curves of muscle rippling along his powerful torso and limbs, indeed the lack of fur seemed almost an enhancement. She watched him move toward the fountain's edge to cautiously kneel beside her. She realized that goose bumps were already prickling his skin and suddenly felt sorry that Felan now had no cover to shield him against the cold air.

"May I see your face in the moonlight?"

"Why?" She asked suspiciously.

"Please?"

Katja finally relented and lifted her tear-stained face to gaze fully into his eyes. The expression in those emerald-azure eyes nearly took her breath away. Felan held her gaze and sighed. "You really are beautiful."

Katja snorted. "What!"

"Katja, have you ever truly looked at yourself? Come, gaze into the water, and see yourself as I see you." He leaned as close to her as she guessed he dared and together they gazed into the pool.

"Gaze and understand what I see: a female blossoming into full adulthood who is loyal and generous toward those blessed to be her friends. You are strong and so beautiful in every form I have seen," Felan said, his voice betraying far more tenderness than Katja expected of him.

She continued to stare at the reflection of her exposed face and shoulders, mesmerized by his words. But then she remembered the vile truth and growled savagely. "And yet this curse is what brought death to my clansmen! The Asheken seek to destroy me and everyone I love because of my ability."

Felan's retort was patient and gentle. "*That* is all the more reason for you to hold your skinshifting gift sacred, Katja. If the deadwalkers wish to kill you or Turn you because of this magic then it means you must pose a threat to them. I often wondered what it was about you that would push them to reveal themselves so soon on Sylvan soil and seek to control or destroy you and your kin. This skinshift seems as good of an indication as any that you are indeed powerful and, quite possibly, a *prophetic* threat against them."

The female frowned. "Felan, how can I possibly be powerful? I can't even control the skinshift when the moonlight strikes me."

"You may not see yourself as strong, but you are. You have had no training to help you deal with the pain nor can you change at will, but still you have improved your human appearance so much that even I can tell no difference between you now and a true human. That takes great skill, whether deliberate or not.

"I can teach you those techniques that you need to end the pain and gain control over your body. It will be difficult, but with a mind as keen as yours, it shouldn't take long for you to learn. This gift is not something of which you should be ashamed; it's a mage blessing just like all the others…you just need to know when and how to use it for the protection of yourself and others."

"You make it seem almost honorable."

"It is! This ability of ours is not an evil; it's merely a tool to be used as we wish. If it were not virtuous, my father would never have used it!"

"Fenris can skinshift?"

Felan cocked an eyebrow and grinned. "Where do you think I inherited the ability? My father can shift into a full wolf; he's the one who taught me how to use my gift. On that thought, which one of your family members could skinshift?"

"I…don't know. It is…it was taboo to discuss skinshifting in my clan."

"Ah, I see. Is that because the skinshifter traitor Fritjof was an original member of your clan?"

Katja nodded. "Felan, if your father turns into a full wolf, why do you turn into a human?"

He shrugged. "The gift manifested itself more powerfully in me than it did in my father. All skinshifters can shift into at least one skin aside from their natural one, but the most powerful ones have two or three learned forms they can use. I have two forms: a human and a wolf. I learned to shift into the wolf first because of my father's tutelage, but I learned to become human on my own soon after he finished my formal education. I've also learned to change at will and, as long as I shift skins at least once during the full moon, I can easily keep my techniques sharp. For some reason, the full moon seems to amplify and renew our skills…Katja, are you well?"

"Sorry…it's just cold and…" She said trailed off Felan's sharp gaze took in her trembling body.

Felan's pulled her into a firm embrace, his arms wrapping protectively around her before she could finish speaking. Katja pushed away from him, confused. She looked into

Felan's eyes and saw the deepest longing spill from their depths before panic changed his expression.

"I'm sorry, that was improper of me...it's just..." he stammered.

"It's...all right; you just startled me," Katja said quickly, panicked and confused by his expressions and by her own jumbled reactions. She didn't know whether she wished to strike him or hug him back.

"Does anyone else know of your abilities?" he quickly changed the subject.

Slowly she nodded. "Lauraisha and Zahra have both seen me skinshift before..."

"That's good. It means we won't have to explain everything to them. We should go back; you are in great need of Zahra's salve and I could use some warmer clothes."

"I thought you could change back at will."

"I can, but I think we should get your first lesson out of the way tonight if you are able, so that you won't have as much pain when you skinshift back at moon's set."

Katja bobbed her head emphatically. "Yes, please."

"Can you walk?"

Katja frowned at her bare feet. "I haven't practiced much on these. The last time I tried running on them, I tore them to shreds."

"Let's not have you run, then." Felan stood and offered a large hand to her. She took hold and used his strength to steady herself as she carefully stood on the new appendages.

"You'll have to remember to walk by planting your heel first then rocking the foot toward the toes...that's it," he said, still gripping her right hand to help her balance.

They walked slowly together through the screen of trees and back toward the main house where the pack had set up the night's camp. Katja stumbled badly once and Felan had to grab her around the waist to keep her from falling. His incredible strength made her suddenly feel like a mouse being tossed about by a bear. How powerful of a mage was he if he kept his werewolf strength even while in human form? Katja kept her face down and concentrated all the more on her wayward feet to keep her scarlet face hidden. Felan noticed her blush anyway and quickly dropped his supporting arm from around her. He would not, however, relinquish her hand nor would he cease his gentle encouragement.

Zahra was the first to wake and see them as they arrived together at the campfire. She gave them both a quizzical smile before rising to stoke the fire.

"I assume you both will need clothes, extra bandages, wash rags, and salve?" she asked.

Felan merely nodded and she was off to search the packs.

"She knows what you are?" Katja asked Felan suddenly.

He smiled. "Of course! I couldn't very well court her without telling her at least some of my secrets. It wouldn't be fair to her otherwise. Even now when we are no longer courting, I still count her as one of my closest friends..."

Katja's shock overwhelmed her tact. "You broke off the betrothal? Why?"

Now it was Felan's turn to flush slightly. "Yes, well...er... you see—"

"Who are y—wait, Felan? You're a skinshifter, too?" Lauraisha's shrill voice cut past the werewolf's sputters. "Why am I always the last to know anything important?"

Their voices had awoken the human, who now sat on her sleeping furs with half of her auburn curls frizzed where she had slept on them. She looked from one to the other of them crossly and then cocked her head toward Katja. "Are you well?"

"She'll be fine; she's just a little unsteady on human feet," Felan said while helping Katja to sit down near the fire. He grabbed two sleeping furs from his gear and draped one around her before using the other himself.

"Could have fooled me!" Lauraisha replied as she moved to sit beside Katja. "The night we escaped to the Glen, she ran just as fast as I did when she was human."

"And how hurt were my feet afterward?"

"Ah, yes, good point."

Zahra came back with the salve and began applying liberal amounts to Katja's raw knees and palms. Felan politely looked away when Zahra and Lauraisha insisted she change into a proper tunic to keep the chill off her chest.

"Even those of us with fur will have to resort to warmer outer clothing if the weather turns any colder," he said as he stared into the distance with his back to them.

"Quite true," Zahra commented. "Mother made sure we all had properly-tailored leggings and cloaks; I think she provided a couple of spare blankets that I can make into extra tunics. I suppose I should get started sewing those items soon."

"Give me a needle and thread and I shall help," the true human told the dryad.

"I think we can hazard a day or two here. We should be safe enough and Katja and I could certainly make the time useful with skinshifting lessons," Felan conceded. "That would give Lauraisha ample time to finish preparing the meat, too."

The werewolf's consensus cinched the decision. Katja and Felan again offered to take watch so that he could teach Katja the basics of controlled her skinshifting. Once the true human and dryad had gone back to sleep, Felan's first lesson began. He started his instruction by shifting into his natural form and then having the human Katja sit cross-legged opposite of him.

"The first thing a skinshifter mage should be able to do is completely feel the form of her body encasing her soul. You should be aware of details like how long your fingers and toes are as well as where your nose sits on your face. For other beings, this information is taken for granted because their features are solidly set, but for us everything about our skins is transitory. Do you understand?"

Katja nodded.

"Good, now we must strengthen this awareness in you and the best way to do that is touch. Fair warning, this will require some contact between us, but most of the feeling practices you have to do yourself...now mirror me."

He held his own right front paw out in front of him with his clawed fingers outstretched. She stretched out her left hand toward his and Felan bent forward until their palms touched. He looked at her and said, "See how much smaller your hands are against my paws? See how the fingers are shaped...the nails are stationary unlike your werecat claws. Memorize these details but keep your hand touching my paw. Notice the color of your skin, the texture of both the back and the front of your hands, and the way the fingers feel when they move…"

Katja concentrated on her own features but found it difficult to immerse herself in the memorization. Her mind kept straying to Felan's paw and its characteristics…the roughness of his palm pad, the softness of his fur around the edges, the way his strong claws gleamed in the moonlight…

"Stop that!" he muttered half-irritably. "The point of this exercise is for you to concentrate on you, not me!"

Katja's scarlet flush of embarrassment caused the werewolf to soften his expression. "Because of our mutual abilities, I can feel your reactions during the lesson. I can help guide you so you know what to sense, but you must focus."

"You can enter my thoughts like Lauraisha?" she said, jerking her hand away in sudden panic.

"No, our bond is not that powerful. Instead I can somewhat sense your emotions, but only when we do these sorts of exercises…Oh, come now, you know I will never harm you or try to assault your privacy. Trust me."

She watched him warily for a moment then finally relented and put her hand against his paw once more. She closed her eyes and concentrated on the form of her hand.

"Good," he encouraged. "Now…no, do not move your focus up your arm yet, we don't need you to advance your concentration right now. Instead focus on your hand and feel its form from the outer skin to the muscles and tendons running underneath and then to the hard bones that give it strength and structure…Excellent! Now, feel even deeper into the very makeup of the bones themselves. Do you feel the liquid flowing in and around and through them? Do you feel both the solid structure and the holes running through it?"

"Yes," she whispered in wonder.

"Well done, now keep that awareness ready in your mind and concentrate to turn the shape of those bones into the shape they must take when you have your natural paws."

"But I don't remember the shape!"

"That is fine, just contemplate the changes…your magic will help you remember the rest. And do not neglect the claws, they are part of the bones…Perfect, now mentally nudge the muscles and cords to follow your bones' example, then stretch the skin around the muscles and do not forget to leave the openings for your claws to extend through. Well done! Now, open your eyes."

Katja squinted at the world around her and her eyes widened in shock. Her left hand was no longer a hand, but her own paw once again. The transformation had earned her only the slightest amount of pain and yet something was wrong.

"I have no fur," she said in surprise.

"No, you do not. But don't worry; growing fur is an advanced technique that I don't want you to try tonight. All in all, you should feel quite proud of this accomplishment."

She smiled at his compliment.

"Now turn the paw back to fit the rest of your human body."

The skinshifter concentrated on her paw again and felt her paw's physical essence all the way through to the bone. She focused to elongate the digits into clawless fingers once more and then pushed her muscles and skin to follow suit. She found the process much easier the second time, but she felt far more exhaustion after this skinshift lesson than she had from the first. She remarked this to Felan, who nodded his head in agreement.

"It's natural to feel weariness after a skinshift. Honestly, I have no idea how you stayed conscious at all during your untrained skinshifts. You should be very proud of yourself for your proficiency. It took me three times before I managed to successfully skinshift my paw!" He laughed.

"Does one always feel tired?"

"Usually." He smiled. "The fatigue will fade with practice. But, be warned, there is a limit to the number of times you can skinshift safely. Each time you try, it will take more stamina to do so. Obviously, skinshifting only parts of your body such as your paws is far less taxing than converting your entire body, but shifting is still a strain no matter when or how you do it. Too much skinshifting in a short time could rob you of even the little energy your heart uses to pump blood through your body."

"I could die?"

"You could die."

"Oh, wonderful!" she snarled and then frowned. How had she acquired Lauraisha's habit of sarcasm?

"Easy now. At this stage in your training, you could die from three to four full skinshifts in a single night. This is why I am teaching you only partial-shifts. My ultimate goal is to see you powerful enough to be able to fully skinshift twice in an hour without harming yourself."

"An hour? As the sundial counts?" Katja was incredulous.

He nodded. "But please don't try that yet."

Katja emphatically shook her head. "I hadn't planned to."

He grinned before continuing his tutelage. "Now, notice that the palm of your hand is now healed of the cuts you received during your full skinshift. We skinshifter mages are blessed with the ability to heal almost any wound because we have the power to essentially reform our bodies. Some are far better at it than others, but the blessing is inherent in all of us. I have a much higher tolerance for pain and can therefore fix more serious wounds such as broken bones. I am not certain of the extent of your abilities, but I expect them to be at least as advanced as mine given the extraordinary talent you've displayed tonight."

"Can we heal others using skinshifting abilities?"

Felan frowned. "The more powerful of our kind certainly could, although it would be at enormous risk to themselves since they are not true harmhealers and therefore lack many skills in comparison to those mages.

"Since you still must change as a reaction to moonset and that will tax you enough, let's cease our practice for now. I shall wait with you and help ease your pain as much as I can during the skinshift. However, I advise that you rest until that time so that you can gather your strength."

The pseudo-human stared at her unlikely mentor. "Thank you," she murmured and bowed her head deeply.

Katja saw Felan smile as he watched her snuggle into her sleeping furs. He then lay down nearby on his own sleeping furs. Katja wondered if he too could sense the moon's set approaching. She yawned and pushed her body deeper beneath the furs. Zahlathra had been so kind to provide them. Idly, Katja pondered the layers of her sleeping furs. The waterproof exterior hide was sewn tightly together to protect its warm, fur-covered interior. She wriggled against the washable, cotton-cloth lining between her and the fur until sleep finally conquered her and cast uneasy dreams over her vision once more…

*

At first all Katja had beheld was pleasant darkness, then an excruciating scream pierced the silence of the dirt-floored chamber where her mind drifted. The room's only light came from a single sprig of incandescent moss, which bathed two deadwalker males in a dim, greenish glow. One knelt over the other's huddled figure, gently stroking his bare back with curved, black claws. The inert ghoul trembled at the Víchí's touch and tried only semi-successfully to stifle his whimpers.

"No, no, this will never do…" the kneeling vampire crooned to his victim. "You have failed to bring her to me twice now…I expected better from you…"

"Master, she knew the revenant's weakness and now she has allied herself with the dryads…I must have more time and reinforcements—" Curqak's reply ended in a deafening screech as the vampire's claws sunk into the small of his back.

"Excuses! These are all you have to offer to me?" the Víchí elder snarled sadistically, exposing his long, needle-like fangs. He jerked his claws free of the ghoul's back and scraped them lightly over his victim's shoulders before continuing his tirade, "Our era of dominion has come at last and my most faithful servant cannot even bring me one scrawny female! I have no time for this, Curqak. I cannot seek out all the stones and the werecat, too. Maybe I should have assigned this task to someone more worthy of my confidence…my grandson, perhaps."

"No, My Lord, no! Give me one last chance. Now that they are on the Sylvan continent, let me take the Gan Ceann with me; I swear to you upon my own sun-stroked head I will not fail again."

The ancient Víchí paused in mid-scrape and stared thoughtfully at the ghoul under his grasp. "So be it. Take the Gan Ceann with you and make haste! Do not let her reach Caerwyn! Do not! Do you understand?"

"Yes, My Master!" the ghoul gasped.

"Good, your loyalty serves you well, Curqak. You should feel honored that I chose to discipline you privately so that you are spared the humiliation of wailing in front of the rest of the camp. Do not expect this mercy again should you disappoint me."

"No, My Lord."

"Now…do you feel you have been punished enough for your disobedience?"

Curqak would not answer immediately.

"Well?" the Víchí hissed angrily.

"N-no, Master," came Curqak's stuttering reply.

"Good." The Víchí master bent low until his hideous mouth hovered just above the ghoul's pointed ear. "I am so pleased that you take responsibility for your actions."

The vampire bit completely through Curqak's ear with his full fangs. The trembling ghoul had let out a bone-chilling shriek that died only with the dream's end…

*

The two humans sat up with screams matching the ghoul's own—startling the dryad and the werewolf out of their sleeping furs.

"What happened!" Felan already had his axe out of its sling as he spun to stare suspiciously at the forest around them.

"Dreams," groaned Lauraisha.

"They are coming…" panted Katja, not sure if the water beading her face was sweat or tears. "Creator, keep us, they're coming!"

"Wait, who is coming?" Zahra said, slowly sliding her sickles back into their sheaths.

Katja looked into Felan's troubled eyes and whispered, "Dullahan!"

XIII
THE ASHEKEN HUNTERS

K atja watched the werewolf stiffen. His lips curled back into a silent snarl and his eyes went wild with fear and hatred.

"Dullahan! Are you quite certain?" Zahra asked, startled.

"What is a dullahan?" Lauraisha asked cautiously.

The werecat nodded. "We saw the ghoul Curqak being tortured by his Víchí master for failing to capture me. They know your mother helped me and the master gave Curqak permission to use the Gan Ceann to track me."

"Dear Creator, keep us!" Zahra whispered in fervent prayer.

Felan studied the Feliconian. "Do you know who Curqak's master is?"

Katja frowned. A faint suspicion nagged the edges of her memory. Hadn't Canuche once told her? Why couldn't she remember?

"If the ghoul has control of the Gan Ceann, no amount of caution will protect us from discovery," the werewolf said grimly.

"What are the Gan Ceann?" the Tyglesean asked.

Zahra ignored her. "I must warn my mother! Did this event just happen tonight?"

"I don't know. Our dreams never seem to follow our own present circumstances. Lauraisha and I have visions from both the past and the possible future, so it's hard to guess when this event actually occurred. It could have been weeks ago or just tonight, but my sense is that it happened sometime in the past fortnight."

"I concur," Lauraisha added.

"If that is the case we must move immediately at sunrise. We dare not tarry here any longer."

"Felan, we would be far safer here," the dryad spoke. "I doubt even dullahan could breach this place, not with the strength of the mage wards guarding it."

"Perhaps. But they would still be able to track us here and surround us. We would be cut off completely from Reithrgar Pass with no path of escape left to us. I would rather risk the open trail than stay here under siege."

Katja bowed her assent as did a still-bewildered Lauraisha. Zahra finally bobbed her head before turning to hug a young aspen.

"Very well, I must warn my mother," the dryad explained.

The others watched as she began to sing and sway against the sapling. Her voice carried no intelligible words, but her enchantment's power prickled the hair on the back of Katja's neck. They watched as the tree began to sway slightly in harmony with Zahra's movements and then in the pattern that she directed. When she finally finished dancing, the tree also ceased its movement. Then a sound like rolling thunder echoed through the ground beneath their feet. The tremor surged away from them—carried onward through other trees' roots toward the Northwest.

Silence fell after a few moments, and Zahra stood waiting with one hand holding the aspen. In time, a reply rumbled back through the roots of the forest and the dryad again wrapped her arms around the tree trunk to feel out the responding message. Several moments passed before the tree and dryad finished swaying, and then Zahlathra's young daughter finally turned back to them—her countenance grave.

"Mother reports that deadwalkers were seen by both dryad and werewolf scouts moving southeast along the main road some two days ago. Felan, your clan and several other races in the general area have evacuated their villages and moved to the protection of the Glen. Mother has her branches quite full of refugees at the moment. She also said that a second wave of deadwalkers is moving down from the north—oddly enough from the general direction of Tyglesea…"

"Lauraisha?" Katja's look toward her human companion was inquisitive.

The princess shook her head, frowning. "I have not one wraith of a clue. My kingdom is corrupt, certainly, but I doubt it's so far gone as to willingly host deadwalkers. Kaylor despises the Asheken with the same passion that he hates mages."

Katja turned back to the dryad princess. "What else did the Queen Mother say?"

"She says to make all possible haste to the Isle of Summons. She fears a siege should the deadwalkers realize the Glen is their preys' main refuge. She has already asked the leprechaun blacksmiths to lace sunsilver into as many bladed weapons as they can; however, it is in short supply."

"Did she report any dullahan moving in our direction?" Felan asked.

"She did not. I will not be able to ask her anything else until we move positions; it is too dangerous to send a second song through the roots now that we know what creatures are set against us. The deadwalkers would have surely noticed our exchange."

"Agreed," said the werewolf.

"What is a dullahan and what are the Gan Ceann?" Lauraisha asked in exasperation.

Katja sighed and finally turned to answer her packmate. "The dullahan and the Gan Ceann are the same type of deadwalker monster," she said. "Has no one explained the Asheken Turning bites to you?"

Lauraisha shook her head.

"Different races can be Turned into different kinds of Asheken depending on what type of Turning bite they undergo and what race they are initially. For example, if humans are bitten with the bite of slavery, they become zombies. This is why I sometimes call them 'sklaaf der seele'. The Feliconian word 'sklaaf' means 'slave' while the word 'seele' means 'soul'. So 'sklaaf der seele' basically means 'slave of the soul'. Do you understand so far?"

"I think so."

"Good," Katja replied, before continuing, "Vampires are

the only kind of deadwalker that can Turn beings into any of the three kinds of deadwalkers: the Víchí elite, their deiner soul servants, and the mindless sklaaf soul slaves. Vampires themselves are usually elves or dryads who have been Turned through the soul-sharing bite. Now not only can elves become vampires through the soul-sharing bite, they can also become deiner ghouls like Curqak if Turned by the soul servant's bite. When given the soul servant's bite, dryads become hags, werecats become nemeans, werewolves become grim, giants become cyclopses, and so forth. Are you still following my logic?"

Lauraisha nodded. "So are dullahan soul servants or soul slaves?"

"The dullahan are deiner der seele deadwalkers who were once centaurs. Centaurs are rather exceptional beings because they are naturally adept trackers who can also travel great distances swiftly. Dullahan keep those same traits after they are Turned, so most of them are pressed into service under the Víchí as prey hunters. Unlike the mindless sklaaf, these undead monsters are extremely cunning and often compete to please their masters and earn notoriety among their ranks. The most elite and brutal dullahan are given the title of Gan Ceann by their respective vampire masters.

"What makes members of the Gan Ceann worse than even regular dullahan is the fact that these deadwalkers can perform Turning bites. While vampires are the only deadwalkers that can successfully perform all three of the known Turning bites, vampire masters will often give their favorite deadwalker servants the ability to use the bite of slavery, the bite of servitude, or both types of bites. Therefore the Gan Ceann hunters are well practiced in both bites and these are the foes we now face."

"What do they look like?" asked Lauraisha timidly.

"According to the legends, they simply look like headless centaurs."

"Headless?"

The werecat nodded. "Their heads are completely severed from their bodies and stuck onto pikes for safe-keeping so that they can be raised at any angle to see around obstacles. Dullahan mainly rely on magically-enhanced vision to track their victims and their shade mages use spells of deception to ensnare their prey in much the same way as a brolaghan shadowshaper."

"Can your roar incapacitate them like it did the revenant and zombies?"

Katja sighed. "Unfortunately not. The dullahan are far too powerful. Legend says they can send almost any offensive spell set against them back on the caster."

"They also are notorious for being able to see past any magical shield," Felan added. "Dullahan are one of the few deadwalkers able to track us to this protected place, and they might even be able to infiltrate the Ring Spell's defenses."

Lauraisha's wide-eyed face blanched.

"As I said before, we need to pack up camp tonight and be ready to leave with sunrise. Katja, you have little time before the moon sets, so prepare yourself to skinshift. If you use the techniques that I taught you tonight to govern the transformations, your skinshift should occur with far less difficulty. Zahra, I need you to check our perimeter for any signs of deadwalkers. Lauraisha, I need you to go through our packs and throw out anything we can do without. I'll be pushing us very hard until we reach Reithrgar, so we cannot afford to carry excess weight."

Zahra and Lauraisha both abruptly scampered off to their allotted tasks. Katja sat down on her furs again, suddenly weary with the approach of moonset and subsequent dawn. Felan knelt close beside her and waited.

"Don't you have some other more important task to attend to?" Katja asked, almost defensively.

"Helping ensure your successful skinshift is far more important than any other assistance I can give right now. I need you alert and strong at sunup so you can protect our flank as we run."

Katja sighed and then closed her eyes. "What do you wish me to do, then?"

"I want you to keep your eyes closed. Focus on the layers of your skin and muscles and bones, just as we practiced. Feel your entire body this time…all the way through the marrow of your bones. Feel each layer of your heart as it pumps and follow its blood flow throughout the rest of your body.

Understand the signature differences in each layer of each organ…

"I know there is a lot to contemplate, but remember that your body will know the natural course of the skinshift. All you need to do is be aware of each change as it happens, understand the process, and control the transformation as much as possible when it occurs. The moonlight will help you. Your body has been storing it since moonrise to help strengthen you for the second full skinshift. Now… concentrate and change."

Katja lay prone to let the dwindling moon rays bathe her and tried to do what he instructed. She felt more than saw the moon sink completely below the horizon and then felt the first spasms begin. As she focused on the first change and began to lengthen her tail, she felt Felan's paw wrap around her right hand. She opened her eyes in surprise.

"Let me lend you some of my strength tonight," he said and closed his eyes to concentrate with her.

The female closed her eyes once more and felt the warmth of his touch grow hotter as the magic flowed between them. She again focused on pushing her tail out of the depths of her flesh and felt bones and muscles lengthen under her attention. Next her hands and feet began to simultaneously change back into paws, then her jaw re-hooked and full fangs sprouted in her maw once more.

As she mentally unraveled the layers of each change, she recognized for the first time what awe-inspiring beauty and complexity her own body held. The Creator had stitched her soul into a beautiful Erdeken form. Whether she was human or werecat on the outside did not matter as long as she remembered the Creator's own strength flowing through her soul.

Even when the frustratingly itchy fur sprouted back into place on her skin, Katja smiled. She was still extremely sore from the changes, but the present pain paled in comparison to the misery she normally endured. Once the skinshift was complete, Katja opened her glowing green eyes and gazed at Felan in amazement. He gazed back and grinned.

"I told you it was a blessing," he whispered, finally releasing her paw.

"It does not hurt as much!" she said, staring at her paws and noting the fur on her body had actually grown back to full length for the first time in her life.

Felan nodded his head. "And even the pain you feel now will be wiped away as you practice your skills. I have no doubt you will soon be able to skinshift at will just as I do."

Katja giggled in sheer joy at her accomplishment and the untapped potential she now recognized in her abilities.

"Come," said Felan after a moment. "We need to help the others check the boundary and pack up the camp. We can't leave any obvious signs of our stay here or the dullahan will be able to track us all the easier."

Katja bowed, suddenly somber. "Felan, I...thank you. You've no idea what this means to me."

He smiled, then rose and offered a paw to her. She took it and used his support to raise herself into a stiff standing position. Then she followed him toward the outbuilding and fountain behind the main house. They had much to do before morning, including lightening their packs, covering their tracks, and masking their scents. Katja doubted these precautions would really help them, but she did them anyway to keep fear from overthrowing her mind.

* * *

The next day's mild sunlight gilded the alternating green and yellow-leafed trees as the pack loped along the windy trail. Despite wearing leather leggings and a woolen cloak in addition to her own full fur, Katja could never seem to feel warm. She ran wearily behind Zahra and the piebald—whipping a pine limb behind her. Her tail had begun to ache from dragging the branch and she kept being distracted from the task of sweeping the road by uncanny red streaks that floated on the edges of her vision.

Several times the pack had to stop as Katja and Felan scouted the surrounding area for enemies. Nothing ever came of their searches, but this did not comfort the werecat, who had the uneasy sense that they were being watched. She would stiffen whenever she heard a bird's frightened twitter or saw a leaf twitch in the cold, erratic breeze.

The horses' nerves fared little better than the werecat's.

They often snorted or flicked their ears back as they scanned the forest around them with wide eyes. Lauraisha and Zahra had to rein them in several times as the packmates loped along the trail to keep them from bolting past Felan in their panic.

The packmates ate on the run and stopped only to water the horses or relieve themselves. Felan's pace pressed the group hard, especially when they passed from the gentler foothills to the rougher mountain trails. By sundown, everyone was thoroughly exhausted and short-tempered.

"I'm hungry," Katja complained.

"It's not safe to hunt here," Felan told her. "We'll have to make do with the rations."

"I'm tired of dried meat!" the human cut in.

The werewolf gave Lauraisha a withering stare.

"It does no good to bully her, Felan!" Zahra growled at him.

The massive werewolf glowered back at her. "Look, we do not have the time or the—"

"Silence!" Katja hissed.

"Do *not* interrupt me!"

"Quiet! Listen!" the werecat snarled.

As the others noticed the Feliconian's wary posture, they fell silent. They moved to the edges of the camp clearing to hide themselves and the horses under the shadows of the beech trees. Felan crouched low beside the werecat's still form, his ears perked in the same direction as hers. Several tense moments of waiting were finally shattered by a low moaning cry issuing in the distance behind them. Its echoes made their hackles rise while etching a cold sweat across their brows.

"What is it?" Lauraisha whispered.

Katja felt the fear garnered in her friend's voice, but said nothing. She simply waited while scanning the gloom under the distant trees. The werecat snarled softly when another chilling cry answered the first from somewhere ahead to their right.

"The deadwalkers have picked up our trail," the werewolf murmured.

No one moved or spoke as a third call replied to the second from far in the distance.

"They are moving," the Feliconian whispered.

He grunted. "We need to determine their numbers and where they are camped."

"You mean to hunt them? Do you honestly think that wise?"

"I'd rather not make our flight blind."

Katja bowed her consent. "Do we seek them now?"

"We?" Felan blinked at her in surprise.

"Do you truly expect me to stay behind when my clansmen's murderers are out there?" she hissed through clenched fangs. "I am not foolish enough to allow you to track them alone. I am the best hunter in this pack and I have dealt with them before. You will need my experience."

The werewolf scowled hard at her before finally bowing his agreement. They whispered their plan to the other two companions and then set off in the direction of the third groaning howl while Lauraisha and Zahra tethered the horses and scaled a large beech tree for safety. Felan took the lead and Katja followed in a half-crouching run. They stopped occasionally to sniff the wind and listen to the sounds of the forest. The Feliconian was the first to catch the deadwalkers' decrepit scent.

"There," she murmured.

Felan stopped and sniffed in the direction Katja pointed. He nearly sneezed for his trouble. They crept around a copse of trees—their ears perked and their eyes darting—and then slunk low toward a shallow ravine leading down from the top of the cliff. They both leveraged themselves onto a grassy embankment just above the ravine using exposed tree roots. After catching their breaths, Felan and Katja cautiously peered over the western edge of their resting place.

Katja again caught the familiar charnel scent and had to hold her paw against her maw and nose to keep from coughing. She saw dark tents erected in the shadows of the pines below her. The zombies' grunts coming from around those tents gave her chills. Then the sound of a horrendous wailing whinny smote her pricked ears and froze her blood. She crept away from the ledge and crouched, trembling until her terror passed. Then Felan motioned her to follow him and the two warriors slunk back to camp, scouting around it along the way.

"Took you long enough," said Lauraisha.

Zahra glowered at the human before turning to Felan. "What did you find?"

"We have a dire problem," he snarled. "Zahra, how familiar are you with the plants here?"

"They whisper to me enough to keep the sproutsinging connection constant. Why?"

"I'm afraid we'll need their vigilant attention tonight."

"So the whispers of fear are true?"

"Quite. We have zombies, dullahan, and perhaps even a few ghouls traipsing around the base of an escarpment roughly two spruce-scores northwest of our position."

"Now what are we to do?" Lauraisha asked.

He frowned. "We'll have to sleep in the trees and let them shield us with their branches."

"That won't be good enough, Felan," the werecat interrupted. "We also must find a way to completely mask our scent and move our supplies off of the ground. There can be no campfire tonight either. Sorry, Lauraisha."

The human sighed in resignation.

"Zahra, are the trees willing to shield us?"

"Yes, Felan, but wouldn't it be more prudent to run?"

He stared into the distance a moment. "No...I think running would be foolish at this point...even with eyes as good as mine or Katja's, the deadwalkers have the advantage in darkness. They would surely discover us if we flee; they might sniff us out here but I would rather stay and fight from a fairly defensible position than risk their herding us into an ambush."

Zahra crossed her arms and stared evenly at the werewolf. "What? You mean like what *I* wanted to do last night when we were comfortably camped within the shadowshaper's Ring Spelled compound?"

Felan gave her a half-heart snarl and rolled his eyes. "Fine, it might not have been the best choice to leave that safety, but we had to try to come as close to Reithrgar as possible, otherwise this is all for naught anyway."

Zahra finally bowed her agreement. "Fine. If we *are* to avoid the dullahan tonight, we will need to make some rather odd adjustments to the trees."

"Such as?"

"We'll need to lie between their roots instead of up in their branches. That will better mask our scents and keep the more fragile branches from cracking under the weight of the horses."

"Well, how do we do that then?"

"You will see," the dryad said while walking over to a large beech just at the edge of the clearing. She put one hand on its rough bark and began murmuring to it. The tree responded by shivering down its length, which loosened the soil engulfing its shallow roots. The roots then moved of their own accord to kick the dirt out from beneath the tree.

Once the hole was deep enough to fit Tyron into, the tree stopped and began threading roots across the space to restrain the soil and reinforce the walls. Meanwhile, Zahra had gone to other trees further from the clearing and murmured to each in turn, asking their consent to "root-hole" each packmate and their gear.

Lauraisha had just managed to convince her finicky horse to enter the first tree's root-lined burrow when the last tree had finished its digging. They slid the sorrel stallion into the first hole and then the tree began weaving a web of roots to form a ceiling upon which litter and soil could be heaped for camouflage.

Zahra covered the root ceiling above Tyron—being careful to leave enough holes through which the horse could breathe—while the others cleaned up the camp and moved their belongings into the burrows. Each companion was buried under a tree until Zahra was the only one left above-ground.

The dryad climbed into the last burrow and murmured a command once the roots had hidden her. At her words, all the area's trees let loose a storm of golden leaves that rained wet upon the forest floor, covering paw prints and smothering lingering smells with their fresh scents. Now entombed beneath the beeches, Katja and the others tucked themselves under their sleeping furs and tried to rest amidst the turmoil of their fears.

* * *

The next morning dawned even colder than the last with heavy frost concealing the ground. Its presence did not hearten the packmates as they scurried around gathering their belongings and once again erasing any sign of their presence from the camp. An overwhelming sense of foreboding loomed over them, which Katja suspected was partially the result of the night's terrors combined with the currently dismal weather.

Throughout the hours of darkness, the werecat had heard the scrape of claws and hooves above her hiding-hole. Deadwalkers had prowled the entire area snuffling out the packmates' muddled scents. Try as they might though, the dullahan had not discovered Katja's companions—or at least they had not discovered a way to get to them. Katja had barely slept during the ordeal and she suspected the others hadn't either. All were more than grateful when sunlight finally dispersed their hunters and allowed Zahra the ability to wake the sleeping trees still confining her fellow Sylvans.

The dryad dug them out and then quickly taught the packmates all how to properly sing their thanks to the trees. They then began sprinting east, eating along the way. Felan led them ever higher into the Nyghe sol Dyvesé mountain range on the trek toward Reithrgar.

The werewolf pushed them ever harder as the weather changed. By mid-morning, heavy clouds clung to the mountains. Their low-hanging tendrils blotted out the sun and wrapped an eerie chill around the travelers. The packmates took this as a grim omen and quickened their pace with Felan in the usual lead and Katja watching their backs. The Feliconian constantly checked for unusual scents and sounds. Although she discovered neither, she still caught the occasional flicker of crimson at the edges of her vision. Unnerved, the werecat tried to concentrate on Zahra and Lauraisha's whispered conversation to calm her mind.

It was about plants and seemed more a way for the two to ease their worries than a serious discussion. Zahra was explaining to the human that although plants had thoughts and feelings, they were not in fact beings with souls. Instead, plants were far simpler in their essence and most possessed less intelligence than many erdeling beasts.

"Then why offer them such respect if they cannot even comprehend the honors?"

"Even the dullest erdeling can understand respect and disrespect. After all, a horse will usually respond far better to a gentle word of praise than a sound whipping," the dryad responded while checking their surroundings.

"True," the human conceded and patted her mount in reassurance. Tyron whinnied in response.

"Besides," Katja added in, "plants are the dryads' prey just as beasts are Felan's and mine. One should always respect what one eats. After all, if the hunted should ever completely perish, so too will the hunter."

"I see. Well, what do you consider worth respect, then?"

Katja laughed. "Isn't it obvious? Everything!"

The werecat's quip put everyone in a slightly better humor, but the packmates' mood sobered again as the air became even colder and they were forced to huddle under their cloaks. The pace slowed as the ascent grew steep and rugged.

"How much farther until we reach our destination?" Lauraisha asked Felan.

"We have a ways to run yet. Once we cross this mountain, we'll need to traverse the edge of Reith Valley before finally ascending toward the pass at Reithrgar."

Katja looked nervously at the swirling clouds. "Do you think the weather will hold?"

Felan did not answer.

By the time the companions were on the mountain's other side, the sun was well past its zenith and snow had begun to fall over the golden grass of the valley below them. They all watched as a blue-black tempest brewed above the eastern slopes near the mouth of Reithrgar Pass and began driving snow in furious flurries toward them.

Felan suddenly stopped and cursed sharply.

"What?" Katja asked.

"We came down the wrong leg of the trail. We'll have to traverse more of the valley than I had planned to make the pass."

"Felan, we can't wade through the storm while out in the open! We need shelter!" Lauraisha yelled over the increasing wind.

A familiar scent whipped past Katja's nose and made her stomach lurch. "Felan, the Asheken are closing in on us! If they find us trapped by the storm, we're worse than dead!"

"Then we have no choice!" Felan snapped.

The male scanned the valley and nodded curtly toward the lone mountain near its center. "There's likely a cave large enough to hold us at the base of that white peak; we'll have to run full out if we are to get there in time. Katja, give me your rope."

The werecat wordlessly untied the sinew length from the outside of her pack and held it out to him. Felan took it and told each packmate to use the rope so they could be sure to stay together even if the coming blizzard should blind them to each other. Felan and Katja tied the rope around their left wrists before passing it to Lauraisha and Zahra, who tied it to their horses' bridles. Thus chained, the companions descended the mountain toward the valley.

As they once again touched level ground, a harsh scream smote their ears over the roar of the wind. The werecat jerked in the direction of the sound and spied a dark-furred dullahan clutching its disembodied head with trembling hands while the head itself screeched in agony.

A dullahan's voice normally caused tremendous pain to any beings unfortunate enough to hear it, but these screams instead gave Katja an odd joy. She saw the others also smiling as they watched the undead monster try and fail again and again to follow them down the mountain path. Katja's grin grew larger as she realized the monster could not attack them. Each time it tried to pursue them, it struck an invisible barrier and scrambled back as if scorched.

"What goes on here?" Zahra said in wonder as the swirling snow obscured their screaming hunter from view.

"I don't know, but let's use this to our advantage," Felan answered. "To the mountain, all of you! Hurry!"

The werewolf set off at a dizzying pace, pulling the party across the slushy ground. As they ran through grass weighed down with white, a screeching chorus built behind them. Deadwalkers had massed upon the road and were wailing their frustration at being blocked from their fleeing quarry.

Felan did not stop until they all were standing at the white rock's base, which jutted above the sea of snow-laden grass.

"This way, everyone," Felan called and ducked around a corner to stand on the leeward side of the peak. He began to yank earnestly on something hidden from Katja's view. By the time Katja realized that the werewolf was wrenching open a door, he had managed to unhook the frozen latch and pulled them all inside out of the storm.

"This is no cave," Katja said as the wind slammed the door shut, plunging them all into dank darkness.

The piebald let out a frightened whinny and refused to move from his position near the door. Tyron stood near him trembling and their fear matched the werecat's own. She could barely recognize shapes in the dimness.

"Lauraisha, would you shed a little more light on the walls for us," the werecat murmured.

Lauraisha pulled Damya's stone amulet from beneath her garments and blew softly on it. The stone glowed with a brilliant blue flame flickering just beneath its surface. The fire illuminated grimy walls and a sluggish center canal channeling water and offal outside through a partially clogged iron grate. Bile rose in Katja's throat at the sight and the smell.

"This looks like a castle's drainage system; it's similar to ours at home," Lauraisha commented while reconnoitering the gloom.

As the stone glowed more intensely, Katja realized that the drainage system was extremely complex—winding around carved stone foundation pillars and mortar-strengthened walls. These walls divided the space in which they stood into both small and large storage chambers. Large casks were stacked in a chamber just behind a stone staircase ahead and glass bottles were stored in racks lining the walls of a side-chamber to the right.

"We should be well sheltered from the storm here and there seems to be plenty of wares to restock our supplies," Zahra said while trying to sound cheerful. But Katja noticed the dryad had both hands gripped white-knuckled around her sickles as she spoke even as the werecat lit a torch.

Something reeked about this place apart from the sewage. Katja detected a stench of old death in the bowels of this place that even the refuse could not cover. Its sinister scent raised her hackles far more than even her previous encounters with deadwalkers had.

"Felan, where are we?" Katja asked nervously after retrieving her rope.

The werewolf didn't answer but instead peered around them while gripping his war axe—his ears pricked forward and his nostrils flaring.

Instead a deep voice answered her, "You are trespassing in my domain."

A tall figure stepped from around an alcove, a metal fighting staff held relaxed but ready in one gloved hand.

"State your purpose here," the muscular male hissed while moving boldly into the stone's light. He was as pale as the snow swirling outside and unbelievably beautiful—like an alabaster visage of an elf prince with broad shoulders and sleek waist-long hair swept back from his oval face and pointed ears. His hair was as dark as a moonless night, yet his eyes were as intense and blue as a hot inner flame. His voice rumbled past two long, white fangs protruding from his upper lip.

Katja's blood froze within her veins when she saw them. "Víchí!" she snarled.

His eyes flashed red at her warning.

XIV

CAERWYN

L eave this place at once!" the vampire snarled.
No one moved except Felan, who bared his own fangs, flattened his ears, and readied his double-bladed war axe. With a growl that would have stalled an ogre, the werewolf launched himself at their would-be assailant and swung the axe with all the power his massive body possessed.

The deadwalker was ready for his attack and flicked the warrior's axe-strike aside with a well-rehearsed parry. He sidestepped the werewolf and drove his blunt staff-end into the small of Felan's back. The werewolf lurched and spun to avoid hitting a wall. Felan evaded the Víchí's second strike and slashed low at his foe's legs. The shorter male jumped high—much higher than he should be able to—and then brought his pole down hard from overhead.

Felan blocked the blow and swung his double-bladed weapon down—trying to break the staff against one hooked sunsilver blade. The staff should have splintered against the axe's superior metal, but it did not. The werewolf growled, kicked the Víchí with a clawed paw, and freed his weapon. The deadwalker lunged even as Felan jabbed him with the axe's spiked tip. The vampire spun to avoid being skewered, but was not swift enough. The spike missed, but the edge of one blade cleaved a bloody gash in the abdominal flesh underneath the deadwalker's leather jerkin and tunic.

The Víchí hissed and swung the staff boldly toward Felan's head. As Felan moved to evade it, the deadwalker switched its course to catch the werewolf hard in the left side. The werewolf feinted to the right to ease the blow, but it was too well placed. Katja heard a sickening crack as several ribs broke.

Howling with rage and pain, Felan attacked again. His next assault put him in worse standing than before as the vampire managed to catch the werewolf's axe handle with his staff. He used the leverage to wrench the weapon out of Felan's grasp. While Felan's sunsilver axe and only means of protection against deadwalkers went skittering off to one side, the vampire used blow after blow to subdue the huge werewolf. Felan fought hard—feinting and slashing with his paws and arms—but his opposition became increasingly futile once the deadwalker trapped him against a stone-walled corner.

Katja had to do something or Felan would die! Before she could move, however, Zahra had already nocked and shot a flaming arrow with her bow. The bolt flew true at the deadwalker's heart. But, before it made contact, fire erupted out of nothingness and razed it in mid-flight. In the increase of light, Katja recognized the deadwalker's face yet she could not think why.

Felan used the arrow's distraction to dive toward his axe, but the Víchí recovered too fast. He spun the weapon away and pinned the werewolf against the wall with his staff across the male's throat.

"No!" The females screamed in unison.

Lauraisha moved as if she were sleepwalking—running toward the vampire and reaching out in an almost beseeching gesture with one hand. The deadwalker flinched as she touched his upswept arm. A flame sparked between them and ignited his glove as he tried to push her away. Felan clawed his way free as the golden flames licked up around the vampire's arm and this time the werewolf successfully retrieved his axe.

A shrill howl froze Felan in the middle of his next attack. A pony-sized white wolf jumped between the deadwalker and the packmates. His snarling appearance from the top of a nearby staircase brought screams from the horses and caused Lauraisha and Felan to involuntarily step back. The huge white beast pushed himself further between the Víchí and the packmates, growling his warnings even as the vampire eyed Lauraisha with appreciation.

"You have some skill, fireforger, but your form is rudimentary at best," he said while frowning at the flames. He then flicked his wrist and the fire jumped to cauterize the bleeding wound on his abdomen before extinguishing itself.

Katja stood slack-jawed. How could a vampire wield fire? Sunsilver weapons could destroy other deadwalkers, but fire was the Víchí's only true bane! More than that, how could Lauraisha forge fire in the first place? She was a dreamdrifter, not a fireforger! Was it a trace of Damya's magic? And since when did wolves—or any Sylvan beast for that matter—ever willingly protect a deadwalker?

Comprehension finally dawned and Katja yelled, "Hold! Hold! Do not strike again!"

Felan and the white wolf ignored her as they both circled back and forth, looking for an opening in the other's defenses. Katja watched them with rising frustration and anger. She felt her rage boil over deep inside her soul and find power in her voice. The werecat's roar shook dust from the overhead beams and everyone turned to stare at her in alarm. She stepped forward, studying the pale male.

"Our sincere apologies, My Sir," she said, "But we thought you a deadwalker. And if you are not one of those villains, then we wish you no harm. It is hard to know friend from foe these days. Tell me, are you Master Caleb?"

The deadwalker's face flashed bewilderment, then hardened into suspicion. "Why do you seek Caleb?"

"We bring tidings from Canuche, former king of the griffins and prisoner to a turncoat's treachery. We must ask your advice and protection from the deadwalkers roaming this land."

"Canuche is dead and the Asheken have not roamed Sylvan soil for centuries. You are not making a strong validation for your actions, werecat," he hissed.

Katja smiled inwardly as Lauraisha shared her thoughts and realized that they both knew this warrior from their dreams. His face had been the one grotesquely reflected in the ancient mirror in the red carpeted room and his mighty staff had been that mirror's ruin.

"It is true, My Sir!" exclaimed Lauraisha. "I am proof of Canuche's continued existence. Were it not for his interference, I would most likely be dead. The healing flame of his altar destroyed the venom from a basel and his power awakened the magic long dormant within my soul."

The uncanny warrior frowned. "I did indeed sense a mighty magic mixed in your touch, but that likely came from the pendant you wear, for I feel its power pulsing even now," he said and pointed to Damya's Keystone, which still radiated blue light from Lauraisha's chest. "If you are being truthful about your encounter with a basilisk's descendant, then show me the fang marks from your ordeal."

With a defiant glare, Lauraisha loosened the ties holding her cloak. She let it fall to her feet as she pulled her tunic and undershirt away from her right shoulder. The male's eyes widened as he saw the rough scars where Katja had cut the fang out of the human's flesh.

A look of deep concentration then stole across Lauraisha's face as she looked into his crystal blue eyes. Katja winced as the human closed their minds' link and she realized that her friend was either probing the warrior's mind or exposing her own mind to his review. Both actions were dangerous and the werecat's hackles rose at the prospect.

The male's face hardened abruptly, then softened—his eyes growing oddly gentle toward the human as something passed between them. Lauraisha's face also altered into a gaze brewed from respect, sympathy, and confusion.

"Dayalan…is that your name?" she asked.

He said nothing, but instead turned his attention to the white wolf. "Bren, see to it that all is prepared for our guests and their mounts. And do not harm the horses. Am I understood?"

The white wolf did not move.

"Bren!"

The beast growled low in his throat before grudgingly giving an affirming bark and then disappearing back up the stairs from whence he came.

The warrior then turned to Felan and the werewolf's eyes narrowed.

"My apologies. Are you greatly injured?" he asked.

Felan's response was a rough grunt as he heaved himself off the wall where he rested. He did not holster his axe. Instead the werewolf held it loosely in his large paws while staring flatly at the suddenly helpful stranger. The male frowned back at him and then turned back to Lauraisha.

"Come, I will take you to Caleb," he said, more to her than to anyone else.

He moved gingerly up the stairs leading out of the drainage cellar. With paws and hands on or near weapons, the four packmates warily followed him into the main castle. They wound their way through several stone corridors adorned with red carpets, immaculate tapestries, and priceless artifacts. Their guide stopped only when he reached a broad set of double doors twice as tall as Felan.

The uncanny male knocked thrice and a voice even deeper than his boomed from the room beyond. "Enter."

The warrior cleared his throat. "We have guests, Father."

"Show them in then, Dayalan."

They all passed through the doors—stepping between carvings of grotesque figures whose facial features had been chipped off and liberally covered with red lacquer and varnish—and into a red-carpeted room lined with shelves that reached to its vaulted ceiling. Myriad scrolls, tablets, and bound books were wedged into the shelves and heaped upon the central table. Despite the room's vastness, Katja felt cramped amidst all the clutter.

The room's lone occupant could not have been a further contrast to the disarray surrounding him. He stood staring at Katja and her packmates with one pale, black-clawed hand pressed upon the table beside him. He was much shorter and carried a leaner build than their guide, but neither fact diminished the intimidation Katja felt in his presence. He had close-cropped white hair slicked back from his angular face and wrinkles sprouting like cobwebs from the corners of his eyes and long-fanged mouth. His visage seemed somehow timeless despite the age lines. His cheeks had a slightly hollowed appearance that contrasted with the blue intensity of his stare. Although lean, his every feature conveyed power and Katja instinctively knew that she stood in the presence of legend.

"Who speaks for this group?"

Stunned silence greeted his question.

"Well?" He asked impatiently.

"I do, My Sir," Katja answered reluctantly.

"Your name?"

"I am Katja Kevrosa Escari of the werecat clan Feliconas, My Sir," she said and bowed deep with both of her paws' palms raised.

"I know that clan well. Many of its members fought bravely with me during the Second War of Ages including, if I am not mistaken, your own parents. I do believe you have your mother's eyes."

Katja felt herself unexpectedly choked with emotion. He had known her mother? She had almost forgotten her mother's eyes were her own.

"My late wife loved your mother in particular. Tell me, how do they fair?"

Katja took a breath to control her emotion before speaking. "They are dead, My Sir."

"Dead? When?"

"Six summers ago, My Sir, when I was but a catling. They were the victims of a rockslide...or so I thought at the time."

"I am truly sorry for your loss. This world is a much dimmer place without their bright souls to fill it. Who reared you after their demise?"

"My two older brothers and my older sister...all of whom are also dead, as is the rest of my clan."

At this, their host's eyes flashed red and he hissed vengefully. His voice was deadly soft when he asked, "How?"

"Deadwalkers, My Sir—"

"Oh, stop calling me that. Call me by my own name, Caleb."

"Yes, Master Caleb."

"Just Caleb is fine," he said testily. "Why would you think deadwalkers are responsible for your clansmen's deaths?"

"Because they have tracked me and also my companions ever since the night of my clan's massacre. They're led by a ghoul who calls himself Curqak—"

"You are sure of this?" their host interrupted, his eyes

widening with shock and then narrowing in loathing.

"Quite certain…Caleb."

"Very well, we will discuss the details of *that* encounter in a moment. For now though, let me meet your companions."

Katja introduced them all and, when pressed, explained her flight to Crown Canyon. She summarized the events of her introduction to Lauraisha, their encounters with Canuche and Durhrigg, the escape to the Glen, their meetings with Zahlathra and Fenris, and the journey since with Damya, Lauraisha, Felan, and Zahra. Caleb listened intently and interrupted only to implore them all to sit and eat as Dayalan, who had gone to better bind his wounds and bring food, returned from the kitchens with a well-laid tray. As Katja concluded the story with their accidental intrusion into Caleb's own castle and the mishap meeting with Dayalan, their host suddenly turned to Felan.

"We must heal you before your body endures any more injury. Dayalan, why did you not care for his wounds the moment you found out their presence?"

"My apologies, Father, but he would not allow me to tend to him nor did they completely explain their intrusion to me."

"And you did the rib-snapping, did you?" the elder shrewdly surmised.

"Yes, Father."

Caleb's eyes narrowed. "You and I will have a talk later."

"I did only what was necessary to protect us, Father. They thought me a deadwalker so I defended myself—"

"Enough!" Caleb's reprimand was as cold as the storm outside.

"Yes, Father." Dayalan bowed his head toward his elder, but his eyes were narrowed.

Caleb turned back to Felan. "This will hurt, but the pain is little penance to pay for the remedy."

"I did not ask to be healed."

"Nevertheless, your body needs aid in weaving your bones back together," Caleb said as he moved Felan's cloak away and gently pressed a hand to Felan's side, his gray brows knitting together in concentration. A pure white light shone around Caleb's claws, and then it seeped into Felan's fur. Katja watched in awe as the wincing werewolf's ribcage realigned itself under the mage's careful concentration.

"There. I have expedited your body's natural healing abilities, but you will still need several days rest to complete the process." Felan bobbed his head in thanks even as Caleb turned to the others. "I would advise you all to keep to the security of this castle until your companion is once again well. If there are indeed deadwalkers outside the valley, as you say, then you all must have full strength before confronting them again."

"Father, what will we do about the deadwalkers?" Dayalan asked.

"When the storm lifts, we will hunt and scrape their decrepit filth off Caerwyn lands." Caleb's fang-tipped grin was a fusion of malice and contempt.

Dayalan's face matched his father's hardened expression and Katja shuddered at the gruesome hunger in their countenances.

"Caleb," she asked awkwardly, "May I hunt with you?"

"Our hunts are not for you, Feliconian."

"I do not fear the fiends," she spat.

"Then you certainly may not join us! Only a fool would be unwary of these monstrosities!"

"Twice I have faced their kind and twice I have survived. I beg of you, let me fight to avenge my clan and my family!"

Although she didn't think it possible, Caleb's eyes grew gentle. "You will have the opportunity for revenge soon enough, but now is not the time. You are strong, Katja Escari, but you are not as yet skilled enough to battle a ghoul as powerful as Curqak when he has aid from the Gan Ceann. You and your companions must train in the halls at the Isle of Summons before you can have any hope of defeating such dangerous enemies. Heed my counsel on this; I hold the experience to know their strengths."

Katja growled sullenly, but finally replied, "As you wish."

Caleb smiled faintly before turning to gaze upon his other guests. "You all must be exhausted from such an ordeal. Come, I will show you each to your quarters. Your bedchambers will be safe enough, but I warn you not to tarry in the unoccupied parts of this house. Caerwyn was built centuries ago by the claws and whips of the Víchí. And, despite my best purging efforts, their evil still permeates some of its corridors."

Lauraisha looked startled and spoke for the first time, "If this place was built by vampires, the deadwalkers will have easy access to us here!"

Caleb's smile was smug. "Only if they have discovered a way past the Ring Spells."

"My sir, why would you live here if vampires built it?"

Caleb gave the human princess a rueful sort of smile. "Because I oversaw its construction."

"That would make you a deadwalker!"

Caleb frowned. "Has no one told you the story?"

"Please bear her with patience, Caleb," Katja exclaimed quickly, "As a Tyglesean, she is ignorant of such matters."

"Ah, I understand." Caleb turned to his son. "Dayalan, these guests of ours will be your charges. See to all their needs and their comfort. However, if there is anything unusual that they require, bring it to my attention."

"Yes, Father," Dayalan bowed his head and Caleb briefly returned the gesture.

Caleb led them through the massive doors into the large corridor once again. As he and Dayalan showed them to their chambers, Katja felt Lauraisha's confused thoughts touch her own. The werecat mentally promised to explain what she knew about this strange place once they were safely sequestered in their rooms.

"Your chambers will be here," Caleb said after bringing them all to a halt in a narrow corridor adjacent to the main hall.

He opened a door on his right. "The females may have this room for their use and you, Felan, will have the room across the hallway. This hall leads straight to the main hall, so you should not have any problems finding your way around this part of the castle. The kitchens are down this hallway to your left and down the second set of stairs.

"We keep no servants in this house so you must prepare whatever you wish to eat yourselves. We do store live prey in the solarium for you to hunt as well as mounds of dried vegetables to eat. If you have any questions, address them to Dayalan. Bren will be posted in this hall for your protection." Caleb gestured toward the approaching white wolf.

Caleb took a breath and gave each of them a piercing stare before continuing, "I know full well that this place piques your curiosity; however, I strongly advise against traversing its corridors unchaperoned. There are places here where even I will not dare set foot alone. If you wish to leave this section of my house, then Bren, Dayalan, or I must accompany you. Is that perfectly understood?"

They all affirmed that they did indeed understand before Caleb and Dayalan bid them a good rest and sent them into their rooms.

* * *

"I despise this! I feel far more like a prisoner than a guest!" grumbled Zahra.

Katja bobbed her head in silent agreement while gazing around the immaculate bedchamber. She jumped off the large canopy bed where she had been crouching beside the other two females and began sniffing around the strange room.

"How long must we stay here?" Lauraisha asked.

"Caleb said we are to stay until Felan fully heals, but I suspect they may keep us here much longer. I shouldn't wonder if they would wish to hold us here indefinitely because we now know their precious secret," the dryad muttered bitterly.

"What secret?" the human asked, raising her delicate eyebrows.

"Where Caerwyn Castle is located, of course! The Mage Council has been searching for this place for centuries—ever since the First War of Ages—and now we find it practically on the doorstep of Reithrgar protected from all eyes by its Ring Spells. That information would be priceless to them."

"I doubt very much that either Caleb or his son would be bothered by the mages even if they knew where to find them," Katja answered after snuffling an ancient tapestry and sneezing from its imbedded dust. "I would wager a king's banquet that the sole reason we found this place is because we were not specifically searching for it and yet we needed a safe place to shelter. That's what this place is…a safe haven for the hunted and the unwanted."

The dryad looked at her quizzically. "Katja, what are you

muttering about?"

The werecat frowned and went back to sniffing the rugs and chair cloths before answering, "Caleb said that he kept no servants in his house, yet Dayalan sent the wolf ahead to make sure all was prepared for us. The wolf could not have changed our bedding or dusted the rooms while we were with Caleb. Dayalan was not absent long enough to do it either, nor would he really be able to accomplish such a task after the beating Felan just gave him."

"What's your point?" the dryad asked.

"My point is that either they were expecting us or there are others hidden here. My nose tells me that the latter is the truth."

"Others, what others?" Lauraisha asked.

The werecat shook her head. "I have no idea; their scents are unlike any that I've encountered before."

Zahra's eyes narrowed. "Deadwalkers?"

"Definitely not."

"Then what would Caleb have to hide, I wonder?"

Katja shrugged and resumed her investigations.

"Who is Caleb or...what is he exactly?" the human queried.

"No one really knows..." said the werecat.

"He is a traitor," the dryad supplied.

"Traitor? To whom?"

"To the Sylvans first, then to Luther and his minions, the Asheken," Zahra answered.

She went on to explain that Caleb was originally the adopted blood-son of the Víchí High Elder Luther who—upon discovering that he could spawn no offspring of his own as a deadwalker—decided to steal a child to raise as his own. Once the child grew to the proper age of adulthood, Luther would then Turn it into a full Víchí. He chose Caleb and trained him into one of the most ruthless vampire warriors in history.

"No one knows exactly what happened to change Caleb's loyalties—although the Sylvan woods are thick with the rumor that the fireforger mage Marga had something to do with it," Zahra explained. "Caleb, who was called Calais at that time, fought faithfully alongside Luther for hundreds of years—killing and Turning whomever he wished. He earned the rightful reputation as the most vicious vampire aside from the High Elder himself. He even challenged and destroyed other Víchí who displeased him, draining their blood to make himself even more powerful.

"Sometime during the Second War of Ages, however, Caleb switched his loyalties and began helping the Sylvan Orders destroy his own kind. Luther had somehow smuggled him onto the Southern Continent to build a deadwalker stronghold here before the war and, in the process of doing so, Caleb had Turned hundreds of innocents into deadwalker slaves and servants to construct this castle. No one yet has solved the mystery of how he managed to keep them hidden from the Sylvan mages' detection."

"It was probably Ring Spells like those that protect this place now…he must have modified them to fit his present alliances after he rejected his deadwalker existence," Katja interjected.

"Aren't deadwalkers always deadwalkers once they are Turned?" the human looked quizzically from the dryad to the werecat.

"Usually," Zahra replied, frowning.

"That part of the legend is a little muddled." the werecat said. "As far as I know, Caleb is the first and only deadwalker in history to ever be Turned Back or Redeemed into his Erdeken form. This reverse transformation was supported by the evidence of his marriage to the legendary fireforger Marga and their apparently successful conception of a son in the years following the Second War of Ages.

"Obviously, there were some imperfections in the conversion back since he still has his red eyes, vampire fangs, black claws, and black-tipped pointed ears. But, as far as anyone knows, he is basically an elf…and an incredibly powerful mage," the werecat finished.

"And it seems his son may have inherited those same eerie qualities as well," Lauraisha commented. "I saw his eyes flash red when he and Felan were fighting."

Katja nodded as she stared through the narrow window at the snow swirling outside. The worst of the storm had blown through and she could just make out the snow-strewn hills beyond the castle walls in the evening light. "It's strange…I would expect Dayalan to be a fireforger because Marga was, but I do wonder why he inherited Caleb's fangs."

"And I wonder if he has the murderous personality to go with those two particular traits."

"Zahra!"

"Lauraisha, don't be so naïve!" Zahra stared scornfully at the Tyglesean. "Just because they are Sylvans now does not make them our allies. I trust each of them about as much as I trust a troll."

Lauraisha cocked an eyebrow. "You do realize that the bow you hold so dear was in fact a gift from a troll, right?"

"Well," the dryad sniffed. "That is…an entirely different matter."

Katja rolled her eyes and flicked her ears. "We're wasting time arguing…"

"If he is keeping deadwalkers in this place, I want to know about it!"

"Like I said before, Zahra, the scents are not those of deadwalkers—"

A knock at the door silenced the Feliconian. She moved cautiously to open it and discovered Felan standing beyond its threshold. She bade him to enter and shut the door again.

"Are you well?" she asked.

"I'm fine," the werewolf said while he gingerly sat down in a nearby chair. "Caleb lent me extra strength not knowing that I am a skinshifter. I should be completely healed in a matter of hours, though I'd prefer to keep that fact secret from our hosts for now. What are you all discussing?"

Zahra grimaced. "Whether or not to actually trust said hosts."

Felan nodded gravely. "They are hiding something from us."

"Or hiding us from something," Lauraisha interjected.

"There is only one way we will know for certain which is the truth," the werewolf said looking around at the three females. "We explore."

"You would have us directly defy our hosts and test their courtesy after we each gave our word of honor?" Lauraisha said aghast.

"Do you have any wiser notions?"

The frustrated human finally shook her head.

"Very well, then; when the storm lets up our hosts will vacate the castle and leave us free to roam its floors."

"What about the white wolf?"

"*The wolf* is coming with you."

Katja's packmates all whirled around to see the source of the new voice. There in the open doorway stood the white wolf Bren. None of them had heard him open the door, but there he was glowering at all of them from its threshold.

"You speak...Shrŷde!" Katja exclaimed.

The wolf's lips wrinkled in a silent growl. "Eloquently."

"My apologies, Wolf. I did not realize you were so gifted."

"My name is Bren; please address me properly," he snapped. "I speak several tongues quite well—better than any of my kin, certainly."

"Are the horses safe?" Lauraisha suddenly asked.

"Of course, but we shall see how safe the rest of you are when the masters of this house return. How dare you dishonor them!"

The wolf's uncanny intelligence and demeanor unnerved Katja. She knew no legend or tale of any Erde beast able to speak the languages of beings. She eyed him warily as she asked, "When will they likely return?"

"It could be a span of days or it could be a span of hours. Largely, it will depend on how soon they can track down and destroy their quarry. Snowstorms can be dangerous even to such powerful mages and they may come to trouble if they find their prey holed up in a cave. Digging out deadwalkers can prove a treacherous task. We shall see if either Caleb or Dayalan require nourishment when they return."

Felan's nostrils flared. "They would not dare to use us as sustenance!"

"You?" The wolf's laughter shook his whole body. "Certainly not! They drink the blood of beasts, not that of beings."

Katja stared in horror at the wolf. "Bren, you are their *prey*?"

If one could call it a smile, Bren was positively grinning. "Dayalan's, actually. I am his bloodmate and will be so as long as he needs me as such. Our exchange of blood helped make me the way I am and gave me the intelligence I hold. I owe him much and he owes me much. We keep each other sane. I do not expect you or any other outsiders to understand, but believe me when I say that they both will do their utmost to help you—if you heed their laws."

Katja drew a breath and stared into the wolf's unblinking golden eyes. "Others live here besides the three of you. Who and what are they?"

"Smell them, can you?"

The werecat and werewolf nodded.

Bren sniffed. "Caleb suspected you might. The others are the Forgotten…the last surviving beings of their respective races. Do not threaten them. They will most certainly kill to defend themselves."

"So Caleb wanted us always escorted for our protection from them, did he?" a seething Zahra surmised.

"Actually it is more for their protection than yours. If your skill" —Bren bowed toward Felan— "is characteristic of this pack's fighting prowess, then all in this castle besides its masters would be under great threat. Most here prefer to spend their days with a plow rather than a sword."

"We do not intentionally harm others unless we ourselves are under threat!" Felan snapped.

Bren nodded. "Truly spoken…but upon meeting the Forgotten, you may change your belief of what 'under threat' truly means."

XV
GLIMMERS OF DARKNESS

Bren shifted his weight uncomfortably as Katja and Felan tracked their quarry within the large solarium. The morning sky outside was a stone gray and the snow drifted mournfully through the chill air—a complete contrast to the relative warmth of the enormous glassed-in room. Katja had never seen so much clear glass set into walls before, so she spent more time investigating the windows than she did helping Felan catch their prize doe.

Finally the exasperated werewolf stomped over to her. "This hunt would end much earlier if two were involved instead of just one. I'd prefer to eat sometime before sundown!"

"It's not yet noon," she replied while absently stroking the black lead molding holding the glass in its place. Caleb and Dayalan had been gone for three days now and she desperately hoped their hunt had proven successful.

Felan blew out his breath in a disgruntled snort and pulled the Feliconian away from the glass. "Come! You have gazed through that clear wall long enough! I'm hungry!"

"Felan, wait!"

"No! You are not going to sit ogling that glass for another moment—"

"Felan, halt!" Katja growled, a mix of aggravation and alarm coloring her voice.

He released her and she immediately bounded toward the opposite end of the vegetation-strewn room. A shadowy figure had caught her eye and she sniffed the air apprehensively as she neared the spot where she had spied it. A strange scent resembling the smell of wet beetles tickled her nose. She halted as the full impact of it overpowered her senses and immediately shifted into a defensive half-crouch.

"I am a faithful friend to my allies and a fierce foe to my enemies. Which are you?" she asked the bushes before her.

For several long, tense moments, nothing but silence greeted her. Then a dark gray face cautiously emerged from the foliage a body-length away from her left paw. Upon seeing it, the werecat gasped. Belatedly remembering her manners, she bowed toward the face and took a step back—beckoning the creature out of hiding. Slowly it shifted out of the plants and Katja beheld its frightening full form.

This being had a humanlike head and body, yet its skin looked far more like that of a hard-shelled beetle or other such wee beast. The armored skin was a glossy black and culminated in a thick arched tail tipped with a venom-laced hook. The tail was that of the legendary manticore—a scorpion's tail. Katja stared at the almond-shaped black eyes and flattened nose. Bren had said that a remnant of the Forgotten races lived at Caerwyn and if his words were true, then she must be looking at a werescorpion.

"Are you one of the girtab?" she asked cautiously, calling the werescorpion by its traditional racial name.

The creature slowly bobbed its head, regarding her without expression.

"I am Katja Kevrosa Escari of the Feliconas Clan of werecats," she said with nervous formally.

"I am Aria, daughter of Paraburus who is chief among the girtab," the stranger finally replied in a voice that recalled the rustling sound of dry leaves.

Katja bowed again and said sincerely that she was honored to meet a member of such a rare race. The girtab frowned in confusion at this and took a step back into the brush, her tail twitching in agitation.

"Peace, Aria," Bren spoke as he and Felan quietly approached. "These guests mean you no harm; they are refugees from the Asheken that Caleb and Dayalan now hunt."

Aria visibly relaxed at the white wolf's reassurance and

then looked questioningly at Felan who, after a moment's hesitation, also bowed and introduced himself. Bren then asked the purpose for her presence in the solarium and the girtab shyly explained that she sought the solarium's solitude because she needed privacy in which to molt her skin. As she said this, Katja finally noticed the foaming lesions running the length of her stomach and chest.

"Do they hurt?" she asked, pointing to the cracks.

"Terribly, but I have learned to endure the changes." Aria grimaced. "I do apologize for breaking the solarium restriction, Bren, but I have little choice today."

"It is understandable…and perhaps best that you did so under these circumstances. Come, Felan. Come, Katja. I apologize, but we must leave Aria to do her skin shedding in peace."

"Please wait a moment, Bren," the werecat said, sniffing her whereabouts again.

She suddenly sprinted toward the center of the solarium and bounded into a stand of short trees. The doe was exactly were her nose claimed it would be and so she pounced on top of it from one of the branches, neatly snapped its neck and back as she landed.

"Show off!" Felan growled when she returned carrying the doe across her shoulders.

Katja grinned and then ripped a hind leg off the beast. She smiled and gave the leg to the speechless girtab. Now she knew yet another being who must feel isolation because of her skinshifting—or skin-molting in this case. The thought stirred a strange sense of kinship for this odd being.

"You may need the nourishment of this while changing skins," she said by way of farewell.

As she and Felan followed Bren up the staircase toward the kitchens, the werecat caught one last glimpse of Aria. The girtab stood looking from the food in her clawed, black paws to the departing werecat with confusion and gratefulness warring across her dark face.

* * *

"A werescorpion? Still living? How is that even possible?" exclaimed Zahra in between mouthfuls of vegetation.

Katja shrugged and tore into the venison once more.

"It doesn't matter to me; I only wonder how many are left," Felan answered while licking his paws. He was always the first one to finish at an eat. Katja surmised that his ridiculous eating speed was because he had the largest mouth in which to stuff his food, but she would never say so out loud for politeness's sake.

A wraith of a smile flitted across Lauraisha's face at the werecat's silent observance before she grimaced in frustration. "I assume this is more history of which I am woefully ignorant?" she asked before taking another bite of baked tubers.

The werecat was pleased to see her friend actually eating with her hands instead of with those silly eating tools she usually used. Honestly, what was the point of using a "fork" to pick up food when one's paws were far more effective? Now, if she could just convince Zahra to stop using her wooden sticks…

Katja swallowed the last of her meat and looked at the human. "Girtab, or werescorpions as they are also known, were one of the original races spawned from the union between the Manticore and Sphinx.

"When the Creator fashioned the world from nothingness, He populated it with many soulless erdeling creatures called beasts…"

"Yes, yes, I know," the Tyglesean princess interrupted. "He then created six powerful beings to watch over these beasts and the world itself: the Sphinx, the Manticore, the Gorgon, the Chimera, the Nymph, and the Hippocampus. I know all that. I also know that the reason that beings can become wiser than beasts because they have souls while beasts do not. What I don't remember is which race belongs to which union of the Six Founders."

Katja thumped her tail pointedly. "Then will you let me finish?"

"Sorry," the fifteen-winter-old mumbled.

Katja nodded and then continued, "The six Founders served the Creator in the protection and nurturing of their world and their subsequent marriages led to the various races of soul-bearing beings now in existence. The Sphinx and the

Manticore's union produced the races of accipions, canis, giants, girtab, griffins, harpies, Tyglesean humans, liopions, ulfrions, werewolves, and, of course, werecats like me that resemble lions.

"The Gorgon and Chimera's union created aspards, basilisks, capanths, Vihouset humans, lamia, satyrs (who call themselves the Pan), sercaps, and werecats that resemble leopards. Most of these 'spotted' werecats belong to the Rosmelan Clan, which I and most of my Feliconian kin call our 'cousin clan'…well, they once did anyway."

Zahra squeezed Katja's shoulder when the werecat's breath caught at the memories of her clan. She cleared her throat and concluded her teaching while the human feverishly scribbled notes on a parchment scrap.

"Finally, the Nymph and Hippocampus's union brought forth the brolaghans, brownies, centaurs, dryads, elves, gnomes, kelpies, kwen, merfolk, naiads, nymphian pegasi, and pixies. Other races of beings such as dwarves, felwolves, hippogriffs, leprechauns, accipionite pegasi, ogres, sea serpents, and trolls emerged from the early intermarriage of the different races until prejudice divided the beings and war broke out among the birthed races. Any queries so far?"

"Am I correct in thinking that a lamia has the upper body of a human and the lower body of a snake while merfolk have the upper bodies of nymphs and lower bodies of fish?"

"Precisely."

"Hmm. Well then, what are aspards and accipions?"

"According to the clan legends, an accipion was a being that looked like an eagle, but with a scorpion's tail and some armored plating along its chest and back. An aspard has the head and body of a leopard, but the tail of a snake. The venom from their bite is deadly."

"Has there ever been a lion-like aspard?"

When neither Katja nor Felan answered, Zahra spoke, "Not to my knowledge, but then I've never met any."

"I thought your clan traded with everyone."

"We do…among the living, anyway."

"What do you mean?"

Zahra explained that the Clan Wars' aftermath saw the complete annihilation of several races including the capanths and sercaps. Widespread decimation of the aspards, girtab, lamia, accipions, canis, harpies, and brolaghans also occurred until the First Mage Council convened to end the killing and award territorial boundaries to the remaining races. The alliance of the Sylvan Orders was born from this long-overdue compromise.

"Girtab are feared by many beings because they are a race of warriors with a reputation of being naturally bloodthirsty and dangerous. Their armored skin and poison-tipped tails also make them especially difficult to defeat in combat," Felan added.

The human frowned. "Small wonder, but are they really as menacing as their reputation suggests?"

"I suppose it would depend on the individual girtab," Katja surmised. "The one we met today seemed just as uneasy with us as we were with her."

Felan nodded his head in agreement, his eyes narrowed in contemplation. "I am curious to know what else lives here besides the werescorpion. Bren indicated that multiple members of the Forgotten Races hold a presence at Caerwyn, so I would assume we shall meet other races, too."

"Will wonders never cease?" Lauraisha said in awe. "None at home would begin to believe my tale."

Katja grinned and then opened the main door of the females' adjoined chambers.

"Bren?"

The werecat heard paws thump across a rug down the hallway. The white wolf appeared from around a corner and loped toward Katja, his claws tapping out a semi-muffled patter on the alternating carpet and stone beneath him. She ushered him into the room and he halted before her with mild curiosity glowing in his golden eyes.

"Would you mind answering some queries of ours?"

He shrugged. "That depends on the questions asked."

"Besides the girtab, what other races reside in this castle and its grounds?"

"That inquiry is best put to the masters, so I shall not answer it."

Katja flicked her ears. "Why?"

"Because the Forgotten Races' safety rests solely in their

anonymity. The less others know of the beings sheltered here, the simpler it is to protect them."

"Hence the secrecy?" Katja asked.

Bren did not answer.

"Hence the secrecy," Dayalan said, entering the room through the ajar door. He paused, looking at their surprised faces.

The werecat's eyes narrowed and her nostrils flared as she checked the strange male's scent. She had not smelled him just now in the corridor, so how could he have escaped her nose when smattered with so much sweat and dried gore? Most of the blood adorning the warrior's clothes wasn't his, but Katja saw that he hadn't finished his mission without scoring several shallow cuts and slashes across his arms.

"I see you all have been busy breaking the rules whilst my father and I were away."

Felan's answering snarl showed every last pointed fang. "We would have been less obliged to do so had we not been held virtual prisoners by your guard dog here."

Bren growled and Katja cuffed Felan hard across the shoulder for his insolence. While she might agree with him, they gained nothing by insulting their uncanny hosts.

Dayalan remained impassive. "I trust your wounds are well-healed?"

"They have. Why? Would you like to have another bout?" the werewolf challenged.

Katja hissed at him in warning.

Dayalan's eyes narrowed and then he turned to the werecat. "You must come with me."

"Why?" she asked suspiciously.

"My father and I will need your assistance to interrogate a *prisoner*," he said, looking pointedly at Felan as he emphasized the word.

"You were successful in the hunt, then?" she asked.

"Partially, at least six of the dullahan will no longer trouble you. However, Curqak and some of his allies slipped through our grasp yet again. We lost Hulus, who was one of our best accipion warriors…and Paraburus was severely injured," he growled, his eyes glinting scarlet. "Come, Katja, we need your talents as a tongue translator."

"Hold! If she must go, then we will all accompany her." Felan took a step forward to place himself between Katja and Dayalan.

"Please, Dayalan, it is important that we support her," Lauraisha added. "We have become packmates, as Felan puts it, and we cannot leave Katja to deal with these monsters alone."

Dayalan frowned and looked from the human to the werewolf and back.

"Very well," he consented. He gazed at Felan and then at Zahra. "Bring your weapons. You will need them."

He led them through the castle to a narrow stairwell that spiraled up the interior of the castle keep. They climbed single-file up the towers' steep steps until at last they emerged onto a walkway surrounding a single stone room built into part of the spire. Caleb stood near the only door in the inner wall and hissed sharply as he saw the procession of beings.

"Why are they all here? I wished for only the werecat to come."

"They insisted, Father, and I do not think them wrong for wishing to accompany her."

Caleb regarded them steadily and then bowed his head.

"Fine, then. But be wary," he said to Katja as he turned to the heavy iron door. "This deadwalker is more dangerous than any cornered and wounded beast. He will try to deceive you, wheedle information from you, or attack you. Mind your tongue and beware of his treachery."

Caleb looked at the others, adding, "Katja, Dayalan, and I will be the only ones to speak to this fiend. If any other being utters even a single word whilst inside this room, I will cast the offender outside the Ring Spells of this fortress myself. Am I understood?"

They each bowed their agreement and Caleb finally unlocked the door. Dayalan held his staff at the ready and entered after his father. Katja draw her sunsilver lytzahn and then entered the gloom beyond the door. Felan, Zahra, and Lauraisha followed her. The huge werewolf shut the door, plunging them into darkness a moment before their eyes adjusted to the dim glow from Caleb's lamp. The guttering flame revealed a lone deadwalker chained to the grimy wall across the small circular room from the Sylvans. The Asheken's face was half-obscured with dark blood and dried muck so it took Katja a moment to realize he was a nemean—a werecat who had been Turned.

The furless fiend slowly lifted his head as the lamplight gained strength. Amber eyes stared hungrily at the true werecat.

"Moarns ljocht en ehre, lytzsibba," he greeted Katja in flawless Felis.

Kajta gasped and covered her maw in horror. For the first time in three months, Katja spoke her clan's native language to another being. "No! It can't be!"

"So you recognize me then? Good." His lustful purr made her ears twitch.

The werecat screamed. "No! You were dead! They could not have Turned you! You were already dead!"

"Katja, what's wrong? Who is it?" Felan asked.

"It's Kayten, my brother," she whispered in Shrŷde.

Kayten, or rather the monster that had once been Kayten, continued to stare at his now-weeping little sister. "I was dead, but the Master's kiss gave me a death transformed. Free me from my bonds, Katja. Join me, join us, and share in our freedom…"

"Never!" Katja snarled.

"Be silent!" Dayalan's gloved hand flew against the deadwalker's face—causing black blood to ooze afresh from one wounded cheek.

"No! Leave him be! He suffers enough!" Katja yelled in anguish.

"Katja…"

"You are not my brother!" she screeched in Felis.

He opened his maw again and his whispers slowly slithered off his black tongue, "You must be so tired of running from us…from me. Come, Katja, I can make it better…I can make you better, stronger—free of grief, of fear, of despair. Come with me and you will see…"

His words were soothing, almost hypnotic. His familiar voice seemed to cast a spell over the room. Somehow the stone reality of the world around her seemed to slip away and Katja was left alone with Kayten engulfed in a shimmering mist.

"What goes on here?" she snapped in panic.

"You are becoming like me…a walker between the shadows of the realms both physical and spiritual."

"You speak blasphemy!"

"Do I now? If you only knew the nature of my being, you would then understand me and understand my power. There is no good and evil, Katja, only life and death and the power pulled between them. In a sense there is only you as life and me as death. You are transient, whilst I am eternal. The power of death is unyielding and ever-conquering. I am its wielder as are my Asheken brothers and sisters. You will join our ranks sooner or later because we as death cannot be defeated."

"I would never wish for your lot in death!" Katja cried. "To be separated from the Creator in life or death is the worst torture conceived. I would never wish that for myself nor have I ever wished it for anyone—not even my enemies!"

For a brief moment, Kayten's detached façade slipped and true terror took hold of his eyes. "Katja! Help me please!" he gasped.

Without thinking, the true werecat ran to the deadwalker and cupped his cheek in her paw. The shock of his cold flesh against her paws sent chills throughout her body. Katja suddenly found herself sitting down, dizzy, as if her very flesh and soul were sick.

The fiend strained against his bonds toward her—his cruel maw twisted in laughter. "Come! Come! Let me free you of your miserable life!"

Dimly Katja heard shouts through the mist and felt paws pull her away from him, but that must be a dream—for now Kayten as a nemean deadwalker was her only reality.

"Come to me, Katja," Kayten taunted. "Come touch me again!"

Katja sat just outside of the deadwalker's reach and blinked hard to clear the waves in her vision. She looked up into his eyes and bored into their decrepit depths with her soul.

Caleb's clawed hand gripped her shoulder hard. "Katja, don't ever do that! He'll Turn you or kill you if he can! Did he harm you at all?"

Katja slowly shook her head, not taking her eyes from her

Fallen brother.

"Kayten, come back to me please," she whispered in deepest love and longing.

At her words, the deadwalker's triumphant laughter turned into a sudden screech. The piercing keen carried with it horrific visions etched in red. Katja watched as twisted crimson and black creatures appeared momentarily around Kayten—their claws digging into his body at odd angles. Then the vision was gone and only Kayten hung limp from his chains as the cold stone keep wavered back into focus.

"Katja, listen to me," Caleb said. "Your show of love has weakened the deadwalker's defenses for the moment. You must press him for information before he recovers and tries to tempt you to your ruin again. Do you have strength enough for the task?"

She nodded and took a breath to steady her nerves. Caleb helped her stand once more and she spoke her questions.

"Kayten...who is your master?"

The nemean slowly lifted his head again and answered in a hollow voice, "Daeryn."

"And who is this Daeryn's master?"

"High Elder Luther."

Caleb and Dayalan hissed their rage even before she had finished translating.

"Why does Luther seek to destroy me?"

"Not destroy! Never to destroy you! Luther is our father; he seeks only to Turn you and give you eternal freedom."

Katja had to stifle a mordant laugh. "Why did he specifically choose me?"

"'Tis not for me to know his will; I only carry out his orders."

"And what are those orders, Kayten?"

The deadwalker hesitated. Katja stared at him penetratingly and willed him to speak. "Kayten, tell me, please?"

"To capture you at all costs and bring you to him alive and unspoiled...he wants to Turn you himself."

"Why?"

"I don't know. But the orders changed once you sought companions. Now they must be secured for his purposes as well—especially the Tyglesean."

Dayalan cursed softly after she translated.

"Who else of our clan has been Turned?" Katja continued.

"None but me."

"And what purpose could Luther possibly have with me or Lauraisha?"

"I told you I do not know High Elder Luther's—"

"Guess," she snarled.

"Katja…"

"Guess! If I am to be Turned, I want to know the purpose for it!"

The deadwalker frowned. "I believe your mage abilities are of great interest to the High Elder; Curqak mentioned something to that effect."

"What could possibly be so important about our mage abilities?"

Kayten frowned. "I know not."

"Why would you ever ally yourself with Curqak? He slaughtered our clansmen, our family!"

Kayten frowned in confusion. "He offered them true power over life and death and they refused him. They had no right to continue their lives…foolish as they were."

"It is hopeless, Katja," Caleb interrupted. "You cannot reason with a deadwalker. Trust me when I say their minds are beyond negotiations or understanding of normal logic."

"How dare you even speak in front of me, blood traitor!" Kayten suddenly lashed out toward Caleb, vengefully fighting his restraints and swearing in the soul-slaves' language of Qak.

"Down, you!" Dayalan snarled and pushed the deadwalker back with the butt of his sunsilver staff. The nemean shrieked and quickly recoiled from the sacred metal's contact.

"Leave him! Leave him!" Katja screamed.

Dayalan reluctantly removed his hold on the deadwalker.

"Caleb, help him! You came back from the depths of Asheken corruption, so you know his pain. Redeem him!" Katja suddenly pleaded.

"Redeem me?" Kayten asked in perfect Shrŷde. He threw his head back and cackled.

His laughter made Katja's fur stand on end. She stood

staring at him in shock. "You wouldn't speak in anything but Felis before! You've never been good at other languages and now you know three?"

"Oh, I'm quite proficient in several now. I just wanted to stir fond memories of home for you." His amber eyes were rimmed in red and his tongue obscenely darted out of his mouth as he cackled cruelly. "Did you like it?"

Katja felt bile rise in her throat. "Kayten…"

"I've delivered my message from the master. I have been faithful until destruction. Do with me what you wish, but know that none can save you. Luther will take you for his pleasure no matter what you do." The deadwalker smiled at Caleb. "He always takes his pleasure in the end, doesn't he?"

"Not if I have anything to say about it!" Caleb thundered. His bare hand was around the deadwalker's neck in moments and both winced at the contact.

The deadwalker gasped and wheezed. "Not even you can protect them, blood traitor! Luther has powers that not even you have yet seen! He will feed off your worthless carcass… as he did your wife's!"

Caleb's hand clenched and the deadwalker's choking became worse. Caleb suddenly released the deadwalker and shoved his head against the cold stones with a crack. Kayten went limp as Caleb strode to the door and opened it.

"We are leaving now!" he snarled and marched down the steps. No one dared disobey him.

* * *

Katja curled up against the cold, stone window ledge and watched the silent world beyond the frosted glass through tear-soaked eyes. Her right paw rested upon the window pane and her left hung as limp as her ears.

"Katja?"

The Feliconian stayed silent as Lauraisha walked into their shared bedchamber.

"Katja?"

"Leave me," she whispered without moving.

"Katja, I just want to talk—"

"Leave me!" the werecat snarled. Vaguely, she registered the hurt in the Tyglesean's gaze.

"You cannot keep hiding from us," the human retorted. "Besides, this is my room, too!"

"Fine, have it then!" Katja hissed and bolted from the room. She would not sit there and be pitied or coaxed or bullied. She had no wish to share her sorrow with anyone, especially not the naïve Tyglesean. Instead of soothing her nerves, the human's sympathy made her furious. Why couldn't she simply leave her alone with her grief? At least Felan and Zahra had shown the decency not to argue with her when she asked for privacy!

"Creator, how could you let this happen?" she screeched and bounded down another hallway. She had no idea of where she was going nor did she care. All she wanted to do was be away from everyone. She stopped to catch her breath only after she had bounded down several corridors and ascended a set of stairs. Panting, she glanced around her.

She was in a completely unfamiliar section of the castle and yet she immediately felt as if she had previously walked this particular tapestry-filled hall. Katja hastily backed against a wall. She hunkered in the shadows between two dim sconces and surveyed the scene with growing apprehension. She knew this place by sight, smell, and fear. She had visited it often in her shared dreams with Lauraisha. It was this hall that led to the red-carpeted room where she and Lauraisha always saw Dayalan shatter the grotesque mirror. Desperately, she wished she hadn't been so careless in her anger.

Katja sniffed the air again and smelled only the familiar must of the tapestries mixed with smoke from the oil lamps. No other being or beast was in this part of the castle and Katja wondered if this section were even used anymore.

The werecat turned her head sharply as voices murmured unintelligibly down the cold corridor. She shifted further into the shadows—sniffing and listening. The unintelligible whispers were issuing from the cracked, lacquered door further down the hall opposite from her. The werecat's neck fur bristled as she crossed the open floor and slunk against the wall toward the disembodied sounds.

Even as she set her right ear against the door, she could not distinguish the hollow voices' echoed words. Katja cocked her head and frowned—her curiosity beginning to override her fear of this uncanny place. Once more she reconnoitered the corridor and saw nothing peculiar, so she slowly slid her face toward the crack to peer inside the red-carpeted room. As her paw brushed the door handle, however, the voices jumped in pitch and the door itself suddenly swung open of its own accord.

Katja had to stifle a screech as she came suddenly face to face with the mirror of her nightmares. It stood in the center of the room with a few large fragments still clinging to the upper left corner of its ornate oval frame. The rest of the mirror, however, lay in shards strewn like blackened corpses across the blood-hued room. Katja gasped as she realized the voices were calling to her from the myriad fragments before her.

Without thinking, Katja walked forward, crouched, and retrieved a shard from the floor. The glass continued to reflect a swirling darkness unlike anything in the room around her. The scene then changed briefly to show Dayalan's staff striking at her before changing again to reflect her own scared face.

"So Dayalan did shatter this mirror. But why would he do such a thing?" she wondered aloud.

A tinkling brought her attention back to the room at large and she realized in horror that the fragments had floated off the carpet and were now hovering in midair around her. The werecat tried to step back into the hallway, but the door shut behind her and her back landed solidly against its varnished surface. The shard in Katja's left paw moved on its own and sliced her flesh. She yowled as her blood seeped into the sliver's surface, staining its swirling darkness scarlet. A gust of wind from nowhere pushed her across the room and the shards began to swirl around her. Then the bloody shard yanked itself out of her grasp and began to whirl with the others.

Katja gasped as the shards spun ever closer to her unprotected flesh.

"Don't touch me!" she roared.

At her command, the fragments jolted back. Then they flew toward the ancient mirror and began to reassemble themselves to form its reflective surface once again. The scarlet sliver was the last to glide into place at the mirror's center. Then the mirror fragments spoke in a chorus of voices.

"Command us, Katja Escari!"

Katja licked her suddenly dry lips. "Show me my brother please," she said hesitantly.

Kayten's image formed in the swirling darkness. He was chained in the dimly lit keep, as dirty and as vile as ever.

"No, no! I mean show Kayten as he once was...before he was Turned!"

"We cannot," said the voices. "We can only show the present or, if you wish, this mirror's direct memory."

"Then can you show me the image that caused Dayalan to shatter this mirror?"

The voices' ire reminded her of the buzz of swarming bees. The fragmented image of Dayalan then appeared before her. She frowned. No, the image wasn't of Dayalan, for Dayalan bore no scar down the length of his left arm as this being did. Rather, this pale creature seemed to be some vile and twisted version of Dayalan—a representation of what he could be if he ever Fell to the Asheken.

"Is this Dayalan?" she asked in disbelief.

"No, it most certainly is not!" Dayalan answered from the room's open door.

"That door was locked against me!"

"As it was against me," the fireforger said quietly, his eerie azure eyes blazing dangerously.

Katja looked at the door lock. It had been melted from the outside. The werecat swallowed hard. The super-heated metal was still hissing under Dayalan's hard grip. She backed away from the reassembled mirror as the fireforger approached.

Dayalan glowered from the mirror to the werecat.

"How did you find this place? How did you reconstruct this?" he bellowed.

"I didn't! I found the room by mistake. When I entered it, the shards on the floor began to swirl around me like angry hornets. Then they just...pieced themselves together."

"Why?" he shouted.

"How should I know?"

"Why did you make it show Daeryn's face!"

"Who is Daeryn?"

"Never you mind!"

The scarlet shard's voice answered, "Daeryn is Caleb's second-born son and twin brother to Dayal—"

"Silence, you!" he shouted at the mirror.

Katja was aghast. "You have a brother? A Fallen brother like mine?"

All at once, the anger left Dayalan's face and was replaced by agonizing sorrow.

"Yes," he whispered.

"Why didn't you tell me? You left me alone while in this agonizing pain when you know the same terror I do! How could you!"

"I have told you now, have I not? Do you honestly think this an easy thing to discuss? How could I be forthright with you? I barely know you."

The little werecat suddenly felt very weak and sank to her knees before the cracked mirror. She stretched a paw out to touch its surface and cover her own anguished reflection. "Kayten, I'm so sorry," she whispered.

The mirror's jagged fissures seemed to liquefy under her touch. Katja and Dayalan both watched in shock as the mirror's cracks disappeared and the shards reformed themselves into a single pane of reflective silver once more. Only one fragment remained—the one that had captured her blood.

"What are you?" Dayalan backed away from the werecat, his deep voice filled with both awe and fear.

"Wraithwalker," the single shard's voice whispered.

XVI

AZURE MERCY

"How did you ever mend the mirror?" Caleb asked while examining its reformed surface. His bandaged hand passed over the frame and Katja winced as she remembered its appearance before Aria had treated the blisters. The girtab's tail venom mixed with parts from the toxic monkshood plant was, ironically, one of the few ways to neutralize the Asheken Taint carried in Kayten's skin. Katja had not understood why she hadn't been afflicted from her own contact with the deadwalker, but she was grateful for her moment of good fortune.

"Katja, how did you repair the mirror?" Caleb asked again, searching her eyes.

"I touched it," the werecat responded in bewilderment. "That was all."

"She certainly did," Dayalan growled.

Katja flicked her ears, but said nothing. Dayalan had been very wary around her in the days following her inadvertent discovery and restoration of the Ott vre Caerwyn. Katja wondered if she had scared Dayalan as much as she had herself with the mirror's transformation. She doubted Dayalan had ever intended to tell her he had a Fallen brother, nor would he discuss the fact now.

She stared at the mirror as Caleb's bandaged hand now passed from his perfect reflection down to the jagged red shard in the mirror's center. She knew from clan stories that the looking glass and its twin the Ott vre Blaec had once allowed Caleb to communicate with Luther at his fortress at Blaecthull on the Northern Continent. When Caleb was Redeemed, however, his fireforger wife Marga found a way to destroy the mirrors' link to each other so that Luther could never spy on the occupants of Caerwyn again.

"And what happened here?" Caleb asked, pointing to the scarlet shard.

"That shard cut me and was stained with my blood before it and the others reattached themselves to the frame."

"It cut you?" Dayalan quickly turned to her, his eyes shadowed.

"Yes, again of its own accord." Katja stared at him evenly and held out her recently sliced right paw.

He took it in a gloved hand and carefully examined the crescent-shaped scab. "It is a clean cut, no sign of infection, and it's shallow enough that it did not damage any tendons or nerves. You will have quite a scar when it heals, though."

"Naturally," the werecat responded dryly and pulled her paw out of his grasp. "Why do you always wear those coverings anyway?"

Dayalan looked at his gloves but did not speak.

"Because he is ashamed of his hands," Lauraisha said as she walked into the room.

"What!" Dayalan thundered.

"Well, you are," she retorted defensively while examining the scarlet shard alongside Caleb. "Otherwise you would not bother hiding them."

For being so naïve in her Tyglesean education, Lauraisha often showed surprisingly keen intuition. Katja looked back at the male and crossed her arms. "Well?"

"Well, what?"

"Are you going to tell us why a fireforger mage would wear gloves that subdue his control over his most powerful weapon or are you going to ignore us?"

"It is none of your concern why I dress the way I do," he snapped defiantly.

"Just as it is none of our concern that you have a Fallen brother like I do?"

When Caleb and Dayalan both glowered at them, Katja realized she had pushed past some unspoken boundary into treacherous territory. Silence hung as a thick wall of tension between them all and Katja swallowed anxiously.

Finally Caleb spoke, "Remove your gloves, Dayalan."

"Father!"

"They have a right to know what company they keep. Do it." Caleb's command was indisputable.

Dayalan glared at his father and then looked at the females with sudden trepidation. The emotion was such a strange pairing with his stern face. When he had finally removed the gloves, both Lauraisha and Katja gasped. Dayalan's hands resembled those of Curqak's—pallid skin stretched around five fingers forged from sharp bone and stringy tendon culminating in curved obsidian-hued claws. Katja could not decide whether to call them hands or talons. The werecat cringed at the sight of the Asheken characteristic and then stared again at both Dayalan and Caleb. Although Caleb's fingers were not as well-clawed as his son's, she immediate recognized the similarities. The black-clawed talons and pointed, black-tipped ears were common traits among deadwalkers. Vampires and ghouls carried these traits along with yellow fangs; however, only vampires bore blood-red eyes.

She looked closer and discovered his hands, ears, and white fangs matched those of his father. His eyes, however, were pale blue—at least for the moment.

"You *inherited* Víchí traits…how is that even possible?" she whispered, dry-mawed.

"I am not evil!" Dayalan whispered, more to himself than to her.

"No, of course you are not," Caleb agreed. "It is I who was evil and it is I who cursed you with Víchí markings. For that, I feel true sorrow."

"Why?" Lauraisha asked, frowning. "Why would you be ashamed to pass to your son the strengths of your enemies without their weaknesses?"

Katja looked at the human, startled, and then comprehension dawned. "That is true! Dayalan probably understands the Víchí as well you do and yet he also has the power to destroy them. He looks like a vampire and yet he seems to have no love of them. He could sneak among their numbers without the slightest suspicion set against him and murder them in their sleep." The Feliconian suddenly smiled maliciously. "He is their perfect predator."

Caleb bowed his head and sighed wistfully. "It is unfair that he would hold such talents for now he must carry the burden of his family and take a path not of his own choosing."

Dayalan smiled toward his father in reassurance. "It is my honor to bear such a burden, Father, for you and for Mother. I make my own decisions and I do choose this path…I will aid Lauraisha and the others in their journey and I swear to you on my own blood that I will find a way to avenge Mother."

Caleb stared at his son sadly. "Do not make promises you cannot hope to keep. Do not be foolish enough to follow your brother's path. There may come a time for revenge, but do not dwell on your hatred for our enemies…if you do so, you may Fall even farther than I did. In the end, I doubt I will have the strength to hunt down my own son…do you understand?"

Dayalan's eyes shut tight for a moment. When he bowed in submission, Katja saw a tear loose itself from his now-scarlet eyes. Caleb meanwhile turned back to the werecat.

"Katja, I am truly sorry, but I must leave a horrible decision to your discretion. Since you are the closest living relative, you must decide what to do with your Fallen brother. You have seen what a monster he has become and knowing the danger he poses to you and to your companions, so you must choose his fate. Either he must remain forever locked in Caerwyn's keep or he must be burned."

"That would be to torment him until death!"

Caleb sadly agreed.

"You cannot! There isn't even a powerful enough fireforger here to perform the proper soul-cleansing needed to be sure his spirit does not cling to this realm and make him a poltergeist!"

"Actually, I can perform the task, Katja," Dayalan said quietly.

"You?"

Dayalan nodded as his eyes returned to their usual pigment of fiery blue.

Katja blinked and tried a different tack. "Caleb, you have to help him! You are the only mage and Sylvar in history to break the slavery of the Asheken curse…can you not restore him just as you restored yourself?"

"Katja, I did not restore myself and I do not possess the power to restore him," the old mage said with surprising gentleness. "It must be the deadwalker's decision to wish to come back to life and not even then would I be able to undo all of the Turning Spells associated with a soul-servant bite. The only way to save him is to burn him, just as it has always been."

* * *

"He's lying! There must be another way!" the Feliconian screamed, her hackles raised and her ears flat in defiance. She was standing in the middle of the bedchamber glaring at her packmates.

"Katja, there is not," Zahra said wearily. "The only way to properly destroy a deadwalker is fire—you know that… we all do. Sunsilver will paralyze them and keep them from reattaching any severed limbs, but fire—real mage fire—is the only way to cleanse their souls and send their spirits on to the Creator's realms of judgment. Otherwise, they will exist here in the flesh forever and feed off of the lives of others to keep up their strength. They are worse than a plague!"

"But this is my brother, my own flesh and blood," she hissed. "He's the only kin I have left!"

"Exactly the point, Katja!" the werewolf growled. "Would you want your own brother confined to the half-life of a deadwalker? To be chained for eternity in a castle's keep with only his own insatiable hunger and hatred as companions?"

"No! Of course not!"

"Then be merciful to him!"

"Felan is right, Katja. There is no way other than what Father suggests," Dayalan said as he stood in the room's doorway.

"Why is Caleb so afraid to try to cure him in the first place? Why will he not at least try?"

"Afraid?" Dayalan's eyes blazed. "My father does not fear anything! Not even Luther! The only one he fears is perhaps himself as he once was, and what he or I could yet become if either of us Fell to the Asheken. Do you not understand that he had not the strength to cure himself? That none of us actually do? Caleb's legendary return from the Asheken darkness was a miracle of the Creator's own doing. It had nothing to do with his talents—great as they are."

Katja snarled obstinately at him, but her ears also perked slightly.

"If you are such a powerful fireforger, why did you leave the deadwalker alive in the first place?" Felan asked, speaking to Dayalan for the first time since Kayten's interrogation.

The fireforger leaned against the doorframe and looked over at the werewolf. "He is hiding something from us. The information he let slip to Katja was inconsequential and meant to distract us from finding out whatever real secret he guards. I must say he is fairly clever. He gave us clues to follow and then insulted my mother—no doubt, hoping to push me or my father into destroying him before he broke and told us his true secrets."

"So the mention of Katja's and my mage abilities is actually of little consequence?" the Tyglesean asked.

"There will certainly be merit in improving your mage abilities once you arrive on the Isle of Summons, but don't trouble yourselves about such matters now. Instinct tells me to doubt the idea that Luther would risk exposure of his activities on Sylvan soil if he wanted you both for your talents alone. There must be another reason he seeks you…is there something significant about your ancestry?"

"Other than my being the youngest Tyglesean princess and hardly worth notice?" Lauraisha's semi-sarcasm seeped through her voice.

"A royal is a royal no matter her birth-rank, Your Highness; however, I was far more curious about how you inherited your fireforging and dreamdrifting abilities."

Lauraisha blinked at him. "You mean only dreamdrifting abilities."

Dayalan shook his head. "No, I meant what I said."

He stepped toward her and asked that she hold out her hand. She did so hesitantly. Dayalan then produced a small golden flame above his left palm and then poured it into her waiting hand. Lauraisha gasped as the flame hit her flesh but did not singe her skin. She, along with everyone else, stared slack-jawed as it danced just above her cupped hand.

"The fire welcomes you," Dayalan said softly, and smiled.

The flame in Lauraisha's hands blazed merrily and then of its own accord turned its golden hue to bright orange. The human's eyes began to water and even Katja could feel the flame's heat. Dayalan's gloved talon scooped up the flame and extinguished it before he looked into her mesmerized eyes.

"When we first met, you instinctively attacked me with fire even though you had never used it before. You know the basics of dreamdrifting and have practiced them for years now. Yet you knew nothing of your fireforger abilities… which means a powerful mage must have kindled them."

"King Canuche's flame," Katja answered for her.

Dayalan's eyes darted to hers. "What about Canuche?"

"When we found Canuche in Crown Canyon, we did so by accident," she explained.

"By falling down a hole into the chamber where his statue resided, if I remember correctly," the fireforger said.

Katja nodded. "Yes, but the reason we fell in the first place was because we were fleeing a pair of basels. One of them was able to follow us down the tunnel and bit Lauraisha before I could destroy it—"

"You really managed to kill one of the basilisk descendants?" Dayalan was incredulous.

"Three of them, actually," Lauraisha interrupted. "She killed the first and the third and I killed the second. Katja, whatever happened to the fourth?"

The werecat frowned. "I think the third snake killed it and then followed us down into the chamber. In any event, the basel attacked Lauraisha before I could kill it. She would have died had it not been for the sphere of fire located on an altar in Canuche's chamber. Lauraisha insisted that she touch it after she was bitten and who was I to argue with a dying being's wish? The fire healed her and, I now suspect, kindled her fireforger abilities, although she never used them until we encountered you."

"Father?" Dayalan turned toward Caleb, who had stood in the doorway listening long before anyone had noticed him. He walked into the room, peering from Katja to Lauraisha and back.

"Did you ever build the campfires while you journeyed?" he asked the human.

"No, we usually did without campfires because they attracted far too much attention."

"You did when we stayed in the shadowshaper mage's dwelling," Zahra reminded her.

"And she used it to smoke and dry meat that night," Felan added. "She did it in a matter of hours with no apparatus to keep the meat and smoke constantly mixed. The whole process would have taken days with proper gear, but for her it took only a few hours to preserve the meat. I thought it was some new Tyglesean technique at the time."

Caleb smiled knowingly.

"Lauraisha's awakening also explains my existence in this realm, honored Caleb," Damya's voice echoed from the princess's stone amulet just before the pyrefay erupted from its depths. She bowed then and floated before him in all her fiery blue splendor.

"A firesprite," Dayalan said wistfully.

"Yes, fireforger, I am called Damya—the untamable flame," she said and flew close to touch his forehead in benediction. The action would have burned any other being, but Dayalan remained quite unharmed. He bowed deeply toward her and whispered his honored thanks.

She returned his bow before turning her attention once more to his father. "Caleb, I have awakened and soon my Keystone brethren will as well."

"It is time?" Caleb asked wide-eyed.

"Indeed. The fulfillment of the prophecies your wife followed so faithfully has begun. Henceforth, the time is ripe for action. I am the First Sign. The second shall come on swift wings."

"What is the Second Sign, My Madam?"

"These Sylvan mages shall witness it among the stones of the Isle of Summons within a month—a Pyrekin's seed shall blossom there upon saving the life of a mage. It shall choose its herald and steward from among the beings gathered there and shall help sear the evil that has taken root among the isle's wise.

"For this sign to occur, you must send these companions to the isle in all haste. The Darkkyn and Drosskin gather against them and their shadows could smite one ere they reach the isle."

"How can we possibly make it through Reithrgar and to the isle now that the pass is snowed under?" the Tyglesean asked.

Caleb smiled. "Reithrgar is one of the southern-most passes, Your Highness; wait another few days and the snow will be cleared. If it isn't, Dayalan's fireforging magic will help warm your way. You will still make slow progress because of the mud, but at least you can traverse the mountains. Without the Gan Ceann or zombies tracking you, your trek should be far safer."

"Did you destroy all of the deadwalkers besides Kayten and Curqak then?" Katja asked.

"Unfortunately, no," the old mage said. "Curqak once again slipped through my grasp. He and two dullahan and perhaps four zombies are all that are left of the original twenty-member party hunting you. They pose little direct threat to you since their numbers are so small, but they could still attempt to ensnare you, so be wary. This is chiefly why I wish Dayalan to accompany you."

"We have taken care of ourselves quite well along our journey thus far, thank you," Felan snarled. "Besides what good can Dayalan do when Curqak can simply send a message to Luther for more support and then find ways to delay us until reinforcements arrive?"

Caleb shook his head. "I doubt he would ask Luther for fresh warriors given his latest blunder with the elite dullahan. In fact, I doubt he will communicate with Luther at all until he finds some way of redeeming himself. To admit failure would be to invite his own execution, for Luther is neither gracious nor forgiving."

Damya agreed with him. "Curqak is currently far too weak to again assume command. Expect any current threats to come from outside of Curqak's influence."

"Honored Damya, what does Luther want with Katja and Lauraisha?" Dayalan asked.

"We must seek those answers from Kayten," Damya said

and then looked at the werecat. "If you wish it, Katja, I will perform the purification for your brother."

"Must it be done?" she asked with tears standing in her eyes.

"To truly free him, yes it must."

Katja stood very still before the Pyrekin and looked into the depths of her flaming eyes. Ever so slowly she bowed her consent, knowing the agony Kayten must endure before he could experience true freedom.

* * *

"You will tell me what I wish to know, Kayten," Damya said calmly.

"Never!" the deadwalker retorted in Shrŷde and then swore viciously at her in Qak and Felis.

The Pyrekin waited out the tirade without even flinching, while Katja was forced to use every ounce of self-control she possessed not to slice the vile tongue out of Kayten's fanged mouth. The companions had been in the keep for hours and yet the deadwalker proved unaffected by their interrogations. He had cursed Damya and Caleb with every question, giving no answers to their enquiries no matter how they might phrase them. At every turn he had tried to anger his enemies into destroying him.

Felan gently placed a restraining paw on the werecat's shoulder as she growled in frustration.

"Do not touch her, werewolf! Your grim filth has no business associating with my sister!" Kayten's eyes flashed.

Katja roared back defiantly and leveled a look of loathing at him. Did she detect a glimmer of smugness in his face? What information was so vital for him to keep hidden? She would find no answers using the present route.

The true werecat closed her eyes and took a deep breath. She banished the deadwalker's presence from her thoughts and focused on her catling memories of Kayten instead. She remembered his infectious grin and laughter, his often-infuriating love of practical jokes, and his valiant loyalty to his family and friends. Deep within her soul, she felt a peculiar reservoir of power unlock and flow through her being. Once her loving memories had overwhelmed her sense of hatred toward the decrepit monster now chained before her, Katja opened her glowing green eyes and stepped forward.

"Look at me, Kayten," she said, finding the name somehow foreign when paired with this broken being.

He did so and hissed in malevolence.

"How did you become a deadwalker?"

His expression suddenly changed into one of zeal. He then began describing the process of the bite and subsequent Turning in gory detail.

"No, I actually meant how and where were you captured?"

"I was taken and Turned while following the stream's flow west of the Feliconas Village."

"West? Why were you traveling west? Our cousin clan lies to the northeast of our village."

"I was hunting you."

Katja frowned. "Before or after you were Turned?"

"Both, Katja. I have hunted you for four full moons now. I hunted you before my Turning because I wanted to protect you, now I hunt you by my master's decree."

"I told you to seek refuge with the cousins!"

"You know I have never really cared to take orders from siblings, Katja. Besides, I could not let such a rare mage go wondering around by herself."

"You were the one who told Curqak I was a skinshifter!"

She had said it as a ruse to keep him talking, but Kayten's sudden wrath at her guess caused Katja to pause. A piece of knowledge previously shared between Canuche and Katja slipped into place.

"You were trying to help me and then you betrayed me when you told Curqak that I was a skinshifter. Luther did not send him after me simply because of my mage abilities, did he?"

Kayten's refusal to speak was the perfect affirmation. A memory came unbidden to Katja's mind of a rockslide and a dark monster sniffing the fragments of Katja's broken fishing spear.

"Luther is hunting me, hunting us, because of our parents, isn't he? Our parents stood against him in the Second War of Ages and then disappeared among our clansmen to raise a family. He found them and had them murdered over six winters ago in revenge for their protection of Sylvans and their defiance toward him. Then he came after our family and clansmen in retribution."

Kayten's eyes shifted to the floor and then back to Katja, but he said nothing.

"Katja," the firesprite whispered in her ear. "Luther would not come after your family simply for revenge…there are too many he would wish to destroy for such a thing. Also, the Sphinx's Maw was shut until perhaps a year ago according to my sources, so no deadwalkers would have been able to set claw on Sylvan soil during that time."

"Unless they were already here," Katja muttered. "There was a deadwalker skulking around on the day of my parents' death. I saw it!"

"Still, Luther is too calculating to send his minions after them only for revenge."

As Damya said this, Katja spied Kayten's gaze flicker across her chest and pay heed to the spearheads and the Feliconas signet crest she now wore. His gaze then followed suit with each of her companions before moving back to their father's crest and finally to the dusty floor.

"He is searching us for something, Damya."

Damya bobbed her head but did not speak. Instead her eyes bore into Kayten's with a frightening intensity. She raised her hand and a rope of fire uncoiled from its depths.

"He seeks the Keystone to which I am beholden that Lauraisha now guards, Katja," she said just loudly enough for the deadwalker to overhear.

Kayten stared startled at her and then drew himself up against the wall. With a leer, he launched himself toward the Tyglesean princess, breaking his bonds in the process. Before he could take another step, however, Dayalan and Damya both drove him back with staff and fire.

"Tell us what Luther wants with Katja and Lauraisha!"

The deadwalker screeched in panic, but said nothing else. Katja growled in frustration.

"Katja, if you touch his skin, he will divulge the truth," Damya whispered.

Katja jerked her eyes to the firesprite in disbelief, but Damya only nodded. Again Katja felt that strange power kindled within her as she looked back at her Fallen brother. She stepped toward him with her right paw partially extended and her left absently fiddling with her necklaces. The deadwalker leered at her, but dared not move against Dayalan's sunsilver staff. Her unsheathed right paw gripped his clammy neck and her verdant eyes bore into his dull amber depths. The contact between skins and eyes proved jolting, but not toxic.

"Kayten, you will tell me what you are hiding." She said it without anger or hate, her soul filled with a calm detachment.

"Never!" he sneered, but his voice suddenly quivered with fear.

"Tell me what I want to know so that your suffering may end in this world."

"You would not kill me!"

"No, Kayten, I never could—"

His face lit in triumph.

"For we both know you are far worse than dead."

The triumph turned to terror.

"Why did Luther's servant kill our parents?"

"Kevros carried a sort of talisman that is sacred to the High Elder," Kayten said, quaking. "Curqak discovered that he had it and plotted to steal it for his Sire. The ghoul caused their deaths and then used the distraction of the rockslide to search for the talisman; however, he never recovered it."

"This past season he looked for it again when the Asheken destroyed the Feliconas Clan. They hunted Kevros and Devra's descendants because Luther believed that one of us had the talisman. He also believed one of us to be blessed with Kevros and Devra's mage gifts and that would mean their descendant was part of a feared prophesy."

"What prophesy?"

Kayten shook his head.

"Do not lie to me!"

"I have not, Katja! I heard Curqak whispering to the head of the Gan Ceann that your and Lauraisha's family lineages are somehow important to the High Elder. It must have to do with whatever prophesies he hopes to undermine.

"Know this, Katja…Devra's blood gives you much strength, but it was Kevros who gave you true power…true dominion over life and death. You were the only one blessed out of all of us siblings with both of our parents' mage abilities and you must be properly awakened by a true warlock before you can appreciate the extent of your dominion."

"Dominion?" she snapped, "Do you honestly think that I would use my gifts for anything other than the protection of others?"

"Katja, those you truly care about are dead. The only one left is me, so will you be Turned in order to protect me from my enemies or will you betray me—the last of the family you love. You have the potential to be a true walker between the realms, a necromancer as powerful as the Elder himself. I feel the ability already growing within you…Join Luther and let him open your mind to the full possibilities of your gifts."

"Never will I join that monster!" Katja snarled at him, her claws coming dangerously close to slicing his jugular as she squeezed his throat.

"Katja, Katja…" Kayten was gasping under her grasp—his eyes filling with true terror.

"No…" she gasped in horror at her own vengeance and unclenched her paw. She backed away from him, tears standing in her eyes. "Kayten…"

The deadwalker pulled himself off of his knees and sneered. "So close you are in life to Turning, your Fall will be swift indeed, lytzsibba!"

Katja massaged her throbbing paw and looked at the panting nemean. Her sudden hatred had evidently made her vulnerable to his skin's poison. She looked mournfully from him to the firesprite. "As a Pyrekin, Damya, you are the best judge of truth…is he being truthful?"

"He utterly believes everything he just told you."

"Very well," the little werecat knelt cradling her left paw as a row of bright blisters puckered across her stinging flesh. "I cannot do that again."

"Nor should you have to," Dayalan said. The packmates all nodded their agreement so that they would not break their vow of silence during the interrogation.

"Hold still, Katja." Damya flitted close to Katja's paw and blew fiery breath carefully over the blisters. The werecat screeched at the sudden pain as Damya's fire seeped into her flesh and burned away the Taint.

"Use your skinshifting abilities to heal the wounds, Katja, then you should be cured of all marks save the mirror's scar. Not even I can remedy *that*."

The Feliconian frowned, took a breath, and concentrated on remaking each layer of her bodily form just as Felan had taught her to do. Her paw changed into a hand and then back to a paw once more—the burned blisters and welts disappearing in the process.

"Come, let us linger with the walking dead no more," Damya said as she glided to the door.

Katja turned to follow her, but the sound of a grunt of pain made her whirl back and instinctively dart sideways as Kayten charged her. He had dodged past Dayalan and pushed through Damya's loose net of fire to attack her—badly singeing himself in the process.

"Katja!" Lauraisha screamed.

Felan was by her side instantly, clawing and snapping mercilessly at the deadwalker while the stunned Dayalan regained his footing. The werewolf drove the fiend back using his massive body as a battering ram and together he and Dayalan pinned Kayten to the wall once more.

"I will destroy you!" the deadwalker screeched at Katja. He made another mad lunge for her despite being pinned again by Dayalan's staff.

Suddenly Katja wished that Felan had brought his war axe despite the werewolf now having little space in which to swing it. Katja screeched in panic as Kayten kicked Felan and sent him rolling. The deadwalker's frenzied strength was like nothing she had ever seen. In that moment, she made her decision and knew it to be right.

"Damya! Destroy him before he kills the others!"

The firesprite was there in an instant, weaving her nets of flame around Kayten. The deadwalker shrieked in agony as Damya tightened the flaming blue threads around his writhing body. Katja could smell the sickening scent of burning flesh and fell to her knees gagging and weeping. Lauraisha and Zahra dragged her to the safety beyond the doorway and held her while Caleb, Felan, and Dayalan stood guard.

"My Madam," Dayalan said quietly while watching the writhing corpse hiss and screech upon the floor. "Will you finish it quickly, so that Katja does not have to watch this?"

"No, Dayalan. You should do it." The firesprite looked back at him. "Quickly, fireforger, for her sake and for his."

"Very well." Dayalan bowed his head once, stowed his black gloves, and raised both talons. Through the doorway, Katja watched him ignite a blue ball of flames within his bare palms and cast it at the swearing and screeching nemean. The blast of heat was unfathomable as the flame hit her Fallen brother. The fire completely consumed Kayten and Katja could swear that the very stones of the floor beneath him glowed red. When it extinguished, only a pile of smoldering ash remained.

Then a wisp of scarlet smoke flowed from of the ashes toward the werecat. Within its depths, Katja swore she glimpsed her brother's once-handsome face smiling at her.

"Kayten…" she whispered in longing.

"It is well, sibba; I love you…I am proud of you…" the wraith whispered.

As he said this, a single ray of sunlight pierced the gloom through one of the keep's arrow slits. Smiling, Kayten vanished into the light, leaving Katja to weep in his wake.

XVII

SCARLET SHARDS

Silence pervaded Katja's world in the days following Kayten's destruction. She spoke to the others only when necessary and preferred to spend most of her time drifting alone from memory to precious memory. She thought not only of Kayten, but also of Kumos and Keepha and Sephna and Sephros and Devra and Kevros and all of her other departed clansmen. She dwelt on memories of the Feliconas Clan's village with its particular smells and sights and sounds. She savored the precious simplicity of its inhabitants' various daily routines.

In the beginning, the shock of Kayten's final death had outweighed her grief and then even her grief began melting away as she remembered the wraith's face smiling in true joy and thankfulness before he was pulled on to the Creator's own realm. In his final moments, Kayten had somehow released her from the guilt she felt over her clansmen's deaths. After all, it was better that they die than be Turned and exist forever, tortured, as Kayten had until his final destruction.

For whatever reason, the Feliconian found it much easier to ponder all that once existed in her life while in the room housing the Ott vre Caerwyn. Often she found herself there before realizing she had wanted to be near the mirror in the first place. How strange that she should seek solitude in a place that was once the focus of her nightmares. She had discovered through this mirror that she shared Dayalan's similar loss of family and it was before this mirror that Dayalan found her sitting seven days after her brother's death.

"How long will you need to mourn, Katja?" Dayalan asked gently upon entering the room.

The Feliconian frowned at the carpet thoughtfully and then stood tall before the uncanny mage. "I no longer mourn my clan," she said perfunctorily. "My sorrow cannot wake them from eternal slumber and therefore my self-pity serves no purpose."

"Then what do you seek from this place? Forgiveness?"

Katja looked toward him, gazing into his troubled blue eyes. "No, Kayten already forgave me."

He continued to search her eyes with a mixture sorrow and fear cradled in his own. "A path of revenge then?"

She smiled gently once realization dawned. "You think I blame you for destroying him."

Dayalan pressed his lips together until they were as pale as the rest of his face. He inclined his head.

"Dayalan, you did what was needed and I am grateful that you destroyed him. Why are you so surprised? Do you think I wanted my beloved brother to exist in that ruined state for eternity? How could I bear such a thing to be done to him in good conscience? I now understand that death—true death—is the only solution to such a torturous predicament."

Dayalan's mouth worked, but no words came. Finally he managed to whisper his thanks and bowed deeply to her.

"No, Dayalan, it is I who must thank you for finally freeing him," she said, returning the bow.

They stared at one another in silence until the Feliconian werecat murmured that she needed answers about her clansmen's deaths. She wanted to discover what plans Luther had for them and for her.

"I highly doubt you will find such answers here, Katja," the mage said, peering over at the mirror.

The werecat scratched her ear and also turned to stare at its shining surface. "No, I suppose not. I thought that perhaps I could think with more clarity in the presence of something that once belonged to Luther—so that I could better understand his methods…"

"You should not wish to understand him, Katja. To understand him is to share in his darkness."

"Have you ever met him?"

Dayalan arched an eyebrow. "Not personally, no…but I know his handiwork—"

"As his grandson, you should."

The male's eyes flashed scarlet and his jaw tightened. "Katja, as a favor to me, please never use such a familial reference for us again."

Katja swallowed. "My apologies, I meant no offence. It's just—"

"I know that you bear no ill intent, Katja, but he is not an ancestor I will ever willingly acknowledge."

"Understood." The werecat bowed. "When you mention Luther's handiwork, what do you mean?"

Dayalan's eyes reddened again. "I was referring to Mother's death."

Katja stared at him. "What?"

"You have a right to know the story so that you understand what evil was done to my family." Dayalan's gloved talons flexed as he spat the words. "You know, of course, that my mother Marga was a very powerful mage whose fireforger abilities I inherited."

Katja half-smiled. "Few besides the Tygleseans would not know about the legendary Marga. Although stories vary as to exactly how she Redeemed the powerful vampire now known as Caleb."

"Does Lauraisha at least have better knowledge of Sylvan history and customs than her countrymen?"

Katja snorted derisively. "Not remotely. I've had to explain much to her this past season; although thankfully she has proved a quick study despite her relative youth."

"Hmm, I see." Dayalan pursed his lips. "The full story of my father's reformation is one I believe he would wish to explain himself."

Katja inclined her head. "As you wish."

Dayalan murmured his thanks. He then explained that for many years before and after he and his twin brother Daeryn were born, his mother served many different clans and kingdoms as the mages' Chief Emissary. She traveled often throughout the Sylvan Realms to hear the petitions of those clans ultimately governed by the Mage Council and would bring their requests before both the council and its governing body, the Ring of Sorcerers.

Several years after Kaylor usurped the throne and closed Tyglesea to almost all outsiders, Marga made her final journey to that country to commune with the Tyglesean priesthood. The priests and priestesses beholden to the Creator were the last mages allowed to practice their arts within the country and so her presence was secretly welcomed among them.

"When my mother became delayed during her return expedition, Father didn't worry—at least not until a fortnight had passed without any sign of her. He dispatched a message by courier pigeon to the priesthood only to discover that she had left the kingdom twelve weeks before she was due to arrive at Caerwyn. Father then alerted the mages on the Isle of Summons of her disappearance and sent scouts along all the roads and back trails around Caerwyn to look for her. Eventually Father, Daeryn, and I discovered what remained of her on a windswept cliff less than five leagues beyond Caerwyn's boundary of protection.

"We found a circle of burnt forest near a cliff's edge where the ashes of both Sylvans and deadwalkers were strewn. The heavy claw marks dug into the ground and trees suggested a desperate fight. Father and I believe that Marga and her guardians were ambushed by deadwalkers and then backed into a trap against the edge of the cliff."

Katja's paw covered her maw as Dayalan spoke. She lowered it to whisper: "Were there any survivors?"

Dayalan shook his head. "None. All we actually found of Mother were charred pieces of her clothes tangled in the half-burnt branches of a nearby tree. The wind must have mixed her ashes with those of the other dead. The bodies that were left were all too unrecognizable due to the fire and the ravens' appetites to distinguish deadwalker from Sylvan, so I incinerated them all in a traditional last rights ceremony, just to be sure of complete spiritual purification and buried the ashes at the pinnacle of Rood Mountain."

"But why would she burn herself?"

"It is the ultimate sacrifice of a fireforger. If we are threatened by an enemy with no chance of escape, we can choose to allow our own fire to erupt uncontrolled out of our soul. The fire would destroy the body and kill us, but it would also destroy all around us —"

"Such as was the case with Aribem's sacrifice to split the continents or the griffins' last stand at Eppon Gue Vale."

"Correct."

"So she sacrificed herself to save her guardians from the deadwalkers?"

"We believe so, although we will never know for sure since those Sylvans who survived the fire were summarily pushed off the cliff and covered with an avalanche of boulders."

Katja's ears flattened. "That death sounds familiar."

"It certainly does have all the qualities of Curqak's particular tastes, doesn't it?"

"You hate the ghoul as much as I," the Feliconian growled.

"Probably."

Katja frowned and absently stroked the mirror. "So what about your brother? Why is he a deadwalker?"

Dayalan cleared his throat. "We don't actually know if or exactly *how* he has been Turned. Daeryn and my father had a falling out after Mother died…"

The werecat watched him shift uncomfortably. "Would it be better if you did not answer?"

His intense blue eyes darted to hers and then quickly dropped to the floor at her paws. "No…no you need to know this in the event that…"

Katja waited, but he did not finish the statement. Instead Dayalan took a long breath and sighed. "Even after we found the ashes, Daeryn believed that Mother was not dead and berated my father for giving up the search. He was convinced that Marga had survived the attack, but that she was captured and therefore somehow remained in deadwalker custody. Knowing full well that Mother would rather kill herself than be held prisoner to the Asheken, Father attributed Daeryn's conspiratorial beliefs to his overwhelming grief. I was instructed to keep close watch on him and prevent him from doing anything reckless if he decided to pursue his erroneous notions."

"How could a fireforger possibly be captured by the Asheken?" Katja asked incredulously. "A fireforger can never be Turned since their soul's fiery magic prevents such a transformation and causes death to both the fireforger mage and the biting deadwalker upon their souls' contact."

"That was exactly my father's point to Daeryn. There would be no reason to capture a fireforger unless the deadwalker specifically wished to destroy itself…"

"And Caleb is, after all, the only one who has ever survived a fireforger's flame," Katja interjected.

Dayalan nodded and continued, "That fact stood out for my brother. He believed that Mother's contact with Father and her birth of us somehow proved her ineffectiveness as a fireforger and that if she were successfully captured by deadwalkers she could be Turned into one. He was at best illogical and at worst insane. I've fought beside my mother before; believe me when I say that I learned my potency from her."

He shook his head. "I should have been with her. She left me behind on that trip so that she wouldn't raise Tyglesean suspicions. She could pass easily enough for a Tyglesean human, but me…" Dayalan's sigh was heavy.

"In any event, Daeryn became more and more obstinate with each passing day. I tried to reason with him, but in the end he would have none of my counsel nor our father's. He began to journey to the outskirts of our borders and beyond. Often, when I followed him, I would find him standing in that charred circle and probing the landscape with his mage gift."

Katja frowned at him in confusion. Then Dayalan explained that, unlike his brother, Daeryn inherited barely a spark of Marga's fireforging gift. Instead he was born with the tendencies of a shadowshaper mage, which was a gift of their father's. Even as a child, Daeryn would often bend the reality around him to suit his purposes—making the brothers' twigs seem like swords or fashioning Dayalan's fire into fantastic shapes and creatures.

"He used the shadowshaper gift to delve between the layers of reality on that cliff—searching for some clue to our mother's death. After weeks of probing, he told me he had found something important, but he wanted to share it with our father first. I never learned what he discovered because he and Father had a horrendous fight that night." Dayalan shuddered. "I walked into the Ott chamber that evening and found my father and brother locked in one of the bloodiest brawls I've yet seen. Of course, I immediately pulled Daeryn off of our father and then he rounded on me for interfering."

As Dayalan shook his head in sadness, the mirror came alive. Katja watched Caleb struggle against a scarlet-eyed Daeryn. Both males were thrashing violently upon the carpet—their claws flailing and their fangs fully extended. Dayalan closed his eyes against the mirror and turned away grimacing while Katja watched the memory play out.

*

Dayalan had just opened the door to stare stunned at the hostility before him. He hesitated only a moment before dragging his twin away from their father.

"Daeryn, are you daft! What do you think you're doing?"

"He murdered her! He murdered her just as he murdered Rhynma!" Daeryn shouted. "I saw him do it as if I were there!"

"What are you talking about?"

"Mother's dead because of him! He let her be taken right off his own land! He made a pact with Luther for peace at the price of Mother's blood!"

"I did not! I could not!" Caleb yelled. "She was my only link to true love and life…"

"Brother, be still! You are not yourself!" Dayalan desperately held his struggling twin against the wall. "What witchery is this? Father would never harm Mother!"

"He loves us even less than he did her! And he loves you, his precious fireforger, more than me! Of course you would defend him!"

Daeryn caught his brother with a fist to the ribs and then flung him off before lunging at Caleb again—screeching obscenities. Dayalan leaped after him, but missed his mark. Caleb, however, was ready for the attack and whipped a shard of wood from a nearby broken chair across Daeryn's path as he charged.

For the first time, Katja saw fear flicker in the son's eyes as he tried to dodge the makeshift stake. The impromptu weapon cleaved a bloody gash in Daeryn's left arm from the wrist almost to the shoulder. He screamed and fell back against the floor writhing in shock and pain.

"Get Aria and Hanna before he bleeds to death!" Caleb

shouted at Dayalan.

Dayalan did not move, but instead stared in shock at his brother and then his father. "You would not —"

"Never!" Caleb said, his voice shaking with anguish as he knelt beside his son. "Now find them and the herbs before the toxin sets in!"

Dayalan sprinted out the door while Caleb bent over his other son.

"Daeryn, I'm so sorry, I—"

"Don't you touch me, murderer!" Daeryn said and scrambled backward to the corner fireplace. He retrieved a sword laying there and held it unsheathed toward his father with his good arm. "You come near me ever again and I will destroy you!"

"Daeryn, I never meant to hurt you, but you left me no alternative!"

"You should have died! It would have been a justice after what you've done to Mother and to hundreds of others."

"I am no longer that Drosskin spawn Calais; don't accuse me of it! I was restored!"

"I will find the truth of this, Father, and you cannot stop me. I looked between the layers of reality and saw your soul's imprint beneath the ashes. You had been there before she met the deadwalkers. You had planned the whole ambush!"

"I never did! I was there mourning the loss of another who had died on that cliff many years before!"

"Liar!" Daeryn drew himself up against the wall and edged toward the door.

"Daeryn, you must let me clean and stitch the wound before the infection spreads!" ·

"You'll not lay a claw on me, Caleb," Daeryn hissed and backed through the door as Caleb cautiously followed.

Running paws and feet could be heard in the hallway outside the room as the two moved past the mirror's vision. Then Katja heard a rush of wind in the hallway and the shattering of glass. A soft moan escaped someone's maw as Caleb's and Dayalan's voices had simultaneously cried, "Daeryn!"

*

The mirror went dark before bringing Katja's haunted face into reflected focus once again.

"And he survived?" Lauraisha asked quietly from the doorway.

Dayalan and Katja both flinched and turned to face her. The male's initial outrage at being overheard instantly dissolved the moment he saw her tear-streaked face.

"He lived, but barely. Certain kinds of wood are toxic to Daeryn and to me. It is the only thing from which we can develop real sickness. Father struck him with a piece from Mother's mahogany rocking chair. Mahogany is one of the worst woods for us, but we couldn't bear to part with it even after she…" Dayalan shook his head. "Anyway, Daeryn stole the herbs and sinew that Aria was carrying and escaped out a window. Father let him go, knowing that no good would come of our chasing him. He always hoped that Daeryn would return…He still hopes."

"Did Caleb kill Marga?" The dreamdrifter's sky blue eyes penetrated Dayalan, heart and soul.

"No," Dayalan said, sorrow washing across his face. "He loved her—loves her still—and will always mourn her."

"So what should we do now?" Katja asked, more than ready to change the subject.

"You shall pack and leave for the Isle of Summons before the pass clogs with snow again. I am to accompany you at least to the Summons Lake's shore." Dayalan crossed his arms.

"Very well." Katja stepped toward the door.

"A moment, Katja," Dayalan said and reached toward the Ott vre Caerwyn. His black glove carefully closed around the sharp edge of the red shard and pulled it free from the rest of the mirror. He held it in his palm a moment before passing it to the werecat.

"This belongs to you, since it cost your blood to conquer it."

"Thank you?" She stared at him in confusion.

"Thank my father, Katja; it was his suggestion."

Katja gazed at the shard in her scarred paw, remembering the pain that it had caused. As she frowned, the shard began to pulse with scarlet light in time with each beat of her heart. Suddenly the half-paw-sized shard hissed as if it were burning and then broke into eight smaller fragments.

"What happened?" Katja asked.

A baffled-looking Dayalan, however, did not answer. Instead Lauraisha was the one to examine the eight shards. As she held one up, the spearhead tucked beneath her garments floated up toward the single shard. The shard then imbedded itself into the center of Durhrigg's spearhead. Then three of the other shards found their way into each of the spearheads hanging from Katja's own neck. One of the three necklaces unhooked itself from her neck and floated to land in Dayalan's open palm.

"Did you...?" Katja queried both Lauraisha and Dayalan simultaneously.

Both emphatically shook their heads. Instead Damya's voice floated from the depths of Lauraisha's hidden sapphire Keystone. "May these shards always unite their keepers even over vast distances. Katja, see to it that all spearheads receive their shards, including Felan's and Zahra's. Keep the shards and the spearheads secret. I will tell you when the time is right to give out the remaining spearheads. Peace and protection to you, mages."

As Damya's voice echoed into silence, Katja and Lauraisha regarded him with astonishment.

"Well, Dayalan," said the wide-eyed princess. "Welcome to our pack."

* * *

While sunlight occasionally won its battle with the clouds, cold gloom ruled much of the first day's journey beyond the lands of Caerwyn Castle. The weather translated into a sort of melancholy that pervaded the minds of each of the packmates. No one laughed or joked; all were simply silent as they trudged along the road snaking up the summits.

Katja passed much of the time watching the road for signs of danger. Occasionally, though, she caught herself glancing back at the lone white peak she knew to be Caerwyn. Shadowshaper spells hid it so well that, although she knew the truth of its shape when inside its own grounds, she now discerned only craggy rock where white spires should extend. When the third attempt to discern the castle through the fog of magic failed, she shook her head to clear the unnatural vision and concentrated on climbing the slope instead.

The ascending hike was even more grueling than the rugged terrain they had scaled while being chased by Curqak and the Gan Ceann. The half-melted ice within the mountain shadows was so slippery that Lauraisha and Zahra had to walk the horses. This needed caution meant that the group barely traversed forty spruce-scores a day, which added to everyone's misery. On the ninth day of this sluggish ordeal, the werecat sighed so heavily in her frustration that Felan looked back at her in concern. She perked her ears and half-smiled to show she was well enough, but the werewolf slowed his gait anyway until they were walking beside one another.

"There will be a full moon tomorrow," he spoke in a whisper too low for the others to overhear.

"I know."

"If you can find some time alone with me, I'll help speed you through the process so that *he* does not notice."

"You have no trust for Dayalan, do you?"

"Very little."

"Damya trusts him, Felan. That is good enough for me."

The werewolf's eyes narrowed suspiciously.

"He destroyed Kayten out of mercy, you know."

"So he says."

"So I say."

Felan growled his disagreement and gazed at her with concern. "And you are sure you are well, Katja?"

"Perfectly," she growled.

"Very well, then—"

"Is this mistrust based on jealousy because he bested you in a fight?"

"I am not jealous!"

Felan's outburst earned them frowns from Lauraisha and Zahra and, although Dayalan did not flick a glance behind him, the werecat saw his torso stiffen slightly. He must have realized they were discussing him.

"I am not jealous," Felan whispered. The females all rolled their eyes at him before facing forward again.

Katja crossed her arms. "Do you have a specific reason for distrusting him?"

"Besides his obvious heritage as a Víchí? No, not in the slightest," Felan growled.

Katja waited out his sarcasm with her ears twitching.

"I just have the sense that he and his father are not being completely forthright with us. That is all."

Katja shrugged. "Is it not their right to be reticent in their own affairs if they so choose? As long as it does not endanger us, I see no harm in their elusiveness."

Felan cocked an eyebrow at her. "Reticent? Elusiveness? Interesting word choices. I do believe Lauraisha's formal education has made quite a strong impact on you."

She shrugged. "You're shifting the subject."

He growled again, but did not argue further. As they walked on in silence, Katja watched Dayalan's back speculatively. There were many things that she did not know or understand about the uncanny mage leading them. Although she felt a sort of kinship to him because of their dual loss of family, the werecat wondered uneasily whether Felan's attitude toward the male was born more of prudence than of prejudice.

* * *

The silvery clouds sheltered any moonlight away from Katja's gaze, but the werecat could feel the glowing orb's eerie sway nonetheless. She shivered involuntarily and then leaned closer to the warm light of Lauraisha's first summoned campfire—willing herself not to change until she could slink away from the rest of the pack. She saw the concern flicker in Felan's azure eyes before he regained his stoic composure and continued his strategic conversation with Dayalan. The two were discussing the expected road and weather conditions along the pass. They both anticipated reaching the stronghold city of Reithrgar—which bore the name of the summit it sat upon—and bartering their passage onward by noon the next day. From the stronghold, it would likely be a good six-day journey to the Isle of Summons if they kept up a brisk walk. Felan's requests that they push it to four days brought vehement protests from the females—especially Lauraisha, who had ripped a hole in her right boot sole that afternoon.

Katja sat on a fallen log close to the firelight and tried

to focus on the conversation, but the moon's seduction was growing stronger. She looked into the fire and thought about the immense effort Lauraisha had spent creating it. Much to the others' chagrin, Dayalan had insisted that Lauraisha practice her budding fireforger skills by lighting the campfire tender so they could prepare the evening eat. Having never consciously produced fire before, Lauraisha was horribly inept at generating even the smallest golden flame. Dayalan, however, would not let her cheat by using flint and steel to start a spark. When she finally did manage to light the tender, her practice session had delayed evening eat by almost two hours. That in turn had caused Katja's current dilemma. She could not slip away to skinshift with everyone still conversing around the fire and so she sat huddled under a blanket in silent misery waiting for the others to seek their sleeping furs.

The werecat's shivering eventually became so violent that even Dayalan took note of her deteriorating condition.

"Katja, are you well?" he asked.

She shook her head, the strain of resisting the transformation materializing as cold sweat streaking her tawny fur.

"I need to lie down," she groaned.

"Here, come with me," Lauraisha said consolingly.

Felan jumped up to assist the human and together they helped her stagger out of the firelight. She moaned as the fire's interfering light diminished and the moonlight hit her in full force from between the clouds.

"Easy, Katja," Felan said, his own voice suddenly husky with concern and the strain of resisting his own transformation. "Just keep hold for a few more steps…just a few more steps."

Once they passed a stand of trees that blocked their view of the campfire completely, Katja lost control and fell onto all four paws. Felan quickly knelt, muffled her cry of pain with his own paw, and then held her protectively as the transformation took hold. Lauraisha watched anxiously until Felan bade her to go pacify Dayalan with a tale that Katja's stomach was upset and that the werewolf would tend to her until Zahra could make the proper medicine to ease her condition. The human finally nodded her consent and then ran to complete her allotted task.

"Peace, Katja. I have you…I will not let go…just focus on the layers of the change and cling to my strength."

She buried her head in his chest and screamed into his fur. "It should not hurt this much! Why does it hurt so much?"

"You've been holding the change at bay so long, so your strength is greatly diminished."

"You also…have resisted…the change," she gasped through flattening teeth.

"And I will continue to do so until you finish skinshifting. I have more experience in controlling my transformations than you. You control your abilities well, but do not expect to become an expert after only a single lesson."

Katja groaned again and was relieved that her blanket's cover kept Felan from seeing her lose her fur as tufts of it began to slough off of her legs. He cradled her upon the pine needles under the shade of the trees until her body completed its transformation and then he cautiously moved from her side.

She opened her emerald eyes at the sense of movement and turned her head toward him. "Where are you going?"

"I have to skinshift too now."

"Good, then we will finally both be of the same race."

Felan swallowed and shook his head in sudden sadness. "Not this time, Katja."

He crawled beyond the tree's immediate shadow into a patch of moonlight. The change took him almost immediately, but Felan did not turn human. Instead of sloughing off, his silky fur actually grew thicker. His back legs and forelegs shrank so that he stood equally on all four reshaping paws while his thumbs shriveled. Next, his maw became a more pronounced muzzle and his torso shrank until it fit proportionally with his limbs. As the last portions of his body completed their skinshift, the dark wolf sat back on his loincloth-covered haunches and looked anxiously at the new human.

Katja finally motioned him toward her and the wolf hesitantly walked toward her. When he stood within easy reach, she put her hand on his neck and smoothed down his fur.

"So this is what you look like as a full wolf," she said in admiration.

The wolf turned his head and gently nuzzled her hand. A deeper version of Felan's voice issued from the creature's mouth. "Do you approve?"

"I prefer you as a werewolf or a human, but you do make a very handsome wolf."

The wolf's lips pulled away from his sharp teeth in a smile. Katja patted his neck again before beckoning him to lie down and be comfortable. The wolf obliged her and put his large head in his paws while Katja rested her head against his shoulder and tried to forget the pain still resonating in her bones.

"You have to skinshift into a human during one moon and a wolf on the next?"

"Yes. If I neglect one form for too long, my skills in that form suffer. As a human, I can't smell or hear as well as I should and, as a wolf, I have less dexterity and flexibility, or strength. I feel almost elderly in this form."

"Strange."

"Indeed." They sat together in silence for a time until Felan spoke again. "Katja, does it really matter to you that we are of two separate races?"

The startled new human looked at the wolf. "I—"

The noise of a twig-snapping thump diverted their attention. Katja and Felan both looked up to see Dayalan walking out of the shadows about half of a spruce-length before them, a cruel leer etching his pallid face. The wind lifted the mage's dark cloak to reveal a leather-jerkin-covered chest, bare arms, and exposed talons. The new human was shocked to see that he had removed his gloves, but then her eyes caught sight of the jagged scar marring his left arm.

"Daeryn," she whispered in sudden fear.

"Found you, changeling," he hissed through fully elongated fangs.

XVIII

TRANSFORMATIONS

Dayalan's brother smiled coldly. "You've been difficult to track, Katja Escari."

"What do you want with me?"

"Your blood loyalty to the Víchí Covens, of course."

Felan darted protectively in front of her, his hackles raised and his own fangs exposed in a snarl. "You will not harm her, Monster!"

The dark-haired mage cocked an eyebrow in surprise, and then spat in disgust. "I see my falíchí of a brother has been busy corrupting more erdelings to do his bidding. Katja, tell your dog to stand down or I will bleed him dry for his troubles."

Katja instead roared as loud as she could.

"Fool!" The vampire's crimson eyes darkened even more. "Defy me and condemn your companions to death."

Katja desperately dipped into her mental link with Lauraisha and announced Daeryn's presence through it. The human, however, did not respond. Katja frantically pushed herself deeper into the bond and discovered that Lauraisha's mind was clouded by an unnatural slumber. Katja's sudden presence there did something to rouse her, but the effect was far from an overall awakening.

"Wake up, Lauraisha! Oh, please wake up! What is wrong with you?" her audible mutter echoed her desperate thoughts. She focused back on Daeryn, who was edging slowly toward them, his hypnotic eyes locked with Felan's.

"You used your shadowshaping abilities to attack the others!" she snarled.

Daeryn's cold gaze shifted to her in surprise. "Very astute, Katja."

"What do you really want of me?" Katja interrupted, glowering at him.

She had to keep him distracted. Neither she nor Felan were a match for Daeryn's strength in their present forms. If this foe was as physically powerful and skilled in combat as his brother, they would need all of the pack to defeat him. Even in this form, Katja could sense her companions' slumbering bodies not two spruce-lengths behind her in the campsite clearing and the knowledge of aid so close yet so incapacitated made the mage roar with frustration. She felt Lauraisha's mind finally drift out of its stupor and mentally screeched at her to wake the others. If the dreamdrifter could break Daeryn's spell and rouse the camp before he attacked, they all might have a chance at life.

"The High Elder wishes to meet you. In truth I, myself, would love to hear the tale of how you slipped through Curqak's grasp not once but thrice in your short lifespan." Daeryn's pale yellow fangs gleamed in the moonlight.

"It is a thrilling tale, I'll grant you," Katja responded, trying to keep her voice even. "But why should Luther purposely seek me out when I am no one of great importance, nor am I a threat to the Víchí?"

"Perhaps you should ask him yourself when you meet him."

Katja began retreating, pausing occasionally to give Felan a chance to adjust his position as well. She kept talking while surreptitiously leading Daeryn toward the camp. She felt Lauraisha trying to stir first Dayalan, then Zahra, and finally Bren.

"Your brother told me much about you, Daeryn...How you turned traitor to him and to your father after Marga died... How they still miss you and wish you would reconcile..."

The dreamdrifter's apprehension flickered through their bond and Katja realized that the others had been more deeply snared in Daeryn's enchantments than Lauraisha.

"Betray? I have betrayed none! It was Dayalan who

betrayed me by siding with that falíchí quisling I once called 'Father' against our mother. Now, enough of your stalling. You will accompany me to Blaecthull. Now."

One of Daeryn's two swords slid out of its scabbard with a hiss as he advanced on Felan. The wolf held his position between Daeryn and his prey.

"Katja, run!" Felan barked and crouched in preparation.

"Felan! No!"

"Go now!" The wolf snarled and lunged toward his opponent.

Katja could not see where Daeryn's right-hand blade struck, but she heard Felan's snarl of fury become a yelp of pain as she sprinted toward the campsite. She gripped her only available weapons, the spearheads, in her hands as heavy steps fell fast behind her. She could feel Daeryn's cold breath on the nape of her neck.

"Lauraisha! Someone! Help us!"

Howling white fur flashed past her and Bren sank his fangs into his former master's left arm. Katja kept running as Daeryn cursed venomously and swept the wolf aside with a deft sword strike to his head and chest. The white wolf went down whimpering and Daeryn raced after her once more.

Through the trees, she could see Zahra draw her bow as Lauraisha finally slapped Dayalan into wakefulness. The dryad let loose two arrows in quick succession straight past Katja's right shoulder. The Feliconian heard a single grunt of pain before Daeryn's black-clawed talon swept around and caught the tender flesh between her collarbone and neck. She screamed in pain as Daeryn jerked her back against him. She tried to elbow him in the stomach and more pain rewarded her efforts as her arm struck his thick-hide jerkin.

"Katja?" Dayalan was on his feet, his eyes wide with shock. She watched them turn to the deepest shade of red she had ever seen.

"Daeryn, release her!" the fireforger hissed.

Instead Daeryn clamped his bleeding left talon around her neck and brushed his lips against her neck. "Stand down, Dayalan, or I will bite her."

"You cannot do this! You cannot Turn her!" His tone was a plea and a statement of fact all at once.

"I can and I will. I have the power, Dayalan, and the blood in her body beckons. Do not tempt me."

Katja nearly whimpered as she felt his icy breath numbing her skin. Fear and unnatural pain paralyzed her. His claws must be laced with venom because her entire left shoulder felt icy from his touch. She gripped the spearhead harder with her right hand and prayed desperately for some distraction that would make Daeryn move his foul fangs away from her unprotected neck.

"Mother would be so ashamed of you!" Dayalan hissed, his gloves gripping his staff. Neither he nor the females dared to risk Katja's life by moving closer, but they all kept their weapons ready nonetheless.

"It is for Mother that I do this, Dayalan, although I would never expect you to understand."

"Release her, you fool! She has done nothing to ever harm you."

Daeryn hissed in malevolence and began to force Katja back with him toward a clearing near their right—keeping himself behind her with his fangs poised to strike should the others attempt an attack. Katja, meanwhile, was mentally conversing with Lauraisha and had discovered that Damya would not answer Lauraisha's silent pleas. The true human's face mirrored the skinshifter's own abject terror as realization struck. No one could save her.

"I will not let you take her, Daeryn. If you try to fly, I will follow and incinerate you."

"You would not dare harm your own brother, coward!" Daeryn spat.

"My brother is dead!" Dayalan screamed it to the sky, his voice ringing with unmitigated loathing.

Katja blinked back sudden tears. "Kayten," she mouthed.

A gray and red shape appeared at the very corner of her vision. Felan, although limping badly, had managed to slink behind them in the left-side blind-spot that Katja's head created for Daeryn. She kept her head steady as Daeryn continued to pull her back toward the clearing, trying to keep herself between Felan and Daeryn's line of vision. The packmates continued to hold their positions and held their eyes firmly on Daeryn, but their bodies all stiffened expectantly.

Felan crouched down on his good front paw and lunged at Daeryn's bleeding left arm. The huge wolf's impact sent both Katja and Daeryn tumbling. For a moment, Katja was free. As Daeryn recovered from Felan's attack, she rolled to her unsteady feet and dashed toward her pack. As one they sprinted toward her, trying to reach her before Daeryn could. The scrape of rawhide, a yelp, and the cracking of wood caught her ears in quick succession and then suddenly she felt an arm snake around her stomach and yank her gasping into the sky.

In horror, she realized that the sounds she had heard were from Daeryn's two huge dragon-like wings unfurling and knocking Felan into a nearby tree. She screamed as she saw the skinshifter's motionless body below her. Daeryn was yanking her further away from help with each powerful sweep of his wings.

"No! I will not go to Luther!" Wildly she struggled, trying to break Daeryn's grasp. She would rather fall to her death than be Turned and forced to serve evil like Kayten.

The vampire snarled and wrapped his arms even tighter around his prey. "Then perhaps you would do well to bond with me instead."

Katja snarled her defiance and then shrieked as Daeryn's fangs pierced her throat. Incomprehensible pain penetrated her senses as his Taint pervaded her body and then invaded her brain through the blood feeding it. The screams of her packmates echoed distantly in her ears until a cold darkness expelled all external awareness. She felt her soul writhe in protest as a new voice spoke inside the depths of her mind.

Bond with me, Katja.

The voice compelled her obedience and yet a part of her soul felt something elementally wrong with its entreaties.

Turn, Katja, Turn…Bond with me and Turn…

The voice was seductive—his words so tempting, like honey dripping from the lips of a lover. The cold darkness deepened and she felt her soul sink with unfathomable weight. In the depths of that darkness, an unquenchable thirst she had never known before was unleashed and raw power ravaged her being. She was changing, awakening, and hungering for more…

"Katja, come back to me!"

Felan? A vision flashed before her of Felan still in the form of a full wolf lying in a bloody heap at the base of a tree. The vision then changed to show Dayalan as he shattered the Ott vre Caerwyn bearing Daeryn's laughing face with his sunsilver staff.

Katja, break his hold! Break Daeryn's hold over you!

Dayalan's deep voice resonated through her mind, but hideous laughter suddenly drowned it out. Daeryn's triumphant pleasure echoed in her mind. He was changing her not into a zombie soul slave or a nemean soul servant, but into the very thing she loathed most—a vampire.

Yes, Katja. Feed me more. More! Let me drain you dry…

Katja tried to push back Daeryn's voice, to fight the cold hunger raging within her, but she was too overwhelmed to prevent the change now consuming her. And the darkest part of her soul craved more. In desperation she cried out to the heavens, "Creator, I love you! I cannot save myself! Save me!"

Daeryn's cold laughter continued to ring in her mind, but sudden warmth seeped back into her bones. The darkness weighing down her soul began to waver and then it cracked as a soothing blue-white light pushed against its barrier. As the hunger died, situational awareness flooded back into her mind. The darkness finally shattered—dispersed by the light. She felt Daeryn's claws still clutching her tightly, but discovered that his fangs no longer pierced her neck. She tentatively opened her eyes and found herself hovering just above the treetops. Her captor was trembling and she heard his mental voice suddenly scream as their souls' connection broke. Daeryn's grip loosened and Katja instinctively knew her moment had come.

She writhed against his grip with all her strength and plunged the spearhead into the chest wound made by Zahra's earlier arrow. Daeryn convulsed and instinctively flew backward—breaking off the spear tip in the process. When he did so, Katja wrenched the remainder of her spear point out of his jerkin and fell.

Katja watched Daeryn flap wildly as the great pines rushed up to embrace her. She did not slam into their limbs as she had expected. Instead the first tree limbs caught and gently cradled her body before passing her down to the next set of limbs. As she was passed from one limb to the other, Daeryn flapped overhead still screeching in pain and hatred. He dove after her, but his pursuit was thwarted by a sudden wall of flames. He avoided the attack only to be struck by a second wave of mage fire accompanied by vine-flailing dryad arrows. Katja's body meanwhile gently touched the welcoming ground just as Daeryn finally retreated shrieking into the night.

Lauraisha was the first to reach her. "Katja, Katja, come back to us! Don't die! Please don't die!"

But another voice inside her soul spoke comfort. *All is well, Katja. Your battle is won; rest now.*

Katja smiled with relief and let incoherence engulf her thoughts. "Felan" was her last conscious whisper.

* * *

Katja's mind drifted in a bath of beautiful brightness. The world around her seemed a liquid filled with every color and reflection of color imaginable.

Is this the Wraith Realm? she wondered.

Not precisely, a strange but gentle voice answered.

She looked around, but saw no one. *Who are you?*

I am the Egg, Katja.

The what?

I am the Emerald Egg...or rather I am the entity borne inside the egg, which you have carried with you since you left the place known to Sylvans as Crown Canyon.

The stone in my pack is an egg? Katja was quite sure she was delirious.

Yes, it is and, no, you are not daft or delirious. I am Pyrekin like Damya, so I am eternal and ephemeral. Also like Damya, I have very limited influence over your world because I am a being of the Wraith Realm. If I am to offer aid to the Sylvan Orders of the more concrete Erde Realm, I must encase myself in a physical body which requires some sort of birth in your world; hence why I am borne inside the egg.

Where is Damya? Why did she not come to our aid against Daeryn?

She did. She was helping to awaken me so that I could protect you if Daeryn bit you. I am far better at dealing with such matters as Turnings than Damya since I am of the same race as the one who originally spawned the Víchí.

You're a drake?

No, drakes are the Drosskin betrayers of our kind. I believe 'dragon' is the more correct Erdeken name for me.

Katja tried to shake her head in disbelief, but the action was impossible. The realization that she currently had no physical body encasing her being sent her thoughts reeling.

Am I dead? she asked in panic.

No, not dead…but I had to cast your body into a deep sleep and separate it from your soul so that you could properly heal. The Erdeken healers' talents should suffice to heal your body, but I need to attend to your mind and soul directly since such terribly indecencies were done to both.

The voice floated toward her mind's eye as an incandescent green mist. Katja stared in awe as a green, triangular dragon head drew itself out of the haze.

Katja would have bowed, if she were able. Instead her voice resonated her utmost respect as she called the dragon by the name its kind gave to themselves long ago: *Thrua'shuille.*

Moarns ljocht en ehre, Katja Kevrosa Escari of the Feliconas Clan of Sylvan werecats. The creature smiled and bowed its head, delicately curving its long neck as it did so. Upon hearing this dragon's true voice, Katja finally understood why "Thrua'shuille" meant "cutting whisper", for every uttered syllable delved beneath the layers of her soul.

By what personal name should I refer to you, honored Pyrekin? the little werecat asked.

I am called Verdagon and the world may know me as such… for now.

Verdagon, she repeated, testing the word with her memory. The name meant green or verdant in archaic Shrŷde and this dragon's essence did indeed remind her of grassy fields freshened with rain. *Moarns ljocht en ehre, Verdagon.*

Come commune with me. We have but a short time before I must rejoin your soul and mind to your Erdeken form; I have much to explain before you return.

* * *

Katja awoke in a strange stone room with dried herbs hanging from its wooden rafters and lit tallow candles set in metal holders along the walls. She was lying under crisp white linen covers on a soft bed of wooden construction. The cold cloth upon her forehead reeked of garlic and monkshood. She coughed slightly as the smell overwhelmed her senses and that sent the room's only other occupant rushing to his feet. Iron screeched in protest as Dayalan wrenched open the chamber door and yelled down the hall.

"She's awake!"

Katja cringed and groaned. "For the love of all things good, Dayalan, not so loud! My head feels ready to split open as it is!"

"My apologies, Katja!"

She grunted, still groggy with dreams. She remembered the dragon and recalled floating blissfully in the Veil separating the Wraith and Erde Realms of Existence. Verdagon's conversations held with her in both Draigas and Felis proved so enjoyable that the werecat almost forgot the cares of the world she had left behind—all but her packmates at least. When Verdagon was finally satisfied that Daeryn's actions had caused no lasting destruction to Katja's soul, he cast her being back into her body and she woke to find herself now very weak.

Lauraisha and Zahra came sprinting into the room.

"Katja!" Lauraisha grabbed her hand with both of hers. "We were sure we'd lost you! Thank the Creator, you are alive and awake!"

"Where am I?" she asked them blearily.

"The Isle of Summons," the dreamdrifter replied.

"But then how did I get…"

"Dayalan flew you here, Katja," Zahra murmured.

She stared at the dryad. She had deep circles under her almond-shaped eyes from a lack of sleep and an excess of tears. Katja looked closely at Lauraisha and then Dayalan. They also looked anxious and exhausted. The male had styled his long, black hair to cover his blacked-tipped ears and there was colored-powder covering the usual pale luster of his face and neck.

"You *flew?*"

Dayalan slowly nodded. "I, like Daeryn, inherited the accursed Víchí wings from our father."

Lauraisha looked over at him indignantly. "Those cursed wings helped us procure a miracle. Without your ability to fly, Katja would be dead…or *worse!*"

Dayalan arched an eyebrow at her vehemence but said nothing.

"Do the mages know who and *what* you are, then?" the Feliconian asked in a worried murmur.

He shrugged. "I was able to land and hide my wings before we were discovered. By some miracle, the Ring member Joce'lynn was the one who found us first. She has kept my family's secrets before and I pray she continues to do so now. My resemblance to my father is so striking, however, that the other mages must suspect who I am. Once they discover *what* I am, I'll not be free of prison stone and bars for long."

"They can't imprison you! You've done nothing wrong!" Lauraisha exclaimed.

Dayalan and Katja both hissed for her to quiet her voice.

"They can," he said. "And, for the safety of all the Sylvans on this isle, they should."

Katja stared at him, stunned by his vehemence. "Why do you stay, then? You fulfilled your promise to your father. You brought us here safely."

"I didn't fulfill my promise! I failed and it nearly cost you your life!" Dayalan shook his head. "No, I'll not abandon you here after the firesprite warned us about an evil on this isle. Besides, even if I wanted to leave, I couldn't do so now."

"Why not?" Katja asked. She looked around at her three troubled companions. "Where is Felan?"

No one spoke as a sapphire-sashed harmhealer master entered the room. Katja had to glance at him twice. The wizened mage looked like a taller, mauve-skinned version of Caleb. Without a word, the elf bowed to Katja and removed her herb-laced cold compress with a pair of metal tongs. Then he began checking the poultices covering her neck and shoulder.

Finally Dayalan cleared his throat. "Master Neha'lyn, is it safe for me to carry her so that she can see them?"

The harmhealer looked dubiously at his patient, but after

washing the excess ointment from her skin and re-bandaging her wounds, he finally agreed. Dayalan gently lifted the Feliconian off her bed, sheets and all, and marched dutifully through the open door and down the corridor followed by the other three beings. Lauraisha lifted a latch three doors down and the party entered the chamber beyond. The scene that met Katja's eyes brought tears to them.

"No...Felan!"

The full wolf was lying on a bed pulled close to the window so that the quarter moon's rays could shine on him. Linen bandages wrapped around half of his body. Bren lay on a bed toward the far side of the room, also heavily bandaged. Neither creature moved as the party entered the room.

"Why is he still a wolf?"

"Probably the same reason you are still human, Katja," Lauraisha answered slowly.

Katja looked down at her smock and sheet-clothed body and gasped as she realized she still possessed hands instead of paws. She looked around wildly until the harmhealer reassured her that it was perfectly natural for gravely injured mages to lose their abilities until their bodies recovered enough strength to use the magic again.

"Natural to you maybe, but not to me!" she growled while staring unnerved at her furless skin.

"Katja, when we finally rescued you from Daeryn, you were near death from loss of blood." Zahra spoke to the Feliconian, but would not take her eyes from Felan's mangled form. "We knew that you would not survive a day without an accomplished healer so Dayalan—at great personal risk—carried you to the Isle of Summons and left you here in the healing houses before rushing back to us. You see, he had to come back to protect us in case Daeryn returned because neither Felan nor Bren were fit to do so."

Lauraisha spoke up. "We knew that you would be safe on the isle, but Bren was still in horrible shape and Felan fared little better. No one at Reithrgar knew how to properly treat wounded wolves so Tyron and the piebald had to bring them here by wagon—much to their discomfort."

Katja mind's image of the horses' precarious predicament made her smile until she looked back at the werewolf. "How many days has it been since the attack?"

"Seven," Dayalan said in a shaky voice. "Felan seemed to be on the mend—at least he stayed somewhat conscious— but Bren grew worse. Zahra did what she could to slow the bleeding from his severed limb, but the body does not heal well when it is so damaged. In the end, Felan tried to use some of his skinshifting abilities to transform and heal Bren's body, but nothing worked."

Katja suddenly understood. Felan had sacrificed too much strength trying to save the wolf and so now he was fighting a battle that Bren had already lost. Katja squeezed her eyes shut determinedly, before gazing up at her bearer.

"I am so sorry, Dayalan," she whispered quietly.

The usually stoic male bent his head and Katja felt him tighten his grip around her as tears clouded his eyes. She nestled against his chest and returned the hug as well as she could before looking from Felan to the healer.

"How weak is he, My Sir?"

"Very. We were hoping he would mend well enough these past days to transform himself, but his current prospects look far too grim. If he has the ability to skinshift, he can help heal himself far better than we can, but I doubt he can live that long—"

"Is there no other skinshifter here who can lend him the strength?"

The healer looked gravely at her. "My dear, no skinshifters have trained on this isle since before the Second War of Ages. You are the only other one here now, and you do not possess the werewolf's immense power. To ask you to lend him enough magic to heal himself would be to assume your death. Just what would that accomplish?"

"There has to be something you can do!" Katja shrieked.

"There is," Lauraisha interrupted. "Pray."

Suddenly the world was winding around Katja's head and she sank dizzily against Dayalan's broad chest. She heard the healer angrily demand that they put her back in bed and could only weakly protest being removed from Felan's side. It was her fault that he was in this condition in the first place and the little skinshifter could not begin to think of the consequences if he died. Despite his racial heritage, Felan had proven himself as good and honorable of a male as any she had ever known. Bren had already lost his own life in the course of trying to protect her just like Kayten and the rest of her loved ones had. How many more noble lives would be destroyed because of her?

Verdagon's mental whisper cut through her bleak thoughts. *Katja, it is not your fault that Felan is so injured; that burden lies with Daeryn. Do not try to blame yourself for his condition or for Bren's death. I cannot have you lost in self-pity.*

I thought it was a dream…

It was not. Verdagon responded. *I am quite real and the time draws near when I will take true corporeal form and help lead the fight against the Asheken. The Sylvans must be ready to annihilate them to the last slave. The massacre of your clan will be insignificant compared to the carnage yet to consume this land if even one Vichi escapes destruction. First, however, we must heal Felan, for his life has a purpose yet in the Creator's plan.*

We?

Yes, Katja, we. You must use my strength to heal your body quickly so that you in turn may help Felan.

How?

My egg is still hidden in your rucksack. Ask Lauraisha to bring the sack to you so that you may guard the egg and nurse from its strength in secrecy. Simply touching the shell should be enough contact to draw forth my magic. Katja, you alone have enough power to restore Felan, but you will need all your strength to complete his healing process without dying yourself.

"How wonderful!" she growled aloud.

Lauraisha looked at her quizzically as Dayalan laid her gently back on the bed. The healer fussed that she was delusional again and began mixing up a concoction of bitter herbs for her to drink. The Tyglesean princess, however, kept looking expectantly at the Feliconian. Although Katja was still too weak to use their mental bond, the true human seemed to know that she was actually conversing to another being.

"Master Neha'lyn, Katja is not delusional; she was talking to me," the dreamdrifter lied.

"How's that?" The elf's gaze moved to Lauraisha.

"She and I share a bond of friendship so deep that we often know each other's thoughts just by glancing at each other's eyes. Katja was commenting on my saddened expression."

"Oh…" Neha'lyn looked from one human to the other and then set his cup down with a thoughtful grunt. Instead he pulled a second cup from the shelf and began to stir different herbs and mulled wine into it while watching Katja speculatively. "This will help you sleep without dreams. You still need more deep slumber to help your body heal and replenish your lost blood."

Katja nodded and then looked at her closest living friend. "Lauraisha, would you bring my rucksack to me? I would like the remnants of my clan close to me while I rest."

"Of course, Katja." The human left the room and returned moments later with the satchel.

Katja pinched her nose and drained the cup as quickly as possible to avoid its bitter taste. She wearily watched her packmates file out of the room and then surreptitiously delved into the rucksack's depths. The hard smooth surface of the egg greeted her outstretched fingers. It warmed to her touch as she rolled it out of the sack. She admired its color — now a breathtaking hue of deep green — as she cradled the sphere against her body and pulled the bedcovers over her shoulders. Only when the Emerald Egg was secure did the little mage dare succumb to sleep.

XIX

FANG AND FLAME

In the dead silence of night, Katja awoke. Verdagon had prompted her to rise and so her mind grudgingly swam out of the depths of slumber. The egg was now extremely warm and she could feel sweat soaking the sheets where her body lay against it.

She squirmed uncomfortably and stretched, then stared at her arms. There was fur on them! Cautiously she felt the crown of her head and discovered that cone-shaped ears were once again properly perched there. The healed werecat sighed in relief. She was herself once more.

Sudden unease prickled up her spine. Katja placed a paw gingerly upon her neck under her bandage and shuddered as she felt the rippled flesh around her fang wounds. Daeryn's bite had left her noticeably scarred. She felt the scabs on her collarbone and snatched her paw away—her breath catching in her throat as she saw the crescent-moon scar on her palm. She had now earned three scars from her two encounters with Dayalan's brother: one from the mirror and the other two from his own body. Her eyes narrowed and her nostrils flared in hatred. She just hoped she had returned the favor when her spearpoint had pierced his chest.

Verdagon's soft whisper caught her attention and dispelled her troubled thoughts. Felan was still in his ruined state of health and she had no time for fear or doubt or even vengeance if she were to help him. Katja kicked off the bed sheets and slipped into the hallway, hauling the egg inside her rucksack with her. She crept to Felan's door, silently lifted its latch, and stole inside. She propped a chair against the door's interior latch before moving to Felan's bed. If her plan failed and she could not cure him without dying herself, she did not want her packmates to break their magic bond while trying to save her. Severing such a bond would surely kill them both.

She found the wolf lying on his side in the same position she remembered from before her healing sleep—his still form faintly illuminated by the waning moon peeking through the room's window. His dressings had been changed, but he continued to bleed sluggishly through the bandages. The shallow gasp that was his every breath made her heart ache.

"Felan, don't die. I could not bear it if you did…" the werecat whispered and felt the egg stir at her side.

She pulled the mottled green sphere from her satchel and gazed at its pitted surface.

"Please tell me what to do, Verdagon," she whispered desperately.

The dragon's thoughts brushed her own and an image appeared before her mind's eye. Quickly she strove to copy it by placing the egg against Felan's partially bare chest and cradling it so that her paws touched the wolf and the egg simultaneously. She closed her eyes and willed herself to transform—not to a human, but to a werewolf. She imagined the reconstruction of bones and flesh necessary for the metamorphosis and felt the energy drain from her body into his as the process began. As the magic flowed from her, Katja pushed her mind deeper into their bond, willing herself to understand the skinshift and its consequences to his body in minute detail. She was so focused on the process that she did not feel the tremor from the door being blasted open behind her, nor did she hear Zahra's initial scream.

"What is she doing?" Lauraisha asked, aghast.

Dayalan yelled, "Katja, cease this madness—"

"Stop her, Dayalan!" Neha'lyn said. "She'll kill herself—"

" —and possibly him!" Zahra shrieked.

Katja ignored their voices and focused on Felan's breathing. The fluid within his lungs was clearing and she sensed precious air delve deeper to replenish the blood coursing through his flesh. She sensed his muscles begin to knit themselves together correctly around mending bones and felt the outer abrasions begin to scab over with the magic. The strength truly began to drain from her then and she knew she could not hold the connection between them long enough to complete Felan's healing transformation.

"Verdagon, help me!" she gasped and felt strong arms wrap around her shoulders—trying to pull her away from the werewolf.

"No, leave me! For his sake, leave me!" she snarled to Dayalan and back-kicked him vengefully.

She felt a surge of power pulse into her from the egg and immediately transferred that power to Felan. As she did so, the werecat felt the scabs on her shoulder and neck open. Blood leaked into the linen robe still covering her furry chest. Beads of sweat clumped the fur upon her face and stung her squinting eyes as she mentally probed Felan's body, knitting deeper wounds together and finishing the minor stages of his skinshift back into a werewolf.

Dayalan's arms fastened around her once more and this time his grip was anything but tentative. Katja tried to fend him off, but such a feat was impossible with her paws currently occupied touching the egg and Felan's chest. She opened her eyes and screeched in protest, then stopped as she saw the fully transformed werewolf's beautiful emerald-azure eyes open and try to focus.

"Felan, come back to me!" she cried as Dayalan drug her away from the werewolf's side.

"Katja?"

Felan's unsure voice shocked Dayalan still for a moment; Katja ducked out of his hold to be beside the werewolf once more. The act caused her horrible dizziness and she felt the blood ooze afresh from her reopened wounds. She tried to steady herself against the bed, but the stone floor rushed up to meet her instead.

"Katja!"

Felan's terrified cry echoed in her ears and her heart, but she could do nothing to comfort him as blackness swept away her mind's awareness.

* * *

"Katja, wake up…Please wake up!"

The werecat's golden-emerald eyes slowly opened to reveal her candlelit sickroom. When her bleary gaze finally focused, she saw Felan sitting beside her bed with his massive right paw wrapped firmly around her own. She squeezed it and gazed at him quizzically.

"How long have I slept?"

"Two days."

"Are you well?"

"Well? You are lying on your deathbed and you ask me if I'm well?" Felan growled at her. She wasn't sure if he wished to strike her or embrace her and, perhaps, neither was he. "Yes, I'm fine—apart from being terrified beyond my senses about you."

Katja shrugged. "I feel better."

"You look better as well…your ears are finally perked." Felan paused and watched her. "I would not have survived had you not given me your skinshifting strength. I have no idea how you managed it, but thank you."

Katja smiled. "I was hardly the one to lend you the power, Felan. It was Verdagon who instructed me how to cure…" She broke off and frantically searched the room. "Oh! Oh, no! Where is my satchel? It held the egg!"

Felan frowned. "Egg?"

"The round green stone that was lying against your chest when you awoke…where is it?"

The werewolf cocked his head and frowned. "Harmhealer Neha'lyn took the stone, Katja. He was extremely excited to find it and said that the Mage Council must be made aware of the stone's existence, although he never explained why. I believe he took it to the head mage in charge of the Department of Archives for safe keeping."

Katja hissed.

"What is it?"

"Neha'lyn is correct about the stone's importance. It's a dragon egg."

Felan sniffed and looked closely at her. "And you are sure you are well?"

Katja bobbed her head emphatically. "I am not daft, Felan. Verdagon—the dragon beholden to the egg—is the Pyrekin who saved me from being Turned by Daeryn. He is the one who also helped me heal you."

Felan sat slack-jawed. "We thought that Damya…"

"It wasn't Damya. According to Verdagon, she actually has little power to halt the Turning process and so she awakened Verdagon to help save me. Dragons apparently are better suited for such work."

The werewolf let out a long breath. "When Daeryn bit you, I thought…we thought we had lost you."

"You were still conscious?"

"Barely. I could see him overhead…I watched as he bit you…" Felan's eyes suddenly held a depth of anguish Katja had never seen. In this moment, he was completely open to her and, in a way, even more vulnerable than he had been before she had skinshifted him away from death.

"I heard you scream my name." Katja blinked hard at the horrible memory of the wolf's body sprawled beside the tree. "It echoed in my mind as he Turned me."

The werewolf was silent, his face filled with contrasting expressions of fear and longing.

"What is it?" she asked gently.

Felan cast his gaze to the floor. "I…I should tell the others you are awake. They will want to know…"

With great effort, Katja sat up. She clung to his paw and searched his downturned eyes. "Felan, please don't leave me again."

Felan's eyes met hers once more as he stood. Her grip tightened on his paw as she silently pleaded with him to stay. He hesitated and then leaned toward her, longing filled his eyes. She could feel his breath curl warm against her face as his nose almost touched hers.

"I don't know what I would do if you'd…" she whispered, her voice suddenly cracking with emotion.

The werewolf peered down at her and then gently rubbed her nose with his own. The cool wet comfort of it caused her to sigh with contentment. When she did not draw away, he sat down on the edge of the bed and gently pulled her into his arms. Felan searched her eyes intensely for a moment, then raised his maw to her ear. "You know I love you."

Katja buried her head against his shoulder and clung

desperately to him.

"Do you love me?" Felan asked, his eyes fragile as she gazed up at him.

"Yes, Felan, I do...I love you," she whispered it in awe as the full realization of her own emotions struck her. "I knew when I saw you lying there battered that I would rather die than live without you. It is why I tried to skinshift you whole again even though I knew the act might be fatal."

The werewolf again pulled her into a firm embrace. Katja nestled against his silky fur then lifted her head to touch the bottom of his maw with her nose. The huge werewolf shuddered at her tentative contact and dipped his muzzle to meet hers. She felt a thrill as his soft lips brushed hers. It was her first kiss.

"Felan..."

He kissed her again, but then Katja pulled away to watch his eyes a moment.

"What of Zahra?"

Felan also leaned back, but his massive arms kept their embrace. "She knows my feelings for you."

Katja frowned.

"She is a friend, Katja, and nothing more—as it has always been. Her mother and my father were the ones who arranged our courtship and it has not met with much success, hence why I no longer wear my Gab Cloth.

"As a dryad, Zahra must choose the lifemate that would best suit her. Such a relationship is extremely difficult on suitors because of the dryads' strong familial ties. Since dryads stay with their own clan and their own birth trees even after marriage, it is Zahra's final decision to accept or reject me based on my merits as a potential improvement to her community. Our parents hoped that we as lifemates would strengthen the bonds between our clans. Zahra, however, knows I have no feelings for her beyond our friendship. She did not wish to burden either of us with a marriage founded out of convenience, so our betrothal was annulled before we all left the Glen."

Katja stared at him in consternation. "Why did you not tell me?"

"You loathed me."

"I did not!"

Felan arched an eyebrow.

Katja cringed. "Very well, I did mistrust you at first. My prejudice…Jierira, I'm sorry."

"I forgave you a long time ago." Felan replied, his gaze gentle.

"Thank you," she whispered and then frowned again. "Does Zahra really approve of this decision?"

The werewolf nodded his head. "I just hope she can find her own lifemate who can love her as properly as she deserves."

"Does she accept me? I do not wish sour feelings to taint our relationship."

He smiled. "Though we haven't discussed it, I think she does. I believe Zahra has known you would be a proper match for me for a while. Now my parents, on the other paw, will probably take some convincing. I still have not informed them of Zahra's and my formal severance and they will most likely throw one impressive tantrum…" He grimaced. "Especially Mother."

"I would think they would rejoice that their son will not be obligated to such a hard life."

"My life with you will fare little easier, Katja, should we choose to be together," he said seriously.

"Because of our difference in race," she said miserably.

"Ah, so it does matter to you."

Katja sighed sadly. "No, Felan. It did. I'll not deny that. But now I have no family to appease, no clan of my own. I fit nowhere and so I have no choice but to take a lifemate outside my own race. Even so, our difference in race will still matter to everyone else."

The werewolf pulled her to him again and licked her cheek in reassurance. She buried her head in the soft fur cloaking his chest, desperate for his comfort.

"If I could turn into a werewolf, I would do so in a heartbeat's time," she whispered.

Felan grabbed her shoulders and pushed her back. "Katja, do not ever wish to give up who and what you are! Your uniqueness is why I love you. I love a werecat and I would not wish it any other way. We will find a way to make this work.

I swear to you on my honor that we will succeed."

"But who would consent to marry us, Felan? If the course of our lives is truly meant to intertwine in such a way, who would dare allow us to be lifemates?"

Felan grew quiet a moment while returning her troubled stare. "I don't know, but the Creator did not bring us together flippantly. He put us together for a purpose and I believe He will reward us as long as we follow His guidance."

"I hope so." She cuddled against his barrel chest again.

"I know so." He held her protectively and bent to nuzzle her cheek.

* * *

The packmates watched in puzzlement as Neha'lyn paced the length of the room, his master mage eye amulet swinging wildly from his flushed neck.

"It's just unnatural! First the werecat survives a deadwalker's Turning, then she heals the werewolf, and now Mori'lyn, our distinguished Head of Archives, is causing hullabaloo in the halls about the werecat's stone being a dragon egg about to hatch! How could you keep this from me?" he yelled at Katja.

"The dragon asked for my discretion," the Feliconian replied, her voice portraying more calmness than she felt. "Verdagon was not ready to reveal himself to the mages yet. Judging from the tumult surrounding the revelation of his existence, I can understand why."

He stared at her in exasperation and then finally sighed. "No matter. If I deem you all healthy enough, the members of the General Assembly of Sylvan Mages wish an audience with you tomorrow."

"What, all of us? That soon?" Dayalan looked up from his sewing. He and Lauraisha had just finished the final stitches in the burial cloth that would adorn Bren once the wolf was laid to rest in the island lake. The quilt had a pieces cut from all of the packmates' belongings including Katja's now-patched rucksack.

"Yes," the elf responded, "every last one of you shall attend."

"Why not just Katja since she is the one associated with

the egg?" Zahra asked as she oiled her quiver.

"Oh, I wonder…" Neha'lyn said sarcastically. "A company of companions involving a human princess, a skinshifter werecat, a dryad princess, a skinshifter werewolf, and a half-breed fireforger is just a touch unusual. Now, throw in the fact that the human princess is a Tyglesean dreamdrifter who enjoys a close bond with the only known survivor of a vampire mauling and who just happens to carry a dragon egg in her pack and you get something truly special!"

"Fine, we get the point," Felan growled at the healing mage and then went back to cleaning his heirloom axe. The werewolf had been sullen for days and Katja suspected his foul mood was a direct result of his frustrated guilt over not protecting her more proficiently from Daeryn. She made a mental note to chastise him later for his unjustifiable shame. After all, he had nearly sacrificed his life for both her and for Bren. She would not allow him to stay in the same snare of undue guilt she had experienced with her own clansmen's deaths.

Katja looked over at Lauraisha. "Well, this was what Canuche originally had in mind and we did promise we would take his plea before the General Mage Council."

The Tyglesean looked up from the last stitches and cocked her to one side. "That we did. I wonder if he anticipated the amazing companions we would take with us."

Katja shrugged, thinking about the strange days and nights they had spent traveling under and over the mountains.

"Canuche? As in the dead griffin king?" Neha'lyn now looked positively frantic.

Katja rolled her eyes. "Jierira, just forget I said anything at all!"

The polished-wood door to the chamber opened then and an apprentice harmhealer came sprinting into the room. "Master Neha'lyn, the mages of the General Council have called for the prophetic companions' presence if they are fit for examination."

"Prophetic?" Neha'lyn grimaced apologetically at Katja and her packmates before curtly bowed his head toward the student. "Thank you, Oeled, I see no reason why they cannot attend the council early. However, please do refrain from throwing around rumored titles so flippantly."

The apprentice flushed deep purple clear to his pointed elf ears and then yelped, "Yes, my teacher!" before bowing and hastily retreating from the room.

"Youth. They're all so excitable." Neha'lyn shook his head and sighed dramatically before looking back at the packmates. "It is odd that they moved the session up so soon. Ah well, I'll lead you to Vraelth. He can then escort you to the Central Assembly Hall where you will stand before the council."

The mage Vraelth was an elegant, twenty-three-winter-old elf with skin as dark as an eggplant's peel and pristine lavender locks swept back from his angular face in an intricate braid. Although he was almost as tall as Felan, his willowy frame was still dwarfed by the werewolf's massive bulk. He introduced himself to them with a formal open-palmed bow and asked each of their names in turn. When all were familiarized, Vraelth thanked Neha'lyn and then led them through the massive stone corridors toward the central portion of the isle fortress.

As they walked, the mage journeyman gave them a brief overview of the various halls' and chambers' uses as they passed near each. The Mage Citadel on the Isle of Summons was part fortress, part mage conservatory with whole wings devoted to teaching initiates specific types of magic and weapons training. The grandiose interior intimidated the simple werecat. Everywhere she gazed, Katja beheld the multihued splendor of marble and granite complementing more solid shades of obsidian, jade, and alabaster. The flawlessly carved passages stood as a stalwart testament to the skill of their ancient sculptors.

As they entered a wide gallery and neared a pair of enormous ceiling-high doors, Vraelth spoke quietly to the packmates, "I will announce you and then take up my post with the other mages. A word of advice: speak courteously and truthfully to the assembly. May the kind Creator bless your words and give you favor."

The journeyman-ranked charmchanter mage bowed toward them once and then turned to the doors. His rich tenor voice sang out a single word of the mage language of Kwaërm in a high, clear note. The doors began to shake, slowly swinging outward. Vraelth then calmly stepped between them and led the companions down a ramp walkway, which led to the floor of a huge amphitheater with terraced walls encircling the stone floor. Seated beings of all shapes and races filled the tiers to overflowing—their simultaneous conversations echoing like thunder inside the vaulted chamber.

The metal doors groaned shut and the resulting clang caused a sweeping silence throughout the room. Suddenly Katja found herself and her companions as the uncomfortable recipients of everyone's attention.

"May it please the General Council of Mages, I have brought those individuals so summoned by this body!" Vraelth intoned. He bowed and strode off the floor—leaving Katja and her packmates alone to bear the brunt of thousands of curious eyes. Katja stared at the tiers of faces and realized the ceiling of this place must be at least a spruce-length high. In all her life, the Feliconian had never seen something so grandiose. The General Council members themselves made up only a fraction of those beings in attendance. The werecat realized that most of the isle's occupants must be present to gawk at the newcomers.

"So it begins," Dayalan muttered under his breath.

"Who requests an audience with this exalted governing body?" the Mage Magistrate intoned.

Overdone much? Katja thought irritably.

Careful, came the warning thought from Lauraisha. *Even whispers are as roars here.*

"I, Zahra Zahlathrazel Etheal, daughter of Queen Mother Zahlathra Ellazel Etheal, Princess of the Zolaramie Tribe, do."

"I, Lauraisha Astrat'a, daughter of King Kaylor and Queen Manasa, Princess of Tyglesea, do."

"I, Katja Kevrosa Escari, daughter of Kevros and Devra Escari, last survivor of the Feliconas Clan, do."

"I, Felan Bardrick, son of Chief Fenris and Vilda Bardrick, member of the Geirgerd Clan, do."

"I, Dayalan Calebson, son of Caleb Luthrial and Marga Amerielle, do."

The verbal dismay that had risen from the council mages with each punctuating name ended in a resounding crescendo of outrage with Dayalan's title.

The silver-haired Magistrate called the crowd to silence with an echoing strike from his sunsilver staff before giving the floor to an older satyr male wearing a Third Rank dreamdrifter adept's pale-lavender sash.

The high-ranked mage stood, sneering at the packmates. "So I am to assume that the half-breed son of an Asheken actually does exist and has been thrust under our very noses this evening? Oh, this is laughable!"

Katja glanced at Dayalan. The muscles of his neck and jaw were taut and his mouth was a slit.

"You forget yourself, Mori'lyn. Do not assume anything to be truth or untruth until it is tested," a human female wearing a flowing white robe, a ruby-hued sash, and a mage-eye amulet said as she also stood. "If he is indeed the legendary son of the Impossible Union, let him prove it."

There was a general murmur of consent among the crowd.

The Mage Magistrate struck his staff for order once again and turned to Dayalan. "Well spoken, Mistress Joce'lynn. Will you confirm your bloodline, son of Caleb?" he asked, his tone neither condescending nor encouraging.

Dayalan's gaze was like ice-tipped granite. "If I must."

"You must!" the dreamdrifter mage Mori'lyn said. Others vehemently nodded their agreement.

Dayalan continued to stare at the Magistrate. He did not move or acknowledge the other beings, not even when their shouts began to overpower the room. With a look of resignation, the Magistrate struck the butt of his staff thrice and the assembly was once again governed by silence.

"Let the vote decide," he bellowed and turned to the five hundred mages seated in the tiers directly behind him. "All in favor of the guest's proof of kinship to the mages Caleb and Marga, show your assent."

In one fluid wave of motion, the assenting mages stood — in numbers too many to easily count. The companions' gazes swept the assembly as members continued standing while each mage council section leader tallied their count. The vote total of "479 assents" was read by the head proctor as that number sat once again.

"All opposed, show your dissent."

Barely more than a score stood and were counted.

"The members' majority have given their assent. Please prove your kinship in the best way you can, Guest Dayalan."

Dayalan bowed his head slowly, but did not speak. Then he grudgingly began to remove his gloves. The audience gasped when he finally thrust his open palms into the air and revealed his black-clawed fingertips—the true claws of a vampire—for all to see. Katja heard him murmur, "Please do not think less of me" to his packmates as his talons grew in size and density until they closely rivaled her own fully extended claws.

"Does this satisfy your curiosity?" he asked the Magistrate.

"An interesting little trick. Do you have wings too or did Marga's womb wash those from you?" Mori'lyn almost brayed.

Dayalan scowled. His eyes went from stormy blue to eerie scarlet. His pale flesh turned as white as a corpse's and stretched more tightly over bulging muscles. His fangs extended out of the corners of his mouth. He threw off his cape and tunic and then hunched his back to free his wings from their folded positions along his spine. Their membrane expanses stretched out over his head, casting his face in deep shadow.

"Truly, you are of Luther's seed!" the Mage Magistrate said, aghast.

"He is a vampire! For the safety of all Sylvans, such fiends are never allowed to live, Magistrate Aver'lyn!" Mori'lyn's voice trembled, but he stared unwaveringly at Dayalan.

Katja and her other companions moved as one to form a tight protective ring around Dayalan. The little werecat was painfully aware of the absence of the others' weapons, which they had not been allowed to take from their rooms. She didn't know what to expect, but she swore she would not lose another companion—especially when he had already saved her life! In her anticipation, Katja instinctively drew on the skinshifter magic flowing through her soul and felt her body try to transform *out* of her werecat form. She shook herself—distracted by the odd sensation—and suppressed the urge to skinshift. Through normal eyes, she saw that Felan stood half-crouched and snarling while Zahra's usually brown eyes now glowed green with her sproutsinging ability and Lauraisha's open palms held crackling yellow flames.

A female centaur wearing a journeyman charmchanter's tan-and-brown striped sash shouted in disbelief and rage, "You would protect this fiend? You must be mad!"

Katja answered her with a defiant roar that seemed to shake the foundations of the room and silenced the stunned crowd.

"Werecat Escari, why do you protect this Asheken?" the ruby-sashed human mage asked while looking bewildered at Katja.

"Since the massacre of my clan, I have been constantly hunted by ghouls, zombies, dullahan, nemeans, and vampires all Tainted by the Abomination's Curse. I can promise you that Dayalan is not one of their diseased breed. He is Erdeken and pure," Katja explained, all the while wondering why the mage would address her only by her surname rather than her clan name or her main name.

The white-robed human frowned. "Son of Caleb, you have proven beyond all doubt that you are Víchí in heritage. But can you prove that you are sanctified of Luther's treachery?"

"I can."

From somewhere in the top tier, a large violet fireball shot forth toward Dayalan's heart. Lauraisha tried to jump into its path, but Dayalan's wing brushed her back—shielding her and Katja from the blast that hit him full in the chest. He staggered back, his body suddenly engulfed in purple flame. Before anyone else could react, Lauraisha reached out and pulled the inferno enclosing Dayalan's body into her trembling right hand. The crowd gasped as Lauraisha arduously closed her fists around the blaze and then extinguished it.

Her voice shook with rage and exhaustion. "You would dare threaten one of my companions—"

"Lauraisha! I fight my own battles." Dayalan hissed. He looked defiantly into the crowd as his still fully clawed right hand extended out—fingers spread and palm up—to be level with his chest. Upon his palm, he produced a small wavering golden flame barely strong enough to light a candlewick.

Mori'lyn sneered. "Is that the best you can do, vampire? I should have expected as much from the half-breed son of a trai—"

Dayalan cocked his head at the satyr and the flame in his hand began to glow brighter. It then turned from one color to another, following the intensity test order of the fireforgers' Flame Refinement system: guttering gold became bright yellow, then brilliant orange, then simmering scarlet, then deep violet, and then a medium blue. The little flame grew hotter with each color and Katja increasingly felt its intensity. By the flame's violet stage, Katja and the others were forced to back away and the blue flame saw even Lauraisha wincing and shielding her eyes. The assembly members stared in awe at the half-breed's impressive display of magical control. Even some of the highest ranked fireforgers had problems presenting a full-scale Flame Refinement—often missing a color stage if their focus wavered for an instant.

Dayalan instructed his companions to move as far from him as they could before he raised the talon cradling the little blue flame over his head. The flame changed again: from medium blue to light blue, then to bluish white, and finally to a brilliant white.

Dayalan now held the highest-ranked flame known among fireforgers, a fiery intensity that rivaled the brightness of the sun. In the flame's brilliant rays, Katja discovered that Dayalan's claws and hair had turned as white as his skin, which now seemed to glitter like new-fallen snow. She looked away, fearing blindness if her gaze remained perched upon him.

"White? You can reach white intensity?" Awe and fear warred within Mori'lyn's voice.

"As you can see, my mother taught me well," Dayalan said with a mirthless smile. His voice was directed toward the Magistrate Aver'lyn, but his gaze held Mori'lyn's until the other looked away. Only then did Dayalan extinguish the flame he held between them.

XX
BLOODLETTING

"Mori'lyn will surely cause you problems; as could Aver'lyn, Yasmina, and Valnic," Vraelth mused. The elf had joined the packmates in their new quarters in the mage-apprentice wing for a discussion of the Mage Council proceedings two days after the event. "I would think that Joce'lynn, however, will be more inclined to aid you should Mori'lyn discover Lauraisha's testimony to be genuine."

"Wait. What about Mori'lyn and Joce'lynn?" Katja asked. She said the names slowly so that she could become more accustomed to referring to high-ranking mages by their traditional suffixed titles of "lyn" and "lynn".

"Mori'lyn will be performing the mental examination since he is both a dreamdrifter of advanced skill and the Mage Citadel's chief historian."

Dayalan cursed viciously. "He'll try to discredit Katja's and Zahra's testimonies through Lauraisha. He might even find and exploit her memories of…" Dayalan stopped dead.

Katja sensed that he was about to say his brother's name and interrupted. "You are afraid that the dreamdrifter might somehow exploit Lauraisha's painful family problems, aren't you?"

All Dayalan could do in front of Vraelth was slowly bow his head in affirmation.

"Family problems?" Vraelth looked at the princess, who turned away from him to stare at the lake harbor outside the room's window.

Katja snarled and then spoke quietly to the elf. "Lauraisha's father is a tyrant who has subjected his children to much abuse and fear. We do not speak of him out of respect to the princess, who has often suffered the brunt of his anger. If you call yourself an ally to this group, I would ask that you also use discretion in this matter."

Vraelth looked genuinely concerned. "Of course, of course. Long have we known of Kaylor's despotic nature, but toward his own children...I'm sorry, I had no idea."

"It's settled then," Katja said and then changed the subject. "What can we expect from Mori'lyn?"

Vraelth sat up straight on the leather divan and stared seriously at the werecat. "Please understand me when I tell you that I have little fondness for the satyr. The love of his life is wine and he can be quite rude to both his pupils and his fellows after he has kissed a bottle or two. I do, however, highly respect him for his vast historical knowledge and superior intellect.

"As an advisor to the Ring of Sorcerers, his word is law for the general population. He would be a formidable foe should he choose to act against you. He is, however, fair with most beings if he likes their race as a whole. Although he may despise Dayalan because of his racial muddling, I have never known him to be unjust to either a human or a dryad."

"And what of werecats or werewolves?" Felan asked.

"Well...it depends on his mood on the day in question."

"Delightful," Katja spat sarcastically.

All will be well, Katja. Don't worry. Lauraisha's thought lit the Feliconian's mind like the warmth of sunlight until she remembered that the packmates would bury Bren's remains the next morning.

* * *

Daybreak dawned bright but cold along the water. The autumn breeze belligerently clawed at the little wooden boat as it plowed through the vast lake's dark swells. The rigging reeked of fish and that, mixed with the constant upheaval of the bow made Katja cringe as she valiantly fought to keep down her morning meal. She dared not complain of her discomfort, however, for fear that she would further upset her companions.

The packmates had set out three days after their meeting with the Mage Council to finally bury Bren. Neha'lyn was kind enough to magically retard the body's natural decomposition until arrangements could be made to hire a boat. Since the isle's limited space made no provision for general cemeteries, Bren's body would have only the lake as its final resting place. Katja did not see the sense of a whole body being buried in the ground or dipped beneath the waves without first undergoing a proper burning, but she respected Dayalan's odd wish anyway.

In an effort to avoid seeing the movements of the pitching watercraft, the seasick werecat turned to watch the others. She spied Lauraisha casually talking to the fishing vessel's captain. After a moment Katja growled with a mixture of envy and admiration toward the human, who seemed completely accustomed to the rolling deck. It was not all that surprising that a being who had lived her entire life near the Westylere Sea could cope with rough waters, but Katja still felt disgust at the other's ease while doing so.

"We're here," Captain Nascius finally called and so the packmates set about preparing Bren's cloth-covered body for burial in the deepest part of the lake.

Before they slid the great wolf into the dark depths, Dayalan commended the wolf for his loyalty, bravery, and friendship. The sailors must have thought such remembrances of a mere erdeling beast quite strange, but those who knew the extraordinary wolf found Dayalan's words rather poignant. All of the packmates spoke a respectful farewell and even Damya twinkled her goodbye from inside Lauraisha's Keystone pendant as Bren's wrapped body slid off the plank into the swirling waves. As the white wolf's rigid form slipped into liquid twilight, Katja saw tears roll down Dayalan's haggard face.

Their way back to shore and subsequent return to their respective chambers was wrapped in somber silence. Dayalan separated himself from the group as soon as their paws touched sand and strode off silently. They made no attempt to follow him as he turned down the stony beach, but Katja's mind still rang with the last of his words to the wolf: "You were the only one to truly keep me sane."

* * *

The days following Bren's funeral were spent busily meeting and making new acquaintances. Many high-ranking mages and island officials came to meet the packmates, which afforded Katja and her companions a sort of distinction among the isle's inhabitants. For the werecat orphan, the experience proved odd—both taxing and exhilarating in combination. Felan and Dayalan too were uncomfortable with the fanfare, while Zahra and, to a lesser extent, Lauraisha, seemed more accustomed to the whole ridiculous situation.

The packmates learned much about the ancient history and current politics of the isle through their frequent encounters with other mages. Some of the mages came to pay their respects to Kevros and Devra's daughter for her loss while others came to gauge the potential of the new mage initiates. Still others came to see the curious half-breed in person, but were always shooed away by the packmates so that Dayalan could mourn in privacy. Their encounters with so many beings left the packmates exhausted at each day's end. While the others seemed to recuperate well each night, Lauraisha and Katja both tossed and turned in the cold sweat ensuing from their dark dreams.

The ancient magic steeped in the isle somehow amplified the range and scope of Lauraisha's abilities. As a result, she and the werecat often dreamt of Canuche's latent words:

When you reach the Isle of Summons, you must tell about your plight as well as mine, but be wary. The mages, who long have remained safe and aloof in their island fortress, will likely doubt your warnings of Asheken attacks. You must stand firm in your convictions no matter who may try to discredit you. Remember that Luther's greatest advantage is his enemies' infighting…

The griffin's words were often followed by a scene of deadwalker destruction such as their ongoing siege of the Glen or their smaller raiding parties destroying villages along the rivers. Often the females saw Daeryn directing zombie attacks, his viciousness growing with each nightmare.

The worst of these dreams came the morning nine days before Lauraisha's examination and found Katja and

Lauraisha both shaking in cold terror. They had dreamt about the destruction of the Great Sphinx who guarded the Northern Passageway and saw Daeryn dealing the deathblow with an uncanny pair of sunsilver swords. Worse yet was watching the villain's red eyes deepening to crimson as he bent and victoriously sucked the last life-flow from beneath the fallen guardian's stony-skinned neck.

"No!" Katja screeched. Then she and Lauraisha knew only the darkness of their opulent Citadel chambers. Katja's scarred paw immediately touched her throbbing neck as she sat up and sprang out of bed. She threw the servants' door open separating her room from Lauraisha's and found the human already standing on the other side.

"Dayalan...Dayalan's face..." Lauraisha panted.

"No, that was Daeryn, not Dayalan." Katja said and put a damp paw on Lauraisha's shaking shoulder.

"No, something is wrong. I can feel him...shivering."

"What?"

"Are you both well? I've never heard either of you scream so loudly," Zahra said as she and Felan stumbled into the human's room, weapons at the ready.

"I dreamt...we dreamt—" Katja stuttered.

"Where is Dayalan?" Lauraisha asked. There was an unusual panic in her voice.

Felan frowned. "I have not seen him for days now, not since we committed Bren to the waves. He had said that he wished to be alone with his grief. I suppose he is in his own den and bed."

Katja stared at Felan. The werewolf's attitude toward the male had changed for the better since their encounter with Daeryn. She suspected the change came because of Dayalan's part in rescuing both of them from death. She wished Zahra's bitterness toward Dayalan had dissolved as well, but at least Felan had softened somewhat.

Lauraisha was violently wringing her hands. "We have to find him, now!"

"What's wrong with him?" Katja asked, suddenly wary.

Lauraisha shook her head again, but did not speak. Instead the dreamdrifter ran off with her shoes in her hands toward the half-breed's private quarters at the end of the corridor—leaving her puzzled companions to sprint after her. They tried the door and discovered it locked. At Lauraisha's frenzied insistence, Felan sighed and broke the latch. They found the fireforger curled up in the farthest corner of his bedchamber with his withered-looking wings unfurled and draped about his tremulous body.

"Dayalan!" Lauraisha screamed and sprinted toward him.

"No, human! Stay away from me!" the large male hissed.

Lauraisha stopped as if she had been slapped and stared in horror at the mage.

"Dayalan?" Katja cautiously crept forward and gasped in horror as she peered at his shadowed face. His sunken eyes were deep scarlet and ruby trails of blood trickled off his pallid chin where his extended fangs had pierced his lower lip. "We must find the healer at once!"

"No! He can do nothing for me, nor can any of you! Stay back if you value your lives!" The male groaned and shook even more violently—his eyes rolling back in his head.

"Dayalan!" the dreamdrifter took a step forward only to be caught and yanked back by Felan.

"Don't go near him, Lauraisha; he will bite you!" the werewolf warned.

"Don't be ridiculous, Felan, he would never do such a thing!" She fought his grasp unsuccessfully while Katja confusedly gazed between Felan and Dayalan.

"Felan?" she asked, wordlessly asking him to explain.

"Do you remember what Bren told us our first night in Caerwyn? He said that he and Dayalan were 'bloodmates.' Dayalan said at the funeral that Bren kept him sane."

"He isn't Daeryn!" Lauraisha screamed.

"Once a deadwalker, always a deadwalker," Zahra quipped. "I guess in his case it should be born a vampire, always a vampire…"

Felan sent the dryad a venomous look. "I never want to hear you utter those words again, Zahra. He saved Katja from death and revealed his existence to the Mage Council in the process. That could have meant his own death, just for being born what he is—a hybrid."

"If his worthless brother hadn't decided to plague us

with his presence, Katja and you would have never had to flirt with death in the first place!" Zahra bellowed.

Felan's massive body towered over the dryad as he glared at her. "Maybe. We would still have had to fight the Gan Ceann instead of Daeryn. How many of us do you think would have survived *that* encounter?"

Zahra's silence was sullen.

Lauraisha looked slowly from the dryad to the half-breed. "What's wrong with him?" she asked in a small voice.

"He's become feral," Katja quietly surmised. "He won't drink the blood of beings, but he still has to sustain himself on the blood of beasts. If Bren called himself Dayalan's bloodmate, then Dayalan must have had to regularly feed on the wolf to survive."

"And now Bren is dead…" Lauraisha said it with tears in her voice and eyes. "Dayalan, how long has it been since you last drank?"

The male did not answer, but slowly raised his head to look at her. No recognition flashed when his eyes met her face, only a devastating hunger.

"Dayalan?" The human trembled.

The half-breed snarled and surged toward her with more speed than Katja expected given his state of health. Felan, however, did not underestimate the warrior. His war axe was unsheathed and held ready as he shoved the females behind him.

Dayalan stopped just short of the blade, panting and swaying slightly on his feet. His ungloved talons twitched sporadically as he stared down his opponent.

"That will not stop me, werewolf." There was both plea and challenge in his deep voice.

Felan calmly stepped forward and rested the flat of the blade against the other's heaving chest. "I don't wish to stop you or end you, Dayalan. There is another way; take another erdeling for your bloodmate. There must be a beast that you can bond with that will be strong enough to withstand your feeding. Do this and spare your friends…spare yourself."

"Bren was the strongest…the only one I dared use. Other beasts—even willing ones—always died. I've killed six… since Bren's death."

"We must take that chance then."

As Dayalan and Felan stared at each other over the axe, an understanding seemed to pass between them. At last Dayalan relaxed and gripped the back of a nearby chair for support.

"Why trust…?"

"Fear solves nothing. It is no fault of yours that you were created this way and yet everyone seems to see you as the source of blame nonetheless. I have had enough of it. You have shown me your honor through the protection of this pack, so I will not doubt you. Now prove me right."

Dayalan bowed his head and slumped heavily against the chair. Felan let the war axe clatter to the ground as he caught the other male and kept him from sliding to the floor. "We have to get him sustenance now!"

"The stables!" Lauraisha replied.

Felan looked at her sharply and finally nodded his head. He threw the languishing fireforger over his massive shoulders, while Katja retrieved the war axe. They all set off at a swift but stealthy pace through the dim corridors of the castle in the direction of the stables.

"What will we do when we get there?" Katja asked Lauraisha in hushed tones.

"He'll have to feed from Tyron if the horse is willing."

"What!"

"Have you any better ideas?" When Katja did not answer, Lauraisha continued, "Tyron is the strongest of any horse I have ever encountered. He is also the smartest. If Dayalan is to survive, he must feed from the strongest beast…so Tyron is the natural choice."

Lauraisha said it matter-of-factly, but Katja could see she was visibly shaking. The werecat wondered whether that came from Dayalan's foiled attack or the prospect of her beloved steed being killed in front of her. Likely, it was both.

In the darkness long before dawn, none were about to see the packmates run toward Tyron's back stall in the stables. Dayalan hung as limp as a corpse from Felan's shoulder and Katja silently prayed that he had not already passed beyond their help. Lauraisha sprinted ahead and hurriedly unfastened the lock on Tyron's stall. The horse looked at her expectantly as they entered and, upon seeing Felan carrying

Dayalan, whinnied softly. Katja felt a whisper through her mental bond with the human and knew that the dreamdrifter was already passing images to the horse—explaining their precarious situation to him in the simplest terms.

"We have little time," Felan muttered as he put the groaning half-bred down against a clean heap of hay.

Katja half-smiled at him in reassurance as she gave the axe back, glad to be rid of the massive weapon's weight. She watched the horse whinny and paw the ground during the exchange with his rider. She envied the human's ability to communicate with her beast. The exchange of body language finished with Tyron cautiously walking toward the prone mage and snuffling his face. Dayalan's gasp caused the horse to jerk back.

"Is he willing?" he wheezed.

"Yes, Dayalan, he is…but you will have to be gentle with him or he will likely buck you across the barn."

Dayalan's chuckle ended in a rough cough. "He'll have to lay on his side, so that this will be easier for me."

The horse did as he instructed with slight coaxing from Lauraisha, and then Dayalan crawled to situate himself near the lower front of the horse's neck. Long white fangs slid forward as he lowered his lips to the vein trailing up from Tyron's deep chest. The horse shuddered as Dayalan's fangs pierced his flesh, but he otherwise lay still as the hybrid began to feed.

Katja gulped as she watched the act and unconsciously reached for her own bite wounds with her scarred paw. Felan saw her gesture and gently laid his paw on Katja's shoulder. Lauraisha wrung her hands and visibly trembled beside them while Zahra stood apart—her body tense with rage.

Dayalan looked up at them from over the horse's body and abruptly stopped his drinking. He stared at Lauraisha with sudden anguish in his scarlet eyes. "Please…don't watch me…do this."

Tears rolled down the human's face, but she would not turn.

"Finish it," she said in the barest whisper.

"No."

"Finish it!" she screamed suddenly.

Tyron raised his head to look worriedly at his mistress and then craned his bloody neck so that he could nuzzle Dayalan's scarlet-smeared face. Dayalan blinked hard, looking from the horse to Lauraisha, Katja, Felan, and Zahra, in turn. All nodded their heads in agreement, even the dryad, so he sank once more to the horse's neck and continued to drink.

Finally, he finished the gruesome task and stroked Tyron's neck in seeming reverence. Zahra wordlessly helped Lauraisha bandage the horse's wound and then began checking Tyron's condition. The horse was weak and would need several days rest before they could be certain of his survival. The same could also be said of the hybrid, who lay panting on the hay-strewn floor with one clawed talon still resting on the horse's flank.

* * *

Despite Dayalan's desperate feeding, the companions had little left to clean once the gruesome deed was done and they soon slunk into the predawn darkness with no one the wiser about their actions. Dayalan took up residence in Felan's chambers so that the werewolf could guard and care for him. The females were forbidden from entering unescorted until Felan judged Dayalan's mental state to be more stable. Katja had mixed feelings about the arrangement since Felan's apartment was just down the corridor from her own. While she trusted the werewolf's judgment, the feeding incident had shaken her. Lauraisha and Zahra shared her apprehension and the human finally consulted Damya on the matter.

"It follows logic that Dayalan would act practically rabid if deprived long enough of sustenance. Unlike you, he is a true predator who must feed from fresh flesh to survive," the firesprite mused.

"And in what part of that comment do you actually expect me to take comfort?" an exasperated Lauraisha exclaimed.

Damya's look was shrewd. "You should realize that this is far beyond my expertise. Verdagon is much better at understanding this sort of thing than I."

"Yes, but he — or rather his egg — has been locked under the supervision of the same arrogant hunza who is to determine Lauraisha's mental candor."

"Katja! Your language!" the human princess said, aghast.

The werecat smiled sheepishly. "Sorry, I'm frustrated and...afraid."

Zahra let out a breath. "Dayalan's feeding frenzy rattled us to the roots."

Damya danced dreamily in the fireplace flames. "I am not surprised. After all, you are used to seeing such wonton ferocity in your enemies, not your allies."

"Do you truly think Dayalan should still be counted as our ally? Even after his foiled attack on Lauraisha?"

Damya stared speculatively at the dryad and then toward the Tyglesean. "To be sure, the hybrid has an almost unfathomable potential for evil just as his father and brother do. I doubt, though, that he will be as foolish as either Caleb in his youth or Daeryn now. However, such things are best to judge in person anyway. Take me to him."

Katja nodded her agreement and then the four crept down the momentarily deserted hall to Felan's chambers. With Zahra's quiet knock, Felan swiftly ushered them inside the low-lit room.

"He's been quiet, sleeping most of the time and sipping occasionally from the wineskin we filled at the stables. Honored Damya, what do you make of him?" Felan asked in a weary whisper.

The firesprite flew to the raised bed where the fireforger slept and watched his even breathing a moment before touching his bare cheek with her tiny burning hand.

"Dayalan, how do you fare?" she asked with obvious concern.

The half-breed's eyes fluttered open and Katja noted breathlessly that they were blue once again.

"Honored Damya, have you come because I failed?"

"You did not fail, Dayalan," she said gently. "Although you did give your companions quite a scare. How do you feel?"

"I feel...very weary, but...where is Lauraisha? Can she still bear to be near me?"

"I am here, Dayalan," the human said tentatively.

He turned his bleary gaze toward her. "Lauraisha! I... How are you?"

"Fine," she said, but her tone was icy.

"How is Tyron?"

"He is…better than I expected…"

"Lauraisha, please forgive me!"

Katja watched tears well up in the hybrid's eyes. For a moment, his eyes' vulnerable glimmer aged his youthful face and he looked like he truly had seen thirty-five winters in this world. The werecat turned slightly to study the dreamdrifter, whose eyes were also welled up with emotion. Lauraisha stared at Dayalan and then her eyes briefly found Damya's. The little firesprite smiled confidently and so Lauraisha finally nodded toward Dayalan. He visibly relaxed. Lauraisha, however, still bore a troubled frown.

Soon after the exchange, the females bid their male companions goodbye and once more congregated in Lauraisha's quarters for private conversation.

"He is still weak and will need more rest before he can completely recuperate," Damya commented as soon as they had all settled.

"He is still dangerous, then?" Zahra asked while pouring mint tea for herself and the other two females.

"Dayalan has always been dangerous, as I have explained before; however, I believe the horse's blood is certainly strong enough to sate Dayalan's unusual appetite."

"Then they will live?" Lauraisha asked.

"I believe they both will, yes."

Lauraisha sighed in relief and gratefully sipped the cup Zahra offered her.

Katja frowned at the flames of Damya's flowing skirt. She felt chill despite the pyrefay's heat on her face and the teacup's warmth in her paws. She couldn't help but compare the memory of the previous night to the memory of her neck wounds. The same scarlet eyes had glared out of both waking nightmares. "Is Dayalan evil like his brother?"

"No, certainly not."

"How can you be sure, Damya?"

"If he had truly fallen to evil, then my greeting touch would have seared his cheek. As it is, he showed no aversion to my touch and therefore must still be free of the Asheken's Taint."

The dryad cocked her head. "You used one of the old Discernment Spells?"

"Very astute, Zahra." Damya smiled and then turned to Lauraisha. "During both wars of ages, Pyrekin acted as righteous wardens—constantly checking the Erdeken ranks for deception. Often times, ghouls would paint their pale faces and sneak among the ranks of mages intent to destroy the Sylvan Orders from within. It takes a ghoul of great theatrical skill and magical power to impersonate a Sylvan mage. They would often shear the black-pointed tips of their ears off so that they looked like humans or else paint them so they resembled elves. The Pyrekin and their most powerful wraithwalker and fireforger disciples would use Discernment Spells intertwined with their magic to flush out the tricksters.

"Of course, we Pyrekin have not practiced such techniques since Zahra's mother's mother was young...not for at least three hundred Erdeken winters, I would say. There were far more of our kind to perform such acts in the olden days and even greater numbers of us in ancient times, but, alas, how our numbers have dwindled. When Verdagon wakes, there shall be two of us finally able to walk in your realm and then we shall begin waking the others..."

Damya sighed. "Forgive me, I must go and rest. Until Verdagon is hatched, it will continue to be difficult for me to stay with you for extended periods. Once he has awakened, my powers in this realm will grow and therefore my time to be with you will also lengthen. Farewell for now. Look for me at the dragon's hatching, but not before."

With one last fiery smile, Damya diminished into a glowing wisp of smoke and curled back into the depths of Lauraisha's sapphire pendant. The human mage regretfully tucked the stone back under her garments and sighed.

"Now what do we do?"

Zahra finished the last of her tea before replying. "Prepare for your interview, I believe."

Katja flicked her ears and cradled her now cool cup in her lap. She had yet to sip its contents and did so now only to steady her nerves.

XXI

SHARD SIGHT

Lauraisha sat biting at the tips of her fingernails in agitation as she and Katja waited outside of Mori'lyn's study. Katja growled softly and then tried to calm her packmate down. The dreamdrifter and skinshifter had both continued their nightmares up to the very day of the human's examination. To make matters worse, Katja had gone through her skinshift barely two days before now and was still somewhat irritable because of her lingering soreness.

On the happier side of matters, both Dayalan and Tyron seemed stronger every day despite their previous troubles. The only truly bizarre part of the healing experience was the deepening level of understanding and communication between beast and being. More than once Katja had to hide a grin as Lauraisha jealously fumed about the increased rapport between her steed and her casual mentor. The stallion began to express himself with a new series of whinnies and snorts and Dayalan had picked up the horse's new mannerisms like a second language while Lauraisha stood in wide-eyed bafflement.

The door across from her opened with a rasping creak, interrupting the werecat's thoughts.

"Well, hurry up, hurry up, dreamdrifter, I have no time to waste. Come!" Mori'lyn said as his portly form pranced through the doorway.

A harried Lauraisha stood and bowed before quickly scurrying after the bombastic little satyr. Katja watched her friend dash through the door and then winced as Mori'lyn slammed it shut behind them. At the door's close, Katja felt a violent ripple in the air around her. A Ring Spell now encompassed Mori'lyn's study so that no sound from within could resonate beyond its walls. Lauraisha's mind echoed Katja's shock at being physically unable to eavesdrop on the conversation. Even Lauraisha's thoughts were vague and so the werecat had to concentrate with all her strength just to catch something more than the human's mood through their bond.

In the beginning, Mori'lyn's presence wafted softly through the edges of Lauraisha's awareness, testing her defenses and comparing her recent memories against the testimonies given by her friends during the General Council of Mages meeting. Katja felt her packmate be lulled into a lucid existence as the intruding mage probed gradually deeper. A foreign sense of irritation slowly began to build in Lauraisha's mind as Katja silently monitored Mori'lyn's progress. She watched shadows of visions dance before her own eyes showing their many close encounters with the Asheken as well as their meetings with each of their current companions.

Then without warning, the human's emotions turned from mere anxiety to outright terror as Katja felt the mage's powerful presence fully penetrate Lauraisha's mind. It pushed past the dreamdrifter's instinctive defenses and plunged into the darkest recesses of her memories. Katja felt the human's thoughts lurch in protest. Sensations of pain exploded through their bond and then the werecat saw not only the sparsely furnished room around her but a vision of frothy water endlessly rippling on top of it. The sensation felt like one of their shared nightmares, but the scene's constitution proved much weaker than usual.

From Lauraisha's mind, Katja gleaned the sense that the water was that of the Westylere Sea. Her suspicion proved correct when the bow of a ship bearing the Tyglesean standard heaved into view. A distant scream hummed in the werecat's ears and she suddenly could not discern if the sound was a part of the vision or of reality. Her mind worked quickly to interpret words spoken in Tygeré.

"No, Father! Please!"

It was a younger version of Lauraisha's voice Katja was hearing and it held the same degree of terror that Katja herself usually reserved for the Gan Ceann. Lauraisha had apparently been watching the sunset in this memory from the bow of one of her father's vessels. Her face, however, had been twisted away from the water's reflective beauty and forced to look into the blotched face of a livid human male.

"You dare defy me! My racing mare Maryssa is priceless and you degrade her with a mere cart horse!" King Kaylor's voice was a hissing whisper punctuated by a strike of his fist to the side of the princess's face.

Even though Lauraisha had braced for the impact, she was still knocked to her knees on the rolling deck. Without a word, Kaylor grabbed her by her dress collar and hauled her into the darkness of the ship's hold below. There in the king's dimly lit cabin, Lauraisha felt her father's cruel touch again and again. Katja began to tremble as her friend's screams echoed in her mind and her ears.

Katja stumbled through the half-manifested vision to Mori'lyn's door and wrenched the latch with all her strength. It did not move—not even a hair's width. Mori'lyn had sealed the door with both spell and key. Frantically, Katja lodged her outstretched claw into the keyhole and tried to unlock the door latch while her eyes still swam with the vision of Lauraisha's childhood torment.

The princess's remembered cries gave way to a brief moment of silence before resuming again in a different scene. Kaylor was still striking and kicking her, but this time they were in a stone-walled room with arrow slits for windows. The scene soon changed again to find an older version of Lauraisha lying on the dusty straw of a small stable stall. Kaylor had partially gagged her, but her terrified voice pierced the air nonetheless as his eager hands began ripping the clothing away from her shaking body. Despite the desperation of her screams and cries, none of the stable hands would dare look at them, much less come to her aid.

With this latest profane event, Katja felt like retching. Lauraisha's desperate thoughts became her own and Katja wondered if she would ever feel clean or safe again. She felt the human's mind growing increasingly turbulent until it seemed to collapse under the weight of the memories. Blackness invaded their bond just as the door clicked and Katja staggered into the room. Lauraisha lay on the floor twitching violently while Mori'lyn held her head in both of his stubby hands. The mage looked up in surprise at the werecat and a crimson haze suddenly smote Katja's vision.

"What have you done to her!" the werecat screeched in rage.

The mage looked at her calmly. "I have done nothing except help the young mage confront her worst fears. It was a bit of a shock for her to undergo such a difficult mental lesson during her first interview with me, but she will be on the mend soon enough. Now could you kindly fetch Neha'lyn? I think the princess will need some quiet rest in the healing ward before she can resume any more tutelage with normalcy."

Every inkling of sense in her body told Katja that this mage should not be left alone with the princess, and yet she had to find the harmhealer. With a roar born of anguish and rage, the werecat kicked Mori'lyn away from the human with a force that sent him tumbling head over hooves into the far wall and then hoisted the limp Lauraisha onto her own shoulders. Katja's sight finally cleared midway down the second corridor and she discovered Neha'lyn in the third. Once she informed him of how Lauraisha had collapsed under Mori'lyn's mental barrage, the angry elf bade her to follow him. Katja found herself feverishly sprinting after the harmhealer—first to his study where they left Lauraisha in Neha'lyn's assistant Oeled's care and then back to Mori'lyn's study to witness one of the fiercest quarrels she had yet seen.

Neha'lyn and Mori'lyn began the shouting match as soon as the elf spied the dazed satyr. Katja, unfortunately, could not understand precisely what was being said since the two were conversing in the elf's native tongue of Lávaloré. From their expressions and gestures she guessed that Neha'lyn was initially furious about the dreamdrifter's treatment of his potential pupil, but she couldn't fathom what happened after that.

Mori'lyn kept pointing from Katja to the laceration she had given him when she kicked him. Finally Neha'lyn seemed to concede something and he turned to Katja. "Come with me, please. We need to move Lauraisha to a more secure location until we can sort out this unpleasantness."

He then ordered Citadel Guardians to take Katja and the still-quiescent Lauraisha not to the healing chambers as Mori'lyn had earlier suggested, but to the isle's underground dungeons.

* * *

Katja?

Lauraisha's distant thought roused the werecat from a dose.

Lauraisha! Are you well? the werecat responded, not quite sure of the human's location.

Mori'lyn and Neha'lyn betrayed us! Lauraisha's reply was a muddled mental grumble.

I'm aware of that. At least they didn't take our possessions. The tone of the werecat's reply was calmer than she actually felt while being imprisoned alone in the dark, but she knew panic would only worsen the situation. She stared at the dim wall in front of her and shifted her weight uncomfortably on the cold stone beneath her. *Lauraisha, where are you?*

I believe I am in the adjacent cell to your right.

The werecat sighed, relieved and somewhat perplexed by their close proximity. *Your thoughts are rather quiet for being so close. Can you sense our packmates' whereabouts?*

I am not powerful enough to push through the dungeon's magical interference, Katja, and after what I just went through—

Yet. You are not that powerful yet. How can you grow your abilities if you do not practice?

And you, of course, practice so often. The human's sarcasm was evident even through the weakness of their link.

I did practice two days ago, as did Felan. Will you stop changing the subject and at least try to contact the others?

Fine. I will do what I can.

Thank you, the skinshifter replied. Her ears flicked in irritation toward the human and toward herself. She felt guilt for commanding Lauraisha so gruffly, but she also knew her mandates would distract the human enough to keep her from dwelling on the nightmarish memories that Mori'lyn had dredged up. Magical communication among any of the packmates existed only as long as the dreamdrifter remained rational.

After a long pause, Lauraisha's unspoken words drifted through their bond again. *I'm sorry, Katja, but I cannot find them!*

The werecat snarled. She scratched her paw irritably and then felt the crescent-shaped scar on her right palm. The memory of its bloody birth flashed back to her mind and she suddenly sat up.

Lauraisha, I want to try something. I have no idea if it will help, but…

Very well, do whatever it is that you are considering. I'll wait.

Katja nodded even though she knew Lauraisha could not see the gesture. She groped around her neck for Durhrigg's spearhead. Holding the blade firmly in her right paw, she stroked the scarlet mirror shard imbedded in its center with her clawed thumb and concentrated. She reached out to Lauraisha simultaneously through their bond and through the shard. Almost instantly, she achieved a level of cognition with the human she had known only in their dreams shared with Canuche.

What did you do? Lauraisha's awestruck mental voice was as clear as if she had shouted directly into the werecat's own ear.

I used the mirror shard and spearhead to increase the power of our communication.

It can actually work that way?

Apparently.

Well, let me experiment with mine, then.

There was another silent pause while Lauraisha tried to track the other packmates through her mind and through her mirror shard. Katja moved her cramped limbs onto the softer section of straw that acted as the cell's makeshift bed, stretched, and waited. Slowly the human's concentration shifted back toward Katja. She had the distinct impression that the dreamdrifter was drawing not only on her shard's uncanny communications abilities, but also on the energy from Damya's Keystone to supplement her strength.

Felan is several chambers down to my left and seems healthy aside from a massive headache. Zahra is on the level of detention chambers just underneath us and has some fascinating mold growing in the straw of her cell bed. Dayalan is being held in a tower in a completely different part of the Citadel and...Caleb is here.

Caleb is here? Are you sure?

Quite certain. And Katja?

Yes?

I can feel Dayalan's hunger rising.

Katja hissed vengefully. *We must find an escape soon then.*

I know. Wait a moment, Katja.

The human's mind drifted away to other thoughts then and, after a while, Katja consigned herself to a bath as she waited. She had just finished licking and grooming the grimy fur on her torso and back paws when the dreamdrifter's awareness finally floated into her mind once more.

Vraelth just came to visit. He had seen Zahra first and then came straight to me. The charmchanter said he wished to aid us. I asked him to take our plea before the Ring of Sorcerers. Since Vraelth doubts the veracity of Mori'lyn's claims, he readily agreed to do so. He also said that Neha'lyn was the one who sent him to us. Apparently Neha'lyn doubts Mori'lyn as well; however, he had no choice but to follow guardian protocols and imprison us when Mori'lyn confirmed that you attacked him.

Did you tell him of Dayalan?

I told him that Caleb should be allowed to see to his son since the half-breed has some odd health requirements. Again Vraelth promised to do what he could.

Katja leaned her head against the cold stone behind her and sighed. *I take it we must wait until aid comes from the outside?*

I'm afraid so.

The werecat growled with all the frustration born of helplessness as she leaned back against her pile of straw.

Lauraisha?

Yes?

Do you want to talk about the memories that Mori'lyn dredged up?

Lauraisha was silent for a long moment. *No, Katja. I never want to talk or think about those memories ever again.*

* * *

A grating sound roused Katja from the depths of her

sleep. The boulder rolled along its track away from the cell's doorway to allow two figures access to enter Katja's prison before grinding shut again. The werecat hid her eyes from the sudden brightness of the smaller figure's candle and sniffed their scents cautiously. One was familiar, but the other was not.

"Katja Escari, we wish to speak with you on a matter most urgent," a female voice issued from the smaller figure's hood. Only the voice's familiarity made the werecat suddenly lower her claws, stand, and bow deeply.

"Your visit humbles me, Your Honor," the Feliconian said as Joce'lynn pulled back her hood. Katja then turned to the other cowled figure. "I am honored to see you again as well, Caleb. Tell me, how does Dayalan fare?"

The ancient mage dropped his own hood and smiled slightly. "Ah, I see you remember my scent. I have yet to see Dayalan; when I do, I shall tell him of your concern."

"Thank you," Katja said while a part of her mind reached through the link beyond herself and stirred Lauraisha to wakefulness.

What? came the human's groggy thought.

Caleb and Joce'lynn are here.

Katja felt relief flow through their link. *Really? Good. Why?*

I haven't the faintest notion, but I will tell you what I dis—

"Katja, leave Lauraisha out of this discussion please."

The werecat stared at Caleb stunned. "You know of our bond?"

Caleb's smile was full of fang. "Of course."

"As does the Ring, Katja Escari," Joce'lynn added. "It was made quite evident to us when you all but smashed down the door to Mori'lyn's office during the Tyglesean's interview."

Katja's eyes narrowed and her nostrils flared in sudden rage. "It was more of a torturous interrogation than an interview, if you ask me."

"And that is part of what we need to discuss with you."

"Katja, we would like to know your perspective on the events of Lauraisha and Mori'lyn's discussion and we expect you to answer honestly without the human's slightest input as to your experiences outside that office."

Katja frowned a moment before finally bowing her head.

She told the princess of their situation and felt momentary sadness as Lauraisha's awareness retreated from her mind. She looked at Caleb and sighed, "It is done."

His azure eyes were gentle as he nodded. "Very well, tell us what you know."

The werecat let out her breath slowly before explaining her impressions. "When Mori'lyn called Lauraisha into his study, I was sitting outside the door. The room was magically shielded from outer influences by Ring Spells, so I could discern little of what happened inside until Lauraisha opened the bond between us. Lauraisha always leaves our mental link open whenever we are faced with anxious or dangerous situations and this was no exception.

"Neither she nor I entirely trusted the mage because of his treatment of Dayalan while we all were being interviewed on the Mage Council floor; however, we did not expect the depth of maliciousness he showed to her during the interview."

"What happened at the council?" Caleb asked.

Katja briefly explained their experience and Caleb's eyes were glinting eerily when she finished.

"They used mage fire against my son? This will not stand," he hissed.

"Please, my dear Caleb," Joce'lynn said, touching the male's shoulder lightly. "Your vengeance will not aid us at present."

Caleb glanced toward her and nodded his head sharply. "I will withhold my judgment for the moment, but I will not allow such offences toward my family to go unpunished, Jocelana."

"I know." Joce'lynn's smile was gentle at his use of her birth name. When she bid Katja to finish her story, the Feliconian described the progression of Lauraisha's emotions during Mori'lyn's manipulative interrogation culminating with her impressions of the human's torturous memories. Although she omitted the more heinous descriptions, her quivering voice and body cued her listeners into her visions' repugnance perfectly. Caleb stepped beside her and wrapped a protective arm around her shoulders. It was an action that Katja found utterly unexpected considering the male's chilling reputation.

She shuddered again and slumped against the mage in sudden exhaustion. "I knew that Lauraisha's father was cruel to her, but I did not realize how dangerous he actually was until I witnessed his actions with my own mind. I never hope to feel that way again."

The silver-haired human tapped a finger on her pale lips and hummed thoughtfully. "You do realize that you are accusing the monarch of Tyglesea of a most odious crime?"

Katja growled. "His being king does not alter the fact that he is a monster as foul as the Asheken. He deserves death just as any rapist in the whole of the Sylvan Orders does for such crimes."

"She does see things in black and white, does she not?" Caleb said in approval.

"Actually the visions were tinged in red," the werecat responded, not comprehending Caleb's quip about her absolute sense of morality.

Joce'lynn looked sharply at her. "Red? When?"

"I have had such visions many times on my journey to this place. Most recently when I burst into Mori'lyn's office, my view of the entire room was bathed in crimson."

Joce'lynn stepped forward and pressed her hand to the side of the werecat's head, gazing intently into her eyes. Suddenly Katja's vision clouded with contrasting swirls of orange, brown, and scarlet until Joce'lynn abruptly broke their contact. The vibrant eddies cleared immediately and Katja was left to stare stunned at the equally shocked Ring member.

Joce'lynn blinked at the werecat in wonder. "Never did I dream it possible…"

"What?" Caleb asked, frowning.

She looked at him. "At long last I have found another of my kind."

Caleb looked from Joce'lynn to Katja and back, his expression unreadable. "I wondered. When she repaired the Ott vre Caerwyn after Dayalan shattered it into hundreds of pieces, I wondered then if it was possible…But you have told me that she is already a powerful skinshifter. Surely she didn't inherit from both—"

"She is both, Caleb."

"You are certain?"

"To the marrow."

"I am both of what?" the werecat asked, look from one to the other.

Caleb ignored her. "Then you know she must be telling the truth about her experiences."

Joce'lynn's eyes narrowed. "Lauraisha must still confirm it before the Ring."

"I know."

"Confirm what?"

"Your visions of her memories, Katja," Caleb said quietly before gazing once more at the Ring member. "We must move quickly to arrange the meeting before this mage Mori'lyn or any of his cohorts learn of this development."

"You fear for their safety should their secrets be discovered."

"And you do not?"

Joce'lynn's expression darkened noticeably in the candlelight. "We will delve to the heart of this matter. Mark my words. I will uncover Mori'lyn's motivations for such betrayal."

She turned to the Feliconian. "Tell none of our visit. Not even Lauraisha is to know the matters we discussion here, nor is she to speak of this meeting to anyone. Your life and those of your friends depend upon your silence. All of your lives could be forfeited if any deduce your importance."

"What do you mean by 'my importance'?"

Joce'lynn's golden eyes suddenly filled with hope and then a deep sadness. "I promise I will answer your queries in due time. The present circumstances are too precarious for me to say more. For now, you must trust our judgment. Caleb insisted that I question you. Because of his recommendation, I have discovered Mori'lyn's deceit and so much more. The mage cannot know that we have discerned his subterfuge."

Katja hesitated and then formally bowed her consent. "But what of Neha'lyn?"

"Don't worry. I will discern his part in this deception soon," Joce'lynn replied.

"Our deepest thanks, Katja. Now you must excuse us. We have much to accomplish," Caleb said.

"By the way, if you do tell Lauraisha or anyone else what has been discussed here tonight, I will know." The Ring member kicked the wall three times with her boot to signal the Citadel Guardians to roll the boulder aside once more.

After a quick exchange of bows, Joce'lynn and Caleb strode from the room leaving a bewildered Katja to ponder their words long after their exit. Hissing in frustration, she began to pace the dark parameters of her confinement. Moving felt good after three days of mostly sitting or sleeping. It seemed that she could always unravel problems better when on her paws instead of her rump.

Why did Councilor Joce'lynn call Katja another of her kind? Joce'lynn was a human and possessed no reputed skinshifting abilities. Joce'lynn's talents lay more in her uncanny ability to discern truth in the behaviors of others. She was famous for her unerring awareness of others' dishonesty. This fact made Mori'lyn's treachery even more disturbing. How had he managed to deceive Joce'lynn about Lauraisha's experiences?

But then perhaps Joce'lynn did have skinshifting abilities that she herself would not reveal to her colleagues for fear of retribution. After all, the title of "Skinshifter Master" had never graced a single member of the Ring of Sorcerers after the Second War of Ages. Many Sylvans, including most members of the Feliconas Clan, considered the practice of skinshifting despicable and therefore formal training for skinshifters was rare outside of the Isle of Summons. If Joce'lynn were a skinshifter in secret, it might explain why she would look at Katja in kinship when so many others would treat the werecat as a leper.

The werecat shook her muddled head and paced to the wall opposite the cell's entrance. Kneeling before it, she squinted through one of the paw-sized breathing holes bored through the speckled granite. She could see nothing, but her nose told her that the fresh air blowing through it still carried the scent of the lake's waters and plants. She lay with her nose over the cold wafts of freedom and wondered when the right to move openly in the wind would be restored to her once again. For now, she let the fresh breeze clear her mind of its confusion.

* * *

Well, what happened?

Sorry, Lauraisha, I don't have permission to tell you.

Why?

The information concerns our safety. The less others know of the conversation, the better.

Very well then, I will do my best not to pry—

No easy feat for you, Kajta sniggered as she took another bite of dried meat left from her evening eat.

Be nice! Lauraisha's response was only semiserious.

Katja chuckled again and tried to reassure her friend that the meeting had seemed to go well.

If it went so well, why are you so anxious?

You have not told anyone else who my recent visitors are, have you?

Who would I tell? My guards?

No, of course not. I just wondered if any of our other packmates know of the meeting.

No.

Good, let us keep matters as such.

Let me guess, this is also for our safety's sake as well? The dreamdrifter's voice was testy.

Yes.

Fine, Katja, I will refrain from sharing anything about your meeting. Now, what else is upsetting you?

Jierira, you are terribly persistent.

Stop changing the subject and answer my query.

Katja sighed. *Oh, I was just wondering if Joce'lynn is a skinshifter in hiding.*

You are "just wondering" several things today. Why would you suspect that?

Katja fidgeted before answering the Tyglesean. *How much do you know about the Skinshifters' Disgrace during the Second War of Ages?*

Roughly as much as you would expect given my background. In other words, nothing but what you've already told me.

Katja scratched her forehead. *Very well, then. At the war's conclusion, several trials were held to punish both Sylvan and Asheken war criminals. During those proceedings, some skinshifters were judged and punished as Sylvan traitors before the Mage Tribunal for their roles as the deadwalkers' spies. These skinshifter mages were in fact Sylvan and their leader Fritjof was a high ranking member of the Feliconas Clan. None of these skinshifters had been Turned into changelings, but all of them had been bribed to gather information for the deadwalkers. The traitors had used their abilities and connections to glean strategic information from among the Sylvan races and then slunk past the battle lines in beast form to deliver messages to the deadwalker leaders.*

Fritjof, himself, was killed in battle before he could be brought to justice, but the clan stories all say that he was at least partially responsible for Canuche's current predicament. In fact, many Sylvans were killed or Turned because of the skinshifter traitors' betrayal during the Eppon Gue Battle and other clashes.

Was Fritjof the werecat we saw in Canuche's dream of the battle?

Katja nodded. *I think so.*

That is horrible! The human's inner shudder reflected Katja's own.

Now you know the vile legacy that I carry within my soul.

You would never betray Sylvans, Katja. You are too pure and too honorable to commit such subversion!

And yet my family and my clan died because of my gift. Sylvans everywhere will fear me for what I am and Asheken will continually try to lure me to their side. There will never be peace for me as long as a single deadwalker roams this world.

Lauraisha sighed. *Nor can there be peace for Dayalan or Caleb, or Felan or Fenris, or Zahlathra or Zahra, or Damya or Verdagon, or me. As long as they remain, Katja, our lives will be fraught with misery. Misery will drive all Sylvans until their Asheken oppressors are destroyed. Freedom from Asheken oppression is no longer only your cause, it is our cause.*

For the first time in many days, the werecat truly smiled. For the first time since the massacre, the last surviving Feliconian felt truly strong. She knew her Tyglesean companion spoke the truth and she felt sudden pride for the human's vehemence. This fight belonged not to one, but to all. And all would be needed to triumph during such a crisis. Because of this, the Feliconian finally felt that she was no longer alone. Although they could never replace Katja's real siblings, her packmates had nonetheless become her second family.

Very well, myn lytzsibba, for our *cause will I fight.*

As will I, Katja. As will I.

For a precious few moments, the skinshifter and dreamdrifter held a mutual moment of joy as deep as their magical bond itself. And then it and Lauraisha's presence were abruptly jerked from Katja's mind.

"Lauraisha!" the werecat screeched aloud as the human's scream echoed in her mind.

The walls of her prison shook with her frantic voice. The dreamdrifter was gone! Simply gone! She could no longer feel any vestige of the human's mental manifestation. It seemed as if an outside force had completely severed their bond in an instant. The werecat frantically paced the room just as her mind raced for some sign of her friend's flight. Tinges of crimson lit the corners of her aching mind, but no other clues presented themselves.

Desperately Katja gripped her shard-infused spearhead and knelt with her face to the air holes. She prayed for the Creator's protection over Lauraisha and asked His aid to find her. Then she focused on the shard itself and tried to push her thoughts through it to the shard hopefully still hanging around Lauraisha's neck. Although the shard itself glowed, nothing else seemed to happen. Katja tried again and again with no success. By the time she allowed herself to rest, she had a piercing headache and nausea in the pit of her stomach.

"Where are you?" the little werecat whispered tearfully into the darkness. The hay beneath her head was soaked by the time exhaustion finally overwhelmed her.

XXII
THE RING OF SORCERERS

G ood evening, Dayalan. How do you fare?"
Katja awoke with a startled shriek. She quickly searched the darkness for intruders, but she was alone in her cell.

"You!" Dayalan's voice was a bestial bark of loathing.

"Now, now, please refrain from any slighting remarks. I came for a service, after all."

"Fangs to whatever you wish, Mori'lyn! You will receive no aid from me."

"My dear mage, I came not to ask a service, but to give one." The satyr's voice oozed smugness. "I have noticed that this prison tower's influence seems to have diminished your mood as well as your magic and I thought some company might bring you joy."

"What have you done...Lauraisha! No!"

Suddenly Katja understood what she was hearing. She peered at her glowing spearhead and realized that it was directly conveying the mages' words to her. Dayalan's slightly distant voice made Katja suspect that Lauraisha's spearhead, not Dayalan's, was the one conveying the spoken exchange.

"Not to worry; she has been senseless but a short while. Once she awakens, I'm sure you two will get on fine together. Oh, and, Dayalan, you look a bit pallid. Perhaps you should take a meal to garner your strength. It would be a pity if you were ill during your council appearances."

The werecat's maw dropped in a silent gasp of horror.

Mori'lyn had discovered Dayalan's weakness through Lauraisha's memories and was going to bait his blood-thirst using the Tyglesean princess.

"May the Creator scorch you as black as the Abomination!" Dayalan's baritone voice lowered even further in hatred.

"Perhaps he may, but not before he strikes you down first, mongrel-born." Mori'lyn's tone lost the charm that had been thinly veiling his malice. "I'll see to that."

"No, Mori'lyn, it is you who will feel death's wrath long before me."

"You really should learn the portent of such impotent threats, Dayalan Luthrial, before you speak them to such an influential mage."

"I am not Luther's spawn!"

"And yet who will believe you after your attempted coercion of me and your brutal treatment of this poor unfortunate." Mori'lyn's mocking chuckle was drowned out by grating metal that sounded like a door being unlocked and opened. His steps then faded out of the werecat's hearing and the door was locked once more.

"Lauraisha! Wake up, please!"

Katja had to catch her breath at the desperation in Dayalan's voice. His words were much louder now, which meant he was either holding the human or he was right beside her.

"Dayalan…what happened…"

"Are you well? Did he hurt you?"

"I think I am—" her voice broke off for a moment. "Your eyes are red."

Katja cursed.

"It is nothing. I am fine."

"Do not touch me!"

"Lauraisha…"

"He sent me here to die! He put me here to tempt you to Turn! Get back!"

The swishing of straw sounded as Lauraisha evidently scrambled back. Katja's mind desperately sought a way to their bond. She discovered no visions and whimpered in fear. At that same moment, Dayalan's appeals gave way to frustration.

"Be still!"

The human stopped whimpering, but her every breath was a raspy gasp. Suddenly the human's vision flooded the surface of the glowing spear shard and the werecat saw Dayalan's gloved talon reaching toward her. The male's haunted eyes glowed scarlet against his colorless face, which bore full fangs.

Lauraisha crouched trembling with her back trapped against the cold stones and could not shrink away from his touch. Dayalan knelt hesitatingly and pulled her into a deep embrace. She trembled in his desperate hold until he pulled back and wrapped his heavy gray cloak around her quaking shoulders.

"I will not allow Mori'lyn or anyone else to harm you, Lauraisha. I swear it."

"You say you would defend me from him, but can you protect me from yourself?"

Dayalan pulled back further, his now-violet eyes full of consternation. "I…I don't know."

"I see."

They both stood and studied each other until Dayalan finally broke the silence. "I am truly sorry. I never want to harm you, but I honestly have no idea how long I can stave off this vile thirst."

Katja felt the dreamdrifter peer past Dayalan's eyes and delve into his stormy soul, searching and confirming the truth of his words. "What do you want, Dayalan?"

"Power." He sighed. "Daeryn and I have always longed for it. We have always sought it."

"Why?"

Dayalan stared into the cramped chamber without seeming to see the walls. "I have not the faintest notion why. Like my father in his own misspent youth, I suppose it is my destined curse to always want power purely for its own pernicious appeal."

"Dayalan, look at me." Lauraisha cautiously pulled his face gently back toward her own. "You have enough power already. You are the most powerful mage I have ever known. The Creator made you with a purpose—he made you a warrior and a leader. You have the power of leadership whether you wish it or not. Now, He has called you to learn the extent of your power by serving others. The greatest leader is always the most humble servant. So humble yourself and submit to His will so that you can accomplish wonders, not terrors."

He sighed again. "You are correct…but power itself maintains its grip on my soul. Vampires have the continual desire to dominate all life and, although my connection with that nature is usually tentative, my mage blood in some ways compounds my power-lust. When I fight with both sides of my being, the mage blood fuels my bloodlust and I teeter on the brink of madness. That was the main reason why Bren was so dear to me. Whether I was fighting or feeding, my mental link with the wolf always helped keep my mind steady. He helped me to remember the value of life. You could say that he was almost my conscience."

"How did you meet?"

"I found him when he was still a pup. His mother actually died defending her den against a bear." Dayalan shook his head. "It was one of the strangest things I have yet seen. The bear must have been senile and sick because it tracked Bren's mother to her den and killed her. Bren and his two siblings had hid nearby, but the bear found them as well. He ate the mother and two pups, but left the third alive. I killed the bear while I was patrolling Caerwyn's borders, and then found Bren hours later. I nursed him back to health; he and I had shared a bond ever since."

Lauraisha bobbed her head. "And now with him gone…"

"Tyron will be a good bloodmate, but it will take time for me to develop a strong bond with him so I have to be cautious." Dayalan looked toward the human. "I am sorry, Lauraisha, to have you involved in this trouble. You should not have to bear such a terrible burden as young as you are. The others should not have to deal with this unpleasantness either."

"How young do you think I am?"

"You look less than half my own age, barely fifteen winters if my eyes judge right."

"I am actually sixteen autumns old now, for I was born at the beginning of that season."

Dayalan inclined his head. "So your birthday coincided

with the middle of this journey?"

"It was, in a way, the reason for this journey. My father tried to assassinate me before my birthday so that I could not seek Royal Title in my country. His soldiers' botched attempt is what prompted my mother and brothers to smuggle me out of Tyglesea."

"Royal Title? Is that like a rite of passage?"

"In a way. It allows me to be a legal adult and to seek an entitled position within the Tyglesean government. Since I am female, I have few rights or privileges within our society, so the Royal Title Law basically entitles me to join the prophetic clergy and blocks the king from marrying me off to whatever idiot he chooses if I enter the priesthood."

Dayalan stood. "Your father tried to kill you rather than let you become a priestess?"

She nodded. "Twice."

"Why?"

"It has to do with a prophesy that some crazy old seer gave long before my birth. She basically told my father that one of his own children would be responsible for the downfall of his reign...that one would become a mage and devout practitioner in a profane religion. My father has no love for the Tyglesean church and so when I wanted to join the priesthood, he assumed that I was the threat and tried to have me eliminated."

Dayalan's dark eyes narrowed. "Kaylor would do well to avoid me then. If ever our paths cross, I promise you that his life is forfeit."

"You'll have to get in line, Dayalan," the werecat muttered.

"Katja?" Dayalan looked utterly confused.

"You heard her, too?"

Dayalan did not answer, but Lauraisha tentatively called the werecat's name.

"I am here, Lauraisha."

The male stared around the room. "Define here."

"I am in my own cell listening to your voices through one of the Ott vre Caerwyn shards."

"The mirror shards can transmit voices?"

"And images, apparently."

"Has Caleb visited you again, Katja?" Lauraisha asked.

"Wait. You've seen Father, too?"

"No, only Katja has."

"When?"

"I doubt she can explain without breaking her oath of secrecy to him and to Joce'lynn."

"When did Katja see both of them?" Dayalan sounded baffled.

"Foul fangs, Lauraisha!" Katja screeched. "You're useless as a confidant!"

"Sorry!" The princess actually sounded abashed.

"Father being here is a small wonder."

"What do you mean?" the females asked simultaneously.

"Before I left Caerwyn, we discussed the possible dangers of my coming to the isle. Father had already decided to pay a visit to this place just as soon as he had finished a little enemy reconnoitering of his own. Ideally, Father's presence here will force the Ring of Sorcerers members to remember a few old alliances. He hopes to push as many mages as possible to declare war against the deadwalkers."

"We have to go to war!" the Feliconian exclaimed. "With northern villages being decimated and the Glen under siege, how can there really be any doubt of that?"

"You forget, Katja, that politics rules supreme here, not logic. Many of the old alliances will still hold true among the Second War veterans, but it will take time and patience—neither of which Father really has—to convince the younger mage generations of war's necessity. Many of them have never seen a deadwalker. I would guess that any under one hundred winters of age would consider vampires to be little more than villains in ancient faeryken tales."

"Do faeryken actually tell tales?" the human asked.

"Oh, pixies tell the best tall tales ever!" Katja replied enthusiastically. "That is if you can get them to sit still long enough to recount one."

"So what happens if your father fails to sway them, Dayalan?"

"We will most likely rot in our cells until our trials are set and then see if we can find justice before a biased tribunal. Of course, that is assuming that we can withstand Mori'lyn's schemes before we seek trial."

Katja grunted. "Well, aren't you cheerful."

"Sorry, but these are the grim facts as I see them."

"I hope your father is more successful than you suggest."

"Creator, keep us, if he is not," Lauraisha added and the others fervently agreed.

* * *

The grating sound of the boulder rolling away from the cell entrance once again roused Katja from her slumber. She wasn't certain when she had fallen asleep, but her groggy mind told her that several hours had passed since Lauraisha and Dayalan's voices had grown quiet.

"We have little time to spare. Katja Escari, gather your belongings and come with me at once!"

After a moment's astonished hesitation, the werecat quickly complied with Joce'lynn's whispered order. The two females and their five mage guardians set off down the detention ward at a brisk pace toward Zahra's cell. Once the dryad was freed, she helped them find Felan.

"Why in a ghoul's bite did you bring along a sample of mold?" Katja asked the dryad once the werewolf had joined their ranks.

"I thought it might be important later," she replied and then continued running down the corridor.

"Katja, where is Princess Lauraisha?" Joce'lynn asked in alarm when they reached her empty cell.

"Mori'lyn moved her to Dayalan's confinements, My Madam."

"Katja, does Mori'lyn know about Dayalan's unusual diet?" Felan asked bluntly.

"He does."

The werewolf cursed sharply.

"He knows what?" Joce'lynn asked.

Katja fidgeted uncomfortably. "Dayalan's odd lineage has given him some unsettling idiosyncrasies."

"Such as?"

"He takes blood as his main nourishment instead of solid food—"

"So the princess is in grave danger of becoming his next meal?"

Katja frowned. "I think he would rather die than attack Lauraisha, or any being for that matter. He's a ferocious fighter when cornered, but he loathes vampires and their murder of beings. He drinks the blood of beasts instead. The white wolf Bren was his main 'bloodmate' as he calls them. When Bren died, Dayalan almost starved himself into madness trying to protect us from his thirst until we convinced him to bond with and gain nourishment from Lauraisha's stallion Tyron. The experiment went well, but Dayalan has not taken a meal since just before the last full moon and not even he can defy the instinct for survival forever."

Now it was Joce'lynn's turn to curse. "The full moon was nine days ago! We'll have to retrieve her immediately for my strategy to work. All of you, put these robes on and follow me. Quickly now!"

After each member had garbed themselves in the proffered mage guardian robes, the Ring member led the companions through the labyrinth of dim corridors and past a narrow door to a pair of spiraling staircases. The limestone stairs wound dizzyingly around each other up to the cells meant to hold the most powerful mage prisoners. There were several points in which the first and second set of stairs crossed and Katja surmised that the purpose behind this was to disorient anyone attempting escape.

Joce'lynn crossed to the first staircase at the third and sixth junctions without hesitation and kept moving. Katja stared after her in astonishment while panting to catch up. The werecat could feel a strange magic pulling at her strength and robbing her of her directional sense, but Joce'lynn didn't seem affected by the force. She was certainly agile for a several-hundred-winter-old human. Of course, the Feliconian knew that mages aged more slowly than normal beings, but she had never appreciated how vast the difference actually was between normal beings—most of which never lived past seventy-five winters—and this spry elder mage now sprinting up the stairs.

Joce'lynn did not pause until they reached the landing just beyond Dayalan's cell. Once Katja and the others finally caught up with her, she immediately motioned them to silence.

"I will enter first, followed by two guardians. Then the rest of you may enter," she said. "Keep your wits about you. Dayalan may be your friend, but he will be your worst foe if he has Turned."

The packmates all nodded their understanding and waited. When Joce'lynn signaled them, they cautiously entered, not knowing what to expect. Zahra was the first to see Dayalan and she gasped when she did. Katja caught the sight and scent of dried blood as she peered past the dryad.

The muscular male was curled like a frightened child against the room's far wall. Dark smears of blood were caked upon his neck and wrists where heavy iron chains had dug into his skin. He stared blearily at the intruders with scarlet eyes and then slowly pointed with an ungloved claw toward Katja's right. Katja looked where he indicated and saw Lauraisha huddled under Dayalan's cloak with her head held in her trembling hands.

"Is she...?" Zahra asked.

"She is Untainted and so is he," Joce'lynn answered for Dayalan.

"How do you know?"

Joce'lynn said nothing but instead looked from the wounded hybrid to the werecat. Although she did not fully understand how, Katja knew the Ring member was correct. Lauraisha had no scent of blood on her. She was unharmed and unmarked. Dayalan had restrained himself before his thirst had reached an irrepressible level. Evidently his last scrap of control was failing him because he had ripped his own flesh against his manacles while trying to reach the princess.

"Take her. Get her out," Dayalan rasped.

Felan nodded curtly and moved to the weeping human's side. Ever so gently, he lifted her into his arms and strode out of the chamber.

"Leave. Let me die now."

Joce'lynn cocked her head. "You would rather perish than live and Turn?"

The hybrid's blood-red eyes found and held her piercing golden gaze. "Yes."

Joce'lynn frowned and turned to one of the five guardians.

"Rorin, I want a healthy winter-old lamb brought from the kitchen pens immediately. You will leave it within the prisoner's reach and you will depart this tower without a word to anyone of your errand. Is that understood?"

"Yes, My Madam. It will be done." The dwarf saluted her with both of his palms up and bowed before leaving.

Katja looked at the Ring member. "A sheep will do little to help him, My Madam. He needs Tyron's blood to ease his hunger and restore his sanity."

"I know. But if he kills the horse during feeding, we will be pushed into this nightmare yet again. The sheep will have to sate his appetite until I can make arrangements for the horse to be moved here, which will be no easy feat considering the stairs it must traverse. The sheep is small enough to be lifted up the food shaft—"

Dayalan's groan interrupted her. "Why…would you do this?"

Joce'lynn stepped toward the male and looked at him without fear. "Despite your desperate thirst, you have yet to yield to evil. I would rather see the lowest bowels of the Abomination's lair than allow a noble son of Marga's to perish. Will you fight for life long enough for me to sway the Ring to allow Caleb to visit?"

His nod caused a fresh trail of blood to ooze down his neck. "I wish to see Father again, if I can."

"Good. We will take our leave and go to the Ring Chambers immediately, then. The Creator's peace be with you."

Dayalan blinked in surprise at her benediction and then replied. "And also with you."

* * *

"The Judgment Hall is just here to our left and the session has already begun. Quickly seat yourselves," Joce'lynn said tersely before pushing them toward the lowest of four ramps. While she hurried up another ramp, the companions slipped furtively through the ramp door and onto an empty bench.

The Judgment Hall of the Ring of Sorcerers looked like a miniscule version of the Central Assembly Hall used by the General Mage Council. Petitioners sat on a bench ringing the floor and gave their requests when the Ring members called them to the floor's center platform. The platform itself was surrounded by three circular tiers rising toward the domed ceiling. Members of the Ring of Sorcerers all sat behind their own platform desks on the first tier while advisors and other high-ranking mages sat on the second tier. General spectators were welcomed on the third—at least during public meetings. Katja gazed at the various Sylvan Orders' decorative contributions to the chamber's banners and remembered that her clan's own communal amphitheater had been based on this very room's architectural design. A pang welled up inside of her as she saw her own clan's crest emblazoned on a banner just to the right of where Joce'lynn sat.

"Fellow Ring Members, I do apologize for my tardiness," Joce'lynn announced once the packmates were seated. "I have brought these prisoners to be questioned regarding the rumors of Asheken activity on Sylvan soil discussed during the General Council of Mages…"

"Rumors!" Katja hissed angrily.

"Quiet, Katja. Let her speak," Zahra said.

The werecat sat scowling and thumped her tail on the bench's underside. She glanced apprehensively at Lauraisha, who was sitting propped against Felan for support and strength. Even though they had traveled many rough leagues together, Katja could not recall a time when the human had looked less like a princess. Although all of her packmates looked suitably disheveled from their imprisonment, the grime-incrusted Lauraisha resembled a half-mad vagabond.

"If it pleases my fellows, I also request that a special magical assessment be performed on the werecat who stands accused of treasonous deception toward the General Mage Council."

Aver'lyn stood upon his stool and spoke, "May I ask, Honorable Joce'lynn, why you wish to have this examination take place?"

"Magistrate, I believe a proper magical evaluation may help discover this female's true intentions."

"Very well, such an act is granted. Now, let us move on to the purpose of this meeting. Will the Tyglesean princess please take the floor?"

Felan moved to help her, but the human shook him off.

Shoving her greasy auburn hair behind her rounded ears, the Tyglesean stepped cautiously to the center floor and bowed.

"Your Excellency," she said to the Mage Magistrate.

"Please state your name and rank for the record." he said while eyeing her disheveled appearance with disgust.

She lifted her head and met his gaze in defiance. "I am Princess Lauraisha Astrat'a of Tyglesea."

Katja heard a nervous cough from somewhere in the second tier off to her left. She glanced up and quickly spotted Mori'lyn. Even from this distance, she could see the satyr was quite ashen under his brown ringlets. The werecat quickly scanned the crowded second tier for Caleb. She found him cloaked in shadow toward the top of the tier about two sections over from where the little traitor sat. Once she caught his eye, she dropped her gaze deliberately to Mori'lyn. Caleb followed her stare and mouthed "Mori'lyn?" when he saw the satyr. At the werecat's confirming nod, the ancient mage's smile was full of fang.

The Ring of Sorcerers' Chief Counselor Si'lyn stood and cleared his throat. "Do you know the charges leveled against you, Your Highness?"

"No, My Sir."

"You were brought before our distinguished dreamdrifter Mori'lyn and found to be untruthful about your experiences discussed before the General Council of Mages. You thus stand accused of perjury when discussing the supposed Asheken invasion of Sylvan territories and inciting panic among the governing mages with your fictitious account. How do you answer such charges?"

"I claim absolute innocence, Your Grace."

"You would deny the validity of the charges set against you?"

"I do deny their validity. Mori'lyn is the one circulating malicious falsehoods, not I!"

Twittering whispers encircled the room and then died instantly at Si'lyn's aggravated gaze. "Your Highness, we are here to discuss your supposed misdeeds, not your opinions of Mori'lyn's actions."

"There are those who can both attest to my integrity and corroborate my story, My Sir."

"If you are referring to the Feliconian werecat Katja Escari," Aver'lyn said, "she also stands accused of perjury. I also highly doubt that a skinshifter mage is in any position to attest to her own integrity—much less any other being's."

That last comment drew simultaneous snarls from Katja and Felan.

"The little elf had better watch his mouth or I will take great pleasure in ramming my axe's butt through his pernicious teeth!" the werewolf whispered.

"Easy, Felan." Zahra gripped the hulking werewolf's arm to keep him seated, but even her jaw was tight.

Joce'lynn addressed the assembly. "Can anyone corroborate Princess Lauraisha's story?"

She looked expectantly toward Caleb, but instead a much younger voice answered from across the room. "I believe I can, My Madam."

Zahra gasped and stood at the sight of the speaker. She was by no means the only one to do so, either. One hundred eyes all stared in amazement as the leather-clad dryad Qenethala made her way from the third tier to the floor. Zahra was there to greet her as soon as she reached the bottom step.

"How did you escape?" she said while hugging the newcomer.

If Zahra's embrace was tight, her half-sister's answering embrace was almost bone-crushing. "I will explain my journey later. For now, I must give you fondest greetings from our mother."

"Is she—?"

"Zahlathra is well…although circumstances in the Glen have become dire. Every Sylvan tribe and clan member within ten leagues of the Glen has sought refuge with us and the deadwalkers have laid siege to our mountain. They cannot pass through the gates, but our food is in short supply.

"The situation was perilous enough that the Queen Mother risked sending three messengers here to plead for aid in case you did not make it through."

"The other two?"

Qenethala sadly shook her head. "Lost to the enemy. I had to pierce Elena with my own sunsilver sickle before escaping."

Zahra bowed her head in sudden grief until the dwarf Si'lyn's high voice brought both dryads back to full awareness.

"Please state your name and your affiliation please, My Madam," Sy'lyn instructed.

"Counselor Si'lyn, I am Qenethala Rahalazel, personal envoy of the dryad Queen Mother Zahlathra Etheal."

"Would you explain to us how you know the young females currently under question?" Si'lyn asked.

"Princess Lauraisha and the Feliconian werecat Katja Escari were guests of the Sol'ece Mountain dryads some four months ago, My Sir."

"What was the nature of their visit?" Aver'lyn asked.

"They were being hunted by zombies, Magistrate. We allowed them to take refuge with us and then smuggled them out of the Glen before the Asheken invaders could lay siege to our mountain home, as they do now."

The tiers were abuzz with whispered conversations once again.

"How, may I inquire, did you escape the Glen if it is besieged?" Aver'lyn smirked as he studied her.

"By the Creator's mercy, I helped escort them along an ancient trading trail well-hidden by shadowshaper magic, My Sir." Qenethala answered.

"I see. And you say Princess Lauraisha and Katja Escari were indeed being chased by Asheken soul-slaves?" Si'lyn asked.

"Yes, Counselor, I was with the group of dryad warriors who defended our main gate as the two rode through. Our vine-arrows were the only things that kept them and their horses from being mauled to death."

"Have you any evidence of these deadwalkers with you?"

"Zahlathra bade me to give you this." With one gloved hand, Qenethala pulled a small pale object from her belt pouch and held it up. Katja's startled gasp matched those of most other mages. It was an ear! It was shaped like an elf's except its pointed tip was slightly jagged with the characteristic dull black spike of a ghoul.

"Well..." Aver'lyn stammered. "Well, this is...certainly the strongest piece of evidence we have yet seen. As to the matter of integrity, Qenethala, would you say that Princess

Lauraisha is an honorable individual who tries to her utmost ability to tell the truth to the fullest?"

"Yes, Magistrate, I would."

"Would you also say this of the Feliconian skinshifter, Katja Escari?"

Qenethala gazed intently at the werecat before answering. "Excellency, I will say this. While I have always been suspicious of werecats in general and skinshifters specifically, the Queen Mother and our elders entrusted this werecat with our lives and sent all of the aid and good will of our kind with her and the human princess in the hope that they would successfully complete their quest. Sir, they did not fail us and stand before you now to warn you of the Asheken invasion, as do I. They should be exonerated for their valor as should Princess Zahra Zahlathrazel Etheal and Felan Bardrick."

Katja bowed her head slightly toward the dryad. She looked around, observing the eerie hush that had overtaken the Judgment Hall at the dryad's words. Qenethala's pronouncement had caused several of attendees to blanch just as pale as Mori'lyn. Katja couldn't blame or belittle them for their fear. She had lived with the nightmare of deadwalkers' destruction for months and now these mages had finally been plunged into the same lurid reality. The fact that all Sylvans would soon be called to war against such horrendous foes was daunting to say the least. Suddenly Katja understood why so many of the mages would rather think her a lying warmonger than face the hideousness of such a reality.

Zahra gave her own corroborative testimony, which was quickly followed by Felan's recounting and a brief summary of Lauraisha's story. Katja was then called to testify and to be formally examined by Joce'lynn. The werecat nervously moved to the center floor and waited as the Ring member calmly stood.

"Katja Escari, I wish to ask you a series of questions. I expect your complete cooperation and honesty when replying. The details that you give are extremely important."

"Yes, My Madam," Katja said under Joce'lynn's piercing gaze.

"At the time of Princess Lauraisha's examination by Mori'lyn, where were you?"

"I was sitting on the bench outside his study, Your Honor. I had waited there with the princess before she went in and I stayed outside the room while they were doing the dreamdrifting session."

"And did you actually see her collapse?"

"No, My Madam, but I did feel it when she did."

"Physically?"

"No, I can mentally feel when she is in pain, and her pain was immense before she fainted."

That comment sent a murmur skittering through the crowd. Joce'lynn and Si'lyn both silenced the crowd and then the female asked Katja to recount her experiences outside the room. The werecat glanced at Lauraisha and, at the princess's small nod, proceeded to tell the events in question. She spared no detail about her visions or about the crimson haze surrounding Mori'lyn and Lauraisha when she burst into the mage's warded study. Her descriptions caused several intermittent gasps and hisses from her audience especially when she explained the strange crimson haze that followed Mori'lyn wherever he walked. Even now it clung to him like a fog and he was not the only one in the crowd on whom that eerie fog settled. As Katja spoke, she noticed that her crimson sight also fell upon one of the highest ranking mages in the room. It vanished so quickly, though, that the werecat wondered if she had imagined it.

Once the werecat's tale ended, Joce'lynn once again stood. "Chief Counselor Si'lyn, I request that you and I form a Bond of Truth around this female."

Si'lyn bowed his consent and then began to charmchant in a soft voice. Joce'lynn meanwhile intently stared at Katja until the little werecat felt that her body might be literally crushed by the force of the wraithwalker's gaze and the charmchanter's song. Katja stood strong through the battering magic for what seemed an eternity. When at last Si'lyn's voice faltered and Joce'lynn blinked, Katja slumped with relief.

Finally Joce'lynn spoke. "My Distinguished Colleagues, can there be any doubt about the quality of being with whom we are dealing?"

"None," Si'lyn said breathlessly.

"But can she be genuinely pure if she is a skinshifter?" the lone centaur Ring Member asked.

"Do not forget, Peha'lyn, that Katja's mother Devra was one of the most powerful skinshifters of the Second Age. She was also reputed as one of the noblest warriors," Si'lyn said.

Joce'lynn nodded. "Besides, I highly doubt Kevros would have taken her as a lifemate if he'd found her to be untrustworthy. Those of us who knew him, know that his judgement of character was almost always accurate."

General murmurs of agreement met Joce'lynn's claim. Katja stared at her, stunned. Her mother was a skinshifter? How could that be?

"I have tested this werecat once before. I can now tell you based on that experience and on this intense collaborative examination that she is a wraithwalker mage of extraordinary ability."

The hall around them erupted in a storm of applause and the little werecat stood in the midst of it utterly bewildered.

XXIII

TREACHEROUS TIMES

There was a sudden outcry from the Second Tier as a scuffle broke out between mages. Mori'lyn had knocked over two other beings in his desperate attempt to escape from the Judgment Hall.

"Stop him!" Si'lyn yelled.

Before anyone else could move, Caleb was flying fast on leathery pinions toward the squealing little satyr. Mages screeched and dove out of the way as he swooped to tackle the coward just in front of the chamber's upper doorway.

Si'lyn took his time silencing the outraged throng. "My compliments, Master Caleb, for that well-timed apprehension of the mage Morinus. You honor us as always with your presence in this hallowed hall."

Katja grinned at Si'lyn's omission of Mori'lyn's rank, but she noticed that the mages nearest to Caleb looked far more terrified than honored by his attendance.

"Now then, distinguished colleagues," the dwarf counselor continued, "since our assessment of this werecat's truth-perceiving abilities is conclusive and her story of deadwalkers has been verified by both physical and perceptual evidence, I ask that the accusations leveled against her and her companions be scratched from the records and their status as guests and pupils of this Citadel conclave be reinstated. All agreed say 'lo aideem'."

"Lo aideem," was the unanimous vote.

"I also strongly recommend that the apprehended accuser

be imprisoned pending questioning about his motives for lying about these companions' testimonies. What say you?"

"Lo aideem," was heard again from all twelve Ring members on the first tier.

Si'lyn and Joce'lynn then performed a Bond of Truth on Felan, which exonerated the skinshifter and further strengthened the packmates' account of the deadwalkers' activities. When the dwarf finally called for a declaration of war, the Ring members unanimously consented.

Once the Ring of Sorcerers' meeting came to a close, Caleb gave the hysterical satyr over to the Citadel Guardians. He then made his way to the floor to congratulate the packmates even as other mages vied for their attention. Talk on the floor ranged from jovial to brooding and Katja felt almost numb in the midst of it. Si'lyn, Joce'lynn, and Caleb made their way through the crowd—dispensing orders as they went—and led the companions away from the Judgment Hall. They all walked in silence through the crowded corridors while mages of all races and ranks hurried past with quick bows. Somewhere in the Citadel, a heavy bell tolled to signal all Sylvans that war was now upon them.

Only when they reached the mage apprentices' residence hall, did Joce'lynn turn to the packmates. "You must wash yourselves and eat. Tomorrow you will begin full training as mages and, I will warn you now, your lessons will be especially difficult because we must train you to readiness for war."

"Honorable Joce'lynn, who will be our instructors?" Katja asked.

Joce'lynn frowned in thought. "Princess Lauraisha will be paired with fireforger Master Nicho'lyn as will Dayalan once he regains his strength. Even with his skill demonstration, I don't relish giving Dayalan any sort of mage rank until I know that he can control his fire and his thirst with equal skill. Now, since our principal dreamdrifting instructor is charged with sedition, we'll have to find another suitable mentor for that craft. Felan will also be especially difficult to train since his skillset is one that has remained untutored for centuries now. I'm sure his skill far surpasses anything that our library tomes have to say on the subject, but we'll see if he can prove me wrong..."

The werewolf grinned at her praise and then asked if he might undertake the rank test so that he could possibly qualify as a mage instructor.

Joce'lynn and Si'lyn both looked momentarily stunned. Finally the dwarf male spoke, "That is actually a perfect idea. The Creator only knows how long we've prayed for a proper one. You'll have to ignore Aver'lyn. Unlike that superstitious buffoon, there are some Ring members who would gladly see skinshifter pupils return to this isle. Very well, you may undergo the examination, but, if you should succeed, you may teach only when a mage adept or master is present until you become more accustomed to mentorship."

"As for you, Katja," Si'lyn continued, "you will be learning the finer points of skinshifting from Felan if he passes the initiate test and Mistress Joce'lynn will instruct you in the ways of a wraithwalker. You will all need advanced combat training which I will leave to Master Caleb if he is willing—"

The ancient mage grinned with full fangs. "I would be honored."

"Also, I think Princess Zahra would do well to take her newly grown mold to Master Peha'lyn for proper sproutsinging scrutiny."

"You all will be staying in the original rooms set aside for you," Joce'lynn said once they had reached the familiar hall. "Guards will be posted outside your doors at all times for extra security. We have no idea if Mori'lyn acted alone in his deceit or if his malicious behavior is part of some grand design by another conspirator—"

"Joce'lynn, really! You don't have to scare the poor mage initiates any more than they already have been during the last few days. Mori'lyn has always done things to suit his own ends and rarely takes orders from anyone else if he can help it. It would be highly unusual for him to have an accomplice to his misdeeds."

"I agree that it is odd, Si'lyn, but that fits the pattern of behavior in this instance. In the many seasons that I've known him, Mori'lyn has never done anything so unscrupulous as to jeopardize his status among the other mages. This whole episode is highly unusual—even for him. It stands to reason, therefore, that nothing is quite what we assume that it is."

Si'lyn rolled his eyes. "Look, we can debate the mage's motives later. You already know that I will grant you full access to him for investigation. If you want guardians posted outside the initiates' doors, fine. I will grant that so long as it is clearly understood that these mages may freely leave their rooms at any time without escort."

The dwarf turned to the packmates. "All the same, I expect the lot of you to be extremely cautious. The last thing I need is for young mages to do something foolish and end up maimed or dead while trying to show off their abilities. Now, I highly suggest that you all get some rest and food for you will surely need both if you're to succeed in your lessons."

"Yes, My Sir," the packmates said in unison before excusing themselves to their respective quarters.

As they left, the werecat saw the two Ring members whispering to Caleb. Dayalan's name was all that Katja could catch before Felan requested that she shut the door.

* * *

"So what is a wrath watcher?" Lauraisha asked after they all had taken much-needed baths and joined together to eat and discuss the day's previous events in the human's chamber.

"Wraithwalker," Zahra corrected her absently as she passed around a plate of bread.

"It's absurd," Katja replied before biting into a succulent lamb shank, her first fresh meal in days.

Felan frowned thoughtfully at the werecat. "I don't think so, Katja."

"Why?" She looked questioningly at the werewolf as he too took some of the meat.

He shrugged and passed a bowl of dried peaches to the dryad. "I just think it's likely you do have the gift based on the way you react to certain things."

"How so?"

"Your shared dreamdrifting experiences with Lauraisha, for one, are extremely unusual. I recall hearing a story somewhere that claimed a wraithwalker could share some mages' gifts for a short time. Of course, Joce'lynn is the only wraithwalker still living other than you, so it's hard to say what is accurate and what isn't.

"Essentially, the Ring member has just proclaimed you to have one of the most powerful mage abilities in our world, and that ranks you with the highest-ranking fireforgers even though you aren't yet trained. Considering your instinctive way of making others tell you their secrets and your deep intuition of other beings' true character, I agree with her assessment. You were, after all, the first in our group to recognize Dayalan as something other than a full vampire…"

"As if that matters now," Zahra grumbled.

Lauraisha scowled at her and then turned her attention to Katja. "So a wraithwalker mage is more intuitive about the good or evil in others?"

"Yes, but there is more," the werecat said. "Legendary wraithwalkers had the ability to see the depths of good and evil in everything. They could often see Pyrekin in their own realm of existence and sometimes even feel the influences of the Wraith Realm itself. They, along with the fireforgers, were the most effective Asheken hunters because they could literally see the evil that the deadwalkers exuded and purge it from them without being as affected by evil's Taint as most other beings are."

"Hence why you weren't seriously injured when you touched Kayten?" the human asked.

Katja frowned. She had been hurt, but not when she'd touched her Fallen brother in love. Only when she'd tried to strangle him in hatred had she felt the Taint's sting.

The Tyglesean frowned. "What is it like to see evil?"

"It's a bit like smelling a corpse." The werecat wrinkled her nose. "I can see a crimson haze or shapes around a particular being, but the color is so foul to view that my eyes often water. Come to think of it, I sometimes smell the evil before I see it, too. It's…strange to explain."

"Did you see evil around Dayalan when you rescued me?"

Katja frowned, suddenly bewildered. "No."

The human bobbed her head then, as if finally deciding something.

"Lauraisha, you cannot expect Katja to catch the presence

of evil every time," exclaimed Zahra. "She'll have to undergo intense training before she is *that* good, and even Joce'lynn misses things."

The human looked from the dryad to the werecat and back. "Why do you hate him so much?"

"Hate who?"

"Dayalan. Since we met, you've constantly scorned him as some sort of leper!"

Zahra's brown eyes suddenly softened with awed bewilderment. "He is a danger to all of us. Twice you have witnessed his depraved hunger and yet you still defend him?"

"I..." tears suddenly glistened in the human's eyes.

Finally Katja intervened. "Zahra, Dayalan is not evil. He may have the potential for great evil, but so do the rest of us. We all can be Turned—I nearly was—but, Dayalan is not his brother. I have seen Daeryn's mind. I almost bonded with it and I can tell you with absolute certainty that where Daeryn has failed Dayalan will succeed."

"Why?"

She frowned for a moment, trying to find the proper words to explain what she felt. "Because unlike Daeryn, Dayalan has felt the enticement of the deadwalkers' power and has forsaken it. Like the rest of us, Dayalan fears their power and the misery it causes more than he fears pain or even death. It's that fear—that hatred of evil—that keeps him noble."

"I too believe that Dayalan would rather die than become such a monster," Felan added.

The dryad cleared her throat noncommittally and changed the subject. "When did Joce'lynn say we each had to meet with our instructors?"

"At nine bells tomorrow morning," Felan answered just as the bell began tolling its evening count of eleven.

"In that event, I suggest we all find our beds. The morning will dawn early enough as it is."

Reluctantly they all agreed, bid each other good night, and sought their own rooms and thoughts. Katja went to sleep that night with a troubled heart. Although she knew that Dayalan would rather die than Turn, she also knew his instinct—by his own admission—was to covet power. Zahra's cynicism was indeed well placed and Katja could not deny that fact.

When the little werecat finally found dreams, their content troubled her even more than her conscious thoughts. Again and again she relived the massacre of her village and the death of her parents. Each remembrance ended with the eerie figure of a manticore on a blood-bathed battlefield staring at her and Kumos's voice whispering, "Beware the traitor or the blood will be your own!"

She did not remember screeching in her sleep, but her cries soon brought Lauraisha to her bedside with a basin of cold water to drown out the nightmares. Her last dream vision was of a crimson-eyed dullahan glowering at Mori'lyn, then Lauraisha's face swam into view.

The werecat sat up shivering. "What happened?"

The apologetic human looked just as haggard as the werecat felt. "You were screaming for your family."

Katja looked past her and saw that the servants' door adjoining their rooms was ajar. It must be thinner than she had originally thought.

"I didn't mean to wake you…again," she said, biting her lower lip.

"It's of little consequence as I was still up."

"You shared the dream?"

Lauraisha rubbed her tired eyes and groaned. "Some of it."

"Jierira, sorry. What is the hour?"

"The bell just tolled twice. Do you think someone put a time-keeping charm on it?"

"Probably," Katja replied and made room for Lauraisha on the bed. "What thoughts finally chased away your dreams?"

The human shrugged.

"Dayalan?"

"I…yes."

"You're worried about him."

She bobbed her head without meeting Katja's eyes.

Katja sniffed the air and cocked her head. "Are you falling in love with him?"

Lauraisha looked positively shocked. "How…how did you know?"

"I know you well enough by now to know when you're

pining for someone."

"If you breathe a word of this to anyone—"

"Lauraisha, who would I tell? More importantly, who would take me seriously? He is twice your age!"

The human hung her head. "I know. There are many marriages between females my age and males his age in my kingdom, but those marriages are always arranged between politically-minded families. I have yet to hear of such a relationship being harmonious."

Katja sighed. "I cannot truthfully say that I approve."

"Do you hate him as well?"

"No, Lauraisha, that is not it at all. I feel that a certain level of maturity is needed before two beings mate for life. I don't believe you are ready for marriage and I know he isn't."

"You told Felan your feelings, did you not?"

Slowly, Katja nodded. "Yes."

"Then how is our situation any different?"

The werecat stared at the human a moment, suddenly wondering if the two relationships actually *were* all that different. *No matter how deeply we might love each other,* Katja thought, *Felan and I are still separated by race and culture. Lauraisha and Dayalan are separated by race, maturity, and Dayalan's thirst. And I have no idea if the male might indeed return the human's affection, but would it really change their circumstances for the better if he does? Most likely, it will only make things worse.*

She ran a paw over her weary eyes. "Are you going to tell him then?"

"Certainly not!"

"May I ask why?"

"Because I have no idea how he would react. Try as I might, I cannot understand him as well as I do anyone else in our pack."

"I'll admit that he is quite the enigma."

"And he is barely sixteen winters younger than my father," the little human muttered while rubbing her temples. She leaned on Katja for support. "Toward the end, in that tower, he almost reminded me of my father...almost."

The werecat wrapped an arm protectively around the human's trembling shoulders. "No good can come of your brooding over him. Trust me when I say that."

"I know," Lauraisha nodded. "May I stay with you until dawn?"

The werecat smiled at the human she had come to regard as a little sister and pulled an extra blanket around the human's shoulders. "Stay as long as you like."

* * *

Morning rays illuminated the thick rug where the human and werecat slept with their pillows before the hearth in Katja's room. The embers of the fireplace were still glowing with a ruddy hue that seemed sulky next to the piercing sunlight streaming through the gap in the heavy green drapes. It was neither the sun's first light nor the embers' last heat, however, that awoke the slumbering females.

Katja bolted upright when the Citadel bell began tolling in rapid succession. Lauraisha was up and wrapped in a robe and shawl a moment later. Together the two of them wrenched the door open and demanded to know what was so urgent from the guardian posted there.

"A mage prisoner of high rank was found dead in his cell this morning," the elf told them.

"Who?" the females asked simultaneously.

"Nothing can be certain yet, but your former companion Dayalan may have had something to do with it. He was found near that part of the dungeons at the same time the Citadel Guardians found the body. No one is certain how he escaped the tower."

"What!"

"That is the rumor. In any event, if the two of you as well as the dryad and the werewolf will all promptly dress, I must escort you to Mistress Joce'lynn."

They shut the door, and then changed into their tan mage robes and black mage initiate sashes. Then they roused Zahra and Felan and told them to dress as well. Katja was, for once, grateful that she had had a full water bath the night before so that she would be somewhat presentable this morning. As soon as the others were ready, the four companions followed the elf guardian to the spell training chamber where Joce'lynn waited. They heard Caleb's raised voice as they entered the vaulted room.

"Jocelana, you know full well that he had nothing to do with it!" the ancient mage shouted.

"What would you have me do, Caleb?" Joce'lynn exclaimed. "Defy the Ring and turn him loose? I have already skirted the edge of treason by allowing him to feed on our livestock! Three did he desiccate before he escaped."

Katja and the others stopped short at the door, not sure what to do. Clearly they were intruding.

"Dayalan is my son, Jocelana; the last of my family. You cannot allow Peha'lyn and Si'lyn to pass judgment on him simply because he requires the blood of beasts instead of the meat of beasts to survive. To do so is a travesty of all things righteous!"

"I cannot continue to protect Dayalan, not when he literally had Mori'lyn's blood on his claws! I am sorry."

"Enough of you, hypocrite!" Caleb hissed.

He stormed out of the room past Katja and the others without even a parting glance. Joce'lynn, meanwhile, stood looking after him and chewing her lower lip. Katja had the distinct impression that the Sorceress was fighting back tears as she watched Caleb go.

With a curt gesture, Joce'lynn finally ushered the packmates further into the training chamber and signaled the guardians to close the massive double doors. Once they had crossed the boundary of the magic privacy ring set in the room's center, Joce'lynn wearily bid them all to sit.

"As you have undoubtedly heard, Mori'lyn was murdered last night while in his cell and Dayalan is the most likely culprit. Before any of you say a word, the facts stand as such: Dayalan escaped his tower early last night and was found this morning with blood on his hands just outside the cell where Mori'lyn died. Thus the Ring believes him to be Mori'lyn's killer."

"But you yourself said that Dayalan was not evil!" Lauraisha retorted.

"Just because a being isn't evil, does not mean he is incapable of a crime, Princess. Some of the vilest acts in our world have been committed by beings with the best intentions in mind. Right now, it's less important for me to determine his motivations than to discover if he did, in fact, execute the mage. I have a few days to confirm the perpetrator and then the Ring will convene to decide his fate.

"In the meantime, we have locked Dayalan up again and have taken extra precautions to ensure that he does not escape a second time. I also must forbid all of you from seeing him until this inquiry is finished."

"What happens if Dayalan is found guilty of Mori'lyn's murder?" Zahra asked quietly.

Joce'lynn cleared her throat uncomfortably. "The punishment for murder is death."

Zahra looked stunned. Tears spilled down Lauraisha's cheeks as the dryad awkwardly held her. Felan and Katja glanced at each other. By his look, the werewolf believed Dayalan's guilt was as likely as Katja skinshifting into a toad. Their attention was diverted, however, when a liopion Ring member and a centaur Ring member entered the room.

Joce'lynn bowed to the new arrivals and continued, "Because of this highly disturbing chain of events, none of you will be able to travel unaccompanied. Also, since I will personally oversee the investigation until this unpleasantness is resolved, I must leave you all under Master Nicho'lyn's and Master Peha'lyn's guidance. I will check all of your progress periodically and, Katja, I will see to your training personally when I am finished with my investigative duties. Farewell for now."

With that, Joce'lynn bowed and strode out of the room. Her absence seemed to signal the beginning of training because Nicho'lyn and Peha'lyn immediately split the companions into groups. Felan and Katja were paired together and instructed to work on refining their skinshifting techniques within the confines of a smaller protective ring while Zahra worked on her sproutsinging with Peha'lyn in another small ring and the liopion mage Nicho'lyn inspected Lauraisha's flame in the main ring.

Katja was grateful for the full coverage that her initiate robe provided her during the skinshifting practice sessions. Even within the ring's protection, there was little visual privacy and that bothered her while in human form. She had difficulty concentrating because she was constantly distracted by thoughts of Dayalan and by the instructors' constant movement within the other two rings. She had never met a liopion, so watching the lion-like being shoot fireballs out of the hooked-tip of his scorpion tail was simultaneously fascinating and unnerving.

The six beings worked in pairs until twelve bells signaled the midday break. By the time the packmates had made it to the main eat hall, Katja was in a surly mood. Sloppy skinshifting had given her a headache and the throbbing became progressively worse while she and the others waited for Zahra to retrieve a mold flask she had mistakenly left in the practice chamber. The dryad's momentary forgetfulness meant that the packmates had a drastically shortened eat period before they had to reconvene for afternoon weapons training.

They entered the weapons practice chamber just as the thirteenth bell chimed. Vraelth greeted them there and explained that Caleb was unavoidably detained, so he would be training them instead. Despite his youth, the elf charmchanter proved to be an excellent instructor in the arts of combat. He used the first third of the training period leading all pupils in basic weaponless fighting techniques and then paired each packmate with another mage initiate or novice based on his or her weapon specialty.

Katja was paired with a centaur in staff combat while Lauraisha and an elf practiced their swordsmanship. Felan found a dwarf as his battle-axe partner and Zahra paired with Vraelth for curved knife and sickle fighting. The day seemed to disappear as Katja worked with her partner Garret to refine her staff skills. After the morning's sinister revelations, it felt so good to just hit something. She had learned some good tricks from Dayalan and put them to effective use against her larger, stronger opponent. She noticed her friends all thriving, especially Zahra, who was already an expert with several different short blades. Even Lauraisha used her sunsilver sword with fair precision. The human's brothers had certainly taught her well.

"Well done, all of you! My special compliments to our new initiates, who have handled themselves so adeptly against some tough opponents. That is all for this day. I will see you all at thirteen bells tomorrow."

The sweaty packmates all bowed to their partners and to their instructor before departing with their guardian escorts for the library. Nicho'lyn and Peha'lyn had both given them evening reading assignments to be finished before their next meeting. Once they all had found the scripts that they needed, they quickly stashed the pile of scrolls and bound books in Lauraisha's room, and then trekked to the mess hall in search of food.

That evening found three of the companions studying their assigned texts in their own rooms. Felan, however, had to revisit the library after the evening's eat so that he could have easy access to the entire skinshifting manuscript shelf. His goal was to skim all of the available texts for any information that might emerge during his instructor qualification examination.

Katja's attempted study lasted only until her head resumed its throbbing. The noon eat had banished the ache, but now it resurfaced with full vengeance. Try as she might to concentrate, Katja could not make her watery eyes focus on the writing in front of her. With an exasperated growl, she rolled up the scroll and stalked into Lauraisha's room.

Apparently, the human was having just as much difficulty concentrating as Katja. The werecat found her curled up by the fireplace staring at the text before her with silent tears dripping down her cheeks.

Lauraisha looked up in surprise when the werecat put a paw her shoulder. "I thought you were studying."

"I thought you were, too." Katja sighed. "So my head aches and your heart aches. Why don't we do some reconnoitering of our own and find out what really happened to Dayalan and Mori'lyn?"

"How? We can't go near them! We cannot even find Dayalan!"

Katja cocked her sore head at the female and held up her shard-imbedded spearhead. "Did you forget that we all carry these?"

Lauraisha stared at her for a moment before recognition dawned. "Oh."

Katja put a paw to her temple in exasperation. "Well, dreamdrifter, why are you waiting? You're the only one who can call to him."

The human looked at her in sudden panic. "What do I say?"

The werecat groaned. "Just ask him the truth and be done with it."

The little human nodded and then closed her eyes to gather her concentration. Katja felt the dreamdrifter's magic build and then flow through the shard, searching out Dayalan's counterpart.

"Dayalan! Dayalan! Please answer me!" Lauraisha shrieked through her shard.

"Lauraisha? What happened? Are you safe? What's wrong?" Dayalan's voice shook with fear.

"Dayalan, tell me you didn't kill him!"

Katja hid her face in her paws. "Oh, that was subtle."

"I did not touch him. Lauraisha, I swear to you on my mother's fire, I did not kill Mori'lyn. Do you believe me?"

"Yes," the human said, bobbing her head emphatically.

"Lauraisha, listen to me...You have to listen to me! You and the others are in grave danger, do you understand?"

Katja lowered her paws and looked at Lauraisha with sudden alertness. Dayalan never panicked. "Dayalan, what are you—?"

"Katja? We don't have time for questions. Just listen. I know what killed Mori'lyn! I was able to fly out of the tower last night to feed from Tyron. The horse conveyed to me that he had heard a scream within the area of the Citadel just below his stables. I left him to investigate and found Mori'lyn dead. Lauraisha, Katja, he looked as if he'd been trampled by a horse. Then I noticed that his neck had been torn open by fangs rivaling mine."

"Are you certain?"

"Trust me. You are all in terrible danger! There is a dullahan on the isle! Where are you?"

"In our own rooms."

"Find Joce'lynn, Lauraisha! She must be warned! None of my guards would listen to my pleas to summon her—"

A scream from Zahra's room stilled the hybrid's voice. Katja tried the servants' door, but it was bolted and magically warded from the inside.

"What's happening?" Dayalan asked.

"Help! Unhand me, monster!" the dryad shouted and the werecat felt the floor tremble beneath her.

"Zahra!" Katja screeched. "Lauraisha, weapons!"

Katja ran to retrieve her staff from her room, and then joined the sword-bearing human in the hallway. Their guardians were all slumped against the wall with slow trails of dark blood oozing down their necks.

"Merciful Creator!" Lauraisha exclaimed as she saw the werewolf, satyr, and two elves twitching in their death throws.

Katja grimaced at the bodies as she tried to open Zahra's locked main door. An odd movement caught the corner of her eye. A dagger came whistling out of its sheath and then stabbed straight at her heart just as she rolled out of the way.

"Get back!" she roared at Lauraisha. "They've been Turned!"

Eerie cackles bubbled out of the fiends' mouths as they drew themselves off the bloody floor gripping their weapons. Katja ripped the spearheads from their leather thongs around her neck and shoved each into position on the end of her bone staff while Lauraisha held her sunsilver saber at the ready. Beyond Zahra's door, Katja could hear shouts and then the shattering of glass as Zahra tried to fend off her attacker.

Whatever happens, Katja, it has been an honor to hunt with you, the human sent out her thought as she took a defensive half-crouch.

Katja smiled at the human's use of the Feliconian endearment. *It is my honor to call you friend and lytzsibba, Lauraisha.*

The werecat and human watched as the two ghouls moved straight toward them while the grim and imp circled wide to surround the Sylvan pair. The deadwalkers' advance was suddenly checked as the human called magic into her sword and bright orange flame lit the length of its blade.

Lauraisha stepped toward the right ghoul while Katja flanked her, all the while watching the ghoul on their left paw. Lauraisha's thrust was parried by her opponent just as the werecat swung her staff to meet her foe's attack. Bone met iron while sunsilver sang against steel. As they fought, Katja and Lauraisha opened their minds to each other and coordinated their attacks to drive the ghouls away from Zahra's door. By the time Lauraisha had landed her first blow into deadwalker flesh, the grim and imp had completed their maneuver and cut the females off from any attempted escape.

Katja used the distraction of the ghoul's agonizing screech as her chance to stab a sunsilver spearhead into her opponent's eye. The narrow blade passed well into the ghoul's skull and sent him writhing to the marble floor in anguish. The strike to his brain did not destroy the fiend, but the sunsilver's essence did leave him paralyzed throughout his entire right side.

Primal rage took hold inside her and Katja roared with the all strength of her soul. Her screech shook the building and momentarily stunned the Turned satyr sneaking up behind her. She turned in time to meet the imp's short-sword strike and then pushed him back with a well-place kick to the chest.

Lauraisha, meanwhile, had used her first successful blow to send flames flicking up the arm of her opponent. The mage fire brought the screaming ghoul to his knees while she circled around him and lopped off his head. The grotesque thing went skittering toward a crowd of mage pupils that had begun gathering in the hall outside their rooms thanks to the werecat's war cry. Beings ran screaming from the flaming skull as Katja, Lauraisha, and their opponents continued their deadly dance.

A few brave shadowshaper mage pupils moved to help until Katja hissed at them to stay back and told the shadowshapers to protect the rest of the group with Shield Spells. The last thing she or Lauraisha needed was for someone to do something foolish and get ensnared as a hostage or, worse yet, to distract her or Lauraisha in a dangerous moment.

"Someone go find one of the Ring Sorcerers!" Katja commanded as she dodged a blow from the imp—his blade whistling just past her chin. Sweat had begun dripping into the werecat's eyes as she and the human dodged and parried their foes' weapons. They were tiring, but their attackers weren't. She hissed at the situation. Neither she nor Lauraisha could hope to survive much longer at this pace without a miracle.

It came in the form of Felan pushing his way through the crowd behind Si'lyn and Joce'lynn. Pandemonium met the mages' arrival as the door to Zahra's room was suddenly blasted out of its frame from the inside. The door hit the opposite wall and shattered into a myriad of oak splinters. Those closest to the blast had to shield themselves from the dangerous debris. Nonetheless a splinter caught Katja full force in the head just as the braying imp advanced from her right flank.

"No, you don't!" Lauraisha yelled.

The human caught the imp on the right side of his chest with a flaming throwing knife just as Katja hit the hard floor. She lay there stunned as a crimson haze flowered in her vision. Then the blurry figure of a centaur bolted out of Zahra's bedchamber into the hallway.

Trapped against the Ring Spells, Peha'lyn turned to face his enraged opponent. He had only a bleeding stump where his left foreleg should have been. The centaur cowered near the far side of the hall as Dayalan stalked bloody and bruised out of the dryad's room wielding Felan's sunsilver battle axe.

"If I have to, dullahan, I will take you one piece at a time!" Dayalan bellowed and advanced toward the other mage, his eyes glowing violet.

XXIV

THE HATCHLING'S CHOICE

Movement on the edge of her vision caught Katja's attention and she turned away from Dayalan's attack of the Turned centaur to find herself eyeing death in the face. The half-paralyzed ghoul had crawled up behind her, an envenomed dagger held in his one good paw. Before he could plunge it into her face, however, Katja instinctively drove her staff toward the ghoul's arm. The spearhead found its mark within her foe's shoulder, throwing off his aim. The werecat hissed as the dagger's tip slashed a shallow gash across her forehead and jerked the staff free of the screeching ghoul. Dizzily, she rolled out of the fiend's reach.

A snarling Felan cleaved the monster's head in two with a borrowed sunsilver broadsword even as Katja reached to remove the door sliver still piercing her left ear. She delved into her soul for the skinshifting magic needed to repair her head wounds and willed herself to change. The ear puncture immediately began to close, but the poisoned gash only foamed and oozed all the more.

"We have to help Zahra," she hissed between clenched fangs as she tried to push herself to a stand.

"I'll see to her; you need to stay still until the harmhealers come!" Joce'lynn said and ran into the room just as Si'lyn assaulted the grim. Katja struggled to stay on her back paws just as the Turned werewolf crumpled to the ground under the duel force of Lauraisha's Wakeless Sleep spell and a barrage of Si'lyn's enchanted oak splinters. Three cleaving blows of Si'lyn's flanged sunsilver mace completed the grim's destruction.

"Katja, are you well?" the dreamdrifter called.

"I'll be fine if—"

"Behind you!"

The werecat could not react in time to avoid Peha'lyn snatching her around the torso and setting his fangs against her neck.

"Come at me again, curs, and the changeling dies!" the dullahan said.

Katja tried to squirm out of his hold, but it was hopeless. The fight and the poisoned cut had robbed her of most of her strength, while desperation bolstered her captor's grip.

"Katja, wraithwalk!" Joce'lynn yelled.

The werecat frantically delved into her soul to open her wraithwalker's sight. Crimson exploded around her for the second time that day as she prepared her mind to attack the evil she saw pervading this Asheken. From somewhere in her kithood, Katja dredged up a memory of her father explaining the Darkkyn beings who first gave the Drosskin and Asheken their tainted power. She recited a crusader's prayer that Kevros had taught her.

"I am a bondservant of the Creator, sanctified by Aribem's dying fire! In the holy names of the Creator and of Aribem, I command you to flee!" she roared at the crimson-covered monsters.

A scream pierced her mind and she saw writhing shapes shred out of the crimson wall before her. Katja repeated the prayer again and again, gaining confidence. The wall of crimson cracked and then shattered. A terrified neigh echoed on the edge of her understanding and Katja found herself crouched before Peha'lyn's prone form. The deadwalker shuddered against the cold stone floor as if he had been struck by a thousand spears.

"How? How?"

Katja stared at him, but did not answer. She looked toward Joce'lynn, who knelt with Zahra in her arms and vengeance sparkling in her glittering eyes.

"Felan, take her to the healing ward and bring Neha'lyn back here immediately!"

Joce'lynn passed the unconscious dryad into the werewolf's waiting paws. The warrior raced away with his precious burden, the borrowed broadsword clanking in its sling along his robed back.

"How severe are your wounds?" Joce'lynn whispered to Katja.

"The one poisoned wound really aches."

"Will you be able to use your special sight to help me interrogate the dullahan while we wait for the healers?"

Katja nodded.

"Good. If the deadwalker tries to harm me while I question him, you are to use your sight to warn me of the attack. Otherwise do not interfere. Understood?"

Katja nodded again and then she felt the Sorceress's magic prickle the hairs on the back of her neck.

"What is your name?" Joce'lynn demanded.

"Pehalius I was born. Peha'lyn I was ceremonially named. Perefaris I am now called."

"Who else have you Turned, Perefaris?" she demanded.

The Asheken tried to turn his face from her probing eyes, but could not. "None."

"Do not lie to me. There are others Turned on this island!"

The deadwalker shuddered. "Only six of us…myself and five others, all of whom I Turned and all of whom are now destroyed…the four guardians in this corridor and the satyr dreamdrifter master."

"Who Turned you?"

"Luther."

Fearful murmurs swept through the crowd.

"When did Luther Turn you?"

"He found me almost two seasons ago during my sojourn to the Westylere Sea."

"What do you know of your master's plans?"

Again the dullahan tried to look away and again Joce'lynn's iron gaze pinned his dull black eyes in place.

"My master bid me to appear as I had before my Turning and spy among my former colleagues. I was to trample any rumors of deadwalkers on Sylvan soil so that his minions could move freely among Sylvan lands. When the time was ripe, I was to then strike whom I wished to Turn and build a mage army loyal to Luther within these walls.

"Mori'lyn was my first successful attempt. But when he proved a liability, I slew him and gave my attention to my new pupil Zahra. I felt it necessary to Turn her for I believed she suspected the truth of what I was. In any event, she would have made an excellent servant since she is one of the most powerful new pupils on this isle."

"But you failed," Dayalan spat vengefully.

The dullahan's answering laugh turned into a horrid wheezing cough. "I may have failed, Half-Breed, but my western counterpart will not."

"Who is this counterpart?"

The dullahan gave a gurgling laugh and Katja felt something in the air shift.

The werecat screeched and lunged in front of Joce'lynn just in time to feel an icy pain spread across her belly. Warm blood flowed through her fur as she tried to keep her flesh sealed around her entrails.

"Katja!" Lauraisha and Dayalan yelled simultaneously.

She saw a knife clatter on the floor in front of her and realized she could not skinshift the wound closed. She groaned in agony, "Knife…Tainted."

"Yes, Changeling, it is," the dullahan sneered. "I was ordered to destroy Joce'lynn if I failed in my main mission, but killing you ought to do just as well…especially after all the trouble you caused me."

While she had the energy, the dying wraithwalker savagely slashed into the deadwalker's marred soul. "Name your western counterpart!"

Perefaris's eyes widened in panic. "Please! I have no knowledge of it."

"Then name the deadwalker's territory!"

The dullahan's tongue moved despite his obvious effort to hold it. "Tyglesea."

"My kingdom? It cannot be!" Lauraisha's voice was a shriek of panic.

Perefaris leered at the princess and nickered. He tried to grab at the werecat, but was knocked back by twin fireballs. Dayalan and Lauraisha watched his abysmal corpse burn with flames kindled in their hands and hatred smoldering in their eyes.

As her packmates helped Joce'lynn drag Katja away from the blaze, she could feel the frostbite sting of poison course throughout her body. Then her vision began to wane.

"I cannot see," the Feliconian whimpered as she held her abdomen together and pondered how similar her fate was to her kin.

Joce'lynn swore. "Where are Felan and Neha'lyn!"

"What can we do?" Lauraisha cried.

"Father, please tell me you have brought the Asheken antidote!" Dayalan said.

"Even if I had, with or without a master harmhealer, there is little hope for her," Caleb's doleful voice responded.

Deep beneath Katja's muddled thoughts, Verdagon stirred. An image of a golden bottle hidden in an ebony box came to her mind and her tongue moved unbidden. "Durhrigg's sword box holds hope."

"Katja, what are you…?"

"Phial," she gasped.

Katja heard feet hurry from her side as the human, Caleb, and Si'lyn all hurried into Lauraisha's room. Then more running steps approached her.

"Katja! Oh, Creator, please no!" She felt Felan's paw cradle her own.

"Move, everyone; let me examine her."

Neha'lyn's cool hands prodded her head and stomach slashes. Katja heard liquid flow into a basin. A cloth rubbed warm water across her bloody fur. The water helped nullify the frigid sensation clawing along her wounds, but she still whimpered from the pain rushing through the rest of her.

"I'm sorry. I can't do much besides making her as comfortable as—"

"Katja, I found the phial!"

"Found what? Let me see that, Lauraisha…" Neha'lyn gasped. "It can't be! Oh, blessed Creator, it is! Katja, listen to me, the poison is in too deep for a topical treatment to be fully effective. You'll have to drink some of this."

Neha'lyn held the phial to her maw and had her drink some of its contents. She dutifully swallowed the elixir and almost retched from the bitter taste. More of the vial's liquid was spread along the werecat's throbbing wounds—its effect almost instantaneous. The werecat sighed as the liquid erased the throbbing in her belly and in her head.

Then the world flooded back through her eyes. Katja groaned as she squinted to adjust to the sudden change in perception. "The light in this hall is too bright," Katja said.

She blinked hard as her stomach laceration began mending itself together before her gaze. Those few mages who had not fled the hall during the fight began to cheer.

"Is the rest of you improving at all?" Neha'lyn asked.

Katja smiled. "The pain in my head is gone; breathing is getting easier as well."

"And your stomach?" Joce'lynn asked.

"Still tingling and itching as if frostbit."

Neha'lyn nodded and offered her one last sip of the golden liquid before giving the half-empty vial back to Lauraisha. The human reverently put the crystal bottle back into the sword case that Durhrigg had given them.

"Master Neha'lyn, what is this miracle?" she asked.

He smiled. "A compote of dragon and phoenix tears, Princess. The Pyrekin Panacea has the ability to heal any wound in the living, no matter how dire."

With Felan's and Dayalan's aid, Katja slowly sat upright. "Jierira, it was bitter!"

"And small wonder, too," Caleb said. "The dragons of legend would cry only if their heralds or stewards died."

Katja gasped. "The egg! We have to find it! Mori'lyn was last to have it so who knows…"

"Katja, calm down!" Joce'lynn said. "You aren't even well yet. Caleb, Felan, we need to move her to a bed so that she can rest. Master Si'lyn, would you please disperse the rest of our onlookers?"

As the two males gently set the ailing werecat on the bed in Lauraisha's room, Si'lyn shooed away the remaining mage pupils. Katja tried to sit up when the two Ring members walked back into the room, but sunk further into the soft bed instead.

"What do we do about the egg?" she asked.

"Did no one tell you that the egg has been germinating in a fire pit since Mori'lyn discovered it?" Si'lyn asked.

Katja cocked her head to one side and frowned. "How did you seize it from him?"

"We didn't need to," Si'lyn said. "Neha'lyn had already told the rest of the Ring about the egg's existence so Mori'lyn had no choice but to turn the egg over to the Ring members. Peha'lyn offered to oversee the egg's transfer to the fire pits, but I took on the responsibility instead since I, as a charmchanter, have a special way with stone." The dwarf shook his head. "Thank the Creator that I did or who knows what the fiend would have done with it! In any event, my own guardians have been stationed around it since its discovery."

"And you are sure it is still there?"

Si'lyn cleared his throat. "I saw it in its proper place just this morning. Besides it has grown far too large for anyone to move it without immense effort. The thing stands taller than Felan now!"

With a sigh of relief, Katja dropped her head against the soft goose-down pillow and finally allowed Neha'lyn to begin cleaning and bandaging her wounds. With the immediate danger eliminated, Dayalan dropped into a nearby chair.

Felan frowned at him. "Are you well?"

The male shook his head and passed the heavy war axe back to its rightful owner. "I will need to visit Tyron again soon. By the way, I hope you had no objection to my borrowing this…I did not exactly have the time to ask—"

"You used it well in Zahra's defense and I thank you for that. What happened exactly?"

"Lauraisha contacted me through our Ott vre Caewyn shards. While I was telling her what I knew of Mori'lyn's death, Zahra was attacked. Once I heard the commotion, I escaped my tower chamber and flew to her aid."

"However did you escape?" Joce'lynn asked, peering at him with suspicion and awe.

"Not to insult you, My Madam, but the mages who originally fortified that tower probably never considered it would hold someone quite like me and therefore they failed to adequately protect the uppermost outside window. The protection spells certainly drained my mage abilities, but I had actually gained natural strength through the lambs' blood. I managed to pick my cell door's lock with a broken piece from my leg irons and break out of the window—"

"That window is framed with solid stone and iron and you were shackled! How could you have possibly broken through either given your condition?"

Dayalan cleared his throat uncomfortably. "Up to a certain point, I grow stronger as my hunger increases, My Madam. That is why I owe you some newly forged manacles and a new window casing. I broke both shortly after draining the third lamb. I had enough sanity to fly out of the tower and gain my full nourishment from Tyron. Of course, then I was caught while investigating Mori'lyn's murder and thrown back into the tower under double guard." Dayalan grimaced then. "It seems I'm more proficient as a warrior than I am as a spy."

Joce'lynn stared at him in disbelief. "If you had enough strength to break a set of well-forged iron chains, why in the First Veil did you allow yourself to be captured? Wouldn't it have been easier to break into the stables, steal the horse, and escape the island?"

Dayalan raised an eyebrow. "And risk further hurt to the Citadel Guardians in the process? What would that prove? Besides, I could not very well flee the isle without making certain that my packmates were safe. These beings have defended and protected me even when I felt the darkest temptations. How could I not help them in return?"

"What happened during your second escape, Dayalan?" Caleb asked, his face unreadable.

Dayalan passed a weary hand over his blue eyes as Neha'lyn began to clean his oozing cuts. "The second escape was easier since I had done much of the difficult work already and since fear for the others' safety fueled my strength. Once free, I came to Zahra's aid. I did not have the time to break into her room using the narrow window there, so I kicked out the larger window in Felan's room and hacked down the servants' door to Zahra's adjoining chamber. By the time I gained entry, however, asp's thorn already covered most of the area and Perefaris had backed Zahra into the room's far corner. She fought valiantly, but she was clearly outmatched."

The group members all stared past him at the now-open side door into Zahra's wrecked room. Thick black vines with thorns twice as long as Katja's own claws had grown out of every single wall in view. Most were hacked stumps, but a few intact limbs still curled ready to impale their next victim.

Si'lyn scratched his wooly beard and whistled. "I'd never thought I'd see the day asp's thorn would actually exist on the Sylvan continent, let alone on the Isle of Summons. Peha'lyn was indeed exploiting the darker side of his magic."

Lauraisha studied Dayalan's haggard face. "Why didn't you just scorch the villain at the first encounter and be done with it?"

"And risk setting the entire room and Zahra ablaze, too? I think not; besides, my mage abilities are still far too weak. I barely managed to lob a scarlet fireball at the fiend after he attacked Katja." The fireforger made a sour face. "I will say that those vines are some of the nastiest vegetation I have ever seen. Zahra did her best to grow a few winding creepers, but those could not hold back the asp's thorn infestation. Even Perefaris had to retreat. Doubtless, it will be some time before the dryad can use her room again. In any event, I suppose you will have me moved to another cell now?"

Joce'lynn looked at him with genuine surprise. "After the service you just rendered, I believe I speak for the entire Ring when I say that you and these other young mages are free to roam anywhere on the isle that you wish."

When Si'lyn heartily added his consent, Dayalan looked from her to him and then hesitantly smiled. "My thanks to you both."

"Will Zahra be all right?" Lauraisha asked.

"Other than a heinous headache and a few lacerations, she should be fine. We'll keep her in the healing ward a few days to be sure though," Neha'lyn replied as he secured the last of Dayalan's bandages.

The fireforger's grin was full of fang. "The dryad scored more than a few of her own strikes before she was knocked out. All three of you females held your own quite well in the skirmish." His deep voice resonated with pride.

"No thanks to me," Felan murmured bitterly as he squatted to stretch his leg muscles.

"You can't be everywhere at once, my friend," Dayalan said.

"If anyone should apologize for negligence in protecting others, it's me," Joce'lynn said, looking morose. "As a wraithwalker, I should have discerned Peha'lyn's evil long before now. I was too complacent to even consider one of my own Ring fellows could be Turned."

"Don't blame yourself either, Jocelana," Caleb growled. "Perefaris was one of the Gan Ceann, greatest of all Asheken deceivers besides the vampires and succubi themselves. Without the telltale head mutilations, you would be hard-pressed to recognize him if you weren't already hunting for him. Among all Sylvans, I alone know the treacheries of their kind."

"Yes, and with that in mind, my dear friend, I do ask your guidance in this unpleasant matter," she responded.

"As do I, Master Caleb," the dwarf added. "Will you help us prepare for one more war against the Asheken?"

Caleb sighed and looked at his son questioningly. With Dayalan's nod, Caleb bowed at his two old allies. "We will lend all the aid we can."

* * *

After Perefaris's destruction, the Isle of Summons' inhabitants began fortifying the Mage Citadel and surrounding township for war with a frenzied urgency. If a Ring member could be Turned, then none save the fireforgers were safe from eternal damnation and not even they were immune to death.

The oppressive gloom was uncanny in such a place of insight, but stranger still was the dim glimmer of hope found in the awed stares that accompanied Katja and her packmates wherever they trod. Within a day after the incident in Zahra's bedchamber, every Sylvan in the Citadel had shared the incredible (and exaggerated) tale of how Katja's cohorts had vanquished the "dastardly dullahan" and his minions. The admiration became so intense that the Ring members had to formally announce a limit to the number of candles which could be lit in honor of the packmates' deceased loved ones at the Aribemasse Remembrance Ceremony during the Winter Solstice.

While the werecat was deeply touched by the outpouring of sympathy, she finally had to adopt a permanently gruff expression anytime she entered a crowded hallway just to avoid being mauled by admirers. Neither Felan nor Dayalan had much trouble dispelling inquisitive onlookers, but the sweet-natured Lauraisha was not so lucky and often found herself signing scroll planks long after the tardy bell had tolled. Zahra fortunately missed most of the publicity while recuperating in the healing ward and, therefore, also avoided much of the newfound fame—a fact which she grumbled about until the day she walked the corridors with the poor human. After that, the packmates tried to schedule their excursions so that they could leave and return together to the relative solace of their new rooms.

Qenethala's news of the Glen Siege was hardly encouraging and so the remaining Ring members quickly passed a series of motions to amass and equip a standing army to aid the dryads and their refugees. The Ring and General Mage Councils called upon every Sylvan blacksmith to begin producing weaponry for the army even as the mages began cleaning and restoring the reserve arms housed in the island's many catacombs. Any mage pupil who had completed twelve seasons' study upon the isle was considered eligible for defensive duty as were regular Sylvans over the age of seventeen winters.

Most of the isle's mages began training overtime in combat skills and spells. Those who were most adept at warfare strategy were given leadership rankings among the newly recruited warriors while younger initiates were sent along with mage delegates to spread the conscription notice among Sylvan villages.

As other mages busied themselves with the preparations for war, the heroic packmates redoubled their efforts to master their respective crafts. Si'lyn and Vraelth began to train Zahra to use basic charmchanting to help broaden her sproutsinging abilities. The dryad thrived under the radical teaching and could soon sing a wide variety of trees, vines, and shrubs from seedlings into manipulated adults in a single instruction session.

Although Lauraisha favored her dreamdrifting gift, she slowly began to work her way from a controlled orange flame intensity to scarlet fire. Once he was deemed healthy by Neha'lyn, Dayalan rotated his mornings between helping to train Lauraisha as a fireforger and working with Joce'lynn even as Katja alternated her studies under Joce'lynn and Felan. Dayalan's regular feedings from Tyron helped calm him considerably and, though he still had bad days, the hybrid regained his normal measure of composure within a fortnight of Perefaris's destruction.

A month into the packmates' training, the first division of the Sylvan army made its way west to secure the frozen Reithrgar Pass. By that point, both Dayalan and Felan had tested for and received all three Novice Tiers, all three Apprentice Tiers, the Journeyman Mage Rank, and their First Adept Rank. The werewolf now proudly wore his First Rank white-orange skinshifter sash over his tan robe while Dayalan wore a First Rank pale yellow sash anytime he instructed Lauraisha. Before Dayalan could undergo the exams for his Second and Third fireforger ranks, however, Joce'lynn insisted that the hybrid undergo wraithwalker integrity training with her so that he could better learn to control his uncanny bloodlust. However, since he had no innate skills in that area of magic, the new education proved excruciatingly slow.

Katja's skinshifter sash also quickly changed from beginning initiate's black through three dark-orange Novice Tiers to her medium-orange First Tier Apprentice sash. The color of her skinshifter sash mattered little to Katja, who had already mastered much of her novice skinshifting techniques while journeying with Felan and the others. What did matter to the werecat, however, was the frustrating task of earning the burgundy Novice Tiers of her wraithwalker sash. Although she had used her gift to free herself from Perefaris, her proficiency in controlling and harnessing her special sight was erratic. Joce'lynn had raised the werecat from the black initiate sash to the burgundy First Tier Novice sash after a month of training, but moving to the Second Tier meant far more work than she had realized.

While she knew it was futile to compare herself with her packmates, Katja could not help but feel a strange mingling of joy and jealousy watching Felan, Zahra, and Dayalan do so well. Even Lauraisha had managed to earn her plum First Tier Apprentice dreamdrifting sash and her light ochre Third Tier

Novice fireforger sash within a day of each other.

When the werecat explained her frustrations to Joce'lynn a month after the Winter Solstice, the mage chuckled and responded that she needn't worry so much.

"You all are doing remarkably well in your training. Judging from the strength of their parents' abilities and tutelage, I am not at all surprised at Felan's or Zahra's immense progress. Dayalan is astounding in his abilities, but again this is not surprising given the magical competence of Caleb and Marga—Creator, rest her soul!

"It is you and Lauraisha, however, who impress me the most because of your limited exposure to magical education. You both have powerful innate gifts, but you have had little practice learning how to harness and direct those abilities. You should feel proud of yourself for accomplishing so much in such a short amount of time!"

"But I've had plenty of magical exposure—far more than the Tyglesean!" Katja argued testily.

"Not really, Katja. Had your mother been alive when you discovered your skinshifting abilities, she would have instructed you much in the way Fenris has trained Felan. If you'd had that preparation at home, you would have come to the isle for perhaps two or three seasons' education before rising from mage initiate to a journeyman or adept mage rank. As it is, Felan's training has helped you understand and build upon the basic principles of the craft, but you still have much to learn.

"Likewise your mental link and your shard link to our apprentice dreamdrifter have somehow hastened your introduction to the ways of wraithwalking; therefore, you have excellent comprehension of the rudimentary principles. More than any other mage initiate, a novice wraithwalker can prove truly dangerous to either evil or to good largely because they usually brush both in their daily dealings with the soul. It is for this reason that our mage rank exams are so grueling."

Since Katja could think of no reply to Joce'lynn's words, she simply bowed in appreciation of the elder mage's advice. Joce'lynn smiled back at her and then frowned when the Citadel bell began tolling an odd pattern of peals.

The Ring member gestured to all of the packmates.

"Everyone please gather quickly!"

"Is something amiss?" Lauraisha asked in sudden alarm as she and Dayalan ceased their fiery duel.

A rapturous joy lit Joce'lynn's face. "The dragon egg is hatching!"

The packmates needed no further prompting to abandon their studies and follow the Ring member's brisk pace out of the training chamber and through the corridors. They hurried through the oldest parts of the Citadel and then down into a lower cavity carved directly from the ancient cavern system under the island. The chamber's exquisite architecture reminded Katja of the carved chamber enshrining King Canuche—clearly ancient dwarven in design.

An intricate system of fire and mirrors lit the chamber along its walls and buttressed ceiling. Dragons, phoenixes, firesprites, unicorns, and other Pyrekin were carved in elaborate detail along the walls and around the cave's natural columns. The whole scene was more awe-inspiring than even the grandest Citadel chambers.

"Quickly take your seats!" Joce'lynn instructed.

She ushered them to a small stone ledge overlooking the egg's position before taking her place on the Ring members' ledge just in front of them. Mages were streaming into the cavern from all entrances, jostling each other for the best views. From her own vantage point, Katja could see the now enormous green egg swaying back and forth in its sandbar cradle among the central fire pits. The top of its mottled shell now stood twice as tall as her! The werecat eagerly watched the egg's swaying motion until her view was suddenly blocked by an ebony-skinned human mage wearing a shadowshaper journeyman's tan-and-ash colored sash.

"What are you lot doing here? This area is meant for ranking mages only. Move along! Move along!"

"Holis, this is the group of young mages responsible for the egg's recovery," Si'lyn bellowed over the general din. "They have earned those seats ten times over. Leave them be!"

The mage stared at the packmates and then at his superior. "These are the mage pupils who fought the isle's deadwalkers?"

"The very same."

Holis looked genuinely embarrassed and bowed deeply to the packmates. "My apologies to you all. If ever you need a friendly guide in Jorn, please call upon me."

"Thank you for the gracious offer," Katja replied.

"Did he say Jorn, as in the capital city of Vihous?" Lauraisha asked as the mage found a seat on a higher ledge.

Katja and Zahra nodded.

"Good. We could use an ally of that kingdom," the Tyglesean murmured.

Katja quietly gave her agreement before turning her attention back to the now violently rocking egg. A muffled tapping could be heard within the shell just as cracks started their jagged descent along its mottled middle. A cheer erupted from the crowd as the first large fissures spider-webbed out from the hatchling's strike point.

"Come on, crack through!" Katja whispered.

Felan surreptitiously put his paw on top of hers in silent support. She rubbed her knuckles against his palm while keeping her eyes firmly fixed on the shell's widening fissures.

"You can do it! Break through!" the werecat growled.

The hatchling sent a small shell shard flying as his nose horn finally shattered through the tough membrane. Little by little, the emerald-hued Pyrekin's efforts were rewarded as his paw-sized hole enlarged into a rift longer than Felan's broad chest. The lower part of eggshell finally gave way and the audience gasped as the hatchling tumbled onto the warm tan sand in front of its egg.

Slowly it raised itself onto four trembling legs and lifted its head. With a great bellow, the hatchling spread his wet wings and greeted the roaring crowd. In that moment, a brilliant green light flashed from the smooth round emerald lodged in the center of the dragon's breast and was answered by a blue flame arching out of the depths of Lauraisha's sapphire.

"Hail to Verdagon, dragon and Pyrekin companion!" Damya intoned.

"Hail to Damya, firesprite and Keystone kin!" the dragon hatchling boomed in reply.

The assembly cheered as Damya flew to the dragonet and embraced him—wrapping her tiny arms around his ivory nose horn. She then turned to address the crowd as she wafted by his scaly side.

"Erdeken Sylvans, hear me!" Her echoing voice silenced the enthusiastic assembly. "The time draws near when Erdeken and Pyrekin will once again be united against our common enemy the Asheken. Two of the twelve Keystones are awakened, but work must be done to recover and free our remaining kin so that their numbers may add to our strength. Verdagon and I thank the small group of mages who brought us to this Sylvan haven. Lauraisha Astrat'a and Katja Escari, we are especially grateful for your aid to the Pyrekin and to your fellow Erdeken in this noble quest. You must be honored!"

Katja's jaw dropped as the Pyrekin both actually bowed toward the section where she and her packmates sat. Many mages inclined their heads as well. The hatchling dragon shook his small body—sending droplets hissing into the fire pits nearest him—and then murmured a question to the firesprite.

At her reply, Verdagon nodded and turned again to the assembled mages. "When a Pyrekin dragon bound to a Keystone gains its Erdeken form, it is customary for the hatchling to choose a herald from among the Erdeken mages. I therefore choose Vraelth Verd of the Aevry clan of elves as my herald. Vraelth, if you are willing to bear such responsibility, please come forward."

There were several shouts of joy and words of congratulations as the awed charmchanter elf made his way out of the viewing tiers and onto the warm cavern sands. Never in the Citadel's history had a charmchanter been selected as a Pyrekin herald. Katja frowned, wondering just what extraordinary qualities the dragon had recognized in the elf. The conversations around her mirrored her curiosity.

"Although I have a capable herald," Verdagon continued, "A dragon must also choose a steward to fly with him into battle. Although I sense bravery in many of those present, I must choose one who has already proven herself pure and strong through hardship. For that reason, I choose the very being who protected me whilst I was still incarcerated in the shell. Katja Escari of the Feliconas Clan of werecats, if you are willing to act as my steward in times of war and in periods of peace, come forward and stand beside me."

For a moment, Katja could not comprehend what Verdagon had asked of her. She sat very still until a slight squeeze of Felan's paw brought her to her senses. She glanced at the werewolf in consternation and then shared the fiery gaze of the Pyrekin dragonet who would consume her destiny.

In an instant, the Feliconian saw the faces of her clan. Verdagon was offering her not only a chance to avenge her kin, but also a way to protect others from sharing their suffering. How could she refuse? And yet she wavered under Felan's warm paw. If she chose this path, she would be at the front lines of every battle in a war where she had already brushed death's doorstep twice. And she could well be fighting away from her packmates for most of the conflict. Knowing now that she loved Felan and that he loved her, could she hazard such a dangerous separation?

The werewolf seemed to sense her unease and squeezed her paw once more. Love and longing pervading his beautiful eyes as he whispered, "Go, Katja. I will wait for you."

She watched him a moment longer and smiled gently as she returned the subtle embrace. With a stately gait, the werecat descended the tiers and stepped across the crystalline sands toward the dragon. She was barely aware of the whispers behind her as she halted and bowed low before the hatchling with both palms raised. Both Vraelth and Damya grinned at her while Verdagon returned her bow.

She stood before him in awe. "But I have no notion of how to be a steward."

The dragon's reptilian lips split into a gentle smile. "Well, graciously face the beings behind you today and accept their accolades for your prowess. When the morrow dawns, I will show you more of the strength born through soaring over adversity."

As Katja waved alongside Vraelth, she smiled fondly toward her companions and recalled the arduous mission that had summoned them all to this magical isle. While her Sylvan brethren still faced an ever-tightening noose of peril, today proved there was still faith held in mage-robe sleeves and Pyrekin wings. After all, if a young skinshifter orphan could win the respect of kings and dragons alike, then anything was possible.

CHARACTERS

PRONUNCIATION GUIDE AND GLOSSARY

The Abomination (ah-BOM-i-nā-shuhn): Drosskin drake; a powerful Litkyn who rebelled against the Creator and was cast to the fringes of the Wraith Realm as punishment for his betrayal. He then enslaved a Pyrekin dragon and used his body to host the Darkkyn's own corrupted soul, thus creating the first Drosskin drake.

King Aedus (Ā-dus): Erdeken human; the king of Tyglesea at the time of the Tyglesean Uprisings. Kaylor murdered King Aedus and his family when he usurped the Tyglesean throne.

The Arbitrator (AR-bi-trā-tor): Erdeken, unknown race; one of the seven mages prophesied to bring about Luther's destruction through use of the Twelve Keystones.

Father Arcos (AHR-kohs): Erdeken human; Manasa's personal priest and advisor who gives Lauraisha Damya's Keystone sapphire. He is imprisoned after helping Princess Lauraisha escape Tyglesea.

Aria (AR-ee-ah): Erdeken girtab, also called a werescorpion; Daughter of Paraburus who lives at Caerwyn Castle under Caleb's protection. The venom from Aria's scorpion-like tail can be used to help mitigate the effects of Asheken Taint.

Aribem (ĀR-i-bem): Erdeken human; the first fireforger

mage ever to exist. He taught his followers how to forge mage fire and use it to destroy deadwalkers. His sacrificial death during a fight with Luther caused the split of the Northern and Southern continents and the formation of the Nyghe sol Dyvesé Mountains.

Arlis (AR-lis): Erdeken human; King Aedus's valet who dies while helping the king's daughter Laura escape Castle Summersted during the Tyglesean Uprisings.

Ashomocos, Ash (ah-SHOH-moh-kohs): Erdeken human; nicknamed Ash by his siblings, Ashomocos is the first son and first-born child to King Kaylor and Queen Manasa of Tyglesea. He is sibling to Prince Tryntin, Princess Kyla, Prince Saldis, Prince Sandor, and Princess Lauraisha. He teaches Lauraisha how to ride a horse.

Aver'lyn (av-ER-lin): Erdeken elf; a dreamdrifter mage master from the Aevry Clan of Elves. He is the Mage Magistrate for the General Council of Mages and the Ring of Sorcerers on the Isle of Summons.

Bren (bren): Erdeling beast, wolf; a white wolf who is Dayalan's bloodmate. Bren can speak some of the tongues of beings, which is quite unusual for a beast. Bren dies while defending Katja and the other packmates from Daeryn, forcing Dayalan to take the horse Tyron as his new bloodmate.

Caleb, Calais Luthrial (KĀ-leb, KĀ-luhs LOOTH-ree-ahl): Erdeken dhampir, formerly an Asheken vampire; Caleb was originally a Toulouse Clan elf Turned by Luther into a vampire. Caleb is the only Redeemed Víchí in existence and terms himself a dhampir because he still carries some of the vampiric traits even though he is once again living. Caleb is the lifemate to Marga and the father of twin sons Dayalan and Daeryn. He is the master of Caerwyn Castle, a powerful shadowshaper, and a weak harmhealer mage.

Canuche (KAN-oo-cheh): Erdeken griffin; king of the Kirni griffin kingdom whose soul was inadvertently banished into a stone effigy by members of the Judas Coven of Víchí during the Second War of Ages. Canuche is a powerful dreamdrifter mage who helps Katja and Lauraisha at the beginning of their journey to the Isle of Summons.

The Creator (kree-Ā-tor): divine; the Creator is the eternal being who created everything else in existence.

Curqak, Solomos (SER-kak, sol-oh-mohs): Asheken ghoul; a servant of the Víchí High Elder Luther. Curqak is responsible for the death of Katja's parents as well as for the Feliconas Clan Massacre. Curqak was originally an elf named Solomos who was first Turned into a ghoul by the vampire Calais. When Calais was Redeemed and became the dhampir elf Caleb, Curqak became Luther's soul servant.

Daeryn Calebson (DĀ-rin KĀ-leb-son): Asheken vampire, formerly an Erdeken hybrid; Daeryn is the son of Caleb the Redeemed and Marga Amerielle. He is the identical twin brother to Dayalan. As second-born, Daeryn is considered a steward of Caerwyn Castle, not its heir. He is a powerful shadowshaper mage and a very weak fireforger mage who looks very similar to a vampire. When he breaks his vow never to drink the blood of an Erdeken being, he is the first being to ever Turn himself into a vampire.

Damya (DAHM-yah): Pyrekin pyrefay or firesprite; the Pyrekin beholden to the Sapphire Keystone. Damya acts as Lauraisha's main spiritual guide and guardian.

Dayalan Calebson (DĀ-ah-lan KĀ-leb-son): Erdeken hybrid; Dayalan is the first-born son of Caleb the Redeemed and Marga Amerielle. As such, Dayalan is the heir of Caerwyn Castle, while his identical twin brother Daeryn is its steward. Dayalan is a powerful fireforger mage who locks very similar to a vampire, but has sworn to only drink the blood of beasts rather than Erdeken beings.

Devra Escari (DEV-rah es-KAR-ee): Erdeken werecat; Katja's mother and a member of the Feliconas Clan of werecats.

Devra was long thought by others to be a weak harmhealer mage. She and Katja's father Kevros were killed in a rockslide when Katja has twelve winters of age.

The Discerner (DIS-sern-er): Erdeken, race unknown; one of the seven mages prophesied to bring about Luther's destruction through use of the Twelve Keystones.

Durhrigg (DOO-rig): Erdeken troll; a collector and hoarder of historical artifacts, weapons, and artwork who lives in the ancient dwarven ruins under Crown Canyon.

Elena (EL-uh-nah): Erdeken dryad; she is the messenger killed during a fight with zombies while she, Qenethala, and another dryad tried to escape the Glen to bring news to the Isle of Summons.

Ella (EL-lah): Erdeken dryad; Ella is a sproutsinger mage who fights against the deadwalkers during the Second War of Ages alongside the famous griffins King Canuche and Nach. She is the mother of Zahlathra and the grandmother of Zahra. The story of Ella and her sister Eliza is one of the more famous in Sylvan history and is recounted in the book *The Dryad's Sacrifice*.

Escos (ES-kohs): Erdeken human; commander in charge of the Fifth Falcon Regiment of Tyglesea. A close friend and ally to Queen Manasa, Escos decides to free Lauraisha and Katja when they are captured by his troops while trying to reach the Isle of Summons. Escos loses his life while battling the deadwalkers that hunt the females.

Evita (Ee-vee-tah): Erdeken human; Evita becomes a courtier at Castle Summersted in Tyglesea and quickly rises to prominence as King Kaylor's suasor (most trusted advisor).

Felan Bardrick (fel-LAN BARD-rik): Erdeken werewolf; a member of the Geirgerd Clan of werewolves, Felan is the son of Chief Fenris and Vilda. He is a powerful skinshifter mage and wielder of his family's distinctive sunsilver battle axe.

Fenris Bardrick (fin-RIS): Erdeken werewolf; Fenris is chief of the Geirgerd Clan of werewolves, Felan's father, and Vilda's lifemate. He is a powerful skinshifter mage.

Fritjof (FRIT-jof): Erdeken werecat; the Feliconian Clan werecat who betrayed the Sylvans by spying on them and then reported his findings to the deadwalkers during the Second War of Ages. He also betrayed King Canuche and turned him over to the deadwalkers.

Garret (GĀR-ret): Erdeken centaur; the mage initiate often paired with Katja for combat training.

The Guardian (GAR-dee-an): Erdeken, race unknown; one of the seven mages prophesied to bring about Luther's destruction through use of the Twelve Keystones.

Holis (HOL-is): Erdeken human; a journeyman shadowshaper mage and an important political figure in the kingdom of Vihous.

Hulus (HOO-loos): Erdeken accipion; a warrior who lives at Caerwyn Castle.

Joce'lynn, Jocelana (JOS-e-lin, JOS-e-lan-ah): Erdeken human; originally named Jocelana, Joce'lynn was originally a Tyglesean human. She is a member of and ruling judge for the Ring of Sorcerers, which governs the General Council of Mages. A powerful wraithwalker mage, Joce'lynn is a war hero from the Second War of Ages and acts as one of Katja's main mentors.

Katja Kevrosa Escari (KAHT-yah KEV-rohs-ah es-KAR-ee): Erdeken werecat; a powerful skinshifter mage, Katja is the youngest daughter to Devra and Kevros Escari and sibling to Kumos, Keepha, and Kayten. She is the sole survivor of the Feliconas Clan Massacre, which was perpetrated by deadwalkers at the beginning of the Third War of Ages.

Kaylor Ryhnus (KĀ-lor RĪ-nus): Erdeken human; the king of

Tyglesea, Kaylor rules by general intimidation and through the scapegoating of mages. He is lifemate to Queen Manasa and the father to Prince Ashomocos, Prince Tryntin, Princess Kyla, Prince Saldis, Prince Sandor, and Princess Lauraisha.

Kayten Escari (KĀ-tin es-KAR-ee): Erdeken Feliconas werecat; he was the youngest son to Devra and Kevros Escari, and a sibling to Kumos, Keepha, and Katja.

Keepha Escari (KEE-fah es-KAR-ee): Erdeken werecat; she is the eldest daughter to Devra and Kevros Escari, and a sibling to Kumos, Kayten, and Katja. She and Kumos are brutally killed by deadwalkers during the Feliconas Clan Massacre.

Kevros Escari (KEV-rohs es-KAR-ee): Erdeken werecat; he is the lifemate to Devra and the father of Kumos, Keepha, Kayten, and Katja. A powerful wraithwalker mage, Kevros acted as the village judge for the Feliconas Clan of werecats for many years until his death.

Kumos Escari (KOO-mohs es-KAR-ee): Erdeken werecat; he is the eldest son to Devra and Kevros Escari, and a sibling to Keepha, Kayten, and Katja. He and Keepha are brutally killed by deadwalkers during the Feliconas Clan Massacre.

Kyla (KĪ-lah): Erdeken human, Asheken succubus; she is the first daughter and third-born child to King Kaylor and Queen Manasa of Tyglesea. She is sibling to Prince Ashomocos, Prince Tryntin, Prince Saldis, Prince Sandor, and Princess Lauraisha.

Laura (LAR-rah): Erdeken human; King Aedus's youngest daughter and Tyglesean princess. Most believe that Laura died when Kaylor murdered the rest of her family with the fall of Castle Summersted during the Tyglesean Uprisings; however, a few beings suspect that she might have successfully escaped the country and sought sanctuary with the dryads at Mount Sol'ece.

Lauraisha of the House of Astrat'a (lah-RĀ-shah ah-STRAHT-ah): Erdeken human; she is the second daughter, sixth-born child, and youngest child of King Kaylor and Queen Manasa of Tyglesea. She is sibling to Prince Ashomocos, Prince Tryntin, Princess Kyla, Prince Saldis, and Prince Sandor. She is a powerful dreamdrifter and fireforger mage.

Luther, Luthrael (LOO-ther, LOOTH-rāl): Asheken vampire; necromancer mage; Luther was originally a Toulouse elf wraithwalker mage. When he was Turned by the Abomination, he became a necromancer and the first vampire ever to exist. Thus Luther is the sire of all Asheken deadwalker races. Among them, he is thus known as the Víchí High Elder and the ruler of the Northern Continent.

Manasa of the House of Astrat'a (MAH-nah-sah ah-STRAHT-ah): Erdeken human; Kaylor's lifemate, the queen of Tyglesea, and the mother to Prince Ashomocos, Prince Tryntin, Princess Kyla, Prince Saldis, Prince Sandor, and Princess Lauraisha. Manasa is largely responsible for Lauraisha being safely smuggled out of Tyglesea after Kaylor hired a pair of assassins to kill the princess.

The Manticore (MAN-ti-kor): Erdeken manticore; he was one of the six Founders of all Sylvan races. The Sphinx and the Manticore's union produced the races of accipions, canis, giants, girtab, griffins, harpies, Tyglesean humans, liopions, ulfrions, werewolves, and, werecats like Katja that resemble lions.

Marga, Marg'lynn Amerielle (MAR-gah, MARG-lin, AH-mer-ī-el): Erdeken human; Caleb's lifemate and the mother of twin brothers Dayalan and Daeryn. Marg'lynn was once advisor to the Mage Council and the Ring of Sorcerers, but she fell into disfavor when she married Caleb. Once she was stripped of her mage rank and title, Marga retired from Isle of Summons politics and moved to Caerwyn Castle. She is presumed dead by all of her family and friends except Daeryn who insists that she is alive and held as Luther's captive at his fortress at Blaecthull in the Northern Continent.

Maryssa (mar-IS-sah): Erdeling beast, horse; King Kaylor's prize racing mare which Princess Lauraisha breeds with a draft horse to produce the stallion Tyron. Lauraisha is punished severely for this act of defiance.

Mori'lyn (MOR-i-lin): Erdeken satyr; originally named Moricz, he is a dreamdrifter mage adept and Head of Archives for the Isle of Summons as well as an adviser to the Ring of Sorcerers. Under the influence of the deadwalker spy Perefaris, Mori'lyn betrays his fellow Sylvans by mentally assaulting Lauraisha and having her, Katja, Dayalan, Felan, and Zahra all imprisoned.

Naraka (NAR-ah-kah): Asheken vampire, succubus; she is Luther's mate and one of his chief deadwalker spies.

Nascius (NĀ-shuhs): Erdeken human; a human of Vihous-ancestry, Nascius captains the boat that ferries the packmates through the Summons Lake for the funeral burial of the wolf Bren.

Neha'lyn (ne-HĀ-lin): Erdeken elf; the harmhealer mage master in charge of the Isle of Summons Healing Ward. Despite his being a Toulouse Clan elf, Neha'lyn is highly respected by both clans of his people for his healing skills and gentle demeanor.

Nicho'lyn (NIK-oh-lin): Erdeken liopion; he is a fireforger mage master and member of the Ring of Sorcerers. Nicho'lyn acts as Dayalan's and Lauraisha's main fireforging mentor on the Isle of Summons.

Oeled (Oh-led): Erdeken elf; an Aevry Clan elf and apprentice harmhealer mage, Oeled works directly under Neha'lyn's tutelage and supervision in the Isle of Summons Healing Ward.

The Pariah (pe-rī-ah): Erdeken, race unknown; one of the seven mages prophesied to bring about Luther's destruction through use of the Twelve Keystones.

Peha'lyn (pe-HĀ-lin): Erdeken centaur; originally named Pehalius; sproutsinger mage master and member of the Ring of Sorcerers.

Paraburus (PAHR-ah-boor-rus): Erdeken girtab or werescorpion; he is Chief of the girtab, charged with keeping the rest of his race safe from outside meddlers. Paraburus and all others of his race live at Caerwyn Castle under Caleb's protection. Aria is his daughter.

Perefaris (PAHR-uh-fār-is): Asheken dullahan; a deadwalker spy.

Qenethala Rahalazel (KEN-uh-thahl-ah ra-HAH-lah-zel): Erdeken dryad; she is Princess Zahra's younger half-sister and the chief messenger for Zahlathra. While she is an important member of her clan, Qenethala is not considered a dryad princess because she came out of Queen Mother Zahlathra's second marriage while Zahra came from the first.

The Renewed (REE-nood): Erdeken, race unknown; one of the seven mages prophesied to bring about Luther's destruction through use of the Twelve Keystones.

Ruthero (roo-THEHR-oh): Asheken revenant; the revenant shade who darkens the skies for Curqak and his allies when they massacre the Feliconas Clan and hunt Katja Escari.

Saldis, Sal (SAHL-dis, SAHL): Erdeken human; nicknamed Sal by his siblings, Saldis is the third son and fourth-born child to King Kaylor and Queen Manasa. Saldis is sibling to Prince Ashomocos, Prince Tryntin, Princess Kyla, Prince Sandor, and Princess Lauraisha. Although he has no mage abilities of his own, Saldis is a great cook and medicine maker. Most of Lauraisha's extensive herb knowledge comes from him.

Sandor, Sandrie (SAN-dor, SAN-dree): Erdeken human; nicknamed Sandrie by his siblings, he is the fourth son and fifth-born child to King Kaylor and Queen Manasa of Tyglesea. Sandor is sibling to Prince Ashomocos, Prince

Tryntin, Princess Kyla, Prince Saldis, and Princess Lauraisha. Of all of her siblings, Lauraisha shared Sandrie's dreams the most while they were growing up. He and Tryntin helped teach her how to hunt and fish.

The Seer (SEER): Erdeken, race unknown; one of the seven mages prophesied to bring about Luther's destruction through use of the Twelve Keystones.

Si'lyn (SĪ-lin): Erdeken dwarf; a charmchanter mage master, Si'lyn acts as Chief Counselor of the Ring of Sorcerers on the mage Isle of Summons. He occasionally acts as Vraelth's mentor.

The Sower (Soh-er): Erdeken, race unknown; one of the seven mages prophesied to bring about Luther's destruction through use of the Twelve Keystones.

The Sphinx (sfeenks): Erdeken Sphinx; she was one of the six Founders of all Sylvan races. The Sphinx and the Manticore's union produced the races of accipions, canis, giants, girtab, griffins, harpies, Tyglesean humans, liopions, ulfrions, werewolves, and, werecats like Katja that resemble lions. The Sphinx was chosen by Aribem to guard the isthmus between the Northern and Southern continents once the two continents were divided. She faithfully protected southern-continent-dwelling Sylvans from the Northern hordes of Asheken deadwalkers until Daeryn slew her in battle at the beginning of the Third War of Ages.

Tryntin (TRIN-tin): Erdeken human; he is the second son and second-born child to King Kaylor and Queen Manasa of Tyglesea. He is sibling to Prince Ashomocos, Princess Kyla, Prince Saldis, Prince Sandor, and Princess Lauraisha. He and Sandrie helped teach Lauraisha how to hunt and fish. Tryntin also secretly taught Lauraisha the basics of fencing.

Tyron (TĪ-rohn): Erdeling beast, horse; Lauraisha's huge sorrel stallion who stands roughly eighteen hands tall at the shoulder by human reckoning. Tyron becomes Dayalan's bloodmate after Bren dies.

Valnic (VAWL-nik): Erdeken satyr; a shadowshaper mage, Valnic is Mori'lyn's political ally and the designer of the Ring Spells protecting Mori'lyn's office.

Verdagon (VER-dah-gohn): Pyrekin dragon; The Pyrekin dragon beholden to the Emerald Keystone. He acts as Katja's main spiritual guide and protector.

Vilda Bardrick (VIL-dah BARD-rik): Erdeken werewolf; a member of the Geirgerd Clan of werewolves, Vilda is the lifemate to Chief Fenris and mother to Felan.

Vraelth Verd (vrālth verd): Erdeken elf; he is a charmchanter mage and an Aevry Clan elf.

Yasmina (yas-min-ah): Erdeken centaur; she is Mori'lyn's political ally and a journeyman charmchanter.

Zahlathra Ellazel Etheal (ZAH-lath-rah EL-lah-zel EE-thee-ahl): Erdeken dryad; she is the dryad Queen Mother, leader of all dryad tribes, and the direct leader of the Zolaramie Tribe.

Zahra Zahlathrazel Etheal (ZĀR-rah ZAH-lahth-rah-zel EE-thee-ahl): Erdeken dryad; a powerful sproutsinger mage, Princess Zahra is one of Zahlathra's daughters through her first marriage and, therefore, in line to succeed Zahlathra as the dryad Queen Mother.

ACKNOWLEDGEMENTS

I have far more people to thank than my memory will probably allow, but I'll do my best. This book was a project of love created over a number of years with the help of so many amazing beings.

Lorelei Logsdon once again lent her expertise as the book's main editor while Sam Armstrong was responsible for the story's initial edits and consistency checks. Thank you both so much for your guidance and enthusiasm!

I must also thank all my beta readers for their help in making Katja's story the best that it can be. My special gratitude, however, goes to Mary Garner, David Gray, Rebekah Kerby, Paul Hostettler, Esther McIntyre, L.W. Salinas, Matt Sears, Jake Williamson, Debby Zuehlke, and Dennis Zuehlke for their extra work to make sure the story would enthrall later readers.

Thank you also to my incredible circle of family and friends who have taught me so much and cheered me on throughout all of life's changes and challenges.

Thank you, Matthew, for supporting me through the many ups and downs of this crazy ride I call a writing career. You are better than the best soulmate and lifemate I could imagine.

Dad, you get the dedication for this book because you are just that amazing. You and Mom have been a constant source of encouragement, wise counsel, and, yes, even edits on everything from my first day of school and on. Thank you for all that you do.

To all of my extended family and friends, thank you for your love and support. Granny, your kindness and graciousness inspire me still. Grandpa, I miss your gentle patience. Granddaddy, thank you for introducing me to our beloved alma mater, Texas A&M University, and for teaching me some of the joys of entrepreneurship. Grandma, whenever I eat a persimmon or fig, I think of your hard working and dedication to see your favorite garden blosscm. Family, you each inspire me in so many ways! Ian, thank you so much for helping me flesh out so many of these characters during all of our talks and for always being there to help me through all of the other crazy things, too. Bekah, words fail me. Just know that Tyron is and always will be your horse. Jake, even though you are no longer in the same realm as I, you should know that I'm still quite proud of my fur.

To my teachers both formal and informal, thank you for your patient guidance and your strong examples. Gloria Wills and Evelyn Roberson, you were the first teachers to help me find the beauty and decipher the meanings of letters strung together on a page. Dr. Deb Dunsford and Dr. Tracy Rutherford, thank you for teaching me writing and graphic design so well. I am forever grateful that my publishing career stands upon the firm foundation of your lessons. To the late Gordon R. Dickson, David Eddings, Leigh Eddings, and Anne McCaffrey, your writing inspired my first characters and, of course, my love of knights, dragons, and crotchety old wizards. To J.K. Rowling, your unforgettable characters and peculiar creatures are the stuff of literary legend. Thank you all for your inspiration.

Above all, I thank God for His overwhelming love and unfailing faithfulness, which have inspired and informed so much of my writing. Jesus, you are my hero, my savior, the breath of my life. Without you, I could literally do none of this. I love you, all of you, so much!

Finally, my dear readers, each and every one of you deserve a standing ovation for finding my work and telling others about it. Writing is a lonely journey when the fruits of an author's labor go unnoticed, so thank you all so much for joining my adventures. May we have many more together!

ABOUT THE AUTHOR

Alycia Christine grew up near the dusty cotton fields of Lubbock, Texas, with a fearless mutt for a dog and a backyard trampoline that almost bounced her to the moon. She fell in love with fantasy and science fiction books when her father first read them to her at age ten. Her love of fiction writing blossomed during her time at Texas A&M University. Alycia's fiction has received wide praise for its unique characters and vivid storytelling. Her award-winning art photography has been featured in Times Square. When she isn't writing or shooting photos, Alycia enjoys long talks with her husband, drinking copious amounts of tea, and coaxing her skittish cat out from under the living room furniture. Find her at AlyciaChristine.com.

AUTHOR INTERVIEW

What inspired you to write *Skinshifter*?
When I was about fourteen, I discovered a book called *Dragonsong* by author Anne McCaffrey and fell in love with the main character, Menolly. That book and character spurred me to write my first fictional character: Lauraisha. I knew Lauraisha's history long before I ever discovered Katja's. In fact, it wasn't until I took a creative writing class in college that I actually met Katja and began writing *Skinshifter* from her perspective.

I originally wrote *Skinshifter* with the idea that I would create an action/adventure story set in a fantasy world populated by lots of unusual creatures. However, with the sudden death of my grandmother in 2005, my perception of the book changed. I saw in Katja's story a tale about losing love and finding hope in the midst of grief. That idea really tugged on my heart, so I felt it was the story that people most needed to read from me.

What influenced your initial decision to become an indie author rather than pursue the traditional publishing route?
I started this journey fully expecting to be a traditionally published author. I wrote two chapters of *Skinshifter* while in college and then wrote the rest of the story's rough draft after work and on the weekends from 2006 to 2009. The next five years were spent intermittently rewriting that book, penning its sequel, and creating various short stories for

possible publication. All of this was done with the mindset that *Skinshifter* would eventually publish when it was deemed "good enough" by the right publisher.

While I had luck traditionally publishing some of my short stories, I sent query letters after query letters about *Skinshifter* to publishers large and small without much success. While there were a few nibbles of interest, no contract offers ever materialized. Somehow a book about love and loss with a werecat protagonist didn't sit well with most editors even though my beta readers had loved every word of it and were demanding more.

Once the advance of technology helped make self-publication easier, I decided to test the indie waters by self-publishing my short story collection *Musings* in 2014. After seeing modest success with that book despite having done little marketing for it, I was convinced that I should go indie with *Skinshifter* as well. So here I am, plunging over the precipice of the indie author writing stream into the publishing pool below me with equal parts anxiety and excitement. I have no idea where this experiment will lead, but I'm so proud that I can finally share Katja's remarkable tale with the world.

Can readers tell you what they think of your stories?
I thrive on the communication from readers. I do happy-dances every single time I read a review. Please, please, please take the time to review not just my work, but every other author's story that you read at your favorite retailers' websites. Readers need each other's informed opinions to help all of us decide whether we want to explore certain works. Honest and fair reviews help keep the literary world spinning.

How can readers keep up with your writing?
Go to AlyciaChristine.com for all the latest updates as well as several awesome extras. I set the website up specifically for the enjoyment of my readers, so please visit! Read my blog, ask me questions, sign up for my newsletter (and its freebies), view my award-winning photography and art, and much more.

What is it about the speculative fiction genre that appeals

to you?

I love fantasy and science fiction for their powerful ability to let me escape from the world around me. As wonderful as this world can be, I often just want to be able explore a completely different realm full of new cultures and unique creatures. Sometimes I really need the opportunity to spend a minute storming a castle wall or riding a dragon in between moving loads of laundry from the washer to the dryer. Reading and writing fantasy allows me to mix magic into the more mundane moments of my life, but it also leaves me grateful that I don't actually have to battle a harpy over the territory of my own bedroom.

How did you become a writer?

I was a terrible reader as a child. Try as I might, I just couldn't make the teacher's patterns of letters make sense as words in my mind. To help alleviate my frustration, my parents enrolled me in special-education classes to boost my reading skills and my confidence. During my homework hours, Dad would read my textbooks aloud as I followed along while Mom corrected my English papers side by side with me. The combination of those three things vastly improved my reading and writing abilities; however, it was my dad's decision to read novels aloud to the family during our vacations that turned reading from a chore into an adventure for me.

My fondness for reading shifted into a passion for writing during my college career when I took my first creative writing and journalism courses as a sophomore at Texas A&M University. Suddenly I had the ability to actively participate in my own written adventures, not just read along while someone else's characters trekked around in their own world.

It wasn't until after college that I began to write in earnest. I wrote sporadically through the years occupied by my first three jobs—learning the fiction writing trade little by little.

Writing, like reading, is always an uphill struggle for me, but the reward of the adventure is always worth the effort of the journey.

What do you plan to write next?

I am so thrilled to have *Skinshifter*, its prequel novella *The*

Dryad's Sacrifice, and *Thorn and Thistle* finished and published now! Now that those are available, I can begin rewriting *Dreamdrifter*, *Skinshifter's* sequel. Then it's on to writing the second novella in the Tempest Maiden series. Right now, I'm weaving some common storylines throughout *Skinshifter* and *The Dryad's Sacrifice* into *Dreamdrifter* to help explain more of the history behind the world of Sylvaeleth. I hope that readers enjoy learning more about the Sylvan world and its wonderful characters in this interrelated way.

An excerpt from the upcoming adventure

DREAMDRIFTER

BOOK TWO OF THE SYLVAN CYCLE SERIES

"Felan!"

It was not a yell so much as a scream that brought the huge human male barreling half-naked into the opulent bedchamber. The full moon's eerie rays illuminated the room through its stained-glass windows, casting everything within it in a blood-tinged hue, including the screaming human now backing away from the source of her fear.

The lioness snarled at the one called Felan in warning just before a pale-skinned male and a green-skinned dryad ran into the room after him. The two nearly trod on Felan's heels when he halted just beyond the servant door.

"Katja?" Felan faltered as he gaped at the lioness.

The skinshifter's emerald eyes met the intruder's troubled gaze, challenging him to come closer and risk the wrath of her claws as she fought to free herself from the jumbled tunic and loincloth now restraining her. She yowled in frustration as she twisted and turned.

The chemise-garbed human pulled on her waist-length auburn hair in agitation as she edged toward the group. "Felan, Dayalan, do something! Katja's gone mad!"

Felan just continued to stare. "I didn't think it possible for her even to become a lioness—not yet, at least! Since she has never skinshifted into erdeling form so fully before, her mind will need some time to gain control over her bestial instincts. Until she does, she's very dangerous."

"Really? We hadn't noticed," exclaimed the dryad. Her

jade-hued lips curled with her sarcasm even as her pale green fingers wrapped more firmly around her sunsilver sickle.

"I suggest we make a slow, steady retreat," the pale-skinned being called Dayalan murmured, nudging the two females protectively behind him as he raised his sunsilver staff into a defensive position.

The skinshifting creature had begun to tear at the cumbersome clothing entrapping her transformed body, her curved claws and fangs shredding both linen and leather with uncanny ease. Malevolent eyes turned back toward the odd cluster of beings slowly retreating through the servants' door as she kicked off the last offending rag. Tail thumping the floor in warning, she stalked the intruders.

She smelled their foul stench all around this strange den. How dare they invade her territory! The lioness focused on the pale elf with long black head-fur. Instinct demanded that she deal with the one called Dayalan first. The breeze from the room's open window blowing the Erdeken pack's scents more strongly toward her keen nose. Katja stopped in sudden confusion, testing the new aromas. Horse blood and wolf fur as well as vegetation tickled her awareness. The scents were familiar, almost comforting, but strange to associate with the beings standing before her.

"Lauraisha, now might be a good time to exercise that uncanny talent of yours," said Felan. He was larger than the other male and smelled more of wolves than of humans.

How odd, the lioness thought.

"I tried!" the human with reddish-brown head-fur whimpered.

The second male, the one that smelled not quite human and not quite elf, gripped his blood-scented staff harder even as he and the others retreated through the door. "Try again."

Her lips curled in a silent snarl at Dayalan's challenge and then relaxed slightly in confusion as emotions not her own brushed the edge of her awareness. Thoughts of kinship and affection floated through her thoughts in contrast to her own raw rage and frustration. The skinshifted lioness's mind dredged up a new well of memories more complex and intense than her bestial instincts could dominate.

Katja stared at Lauraisha and cocked her head,

remembering a pile of fish and a curious contraption of string and stick used to catch them. She turned her gaze toward the green-skinned dryad, and remembered her red hair aflame with the setting sun's rays as she strode toward Katja in the royal linen garb of her odd feminine race. Of the tallest human saturated with wolf scents, she remembered another full moon's night when he had comforted her after her skinshift by an artificial water spring…a fountain, it was called. But the half-human who reeked of horse blood brought forth memories of vile red eyes and crimson-streaked fangs. Flashes assaulted her mind of his face contorted in gleeful lust as he drank his fill of blood from a horse. The lioness crouched in sudden hate and fear, her guttural growl forming a single snarled word: "Víchí!"

She roared and launched herself at the deadwalker fiend before he could close the door against her.

"Katja! No!"

The human Lauraisha flung herself in front of Dayalan, a hand raised against the lioness. A blast of scarlet flame burst from her delicate fingertips, searing the lioness's golden fur. Katja felt the terrible heat even as her claws sliced skin.

"Lauraisha!" the Víchí and dryad screamed in unison.

"I'm bleeding…" the human fireforger murmured. She stared in dumb fascination at her tattered arm and chest before crumbling to the floor.

With her eyes squinted in agony, the skinshifter snarled as Dayalan knelt over the Tyglesean princess's still body. The vampire snarled at the werecat through elongated white fangs, his eyes glowing scarlet as he watched her. Both the huge human and the dryad princess flanked him with their weapons ready so that Katja could find no opening through which to attack again.

The skinshifter roared at them in rage, her voice nearly rattling the teeth in their maws. Then she finally found words. "Turncoats!"

"Who's the traitor, Katja!" Felan, the skinshifter mage, shouted. "Look at what you've done to her!"

Katja focused on the blood-streaked human near the great skinshifter's bare feet. Cold recognition doused the lioness's ire. She had often considered this human princess to be her dearest friend and sister—when her thoughts were coherent.

Lauraisha, she thought. *No!*

She watched with sudden fear as Dayalan stripped his gloves off to reveal black claws. A strange mix of expressions washed across his pallid face as he knelt to apply pressure to the now unconscious girl's wounds—anger, fear, and a terrible hunger. His talon-like hands began to tremble as he held them against Lauraisha's slashed chest.

"Zahra..."

The dryad princess glanced at the half-breed enigma questioningly.

"Bring bandages, rags, anything so she won't bleed to death."

The dryad blanched a paler green than usual and sprinted into the neighboring bedchamber. She returned moments later with linen bed sheets, a satchel of herbs, and a dagger. As she knelt beside Dayalan to examine the damage, the rug underneath Lauraisha turned from pale green to a sickening maroon.

"There's no organ damage, just semi-deep gashes..." Zahra whispered.

Together she and Dayalan shredded the cloth and bound the princess's chest and left arm while Felan stood watch over a now mewling Katja. From somewhere in the dark recesses of the lioness's mind, a baleful voice as deep as Dayalan's began laughing.

How brave are you now, little changeling? Now that I have taught you true fear?

Katja stared, startled, at Dayalan, but he had not spoken. She looked at her victim and swallowed hard. The lioness backed away from the carnage. She was suddenly chilled even though the skin of her shoulder still felt afire. "What done?" Katja asked in broken Shrŷde.

"What indeed, Katja!" snapped Dayalan.

The lioness scooped up her own torn clothes with her maw and laid them at Felan's bare feet.

"Me...skinshift wounds close?"

"After you went to the trouble of opening them in the first place? No, absolutely not!" Felan snapped after a moment's work to comprehend her. "I'll heal her—if you can control your wretched instincts long enough for me to turn my back on you."

Katja flinched at his harsh rebuke.

"I'll watch her, Felan," Dayalan said while Zahra mixed an herb poultice to use in soaking the human's bandages. "Come quickly!"

The males exchanged places and the skinshifter mage laid his large hands on the female. After a last baleful look at Katja, Felan closed his eyes and gained an expression of profound concentration. His hands seemed to almost seep between the flesh and bone of Lauraisha's sternum. A curious scent of spicy warmth pervaded the room.

Katja perked her rounded ears and prayed silently for the Creator's aid. Her erdeling instincts still screamed at her to defend her territory, but her true mind now dominated and, though she beat her tail restlessly, she maintained her low crouch under Dayalan's wary eye.

A curious blue light glowed beneath Felan's palms, and suddenly Damya erupted from the amulet between his pressed fingers. Without a word, the firesprite also laid her tiny hands in healing upon Lauraisha's ravaged chest and arm. Together they closed the gashes, lacing the female's small body with skinshifting and fireforging magic.

The Mage Citadel's bell tolled once as they finished their work. Zahra unwound the seasoned bandages and added fresh poultice to the angry red scars. Although the healing had succeeded, Lauraisha still did not wake.

"She has lost too much blood," the little blue firesprite whispered, gently smoothing the female's hair out of her ashen face. "Best to get her to the Healing Ward now that you can safely move her. She could yet come down with sickness before this is finished."

"Will she live?" Katja asked and suddenly felt four sets of scornful eyes upon her.

"As long as her body can remake the proper fluids, yes," Damya answered. She surveyed Katja with a cold glare as Felan began to move the human princess. "She will need time to heal fully, and time is a luxury we do not have. Thanks to you, we will have to postpone the upcoming expedition once more and risk more lives in the process."

Katja mewled. "I am sorry, so sorry."

"Zahra, call the guards!" Dayalan's flames flared. "Tell them to get this changeling out of my sight or I will finish the scorching that Lauraisha began!"

The whimpering lioness pushed past Zahra as she opened the bedchamber door to yell for aid. Katja dashed down the granite corridor, evading guardians and mage pupils alike as Daeryn's triumphant laughter echoed through her thoughts.

Dreamdrifter
Available soon in print and e-book versions.
Find out more at AlyciaChristine.com.

THE DRYAD'S SACRIFICE

THE SYLVAN PRELUDE SERIES FIRST NOVELLA

The warm autumn light filtered through the trees as we made our way out of the swamps and onto the rolling hills preceding the Nyghe sol Dyvesé Mountains. The Hunter's Path led us northeast just beyond the hawthorn hedgerows marking the werewolf clan territory borders. Occasionally, we heard the long double-howl of a sentry as he marked our progress along the outskirts of his race's domain. Twice we glimpsed a furry gray face peer around vegetation at us before silently disappearing.

Eliza expected a challenge, but none came until we reached the Nyghe Gap within sight of the pine-cloaked mountain range itself. As we neared the narrow gorge, Eliza and I spotted a lone werewolf standing before the entrance of the gap's only bridge. Like all the others of his odd race, the male stood upright on his back paws and gripped his battle axe in clawed front paws that looked almost like hands.

"Do we draw our weapons?" I asked Eliza.

She subtly shook her head. "He might appear to be alone, but he is not. Keep your sickle within easy reach, but do not draw it unless absolutely necessary. If you show aggression, the pack will respond in kind. The last thing we want to do is incite a clan war."

I nodded as she greeted the muscular male. "A golden morning to you, My Sir."

"And to you, My Young Madam," he said, returning

our bow of greeting. "I am Fenraz of the Geirgerd Clan of werewolves. What brings you to this hallowed place?" The werewolf towered over both of us, the bottom of his ribs stationed just level with Ella's forehead. He was covered from his pointed ears to his clawed back paws with shaggy black fur. He was clearly a formidable gatekeeper, and yet his keen pair of golden-green eyes peered at the pair of us with a strangely gentle curiosity.

"I am called Eliza; this is my sister Ella. We have come to lay a Sol'ece flower in tribute at the mouth of Aribem's Spring, My Sir."

"Ah, you are on quest then."

Eliza nodded. "We are."

"So young," Fenraz frowned. "So young a pair to be granted such a perilous task."

Eliza and I watched him silently.

"By what right and privilege do you seek the Sylvan Savior's hallowed mountain?" the black werewolf finally asked us.

"By the grace allotted to us through Aribem's fiery sacrifice."

The werewolf bobbed his head. "Correct. You may proceed. A word of warning, however: we who guard the mountain have seen odd things occur of late."

"What have you seen, My Sir?" I asked. Eliza and Fenraz glanced at me with stern eyes and I ducked my head in silent apology. The youngest attendee of any inter-clan meeting was expected to remain silent in deference to her elders. My fear had caused me to break tradition.

Fenraz turned back to Eliza and continued. "My scouts have spotted strange migrations along our borders: humans, centaurs, even an elf or two. Always at night do my packmates spy them and always they hide when they sense the warriors' scrutiny."

Eliza crossed her arms and frowned. "A band of rovers, perhaps?"

The hulking werewolf shook his shaggy head. "Doubtful. I've never known nomads to take in any kind other than fellow humans. My guess is that they are a band of slavers trying to thread their way back to Tyglesea without being caught." He let off a low growl. "If I find them in my clan's territory, I'll be happy to upset their schemes. However, the two of you should use caution. They may travel north of here and our truce agreement with the Feliconian werecats prevents us from straying into their territory."

I gave Eliza our map when she gestured for it. She unrolled it for the werewolf's review. "But we will not need to enter werecat territory to reach the mountain, will we?"

Fenraz nodded and traced the faded map's trail lines with a clawed finger. "You'll skirt the southern tip of it once you enter the foothills. The mountain itself may be open to pilgrimage, but it is still encircled by Feliconian lands."

Eliza let out a weary breath. "Our flower bud has already begun to open. Creator keep us if it fully blooms—or worse, withers—before we reach the spring."

Fenraz nodded. "I will delay you no longer, but be mindful of my warnings."

"We will. Thank you, My Sir," Eliza replied and I firmly nodded my agreement.

We made our way slowly across the rickety bridge spanning the gorge. It took all my self-control to keep me from running across that rotted wood and rope skeleton just to breathe easier on solid ground again. As I carefully placed one sandaled foot after another, I suddenly understood how beings had so easily died during this bridge crossing. If I looked between the boards for even a moment, I could clearly see the world drop below me into a chasm of splintered rock. Our deaths here meant free falling through air to collide with either churning river water or slabs of feldspar. I shuddered and once again suppressed the urge to race back to solid ground. Any quick movement could tip the rope bridge and bounce us over the side. Eliza must have felt my trembling as we clung to the ropes because she told me to keep one hand on the guide ropes and the other firmly fixed on her shoulder. The contact reassured me a little, but not enough.

We were about three-quarters of the way across the bridge when a gust of wind caused the abominable contraption to sway. Eliza lost her balance and tipped sideways against the ropes as the bridge bucked and rolled. Before I knew what was happening, my body was tangled within the bridge's right-side netting and the hand that had been holding Eliza's shoulder now gripped the left strap of her pack.

"Don't let go!" she screamed as she dangled below me, clutching the bag's other strap with both hands.

Despite being well-sewn, the pack was not made to withstand this amount of pull. Tears stung my eyes as we heard the pop of her strap's first seam.

"Climb!" I ordered her.

"I can't!"

"You can! Climb!"

Another louder snap resounded above us and I felt my body lurch as a rope loosened around my captive arm. I thrust it toward my sister. "Grab hold!"

"If I move, I could break the strap!"

"If you don't move, it will break anyway! Move!"

She nodded and began to inch her fingers up the strap toward her pack's main flap. If she could catch hold of the opening, she could spill the pack's supplies, lighten the load, lessen the strain on the straps, and shorten the distance between us. Her fingers snagged the bag open and Eliza ducked her head as supplies pelted her body on their way to the gorge floor. I heard a second pop just as her fist found purchase around the knapsack's opening. The strap I was now clutching with both hands had begun to loosen.

"Hurry!" I yelled.

She gripped the bag and swung her left hand up to grab the strap I was holding. The action ripped the pack and strap apart. I screamed as I felt the strap slice against my raw palm. Our left hands clutched the same straining strap while our right hands flailed. Our hands touched, stretched, and finally locked around each other's wrists just as I felt the second rope give way under my chest. We lurched downward and I screamed again.

We heard a forlorn howl echo across the gap. Eliza and I turned our heads in the direction and spied the werewolf elder watching us from the bridge entrance.

"Fenraz! Help us!" I yelled.

Four of Fenraz's packmates were gripping the anchoring poles of the bridge to keep them from ripping away from the side of the ridge.

"We can hold it but for a moment more!" he shouted. "Try to reach the ledge!"

He pointed to a narrow precipice of rock rear us.

"I see it!" Eliza shouted back.

She looked up at me and I saw that the fear in her eyes matched my own. "I am not going to lose you today!" I said. I squeezed my fist around her wrist. "On my third count, let go of the strap and catch my hand."

She nodded.

"One, two, three! Grab it!"

She did. The strap followed the pack into the rapids far below us as she gripped my arms and swung in midair. A second gust of wind caught our tangle of a bridge and rocked it hard. Sweat slicked our raw hands and stung inside the welts wrought by the straps. I winced as I felt her weight shift under me.

"What are you doing?" I screamed as she twisted and kicked in my grip.

"Neither you nor the bridge cannot hold me much longer. I have to swing into that ledge!"

"It's too far from us!"

"No it isn't. I've swung between tree boughs that are much farther apart than this distance. Believe me; I can do this."

I didn't, but what other option did we have?

"Count to five and then release me," she said.

"No!"

"Ella, your grip is already slipping. Do this before we lose all strength."

"I—"

"Do it!" she ordered.

I pushed back the tears and nodded. "Yes, My Madam."

"One..." she said and kicked backward against my hands. She then flung herself into a forward swing.

"Two..." She used her momentum to kick backward harder to make her next forward swing bigger.

"Three..." I could feel my grip slipping and clinched my fingers hard against her skin as she kicked and swung. The movement was almost more than I could bear.

"Four—"

"I can't hold it!" I cried. "Release, release!" I stared in horror as I lost my grip in mid-swing. My wrists cramped as she let go. She had managed to hold on almost to the end of her swing, but now she was dropping away from me—hurtling down and toward the gorge wall simultaneously.

"Eliza!" I screamed.

The ropes twisted around my thighs and legs now lengthened and snapped just as I reached up to grab hold. My legs and feet came free and I screamed as my body tumbled past my outstretched arms.

"Ella! No!"

The force of the fall caused the first and second ropes to slip through my grip, but a third saved me from death. I looked around as I dangled from the bridge by my right hand. My precious sister had made the leap to firm ground. She was safe! I heaved a sigh of relief before staring up at my new problem.

Only one rope held me away from death's sway and it was fraying rapidly. The potential break was less than a limb's length away from me. On the other side of that strain, the rope was still tied to the rest of the bridge, which meant it could more likely support my weight—if I could get to it in time.

"Hurry, young one!" Fenraz yelled across the chasm.

I wiped the remaining sweat off my palms and began to climb hand over hand along the rope as quickly as I could. As I did so, I watched Eliza scramble up the rock face above the ledge. I knew she would likely try to climb along the bridge to get to me, which I could not let her do. We had no idea if the damaged bridge could still support both of us. I moved faster. The rope drooped with my weight and still I moved faster. Hand over hand, twig-length by twig-length, I moved. The rope had unraveled to a mere set of strings by the time I crossed it. Its final snap happened just as I tightened both hands on the sound section. Suddenly I was swinging through the air toward the same ridge as my sister—except I was much closer. I was so close that my shoes scraped the ledge as I swung and I had to let go of the rope to avoid crashing face-first into the cliff. My tumbling stop was less than graceful, but I was alive.

"Ella!" Eliza practically slid down the cliff section that she had just climbed to embrace me.

"I'm fine, sister. Just scraped and bruised," I said between hugs.

A sudden crash startled us and we turned to see the entire gorge bridge break away from the far ridge where the werewolves had held it fast. The twisted contraption slammed into our side of the gorge, broke its last ties, and plummeted to the world far below us.

The Dryad's Sacrifice
Available as an e-book now.
Find out more at AlyciaChristine.com.

WHAT WILL
ALYCIA CHRISTINE
WRITE NEXT?

From Thorn's newest exploits on the high seas to Katja and Ella's latest battles against the cursed deadwalkers, more pulse-pounding adventures are racing your way!

Dreamdrifter
Book Two of the Sylvan Cycle series

The Vampire's Redemption
Second Novella of the Sylvan Prelude series

Sloop and Sword
Second Novella of the Tempest Maiden series

and more!

Can't wait to read what comes next?

Sign up for the **newsletter** to:

Get FREE books
Learn about the latest releases
Get access to exclusive content and more!

AlyciaChristine.com/news

www.ingramcontent.com/pod-product-compliance
Lightning Source LLC
Chambersburg PA
CBHW020505260626
47156CB00006B/1877

CHRYSALIS

Book 2:
Keeper of the Sphere

D M Youngblood

Cover and interior artwork designed by Farah Evers Designs
www.faraheversdesigns.com

Editing by Jen Whitten Consulting
www.jenwhitten.net

D M Youngblood
Visit my website at www.dmyoungblood.com

Printed in the United States of America

First Printing: May 2020
Wyked Words Press

ISBN 978-1-7325331-3-4

PRONOUNCIATION GUIDE

Aes Sídhe	People of the Fairy Mound	Ice SHEE
Arddhu	Old Welsh for "Dark One"	AR-thee
Beltaine	Beginning of Summer	BEL-tin-uh
Bodhrán	Irish frame drum	BAWE-en
Bricriu	"Poison-Tongue" Warrior, satirist, poet, and troublemaker	BRIK-roo
Claíomh Solais	Irish for "Sword of Light"	KLOH-solay
Cromm Crúaich	Crooked Lord of the Mound	Krom—KROO-ack
[The] Dagda	Old Irish for "The Good God"	DAH-dah
Féth fíada	Irish for "Cloak of Concealment"	Feh FEE-oh-ah
Goibhniu	Irish for "Divine Smith"	GAHV-nu
Imbolc	When sheep come into their milk	IM-o.-uhg
Litha	AKA Midsummer; Summer solstice	LEE-ha
Lugh	Old Irish for "Shining One"	LOO
Lughnasadh	AKA Lammas; Festival of Light and first harvest	LOO-na-sah
Mabon	Autumn equinox and second harvest	MAH-ben
Midir	Son of the Dagda	MIDH-ar
Oidreacht	Irish for inheritance, heritage, or legacy	EYE-rawckt
Ostara	Spring equinox	AUS-tah-rah
Samhain	Final harvest and start of Winter	SOW-en
Siobhan	Irish form of Joan	Shiv-AWN
Tír na nÓg	Irish Otherworld Land of the Young	TEER-nah-nōg
Túatha de Danann	People of the Goddess Danu	TOO-ath-a day DAH-nan
Yule	Winter solstice	YOOL

PROLOGUE

ROD HANGS UP the phone and leans back in his sumptuous black leather executive chair with a contended sigh.

With that call, the acquisition is finally complete. Now, he's officially the most powerful man in the country—even more so than the president. Not many people know that same president is in Rod's pocket.

As is more than half of Congress.

It's incredibly satisfying, having this kind of power. Sexually stimulating, in fact, since he feels himself growing hard.

He can't contain his grin.

On a whim, he retrieves the special cigar from his top right drawer. It's been waiting patiently for just such an appropriate moment as this. With his gold-plated cutter, he clips the end delicately and passes the cigar under his nose to inhale the tobacco's spicy aroma.

Smoking hasn't been allowed in the building for over thirty years, but who's going to tell him he can't? It's *his* building, after all, as well as the entire city block it sits on.

He props his bespoke Italian leather shoes on his desk, lights the cigar, and puffs away, savoring the rich roasted-meat flavor of the tobacco. He watches the smoke curl toward the ceiling tiles before studying the cigar. He squints, looking for any traces of blood that may still be on it. It'd last been in the hands of a Mexican drug lord who'd had more money than brains. Especially at the end, when those brains had been splattered all over the polished marble floor of his luxurious hacienda.

Rod shrugs; it really doesn't matter. A little blood never hurt anyone, and maybe it adds extra spice to the flavor.

Leaning his head back, he muses on his accomplishments. It's taken far too long to get to this point. He would've solidified his empire at least ten years earlier if Thomas had partnered with him like he was supposed to. But no, the asshole had to go and get all high and mighty on him. All *moral*. He'd really been left with no choice, and the goons he'd hired had exceeded his expectations. The fire had destroyed every scrap of evidence. True, it was unfortunate Thomas hadn't been alone in the house, but who knows what he'd told his wife. It was probably for the best that they'd both been taken care of at the same time.

Two birds with the same stone and all that jazz.

The only potential loose end had been their daughter, who'd been away at college at the time. But the goons who'd investigated her were clear: she's just a bubble-headed accountant out in Arizona. Certainly not a threat to *him*.

His phone buzzes and rudely interrupts his reverie.

"Mr. Hartsfield, Mr. Malsumis is here to see you."

Rod almost chokes on his cigar smoke. Malsumis wasn't expected. Not today. Not now.

"Uh... thank you Lana, I'll just be a minute—"

"Sir, you can't—" Lana is cut off as the office door opens.

"Rod, Rod, Rod." Malsumis closes the door behind him, his voice deceptively quiet. "You've been a very bad boy, not returning my calls." He doesn't wait for Rod's invitation—or permission—to sit in the guest chair. His dark suit is impeccably tailored, his long black hair neatly bound at the nape. With one long leg crossed over the other, he has the appearance of a high-class, successful businessman.

As long as one doesn't look at his otherworldly eyes, that is.

"I—I've been busy. Working on the acquisition." Rod hates how his voice shakes.

Malsumis grins, but there's no humor in it. "The minute you don't have time for me is the minute our little arrangement is over. And when that happens, your debt comes due." He sighs dramatically and shakes his head. "We've been through this before, but I suppose another reminder can't hurt. Something a bit more... meaningful... perhaps."

Rod impatiently waves away the smoke in his eyes and rests the cigar in a crystal ashtray, desperately trying to ignore how bad his hand trembles. "No. Please. I'm sorry. I didn't mean... I didn't forget. I've just... been busy." His excuse sounds lame even to his own ears. He's sure Malsumis won't buy it despite it being the fucking truth, for once.

He knows better than to lie to Malsumis.

But Malsumis just shakes his head again and focuses on Rod, his eyelids half-closing over his strange glowing red-gold eyes.

And just like that, Rod has no control over his body. His left hand jerks as it places itself palm-down on the cool glossy surface of the desk with the fingers spread.

Rod's heart pounds in his ears and his breathing quickens as his panic sets in.

Last time, Malsumis had squeezed his throat for several minutes, until he'd almost passed out. He'd had a sore throat for days afterward and had to wear a scarf around his neck to hide the angry red marks. Thankfully it'd been winter, so he'd been able to pass it all off as the effects of a nasty cold.

This time feels different.

Without taking his eyes from Rod, Malsumis draws a small object from inside his jacket. He brings it to his lips and whispers to it.

As Rod watches in horrified fascination, the object comes alive and grows to twice its original size. Long spider legs unfold from a dog-like body and its tiny fluff of a tail wags furiously at Malsumis in obvious excitement.

Then it turns its head and focuses its malevolent, blood-red eyes on Rod.

With a single leap, the creature lands on the desk near Rod's hand and begins eating his little finger.

The pain is excruciating.

He opens his mouth to scream but no sound comes. Blood pools obscenely on the desk's polished ebony surface as the creature continues its gnawing. Rod's stomach lurches at the strong metallic odor filling the air. The thing's sharp teeth make easy work of his finger bones, and the crunching noise is much too loud in the breathless silence.

The room spins, but Rod can't take his eyes from the creature.

When the slurping starts, Rod thinks he's about to lose his prime rib lunch, along with the three gin and tonics.

Luckily, his stomach just rolls.

The creature has eaten Rod's entire finger to the base, and now it squats over his hand suggestively. Before he can form a question in his mind, it releases a stream of yellowish liquid that burns like acid.

Rod's vision is filled with bright lights, but he doesn't lose consciousness. After a moment, he blinks as his vision returns to normal.

The liquid, whatever it was, has cauterized the wound. At least he won't bleed to death.

But it's also taken the polished finish off that part of his desk, leaving it pitted and corroded.

The creature's tiny clawed feet make a scratching noise as it scurries around on the desk, lapping up the last of the blood with its long tongue. Its tail is still a wagging blur. Rod swears he hears a tiny satisfied belch before it leaps back to Malsumis, where it once again becomes a small inanimate object and is stowed away in a jacket pocket.

"Perhaps now you'll remember to take my calls promptly." Malsumis speaks politely. Conversationally, as if he'd merely chided Rod instead of tortured him.

But with those words, Rod is released from the immobility spell that held his throbbing hand against the desk. He clutches it to his chest and stares at Malsumis with wide eyes.

Malsumis raises his eyebrows.

Obviously, he expects a reply.

"Y—yes, sir." Rod's voice breaks but he doesn't care.

Malsumis smiles. "Good boy. Now, if you'll excuse me, I have some other business to attend to." He rises gracefully and leaves without another word.

After the door is once again firmly closed, Rod clears his throat. His hand shakes so badly it takes two tries to successfully stab the intercom button on his phone. "Lana, I am not to be disturbed for the rest of the day."

4

"But, Mr. Hartsfield—"

"*For the rest of the day, Lana.*" Snarling from the pain, he disconnects the intercom and draws a deep yet shaky breath.

He doesn't give a shit what meetings he's bailing on. He can barely think at all through the agony coursing through his hand.

Wait—doesn't he have a bottle of painkillers somewhere here in the drawer? He fumbles it open and roots around. Goddammit. Where the *fuck* is it?

Ah. There. In the back. He grabs it and fumbles again, almost dropping it. Goddamn child-proof caps. Finally he shakes out two pills and dry-swallows them with a grimace.

After a second thought, he takes two more.

He leans forward and rests his head on his arm while he waits for the pills to kick in.

He realizes he significantly underestimated Malsumis. Before he partnered with him, obviously he should've done better research on who this fucking deity really is.

Just what the hell did he get himself into? His empire has come at last, but at what cost?

CHAPTER ONE

"**S**QUEEZE HARDER, DEE," Mike commanded.

Compressing the hard rubber ball was supposed to build muscle memory, strength, and dexterity in my left hand so it could be as useful as my right hand had been. But no matter how hard I tried, I didn't feel any give in the ball when I squeezed it.

I'd only been back home for two weeks, but in that time Mike had been relentless in pushing me to improve my left hand's abilities. But it wasn't just working with the rubber ball; it was also practicing my handwriting and printing, typing one-handed, and using my weapons effectively.

"Harder. As hard as you can," Mike said.

Sudden rage filled me. "I *am*," I snarled as I threw the ball.

It was a shitty throw. The ball just bounced along the floor and rolled to a stop in the corner with the dust bunnies.

My aim was way off, but at least I hadn't hit him or Kevin.

Maybe I should've put a magickal boost into it.

But then, just my luck, it would've gone through the wall.

Mike rubbed his forehead. "Look, I get it. I know you're frustrated. I know you're probably tired of this. But if you don't take it seriously, you won't be able to hold your weapons for longer than a few minutes, and that's just not long enough. In a battle, you might need to maintain your grip for hours. And then there's being able to slash and stab with your knife and sword. And before you ask, no, you can't just hit them with

CHRYSALIS

fireballs. We've discussed that at length over the past year." He sighed. "We've lost too much time. The clock is ticking, and we need to get you up to speed with your left hand as soon as possible."

I sighed too, and my anger left as quickly as it'd come. "I know, I know. I just... didn't think it would be so hard. This goddamn ball—it's like I'm squeezing a rock."

While we'd been talking, Kevin had retrieved the ball, and now he handed it to me with a tiny smile of encouragement.

So I swallowed my frustration and got back to it.

Squeeze, squeeze, squeeze.

Wait—what was that? Was that a tiny bit of give just then?

With renewed hope and energy, I squeezed the ball a few more times, but now my hand ached.

"Okay, that's enough for now." Mike plucked the ball from my hand. "It's lunchtime. I'll fix up some sandwiches."

Kevin and I followed him to the kitchen and sat at the granite island. I gingerly flexed my sore fingers as I watched Mike make one of his specialties: grilled cheese sandwiches. But he didn't make them the same way my mom had, back when I was a kid.

Oh, no.

Because he'd had professional chef training before becoming my Assistant, he made a gourmet version of the classic, using thick slices of rustic homemade bread and savory slices of white cheddar cheese. Before placing the sandwiches on the cast-iron griddle, he'd brushed both sides with soft, European-style butter for richer flavor.

It was one of my favorites, and he knew it.

The tantalizing aroma filled the kitchen, and my stomach rumbled.

Before long, he set three plates on the granite, and I concentrated on my lunch.

"Today, you'll be working with knives," Mike casually mentioned before digging in to his own sandwich.

I winced.

Three times a week, Kurt showed up and made my day a living hell.

I'd worked with him last year to learn combat fighting, but that'd been when I still had my right hand. Now, of course, I had to relearn almost everything all over again. This time with my left hand.

Knife days weren't so bad. No, sword days were far worse.

It hurt to grip my sword with one hand; even though it was only a Celtic short sword, it was still heavy and difficult to hold in my weaker, non-dominant hand.

And I was clumsy. My movements were jerky, not fluid and smooth like they'd been last year.

When I'd had both my hands.

And this was why Mike made me squeeze a hard rubber ball three times a day, every day.

I knew I'd get better with time and practice, of course. But just as Mike had pointed out, we didn't really have the luxury of time. Being Cromm's prisoner, then waiting around on Arddhu's world until I'd finally reclaimed the Sphere... that'd all been time we couldn't afford to waste. It'd set me behind on my mission: to gather allies, remove all the assholes who were causing environmental damage, and heal Earth.

"But," Mike's voice interrupted my thoughts. "Before he gets here, I have a little surprise for you."

Ooh. I *loved* his little surprises.

During my training last year, they'd been useful gifts to reward certain milestones, because apparently he preferred the carrot rather than the stick. My knife, pistol, and sword had all been such *little surprises*.

I'd nicknamed my sword Ire since its actual name, *Oidhreacht*, was a bit of an Irish tongue-twister. Long ago, it'd belonged to Siobhan, a warrior Keeper. Mike had somehow tracked it down and had it restored.

His lips quirked at my obvious excitement. "After lunch."

Naturally, I wolfed my sandwich in record time and then sat impatiently while the guys finished theirs.

Kevin helpfully cleared the dishes while Mike left to fetch his surprise, and I scratched at my itchy stump. Sometimes I could've sworn I felt a sharp stab in my right hand, which wasn't there anymore. I knew it was phantom limb pain, but knowing that didn't make it go away.

Mike returned a moment later and set a curious long black case on the granite in front of me, then stepped back.

I lifted the lid and stared at the contents, not really sure what I was seeing.

Snugly fitted into dense gray foam, the object seemed to be a glove or sleeve of some kind. Its strange metallic mesh fabric gleamed dully in the kitchen light. Sleek and striking, it was futuristic-looking in deep black and charcoal gray with bright red accents.

I met Mike's eyes. "What is it?"

"It's a prosthesis. To replace your right hand."

What?

I stared at the object again, and now my eyes made sense of what they saw.

Carefully lifting it from the foam, I studied it with renewed interest.

It was surprisingly lightweight, and it wasn't cold to the touch, so maybe the mesh wasn't metal after all. Maybe it was carbon fiber? I'd read about some fantastic innovations being made with 3D printers and carbon fiber these days.

But this went far beyond anything I could've ever imagined.

The fingers were exquisitely crafted and fully articulated, just like the real thing. The inner workings were hidden behind a softer, finer version of the mesh fabric, which closely resembled skin. Several complicated-looking wires and connectors dangled freely from the open end, and I wondered what they connected to.

Mike took it from me and, while untangling the wires and connectors, said, "The firm's been working on this for the past few weeks."

I did some quick calculations in my head, and was stunned to realize they must've started this project while I was still on Arddhu's world, waiting for the poultice to free the Sphere.

"This is just the prototype." He continued to talk while he opened a foil packet, wiped the area above my stump with a small alcohol swab, then gently blew on it to dry it quickly before pressing the sticky connector pads to my skin. "It's not one hundred percent functional yet, but the team needed a quick fitting and initial test. And I wanted to get your feedback. By the way, in the final version these connectors will be hidden inside the sleeve. That's how the prosthesis works. It communicates directly with your nervous system."

"My nervous system?" I echoed, confused.

He nodded. "Your brain will control the fingers and wrist, just like with a real hand."

I still didn't understand, but he didn't explain further as he slipped the device over my stump and adjusted the Velcro strap so it fit snugly but not too tight.

"When I power it on, the fingers will flex in the startup sequence, but they won't do that in the final version."

He pressed a tiny red button I hadn't noticed until then, and the faint whirr of a motor seemed loud in the quiet kitchen. But the fingers didn't move smoothly; they jerked a bit, which reminded me of androids I'd seen in a movie.

"Whoa," Kevin breathed. "That's so fucking *cool*."

I'd almost forgotten he was even there, he'd been so quiet.

"Okay." Mike sat on the stool beside me. "So, how does it feel? Too tight? Too loose? Is it comfortable? Too heavy?"

I waved it around a bit, marveling at the technology. I barely even felt it, it was so light on the end of my arm. "No, it's good. Yeah, it's comfortable. No, it's not heavy at all."

"Good. Now, let's test the functionality. I want you to concentrate on making a fist. Pretend it's your real hand, and let your brain tell it what to do."

Skeptical, I stared at it and sort of silently formed the command, similar to how I'd first learned to use my magick last year. Before it'd become second nature.

Nothing happened.

Before I could try again, the motor whirred and the fingers slowly curled into a fist.

Oh wow. I couldn't contain my grin.

Without waiting for Mike's instruction, I sent it a command to relax, and watched as the fingers opened and returned to their original slightly-curved state.

"That is *awesome*," Kevin murmured softly, almost reverently. He loved technology and gadgets, so I could tell just from his voice how fascinated he was.

I repeated the process again, and this time there was no delay between my thought-command and the action. It was smooth and instantaneous. And there was less jerkiness.

"Excellent," Mike said. He pressed the little red button again, and the unit powered off. "That's all for now. I'll let the guys know this test was successful, and the fit is good. They'll put the finishing touches on it." Gently, he removed the sleeve from my stump and disconnected the electrodes, then placed it back in its box.

Unexpectedly, I felt a sense of loss. That little taste had been like a drug, and I already wanted it back on. And for much longer. My mind raced with the possibilities, and I wanted to see what it could do.

"When? When'll it be done?"

He grinned at my naked enthusiasm and stood. "I knew you'd be impatient once you saw it. Probably not for a couple of weeks or so. It's been their top priority, but it'll still take some time to finish up."

Ooh. Maybe I'd get to show it off at the Finn's Cove Midsummer Festival, which would be around then.

Unlike his surprises of last year, this was a *really big deal*. On impulse, I stood and hugged him.

"Thank you," I murmured.

"You're welcome." His eyes warmed, then his mouth quirked as he pulled away. "I bet you won't be this happy when it's finished and I'm making you work extra hard to learn how to use it."

"I'm not worried." I grinned. "It'll be fun."

"I could crush your sternum right now, if I so wished." Kurt's smugness was infuriating as he towered over me, one large foot firmly planted on my chest.

His ice-blue eyes and close-cropped, almost-white blonde hair gave him a distinctive and intimidating appearance. As did his broad chest and thick leg muscles, which looked sort of freakish from my current point of view.

Which was, once again, flat on my back on the padded floor of the training room.

He'd disarmed me in record time. My knife was at least ten feet away and well out of my reach—unless I teleported it to my hand so I could stab him in the foot. The one that wasn't holding me down.

But technically, that would be cheating. Because Mike didn't want me to use my magick during these sessions.

Just like last year, he wanted me to learn to use ordinary weapons instead of magick in my combat training. He'd said he didn't want law enforcement finding evidence of magick use if I ever needed to defend myself. I sort of saw his point, but then again it hadn't mattered last year, with Cromm. I hadn't been able to use any of my training against him, and I hadn't had any of my weapons with me. So it was still a sore subject as far as I was concerned.

Kurt pressed his foot down a little harder, and I groaned. "I know, I know." After a few more seconds to make his point, he finally released me and extended a hand to help me up.

Yes, he was infuriating, but he knew his shit. There really was no one better to learn this stuff from.

I accepted his help and got to my feet.

As usual, Mike sat in the folding chair in the corner, watching without comment. Kevin wasn't allowed to observe these sessions because Mike knew he'd be an unnecessary distraction for me.

And I had enough of those already, as evidenced by my poor performance today.

Kurt frowned. "You are worse today than last week. You must focus."

Easy for him to say. He wasn't the one with PTSD.

Today's session had been trouble right from the start. Within the first five minutes, the ceiling lights had twinkled on Kurt's blade and the next thing I knew, I was in the middle of a flashback to what Cromm had done to me.

… a small steel blade—like a scalpel—glinted in the light. At least it wasn't the machete-thing he'd used to cut off half my arm, but this one looked wicked-sharp

and scary in a different way. Cromm applied the blade to my thigh, slicing into the top layers of my skin, then slowly brought the blade down to remove an entire patch of skin. I screamed as the intense, burning pain seemed to last forever. Tears trickled from the corners of my eyes and slowly rolled down the sides of my face and into my ears...

"Dee?" Mike's sharp voice had cut through my terror and brought me back to the present.

My legs had trembled and started to give out. Mike had quickly helped me to the folding chair, then offered me a bottle of water. I'd drank almost half of it before I'd set it down with a shaky hand.

Yeah, working with knifes wasn't what it used to be.

That fucking asshole Cromm had really messed me up, mentally.

"Better?" Mike had asked, after I'd done my breathing exercises to calm myself.

I'd cracked my neck and rubbed it. "Yeah."

"Ready to get back at it, or need more time?"

My temper had risen and I'd blurted, "Y'know, none of this mattered when I was up against Cromm. Sure, I didn't have my magick, but I couldn't do any of this shit anyway. Because *he* had magick. And it would've been like an ant trying to take out an elephant. So what's the big deal? Why can't I use my magick here?" During the last, I'd directed my words to Kurt, who'd silently looked at Mike.

Reluctantly, so had I.

He'd sighed. "We've talked about this. *Many* times. It's not about whether you have your magick or not. It's about knowing how to fight against *humans*. Remember: we don't need the attention that would come from you blasting someone into red rain."

"Yeah, yeah, yeah." Always the same answer. It was like he wasn't really listening to me.

Or maybe he just didn't care what I thought.

So I wasn't surprised I wasn't doing too well in this session.

When I didn't reply to Kurt's criticism, he shook his head, retrieved my knife, and offered it to me, handle-first. After a moment's hesitation, I took it and gripped it firmly.

Once again, we faced off in the middle of the room.

Each of us held our blades in front of us, and Kurt shifted to my right. My weaker side. Naturally, this forced me to shift my own position, to keep him in front of me.

But I wasn't too concerned about getting wounded, since I could heal cuts fairly easily. We'd both had a lot of cuts last year, but not many so far this year. That'd probably change as the training sessions progressed. Despite ending up on my back several times, I thought Kurt was taking it easy on me today.

While I'd been inattentive, he'd moved almost too quickly for my eyes to follow, and he'd slashed my upper arm. I grimaced at the sharp stab of pain, then my anger spiked and I reacted without thinking. Before he'd even completed his follow through, I slipped under his guard and stabbed his midsection. His eyes widened a fraction and he stepped back. We both glanced down at the stark bloom of red on his spotless white tank top.

"Hold," he commanded. He sheathed his knife, then pulled off his shirt to inspect the wound.

Unlike the forearm cut I'd given him earlier in our session, this one was wider and deeper—and actually worse than the slash he'd just given me.

I winced, then wiped my blade on my shorts before I sheathed it. I stepped close, held my palm over the cut, and sent healing energy to it. The edges of skin knit together neatly, not even leaving a scar.

Kurt wiped the blood with his shirt and carelessly tossed it at his duffel bag near the wall. He studied me for a moment, and his eyes warmed a few degrees. "Well done. That is all for today." With a nod to Mike, he grabbed his stuff on his way out.

As Mike and I followed, I healed my own cut. It'd been shallow and had barely bled.

"Nice move," Mike said. "I didn't expect that at all. Obviously, neither did Kurt. You may want to remember it for future use."

"Thanks." I didn't look at him, didn't want him to know it'd just been a lucky strike. I hadn't planned it, and I sure as hell hadn't known what I was doing at the time. It'd been pure reflex.

Grabbing two beers from the fridge, I handed one to him and sat at the kitchen island. He leaned against the counter, and we both took a long swallow.

That first taste of a good beer after physical activity was simply the best.

"Do you think the team will have the prosthesis done in time for the Midsummer Festival? I'd love to wear it." Before he could answer, I continued. "It's been all work and no play ever since I got back. I'm more than ready for some fun."

He studied me for a moment, and I couldn't read anything in his expression. Then he shook his head. "Sorry, but I'm going to have to say no on this one. You're not ready. Physically *or* mentally."

What?

"Bullshit. I'm ready. I'm going." I hated how childish that sounded.

Unlike some of the other festivals that required me to perform a ritual as the avatar of the Goddess, Midsummer was just a big party. So I'd been sure I could attend this one. After all, I'd missed both the Yule and Imbolc festivals because of Cromm. Then I'd also missed Ostara and Beltaine when I'd been stuck on Arddhu's world. So at this point, the people of Finn's Cove hadn't seen me since last Samhain.

Some Lady of the Cove I was.

His eyes held little sympathy. "No, Dee." Then his voice softened a bit. "Look, I know you've been working hard. And I've been working on something to alleviate some of that. But forget about Midsummer. Concentrate on your training for now, and we'll make the Lammas Festival in August. I promise."

I desperately tried to come up with another argument, but I couldn't.

When I didn't reply, he added, "You had fun there last year. And it's only six weeks away, more or less. It'll come in no time."

Oh yeah, I'd had fun at the last Lammas Festival. Right up until he'd gotten jealous of the male attention I'd received from the hot young Irish lads.

And then I'd thrown him across the room. Accidentally, of course.

In the silence, he said, "And in the meantime, you've got the pool." He hesitated, then softly added, "and the spa's fixed."

That was great news. I'd missed my spa. After my training sessions last year, I'd spent almost every evening in it, letting its soothing jets massage my tired and sore muscles.

Forgetting about Midsummer for now, I said, "You never did tell me how it got broken."

Now he didn't meet my eyes. "It was an accident."

"Must've been a helluva accident." There'd been a huge crack in the floor and several tiles on the side had been broken.

He nodded but didn't reply.

"Did anyone get hurt during that accident?" I pressed.

He hesitated then shook his head, still not looking at me.

My pet theory was that he'd taken his frustration out on the spa, since that'd been where I'd disappeared from. But he didn't seem too interested in confirming my suspicions anytime soon.

I was patient; I could wait. He'd probably slip up eventually and give up the details.

We drank in silence for a while, and I let my thoughts wander.

Although I really did enjoy the pool and loved my backyard paradise, it wasn't the same as going to a party. I'd never even had a chance to celebrate my birthday earlier in the year because of Cromm.

Somehow, everything always came back to that asshole.

And even though I'd looked forward to the Midsummer festival for so long, I had to admit my training sessions left me exhausted more often than not, and I still wasn't sleeping well because of the damn nightmares.

If that whole Cromm thing had never happened, we'd have had the alliance meeting months ago, Earth's enemies would've been removed by now, and we'd probably be well on the way to healing Earth.

Which reminded me...

"Any news about Cromm?" I asked.

With a little luck, as long as his golden monument didn't get rebuilt on Earth, he couldn't come here. When Lugh had defeated and banished him centuries ago, that'd been quite clear. So far, I was safe from him.

But the same couldn't be said of his minions.

"Not a peep," Mike replied. "He's laying low. Almost as if he's fuming somewhere with his tail tucked between his legs."

"Somehow I don't think that's his style."

"But it's probably what he wants us to think."

"What about any of his allies?"

16

"Arddhu said no one will even admit to knowing him."

"You don't suppose he's planning something for Lammas or Samhain? Maybe some kind of attack at Finn's Cove?"

He shook his head. "I thought about that, but anyone he sent there would have a hard time pulling anything off."

Huh? "Why?"

He hesitated before replying. "The people of Finn's Cove are formidable enemies. They can take care of themselves."

I almost choked on a mouthful of beer. "*That* bunch of peaceful old Pagans?" Ridiculous.

"Oh, you'd be surprised at what they can do."

Now he's being cryptic? After everything that'd happened? Everything we'd been through?

I studied him with one eyebrow lifted. "Care to elaborate?"

He met my gaze steadily. "No."

"Then why'd you even say anything?"

He didn't answer, just drank his beer.

"You sure have changed." I hadn't meant to say it out loud, but I hadn't bothered to try and keep my tone light.

But it definitely got his attention.

"What's *that* supposed to mean?" His eyes narrowed.

I drank my beer and thought about what I wanted to say, refusing to be rushed into a stupid answer.

He'd always been evasive when he wanted to be, but ever since I'd returned from Arddhu's world he'd seemed different. He'd loosened up in some ways, like the more casual way he spoke now. But he kept me at arm's length more, kept his distance. We'd begun to grow close at one point last year, before the whole mess with Cromm.

Or maybe it'd actually changed when I'd started screwing Kevin.

"You're different now," I finally said.

"So are you," he shot back.

Yes, I was. Besides the almost-constant exhaustion from not sleeping well, I was more impatient and easily angered. I'd lost interest in most of the things I used to enjoy, back when I'd just been an accountant; things like working with my herbs and crystals, and reading the latest bestselling novels. I longed for the deep sense of peace I'd had before this whole Keeper thing had turned my life upside down.

"Duh. I've been through some shit, in case you haven't noticed." The words had come out a bit more harsh than I'd intended, and I forced my voice to soften. "Cromm... well, *everything* changed me."

He winced. "Shit. Yeah. Of course it did." Then, thankfully, he changed the subject. "Were you planning on bringing Kevin with us for Lammas?"

"Yeah. Why? Is that a problem?"

"No. He'd be useful to have around in case Cromm—or his minions— did try something, after all."

I knew Kevin had powerful magick, but how much of a fighter was he?

As if reading my thoughts, Mike added, "At the very least, he could get you out of any danger quickly because he doesn't need a portal to teleport. He's got impressive magick, but maybe it'd be a good idea to have Kurt evaluate his mundane combat skills. Just in case."

I couldn't help but laugh. I knew all too well what one of Kurt's *evaluations* were like, having been through it myself, last year. "Ooh, I'd pay to watch that."

His grin was wolfish. "Then I'm sure you wouldn't mind him sitting in on *your* sessions."

Oh no. Not a good idea. I sure as hell didn't need him distracting me with his gorgeous and sexy self. "Um, never mind."

He smirked. "Thought not."

He was so insufferable sometimes.

Settled comfortably in the spa later that evening, I groaned softly as the jets pounded my sore muscles. When I boosted my natural healing with a bit of energy from my reserves, the aches disappeared completely. I finally relaxed and even felt slightly sleepy. My eyes closed and I drifted, my mind quiet. For once.

"Can I join you?" Kevin's voice was soft, tentative.

Cursing silently, I looked up at him, standing by the spa steps. "Sure. But just so you know... I'm not ready for... anything... just yet."

"Understood."

He made his clothing disappear, and I quickly looked away. But not before I clearly saw his beautiful body, and the memory of last year's hot sex made my face flush.

Not that I had any false modesty; I just didn't want to be tempted. Although I expected to resume having sex one of these days, I really wasn't ready. For a number of reasons; one of which was how self-conscious I was about the scars Cromm had left on my body. I'd been careful not to let anyone see me naked since I'd come back home. I even wore an old tee shirt and shorts in the pool instead of my swimsuit, since the shorts covered my thigh, where Cromm had taken a slice of my skin.

But another big reason was Kevin himself.

He'd apologized profusely and given me reasonable explanations for the things he'd done, but it still bothered me that he'd cast a compulsion spell on me for uninterrupted sex. And although I'd forgiven him because he'd helped rescue me, it all still seemed a bit too fresh, as if it'd just happened.

Instead of six months ago.

I hadn't scooted over for him to sit next to me, and smart guy that he was, he took the hint and sat across from me.

Which brought to mind *that* night, when he'd sat there. Before I'd convinced him to be my ally and he'd unexpectedly ported us to his world to seal the agreement. Where he'd then cast the compulsion spell.

I shivered despite the heated water surrounding me, but they weren't the good kind of shivers.

Then the flashback hit me.

... his wide grin was the last thing I saw before vertigo and darkness took over. When my vision cleared, I was on my back in an enormous bed and Kevin loomed over me, his face twisted in lust as he pounded away inside me.

"I'm sorry." Kevin's soft voice brought me back. "I know you're remembering that night."

I blinked and met his eyes, and I couldn't help but see the sadness there.

Yeah, he'd known exactly where my mind had gone.

And if he hadn't taken me off Earth, Cromm's minion wouldn't have abducted me. So in a way, Kevin had been responsible for everything that'd happened after that. All the pain and torture.

"It'll take time," I said, just as softly.

"I understand. I'll wait as long as I have to. I won't rush you."

It was as if he knew I wasn't only talking about the flashbacks and bad memories.

As much as Mike and I had changed since last year, Kevin had changed even more. Where was the arrogant asshole I'd first met? This Kevin was kind. Considerate. Compassionate. And not a bit selfish.

It made me wonder: could I truly trust this version of him?

He studied me for a moment longer, then leaned his head back with a sigh and closed his eyes. "I'd forgotten how good this feels."

Taking advantage of the moment, my eyes roamed over his gorgeous face. His long dark hair, unbound except for the small braids at each temple, fanned out on the water's surface like some exotic seaweed.

He laughed softly, and it had an immediate effect, sending a jolt of pure sexual heat through me.

"Stop staring at me." He hadn't opened his eyes. He just knew.

He always knew.

"Sorry," I shrugged. "Can't help it. You're beautiful."

His soft lips curved in a sweet smile, but he still didn't open his eyes. "Thank you."

Forcing my own eyes closed to stop staring at him, after a moment I finally relaxed again and sighed in pleasure. "I've missed this so much. Especially with all the training."

"You've been working too hard. You're not having any fun."

"I know. Mike can be a real jerk sometimes." I'd said it lightheartedly, jokingly; I should've known better.

"*He's an asshole.*" He'd snarled the words, making me jump from the sudden change in tone.

We stared at each other. His eyes glittered with fury, green fire in the dim landscape lights.

"He's doing what he has to do," I said, keeping my voice calm.

"He's *hurting* you," he growled.

Was that what this was about? He was concerned for me?

"He's doing what he *has to do*," I repeated, but this time with iron in my voice.

His jaw clenched, but after a moment he took a deep breath and released it. He shook his head and visibly calmed himself. "Fine. Alright. I'll let it go. This time."

I nodded but didn't reply. The fact that he'd unexpectedly become so fiercely protective of me was enough to think about for now.

Until another thought popped into my head and I decided to pursue it.

"What exactly happened last year? To this spa? Do you know?"

He just stared at me for a few seconds. "I'm not surprised he never told you."

"Why?"

A shadow of a smirk was there and gone as fast as my eye blinked. "The three of us had already started working together to try and find you. He was so concerned about you and seemed so reasonable, I made the mistake of coming here to try and help him, since I knew how he felt about you. But he went berserk, flew into a rage. Accused me of taking you against your will, all sorts of nasty things. See, he'd watched the security recordings and seen us that night. But of course, there was no sound, so he hadn't heard us make our deal. So he had no idea what actually happened. He just assumed." He took a deep breath before continuing. "When I turned away from him, he attacked me. Well, he tried to. I'm not stupid. I had my shields up, so the sledgehammer just bounced off me." He winced. "Unfortunately, it landed in the spa and cracked the bottom. Neither of us noticed it leaking until much later."

Sledgehammer? Holy fucking hell.

While he'd related the story, I'd stared at him with my mouth open, but now I had questions. So many questions. "That can't be the end of it. What happened next?"

He smirked. "I blasted him with my magick. Mostly defensive, though. I just wanted him to leave me alone." He winced again. "Unfortunately, some of my fireballs missed and hit the tiles in the spa." He cleared his throat and continued. "After I knocked him down a few times, he finally asked for a truce, and I gave it to him. He never pulled that shit on me again."

Fuck.

I'd assumed Mike had taken his anger out on the spa, but I'd been wrong. So, so wrong.

Remembering back to when I'd been on Arddhu's world after my rescue, I'd thought it strange how Mike and Kevin had suddenly seemed to get along. I'd asked Mike about it, and he'd simply told me they'd worked it out.

So *that* was how they'd worked it out. No wonder Mike had never told me; it sounded like Kevin had kicked his ass.

But I still had one big question...

"Getting back to what you said. About knowing how he felt about me. What do you mean?"

He snorted. "Oh come on. Don't be so dense. You're smarter than that." He paused, and I didn't know if it was because he was choosing his words carefully or for dramatic effect. "He's wanted you for himself, right from the beginning."

Mike? *Want me?* That was absurd. He'd never treated me like anything more than a friend or coworker. Sometimes, I'd even felt more like an enemy.

I'd been about to tell him no, he was wrong. But then again, there was what'd happened at the Lammas Festival last year: Mike's jealousy and the blow-up that'd ended with me throwing him across the room.

Maybe there was some truth there, after all.

And what about the security recording he'd watched? I'd been so sure there weren't any cameras near the spa. It took almost all my willpower to resist the urge to look for them right this instant.

My face grew warm as I realized he'd seen me step naked into the spa countless times. Had the rest of the security team watched, too? Hell, if I'd known I was on camera, I would've worn my swimsuit.

And where else had cameras been hidden? Would I find any in my suite?

"So now you know." Kevin leaned his head back and closed his eyes again.

"Yeah." Now I knew.

But what I did with the information—if anything—would be a different story.

CHAPTER TWO

FOR THE NEXT couple of weeks, mindful of Kurt's criticism during my last session, I stepped up my efforts to stay focused during my training sessions. He seemed satisfied with my progress, especially when I'd given him more wounds than he'd given me.

But I didn't let it go to my head. I couldn't. Kurt could easily kick my ass, and I couldn't let myself ever forget it.

I'd also continued practicing my writing, and had made significant improvement typing with only my left hand. Completely by accident, I'd discovered I could work my laptop's touchpad with my stump, and with a little practice, I could even press the mouse buttons with it.

Not that I had much to type. But it made internet searches a helluva lot easier.

And I was doing a lot of internet searches, looking for ways to eliminate the nightmares and flashback triggers, and how to deal with phantom limb pain.

So far, I hadn't found anything useful.

I'd even asked the one entity who'd done so much for me last year, thinking she'd have a solution.

"*Greetings, Anu.*"

"*Greetings, Deirdre. Much love.*"

"*Much love. I need your help. Can you take away these nightmares I keep having?*"

"You must heal, Deirdre. Healing will take time."

"Yes, but... isn't there anything you can do? Or what about for when I still feel pain in my right hand, even though it's not there anymore?"

"I am sorry, Deirdre. You must heal."

I'd wanted to throw something, then.

One morning at breakfast, before my scheduled training session, Mike mentioned that Kurt's evaluation of Kevin's combat skills went quite well.

"What does that mean?" I asked.

After a slight hesitation, he replied, "Let's just say he can more than take care of himself." He wouldn't explain any further, which left it to my imagination.

When I saw Kurt later, I stared at the dark purple bruises on his arms and throat.

In all the sessions I'd ever had with him—this year and last—I'd never bruised him. Sure, I'd cut him, and I'd struck him more than a few times. But for whatever reason, he'd never sported the multicolored evidence of those hits like he did now.

"Would you like me to heal those?" I asked Kurt, nodding at his wounds.

He met my gaze evenly. "Thank you, but no. I require no healing just now."

Of course, this just made me even more curious about Kevin's abilities and skills.

The days continued in a haze of workouts, training, and trying to heal myself—inside and out.

Then one day, Mike set the long black box in front of me once again.

I'd sort of forgotten all about the prosthesis.

For the most part, it looked the same as when I'd last seen it, but this version was longer, the connectors no longer dangled from the end, and the Velcro strap was gone.

It looked like a futuristic invention for a science fiction movie. Or maybe like something a comic-book superhero would wear to fight crime and battle nasty evil dudes.

Without waiting for any prodding from Mike, I slipped it over my stump. The edge of the sleeve almost reached my elbow now, and it fit my entire forearm snugly but not uncomfortably. It was also much quieter; I barely heard the soft whirr of the motor as it automatically powered on as soon as it was in place.

Just as I'd done last time, I sent the unit a mental command to make a fist, and this time the fingers curled obediently without any lag at all. The movement was smooth and quiet, with none of the jerkiness of the prototype.

It was truly amazing technology, and it probably cost a fortune to design and build.

And for just a moment, I felt unworthy.

Not many amputees ever got this kind of opportunity, and the only reason I did was because I was rich and knew someone who was well-connected. It'd be nice if we could make this design available for local amputees at no or low cost to them. I made a mental note to talk to Mike about it.

For now, I focused on repeatedly making and unmaking a fist and stared at it in wonder. I had no idea how the thing functioned technically, but it was amazing.

Without a word, Mike got a beer from the fridge, the bottle opener, and a kitchen towel. He set the beer and opener in front of me, but kept the towel as he sat down again with a tiny smile.

I frowned at the towel, then set my jaw with determination. He might not have any confidence in me, but I'd prove him wrong. He wouldn't be wiping any beer off himself.

As soon as I reached for the bottle with my left hand, Mike shook his head. "No. Use the prosthesis to hold the bottle."

"What? Why?" Back in the old days, I'd always held bottles in my left hand and used the opener with my dominant hand—my right. Since losing my right hand, though, I'd held bottles between my legs and used my left for the opener. I'd assumed I'd revert back to the old way, even with the prosthesis.

"You need to learn how to use and control it in every situation. This is a good test."

I sighed but managed to not roll my eyes. "Fine."

It was a simple task, really, broken down into steps: hold the bottle with the prosthesis, use the opener in my hand to take the cap off, lift the bottle, tilt it and take a drink, then set it down.

But as I sent the mental commands, I quickly realized the task consisted of several even smaller steps that required the commands to be communicated individually to the prosthesis. First, close the fingers around the bottle. Keep them closed while applying pressure against the bottle—but not too much. Not enough to break the glass. Hold the bottle in place while using the opener in my left hand to pry off the cap. Only then could I begin to bring the bottle up to my mouth for a drink, which would require several more small steps.

Despite it being more complicated than I'd first thought, I managed to get the first part done without incident—although the bottle slipped a bit when I started working on removing the cap. I tightened the fingers' grip a tiny bit and that worked.

By that point, I was more than ready for a drink. Hell, I'd never worked so hard for a sip of beer in my life.

"Great," Mike said. "Now, sit on your left hand."

What?

"Why?"

"So you aren't tempted to use it during the rest of this exercise."

I groaned but complied.

Just as I started to lift the bottle to my mouth, it slipped. Intending to set it back on the counter before trying again, I misjudged the speed of the movement and accidentally slammed the bottle on the granite. Thankfully, it didn't break, but I'd tensed up, expecting shattered glass and beer everywhere.

I forced myself to relax and take my time.

Besides, he wasn't going to have to use that fucking towel.

"By the time we reach our mid-thirties, we take our muscle memory for granted," Mike softly said. "You're having to learn it all over again, this time with a prosthesis. Take your time. And don't worry about making a mess."

Yeah, 'cuz you have a towel, I almost growled at him.

When I felt the bottle slip on my next try, I commanded the fingers to grip a little harder. I added pressure bit by bit until the bottle stopped slipping.

Slowly, I brought the bottle to my lips and drank a long, hard-earned swallow.

Which promptly broke my concentration.

The bottle slipped again, spilling beer down the front of my shirt before I successfully corrected my grip.

Carefully, I set the bottle on the counter and relaxed the prosthesis. Sweat tickled my temple, so I wiped it away with my sleeve.

Dammit, this shouldn't have been that difficult.

Mike handed me the towel, and I dabbed at my shirt.

"Don't be so hard on yourself. You did great. I purposely gave you a tough test." At my scowl, he continued. "The condensation on the glass bottle makes it slippery and a challenge. Just like human skin sometimes has difficulty dealing with wet, slippery objects, so does your prosthesis."

"So you set me up to fail."

"No, not at all. I wanted to see how well it—and you—performed in that specific test. Besides, it's something you'll need to keep in mind."

I tossed the towel on the granite. "You could've told me."

"Then it wouldn't've been a fair test."

"So what you're saying is: it's a design flaw."

A corner of his mouth quirked. "Not unless you think human skin has the same flaw."

"Maybe it should be *better* than human skin," I countered. "Maybe you should've asked for my input on the design."

"I suppose we should have." He laughed, then sobered. "We'll work on some easier tasks, and when you're ready, we'll try this one again."

He got a notebook and pen from a drawer and placed them in front of me. "I want you to practice writing for half an hour every day, after you've finished your left-hand practice. It'll help you to master fine motor control, which is the basis for learning other movements."

Ugh. More writing practice. At this rate, I'll run out of magazine articles to copy. Maybe I'll have to start using books.

Not saying a word, I grabbed my beer—with my left hand this time.

27

"Now," he continued. "A few other things you need to know. Yes, it's waterproof, but only to a certain extent. So take it off before you shower, and don't wear it in the pool or spa." He stood and got another beer for himself. "Right now, it's powered by a couple of special batteries. Ideally, any movement of the prosthetic will negate the energy discharged. But the team is working on a module that will tap into the energy reserves stored by Anu. They wanted to wait until that was finished, but I wanted to get it to you now because the sooner you start working with it, the better. The only problem is, the batteries don't last long. They'll stop holding a charge after about a week or so."

"So I'll need to change them?"

He nodded, then pointed to a drawer on the kitchen island. "There's a three-month supply in there. Put the old ones in the little box marked *used*. The new ones go into a small compartment just inside the top of the sleeve. You can't miss it. It's got a big battery symbol on it."

"How long until they have that module finished?"

"Around six to eight weeks." He took a swig of his beer before continuing. "The team put a governor on the hand strength while you're still in learning mode. That's for your protection as well as anyone else's. We don't want you accidentally crushing bones when you shake hands. After you're proficient at controlling it, we'll remove the governor so you can take advantage of that strength as a weapon in a fight—"

"Oh wow, it's done?" Kevin burst into the kitchen and sat next to me, completely ignoring the fact he'd rudely interrupted Mike.

"Yep." I wiggled the fingers at him.

He cocked an ear. "I can't even hear it." He looked at Mike with a measure of respect. "Your team did a fantastic job."

Mike nodded, face impassive. "Thanks."

"Anything else I should know?" I asked, getting our conversation back on track.

"Not really. Just use it as much as you can to get used to it as quickly as possible. I expect to see you wearing it almost all the time. You'll also be wearing it in training sessions from now on, so you'll get some practice with weapons—but don't worry. You'll still be working with your left hand, too."

Great. Double the workout. Double the fun.

"Oh—one other thing: it automatically shuts off when disengaged, so that'll save on the battery life and you won't have to remember to manually shut it off. Any questions?"

I glanced at the prosthesis. "Um, yeah. How do I take it off? Just pull on it?"

"No." He showed me the tiny button that disengaged the locking mechanism, and the sleeve easily slipped off my arm. The soft whirring stopped.

I immediately put it back on.

He stood. "Don't forget: half an hour of writing, every day."

"Yeah, yeah, I got it."

"I need to go over some stuff with the security team before Kurt gets here, so I'll see you later."

He'd already turned away. "Hey," I said, to stop him. When he looked at me, I smiled. "Thanks."

He returned my smile, then left.

Kevin's hand hovered over the prosthesis. "May I?"

"Sure."

He stroked the mesh on the sleeve and his eyes widened. "It's warm."

"Yeah. I think it's carbon fiber or something. It's too light to be metal. And it's never cold like metal usually is."

But then again, that was true of my bracelet too; it looked like silver metal, but it didn't get cold and it didn't set off metal detectors, as I'd found out last year when flying back from Ireland. Were the two materials related in some way?

"This finer mesh—here, on the fingers—is fascinating."

When Kevin's fingers brushed those of my prosthesis, I gasped.

I'd felt his touch.

But that was impossible, unless he'd used magick.

"Are you doing that?" My voice was barely a whisper.

"Doing what?" His confusion was obvious.

"Using magick on me. I can feel your fingers touching my prosthesis."

He shook his head. "No, I'm not using any magick. Maybe it's part of the phantom limb sensations you get."

29

"Maybe." Had my brain just imagined the sensation when my eyes saw his fingers touch the prothesis?

"Maybe they'll start to go away now that you have this." He tapped the prosthesis, and again I felt it.

It was unnerving.

"I hope so." I picked up the pen and fussed with it, trying to get it into the right position for writing. Porting a random novel from my suite, I put the pen to the paper with a sigh. "Well. Guess I'll get started."

"All I'm saying is, you have to keep trying." Mike punctuated his words with his fork. "There has to be *something* that'll get rid of those nightmares. Your performance is suffering."

The two of us were eating breakfast at the kitchen island. Kevin was either still sleeping or he just hadn't come out of his room yet, so Mike had made a quick ham and cheese omelet for each of us.

The nightmares were getting worse. Everyone around me knew I had them, but not everyone knew what they were about because I wasn't comfortable discussing how Cromm sliced my body like a butcher slicing bacon. These happened at least five nights a week now, up from three or four.

And although I spent several hours every week doing internet searches for potential herbal potions or obscure biofeedback techniques, nothing I'd found had worked. I'd even tried different combinations of my crystals, slipping them under my pillow, but they didn't help either. I kept feeling like I was missing something simple, though; as if it were just on the tip of my tongue.

Anu continued to tell me I just needed to heal. It made me want to scream with frustration.

"The longer this goes on," Mike continued, "the worse you're getting. You're too distracted, like you can't focus or concentrate. This will make you vulnerable if and when someone attacks."

"I know, I know, I know." I set my fork down on my plate with only half my food eaten. My stomach was a bit queasy this morning, probably from compounded lack of sleep.

"Maybe it's time to see someone," he added softly.

"See someone?" I echoed, not understanding his point.

"Y'know. A therapist, maybe."

Oh. That.

I imagined trying to tell a therapist about everything I'd been through, and I almost laughed. I shook my head. "No."

"We'd get someone recommended by the firm, so you wouldn't have to... well, you know, you could be honest about everything that happened."

Of course the firm would have someone. Was there anything or anyone they didn't have at their disposal? But I shook my head again. "No. That's a last resort. I'm not ready for that yet."

By telling it to someone else, I'd relive it. Nat had suggested I try keeping a journal, but that'd only relive it all, too. I just couldn't face that. Not yet.

He sighed. "Well, give it some thought. And just let me know when — *if* — you're ready."

"I will. Definitely."

"Now, we need to talk about the alliance meeting," he said.

I nodded, grateful for the change of subject. "I think we should probably have it soon. Like maybe a couple of weeks after Lammas. What do you think?"

"That should give us plenty of time."

Really, I couldn't believe it was July already. I'd lost so much time between Cromm's world and Arddhu's world, then the past couple of months had been a whirlwind of training, workouts, and practice of some kind or other. Now, it was the middle of monsoon, the rainy season in Arizona. Dust storms were common, and almost every night was a spectacular lightning show as the thunderstorms moved into the valley. Sometimes the rain was torrential, coming down in heavy sheets so fast the ground couldn't soak it up and leaving small ponds on the property. The normally dry wash that meandered through the desert beyond the house ran with muddy water for days afterward.

Unfortunately, that meant my spa time was reduced considerably. But so was Mike's ability to spy on me, if he still used the security camera nearby.

"Where should we have it? I'd hate to ask Arddhu to host it." I looked around me at the main living area, which was big but not *that* big. "I can't imagine trying to have it here."

"No, it should be here, but not *here*." He studied the view through the window wall. "There's that huge empty patch, east of the house. We could get one of those VIP tents like they have at the annual golf tournament."

"A *tent*?" I'd never been to the golf tournament, so I didn't know what he meant.

He nodded. "From the inside, you'd never even know. Paneling on the walls, carpeting on the floor. They even have bathrooms. We'll get a conference table and chairs, a few sofas and armchairs. Food and beverage service. Full bar. It'll be classy. You'll see."

"And air conditioning?"

He laughed. "Of course."

As I thought it over, I wondered if providing food would open us up to the risk of being poisoned. "Who can we trust to do the food and beverage service?"

"The firm will take care of it."

Of course they would. The firm seemed to have an unlimited number of resources.

"How many guests are coming?"

"Last time I checked with Arddhu, he said about ten."

I almost choked on my coffee. "*Ten*? Why? How?"

"He's been busy. Most of the deities he's talked to have pledged their assistance on his word alone."

"Oh gods. I can only imagine what he's been saying about me."

He laughed. "Nothing that isn't true, I'm sure. You know how honest he is."

"Oh, just like the people of Finn's Cove? If I remember right, the fishermen swore they caught more fish whenever I visited the village. And some sheep farmer said his flock needed almost constant shearing." I shook my head. It was insanity.

He smirked. "We can't exactly prove them wrong, can we?"

"Morning." Kevin greeted us as he entered the kitchen and poured himself a cup of coffee.

We returned his greeting while he sat next to me. His hair was still damp from the shower and he smelled like spiced vanilla.

"Okay, so what do you need me to do?" I asked Mike.

"Keep doing your training and workouts, and practicing your writing."

Dammit. I'd hoped to get a break from all that and help with the event planning.

He stood. "I'll track down the tent company and get that ball rolling. We'll talk more later."

After he left, Kevin surprised me by clearing the breakfast plates and loading the dishwasher. "What's a tent for?"

"For the alliance meeting. We're going to have it here, a couple of weeks after Lammas. That's Lughnasadh to you." I'd gotten used to the English name for the early August harvest festival because that's what Finn's Cove called it. But Kevin and the rest of Ireland referred to it as Lughnasadh in honor of Lugh, an ancient Irish deity.

The same ancient Irish deity who'd banished Cromm from Earth centuries ago.

I clenched my teeth and fought off a flashback.

Kevin didn't seem to notice. He topped off our cups with the last of the hot coffee. "By the way, what're we doing for it? Party? Ritual?"

His use of *we* broke through my discomfort. I shook it off and concentrated on the question.

"Finn's Cove always has a ritual and a festival. As Lady of the Cove, I'm an active participant in both." I hesitated, then met his gaze. "Did you want to come with us?"

"Absolutely." His quick grin faded just as fast as it'd appeared. "I used to have a big bash at my place every year, but now... here .. well, I wasn't sure."

He'd left his world last year to come stay on Earth with me, and I often wondered if he missed it. Missed being the one in charge, the god of his domain. Here, I was technically the one in charge, although I deferred to Mike more often than not since he could be such a dick about it. It was just easier than fighting all the time.

I smiled. "It'll be fun. You'll see."

We drank our coffee for a moment, then he spoke softly. "I can help you, you know."

My brows raised, I turned to him. "With what?"

"Sleeping better."

Shit. He just never gave up.

I sighed and couldn't keep the annoyance from my voice. "I told you: I'm not ready yet."

He shook his head. "No, not... that's not... what I mean is, I can give you a spell to sleep peacefully through the night. No more nightmares."

Oh. Like he'd done for me on Arddhu's world. *That* was the damn thing I'd been missing all this time.

I felt like an idiot.

"That would be awesome." I smiled in apology and checked my watch. "But it'll have to wait till later. I have to change and meet Kurt in a few minutes."

"No problem. We'll meet up later and go through it."

"Thanks," I murmured, and lightly brushed his lips in a quick kiss.

For the first time in weeks, I walked away with a spring in my step.

And I just knew everything was going to get better.

CHAPTER THREE

A T LUNCHTIME a few days later, I sank onto a stool at the kitchen island with a groan. Today had been sword day, and I had more than a few bruises on my body from the flat of Kurt's blade, where he'd snuck in under my guard to prove a point.

For the past several sword days, I'd been switching between using my left hand, the prosthesis, and both. At first, using my prosthesis had been really awkward; not only did I have to concentrate on maintaining my grip, but then I also had to make effective movements. Luckily, my brain had adapted quickly so I didn't have to focus so much on the mechanics anymore.

Almost like a real hand.

"You've really improved," Mike said while he finished piling sliced meat and cheese on fresh rolls. He served the sandwiches with a side of creamy coleslaw and a large pickle spear.

Pleased with his praise, I grinned and dug in to my food.

I'd even gotten much better at eating with my prosthesis; at first, I'd kept dropping my fork or crushing the bread on my sandwiches. It'd taken a while to fine-tune how to grip objects with the right amount of force.

For that, I had Kevin to thank. The sleep spell he'd taught me had worked wonders, giving me regular, restorative sleep again and improving my performance exponentially.

Between bites, Mike gave an update on the meeting arrangements.

"The tent is booked. It'll be delivered and set up a few days before the meeting, furniture included. The portable air conditioner will be hooked up the day before, to get the interior nice and cool before anyone arrives. Food and beverage service is handled; I requested a staff of ten. The firm is going through final selection and reviewing background checks as we speak."

"Great. Thanks, Mike. You're awesome."

He'd tried to hide his satisfied smile behind his sandwich, but I'd caught a glimpse.

After lunch, we headed out to the small shooting range, set up a few hundred yards past the backyard.

Out here, the relatively flat land was dotted with saguaros, wild mesquite trees, and creosote bushes. The cicadas loudly buzzed their summer song, and I breathed in the unique perfume of the desert. As much as I loved—and missed—Ard na Mara, the Arizona desert would always be my favorite place in the whole world.

The shooting range was minimalist, just some hay bales for the targets, a table to lay weapons and ammo, and a shade cloth stretched overhead to provide some relief from the bright sun. Most of the security team used the range often, since they didn't have much else to do.

For some reason, Kevin was the only one who never used it. Firearms didn't hold much interest for him, which surprised me. I would've thought he'd be fascinated by the modern technology, but when I'd asked him about it once, he'd just grimaced and shook his head.

Now, Randy and Joe had just finished up using the range, and they nodded at us as they headed back to the guesthouse that served as their base of operations.

While I loaded the magazine for my pistol, Mike set out our ear and eye protection and other gear.

"So is Kevin coming with us for Lammas?"

"Yep." I adjusted my goggles.

"Good." He'd already loaded his pistol, but stepped away for me to go first.

Setting my ear protection in place, I thumbed off my safety and gripped the pistol in my left hand, using my prosthesis to steady my aim in the proper technique I'd learned last year. I didn't rush my shots, but I also didn't take too long, either. After all, this was for combat training; in that type of situation I wouldn't have time to linger between shots.

After my mag was empty, I set my pistol on the table and waited as he replaced the target with a fresh one.

He spread my target on the table and I slipped off one side of my earmuffs so I could hear.

He whistled low and softly, and I stared in disbelief.

Every shot was in the head. I'd never done so well before.

"Very nice work. You've gotten a lot better."

"Well, I have a great instructor."

He grinned, and I caught the flash of challenge in his eyes before he turned away and slipped his protection on. I readjusted mine and watched as he aimed and fired.

He laid his target on top of mine, and I studied the neat pattern.

All but one were in the head. The last was in the throat.

We'd be a lethal pair in a gun fight.

"Didn't beat me," I goaded.

He shrugged. "I'm not worried."

In the next round, I missed two shots when sweat dripped into my eye. It was enough to put Mike in the lead, but he didn't gloat.

In the final tie-breaker round, I didn't miss any, but I wasn't as good as I'd been in the first round, either. Two were in the head, two in the throat, and the rest were in the torso.

He crowed with pride, annoying the hell out of me, before he checked his watch and sobered. "I have a conference call with the firm. Why don't you practice your magick for a couple of hours? Don't worry about the pistols; I'll take care of cleaning them."

He headed back to the house and I stayed near the range, where a pile of rocks beckoned.

I disintegrated several rocks to practice my destructive powers, then used a sharp fragment as a knife to cut my arm. After I healed it, I drew a bit more energy from Earth and began teleporting around the property.

Unfortunately, I startled two more members of the security team on their rounds when I suddenly appeared only a few feet from them.

"*Shit*, Dee. You could've been *shot*," Nat scolded, holstering her pistol. Her anger was palpable, but I also saw a touch of fear in her eyes. Fear of me? Or fear that she could've hurt me?

"I know. I'm so sorry." I sighed, then pleaded with her. "Please don't tell Mike. I don't need another lecture from him. I promise I'll be more careful from now on. I'll stay closer to the house when I'm practicing."

Nat scowled, but Jason grinned at me and tossed his long, glossy black mane of hair. Somehow, he always reminded me of a beautiful wild horse.

"Alright, just this once." Nat finally agreed, but she didn't look too happy about it.

"Oh, thank you." I breathed a sigh of relief. "I owe you one."

Now she grinned. "Yeah, you sure do."

Quickly, I teleported to the shady patch of soft grass between the pool and the back of the house. I ported my sword from my room and practiced the latest movements I'd learned from Kurt and Mike. After a while, I added some from Siobhan's memories. She'd had smallish hands like mine, so both the prosthesis and my left hand fit together comfortably and easily on the grip. When I trained with the guys, they wanted me to use a one-handed grip—switching between my left hand and my prosthesis—to build strength and endurance, but when I practiced alone, I used a two-handed grip for better control and confidence.

By the time I was done, about forty-five minutes or so later, sweat ran freely down my neck and face. I ported my sword back to my room and headed to the pool for a refreshing dip. I disengaged my prosthesis and laid it on the decking, then waded in and sat on the built-in seat. My tee shirt and shorts were a bit more restrictive than a swimsuit, but I didn't plan on swimming. Just relaxing.

The day was beautiful, but it'd turned oppressively hot and muggy. The sky was deep blue and cloudless except for far to the north, where thunderheads had formed. A dust devil whirled through a corner of the property before dwindling to nothing and settling into the dirt of the desert. A soft breeze rustled the trees and bushes; birds sang and bees buzzed. Under it all was the steady drone of the cicadas.

It was peaceful. Just the way I liked it.

I leaned my head back, sighed, and tried to relax.

But I couldn't.

Somehow, this felt like the calm before the storm. Soon, moments like this would be few and far between as things really ramped up. As busy as I'd been over the past couple of months, I knew I'd be even more so after Lammas and the alliance meeting. But at the same time, I looked forward to finally starting the mission from the Goddess. I was tired of the endless delays.

With a little luck, this time nothing—or no one—would get in the way.

On Lammas morning, the three of us met at the portal. Thank the gods I didn't have to fly to and from Ard na Mara anymore. I'd never been a relaxed flyer, and too much time was lost on the long flights anyway.

Mike and I reached the center of the portal, but Kevin hadn't moved from outside of it.

"Well? Aren't you coming?" I tried to keep the impatience from my voice.

"What exactly is this? What are you doing?"

"Porting us to Ireland. Duh."

He frowned, but finally joined us.

I spoke the incantation and visualized Ard na Mara and the wind whipped the dust around us.

We arrived in the afternoon, and despite the abundant sunshine it was at least thirty degrees cooler.

"That really was some beginner-level shit, you know," Kevin said.

"Yeah, I know. Because I *am* a beginner. Remember?"

He shook his head. "Why don't you just hold the portal open for us, like Arddhu does?"

"Because I don't know how to do that."

"Then I'll show you when we leave."

"Fine," I snapped.

"Alright, you two, let's get going." Mike had kept his voice mild, but the clench of his jaw afterward betrayed his irritation.

"Wait," I said. I turned away from them and stood in the center of the stone circle with my eyes closed, breathing in the green scent of the woods and the salt tang of the ocean.

It felt like I hadn't been here in years instead of only a few months.

I'd missed the place more than I'd realized.

After a moment, I joined them and we silently walked single-file on the path to the cottage.

The meadow and garden were well-tended. Donal was doing a fine job of keeping everything tidy in my absence. And the wards I'd placed were undisturbed.

But as we passed the garden, a twinge of guilt made me look away. When I'd first seen it last year, I'd expected to be tending it often, and I'd looked forward to having a true witch's garden for the first time in my life. I'd expected to spend time working in it, harvesting the herbs and making potions.

Being more of a witch, like Maggie had been.

Instead, I spent all my time training.

Would it ever end?

Maybe after the mission. After I healed Earth, maybe I could settle down and do all the stuff I wanted to do. Maybe even restart Maggie's brewing operation and give Garrett some friendly competition.

"I'm going to check on my place," Mike said. "I'll be back in an hour or so."

"You uh... going for a run?" I wasn't sure if Kevin knew that Mike was a wolf shifter, but if he didn't, it wasn't up to me to divulge the secret.

"No." He barely glanced at Kevin before continuing on the path through the woods.

Shrugging, I went to the back door and spoke the spell to unlock it, then stepped inside. I'd packed a bag of snacks for this overnight trip, and now I put the food in the fridge.

When we'd talked a couple of days ago, Mike had wanted to just teleport right back to The Hacienda after the festival, but I'd wanted to stay overnight. I so rarely got to see Ard na Mara these days, and I looked forward to some time here. Then we'd talked about him staying at his cottage so Kevin could take the second bedroom here, but Mike had insisted on staying in what he considered *his* room.

So Kevin would either have to sleep on the couch or with me, and I wasn't sure how I felt about that. We'd never slept together, and part of me wondered if he snored or drooled on his pillow. Did he talk in his sleep? Walk in his sleep?

Maybe he didn't really sleep at all. Did gods and demi-gods sleep?

While I'd been distracted, Kevin had drifted to Maggie's cupboard and now stood quietly studying the various bottles of potions and jars of herbs.

"This place hasn't changed in decades," he murmured.

He and Maggie hadn't exactly been friends, but they'd worked together enough for him to be somewhat familiar with her cottage. And no, I hadn't changed a thing since it'd become mine.

Well, except for the bed sheets.

"She was an incredible woman," I said, stepping closer to him and the cupboard. "I have her knowledge and memories, you know."

He turned toward me. "Yeah, I know. She and I weren't close, but I truly respected her. And she was quite accomplished with potions."

My eyes scanned the bottles and jars wistfully. "I haven't had a chance to really get into any of that. Mike's kept me too busy with training and practicing."

"You know how I feel about that." His voice was low with anger. "He's working you too hard. You never have any time for anything else. He even interrupted your meditation session the other day. Seriously—who does that? Back in the old days, he would've been flogged for less." He pressed his lips into a thin, angry line.

I sighed. "Look, I get it. Really. And yeah, sometimes I'm pissed about it, too. I feel like I haven't had fun in forever. But I lost so much time because of Cromm, and Mike's just stressed about that. Even though we didn't really have a strict deadline, I feel like we're behind schedule and I have a lot to make up. So c'mon, let it go. Please."

His eyes searched mine, then softened. He stepped closer and lightly ran his thumb along my jawline. "Okay. For you, I'll let it go."

He leaned forward and kissed me softly, sensually. He tasted of peppermint.

But when he pressed himself against me, I gently pushed him away. "Kevin..."

He leaned his forehead against mine. "I know. I wasn't... I didn't..." He sighed. "I'll wait as long as I have to." He stepped back and seemed to force brightness into his voice. "So when do you have to start getting ready?"

The festival would begin at sundown, like most Pagan holidays.

"In a couple of hours. I wanted to go down to the beach for a bit. Want to come along?"

"Sure."

He followed me on the path to the cliff, but once there he insisted on being first down the steep and narrow stone steps, just as Mike had done last year. Was it a guy thing? Did they both expect me to stumble and fall? I didn't think I was particularly clumsy.

The sea birds whirled and squawked overhead as we got to the bottom and headed to the beach through the rocks and tall sea grass.

"You know, we could've just ported down here." He almost shouted so I could hear over the waves crashing ashore.

"I know. But it's not the same. Besides, I wanted the exercise."

He shrugged and we continued on to the sandy beach, a tiny piece of paradise surrounded by cliffs.

Mine.

I drew in a deep breath and inhaled the unique combination of smells: fishy saltwater, sun-warmed sand, and fresh, clean air.

Unlike the last time I'd been here, I didn't take off my socks and shoes to walk on the sand. I remembered how cold the water was and made sure to stay away from its reach as I walked along the beach with my head down, searching for the elusive blue glass beads that Mike had told me sometimes washed ashore after storms.

But all I found were long strands of drying seaweed, pale pieces of driftwood, bits of sun-bleached fish bones, sea shells, and lots of stones worn smooth from the constant friction of the water.

No little treasures today.

Lifting my eyes from the wet sand, I glanced at the rocky cliff face ahead, then frowned and looked again.

Something didn't seem right, and it took me a moment to figure out why.

A long vertical shadow began halfway up the cliff and zigzagged down to the sand. But from the position of the sun, which fully illuminated the cliff, there shouldn't be a shadow there at all.

"Dee?" Kevin called from several yards behind me. "You okay?"

"Yeah," I replied over my shoulder. "Do you see that?" I pointed at the shadow.

In a moment he was beside me. "See what?"

"That long dark line there. It seems odd."

While I waited for his answer, I sent out a probe, but it didn't sense anything threatening or alarming.

Oddly, just an impression of peace.

"I'm going to check it out." I started forward, but his hand on my arm stopped me.

"I don't think that's a good idea."

"Why not? This is my property now. I should know everything about it."

He hesitated, still frowning at the shadow. "I don't like it. I think we should go back."

I shook my head. "I'm just going to take a closer look. That's all."

He sighed. "Well, I'm not letting you go alone. And be prepared to port away immediately if a wild animal attacks."

By the time we stopped only a few feet away, the explanation for the long dark line had become obvious: a wide crack in the cliff face that led to darkness.

The fissure could be the entrance to a cave.

"Now I suppose you want to go inside." He sounded resigned.

"Just a little. Y'know, I could swear this wasn't here last year. I would've noticed it."

"Hold on a sec. Let me make some light." He formed a ball of light in the palm of his hand and sent it floating ahead of us.

Ooh. Neat trick.

"And let me go first, just in case," he added.

Following him, I watched my step on the upward-sloping ground. Nothing would piss me off more right now than if I accidentally fell and broke a leg.

Or my neck.

Once inside, the ball of light rose above our heads and hovered in place. Far above us, a natural hole in the ceiling let a spear of daylight in. Between it, the opening behind us, and Kevin's ball of light, the entire chamber was somewhat revealed.

The floor was level, clean, and dry. The absence of typical beach debris such as driftwood or fish skeletons made me think the tide didn't rise high enough to flow in here. There weren't any animal droppings that I could see, so I didn't think the cave was used as a den. In fact, the floor was clean enough to seem as if it'd been swept by a human recently.

In the center of the chamber, a shallow circular depression was surrounded by stones which resembled a fire ring, but it was empty of either ashes or wood. Several large, flat rocks surrounded the fire ring and lined the walls, and I couldn't help but think of them as beds and seats that'd been strategically placed by someone with super-human strength.

Okay, so maybe my imagination was just a bit overactive.

Off to one side, a small natural pool softly glowed blue-green and drew my attention. Its unnatural light reflected eerily on the wall behind it.

I stepped closer, Kevin close at my heels.

"It's the rock," he murmured. He studied the hole in the ceiling. "It must be phosphorescent."

"So it glows in the dark." I'd read about such natural features, but never seen anything like it in real life.

He nodded distractedly, frowning as he peered into the pool's depths.

I craned my neck to see, too. The water was so crystal clear I easily saw the bottom of the pool and every detail of the sides and bottom, which were veined with the phosphorescent material. It didn't seem to be deep, but looks could be deceiving.

But those veins weren't anywhere else; the floor, ceiling, and walls of the chamber were plain rock.

I couldn't smell the water at all, although the rest of the chamber had a dry, slightly musty odor. "That can't be sea water," I said. "It doesn't smell fishy."

"And it's too clean," he agreed. He squatted and cupped his hand in the water, then tasted it. "It's spring water."

A spring? Here, so close to the ocean? I didn't know much about that sort of thing, but it seemed odd.

Turning away, I approached the fire ring. I hadn't noticed it before, but beside one of the large rocks a neat stack of firewood had been laid. The bowl of the fire ring was blackened from use, so *someone*—or several someones—had used this chamber often.

Suddenly I was surrounded by a deep sense of peace, with a hint of something more that came to me in a scrap of a feeling instead of a coherent thought.

Sanctuary.

This was a safe place. Safe from who or what, I wasn't sure. Maybe something or someone, or everything and nothing, in particular.

But when I probed Maggie's memories, I found none about this place. I didn't understand; how could she *not* have known it was here?

Kevin's soft voice interrupted my thoughts, and it echoed in the chamber. "Ready to go back?"

There was no reason to stay. But I was reluctant to leave. I longed to arrange the firewood in the ring, light it, and perch on one of the nearby rocks. Maybe commune with the gods.

I shook it off and nodded, following him back through the opening.

Outside the cave, he carelessly waved a hand and the ball of light disappeared. He quickly pulled me against him, and before I'd even opened my mouth to protest, we were back in the kitchen of the cottage.

Oh.

I'd thought he was getting frisky, but he'd only ported us.

"I could've done that," I snapped, then immediately hated how petty I'd sounded.

Thankfully, he didn't seem offended. "I know. But I thought of it first." He grinned.

Of course my stomach growled just then. He immediately sobered and pointed to the table and chairs. "Sit. I'll get the food."

Obediently, I sat while he took the snacks from the fridge and set them on the table with a frown. "This is all you brought?"

"Well, yeah. We'll eat a real meal later, at the festival. This stuff is just for taking the edge off our hunger."

He shrugged, and doled out an apple for each of us, some pita crackers, and cubes of cheese.

By the time we were finished, Mike hadn't returned, but I wasn't worried. He didn't really have a role to play at Lammas, so it didn't really matter when he showed up—although I hoped he wasn't late, like he was last year.

Checking the time, I stood. "I should start getting ready."

Kevin's voice was low and he wouldn't look at me. "I could help you."

Oh hell no.

Now he met my gaze with a hand placed over his heart. "I promise I won't do anything to disrupt your preparations." He glanced pointedly at my prosthesis, which I'd need to remove. "You could use an extra hand, right?"

Shit. He had a point. I actually *could* use some help. Although I'd gotten much better using my prosthesis for everyday tasks, I still hadn't attempted braiding my hair with it. The thought was daunting.

And it wasn't like he'd never seen me naked, just not since last year.

Before Cromm.

And before the scars.

"Fine," I replied. "But I'll hold you to your promise. If you break it, I'll port you off the cliff." I gestured vaguely out the kitchen window.

He flashed a grin. "Deal."

With the Lammas Oil from Maggie's cupboard, I headed up the stairs to my room, and he followed. I disengaged the prosthesis and left it on the bed, then ran the bath. After I added a few drops of the oil, the small bathroom filled with the essence of late summer: sunlit fields of ripening grain, crisp starlit nights, and golden warm sunshine.

It was hard to believe it'd been a whole year since I'd performed this routine.

Back then, I hadn't known what to expect; even though I'd had Maggie's memories of the Lammas Festival and ritual to refer to, it'd been a different experience for me.

Especially when Mike had pissed me off and I'd thrown him across the bedroom afterward.

Accidentally, of course.

I shook my head to clear it; I'd distracted myself long enough. It was time to undress.

Keeping my back to Kevin, I pulled off my shorts and tee shirt and left them in a pile on the edge of the threadbare rug. I stepped into the water and quickly turned to lower myself into the water.

His gasp was loud in the small room.

Despite my efforts to hide it, he'd seen the evidence of Cromm's cruelty on my body.

I hunched forward in the water and didn't look at him. I didn't want to see pity in his eyes.

Without a word, he knelt beside the tub and sponged the bath water over my shoulders and back.

I silently thanked him, but before I could focus on preparing for the ritual, my mind flashed back to when Zara had bathed me during my imprisonment in Cromm's palace. I pushed the memories away and forced myself to relax.

As he continued his ministrations, my mind opened and my consciousness retreated. I was almost ready to accept the presence of the Goddess.

Kevin helped me step from the tub, wrapped a soft, thick towel around me, and started drying my legs with another.

By now, I was beyond caring that he got a close look at the ugly scar on my thigh, but I knew what he saw: a paperback-sized rectangle of shiny, puckered skin.

He was gentle with the area, and after he stepped away, I finished drying myself. I took my hairbrush to the bedroom and reached for the prosthesis, but he stopped me with a light hand.

"Let me brush out your hair."

Well, why the hell not?

I nodded and sat on the edge of the bed with my back toward him, holding the ends of the towel closed with my hand.

His long, steady strokes almost made me moan; I'd forgotten how good it felt to have my hair brushed.

All too soon, his soft voice intruded on my stupor. "How do you wear it?"

"Braid each side. Make it into a crown and pin it. Leave the rest loose."

"Where are your hairpins?"

"In the box on the dresser."

He followed my instructions to the letter. No one would know I hadn't done it myself.

After I attached my prosthesis, he turned his back to give me privacy without being asked, and I dropped my towel.

Once again, I wore the butter-yellow dress with its paprika sash. I stared at my right arm in dismay.

The short sleeves of the dress exposed my prosthesis for everyone to see.

Not too long ago, I'd looked forward to showing it off. Why was I self-conscious now?

Well, there wasn't much I could do about it.

Since I'd never recovered the sandals I'd left under the oak tree last year, I decided to keep it simple and go barefoot. After all, this wasn't Arizona; there was no chance I'd burn my feet on scorching pavement here.

Foregoing makeup, I was done in less time than I'd expected.

"You can turn around now," I said.

Kevin's eyes roamed over me with obvious appreciation. These days, I mostly wore jeans or shorts and tee shirts for comfort and ease, but it was nice to dress up once in a while.

"You are so beautiful," he murmured, then glanced down at his jean shorts and tee shirt. "I think I should probably wear something a bit more appropriate."

"What—"

I'd started to ask what he'd brought, but I'd forgotten he didn't pack clothes like a normal person did.

No, he did what demi-gods did: he used magick.

Instantly, his appearance changed. Now he wore a dark green tunic with intricate Celtic knotwork embroidered in gold thread, and soft trousers in a darker green that was almost black. Leather boots completed his ensemble.

He'd also brought his warrior braids back.

All with just the wave of his hand.

I really needed to learn how to do that.

Looking at him, my mouth went dry. He was gorgeous, every inch a glorious Irish demi-god in his prime.

He smirked at my appreciation. "I thought you'd like this. It's traditionally what I wear for feasts."

I didn't reply. What could I possibly say to that?

We went downstairs to the patio, and only waited for a few minutes before Mike appeared on the path through the woods. He wore the same dark pants and white silk shirt he'd worn last year.

I watched his eyes flicker over Kevin, alternating between detached assessment and wry amusement. A ghost of a smile flickered on his lips before he stilled with his head cocked.

"They're coming."

Oh. Of course, his hearing was better than ours because of his shifter blood.

I faced the path, with Kevin on my right and Mike on my left.

A moment later, the voices of the village women echoed through the woods as they sang the harvest song. Another moment passed, and they were visible at last, headed straight toward us.

I took a deep breath.

Here we go.

CHAPTER FOUR

SOMETHING WAS WRONG.

Maura, the elderwoman of Finn's Cove, had smiled at me kindly, her eyes sparkling in the twilight. But when she looked at Kevin, those sweet eyes flashed first with disbelief, then fury. She raised her hands as if to attack him.

The rest of the women broke off their song and stared at her for a moment in shock before frowning at Kevin.

I quickly searched through Maggie's memories, but found none of Maura using combat fighting techniques or defensive magick. But if what Mike had hinted at was true, she could be a formidable opponent.

Naturally, Kevin had immediately assumed a fighting stance. His hands were also raised, to counterattack. His eyes, sharp and wary, watched Maura closely but he'd clenched his jaw and pressed his mouth into an angry line.

I spared a glance at Mike; although his eyes were fixed on Maura, he didn't seem too interested in diffusing the situation.

Guess that was my job, then.

"No, Grandmother." Hopefully, the honorific showed her the appropriate respect due her. "He is welcome here." My voice was calm, but strong and confident to reinforce my authority as the Lady of the Cove.

Maura's eyes shifted to mine and she studied me carefully. "Are you quite sure, child?"

"Yes." I replied without hesitation. "I am absolutely sure."

Her eyes darted back to Kevin for a tense moment, but she finally relented, lowering her hands and signaling the women to resume their song.

Kevin relaxed and took a deep breath, and his hands dropped to his sides.

Without another word, Maura began the ritual by pouring an offering to Earth before handing the cup of potion to me.

Its bitterness slid down my throat, and my mind receded further.

Just like last year, Maura led the procession to the village. Behind her, Kevin stayed at my side, and since the path was narrow, Mike was forced to walk behind us. The village women followed, their sweet voices echoing through the woods.

We paused at the same farmer's field as last year, to cut the first sheaf of grain for the symbolic sacrifice to the Goddess, and then continued to the village green.

When we arrived, it was too quiet. The tension was thick, almost tangible. The villagers stood to one side and stared at Kevin with hostility, and some of the older men held their walking sticks like weapons. Even some of the younger men seemed eager to fight.

Oh no. This wasn't good.

Silently, I begged Kevin not to do anything stupid to set anyone off. Maura had just nudged me to do my part of the ritual, and that had to come first. Afterward, I'd see what I could do to fix this.

The sheaf of grain flared brightly in the bonfire, and without another word Maura turned and disappeared into the darkness beyond the torchlight.

This year, no dogs or kids chased each other around the food tables. No laughter lightened the mood. Even the musicians sat quietly, as if unsure whether to play or not.

The potion wore off, and my senses returned in a rush. It dawned on me that the Goddess hadn't filled me with Her presence, like She had last year. It shook me more than I cared to admit, and my earlier calm confidence became deep unease.

What did it mean? Was She angry with me?

Mike found a table for the three of us and insisted we stay seated while he fetched our food.

"I guess I should've just stayed home." Kevin's voice was low. "I can feel everyone's hatred. It's crawling on my skin like ants."

"Their opinions won't change overnight. They'll come around." I studied him in the firelight for a moment, while his gaze was focused on the table in front of him. "By the way; why *do* they hate you so much?"

He still wouldn't look at me. "Not here. Not now."

Hmm.

Then Mike arrived with three full plates of food. He'd somehow managed to carry them without dropping or spilling anything, which was amazing. But he quickly left again, this time for the drink station.

At least there was one good thing in all this: with everyone so preoccupied with Kevin, no one seemed to notice my prothesis.

Garrett suddenly appeared in front of me; I hadn't even seen him walk my way. His normally warm eyes and smile were icy as he glared at Kevin, who kept his eyes on his plate.

"Beg your pardon, Lady, but what's *he* doing here, then?" Garrett snarled. His hands were balled into fists, and I'd never seen him so threatening.

I laid my hand on his arm. "Garrett, please. He's not... he's Kevin now. He's an ally. And a friend."

The scowl hadn't left his face, but a tiny flicker of doubt appeared in his eyes, and I decided to press my advantage.

"You—and the others here—may not be aware of this," I started, "but after Samhain last year, I was kidnapped and tortured." I held up my prosthesis, and his gaze flicked over it with interest. If he hadn't known, then probably none of these people knew. As the owner of the village pub, he'd be the perfect person to spread the word. "Kevin helped rescue me. He's an ally," I repeated.

After a long, measured look at Kevin—who remained focused on his plate—the animosity drained from Garrett's face, and I knew he'd come to a decision. Gently, he took my left hand in his and raised it to his lips.

"Please forgive me, Lady. I'll make sure the others know."

At the change in Garrett's tone, Kevin lifted his head in surprise. After only the briefest hesitation, Garrett nodded to Kevin. Kevin blinked and returned the nod.

"Thank you. I knew I could count on you." I gently squeezed Garrett's hand.

With a final smile at me, he turned and left just as Mike arrived with our drinks.

"Thank you for that," Kevin murmured.

"Be patient," I replied, just as quietly. "Things will work out. You'll see."

After handing out the drinks, Mike sat. "So was that about what I think it was about?"

"Yeah. Hopefully everyone will chill out now."

He raised a brow but didn't reply.

As I ate, I noticed Garrett was already making the rounds among the villagers, and I almost smiled at the sense of accomplishment I felt. After all, I'd handled this situation without so much as a word of help from Mike. Which, on the one hand, showed how much I'd grown and changed. But on the other, it raised a big question: why had Mike been backing off on things that, only a year ago, he would've insisted on handling himself?

By the time I finished my food, the overall level of tension had dropped considerately. I finally relaxed, as did Kevin, who smiled at me. Now the band warmed up with their fiddle, bodhrán, and whistle then launched into a rousing jig.

But I didn't feel like dancing anymore, and it sucked. For weeks I'd looked forward to having some much-needed fun, but now that it was here I was too tired.

Without a word to anyone, the three of us slipped away and headed back to the cottage.

We walked in silence on the path through the woods, lost in our own thoughts.

It was a gorgeous evening. A slight breeze rustled the leaves above my head and brought the salt tang of the ocean inland. The half-moon was bright enough to cast shadows, and an owl hooted somewhere—a lonely sound echoing in the dark woods.

We were several hundred feet from the bridge over the creek when a ferocious growl split the calm night and stopped us in our tracks.

From the darkness, an enormous beast charged straight toward us.

The creature was easily twenty feet tall, with leathery gray skin and menacing yellow eyes. Long strings of saliva dripped from wickedly-long fangs that seemed too sharp and too white. Some sort of tattered remnant of clothing barely covered its hairy body, and it carried what seemed like a small tree in one meaty fist, brandishing it like a club. The creature smashed it on the ground a couple of times and roared again, and I felt the vibration in the soles of my feet.

If it wanted to scare us, it was succeeding, because I was petrified.

One swing of that makeshift club would smash me into a gory mess.

My mind frantically considered—and promptly discarded—various ways to get out of this mess.

The creature continued toward us—wait, no, he was focused only on *Kevin*—in a shambling but surprisingly fast gait. As it came closer, the most god-awful smell hit me and my stomach rolled. It smelled like rotten cabbage.

Or what I *thought* rotten cabbage smelled like, since I'd never actually been around any. Yet.

When the beast was almost on top of us with its club raised high, Mike stepped forward and placed himself between the creature and Kevin and I.

"*Stop, Petelorionitis!*" Mike's voice was a sharp command that immediately halted the creature's charge.

It stood for a moment, uncertain, the club still raised in readiness for smashing. Then, it slowly lowered the club and pointed it at Kevin. The creature growled roughly, but I was able to understand the one word it spoke in its gravelly voice: "Enemy."

I glanced at Kevin. He held a long, wicked blade in his hand—now where had *that* come from?—that began to faintly glow blue.

"*Not* enemy." Mike was stern, uncompromising. "Friend. Ally."

"No." The creature shook its shaggy head. "Always enemy."

"Not anymore. Friend. Ally." Mike repeated his words calmly but firmly.

If I spoke, would it help or hurt the situation?

There was only one way to find out.

54

"He is our ally. We speak the truth." Thankfully, my voice was only a tiny bit unsteady.

The creature's yellow eyes shifted to me, and I forced myself to keep my gaze locked despite my terror. Then it moved on, to study Mike again. Then back to Kevin. Finally, the tension left its shoulders and the tree-club dropped to the ground with a heavy thud that shook the ground.

With a heavy sigh, the creature shrunk down in size and became... Pete the Troll.

What the hell? That huge ugly monster had been *Pete?* Friendly little Pete?

Back before this whole Keeper thing started, I'd thought trolls were like the ones I'd seen in movies: huge, nasty, and mean. Then I'd met Pete—nice, friendly, and sweet Pete—last year. I'd thought the movies just had it all wrong.

Now I understood.

Apparently, trolls transformed when they were angry. Sort of like how the scientist became the big green dude in the superhero movies. But at least Pete wasn't naked like that guy. Thank the gods I hadn't had to see that.

Pete was now dressed in his usual clothing. The strange tattered garment he'd worn as Angry Pete was just *gone.* Must be that weird magick thing again.

"Sorry, Lady," Pete said, twisting his hat in his hands. "I didn't mean to frighten you. I saw *him* and just... well, anyway, I'm sorry."

I glanced at Kevin again, wondering what the hell he'd done to generate such hatred from everyone here.

"It's okay, Pete. Apology accepted." Honestly, I really didn't know what else to say at this point. Just when I thought I'd seen everything, something like this happened.

Pete nodded at Mike, then, after a slight hesitation, he nodded at Kevin before plunking his hat on his head and scampering under the bridge.

I had to remember to stay on Pete's good side.

After a moment, we shook off the experience and continued over the bridge on the path to the cottage.

When we'd left the bridge far behind, I asked Mike, "What was that you called him? I didn't even know that was Pete."

"Petelorionitis is his full name. Pete's his nickname."

It sounded like a rare and deadly disease to me, but I didn't say that. "I had no idea he could... grow... change... like that. He was *huge*."

"When trolls go into battle, they change their appearance," he explained. "I've seen some even bigger. Older trolls, mostly, because Pete is still relatively young. But there's a downside to that form: it takes a lot of energy to maintain. That's why they usually consume their opponents in battle." After a slight pause, he added, "Whole."

My imagination went into overdrive then, hearing the snap and crunch of bones in that huge maw of needle-sharp teeth. My stomach was just a bit queasy.

"Thank you both for defending me." Kevin's voice was soft, but it still brought me out of my gruesome thoughts.

"That's what allies are for." I noticed his sword was gone. "So what happened to your sword?"

"I sent it back to my roaming room."

"Your what?"

He flashed a smile. "It's like a fold of space that I use to store things in. Sci-fi and fantasy nerds would call it a *pocket universe*, but it's not. Not really."

"A universe in your pocket?"

He snorted. "No. You're thinking too literally."

"Never mind." I shook my head, but it actually sounded like a cool thing to have.

At the cottage, Mike said goodnight and went up to his room, leaving Kevin and I standing in the living room a bit awkwardly. I studied the couch dubiously. Although I'd napped on it once or twice, it didn't look comfortable enough for a full-grown man to sleep on for a full night.

I turned away. "I should find some sheets and a blanket."

He stopped me with a hand on my arm. "Can I sleep upstairs? With you?"

Of course he'd want that instead.

As if expecting me to protest, he quickly added, "Just sleep. I won't pressure you for anything else, I promise."

As I hesitated, he stepped closer.

"I... I hate to admit this, but I just want... need..." He sighed and tried again. "I just don't want to be alone tonight."

Damn. He'd said the one thing that would convince me.

"Okay," I nodded.

He followed me up to my room, but it wasn't as if he'd never seen it before. Last year, he'd sort of ambushed me here after my shower. It was how we'd first met, actually. Back when he was an arrogant asshole.

Now, with a wave of his hand, he changed into loose sleep pants and a tee shirt.

"Can you show me how to do that?" I asked.

"I'm not sure you'd be able to."

"What do you mean? Why wouldn't I?"

He shrugged. "It's not something just anyone can learn. It's not spell craft. It's more like porting without a portal: either you can do it, or you can't."

As I headed to the bathroom to change, I grumbled under my breath.

When I came out, I expected to find him tucked into bed, but he'd settled into one of the big armchairs by the fireplace. It looked even more uncomfortable than the couch downstairs.

While I hung my dress in the wardrobe, I made a decision.

"You can share my bed, if you want." My voice was quieter than I'd intended. Was I nervous?

He searched my eyes and shook his head. "I don't think that's such a good idea."

"Why not?"

"You know *exactly* why not." His eyes flashed green fire.

I sighed. Now that I'd made up my mind, I didn't appreciate the rejection. So I went to him, took his hand, and tugged him toward the bed. At first he resisted, but when I boosted my strength magickally and pulled harder, he finally gave in.

We snuggled under the covers, my head resting on his chest and the comforting steady beat of his heart in my ear. He held my hand against his chest, and gently stroked my hair with the other. My eyes closed as I relaxed.

It felt good. *Better* than good. It felt amazing.

His breath stirred my hair, and my mind wandered.

When was the last time I'd been held and touched like this? I couldn't remember. Maybe it'd been last Lammas, when Mike had held me through the night.

After I'd thrown him across the room.

That must've been the last time; only a couple of months later I was imprisoned on Cromm's world, isolated for long periods of time and craving the touch of another human being. And even after my rescue, no one had seemed to know exactly how to deal with me and my new problems, so they'd left me alone more often than they had before I'd been taken.

A lump formed in my throat as I thought of all the times I'd needed this kind of contact but had been too fucked up to ask for it.

But this... this was a damn good start to fixing all that.

My mind drifted for a while, until it began replaying the events of the evening. And an unanswered question came back to me.

"So can you tell me now?" I asked softly. "Why the people of Finn's Cove hate you so much?"

After a moment, he replied, just as softly. "Once upon a time, long, long ago, there lived an asshole who went by the name of Bricriu of Ulster. As a satirist, he loved to ridicule the rich and famous nobility of Ireland, as well as their pompous ladies. But after a while that grew boring, so he became a brigand. A thief, a cheat, a marauder, a bandit. I—he—stole sheep and cattle from farmers. Seduced their daughters and left them with babes in their bellies. Got drunk and trampled widows' vegetable gardens. Toppled buildings in the middle of construction. That sort of thing." He drew a breath to continue, and his stroking of my hair slowed, as if he were lost in the story. The memory.

"Then one day, during his travels in Munster—that's this part of Ireland, by the way—he came to a small harbor village that he didn't bother to learn the name of. He stopped at the tavern for food and drink, and if the tavern keeper had a pretty daughter, a roll in the sheets. If he were lucky. Somehow, he got caught up in a discussion among the menfolk, who were placing wagers on who'd be the one to successfully track down and kill a vicious wolf who'd attacked one of the villager's children. Poor babe had been partially eaten, they said."

I gasped but didn't comment, and I fought the urge to look at him. I had the strange idea that if I looked at him, he wouldn't continue with his tale.

"Well into his cups by then, Bricriu decided to take on that wager. After listening to the conflicting accounts of the wolf's appearance, he set out on his task. If he'd been smart and sober, he would've stuck to tumbling the tavern keeper's daughter. But alas, that was not to be."

It was fascinating, the way he'd reverted to more of an old-fashioned manner of speech and his accent had grown more pronounced, as he spoke. And under my ear, his heart beat had quickened.

"The night was a bit chilly, but a bright, full moon was high in the sky, so he could see quite well. As he walked the path through the woods, a snarling shape suddenly appeared from the darkness and rushed at him. He struck at the beast with his heavy walking stick and heard a sharp crack. The creature collapsed and lay whimpering, and he thought himself quite lucky that he'd managed to complete the task so quickly and easily."

By now, he'd completely stopped stroking my hair. Instead, his hand had dropped to my shoulder, where it gripped me almost painfully. But I didn't want to interrupt, so I did my best to ignore it.

"As he approached the creature, it snarled at him and pawed the ground desperately, but didn't run away. Surely his luck was in. And then..." He drew another deep breath. "And then, the moon showed him his prey. Too small for a wolf, really. And with a beautiful reddish coat, it could only be a fox. A closer look—but not too close; after all, he had to stay clear of those snapping jaws with their needle-sharp teeth—showed the fox to be heavily pregnant. A female, then, and surely dying. Her poor head was smashed in, and blood soaked the ground around her. Still she snarled and snapped at him, and he stumbled backward in shock."

Now his heart pounded in my ear, and my mouth had turned dry.

"He told her he was sorry, over and over, but there was nothing he could do. 'Twas before the cattle raid, you see, so I—*he*—didn't have any magick yet. He could not heal her. Could not fix his mistake. And the gods ignored his pleas." He swallowed and took another deep breath. "He crouched there, as close as he dared, crying and apologizing, and when he finally blinked the tears away and looked at her, she was gone. Well, the *fox* was gone. In her place... she'd been a shifter, you see. Her human body, full with child, lay unmoving in the moonlight. Only later, *much* later, did he find out she'd been the beloved wife of the tavern keeper. In a tiny village known as Finn's Cove. She wasn't supposed to be there, you see. She'd been cooped up for so long with the babe growing in her belly, she'd been desperate for a little run."

Now, I couldn't hold it back any more. I propped myself up on my elbow and looked at him. As he met my gaze steadily, I wasn't at all surprised to see his face was streaked with tears.

"Oh gods," I breathed. "Poor Garrett. He must've been insane with grief."

"Garrett?" He frowned. "He had nothing to do with it." When I blinked in confusion, he explained, "This was long before Garrett's time. Someone else owned the tavern."

I should've known better than to assume. I knew Kevin had lived for roughly a thousand years, which meant Finn's Cove was much older than I'd thought.

"Oh, but now's the best part," he continued. "See, those men at the tavern had known *exactly* who I was, and they'd set me up. Maybe I'd wronged someone's kith or kin, I dunno. That part I never did find out. Oh sure, 'twasn't all lies. There *was* a ferocious wolf, but he'd been sitting right there among the men. He was a shifter too, y'see. There'd been no vicious attack on a wee one. It'd all been a fairy tale, with one goal in mind: to lure me out so he could attack and kill me. Get rid of me for good."

I blinked away tears.

"So of course, the good people of Finn's Cove had cause to hate me, didn't they? I murdered one of their own. A woman and her unborn child, no less."

"I'm so sorry," I murmured.

He took a deep breath and let it out, staring at the ceiling. "He ran back home with his tail 'tween his legs and never ventured out of Ulster again. Well, until he got trampled by a bull and woke up a demi-god."

"Is that when you decided to change? Be a better person?"

His bitter laugh sounded odd. "Oh, I tried. Believe me But too many people wouldn't give me the chance. After a while, I gave up. Just stayed on my own world and minded my own damn business."

A fragment of Maggie's memories came to me, and I frowned. "But you helped Maggie find a lost child. Here, in Finn's Cove. Surely that helped a bit?"

He met my eyes again, this time with a sad little smile. "No one knew it was me, love. That was one of the conditions of my help."

I cocked my head. "Whose? Yours or hers?"

"Mine, of course."

I shook my head. What a mess.

Again, he took a deep breath and released it. "So, now you know."

Impulsively, I leaned forward and kissed his cheeks, tasting his salty tears. Then I moved to his lips, and after a moment's hesitation, they parted. I kissed him softly, deeply, then rested my forehead against his.

"I'm so, so sorry," I said. "I know it doesn't mean much coming from me, but I just wanted to say it."

"What?" He pulled me away to look at me sharply. "Of course it means something. It means *everything* to me. You are, after all, the Lady of the Cove."

His eyes were deep green pools I could get lost in, and the moment had turned even more serious. To lighten it up a bit, I tried for a playful tone. "Careful. If someone didn't know any better, they'd think we were in love or something."

He studied me for a moment longer, and his look softened. "Yeah. I guess we're just two crazy fools, then, aren't we?"

I didn't answer; I was too busy kissing him.

In the morning I woke refreshed, feeling better than I had in weeks. I untangled myself from Kevin's arms and legs and stretched, then sat on the edge of the bed and stared at him while he slept on, undisturbed.

His long dark lashes fanned on his cheeks, and his mussed hair begged for my fingers to smooth it. The sheet was bunched around his hips, leaving his chest bare to invite my kisses.

He was simply too gorgeous to be considered simply handsome. How the hell was I so lucky to have this gorgeous demi-god in my bed?

And yet, I couldn't let myself forget he'd been such an arrogant asshole last year, even though he seemed to be the perfect boyfriend now.

Wait—where had *that* come from?

He *wasn't* my boyfriend.

Nope. No way.

Irritated, I slipped out of bed, grabbed my clothes, and headed to the bathroom.

As I dressed, I thought back over our night of sex.

We'd started out slow and gentle, but ended wild and filled with raw pent-up need. Thank the gods for Kevin's soundproofing spell.

And in the darkness, I hadn't cared one bit about my scars. It'd also helped that he'd kissed each one almost reverently.

Afterward, as the sweat dried on our bodies, we'd snuggled and finally dozed.

Now, catching myself in the mirror, I almost laughed at the dopey grin on my face.

I left the bathroom and found him sitting on the edge of the bed, dressed in fresh jeans and tee shirt, and waiting for me.

"Morning." His sly smile sent a shiver through me.

"Morning." I stepped between his legs, lifted his face, and kissed him.

He always tasted of peppermint.

"You shouldn't start something we can't finish," he murmured against my lips.

"Mm. Good point." Reluctantly, I pulled away.

I threw my few things into my bag and we went down to the kitchen.

The aroma of coffee was strong in the small room. Mike leaned against the sink, eyes flicking between me and Kevin without emotion.

But with his enhanced wolfie senses, he could probably smell Kevin's scent all over me. Maybe I should've taken a shower.

Feeling my cheeks heat, I mumbled a greeting and poured myself a cup of coffee.

On the kitchen table, the bagels I'd brought were misshapen and sad-looking. I stared at them and sipped my coffee, and my stomach took the opportunity to growl loudly in the quiet room. It seemed like a good excuse to go to the pub for breakfast.

"Let's go to Garrett's," I said.

"Uh... do you really think that's a good idea?" Kevin frowned.

"It'll be okay. You'll see." I had more than enough confidence for both of us.

And if anyone said anything different, I'd just deal with them.

He offered to port us there, but I shook my head. "I'm not here often enough. I want to enjoy the walk."

So far Mike hadn't said a word, but at least he'd thought to turn off the coffeemaker before we left.

Oh, but it was a beautiful day. The breeze was cool but the sun was warm, and only a few puffy white clouds dotted the deep blue sky. Last year, Mike had been convinced I controlled the weather here, that I'd been keeping it sunnier and warmer than was typical for southern Ireland.

But if he was right, I sure as hell didn't know *how* I was doing it.

We were quiet on the way to the village, each of us lost in our own thoughts, I supposed. At the bridge across the creek, there was no sign of Pete, and I wondered if he was okay.

The pub was nearly empty and we didn't attract much attention, which Kevin probably appreciated. When Garrett looked up from the bar, he greeted us with a huge grin. It slipped just the tiniest bit when he saw Kevin, but he recovered quickly, and Kevin seemed relieved and pleased at the warm welcome.

All three of us had the day's special, the Full Irish Breakfast: crispy bacon, savory sausages, fried potatoes, and eggs, all served with crusty brown bread still warm from the oven with creamy, soft butter on the side. A pint of Garrett's signature harvest brew complimented the meal perfectly.

But as I looked over my plate, I didn't recognize the odd round things. Two were a light tan color but the other two were dark, almost black.

"What are these?" I poked them with my fork.

"Black and white pudding," Mike replied. At my blank look, he explained. "It's basically ground pork, oats, some spices, and salt. A bit of pig's blood makes the black pudding its dark color."

63

I stared at it dubiously. *Blood?* Eww.

"You'd be surprised how tasty it is," Kevin said. "Try a bite of each, and if you don't like it, I'll eat it."

Well, why not?

First, I tried the white pudding, and he was right; it was quite tasty. Then I cut a smaller piece of the black pudding.

If I hadn't just been told it had pig's blood, I'd never been able to tell. Other than being a bit too salty for me, it was surprisingly flavorful.

"It's not bad," I mumbled around a mouthful.

Mike nodded, but Kevin seemed a bit disappointed he wouldn't be getting my portion after all.

The meal was heavy and filling, but it was delicious, and it fed more than just my stomach.

It fed my soul.

The harvest ale, on the other hand, was light and refreshing.

We didn't stick around after we finished. We weren't exactly in a hurry, but we were ready to go back home. Mike paid the tab, we gave Garrett our praise, and took our leave.

On the way back through the woods, my face was tilted to soak up the sun filtering through the green canopy of leaves. Mike grabbed my arm and pulled me to a stop.

Pete stood near the bridge with his hat in his hands.

Last night, I hadn't seen him clearly enough to notice how much he'd changed since last year, but now I did.

Gone was the grubby little guy I'd first met. His grizzled beard was neatly trimmed, his unruly hair was cut, and he sported clean clothes. Even his wide-brimmed hat was new. His face and hands were spotless, too.

"Greetings, Lady. I... uh... just wanted to apologize again for last evening." As he spoke his gaze moved from me to Kevin to Mike then back to me again. "I've been letting others know that Bricriu is an ally now."

"Kevin," I gently corrected. "His name is Kevin now."

"Ah. Yes." He nodded. "Kevin."

"Apology accepted." Kevin's voice was respectful.

Pete nodded again, now seemingly unsure of himself as he opened and closed his mouth a few times, somehow reminding me of a fish.

"You look very handsome," I told him, hoping to set him at ease.

His cheeks flushed but he lifted his chin. "Thank you, Lady. I did as you and the Goddess bid, and I must thank you for that." He grinned and fiddled with the hat in his hands. "See, I met the sweetest girl troll on the library's computing machine. It is impressive magick. We speak using something called *chat*. Her name is Petunia. She even sent me a picture. She's very pretty, and she's coming here to stay. Um, today."

That was by far the most words I'd ever heard him say.

Impulsively, I knelt and hugged him. It was a little bit like hugging a child, except for the beard tickling my neck. After only a second's hesitation, he hugged me back.

"Oh Pete, I am so happy for you both."

But when I pulled away, he became shy once again, fidgeting and hesitant. "Could... could I ask a favor, Lady?"

"Of course."

Once again, his mouth worked soundlessly for a moment. Then he blurted, "Could you marry us?"

I smiled. "It would be my honor to marry you and Petunia. When is the ceremony?"

"Today. At sundown."

My smile slipped. We'd planned on leaving for The Hacienda as soon as we got back to the cottage, but it'd be nighttime there and it wasn't like we had anything planned. I looked up at Mike. "Can we delay our trip back?"

He smiled warmly, in a way I hadn't seen in far too long. "For this? Absolutely."

To Pete, I said, "Then it's set. We'll meet you at sundown—uh, where?"

"Right here at the bridge, Lady." His eyes sparkled with joy. He threw his skinny arms around me and hugged me with surprising strength. "Oh, thank you, Lady. I can't wait for you to meet her."

Gently, I pulled away from him and stood. "We'll see you later, then."

He quickly scampered under the bridge, and we continued on our way.

How in the world did he manage to stay clean under there? And was there enough room for another troll under such a small bridge?

"Will he need to move? Or get a bigger bridge?" I mused aloud.

Mike shook his head. "He doesn't actually live under there. It protects a portal to his home world."

I stopped walking. "Wait—so he actually lives in another dimension?"

He nodded.

Dimensions. Realms. Worlds.

I didn't know if I'd ever truly understand all this, but I definitely recognized the cool factor of it all.

CHAPTER FIVE

"**S**O. HOW THE hell do I marry two trolls?" I sat with Mike and Kevin at the kitchen table with my chin propped on my hand. The three of us shared the bottle of Irish whiskey from Maggie's secret stash.

I was kicking myself for not asking Pete for guidance on what he expected me to do for his wedding. I'd checked the memories and knowledge from the other Keepers, but there was nothing there. And even if there were internet service here at the cottage, I doubt I'd find anything on the topic of troll weddings.

Mike shook his head. "Sorry, I don't have a clue. My knowledge of trolls is limited to pretty much what I've already told you."

"If my memory is correct," Kevin said, "I think it's not much different from a standard human handfasting."

As one, Mike and I swiveled our heads toward him.

He seemed lost in thought, tapping a long finger against his chin, and hadn't noticed our astonishment.

"Go on," I prompted.

"Well, uh, let's see... " He cleared his throat and began ticking items off his fingers. "They say their vows to each other. You ask for a blessing from the Goddess. You tie a cord or ribbon around their wrists, then invoke the elements. Something like: *Sky above us, Earth below us, Sea surround us, and Sun upon us; you are now joined together as one with the blessing of the Goddess.*"

Oh. That was actually quite beautiful.

"Okay," I nodded. "Does it matter what type or color of ribbon we use?"

"Traditionally, red is used for handfastings. But I'm not sure if they—trolls, I mean—prefer one color over another."

If I remembered correctly, I'd seen some lengths of ribbon in the drawer of Maggie's cupboard, and got up to look. "Let's see what we've got in here."

There in the back, behind a small box of rubber bands, were several neat bundles of ribbon in assorted colors. I even found a length of silky red cord.

"Red cord and ribbon in different colors, check." I placed the bundles on the table and took a sip of my whiskey.

"Should we have some kind of celebration dinner for them?" I mused.

Mike shook his head again. "From what I understand, human food isn't part of their normal diet. Trolls are foragers when they're not in their battle form, so they eat whatever they find in the forest: grubs, mushrooms, animals—dead or alive—and sometimes just bark and leaves."

Eww. Gross.

Kevin spoke up. "If you have a bowl or something I could use, I'll go and find some grubs and mushrooms. Maybe I'll even get lucky and find a rabbit or two."

Better him than me. Since I wasn't familiar with the local species, it'd be just my stupid luck to pick poisonous mushrooms.

Hell, who was I kidding. I wasn't sure I could tell the difference with Arizona mushrooms, either.

I rooted around in the kitchen cupboards and finally found a large plastic bowl with a snap-on lid. It looked ancient, but serviceable.

"Perfect." Kevin smiled as if he actually looked forward to his task.

I shook my head. "While you're out foraging, I'll pick some wildflowers from the meadow and make a bouquet and crown for the bride."

Mike stood. "And while you two are doing all that, I'll get a bottle of mead from Garrett for a proper toast."

"Could you also get some dinner for us, too?" I asked. All the snacks were gone—except for the lumpy bagels, which I purposely didn't mention.

He nodded, and we all went our separate ways.

A couple of hours later, we met up again in the kitchen.

Garrett had given Mike a bottle of his special occasion mead, with a warning that it'd be potent. He'd also thoughtfully included a stack of small plastic cups. He'd boxed up a large order of crab cakes for us to share, and they smelled delicious.

Kevin removed the bowl's cover and proudly showed off his foraged feast: fat gray grubs wiggled enthusiastically among the earthy brown and white mushrooms. Noticing my grimace, he teased, "They're an excellent source of protein, y'know."

"No thanks. I'll just stick to the crab cakes."

Kevin smirked but didn't reply as he re-covered the bowl and set it on the counter beside a small unmoving sack. I assumed he must've been lucky after all, and found a rabbit.

I placed my contributions nearby; the colorful bouquet of summer blooms was accented with a few spikes of tall grasses, but the matching flower crown hadn't been easy to make since I didn't know how big Petunia's head was. So I'd estimated Pete's size and hoped for the best. Maybe these modest items would make her special day a little bit brighter.

Mike found a wicker picnic basket on the shelf in the laundry room, and it was the perfect thing to carry everything in. Packed and ready, we had plenty of time to enjoy the crab cakes.

The tender and juicy fresh crab had been skillfully combined with savory seasonings and nicely browned. The lemony mayonnaise sauce was tasty, and paired well with the crab.

So far, everything I'd tried at Garrett's had been fantastic.

When we arrived at the bridge, the sun had just dipped below the trees and backlit them in bright yellow-orange. Kevin set the basket and sack down, and we stood quietly waiting for the couple to arrive.

Close to the eastern horizon, the cloudless sky was almost lavender, but gradually shifted to a dark blue directly overhead.

"The magick hour," Kevin murmured.

"Twilight." I nodded, acknowledging the alternate term he'd used.

Within moments, stars appeared in the darkening sky, but the moon hadn't risen yet. The shadows closed in around us, and I could've kicked myself again, this time for not even thinking about bringing a flashlight or lantern. We'd have a hard time seeing each other in the dark.

As if reading my mind, Kevin created a ball of soft white light and floated it above us. The shadows receded, and before I could thank him, I was distracted by movement to my left.

Pete appeared from behind a sturdy old oak, dressed in a suit that could've been considered dapper if it weren't such a bright neon blue. But he'd left his hat behind, opting for a neatly combed appearance instead.

He bowed to me. "Good evening, Lady." The guys each got a simple nod. "Michael. Kevin."

"Good evening, Pete," I replied, while the men returned the nod.

"Miss Petunia will be right along. She had a bit of a fuss with her hair."

I could relate. "Is it something I can help her with?"

"No, Lady—ah, here she comes now."

The three of us turned toward where he'd indicated.

Petunia was roughly Pete's height and build, but that's where the similarities ended. Unlike his pale and rosy-hued skin, hers had a greenish tint. Her hair was piled on top of her head in an enormous blue spire that reminded me of some cartoon character I'd seen somewhere.

I blinked as I realized that in fact, her hair was the same bright blue as Pete's suit.

She wore a light pink dress with a train, which gathered dirt, leaves, and twigs as it trailed along behind her on the forest floor.

But it was her face that captured my attention, and I tried not to stare.

Unlike Pete, whose face mostly looked like a scaled-down human's, Petunia could easily be mistaken for a large, upright-walking frog.

Her thick, full lips protruded from a somewhat flat face below a wide nose. Her huge eyes gleamed yellow, and she didn't have much of a forehead. As she came closer, her lips opened wide and exposed a row of tiny dagger teeth.

I'd taken an involuntary step back before I realized she was smiling.

Beginning with me, Pete introduced us.

"I am so pleased to meet you." Unfortunately, I couldn't think of anything better to say.

She chittered and chirped in an unfamiliar language, her voice piercingly high.

"She hasn't learned English yet," Pete explained apologetically, then translated her greeting. "She says she is honored to meet the Lady of the Cove."

Mike said pretty much the same thing I did. But when Kevin was introduced, he bowed deeply from his waist and spoke a string of incomprehensible words.

Pete stared at Kevin with wide eyes, but Petunia chittered again. Her skin turned an even deeper green, and her smile spread almost around her entire head.

It would've been scary if I didn't know better.

Hell. Who was I kidding? It was *still* scary.

Pete inclined his head to Kevin and I saw deep respect in his eyes. "I am truly grateful for your kindness and courtesy."

I raised my brows at Kevin, but he ignored me and spoke directly to Pete.

"We brought several choices for your binding." He spread the bundles of ribbon and cord across the top of the basket. While the couple conferred, I quietly asked him what he'd said to Petunia.

"I just told her I was honored to meet a member of the Kociewie Clan. And that she looks as lovely as spring twilight."

I tried not to let my jaw drop. "You speak her language?"

He shrugged. "Only a bit. It's an informal dialect of Polish Troll-verse that I'm not completely familiar with. But I used a more formal version, thinking she might know it. I was lucky that she did."

Truly, sometimes I really didn't know what to think about him.

Pete and Petunia chose the red silken cord, and I wasn't really surprised; it's what I would've picked, too.

I retrieved the flower crown and bouquet I'd made, and the crown was a perfect fit, although I had to drop it down onto the spire of her elaborate hairdo as if playing some bizarre lawn game.

Thank the gods I didn't break out in inappropriate laughter.

All seemed to be in order, so I asked, "Shall we begin?"

The couple stood facing me, while Mike stood beside Pete and Kevin stood beside Petunia.

I took a deep breath and began the ceremony I'd cobbled together earlier, incorporating Kevin's suggestions as a guide. I measured my words carefully, so Pete could translate to Petunia without falling behind.

"Pete and Petunia, we are gathered here today to celebrate the beginning of your life together. Before the Goddess and the Elements, and as the Lady of the Cove, I ask you now to pledge your devotion to each other."

Petunia turned toward Pete and chittered for several minutes, but he didn't translate her words.

Actually, he didn't need to; we really didn't need to know what they vowed to each other.

After she finished, he spoke to her in the same language for a minute or so. They faced me again, which I took as my cue to continue.

"Pete and Petunia, you have pledged your devotion to each other before the Elements and the Goddess, who will now bless this union."

If She even heard me, that was.

Closing my eyes, I swallowed my sudden panic.

Shit. Why hadn't I thought of this sooner? What if She didn't respond? I hadn't talked with Her since last year, and She hadn't bothered to attend the Lammas Festival the night before.

I took a deep breath and plunged on, willing my voice to remain strong and steady.

"My Lady, I ask You to bless this union between Pete and Petunia. Great Mother, Goddess of All, please bestow Your blessing upon this couple on their marriage day."

In the silence, my heart raced, and I swear I heard a leaf drop nearby.

"*Deirdre, I am here.*" Her melodic voice in my head sent blessed relief rushing through me.

Then I felt Her as I was filled with Her presence. When I spoke, it was with Her voice. And somehow, everyone understood Her without a need for translation.

"Pete and Petunia, may your days be filled with love, laughter, and bounty. May your nights be filled with passion and pleasure." She lifted my left hand and touched two fingers to each of their foreheads. "I hereby give you My blessing for your joyful and fertile union."

Then She was gone, without another word.

Damn. I would've appreciated some kind words from Her, something that let me know She wasn't disappointed in me.

Oh well. I had a job to finish.

I looped the red cord first around Petunia's wrist then Pete's, and tied a loose knot.

"Sky above us, Earth below us, Sea surround us, and Sun upon us. Pete and Petunia, you are now joined together as one, with the blessing of the Goddess and the Elements. Go in peace and love."

Immediately, they hugged and kissed, and we awkwardly stood waiting for several minutes to congratulate them.

Without warning, Petunia shoved her bouquet into her mouth and devoured it, stems and all.

My jaw must've dropped; Pete looked at me, frowned, and cocked his head. "Lady, I thought you knew. It's traditional for the bride to eat fresh flowers for her first meal. Wasn't that why you gave them to her?"

I could've lied, but what was the point? He'd already seen my shock. "Uh, no. Actually, I had no idea. It was just a lucky guess."

And it was another detail I'd have to remember if I ever again had to marry two trolls.

Kevin uncovered the bowl and offered it to the couple. "We brought a little something to celebrate your wedding."

Petunia squealed in delight, and they both began scooping handfuls of the grubs and mushrooms into each other's mouths. In a matter of seconds the bowl was empty, and this time I made sure my mouth didn't hang open even though I was just as shocked as earlier.

Kevin took the bowl and set it aside, then pulled a limp furry body from the sack for each of them.

I don't know what I'd expected, but it sure as hell hadn't been *this*.

They ate the rabbits whole. And raw.

My stomach lurched as blood ran down their chins. In the quiet of the evening, I clearly heard the crunch of bones as they chewed enthusiastically, and somehow I managed to keep my dinner in my stomach.

Kevin stood grinning with pride at their obvious enjoyment of his foraging efforts, and Mike didn't seem bothered at all. He poured the cups of mead and handed them out, and we toasted the new couple.

The mead wasn't as sweet as I'd thought it would be; it was smooth and rich, with hints of spice and berries. True to Garrett's word, it had a kick: it went straight to my head, making me woozy.

But surprisingly, it settled my stomach.

Pete turned to us, eyes shimmering with tears. Even though I kept my eyes locked on his, I still clearly saw the blood that covered the lower half of his face and dripped from his beard.

One thing was for certain: I'd never see him the same way after this trip.

"Thank you all for making this my best day ever." His voice was choked with emotion, and he met and held each of our gazes in turn. "I owe you each a boon. Simply name it."

I opened my mouth to protest—after all, it'd been an honor to perform the ceremony—but Mike's hand on my arm stopped me.

"When next we meet, we shall name our boons." Mike's voice had a formal sound to it, as if giving a ritual response.

Pete bowed to us and turned to Petunia. We took that as the signal to leave, so we began gathering our stuff.

Until the emphatic grunting turned my head.

Pete and Petunia were on the ground, a pile of discarded clothing nearby.

Were they—having *sex*? Right here, in front of us?

Averting my eyes, I quickly started toward the cottage. Kevin's ball of light conveniently floated past me to light the path and we took our leave.

Halfway to the cottage, I could *still* hear them.

Apparently, I knew nothing about troll life.

"Wow. Just... wow." I shook my head, then burst out laughing.

Kevin joined in, then finally Mike.

"You did good, though," Mike said when he could breathe again.

"You sure did," Kevin agreed.

"Are we going home now, or waiting until morning?" I asked.

"I don't think we need to stay another night, do you?" Mike replied.

"Not really."

"Then let's leave now."

As I returned the unused ribbons to Maggie's cupboard, Mike washed the bowl and plastic cups, and Kevin fetched my bag from upstairs. Then we were on our way to the stone circle.

The moon had just risen but it wasn't bright enough to light our way, so Kevin created another ball of light.

"Can you teach me to do that?" I asked.

"Sure."

As we walked, he repeated the spell for me, and by the time we reached the stone circle I'd created a tiny spark of light.

"You just need to practice," he encouraged. Then he gave me the spell to open the portal and keep it open, which I'd almost forgotten about.

Unlike when I used the portal, the wind stayed calm with his spell. If I didn't know better, I wouldn't even know the portal was active, since there wasn't any obvious indication it was open.

"Mike, you should go first," Kevin said. "Dee, count to six before you follow. I'll be right behind you, and we'll close it from the other end."

Mike stepped into the bare patch of earth at the center of the stone circle, and disappeared. I counted to six and followed—and was immediately blinded by the midday Arizona sun.

Quickly, I stepped out of the way for Kevin. As soon as he appeared and stood next to me, he spoke the spell to close the portal.

"See?" he said. "Way easier. And not so windy or dusty."

And because the destination was named in the spell, this method would work for someplace I'd never been, unlike my method, where I'd had to visualize where I'd wanted to go. "Yeah. Much better. Thanks."

As we walked to the house, sweat trickled down my back. Somehow, I kept forgetting the temperature difference. If I wore shorts here, I was too cold when I got there; if I wore jeans there—like now—I was too hot when I got back.

But it still beat flying.

The alliance meeting was less than a week away.

The VIP tent had been delivered and set up on the garage side of the house, so it didn't spoil the backyard view and wasn't visible at all from the window-wall.

The delivery crew was still inside, arranging the furniture according to the layout we'd provided and putting the finishing touches on the décor.

I wasn't surprised that I was already nervous. This seemed like the most important meeting of my life, and I knew absolutely nothing about the proper diplomatic protocols for gods and demigods. After all, it wasn't like there were guidebooks available on the subject. And with a little luck, there wouldn't be any fights or arguments among the allies—most of whom I hadn't even met yet.

After lunch, Mike cornered me with a thick folder in his hand.

"If you have a few minutes," he said, "We need to go over some things."

So I sat on the sofa, and after a second's hesitation, he sat next to me instead of in the chair.

"Arddhu's concerned that someone at the meeting may be one of Cromm's spies."

I frowned. "I thought he knows everyone?"

"He does. But until we know for sure who we can trust, he's going to enchant an object for you to wear. It'll block any spells against you or attempts at mind magick."

Damn. Too bad I hadn't thought of that myself.

"He'll bring it the morning of the meeting." He handed me the file folder. "This is your homework for the next few days. I expect you to study the material and commit it to memory, because I'll be testing you on it."

I almost rolled my eyes, but instead opened the folder and flipped through the pages.

Each ally that was expected to attend the meeting had his—or her—own one-page summary that gave current name, other known names, identifying traits, and descriptions of magickal abilities.

I skimmed the first page with growing alarm.

Name: Ares, Greek God of War

Also known as: Aris, Enyalios. Mars to the Romans, Hadur to the Hungarians, Onuris to the Egyptians, Laran to the Etruscans, and Verethraguna to the Persians

Birthplace: Thrace

Residence: Olympus

Significant others: Enyo and Aphrodite (principal consorts)

Immediate family: Zeus (father); Hera (mother); Eilithyia (sister), Hebe (sister), Athena (half-sister); Artemis (half-sister), Phobos (son); Deimos (son); Eros (son); Anteros (son); Harmonia (daughter); Adrestia (daughter)

Weapons and armor: spear (primary), sword, shield, helmet, four-horse chariot

Abilities: exceptional strength, superior fighting ability, self-healing

Associations: dogs and vultures

Other: unpopular; extremely cruel, brutal and destructive; hair-trigger temper

There was more, but I'd seen enough for now.

"According to this," I tapped the page, "Ares isn't a very good prospect for an ally. It says here he *tends to lose control in battle* and is *unpredictable*."

"If Arddhu trusts him, so should we."

"But I thought we wanted allies to heal Earth." I flipped through the pages again. "These are all war gods and goddesses, not nature deities."

He cocked his head. "We have to defeat Earth's enemies first, remember? Which means battles. And war. That's why we need these allies now. Afterward, when we're ready to heal Earth, we'll enlist Elementals and Earth deities."

That made sense. But exactly *why* were they helping us? Just for goodwill, or would they expect something in return? Those were probably questions for Arddhu.

"Okay." I flipped the folder closed. "I can't believe Arddhu actually knows all these guys personally."

A corner of his mouth quirked. "He's the one who gave me the info on each. All I did was type it up for you so it was easier to read." Now his eyes narrowed. "By the way, what're you planning on wearing?"

Suspicious, I asked why.

"Because you have to make a proper first impression." He stood. "Show me your wardrobe."

"You've got to be kidding me."

His gaze was unwavering. "Nope."

He followed me to my suite, and I performed an exaggerated game-show host flourish in the doorway to my closet. He didn't react, just swept past me.

After a few minutes, he selected slim-fitting black pants, boots, and a dark red short-sleeved top.

"Uh, no. I'm not wearing that shirt." I showed him the long-sleeved black one I'd chosen specifically to cover as much of my prosthesis as possible.

But he shook his head. "You'll wear this one." Then his tone softened. "Look. I get it. You're still self-conscious about your prosthesis. But this meeting is important. You have to show them your strength—your *power*—and that you're ready and able to lead them. Don't forget, these are all battle-hardened gods, and they'll respect you more if you demonstrate that you are one hundred percent invested in this effort."

Yeah. I was well aware of the concept of *skin in the game*.

Except in my case, it was literal.

"But—"

"No buts. Hell, I'd rather you wore armor... hmm."

I knew that look on his face, I'd seen it often enough: he was up to something.

"Oh no, you don't," I interrupted his thought process. "I am *not* wearing armor to this meeting."

"No, not to this meeting. We don't have enough time to get something like that together this late. But it does give me an idea. You should have some type of armored suit for later, something for battle. I'll get the dev team on it."

Shit.

He left so quickly, he didn't see me roll my eyes.

Just what I'd never wanted: a suit of armor. In Arizona. I'd probably pass out from the heat before I'd ever get a chance to use any of my fighting skills.

But his words echoed in my mind: *something for battle.*

It wasn't like I didn't know that day was coming closer. It was just a bit of a shock to hear it out loud.

And it didn't matter if I didn't think I was ready; I had to be. Because I'd have to eliminate the threats to Earth before I could heal her. And even though the war gods and goddesses would be helping, the Goddess had given *me* that mission.

The buck, so-to-speak, stopped with me.

CHAPTER SIX

T HE MORNING OF the alliance meeting was one of those absolutely gorgeous Arizona days that we residents bragged about; one of the reasons we lived here.

The temperature was expected to stay in the mid-nineties, which was a bit unusual for early September, when triple digits were more common. The sky was a deep, cloudless blue that was a hallmark of low humidity, which made the foothills sharp and clear in the distance. There was no wind to stir up the dust, just a gentle breeze that made its own music as it passed through the mesquite and palo verde trees.

If this signaled that the monsoon was over, it'd been one of the driest on record.

But it should make for a most pleasant environment for our visiting allies.

A cocktail reception was scheduled for three o'clock, with the meeting immediately following at five. Chefs from the firm were preparing the food somewhere offsite, but it'd be delivered well in advance of the allies' arrival.

It'd be a busy afternoon and evening, but for now it was the calm before the storm.

Mike, Kevin, and I had a leisurely breakfast, then Mike grilled me one final time on the dossiers I'd memorized.

Arddhu arrived promptly at ten.

"Be welcome, Great One." I bowed my head in formal greeting.

"It is a pleasure to see you once again, Keeper." The corners of his warm brown eyes crinkled as he smiled. His longish dark hair didn't quite cover the two nubs of antler protruding from the top of his head. From experience, I knew they grew large and intimidating when he felt threatened.

He had a formal way of speaking that I started to pick up in my own speech patterns the longer I was around him. He didn't spend enough time among humans to understand many of our customs and idioms, either, so it seemed I was always explaining things to him.

But I didn't mind too much. After all, I hadn't seen him since I'd left his world after my rescue from Cromm's palace. I'd planned to return—especially to spend time in his extensive library—but Mike had kept me so busy, I'd sort of forgotten all about it.

Now, he reached for my hand, and I placed my prosthesis in his. He glanced down in surprise and studied it with intense interest.

"Ah, so this is the new limb. It is well made, Michael.' He raised his eyes to mine. "And from what I understand, you have done quite well learning to use it effectively."

Mike must've been keeping him up to date on my progress.

Gently, I squeezed his hand with my prosthesis, a level of control that would've been impossible for me a month ago. But I'd spent long hours over the past couple of weeks working hard to achieve that level of proficiency.

After all, I didn't want to crush any of the gods' hands when greeting them.

"I'm better than I was, but not as good as I will be." I smiled wryly.

"Don't let her fool you," Mike said. "She's become quite accomplished in a very short period of time."

"I have no doubt you will acquit yourself fittingly." He'd probably only squeezed my prosthesis as a reflex, but I felt it.

Just like when I'd felt Kevin's touch.

One of these days, I had to mention it to Mike. Along with a bunch of other things I kept meaning to talk to him about but kept forgetting.

With a smile, he released me and performed a short bow to Kevin. "Well met, Bricriu."

He'd probably never stop calling him by his old name, but Kevin didn't seem to mind much, coming from Arddhu.

"Well met, Great One," Kevin said with a full bow, from his waist.

I indicated the sofa and chairs in the living room. "Please make yourself comfortable. May I offer you any refreshments? Some Polish mead, perhaps?"

He'd shown such a fondness for that particular mead at our first meeting last year, I always made sure to have some on hand for him.

"That would be most welcome, Keeper."

Not too long ago, his use of my title would've sent me into a flashback since Cromm had used my title like that. But now I hadn't even flinched, and it was a measure of how far I'd come, how much I'd healed.

I poured a small glass for each of us, well aware that alcohol was typically consumed at any and all hours of the day when gods and demigods were involved.

Mike and I, of course, had adapted.

We sat and sipped for a moment, and Arddhu savored the rich flavors of honey and berries before he set his glass on the nearby table and brought a silk-wrapped object from his pocket. "This is the item I have enchanted for you to wear during the meeting. It will prevent any spell or attempt to magickally breach your person."

He unwrapped the object and presented me with a small, delicate ring. Not too fancy to draw attention, it was shiny silver with a filigree setting that cradled a jewel so dark it was almost black. When I held it up to the light, it was a deep crimson.

Figuring it probably wouldn't work if I wore it on my prosthesis, I started to slip it on my ring finger, then stopped. Not that finger, it didn't feel right. Instead, I put it on my middle finger and wasn't at all surprised when it was a perfect fit.

That weird magick thing again.

I didn't know what I expected; maybe a sensation of being shielded. Or maybe something similar to how a warding spell feels when it's walked into: like a feeling of heavier air, or higher air pressure.

But I didn't feel anything at all.

"How do I know it's working?" The question had popped out before I could stop it, and inwardly I cringed at questioning Arddhu's skill.

But he didn't seem to take offense. He just smiled. "Bricriu, would you do the honors?"

"Of course." Kevin leaned forward. "How about a basic fireball, for starters?" He created a small ball of red light and, instead of throwing it at me as he'd do in battle, he gently pushed it toward me.

Surprisingly, Mike didn't object.

Reflex made me flinch when the fireball was only a couple of inches from my body, but it hit an invisible barrier and simply vanished. I hadn't felt anything more than a slight warmth against my skin as the shield had done what it was supposed to do.

"And now, how about a compulsion spell?"

His words triggered a flashback, to the compulsion spell he'd put on me last year to keep me from leaving his bed while we'd had sex for what'd seemed like hours.

Before I'd been captured by Cromm.

"Dee?" Mike's voice had risen with alarm.

"Hmm?"

"Are you okay?"

"Oh. Yeah. Sorry, I was lost in thought for a minute."

Mike turned to Kevin. "What did you compel her to do?"

Kevin's mouth quirked. "Bark like a dog."

Obviously, the ring had completely blocked that silliness.

"Was that demonstration sufficient to answer your question?" Arddhu asked.

"Yes." I knew I shouldn't have doubted him, but I did feel much better seeing the ring in action.

Arddhu sipped his mead, but I'd caught the hint of a satisfied smile he'd tried to hide.

"How long will the enchantment last?" I asked.

"It is permanent. But be aware, if you wear the ring at all times, it will sip a tiny bit of your energy to maintain its readiness. After an attack, it will require additional energy to replenish itself to full effectiveness."

I stared at the ring, then realized its filigree pattern echoed the swirls of my bracelet. Had Arddhu intended them to match? Or was this more of the weird magick thing again?

"I'd like to show you the tent," Mike said to Arddhu. "And I'd be grateful if you could scan it for any spells."

"Of course. Bricriu, may I request your assistance?"

While the three of them headed out to the tent, I sat back in my seat and fiddled with the ring.

Why hadn't I thought to ask Anu to create a shield like this for me? It embarrassed me to admit it, but sometimes I forgot she was even there.

Which wasn't good.

"*Anu, how are you doing?*"

"*I am fine, Deirdre.*"

Was she offended at Arddhu's ring?

Before I could ask, she replied.

"*Do not concern yourself, Deirdre. I am not offended at the Great One's gift. All is well.*"

"*I'm sorry I didn't ask you first, though.*" I had to say it.

"*Your mind has been filled with many important details. Do not trouble yourself. The Great One's gift is precious.*"

"*You're precious, too, you know.*"

A brief hesitation before she replied. "*Gratitude, Deirdre. Much love.*"

"*Much love, Anu.*"

My thoughts turned to the flashback I'd just had; I'd have to make sure that didn't happen during the meeting later. I couldn't show any weakness, especially not this first time. Maybe after they got to know me better it wouldn't matter so much, but this first meeting was crucial. I needed to be strong, confident, and keep my wits about me.

The guys returned just as I'd finished rinsing my glass in the kitchen sink.

"We got the all-clear," Mike announced. "We're good to go." Which meant no spells or oddities had been detected in the tent or anywhere in the vicinity. It was safe to proceed with the meeting.

"That's great."

It would've sucked to cancel at the last minute. Especially after so many delays.

"I'm serious," Kevin quietly said to Arddhu. "C'mon, let me show you." He pulled Arddhu toward the hall, and they disappeared around the corner.

I shot a questioning look at Mike.

"He's going to show Arddhu how to use the internet."

Oh no.

Poor Arddhu.

Mighty God of Nature and the Forest he was, but he wasn't good at technology. He never used it. But Kevin kept hoping Arddhu would someday embrace it and maybe even install it on his world.

I wasn't so sure.

When I'd visited last year, he hadn't even had electricity; everything had been powered by magick.

"The additional security showed up while we were out there," Mike said.

"Good," I nodded.

In addition to our permanent six-member team, Mike had requested an extended temporary team of ten sent from the firm. They'd be backup for our own team and provide complimentary security for each of the attendees. The last thing we'd ever want would be an attack on any of the allies. Each probably had his or her own bodyguards, but it was a show of good faith for us to provide that extra security while the allies were here, on our soil.

And, according to Arddhu, most of them had never been here to Arizona, so everything had to be perfect and make a good first impression.

"Nervous?" Mike asked.

"Hell yeah."

He flashed a quick grin. "You'll do fine. Pay close attention to what Arddhu does. Concentrate on welcoming each ally. And stick to the agenda. I'll handle everything else."

"Oh, so you're doing the PowerPoint presentation then?"

He laughed. "I can't believe you actually thought we were doing that."

It'd been a running joke for the past couple of weeks. We'd playfully argued about which of us was doing a set of slides for an old-school projector screen.

He hadn't known I'd only pretended to be serious about it. After all, I knew this wasn't a corporate or business meeting. No, this was going to be a bunch of humans and non-humans sitting around an enormous table discussing the best way to remove the threats to Earth.

"You have to admit it was funny," I pointed out.

"Oh, it was. Especially when you said you expected one or two of the allies to chase the laser pointer. Like cats."

We both laughed this time, and I relaxed.

But I couldn't stop fidgeting with the ring on my finger, spinning it around and fussing with it. I rarely wore jewelry, especially rings. This one felt alien and conspicuous.

Arddhu and Kevin came back to the kitchen.

"We'll try again," Kevin said.

The look on Arddhu's face told me that wasn't likely.

"We have some time yet until the meeting," Arddhu said. "I suggest we review the agenda and discuss our expectations."

Once again, we got comfortable on the sofa and chairs, this time with bottles of water instead of booze.

"Well," I started, "my expectations are that I'll welcome each of the allies and schmooze them a little. Then we'll go over the agenda and decide how to proceed with removing the threats. Then we'll adjourn."

His brow furrowed. "What is this *schmooze*? It sounds... risqué. Please tell me you are not planning to couple with them."

I almost spit out my water.

From the corner of my eye, I saw Kevin cough and quickly turn his face.

"Gods, no. It means... make a good impression. Spend a few minutes of time with each of them. Compliment them a little. Make sure they have something to drink. Pay attention to them. That sort of thing."

His face cleared. "Ah, I see. Yes, that is a good plan. And you have committed to memory the information I provided to Michael?" I nodded. "Excellent. As I perform the introductions, you will have the opportunity to think of the material for each ally and perhaps make a personalized comment. Many have been quite eager to meet you."

My turn to frown. "Why is that?"

"You are unusual." His eyes twinkled. "You are the first *American* Keeper of the Sphere."

Oh not *that* shit again. It'd been what had pissed Arddhu off about me before we'd ever met. And apparently it made me a novelty among the immortals.

Yay me.

Mike spoke next, ticking items off on his fingers. "The agenda is as follows: state the overall goal. List the viable methods to attain the goal. Discuss the strengths and weaknesses of each method. Solicit feedback from the group. Revise the methods as necessary. Select the method. And, finally, begin planning to execute the method."

A tiny line formed between Arddhu's brows. "Perhaps we should make one small change: we should not be too detailed in the plan just yet. We are still not certain if Cromm has allies among the group."

"But how will we know?" I asked.

Before Arddhu said a word, Mike replied. "Kevin and I have a few ideas on that, but we haven't finalized anything yet. We'll just have to be cautious and keep it to a high-level discussion only. Generalities, not specifics."

"Will we still get into logistics? Like, who'll be responsible for what?" In my earlier discussions with Mike, I'd been tasked with distributing responsibilities. But if we weren't going to do that at this meeting after all, I needed to know.

Now Arddhu replied. "We will only assign leadership roles to trusted allies at this time. Not everyone will have a leadership role."

"So you'll assign the tasks then. Instead of me."

He nodded.

Great. One less thing for me to worry about.

Kevin spoke next. "And we need to make sure we don't discuss who the targets are. That way we won't tip off Cromm or any of his cronies. Especially if they're working with the targets."

I nodded.

"Any questions?" Mike asked.

"I have one," I said. "Will everyone be in a human-like form? Or will anyone look... um... scary?"

Arddhu answered. "I have requested the non-human allies to appear human for this meeting. Specifically with two eyes, two arms, and two legs."

Oh, thank the gods I didn't need to worry about the proper etiquette for greeting someone with three eyes or six hands.

CHAPTER SEVEN

THE BLACK PANTS fit well, and although I was still self-conscious of my prosthesis being so visible, I had to admit Mike had been spot-on with his clothing choices for me. I was comfortable and the pieces were flattering. I'd swept my hair back in a low ponytail and kept my makeup minimal.

The overall effect, I hoped, presented me as attractive yet not too much so, and tough yet poised.

Worthy of leading the allies.

After I finished dressing, my bootheels clicked on the marble floor and echoed in the high-ceilinged main room. The butterflies in my stomach were having a field day, but I was sure they'd settle down once the meeting was underway.

Same way they used to do after a job interview had started, back when I'd been just an accountant.

Arddhu, Mike, and Kevin stood talking at the kitchen island, and all three broke off and turned toward me when they heard me approach.

"You look great," Mike said. His smug smile told me he was well satisfied with his choices. He was sharply dressed, in black trousers and a dove-gray silk shirt.

At first, I was uncomfortable with the heat in Kevin's eyes as he shamelessly looked me over, but then I lifted my chin and returned the compliment with my own once-over. I'd become so used to seeing him in jeans, shorts, and tee shirts that I'd almost forgotten how gorgeous he looked when he dressed befitting his demi-god status. His trousers were dark green, and his tunic was a shade lighter and richly embroidered with Celtic zoomorphic figures in gold, silver, and bits of red thread. The sides of his gleaming black hair were bound in warrior braids, but the rest lay in waves over his shoulders.

But it was Arddhu's reaction I wasn't prepared for.

His blatant head-to-toe appreciation of my body made me fidget with awkward self-consciousness, and I knew I was blushing again.

"Perfection." His voice was a soft, silky croon—a tone I'd never heard from him before now. I decided to ignore his compliment, since I had enough to worry about.

He, too, wore clothing befitting his god status: soft dark trousers and a forest-green tunic with Celtic knotwork embroidered in gold. His antlers rose from his head roughly six inches in a stately but non-threatening display of power.

As the four of us headed outside, he gently took my arm. "Remember: observe the manner in which I greet each ally and simply copy it." Thankfully, his voice had returned to its normal tone, and I relaxed a bit.

Earlier, he'd opened a portal nearby for the convenience of our guests. Even though I assumed some of them didn't need one to travel between worlds—like Kevin—Arddhu had requested the portal be used by everyone attending this meeting, as a gesture of goodwill.

We didn't want the allies popping in just anywhere and at any time; security would've been rendered useless.

Half of our security team stood ready to direct the guests as they arrived. They seemed a bit uncomfortably warm in their dark suits, but we wanted to project a professional image, even in the intense afternoon Arizona sun.

Since we had no idea how long this thing would last, we tried to prepare for the worst. We had plenty of food and drink—even for gods of legendary feasting status—and the other half of the security team was resting so they'd be fresh for the next shift, if we needed one.

Now, the four of us entered the tent, where we'd greet the guests in something like a standard receiving line.

It was cool and inviting, and I was impressed. As Mike had said, it was classy and refined, for a temporary setup.

The far end of the enormous tent held the large circular conference table and chairs. The near end had a variety of plush sofas, armchairs, and glass-topped tables arranged in a pseudo lounge for the cocktail hour. Along the left wall, cloth-covered tables held warming trays of prepared food, with the staff of servers stationed behind. A full-service bar was tucked in the corner with two attendants. Cases of beer, wine, and liquor were neatly stacked against the wall nearby.

The walls were dark wood paneling, and thick carpet in a striking shade of dark red covered the floor.

Good color to hide blood stains.

"The bathrooms are over there." Mike pointed to two dark-wood paneled doors on the right-side wall. "They're huge, by the way. And very fancy."

I shook off my morbid thoughts and smiled at him. "It all looks great."

"It did come out nice, didn't it?" He glanced around, obviously pleased with his efforts.

I glanced at the large clock over the entrance and my heart jumped into my throat. "Is that the right time?" Shit. My voice had actually *squeaked*. I cleared my throat and fussed with my prosthesis.

Mike checked his watch. "Yep." His gaze met mine. "Relax. Think of it as a party. Well, the first part, at least. It'll be fun."

"This isn't exactly my idea of fun."

"I know." He smiled. "But it is to me."

At his direction, the four of us got into position: Arddhu closest to the door with me next, then Kevin. Mike stood opposite with a tablet to mark each attendee's name off the list.

I took a deep breath and exhaled slowly, trying to calm the frantic butterflies in my stomach. Arddhu caught my eye and smiled reassuringly.

The door opened.

Show time.

And just like that, the butterflies went to sleep and an eerie calm settled over me.

Arddhu greeted the first guest warmly, taking both hands in his and speaking a few foreign words before turning to me.

"Deirdre, I present to you: Ares of Olympus. Ares, this is Deirdre Connor, Keeper of the Sphere."

So this was the legendary Greek God of War with a nasty temper. He was incredibly tall. His dirty blonde hair was thick and wavy to his broad shoulders. Golden armor gleamed under the fluorescent lights—gods, it'd be blinding in direct sunlight—and his knee-length leather kilt bared his tanned, muscular legs.

His head was tilted slightly backward in a haughty, down-his-nose glare. His gold-flecked light brown eyes dropped to my chest before returning to hold mine, which I made sure remained steady and unblinking.

I wouldn't let him intimidate me.

When I took both his hands in mine as Arddhu had done, Ares bent his head and stared at my prosthesis for a moment, then met my gaze with new respect.

"Be welcome, Ares of Olympus." My voice was firm and confident. "Thank you for attending today. Please help yourself to the refreshments, and I will speak with you shortly."

"I look forward to it, Keeper." His voice was deep and melodious, and he dipped his chin in a gracious nod before moving off.

Next was his half-sister, Athena. Known as the Greek Goddess of War, she was most famous for her expertise in battle strategy. She was gorgeous, and just as arrogant as Ares. Not quite as tall as him, she still towered over me by several inches. She, too, wore golden armor with a short kilt, but her breastplate was cut so low it showed the tops of her generous breasts.

Highly impractical, but definitely sexy, like something from a video game. So, it was probably ceremonial armor, then.

Her long, dirty-blonde hair tumbled in waves over her shoulders, and her eyes were stormy gray with gold flecks.

"Keeper." Her voice was smooth and rich as she nodded imperiously to me after Arddhu's introduction.

Oh joy. This was going to be a barrel of fun.

Not.

Ignoring her attitude, I welcomed her with as much warmth as I could muster, and she moved along with a thoughtful expression.

Next was Reshep, the imposing Egyptian God of War and Military Operations. He had to be almost seven feet tall; my neck strained to properly meet his eyes. His beard was neatly-trimmed along his jawline, but grown long enough in the center to braid and decorate with colorful beads. His deep brown skin glowed with a rich sheen, and his curly ebony hair was cut short in almost a modern military style. He wore a flowing caftan of multi-colored stripes, and an elaborate headdress that featured an animal skull of some kind. Its hollow eye sockets seemed to stare right through me. With difficulty, I suppressed a shiver of unease.

His dark eyes critically assessed me from head to toe, rested on my prosthesis for a moment of interest, then finally returned to mine. When we clasped arms as he'd done with Arddhu, his grip was strong and his muscles were firm.

"Pleased to meet you at long last, Keeper." His soft voice was deep, with only a slight accent. His full lips curved in a slight smile, which had transformed his stern expression into something almost resembling friendliness, before he moved on.

Tyr, the Norse God of War and Heroic Victory, was next. He was shorter than the others—hell, *everyone* was shorter than Reshep—and although he could be described as stocky, if the hard muscle of his arms was any indication, the rest of him was probably all muscle, too. His biceps were roughly the size of my thighs, and bulged obscenely from his sleeveless leather armor. He wore brown trousers and boots, and his russet hair was shorter than I'd expected, although not as short as Reshep s.

"I look forward to many victorious battles, Keeper." His gravelly voice boomed, and I couldn't miss the pure excitement in it. Nor that in his sparkling bright blue eyes. So far, he was definitely the most enthusiastic to be at the meeting.

Unfortunately, Kali, the Hindu Goddess of War, had sent a representative instead of attending in person. Maybe she was just super busy with all the wars and chaos going on in the world, or maybe I just wasn't important enough for one of the biggest names in war councils to attend this initial meeting.

Regardless, Arin, her male representative, seemed a bit shifty-eyed; he never allowed his gaze to rest on any one place for too long. But he was unfailingly polite, and even seemed warm and friendly toward me. He wore a cream-colored silk tunic with intricate gold embroidery down the front opening and on the hems, and matching trousers. His head was also wrapped in gold-embroidered silk.

"Great Kali sends Her deepest regrets," he said, rising from a small bow. "However, She has authorized me to speak on Her behalf."

As Arin moved on to mingle with the other guests, Arddhu spoke quietly in my ear. "Do not be overly concerned. She always does this. She will attend our next meeting."

Oh. She was *that* kind of goddess.

The next guest was Nayenezgani, the Navajo God of War and the Slayer of Alien Gods. I'd bet he had some fascinating stories to tell.

Unlike the others, he wasn't in traditional clothing or ceremonial armor. Instead, a beautifully tailored black silk suit draped his long, lean body extremely well. His raven hair was unbound except for a brightly colored head wrap, and it fell down his back in a smooth curtain.

Also unlike the others, he kept his dark eyes fixed respectfully on mine.

Okay, so I was impressed.

Belatucadros, the British God of War and Destruction, was the last to arrive. Another impossibly tall man, he was built like a tank, his body all solid muscle. His Roman-style leather kilt and chainmail shirt looked heavy, but he didn't seem to notice or care. A metal-studded leather helmet was tucked under one arm, so he offered his free left hand in a relatively modern handshake. His light brown hair was cropped short, and his ice-blue eyes were sharp. He seemed to miss nothing, taking in my prosthesis with a quick appraising glance that I'd almost missed. His demeanor spoke of a well-trained general: no-nonsense and highly organized.

With the initial greetings over, I glanced at the room and realized it was filled with men. Too bad Athena seemed like such a bitch. I could've used a bit more female representation at this point.

Oh well. Time to schmooze.

Slowly, I made my rounds among the guests, being courteous and complimenting them enough but not too much. No need to give them even more inflated egos.

Unfortunately, more than one mistook my friendliness for flirting, which forced me to politely—but firmly—decline their bold propositions. Almost as a rule, they openly leered at my body and made me feel like a piece of meat on display.

And each was fascinated with my prosthesis, boldly handling it as if it weren't attached to me and turning it this way and that. One or two stroked it suggestively, then chuckled when I pulled it away from them with a grimace.

They couldn't possibly know I'd felt those unwanted caresses.

Even Arin, Kali's stand-in, wasn't immune; where he'd been respectful when we'd first met, now he brazenly eyed my chest with a smirk.

Were these immortals just testing me, or were they really just a bunch of lecherous louts?

But there were two exceptions: Reshep and Nayenezgani. They were the only ones who consistently met my eyes and were respectful, never once saying anything even remotely rude or improper. And Reshep was the only one who asked me thoughtful questions about Arizona, as if he really wanted to know.

"In early summer here," I explained, "it's probably a lot like Egypt. Hot and dry. But by late June or July, we have monsoon storms that—"

Loud voices interrupted me. Annoyed, I turned toward the commotion.

There. Near the bar, Ares and Athena were in a heated argument.

"You fucking *bitch*," he snarled, his face inches away from hers and hands curled into fists. "Don't you *dare* tell me what I can and can't do."

Shit. This wasn't good. The meeting hadn't even started yet and there was already a fight?

But before I'd taken a single step toward them, Arddhu was already there. He smoothly intervened, and after a moment of speaking quietly to both of them, anger had given way to smiles and laughter.

Thank the gods for Arddhu's tact and diplomacy. If I were lucky, I'd learn a lot from him.

Instinct made me glance at the clock: it was time to convene the meeting. Making my excuses to Reshep, I drained my cocktail glass and headed toward Arddhu. Along the way, I caught Mike's and Kevin's eyes and tapped my wrist as if I wore a watch.

They nodded and started making their way to Arddhu.

"Time for the meeting," I said to Arddhu.

"Yes." He smiled. "Why don't you get everyone's attention?"

I took a breath and raised my voice. "Excuse me."

No one even turned their heads.

Well, except for Reshep. His dark eyes were fixed on me in an almost unsettling way.

I cleared my throat loudly and used a bit of magick to boost my voice. "Attention, everyone."

This time, only Tyr noticed.

"Fuck me," I muttered. "It's like herding cats."

Arddhu coughed over a laugh but recovered quickly. "Perhaps I should... if you would allow me?"

"Yes, please."

He took a step away. "May I have your attention, please." His voice boomed throughout the tent, and immediate silence descended as every single person stopped talking and turned toward us.

Of course they did. Typical.

My jaw clenched as my anger flared.

"The meeting will begin shortly," he continued, and pointed at the conference table. "Please move to the table and find your seat. Thank you."

The guests headed toward the table, but Athena pushed her way through them until she stood in front of me. "Where can I pee? I have to pee before we start this thing."

Without a word, I indicated the bathroom doors, and she rushed off.

As we walked to the table, I couldn't help it. I complained to Arddhu. "It just figures. They listened to *you* but completely ignored *me*."

"Do not be upset." He patted my shoulder. "They will come to respect you."

I eyed Ares, who was staring daggers at Tyr. "Will any fights break out?"

Arddhu shook his head. "I took special care with the seating arrangements."

Of course he did. I hadn't even given it any thought.

I laid my hand on his arm. "Honestly, I don't know what I'd do without you."

His lips curved in a smile, but somehow it seemed sad. "Someday, you will no longer need me. But for now, I am enjoying your belief in my importance."

Somehow I doubted that, but didn't reply.

Although the food tables were untouched, the booze was a hit. The guests hadn't even been seated a full minute before the servers were distributing refills.

Damn. I hoped we didn't run out.

Athena hurried to the table, then prowled alongside, looking for her name. She sat next to Reshep and grinned at him.

Mike sat on my right, Arddhu on my left, and Kevin to his left. The table was configured with several wedge-shaped sections that were arranged in a circle, which allowed everyone to easily see each other.

With everyone seated, I couldn't help but notice the two empty spots.

"Who are the no-shows?" I whispered to Arddhu, pointing with my chin.

"Marisha-Ten and Begtse."

Huh. The Japanese Goddess of War and Victory, and the Tibetan Lord of War.

"Should we be worried?"

"No, but I will contact them for an explanation. They had both agreed to attend."

The noise level rose as everyone chattered to each other, and I had the beginnings of a headache.

"Attention, please," I said.

Once again, everyone ignored me. Except Reshep. Again.

Had he even taken his eyes off me once, this whole time?

My anger flared again. I stood and tapped my pen against my drink glass.

The sharp ringing cut through the chatter surprisingly well, and now conversations broke off as heads swiveled toward me.

"Thank you." I flashed a smile, then sat and folded my arms on the table. As I spoke, I took care to make eye contact with each of them. "Welcome, allies, to this first meeting of our war council. In this session, we will discuss our objective and the methods to reach that objective. We'll also select one or more of those methods to focus on. But before we begin, does anyone have any questions?"

Most of them only glanced at each other, but Tyr spoke. "Yeah. What's *he* doing here?" His finger rudely pointed at Kevin.

We'd anticipated that question, and Mike had briefed me on the best way to respond.

"As most of you know, I was captured by Cromm Crúaich last year," I began. Almost everyone's eyes flicked to my prosthesis. Except for Tyr, who still scowled at me. I met his gaze calmly. "Kevin helped rescue me and is a sworn ally."

"So he's not Bricriu anymore?" That came from Belatucadros.

"No," Kevin answered. "I changed my name a long time ago, when I... stopped being an asshole." *Unlike you*, he left unsaid but was quite clear in the tone of his voice.

Shit. Those two had history?

And Tyr, too—had Kevin pissed off every pantheon of gods in existence? Ugh.

Most of the attendees turned to each other and murmured, but it was time to nip this in the bud.

"Are there any other questions before we begin?"

"Yes." Mike replied. "What's the objective?"

The murmurs immediately stopped, and I flashed him a quick smile of gratitude for helping me to get the group back on track.

"To remove the enemies of Earth."

Chaos erupted.

"Everyone, please." Once again I tried to regain control of the meeting, and once again, I failed.

Tyr and Athena loudly argued, and Belatucadros and Ares looked close to a fistfight.

None of this helped the headache that was steadily taking over my entire head.

Arddhu just sat there calmly observing the chaos and didn't lift a finger to help rein in these immortals he supposedly knew so well.

My anger spiked, and without thinking, I stood and slammed my fists on the table.

"*Enough!*" My voice thundered through the tent.

With a crash, my section of the table split into several pieces and fell to the floor, scattering my pen, papers, and notepad.

Dammit. How much would we be billed for *that*?

I shook my head; I didn't think I'd magickally boosted my strength, but I must have. There was no way I could've broken a conference table otherwise.

But at least there was silence now.

Blessed silence.

Because everyone's disbelieving eyes stared at me or the broken table.

And in that silence, the tent's door banged open.

"Who the *hell* thought it was a good idea to have a *war council* and *not invite me?*"

An unfamiliar female voice roared, the Irish accent unmistakable. Some of the allies visibly cringed. Just before the door quietly closed I heard the security team scuffling outside, and I turned to see who had crashed our meeting.

She stalked toward us, eyes on fire with fury and long dark hair blowing around her head as if in a storm. Dressed head to toe in black, her long open tunic flapped like wings.

Oh. I knew *exactly* who this was.

The Morrigan, Irish Goddess of Battlefield Death and Chooser of the Slain.

She hadn't been on the guest list.

And we'd just pissed her off.

Shit shit shit. This was so not good.

It was never a good idea to piss off a Goddess.

Arddhu sat like a deer in the headlights, his eyes wide in shock.

Ooh, there was a story there.

But goddammit, his expression meant I'd get no help from him.

Fine. I could handle this myself.

Maybe.

"Please accept our most sincere apologies." Thank the gods my voice was strong and even. "It was a simple error and no disrespect was intended."

She turned those fiery eyes on me, and I almost took a step back before I squared my shoulders, forced myself to stand motionless, and met her gaze.

"And just who the hell are *you*?" Her voice growled menacingly.

"I am Deirdre Connor, Keeper of the Sphere."

Abruptly, the fire in her eyes winked out and now they appeared mostly normal, although they were so dark they looked black.

"So *you're* the new Keeper." Her gaze raked me from head to toe before she seemed to dismiss me. Much like the other immortals had.

This was really starting to piss me off.

Feeling defiant, I raised my chin, shifted my shoulders back, and stood as tall as I could in my three-inch heeled boots. "Yes. I am."

Too bad I couldn't grow like Pete the Troll.

"Nice to finally meet you, Keeper." She grinned.

The tension in the room immediately eased, but I didn't relax just yet.

I smiled stiffly in return and indicated the empty seats. "Please join us. A server would be happy to bring you whatever you'd like to drink."

"Really? *Whatever* I'd like?" She sat and smirked at the server. "Do you have fresh blood?"

Knees weak, I dropped into my chair. She had to be joking.

I braced myself for some wise-ass god to say, *what? There's blood available and you didn't tell us?*

The server dead-panned, "Sorry, ma'am. We're all out."

Morrigan pouted. "Pity. I'll take an Irish whiskey then."

Of course she would.

The server dashed off to get her drink, and she greeted the others around the table with a polite nod. But when she saw Kevin, her eyes sparkled and she blew him a kiss.

Huh. For once, someone *didn't* hate him.

I looked at Kevin with a raised eyebrow.

He was actually *blushing.*

Oooh.

There was another story.

But it'd have to wait for another time.

Bending, I retrieved my notebook, pen, and papers from the floor and held them in my lap.

"So, what'd I miss?" she asked me.

"Actually, nothing. We'd only just started, and I'd just stated the objective for this council."

"Which is?"

The server brought her drink, and she threw it back in one swallow and indicated a refill. She leaned forward and folded her arms on the table, gaze locked with mine.

"To remove the enemies of Earth."

"Bold." She smirked. "I like that."

Damn, but I liked *her*. She was a welcome change from this room full of arrogant males.

"And just how do you plan to accomplish such a thing?"

"Actually, that was our next topic for discussion."

"So I was just in time. How fortunate."

And with that, the meeting was back on track. Interestingly enough, everyone stayed respectful and polite, but I had no idea if it was because of my violent outburst or the Morrigan's presence.

Maybe it was a bit of both.

By two in the morning, my headache was fierce, and I was having trouble staying focused on the discussion. I was exhausted and irritable, but at least we'd finally hammered out a plan that everyone had agreed to.

No minor feat.

Reshep was appointed mission commander, since he was the expert on military operations. As our strategist, Athena was second-in-command. Both of them would assign subordinate roles.

Kevin became my lieutenant, primarily responsible for herding this group of unruly deities. This made Mike happy, since it removed my biggest source of distraction and allowed me to focus on the more important issues, like getting battle-ready.

For his part, Kevin seemed pleasantly surprised but appreciative of the added responsibility.

Thankfully, none of the allies balked at these appointments.

After we adjourned the meeting, the allies made a mad dash to the food tables like a swarm of locusts, and it was then that I remembered that traditionally, feasting took place *after* business had been concluded.

I wished I'd thought of it before, and had the food brought later instead of having it sit around for hours.

But in only a matter of minutes, the warming pans were empty. Nothing but crumbs remained by the time I got to the tables. My stomach growled loudly, and I sighed. I'd have to just eat something quick back at the house, after everyone was gone.

"Sorry, ma'am," one of the servers said.

I'd just opened my mouth to reply when Tyr's voice boomed through the tent.

"Where are the wenches? Bring on the wenches!"

What the hell?

Kevin had reached my side and smiled sheepishly. "Uh... it's traditional to offer the company of women after the feast of a war council."

I rubbed my forehead and sighed again. Could this fiasco possibly get any worse?

"Tell you what," he continued. "I'll take them to my world. There are plenty of wenches—um, *women*—for them there, and they're welcome to use my palace for their... um, fun."

Before I could thank him, he moved off and drifted easily among them, letting them know the plan. I watched as he gathered the men to escort them to the portal.

Then the Morrigan eased close to him and seductively rubbed her body against his while she whispered in his ear.

The look on her face was nothing but trouble, and when he turned to her with his sly smile, the surge of jealousy in me was about to spiral out of control.

For some reason, the inside of the tent felt stiflingly hot. Or maybe it was just me.

"Dee, we need you." Mike's firm hand on my arm drew me back to the conference table, where Arddhu, Reshep, and Athena waited to discuss our first mission.

I glanced over my shoulder, but the large group had left the tent. I had no way of knowing if the Morrigan had gone with Kevin and the guys or not, but that roiling jealousy inside me snarled *of course she did*. My mind immediately pictured a frenzied orgy at Kevin's place, and the Morrigan fucking my boyfriend in the middle of it all.

Why did I keep thinking of Kevin as my *boyfriend*?

Ugh.

"Dee. I need you to focus, please." Mike's sharp voice cut through my thoughts, and I reluctantly turned toward him.

"Oh. Yeah. Sorry." I shook my head to clear it and turned my full attention to the small group waiting for me to get myself together. Why was I struggling so much?

"Remember last year, when Kurt and I told you you'd need to learn the rest of your training in actual battle?" Mike waited for my nod to continue. "Well, it's time for your first combat mission."

What? Already? I'd expected to be in a supporting role at first. I'd thought someone else would do the actual fighting.

"But—"

"This is the target." He distributed a handout to each of us, and I immediately recognized the smug asshole in the photo, since he was famous.

Or infamous, more accurately.

Roderick Hartsfield III, the biggest name in oil and natural gas exploitation. He was almost solely responsible for massive destruction to the Amazon rainforest, the decline in ocean life off the coasts of multiple continents, and the widespread ecological devastation in Africa and the Americas.

A billionaire several times over, he regularly boasted in interviews how powerful he was, even more so than our own president. He was close personal friends with the Chief Justice of the Supreme Court, and most likely used that relationship to influence favorable decisions for himself and his cronies. It was widely rumored he had most of Congress in his back pocket, and the proof of that was in the legislation recently passed for the benefit of himself and his business interests.

At the expense of everyone else, and of the planet itself.

"We'll only take a small force," Mike continued. "Maybe two from the firm and a couple of our own guys for backup—Jason and Randy, probably. But we can't storm a Manhattan skyscraper. That would be insane."

"And idiotic," Reshep added.

Arddhu spoke up. "The easiest solution would be for me to open a portal to the target's office."

"Brilliant," Athena said. "So the team ports in, the Keeper beheads the guy, then everyone ports out. So simple it's beautiful."

"Wait. *Behead* him?" I'd almost choked on my drink. "Are you kidding me?"

"Well, you can't blow him up with your magick," Mike explained. "Remember, he's human, so I want you to use your weapons and training. And we can't have a long, drawn-out fight. The longer we're there, the higher our risk of being interrupted and arrested."

"Just a quick and dirty deed," Athena agreed.

"It is also the traditional method of execution," Arddhu added.

Stunned, I didn't comment.

Mike frowned at whatever expression he saw on my face. "Don't tell me you have a problem with killing."

That wasn't the issue. Ever since the Goddess had assigned this mission to me, I'd given it a lot of thought. I'd known I'd be taking lives, because there's really only one way to remove a threat. And I didn't belong to any religion that had a prohibition on murder.

"No, I don't have a problem with killing," I finally replied. "I just... don't feel ready for this. My training has been for fighting in combat, not beheading anyone."

"Yes, you *are* ready," Athena argued. "Michael has assured us this is so. You probably just don't realize it."

I appreciated her vote of confidence, but it didn't make me feel any better.

Mike ignored her and replied to me. "Okay then. Starting tomorrow, we'll do dry runs of the scenario to get you this specific training. We'll use one of the extra rooms as a staging area." Then he turned to Reshep. "I'll ask the firm to get us the target's schedule and the details of his office, such as the layout and what floor it's on, so we can plan accordingly."

He hadn't once used Hartsfield's name, I'd noticed. He'd only referred to him as *the target*. Maybe it kept him dehumanized. I supposed it was easier to think of killing a target rather than a person with a name.

"Any questions?" Mike asked.

"Yeah," I said. "When do we do this?"

"In a couple of weeks. As soon as we have all the info we need."

"And who will block any technology in use?" Athena asked. "Security systems, cameras, communications. That sort of thing."

Mike again turned to Arddhu. "Can you talk to Kevin about a spell for that?"

Arddhu nodded. "Of course."

Still too stunned to think clearly, I finished off my drink and got another, hoping to tap into some liquid courage.

But then I thought about all the training I'd been through, both last year and recently. All the hard work I'd put in had been leading to this, and I knew I was good with my weapons. Also, I wouldn't be alone; I'd have backup. People I trusted would have my back.

What could possibly go wrong?

CHAPTER EIGHT

"SO. WHAT'S THE deal with you and the Morrigan?"

I hadn't planned on asking Kevin that question, but it'd been bugging me for the past couple of days, ever since the alliance meeting. The two of us were in the training room working through a session of tai chi, and I'd just wanted to know.

Needed to know.

He smoothly transitioned into White Crane and calmly replied, "We've known each other for a very long time."

I'd been only a second behind in my own White Crane, and I kept my voice neutral. "What I mean is, are you two a thing?"

He stopped abruptly and faced me, frowning. "What?"

Mirroring him, I shrugged. "I'm just asking. It's no big deal if you are. But just so I know. I don't want to step on her toes. Uh, her territory. So-to-speak." Shit. I was babbling. I hated when I did that.

He stepped close and cupped my face in his hands. "Dee. No. There's nothing between her and me. Yes, there was once, but that was a very long time ago. As in, at least four hundred years. And I'm not her territory. Never was, never will be."

Truth, my witchy-sense declared.

"She was all over you after the meeting." *Shit.* I couldn't believe I just said that.

"I know. But I'm serious. There's nothing between us now. She can try all she wants, but I'm telling you the truth and you know it." His eyes held mine. "Besides, you know how I feel about you."

Another truth.

He leaned close and kissed me, and it was glorious. But why did he always taste of peppermint?

"That isn't tai chi."

Mike's voice startled me and I broke away from Kevin, suddenly shy of showing affection in front of him. "Uh, sorry," I mumbled.

He shook his head, then smiled. "Don't apologize. I was just messing with you. But it *is* time for sword practice." As he spoke, he tossed my sheathed sword to me, then took a practice swing with his own.

I groaned. Even though my hand and arms didn't hurt as much as they used to after sword practice, I still hated it.

But then again, it was a good excuse to spend time in the spa.

Fair compensation.

Kevin knew better than to sit in on my practice sessions; Mike didn't like the distraction. So he nodded to me and left the room, quietly closing the door.

Mike and I warmed up individually for a few minutes, then we began lunging, pivoting, and parrying. The clang of metal on metal seemed loud in the room, but then again it always did.

Since I could heal wounds, neither of us shied away from slashes. But we didn't exactly try to kill each other, either.

Even so, by the end of the hour's practice we were both sweaty, bloody, and exhausted. I pulled energy from my reserves and healed Mike's cuts first, then mine. He probably could've healed his own because of his shifter blood, but I still did it as a courtesy.

"Let's take a short break," he said. He propped his blade near the door, got two bottles of water from the mini-fridge, and sat on the floor against the wall.

I joined him, setting my sword beside me.

"You've really gotten pretty good."

The note of admiration in his voice made me sit up a little straighter.

"I don't worry about you as much as I used to," he added.

"Bullshit," I said, then we both laughed.

"What I mean is, I know you'll hold your own in a fight."

I drank my water and thought about that for a moment, remembering when I'd first started training with Kurt last year. I'd been clumsy, hesitant, and tired quickly and easily.

I'd come a long way since then.

"Thanks," I finally replied.

"Ready for scenario practice?" He launched his empty water bottle at the small waste can, but it missed by several inches. He sighed heavily, but I grinned.

"Sure." I could've let him pick it up, but I did something a bit more fun: I used my magick to lift the bottle and drop it into the can, which earned an eyeroll from him on his way out the door.

Picking up my sword, I followed him to the office.

A dummy was set up in an old chair at a desk facing the wall. Just a basic setup, since we didn't know the exact layout of Hartsfield's—uh, the *target's*—office yet. With this design, I'd approach from behind.

Mike stepped clear as I got into position. Turning my blade so I'd strike the dummy with the broad side instead of the edge, I made my first swing. As my sword hit the buckwheat-filled dummy, the impact shuddered up my arm in a different way than when I'd practiced with Mike.

This was like hitting something dead, somehow. I didn't think I'd ever get used to that.

"Good. Again," Mike said.

After a few more, he had me hit from the opposite side, using my prosthesis to drive the swing instead of my left hand.

Back and forth, switching between the two, I hit the dummy for what felt like an hour, until I was exhausted again.

Finally, he called it quits. "Okay. That's enough for today."

Thank the gods.

"Are you hungry? I can make something."

"No. I think I'll go soak in the spa for a bit."

For a moment, he seemed reluctant to leave, almost as if wanted to say something more. Then he shook his head and held the door open for me. "Okay. Maybe later then."

"Sure." I left my sword near the door and headed to the spa.

CHAPTER NINE

"**I** LOOK RIDICULOUS." I tried to grab the fabric creeping into the crack of my ass, but my fingers slipped again and again. It was some weird stretchy stuff that was slick like nylon, and wouldn't let me get a grip on it.

To my dismay, Mike had made good on his threat of having an armored suit made for me. But instead of being what I'd expected—shiny plate metal or chainmaille, like something worn at a medieval festival—it looked like an outfit a comic book superhero would wear.

Charcoal gray with black and red accents, it hugged my curves and left little to the imagination. On each side of the long front zipper, semi-rigid sections covered my chest and abdomen, protecting vital organs. And although the fabric was thick, it was also lightweight and breathable. I wasn't overheating, it didn't restrict my movements at all, and was surprisingly comfortable.

Except for how it kept riding up into my ass crack.

Oddly, the design team had chosen to leave my right arm completely bare all the way to my shoulder, but my left was completely covered down to my wrist. Most likely, it was to show off my prosthesis.

Mike had also found some new lightweight all-terrain boots with a thick but low heel that were exceptionally comfortable.

For the first time in my life, I was fully armed. My pistol was holstered on my left thigh with spare mags in a belt pack on the right. My knife was sheathed on my right hip, and Ire was in a baldric on my right for a left-hand draw.

I'd probably get a ton of attention at a comic book convertion—but most likely, unflattering.

My hair was in a tight ponytail to keep it off my face and out of my way, and I wore no makeup.

Arddhu had insisted I keep the ring he'd enchanted for the alliance meeting, so it glittered darkly on my left middle finger. Anu had completely filled my energy reserves, so I'd have plenty to draw from no matter what happened.

But I truly felt like I was an imposter superhero.

"No, you look *fucking sexy*," Kevin said. His eyes flashed with emerald fire, making me blush.

Then, he stepped back and snapped a photo of me with his new smartphone, and I rolled my eyes.

Oh, for fuck's sake.

It was a damned good thing he wasn't going with us on this mission; he'd be a terrible distraction.

He wouldn't be near any action, either; he'd work with Athena and Reshep to manage the coordinated attack on the target's global holdings, so he was dressed casually in jeans and a tee shirt.

According to the plan, while I was at the target's office doing my beheading thing, all of his assets—drilling rigs, refineries, warehouses, and other facilities—would be destroyed. Our guys would try to minimize loss of life, but their mission was clear: take out everything the target owned so it couldn't be rebuilt or salvaged.

"I agree with Bricriu." Arddhu's voice was low and breathless, and a new look in his dark brown eyes made me blush even more.

It was one thing to be drooled over by such an esteemed god, but it was another thing completely when he was also the Consort to the Goddess. He *had* to know She'd find out—didn't he care?

"As long as you can move freely and you're protected from magick, blades, and bullets, that's all I care about," Mike said, bringing me back to more comfortable territory.

He wore tactical gear like I'd seen in action movies, but Arddhu wore his usual tunic and trousers.

So I was the only one dressed in a ridiculous catsuit. Yay me.

"Are we ready?" Mike asked.

"I guess so," I mumbled, still trying to pick the fabric out of my ass crack.

He moved fast, so fast I hadn't even seen it. He was just *there*, an inch away as he lifted my head with his fingers, and he wasn't exactly gentle. "No guesses. *Are you ready?*" His voice was sharp, commanding.

My stomach was full of manic butterflies, but I held his eyes and answered in a firm voice. "Yes. I'm ready."

I'd probably calm down once the mission was underway, just like I used to do at job interviews.

Or maybe not. People didn't usually die at job interviews.

Fuck. I was going to kill someone. In just a few short minutes.

Don't think about it, I told myself. *Just do it.*

"Okay. Let's go." Mike led the way to the portal site.

According to the intel we'd received from the firm, the target had a clear schedule for an hour, then he'd be in a meeting. Right now, he should be sitting in his office either plotting the end of the world on phone calls or doing whatever it was a rich asshole did.

Maybe even screwing his secretary.

Jason and Randy waited at the portal site along with two other guys from the firm I'd never met before. All were dressed in tactical gear.

Jason's dark eyes swept me from head to toe with obvious appreciation, and my cheeks flushed again. His long black hair was bound into a tight nub at the back of his neck but that did nothing to detract from his glorious good looks. Sometimes I still wondered if I'd made the right decision not pursuing a relationship with him.

Except for Arddhu, the rest of us looked like a cast filming a scene of commandos in an action movie.

I had to shake myself. *This is real. We're on our way to kill someone.*

Correction: *I'd* be the one doing the killing. And if we were lucky, no one but the target would die today.

"On the count of three," Mike said. When he finished, Arddhu opened the portal and spoke the spell he'd gotten from Kevin to disable all technology.

Jason and Randy went through first, followed by the other two guys, to secure the location. I followed Mike, and Arddhu was last. The portal would stay open until we returned.

After a few seconds of vertigo passed, I took in the scene.

The two guys from the firm stood a couple of feet away with their rifles pointed at the target, who sat behind his enormous desk. Despite being quite a large man, that desk made him seem petite. His eyes were huge in his round face, and his mouth hung open.

But he wasn't alone.

Someone sat in one of the guest chairs, facing away from us.

Shit.

None of us had expected the target to have company. Unless someone other than me had thought maybe we'd catch him getting a blow job from his secretary.

Slowly, the stranger turned in his seat to look at us.

Jason muttered something I didn't catch and stepped backward with wide eyes.

"What—" I started, but Mike's hand on my arm stopped me.

"Well, well, well," the not-target said. His deep voice sent shivers up my spine, and they were definitely not the good kind. He reminded me way too much of Cromm, and I shuddered.

"What have we here?" he asked. Slowly, smoothly, with his arms hanging loosely at his sides as if to prove he was no threat, he rose and moved to stand beside the target.

"What are *you* doing here?" Jason snarled.

Jason seemed to know him. Or at least, know *of* him. Should I? I searched the Keepers' memories in my head but found nothing. Who *was* this guy?

He ignored Jason's question and swept each of us with his cold gaze. Then, as if he'd read my mind, he held my gaze and answered my unspoken question. "Please allow me to introduce myself. I am Malsumis."

"Evil God of Chaos and Tricks," Jason spat. "He belongs to the Algonquin people." He'd finally raised his rifle, but didn't aim it at the target. He aimed at Malsumis.

This god was definitely not supposed to be here, and although a complete list of the target's known associates had been included in the briefing materials, there'd been nothing on Malsumis.

Arddhu stepped forward. "We have no quarrel with you. You may leave in peace."

Malsumis laughed.

"No," Hartsfield said. His voice was unsteady but somehow it still sounded arrogant. "He stays. He's been helping me."

Mike's hand tightened on my arm, and all hell broke loose.

Malsumis threw red energy bolts at Arddhu, who dodged them and returned fire. Malsumis continued firing, and one bolt missed Arddhu by only a couple of feet but directly hit one of the guys sent by the firm. He dropped his weapon and fell to the floor screaming. The energy consumed him in seconds and left only a charred pile of remains where the man had been only seconds before.

Hartsfield stood and braced himself on his desk as he started toward the door, but he didn't get far. Randy smashed his rifle butt into the target's face, and Hartsfield landed in a heap with both hands cradling his broken nose. Blood gushed between his fingers.

A woman's high-pitched scream cut through the chaos, and I turned toward the sound. Dressed in a plain skirt and blouse, a pretty blonde stood in the doorway, her wide eyes taking in the magick battle between Arddhu and Malsumis—until Mike roughly pushed her out of the room and slammed the door in her face.

Hartsfield's secretary, probably. With a little luck, she hadn't seen any of us well enough to give an accurate description to the cops she was probably calling right now.

"*Do it now.*" Arddhu's commanding voice rose above the pop and sizzle of the energy bolts.

Mike pushed me toward the target, who was now sitting against the wall beside his full bookcase. Over his blood-covered hands, his eyes met mine.

"Who—what—" He stuttered, voice muffled and nasal, and seemed close to panic.

In contrast, mine was steady. Strong. Confident. "I am Deirdre Connor, the Keeper of the Sphere."

His eyes widened then narrowed, and he barked out a laugh. "*Deirdre?* Lester's kid? Shit, I haven't seen you since you were three years old. You're all grown up." Even in his state, his gaze lingered on my curves disgustingly.

It made my stomach turn.

Then his words registered in my brain, and I took a step closer, frowning down at him.

"How do you know my father?"

"He was my partner. He—he was going to turn me in. To the cops."

His... partner? He'd worked with my dad?

My dad was going to turn him in?

That meant...

Oh gods.

It hadn't been an accident after all. My parents had been *murdered.*

I stared at him. "You killed him. And—and my mother too."

"Best thing I ever did." He grinned then, mouth and teeth covered in blood. It made his grin seem even more twisted and macabre.

"Hurry, Dee," Mike urged.

I shook off my shock and outrage, and rushed my prepared speech through a clenched jaw. "Roderick Hartsfield the Third, the Goddess has judged you guilty of crimes against Earth." I drew my sword and Hartsfield—*the target*—sucked a noisy breath into his mouth.

"You are hereby sentenced to death for your crimes."

Gripping Ire before me, I hesitated, and he laughed hysterically.

It wasn't because I didn't want to kill him, because I did. Fuck yes, I wanted to kill him, fifty times over. The fucker had killed my mother and father.

But with him sitting on the floor against the wall, I wasn't sure how to angle my blade for a clean strike. I'd only practiced with a dummy sitting in a chair and striking from behind.

115

"What's wrong?" Mike asked. I barely heard him over the escalating noise of the battle between Arddhu and Malsumis, and the shouts from beyond the office door.

Before I could answer, somehow Jason had figured out what I needed and sprang into action.

Slinging his rifle over his shoulder, he roughly grabbed the target and hauled him upright, then thrust him face down over the arms of the guest chair. He easily held him in place with a knee in the back, and now the target's head was positioned freely for a clean strike.

Time slowed.

The roaring in my ears made everything around me seem distant even while I became hyper-focused on the target. Arddhu's shouts seemed far away, but the tiny unshaven hairs on the back of the target's neck were sharp and clear.

I took a step closer, raised Ire in a two-handed grip, and swiftly brought it down.

Hot blood spurted everywhere, and I flinched and blinked as some of it sprayed my face. Within seconds, it'd drenched the carpet and filled my nose with its sharp metallic smell.

For just a second, I flashed back to when Cromm had cut off my right hand. My blood had gushed into a spreading pool on the stone floor of his torture chamber.

With effort, I blinked and returned to the present, wondering who the hell was screaming bloody murder.

It was the target.

He was screaming and struggling, flopping in agony. Jason was having trouble holding him down.

Shit. I'd fucked this up. The cut, although deep, hadn't done the job.

So much for a quick beheading.

Wrenching my blade free—not really caring how much more pain I caused—I struck again, this time with a boost of magickal strength.

The screaming abruptly stopped. The target had finally shut up.

His head bounced and rolled across the floor, spreading more blood on the carpet along the way. For just a few seconds, the body continued to jerk and twitch until it finally lay unmoving across the chair, and Jason straightened.

Unfortunately, my blade had gone all the way through the neck and become embedded in the floor.

Maybe I'd boosted my strength a bit *too* much.

Goddammit.

I tried to pull Ire free, but it wouldn't budge. It felt like it'd stuck in the subfloor, which was remarkable. I hadn't realized I could be that strong.

"Dee. We gotta go." Mike's voice was unsteady with urgency.

"I know." I used another boost of magickal strength to free my sword, bracing myself so it wouldn't fly up and hit my head. For just a second, I stared at the blood and other matter on the blade, then quickly wiped it on the target's suit.

Jason met my eyes and nodded once, then Mike yanked me toward the portal.

I glanced over my shoulder at Arddhu's battle with Malsumis.

Malsumis was in rough shape. His face and body were covered with scorched spots where he'd taken hits from Arddhu's energy bolts. As I watched, he staggered as yet another bolt hit him. His return fire was wild and sloppy, and it'd been a miracle none of the rest of us had been hit.

But the fucker was still on his feet.

Arddhu had taken some hits, too, and was badly wounded. I'd never seen him so tired; he looked like his legs would give out at any moment.

Oh no. Was Malsumis that powerful?

The portal had been left open for a fast exit, but as Mike pulled me toward it, I dragged my feet and resisted. How could we leave Arddhu and the others behind?

"Go," Mike growled. "Get out of here."

"No, I—"

"Dammit, Dee, *go.*" And he shoved me. *Hard.*

I stumbled through the portal and lost my balance, hitting the dirt and rolling a couple of feet. Somehow I didn't impale myself on the sword still in my hand, although my bare right arm got scraped raw on the rough gravel. I barely registered the pain.

Then Randy was there, helping me up and pulling me further away from the portal. He kept one meaty hand clamped like a vise on my arm.

Probably on orders from Mike, who knew I'd try to go back through.

It must've been only a minute, but it felt more like an hour by the time Mike and Arddhu came through. Just before Arddhu closed the portal, I heard a burst of gunfire erupting on the other side, then he fell to the ground with a gasp that was way too loud in the sudden silence.

Not even the birds sang.

"Wait—no—what about *Jason*." My voice was hoarse.

Mike shook his head. "He and George took on Malsumis so we could leave and close the portal."

George? Who the hell—oh. He must've been the other guy from the firm. I'd never even bothered to introduce myself to either of them.

"We have to go back." I tried to take a step, but Randy tightened his hand on my arm. It was almost painful now.

Mike shook his head again.

"But they're probably still alive... "

"No, Dee. They're not." His voice was clipped, stony.

The grief in his eyes told me what I didn't want to believe: they'd been killed by Malsumis.

In that moment, everything crashed down on me.

Two more deaths. Three in total.

All of them my fault. Because I'd fucked up the execution. It hadn't been quick enough. If I'd been better, faster, they'd still be alive.

I'd never even thanked Jason for making my first kill easier for me.

Randy let me go and helped Mike get Arddhu to his feet.

"Let's get back to the house," Mike said to me over his shoulder, as he and Randy half-carried Arddhu between them.

I barely registered his words, but my feet moved automatically and I followed, not caring one bit about the flies attracted to the congealed blood covering my suit.

CHAPTER TEN

STANDING UNDER THE shower's steaming flow, I scrubbed the skin on my right arm until it was tender and pink. Although the water ran clear as it circled the drain, I still felt dirty.

I'd left the gory armored suit in a heap on the bathroom floor. Luckily, I remembered at the last minute to take off my prosthesis. I'd worry about cleaning the blood and dirt from both of them later.

When the tears came, I was surprised.

But at the same time, I wasn't.

I knew I didn't cry for the target. Hell no. Part of me was still in shock that the cause of my parents' deaths had been actual murder instead of accidental, as I'd believed for so many years. And I sure as hell didn't care I'd caused the target excruciating agony before he'd finally died.

Mostly, I cried for George and the other guy sent by the firm, the one whose name I'd never even known.

And I cried for Jason. Beautiful, sweet Jason, who, as one of his last acts, had helped me perform the execution. *Helped me do my job.*

Lastly, I cried for myself.

Never in my entire life had I ever felt like such a failure as I did right now. After all, if I'd done my job right, they'd all still be alive. And Arddhu wouldn't be resting somewhere badly wounded, maybe even dying, for all I knew.

How the hell was I supposed to do dozens of these executions when I couldn't even do *the first one* right?

And how many others would die because of my incompetence?

Unexpectedly, a sense of comfort and peace flooded me.

"*Deirdre.*" Anu's voice was soft and soothing in my mind. "*You must not blame yourself. It is Malsumis who is at fault.*"

I was grateful for her efforts, but I wasn't ready to blame anyone else for my failures. Remaining silent, I drew a shaky breath and let the water cascade over me.

"*Malsumis caused the death of your friends,*" she insisted. "*It was not your fault.*"

She did have a point. If Malsumis hadn't been there, everything else wouldn't have happened. If he hadn't been there, my botched execution wouldn't have mattered. Only the target would've died.

"*This was your first kill, correct?*"

"*Yes.*"

"*Removing the rest of Earth's enemies will be easier.*"

Somehow, I doubted that. But I appreciated her words of comfort nonetheless.

"*Thank you, Anu.*"

"*Be at peace, Deirdre. Much love.*"

The water finally ran cold. I shut it off and wrapped a towel around me before drying my tears and blowing my nose. In the mirror, I studied my face and neck for the specks of blood I was sure I'd missed. But there weren't any.

So why did I still feel so *dirty*?

Numb, but at the same time empty and hollowed out, I dressed and sat on my bed. The mission replayed from start to finish in my mind's eye, over and over, in a loop.

I shook my head and tried to clear it.

Was this what every mission would be like?

And who'd die next? Mike?

No.

Numbness gave way to anger as I roused myself.

No more deaths. I'd make sure of it.

Somehow.

My stomach rumbled loudly, and I knew I had to eat something. Even if it came back up again afterward, I *had* to eat.

I left my suite, bare feet padding quietly on the cool tile. I probably looked rough, with puffy red eyes and blotchy skin. My wet hair hung loose and dripped water down my back. My blood-crusted prosthesis was still on the bathroom counter, so my stump seemed more conspicuous than usual.

Mike and Kevin sat next to each other at the kitchen island, heads bent and talking quietly. Mike heard me first, with his sensitive wolf shifter ears, and turned to watch me approach. I recognized concern and kindness in his eyes, with a bit of wariness.

He'd stripped down his tactical gear to just the black tee shirt and pants.

Kevin looked like he'd gone through hell too, but he'd immediately stood and enfolded me in his arms. He didn't say a word; he didn't need to. He just held me close, and I rested my head against his chest.

Until that moment, I hadn't known how badly I needed that hug. It was comforting. Soothing.

But the tears threatened to start flowing again, so I pulled away.

"Thanks," I murmured. "I'm starving," I said to Mike.

I'd barely finished saying the words before he was up, pulling stuff from the fridge. "I'll fix something."

I sat on one of the stools. "How'd your thing go?" I asked Kevin.

"Good. We destroyed everything the target owned. No losses on our side, but there were a couple of employees who... were in the way." When I didn't comment, he continued. "We got his family out before we leveled the mansion. And his two vacation homes in the Caribbean were empty."

"What'd you do with his family?"

He glanced at Mike before he replied. "The firm took custody of them."

Oh.

I didn't know if that was good or bad.

Did I really care?

Not really.

"If it went so good, why do you look like shit?"

"It wasn't that... I mean, sure, it was hectic. I did a lot of coordinating with a bunch of different teams, but that part was actually kind of fun." He paused. "I guess I'm worn out from healing Arddhu."

Shit. How could I have forgotten? "How is he?"

"He'll be fine with a few hours' rest. He's resting in my room right now."

Thank the gods. I nodded, relieved. "You heard what happened?"

Mike answered without turning from the stove. "He's had a full briefing."

"Yeah," Kevin replied anyway. "I've never heard of this Malsumis guy, but he sure did a number on Arddhu." His eyes softened as he changed the subject. "How are *you*?"

I didn't need to look at Mike to know he was listening closely. I shrugged. "I'm... okay, I guess."

Then Mike set a plate in front of me. His infamous grilled cheese sandwich, one of my favorites. And some of the best comfort food I could have right now.

I gave him the best smile I could muster. "Thanks."

He nodded and leaned against the counter. "I've got the firm looking into Malsumis. With a little luck, he'll show up somewhere soon, so we can nail him. And we'll need better intelligence so we don't have the same situation. But that's for later. When Arddhu wakes up, we'll have a mission post-mortem."

Mouth full, I just nodded, and he began cleaning up the pan he'd used. Kevin rested his hand lightly on my thigh and stayed silent.

After I finished my sandwich, I pushed my plate away and wiped the butter off my fingers.

"By the way," I said. "How do I clean that armored suit? It's covered in dried blood and dirt, so I left it on the bathroom floor. And my prosthesis, too, has blood on it."

"I'll take care of both." Mike placed my dirty plate in the dishwasher and headed to my suite.

Kevin's fingers gently cupped my chin and turned my face toward him. "No offense, sweetheart, but you look like shit, too."

I couldn't help but smile. "Gee, thanks."

"I think we should go to bed."

I sighed. "Kevin..."

He lifted his hands in surrender. "I don't mean sex. I need to recharge from healing Arddhu. But since my bed is currently occupied, I thought..."

Oh.

I raised my eyebrows. "What's the matter? You don't want to sleep with Arddhu?"

A corner of his mouth quirked. "Not particularly, no. He snores. And kicks."

"Interesting that you'd know that," I teased.

Just then, Mike came back with the suit and prosthesis, but headed straight through to the laundry room without a word.

Truth was, I was exhausted. Between the stress of the mission, all the emotions, and now a full stomach—which so far seemed to be holding on to the food just fine—I was ready for rest, too.

"Okay," I agreed. "You talked me into it."

Before I could even move, he ported us to my bed. It took a moment to get settled, then he spooned me and rested one hand on my hip.

He was solid. Warm. Comforting.

I didn't think I'd be able to sleep, though. In the silence, the mission looped yet again in my mind.

Jason's shocked eyes staring at Malsumis. Red energy bolts zinging everywhere. The guy from the firm—the one whose name I didn't know—turning into a pile of ash. The target's screams. Blood spreading on the tan carpet, turning it reddish-brown.

Then Kevin whispered something I didn't catch, and I sank into blissfully deep sleep.

"Why did you hesitate?"

Although Mike's voice didn't seem accusatory, I couldn't help but feel I was being interrogated, and it was hard not to become defensive.

For this first mission post-mortem, we were joined by Arddhu, Kevin, Randy, Reshep, and Athena. The living room seemed crowded, and I wondered if maybe we should've used the VIP tent instead.

When I'd last seen Arddhu, he'd been a mess, but now he seemed fine. Kevin's healing had worked wonders.

"Because he—the target—was sitting on the floor against the wall. I'd expected to perform the execution with him in his chair, so it was a weird angle. I just didn't know how to make the strike effectively."

"Which is why Jason did what he did," Randy pointed out.

I nodded at him and turned back to Mike. "Besides, it wasn't like I practiced anything other than him sitting in his chair and me approaching from behind."

Mike's eyes narrowed at my words, and in my peripheral vision Arddhu and Reshep exchanged a glance. Maybe I'd been a bit too harsh. But no one else said anything, and before I could, Mike fired off another question. "Why did it take two strikes?"

"In hindsight, I don't think I put enough muscle into the first one. I actually thought my sword would cut through easier."

He shook his head. "It's a sharp blade, but it still has to go through bone, cartilage, and muscle."

"And fat," Randy added.

One corner of Mike's mouth quirked. "He did have quite a bit, didn't he?"

A few chuckles at that.

"Okay." Mike grew serious again. "Over the next few days, we'll work on different angles for the strike so you are better prepared for any target's position when we arrive at the scene." He wrote on his notepad. "We'll also set up some better practice dummies to help you determine the required force."

He paused, but I didn't say anything.

Reshep spoke. "How do you feel?"

"I'm fine." The words were automatic.

Mike studied me for a moment before clarifying Reshep's question. "This mission was supposed to be a slam-dunk to reinforce your training, and boost your confidence in your abilities and skills. So even though it didn't go as planned, how do you *feel*?"

Oh. I hadn't given that much thought.

"Give me a minute."

Despite the lives lost, Arddhu's injuries, and needing to magickally boost my strength for the killing blow, I was actually satisfied with myself and my performance for several reasons.

First, I didn't chicken out.

I'd remembered what to say.

I didn't get distracted.

And all things considered, I'd handled the shock of learning he'd killed my parents pretty well. After all, they'd been dead for many years. And now so was their killer. In a way, I had closure.

Overall, I felt damn good about myself, so that was my answer.

"I feel really good about myself and what I can do," I said to Reshep. "I know I need improvement in some areas, but at least I know I can get the job done."

He nodded, seemingly satisfied with my reply.

"Now, one last thing. An observation." Mike's eyes held mine. "I thought you handled it very well when he said he'd murdered your parents."

Well that was something. Coming from him, anyway. It was nice to have validation.

"Thanks." I flashed a smile.

He turned to the others. "Does anyone else have any questions? Or concerns?"

In the brief silence, Athena's voice was eager. "When's the next one?"

Mike nodded. "The firm is gathering the intel now. And we'll take a little extra time with it to make sure it's complete. We don't want another mission ending up like this one."

Kevin spoke up. "I've actually got a couple of ideas on that. What if, before Arddhu opens the portal, I pop in, look over the situation, then pop back out again? Of course, I'll cast an invisibility spell so no one can see me, but I'd be able to warn you if Malsumis—or someone other than the target—is there."

I thought it was a brilliant idea, but Arddhu objected. "If Malsumis or another god is there, he will most likely detect your presence despite an invisibility spell. And then you will have warned the target as well as put yourself in danger."

Shit. He had a good point.

Then I remembered how, before I'd met Arddhu last year, he'd somehow spied on me in my bedroom. At least, that's what Kevin had told me at the time. Now, I wondered if Arddhu could do something like that with the targets. I opened my mouth to ask but quickly shut it again. I didn't really want to disclose that little tidbit in front of everyone. Maybe I'd ask him later, in private.

Kevin frowned. "Just how many of the targets do you think are working with beings like Malsumis?"

Mike replied. "I think at this point, we have to assume it's all of them."

"*Shit.*" Oops. I hadn't planned on saying that out loud.

"That's exactly what I was going to say," Kevin said, and flashed a grin at me.

"The good news is," Mike added, "if we prepare for each mission correctly, it shouldn't matter even if someone else is there. And since beheading will continue to be the method of execution, if the targets *are* working with any deities, they can't be healed."

Right. Because not even a deity could heal someone who'd been beheaded.

"I have a suggestion," Arddhu said. As everyone turned to him, he continued. "Assign Kevin to the execution team. Choose someone else to oversee the asset destruction teams."

It took me a second to realize he'd actually called him *Kevin* for the first time. Up until now he'd continued using Bricriu.

Of course, Kevin had noticed. He stared with wide eyes at Arddhu, then they shared a respectful nod.

"But if he's not going to do the invisible spying, why bother?" Athena asked.

"If I become incapacitated and unable to close the portal, he can," Arddhu stated without emotion. "He can also port Deirdre to safety without requiring a portal, if the need arises."

"Why can't you just show someone else how to do that?" Mike asked.

Kevin shook his head and answered. "No offense, but it's not something just anyone can learn to do. You need to have the magickal ability to begin with. Everyone in this room needs a portal to move between worlds except for me. It's one of my unique abilities."

Eyebrows raised, I glanced at Arddhu, Athena, and Reshep in turn. "Wait—all of you need a portal?"

They all nodded.

Huh. Interesting. A demi-god could do something that a bunch of ancient gods couldn't. Who would've guessed?

"Okay," Athena said. "I second that Kevin is added to the execution team."

Reshep agreed, and although Mike wasn't happy about it, he had to agree as well. Both Arddhu and Kevin had made compelling arguments.

I'd just have to make sure he didn't distract me.

"All right," Mike said. "That's settled. Kevin, you're on the execution team from now on. And I think we can try your invisible spying thing. See how it goes. Reshep, could you please assign someone else to coordinate the other teams? Maybe Belatucadros?"

Reshep nodded. "I will do so after we finish here. But I would prefer to assign Begtse." He paused, as if choosing his next words carefully. "Belatucadros... is better suited to continue as leader for his asset destruction team."

"I completely agree," Athena said. "Bel is excellent at destroying assets, but he's not very good at planning, organization, or working with other team leaders. We need him to stay put."

Wow. So much for me thinking he was an efficient military guy.

"Okay. Got it." Mike nodded, still making notes. "Now, does anyone have any other business before we adjourn?"

"I do," Athena said. "Can someone *please* talk to Tyr? He keeps picking fights with my brother and it's really getting on my nerves."

Was I the only one thinking it was more likely to be the other way around? From what I'd seen at the alliance meeting, Ares was always spoiling for a fight.

"I'll take care of it," Reshep said.

"Anyone else?" Mike asked.

"Me," I said. "Are there some safety glasses I can use?" At Mike's blank look, I stumbled on. "When I made the strike... the blood... it... uh, I don't want it getting in my eyes, and some came pretty close today."

"We'll figure something out." Mike made another note on his pad. "Is that it?"

Finally, everyone nodded.

And with that, we were done with our first post-mortem.

While Randy, Athena, and Reshep stood and exited, Mike, Kevin, and Arddhu remained seated. I brought the bottle of Irish whiskey and four glasses from the bar and poured two fingers' worth for each of us.

Mike switched on the flat screen television and flipped to a national news channel.

The split-screen featured a male anchor in the studio on the left, and an on-scene female reporter on the right.

The anchor was speaking to the reporter. "... no, Samantha, we don't have any other information at this time. You're at the scene, what can you tell us about what's happening there?"

The caption on the bottom of the screen stated Samantha was located at Hartsfield's office building. Behind her, yellow crime scene tape fluttered in the breeze and kept the entrance clear for the first responders, who bustled in every direction. Blue and red lights from the emergency vehicles flashed against the building's façade.

"Joe, I haven't been able to get official statements from anyone here. As you can see, we're being kept far away from the building. The chief of police arrived only a moment ago—" she looked off-camera as if listening to someone, nodded, then returned her gaze to the camera. "We've just been told there will be a press conference in about an hour. Hopefully we'll get some answers then. Back to you."

"Okay Samantha, we'll check back with you a little later." The feed from the scene ended and the studio shot took over the entire screen. The anchor looked directly into the camera. "To recap for those of you just joining us: earlier today, police were called to the Hartsfield Building, where the decapitated body of Roderick Hartsfield the Third was discovered in his office. There was evidence of a struggle, and the remains of three other bodies who have not been identified. His secretary, whose name has not been released, is in protective custody at a local medical facility.

"We've also learned that while the alleged murder was taking place, all of Hartsfield's facilities around the globe were destroyed in an apparent highly coordinated attack of ecoterrorism. There's been no official word from any group claiming responsibility, but the terrorists were apparently very well organized and professionally equipped. Initial estimates show the destruction was complete. At this time, we don't know if there were any casualties at those facilities.

"We turn now to George Frost, a former counterintelligence and terrorism expert at the Federal Bureau of Investigation..."

The screen went blank as Mike shut it off.

"Oh great, so we're *terrorists* now?" I hated the shrill note in my voice, but I sure as hell hadn't expected *this* to be the fallout from the mission. I slammed my whiskey in one swallow, then coughed as it burned my throat and made my eyes water.

"Well, they're not exactly wrong," Mike said. "It does, by definition, fit the *terrorism* label. And we knew there'd be consequences."

"Yes, I knew there'd be consequences. I just didn't think it'd be... labeling us as terrorists." My voice rose with my frustration level, and I forced myself to take a deep breath.

"No one knows it was us," Kevin pointed out.

"It's just a matter of time before they find out. Then I'll be on a *Wanted* poster on the post office wall." I refilled my glass and leaned back in my chair.

"Dee—" Mike started.

"Don't you dare tell me to calm down." I pointed a finger at him.

"I wasn't going to." His calm, steady eyes held mine. "We're fine. They can't identify us. Remember, Arddhu disabled the cameras and communications before we even went through the portal. And the firm has already scrubbed identifying information from the systems for our casualties. No one will ever tie any of the missions back to us."

I rubbed my forehead and tried to remember if I'd touched anything in that office with my left hand. Did they already have my fingerprints?

"I just can't believe this shit. I never thought I'd be called a *terrorist*."

Kevin shrugged. "I've been called worse." He calmly sipped his whiskey.

Despite everything, I laughed.

Yes indeed, he'd been called worse.

Even by me.

Arddhu had been quiet until now, and he leaned forward. "Deirdre, this was to be expected. However, it will become worse as the missions continue. You must prepare yourself for the turmoil to come." He turned to Mike and gestured at the blank television. "Perhaps we should no longer use this device after the missions."

Mike nodded. "You've got a very good point. I'll keep tabs on the media coverage privately. If anything becomes troublesome, I'll have the firm deal with it."

Oh, so *that* was their solution to my concerns? Just cut me off from the news coverage, and everything was hunky-dory? My anger spiked again and I fumed in silence, sipping my whiskey.

Arddhu nodded and stood, placing his glass on the coffee table. "I must take care of some issues on my world. Contact me if you require my assistance before the next planning meeting."

He hadn't finished his whiskey. Not wanting it to go to waste, I downed it.

"Whoa, slow down," Mike said.

"I don't want to."

He studied me, frowning. "Okay. Spill it. What's bothering you?"

I could've played the *nothing* card but that really wasn't my style. "I think your answer to this is shit. Hiding the news from me just because you don't like how I react to it? That's bullshit and you know it."

He sighed and ran his fingers through his hair. "What else do you want me to do? Dee, you can't get upset like this after every mission."

"Besides," Kevin added. "Why do you care what those people say? They're not talking about *you*. They don't even know it was you. And they never will."

Dammit. Why did he have to be so logical?

"Look," I said. "I know it doesn't make sense to either of you. But I just wasn't prepared. That's all. I'll be fine. I just have to adjust."

And with that, I set my empty glass on the table next to Arddhu's and went to my suite.

CHAPTER ELEVEN

"**T**RY IT LIKE this," Kevin said.

He and I were in the training room, where Mike had set up another simulated office environment. A practice dummy sat in an office chair behind a desk facing the door, similar to Hartsfield's setup.

Unlike the buckwheat-filled dummy I'd practiced with prior to the first mission, this one was molded impact-resistant plastic with articulated arms and legs. It even had a somewhat realistic head that moved, with painted blue eyes and sculpted brown hair. Although I'd expected Mike to dress it in a suit for authenticity, he'd used an old pair of sweatpants and a ripped tee shirt instead. Its hands rested on the desk as if it were about to actually do some kind of work.

Now, Kevin demonstrated an angled downward stroke with his sword—which he'd pulled from his handy pocket dimension, of course.

The head of the practice dummy popped off, bounced on the floor, and rolled to a stop several feet away. The rest of the body slumped to one side of the desk chair, its arms dangling toward the floor.

"Uh, oops." He retrieved the head and tried—unsuccessfully—to put it back on the body. His stroke would've been a killing blow for a human, but it only smashed the side of the dummy's neck in and broke the mechanism that attached the head to the body.

Not so impact-resistant, then.

I couldn't help but laugh. "Mike's not gonna be happy. That's the third one we've broken this week."

They probably weren't cheap, either.

"Well, he should've expected to go through a few of these." He set the head on the floor by the wall and arranged the dummy's hands on the desk again. "We can still use this one. Just hit the body instead. It's the move you need to practice, not specific anatomy."

I sighed. My arms were sore and tired from all this sword swinging.

But I raised my blade and struck downward, in my best imitation of his move.

The torso cracked open and sand spilled on the floor.

"I guess we'll need a new one after all," he said. "But that was much better. You've improved tenfold since your last mission."

His praise made me stand a little taller and straighter.

A quick knock on the door before it opened, and then Mike was there taking in the mess with a single disgusted glance. "I see I'll have to place another order."

"Maybe you should ask for a volume discount," I joked.

He frowned and ignored my comment. "Arddhu, Athena, and Reshep are here for an impromptu briefing." He paused. "We have news on Malsumis."

Kevin sent his sword back to its pocket dimension while I sheathed mine and left it in the training room. On my way to join the others in the living room, I grabbed a bottle of water from the fridge.

Mike opened a file folder and began the briefing. "Malsumis, as we know thanks to Jason, is the Native American—Algonquin—deity known as the God of Chaos and Tricks. Apparently, his main goal is to cause the end of mankind. Hartsfield said Malsumis was helping him, but the firm hasn't been able to determine exactly what he was helping him with."

"He was eliminating obstacles to Hartsfield's domination of the fossil fuel industry," Reshep said. "That is some of what we—Athena and I—have learned since the mission."

"Great." Mike nodded and continued. "We've also discovered that Malsumis is a confirmed ally of Cromm Crúaich."

At the mention of Cromm, I fought—quite successfully—the flashback to my captivity, and was able to stay focused on the discussion. My confidence went up a notch.

Someone made a rude noise, but I wasn't sure who. If I had to guess, it'd probably been Kevin.

"So it would seem their goals are aligned," Arddhu said. "It is my belief that Cromm also longs for the end of human kind."

"Somehow, I doubt that," Kevin said. "Cromm seems like the type of guy who wants to keep a few live ones for slaves."

"Or playthings." My voice was low but seemed to echo unnaturally, and I shuddered.

Reshep broke the uneasy silence. "Have you discovered where Malsumis is now?"

Mike shook his head. "The firm is still working on it. I'm hoping we find him before the next mission, but we need to prepare for the possibility that we might not."

"When is the next mission, by the way?" Athena asked. "At the post-mortem, you said it'd be in a couple of weeks, but it's been longer than that."

Mike nodded. "I was hoping to get more info from the firm by then, but I didn't. We can discuss it now, if you're all okay with that." At everyone's agreement, he handed a briefing sheet to each of us. "Here's the next target."

The face in the photograph surprised me, but not because I knew the target.

"Rhonda Anne Sitwell," Mike said.

I hadn't expected a female target, but I really shouldn't have been surprised. Women could be just as nasty as men, after all.

Sometimes even more so.

"Founder and CEO of Sitwell Industries," Mike continued. "World's largest plastics manufacturer, with dozens of facilities. Here in the States, they've been fined by the EPA at least a hundred times, with no effect whatsoever. Not even on their profit margin, which has remained healthy despite the increased global awareness of the environmental impact of plastics. They have thirty-three Superfund sites, mostly in the South and Midwest."

At the blank looks in our group, he explained. "If you're not familiar with Superfund sites, they're places contaminated with toxic substances that require extensive cleanup efforts. One of the most famous was in the nineteen seventies at Love Canal, near Niagara Falls, New York. For decades, it'd been used as an underground waste dump for caustic chemicals. When the town expanded, schools and houses were built over the dump. But construction had damaged the containment system and the chemicals seeped into the groundwater. People got sick. Hundreds of babies were born with serious defects. Eventually, the town was evacuated and houses were demolished as part of the cleanup efforts. And, if any of you are curious, it was removed from the Superfund site list not too long ago. Which means it's been cleared for redevelopment. New houses have been built."

In the stunned silence, Mike paused for a drink of water, then he took a deep breath and concluded his briefing. "In the past five years, Sitwell's lobbyists have been responsible for the rollback of just about every environmental protection law passed in the last fifty years."

Which meant we could expect many more Superfund sites from just her company alone.

The implications of only one corporation having so many of these sites was disturbing, and really put a different perspective on my mission.

Fucking insanity. It had to end.

According to the handout, the target wasn't married and didn't have any kids. Apparently, she'd devoted her life to her company and the effort to make herself even wealthier.

While destroying Earth in the process, of course. I shook my head in disgust.

Mike handed another sheet to Reshep and Athena. "This is the list of current assets and facilities."

Athena immediately began studying it, but Reshep only briefly scanned it and said, "I'll call the team together and start planning the demolitions."

135

Mike nodded. "To answer Athena's question: I'd like to schedule the mission for next Tuesday. The target will be at a leadership retreat with her top team members, which is convenient for removing all of them at once. But we'll need a bigger team to handle the increase in targets."

My heart leapt into my throat.

A week.

I only had a week to get my shit together for this one.

Then the rest of what he'd said registered.

More targets.

"So how many targets, total?" I asked.

"Eleven."

Oh gods. It'd be a disgusting bloodbath with that many beheadings.

"Wait—I'm supposed to behead *all of them*?"

Mike shook his head. "No, you just take care of the main target. The extra team members will deal with the others."

Oh. Whew.

"Could I make a suggestion?" Kevin asked. Mike nodded for him to continue, but Kevin glanced at me first. "Dee has improved quite a bit since her last mission, but I'd like to ask the Morrigan to spend some time with her before Tuesday."

Mike frowned and didn't bother to hide his annoyance. "I can't imagine why. She's already been trained in combat techniques by the best instructor in the field."

I knew Mike thought highly of Kurt, but he just couldn't be in the same league as the Morrigan. She was the Goddess of the Battlefield, after all.

"I know," Kevin replied. "But I've had time to make several observations, and I think the Morrigan might have some specific tips for Dee that we—*as men*—have been missing."

His emphasis wasn't lost on anyone, least of all Mike. He appeared thoughtful, and both Arddhu and Reshep nodded in agreement. I glanced at Athena, but if she'd felt offended at how her own famed battle prowess had been ignored, she didn't show it.

"Y'know," Mike said. "You just might have a point there. I hadn't thought of it quite like that."

Wow. He'd just come close to admitting he was wrong. I ducked my head and studied my prosthesis to keep the smile off my face.

And then I remembered I'd wanted to ask Mike something about my prosthesis, but I'd kept forgetting.

Kevin continued. "They both have similar body types, and the Morrigan may have discovered some techniques over the centuries that work for her—and maybe they could work for Dee, too."

Of course. Because if there was anyone who could behead an opponent in just about any position, it had to be the Morrigan.

"Can you ask her?" Mike asked.

"I'll get right on it."

"Great. Thanks." Mike glanced at everyone. "That's it, then. Unless anyone has something else?"

No one did.

But as everyone else left, I called Mike back. "I wanted to talk to you about something. It's not related to the missions."

He sat again. "Okay."

I held out my prosthesis. "This is remarkable, you know. It's been a complete game-changer for me. And I know how lucky I am to have it."

He smiled. "It's definitely a wonderful piece of advanced technology."

I nodded. "Is there a way we can have more of these made? For amputees?"

Now he frowned. "You mean, for a charitable organization?"

"Yeah."

He gazed into the distance and softly tapped his pen against his notepad. "Hmm. I don't see why not. And I'm sure there would be some tax advantages, too."

From my accounting days, I knew there would be. But that wasn't the important thing for me. "I just think it would be awesome to help others that aren't as lucky as me. Maybe we could pick a veterans group first."

Now he met my gaze with a hint of something I'd never seen in his eyes before now, something like admiration. "It's actually a damn good idea, Dee."

I grinned. "I thought so, too."

"Oh, that reminds me." He pulled something small from his pocket. "The module to replace the batteries came. It'll only take a minute to install."

So I took off the prosthesis and watched as he opened the small battery compartment just inside the sleeve. He removed the special batteries and slid the module in. Peering intently inside the sleeve, he fiddled for a moment then handed the prosthesis back to me.

I slipped it on, but didn't feel anything different. This module was supposed to somehow tap into my energy reserves instead of using batteries for power, but I didn't even feel the slightest bit of pull from my reserves.

And I was glad I'd never told him about the day I'd forgotten to change the batteries. The prothesis had been completely nonfunctional and I'd been worried at first. Thankfully, I'd never forgotten to change them again.

"By the way," Mike continued. "I just removed the governor. I figured you've proved your proficiency and it wasn't needed anymore."

I didn't know what to say. The governor had been limiting my strength. Now, I could snap someone's bones with just a squeeze.

"Thanks," I finally said.

He smiled. "Just don't go crazy with it, okay? I don't want any complaints about you crushing someone's hand during a handshake."

"Not unless I'm supposed to, you mean," I pointed out, and we both laughed.

CHAPTER TWELVE

"**I** STILL THINK it'd be a better idea just to take her with me," the Morrigan said, not letting it go.

She wasn't opposed to showing me some of her battle tricks, but she thought getting me onto an *actual battlefield* would be the best learning experience.

As he'd said he'd do, Kevin had asked her to show me anything she'd learned over the centuries that could help me behead my targets more efficiently, no matter what position they were in. She'd expressed interest but had wanted to discuss it with Mike before committing herself.

And that's when it'd turned into an argument.

"For the last time, *absolutely not*," Mike growled. "We need her in one piece for these missions, not mortally wounded on one of your battlefields."

The Morrigan shrugged, unperturbed. "Of course that's always a risk. But it'd be an honorable death, regardless."

I couldn't tell if she was teasing him or not.

"I said no, and I mean it." Now Mike's eyes took on the golden glow that meant he was in danger of losing his temper. And possibly letting his wolf take control.

She smirked. "Oh, Michael. Don't be so melodramatic. Of course I wouldn't let our precious Keeper come to any harm. Remember, I said you could come along."

"We don't have time for that," he snapped. Then he inhaled slowly, trying to calm down. "Please, just do as I asked."

She looked straight at me. "And what does our Keeper want?"

Just as I'd opened my mouth, Mike replied. "*Goddammit*, Morrigan, she wants the *same thing*."

She hadn't taken her eyes from mine, and hadn't even flinched at his outburst. "Is he always like this? So rude and bossy?" She completely ignored him now, and Mike's face started to turn an odd shade of purple I'd never seen before.

Easy answer. "Yep."

"Who's the boss here, you or him?"

"I ask myself that very same question all the time."

One corner of her lips quirked up, and I couldn't help but grin.

I really did like her. From outward appearances, she seemed around my own age even though I knew she was centuries old. It almost made me think of her as the sister I never had.

And I hoped she'd say yes to helping me, so I could spend more time with her. I had a feeling I could learn a lot from her.

"Will you two knock it off?" Mike barked. "We don't have time for this."

She shrugged again. She had such a wonderful way of not letting anything he said or did get to her.

Maybe I should try it.

"Fine," she said. "Yes, I'll work with the Keeper."

Mike's eyes returned to their normal appearance as he calmed down. He wasted no time escorting us to the training room.

A new practice dummy leaned forward over the desk, head bent as if writing a note.

Or maybe it'd just fallen over and nobody had straightened it.

The Morrigan called in her sword from somewhere and unsheathed it. I'd been about to ask if she, too, had a pocket dimension, but the sight of her sword took all the words from me.

The blade was almost twice as long as mine, with runes of power deeply etched into the steel. It glowed a faint and eerie green, and it was a *monster*. How the hell could she handle that thing?

Unsettled and less confident than just a few minutes ago, I unsheathed mine. It looked pathetic in comparison.

There was a joke in there somewhere about comparing our swords like men compare their dicks. But I was able to hold it back.

She studied my sword with a wistful smile. "Ah, Oidhreacht. I haven't seen her in ages."

"You—you know it? Um, *her?*" I'd never referred to an inanimate object using a gender pronoun before, but somehow it fit.

Her smile widened. "Siobhan was one of my favorite warriors, back in the day. I called in a few favors with the smith to have him craft that blade." She ran her fingers lightly but lovingly along the smooth metal. "Of course, I know it's not the same blade. Michael, please tell whomever restored it they did a remarkable job."

He nodded, but motioned impatiently for us to start.

Wow. Bossing around the Goddess of the Battlefield? Ballsy.

But she didn't seem to mind, and we got right down to business.

She used a two-handed grip on her sword, knees slightly bent and spine straight. "Start with a proper stance."

I didn't mention I already knew about stance. I'd already set up in the same position, so when she glanced over she nodded with satisfaction.

"As you prepare for the stroke, take a deep breath and hold it. Exhale as you follow through. And keep your eyes on the blade path, so you can make any small adjustments as necessary." She approached the desk with the sword turned to strike with the flat instead of the sharp edge.

That was her big trick? Breathing a certain way?

But when she pivoted her torso from left to right, putting the power of her body into her swing, I realized I'd been hasty in my judgment.

No wonder my arms had always been so sore after practice. They'd been doing all the work, and it'd been totally unnecessary.

The dummy's head popped off and hit the wall next to Mike—who flinched and stumbled away awkwardly but comically—before it bounced on the floor and rolled to a stop.

"Your turn." She stepped away.

Mike retrieved the head, set it on the rod, and shoved it down into place.

Ah, so he'd found a new model. Apparently, one with a proper removable head.

I stepped up to the desk, took a deep breath, and held it. Copying her movements, I used the flat of my blade and pivoted, keeping my eyes on the shiny metal instead of the dummy. Just as she'd instructed.

Unfortunately, I smashed the side of the head in, and now it tilted drunkenly. But it'd stayed on.

Mike's sigh was loud in the quiet room.

How much did these dummies cost, anyway?

"So what did I do wrong?" I asked the Morrigan.

She repositioned the sword in my hand, moving my prosthesis further back on the hilt. "Try again."

I repeated all the steps, and heard the pop of the head before I watched it bounce around the room.

"Holy shit. It worked."

"Of course it did. You were treating your fake hand like a real one. It's not. You need to use it differently. Take advantage of its strength. Its power."

Why hadn't Mike ever told me any of this? I studied my hand position closely to memorize it.

"Besides," she continued. "You're short like me. You have to use the power of your body to compensate for the lack of leverage from your short arms. I'm surprised no one ever explained this to you."

I barely resisted giving Mike a pointed look, but I adored her honesty. And since Kevin had told me there was nothing romantic between them anymore, I didn't feel jealous. She was a remarkable woman, and I really liked her.

While we'd been talking, Mike had replaced the head on the dummy. I repeated the movement and got the same result, except this time he managed to catch the head as it flew toward him.

"Time for something different," he said. He replaced the head and rearranged the dummy into a new position. Now it leaned back in the chair with its head cocked to one side, as if on a phone call.

If it really did have a phone against its head, I'd hit it instead of the neck.

Unsure, I looked at the Morrigan for guidance.

"Doesn't matter." She shrugged. "Same movement. But reversed. Hit the other side."

One advantage of keeping my eyes on my blade was I didn't get hung up on the position of the dummy's head.

And again, it worked.

This time, Mike pulled the dummy out of the chair and propped it against the wall with its hands in front of its face. As he stepped away, it slumped forward slightly but otherwise held its position.

Which was pretty close to how Hartsfield had been sitting when I'd hesitated, and I did it again now.

"It's still the same movement," the Morrigan said. "Just relax your knees more so you're lower to the floor, and shift your position so your strike hits the front of the neck."

Still doubtful, thinking my sword would bury itself in the wall, I followed her instructions anyway.

And again was amazed, as the head popped off.

Mike set up the dummy in six more positions. Each time, the Morrigan's technique worked.

I should've never doubted her.

"Thank you." On impulse, I hugged her with my free arm. "This is *exactly* what I needed."

Now, I wasn't so nervous about the next mission.

She patted my back awkwardly. "Oh, you're welcome. Are we done now? I'm thirsty and ready for some fun."

I'd assumed she'd asked Mike that last question, but when I glanced at her, her eyes were on me with one brow lifted expectantly.

"Uh, sure. Fun sounds like... fun."

"That actually depends on what your idea of fun is," Mike wryly said as he replaced the dummy's head for the last time.

The Morrigan laughed, full-throated and sultry at the same time. "Oh, nothing bad, I promise. I was thinking maybe just some feasting and drinking." Her eyes sparkled with mischief as they raked him from head to toe. "Or maybe some sex, if you're interested."

He actually *blushed*. "Uh... yes to the feasting and drinking. No on the sex. Sorry."

Well now. *That* was interesting. Why wouldn't he want to hook up with the Goddess of the Battlefield?

He turned and left the room. Before she took a step to follow, I laid a hand on her arm and spoke quietly. "I have a favor to ask..."

"Certainly." She'd hesitated only a second, but kept her voice just as low.

Damn, she caught on quick.

"Would you teach me battle magick?"

Her gaze sharpened. "You aren't trained in that?"

"No. He—Mike—doesn't want me using magick when I fight. So we... uh, we'll have to do it without him knowing about it."

Her frown deepened, but she didn't get a chance to respond.

"You two coming or not?" Mike had reappeared in the doorway.

"Of course," the Morrigan replied smoothly. As we walked toward him, she turned to me. "It would be my pleasure, Keeper."

Both of us ignored his questioning look as we swept past.

"And what is this set of cards worth?" The Morrigan showed her five-card spread to Mike and I, and I stared in disbelief.

Royal straight flushes were incredibly rare, and yet she'd pulled one her first time playing poker. What were the odds?

"That, my friend, is worth the pot," I said. "It's the winning hand." I tossed my cards, which contained a normally decent hand: two pair, kings and tens.

Mike snorted in disgust and threw his cards face down on the counter so we couldn't see what he'd had. "Are you sure you've never played before? And that you're not manipulating the cards?"

She laughed. "No, Michael. I don't lie or cheat." She turned to me. "So what do I do now?"

"Take the pot." I pointed to the pile of Goldfish crackers on the counter. It'd been hard not to munch on our chosen form of currency during our game; they were tasty.

"Excellent. These are quite delightful," the Morrigan said, and swept the pile toward her.

Irish pub music played on the living room speakers. Mike had cooked dinner for us before we'd started drinking, then he'd had the bright idea to teach her how to play poker.

She'd proved to be a fast learner; we'd started with five-card draw but quickly moved on to wild cards, seven-card stud, and dealer's choice.

I had no idea where Kevin was, but he'd probably be bummed that he'd missed this little impromptu party.

She stood. "I'll be right back. Must drain a vein, as they say."

I snorted with laughter. I'd only heard guys say that when they had to pee, it wasn't usually what women said.

Damn, but I really liked her, and I hoped we'd be friends for a long time. She wasn't anything like I'd expected, and I'd even forgiven her for being so handsy with Kevin after the alliance meeting. After all, I couldn't blame her. He *was* gorgeous.

Mike set another beer in front of me and refilled his and the Morrigan's glasses with Irish whiskey.

"She's fun," I said.

"Yeah, she can be."

Of course, she probably wasn't so much fun when she was in battle mode.

He took a sip. "So what were you two whispering about earlier?"

Hah. I'd wondered when he'd get around to asking about that.

"Nothing much. I just asked her for some help with female stuff. If you really want to know..."

There was one interesting thing I'd learned during my working years: most guys hated hearing about female stuff such as periods or body part issues. I knew if I used that old tactic right now, he'd drop the subject.

And I was right.

"No, no. That's okay," he waved it away. "Glad she can help you with that."

I wasn't sure how much time I had before she came back, but I was just tipsy enough to push for an answer to the question I'd had all evening. I leaned closer. "Why don't you and her... you know... do it?"

He almost choked on his whiskey. "I can't believe you just asked me that."

I grinned. "You two *should* do it. I'll bet she's a lot of fun in bed."

Now he turned scarlet and wouldn't look at me. "Dee, drop it."

"C'mon. How long has it been, anyway? You've got to be horny as hell. You should get some. It might even make you less grumpy."

"I said, *drop it*." He snarled at me, but still wouldn't meet my eyes.

"Drop what?" The Morrigan breezed into the room.

"Nothing," he said.

"His pants," I said.

Oops.

I'd probably had way too many beers.

"Michael knows all he has to do is ask and I'll be on him like a bitch in heat," the Morrigan crooned.

Abruptly, he stood and left the room without another word. He'd even left his whiskey.

"Ooh, touchy," I said.

She sat with a sigh. "He's always been like that. I do love teasing him, though."

Again, those hints of history between them. Maybe someday I'd find out more.

Then again, I was just drunk enough to ask right now.

"Were you two a couple?" I blurted.

She laughed. "No. We've only been good friends. And like I said, I love to tease him."

Oh.

She drank her whiskey and took Mike's glass for her own. "Now, where were we? Whose deal is it?"

Poker wasn't as much fun with only two people, but it was still enjoyable.

Eyeing the pile of Goldfish in front of the Morrigan, I shuffled the deck and grinned.

This time, we had a much larger team for the mission at the leadership retreat; fifteen elite soldiers were sent by the firm, and they waited at the portal. Each was probably decked out in the requisite tactical gear, of course.

Our own security team remained on duty—and safe—at The Hacienda.

Arddhu, Kevin, and Mike met me in the kitchen. Arddhu wore his leather armor, and Mike was in his tactical gear again. This time, Kevin wore it, too, and I didn't know if it was his idea or Mike's.

Once again, I wore my armored suit. I'd sort of gotten used to it creeping up into my ass, so it didn't bother me as much this time.

Without a word, Mike handed me a sleek black case. Inside were the safety glasses I'd requested after the last mission. Aside from the general ick factor of getting a target's blood in my eyes, I sure as hell didn't want to catch any weird disease that I wouldn't be able to heal.

But these weren't like any safety glasses I'd ever seen; extremely lightweight and crystal clear, they had zero distortion. And they were surprisingly comfortable.

We joined the soldiers at the portal and followed the procedure Kevin had proposed at the last post-mortem: he cast an invisibility spell on himself and transported to the location.

He was back in only seconds with a thumb's up, which meant Malsumis—or anyone other than the target—wasn't at the location.

We were good to go.

From there, the mission proceeded like the last one.

Arddhu opened the portal and used Kevin's spell to disable security and communication devices. The soldiers quickly went through. I was third from last, and by the time I arrived, the location had been secured.

The target sat at one end of a large conference table. Her eyes were wide and her mouth hung open in shock as she stared around her. Each member of her leadership team had a soldier's firearm against his or her head, and would fire when I made my kill.

From the mission briefing Mike had given the day before, I knew they had silencers on their weapons to reduce the need for ear protection, and that the bullet fragments couldn't be traced back to the firm. Or us.

Without hesitation, I stepped closer to the target, drawing her attention and holding her gaze.

"Rhonda Anne Sitwell, you have been judged guilty by the Goddess of crimes against Earth."

She continued to sit in stunned silence until I unsheathed my sword. She gasped then, and the stench of loose bowels filled the air.

"You are hereby sentenced to death for your crimes."

"Wait—" she started.

But I didn't.

My stroke was just as the Morrigan had shown me. Just as I'd practiced.

And it was quick and clean, even though everything seemed to move in slow motion.

The head dropped onto the conference table and rolled off the edge. Some of the target's blonde hair, which had been so neatly pinned up, had come loose. Covered in blood, the tangled locks stuck to one white cheek in a grisly pattern. The torso fell forward and leaned against the table. Blood gushed from the gaping neck, drenching the papers and laptops nearby.

The soldiers had fired their weapons at the same time, and now each of the target's leadership team members slumped in their chairs in various awkward poses. Their heads were a gory mess from the large-caliber bullets, one used per person.

Despite the silencers, my ears buzzed from the noise—which meant others in the building would've heard it, too, and the police had probably already been called.

Taking in the scene, my stomach lurched.

In hindsight, I probably shouldn't have eaten breakfast earlier.

Blood was everywhere. The room was thick with the smell of it.

But the blood wasn't the problem; I'd seen enough of it by now to not be bothered too much.

It was the other stuff, stuff I hadn't seen before.

Swallowing convulsively, I stared at the disgusting brain matter scattered everywhere. And then the overwhelming stink of shit and piss hit me.

Turning away, I vomited onto the carpet, which added to the mess already there. Even with my eyes closed I could still see it all in exquisite detail, and I continued retching even after my stomach was empty.

Finally, shaky but clear-headed, I straightened. One of the soldiers handed me a napkin soaked in ice water. I nodded my thanks and wiped my face and mouth, but didn't know what to do with the used napkin. The soldier helpfully held his gloved hand out, palm up, with a smile.

"Thanks," I muttered, and handed it over.

Keeping my eyes focused on my blade, I cleaned it on the target's clothing before sheathing it and heading toward the portal.

As it turned out, I hadn't needed those safety glasses after all. Somehow, not a single drop of blood had touched any part of me.

Maybe my strike had been more effective? More efficient?

But as I went back through the portal, I felt oddly disjointed and disconnected.

The whole thing probably hadn't even taken five minutes, and had been so much easier than the last mission.

Too easy, maybe.

"You did quite well, Keeper," Arddhu said. He smiled at me, eyes shining with pride.

"Thank you," I replied automatically. I still felt strange, completely numb despite the gory conference room continuing to play on a loop in my mind.

The usual group had gathered in the living room for the post-mortem: Arddhu, Athena, and Reshep on the sofa; Mike and I in the side chairs; and Kevin cross-legged on the floor, propped against the wall under the flat-screen television. He'd been unusually quiet since we'd returned.

"I agree," Mike said. "The whole mission just took a little under five minutes. Although technically I could tack on an additional four minutes for the time it took to take care of the DNA sample."

DNA sample?

Oh. He must mean... my puke.

I felt bad for whoever had drawn the short straw on *that* duty.

"Maybe next time I shouldn't eat before we go," I suggested.

"Not a good idea," Mike immediately disagreed. "We need to be prepared for anything. If something goes wrong you'll need that extra energy."

I closed my eyes but the scene was still there, as if burned into my retinas. So much brain matter... I shook my head and tried to focus on the discussion.

"You get used to it." Kevin's voice was low, as if meant only for my ears.

I met his gaze steadily but didn't reply. His eyes seemed haunted, and I realized he should know about getting used to it. He'd seen his share of blood-soaked battlefields back in the old days, when they were much worse than anything we had now.

Probably worse.

But the sympathy I also saw in his eyes made me want to scream with frustration.

I didn't want sympathy. I didn't know exactly *what* I did want, but I knew what I didn't.

Instead of screaming, I just nodded and took a long sip of my drink: a strong gin and tonic, not my usual choice of alcohol. But I'd wanted something crisp and clean to clear my mouth and nose of that horrid smell.

Unfortunately, it wasn't working too well. That smell was still there, buried deep in my nasal passages.

"We had no losses this mission, which is exceptional," Mike continued.

I clenched my jaw to keep a bark of wild laughter from escaping.

Oh yes, so exceptional.

"Indeed. It was quite efficient," Arddhu added.

Him too? Ugh.

So far, Athena and Reshep had also been subdued.

Mike cleared his throat. "Based on this success, I don't think there's anything that needs improvement for our mission planning. Overall, it went extremely well. It should be the model for future missions. We should all be proud."

"*We?*" This time, I couldn't stop the wild laughter. All eyes were on me as I neared hysteria and only forced myself back from that edge with sheer willpower and several deep breaths. As quickly as it'd started, the madness ceased and the strange disconnectedness I'd been feeling was replaced by anger.

No, not anger. That was too mild a word for what I felt now.

It was *rage*.

My heart raced as I stared at him incredulously.

"You keep saying *we*, but I don't see you getting *your* hands dirty."

His wide-eyed surprise quickly became fury. Leaning forward in his seat, his eyes narrowed and started to glow. "Oh, is that what you want? You want me to get my hands dirty? Fine. So be it."

We glared at each other in silence. My mind flashed back to when I'd thrown him across the room at Ard na Mara, and I pushed it away. As satisfying as repeating that action might feel right now, the rational part of my brain knew it wouldn't help the situation.

"Michael. Deirdre. What is this?" The concern in Arddhu's voice was obvious.

"Nothing." I shook my head. "Never mind."

"Oh no, it's not *nothing*." Mike bit off each word. "If Dee—the *Keeper*— wants me to take a more active part, to get my hands bloody, then that's exactly what she'll get." Abruptly, he stood. "This post-mortem is concluded. I'll get you all the brief on the next target in a couple of days."

He turned and stalked out of the room.

And my anger went with him, leaving me exhausted.

I closed my eyes and rested my head in my hands.

We'd butted heads before, but we'd usually been able to work it out. This time, I wasn't so sure. He'd never spoken to me like that before, and especially not in the presence of others.

What had I done?

A gentle hand rested on my knee. "You okay?" Kevin had moved to my side.

"Yes. No. I don't know." I sighed and opened my eyes. "I guess this has been harder on me than I thought it'd be. I'm sorry, everyone. You shouldn't have had to sit through that."

Reshep and Athena shared a glance, then he spoke. "These things happen. It is not unexpected. However, we did not have an opportunity to discuss the destruction of the assets and facilities. It, too, went well. Please pass that information on to Michael."

I wasn't sure exactly who he was talking to, but Arddhu nodded, so I assumed he'd give Mike the message.

Reshep stood, with Athena also rising a half-second later. "We look forward to the next successful mission," he said. They left for the portal.

Kevin took my empty glass and refilled it with another gin and tonic. After Arddhu declined another drink, Kevin got a beer for himself and plopped on the couch.

"This is probably an unpopular opinion," he started. "But for what it's worth, I think you're right, Dee. He needs to have skin in this game, too. It can't just be you."

"Kevin is correct," Arddhu said.

I still felt a tiny shock every time he used Kevin's new name. After all, he'd continued using his old one for so long. It was a good indication of just how far Kevin had come in his redemption journey, and if I wasn't so fucked up right now, I'd be truly happy for him.

But then I realized: they'd both just agreed with me. So maybe I wasn't as fucked up as I thought.

"I had planned to mention it myself after one or two more missions," Arddhu added.

Oh thank the gods, it hadn't just been me.

The validation warmed me down to my bones.

Oddly enough, I felt tears prick my eyes, and I could only stare at them for a moment.

"Guys. You have no idea how much better that makes me feel."

Arddhu held my gaze. "We all have noticed something amiss. It was not just you." He seemed to hesitate, then continued in a soft voice. "It bodes well that you are beginning to assert yourself. You are coming into your full power and position. Michael must understand his role is changing. He is your Assistant and not—as you say—your boss."

I raised an eyebrow. "Have you been talking to the Morrigan, by any chance?"

He quirked a small smile. "She and I have spoken, yes. And I agree with what you have asked of her. That was very insightful. I am quite pleased at your continued progress."

"What'd I miss?" Kevin asked, glancing from Arddhu to me.

Cautiously, I eyed the hallway. If Mike was still around, his wolf shifter ears would hear anything above a whisper. "I'll tell you later."

He seemed to understand why I'd hesitated, and nodded.

The three of us sat quietly for a few moments, each lost in our own thoughts.

As much as I hated keeping secrets from Mike, I *was* the Keeper and I needed to own these missions. Which meant doing as I saw fit, even if it went against what Mike wanted. So even though I felt a twinge of guilt for asking to learn battle magick behind his back, I knew without a doubt it was the right thing to do. After all, I couldn't always depend on having my sword, pistol, or knife with me in a bad situation. And if I got caught in that kind of thing I probably wouldn't care about breaking Mike's rules anyway. Because I'd be more interested in surviving.

Arddhu drained his glass and stood. "I must go. Please do not hesitate to contact me if you need any assistance." He nodded at Kevin and left for the portal.

Finishing my drink, I stood and stretched. My neck cracked loudly and I winced. It'd been a few days since I'd last been in the spa, and my muscles were achy from tension. On impulse, I headed toward the window-wall.

"I'm in dire need of the spa tonight." Over my shoulder, I glanced at Kevin. "Want to join me?"

In a heartbeat, he was at my side. How the hell did he move so fast? Had he just teleported?

"I thought you'd never ask." He'd used the tone of voice that sent shivers up my spine.

The good kind.

At the spa, I unfolded the screen I'd bought to block the view of any security cameras mounted on or near the house. Sure, they could be hidden in other places, but I didn't want to completely surround the spa because it'd spoil the view and the atmosphere. But at the same time, I figured the house was the most logical place for cameras, and didn't want to take any chances.

I didn't want Mike watching me and Kevin again.

We both stripped—well actually only I did, since he just waved a hand to make his clothes disappear—and I carefully removed my prosthesis before I stepped down into the spa. Kevin was close behind.

Oh gods, it felt so damn good.

I hadn't realized how tense my muscles were until they relaxed under the soothing heat and massage jets.

Beside me, Kevin leaned close and whispered in my ear. "So what's the Morrigan doing for you?"

Somehow he'd made it sound dirty, and I shivered again.

I whispered the answer in his ear, just in case Mike could still hear a normal voice despite the noise of the jets and bubbling of the water.

He laughed, which wasn't the reaction I expected, to be honest.

"What Arddhu said makes perfect sense now." He looked at me, eyes sparkling with mischief in the landscape lighting. "And for the record, I also agree. One thousand percent."

I couldn't help but smile.

This was validation from *three* respected associates, including the Morrigan, that I was doing the right thing.

It felt good. *Real* good.

"So why's it funny?"

His lips curved in a sly smile. "Because I fucking *love* it when you defy him." He'd kept his voice low, and it sent yet another shiver through me.

He'd made it clear to me for quite a while now exactly how he felt about Mike, so I shouldn't have been surprised how much he enjoyed this.

Now, he rested his head against the spa and closed his eyes, giving me the perfect opportunity to study his gorgeous features, something I never could resist doing.

Strong jaw, long dark lashes, and full sensual lips. His long hair was bound at the base of his neck tonight, but usually when we were in bed it fanned out onto his pillow like black silk and made me want to bury my face in it.

"You're staring at me again." His voice was a soft caress.

"I can't help it."

"Mmm."

"You know damn well how gorgeous you are."

Another slow smile.

Oh yes, he knew.

"And you know what you do to me." My confession was barely above a whisper.

He cracked open one eye and focused it on me. "And just what do you think you do to *me*? Hmm?"

I rolled my eyes. "Yeah, I know I make you horny."

Both eyes opened now, and he straightened. "Girl, you do a helluva lot more than that."

"Oh really?" I snorted. "What? I make your stomach roll over?" Spoken, it sounded way more idiotic than it had in my head, and I cringed inside.

He shook his head, frowning, and suddenly became quite serious. "Far from it. When I think of you my heart skips a beat. When I see you, butterflies dance in my stomach. When I touch you, my blood heats. And I have to fight every impulse to take you in my arms and never let you go."

I remembered then: he'd been infamous for both satire and poetry.

A warrior poet with his fancy words.

"So this isn't just for fun anymore?" I whispered.

His hands found mine under the water. "Dee, this hasn't been *just for fun* in a long time. Since... well, since before Cromm." He paused, head tilted. "Actually, now that I think about it, it's *never* been just for fun. At least for me."

Truth. My witchy-sense was absolutely clear on that.

Stunned into silence, I stared into his eyes—those deep pools of emerald green that I could almost get lost in.

He blinked then, and the spell was broken. He took a deep breath and released it slowly. "Hey, it's okay if you don't feel the same way. I told you that on Arddhu's world. After your rescue. Remember? I still mean it." He shrugged. "But you asked."

I freed one hand and touched his cheek. "I know. I remember. And I..."

Shit. Was I really going to do this? Was I really going to bare my heart to him?

Well, he'd done it first, hadn't he?

"I think... I *do* feel the same." I'd finished in a breath, as if saying it any louder would make it not true.

"Do you—do you really mean it?" The hope in his voice was naked and raw, and it made my heart do a weird little flip.

"Well, it's sort of funny." I found his hand under the water again. "After the alliance meeting, when I saw the Morrigan rubbing herself all over you, I—I actually got jealous. And it surprised the shit out of me. The next thing I knew, I thought of you as my boyfriend. And that shocked the shit out of me even more. Then, when you told me about why the people of Finn's Cove hated you so much... well, I guess what I'm saying is... I guess we're a couple."

He pulled his hands free of mine and held my face, getting my cheeks wet but I didn't care. "Do you know what you've just done?" I shook my head—or tried to, but his hands prevented that. "You've just made me the happiest man in the universe."

And then he kissed me. The kind of kiss that made my toes curl and my heart race. The kind that wasn't foreplay, but somehow more.

Was this love?

Shit. Maybe it was. *Fuck me.*

CHAPTER THIRTEEN

"I 'M ROASTING IN an oven," the Morrigan complained.

I snorted. "Nah, it's just Arizona. Trust me, it's a lot worse than this in July and August."

Despite my flippant attitude, I was covered in just as much sweat as she was, as we stood in the relentless heat of the late morning sun under a gorgeous deep blue cloudless sky.

Normally, late September temperatures were in the high nineties, but today was unseasonably warm, nearing one hundred and twenty degrees. Thankfully, the monsoon was almost over, so the humidity was only around twenty percent. Any higher would make what we were doing out here unbearable.

She and I were working on my battle magick, far away from the house. I hadn't wanted to use the training room for several reasons. The main one being, of course, because I was hiding this whole thing from Mike.

Even though I hadn't really seen him around lately, not since our blow-up at the last post-mortem.

"I don't know how you tolerate this heat." She fanned herself dramatically.

I shrugged. "You get used to it after a while. Your blood thins out and you adapt."

She shook her head and took off more of her clothing, down to her sports bra and skimpy shorts. I doubted she'd put on any sunscreen and I frowned, not only concerned that her pale skin could get blistered by the time we were through, but also at the strangeness of an ancient goddess wearing a modern sports bra and short shorts.

Then again, did immortals even get sunburned?

I, on the other hand, had dressed sensibly: a loose-fitting lightweight cotton shirt and shorts. And I'd used plenty of sunscreen.

She stilled and stared off in the distance with alarm. "What the hell is *that*?"

Given her reaction, I expected to see something threatening, but it was relatively harmless.

"Oh. It's just a dust devil." The miniature column of dirt was about one hundred yards away and slowly spinning toward us. I'd learned about this phenomenon soon after I'd moved to the state.

She snarled and raised her sword as if to fight it, and I had to bite my lip to keep from laughing.

Probably not a good idea to laugh at the Goddess of the Battlefield.

"It's not really a devil. It's just air," I quickly explained. "A dust devil forms when there's a pocket of warmer air called an updraft. It starts to rotate and picks up dirt from the ground. It'll stop in a minute or so."

Sure enough, it spun itself out and disappeared.

"Whatever." The Morrigan wiped sweat from her brow and sighed. "Let's get back to work."

She faced me with her sword raised, then put her personal shield in place so I didn't need to worry about injuring her.

My prosthesis gripped my sword, since I needed my left hand free.

The Morrigan began her attack. I blocked her sword with mine then blasted a fireball at her. It disintegrated when it hit her shields, but she was already moving, getting another strike in. Thank the gods she wasn't using her full strength or speed. No, she was taking it easy on me for this first lesson in battle magick.

After about ten more minutes of these blocked strikes and energy blasts, I was tiring and she knew it. Taking advantage, she slipped her blade past mine and batted it away. Ire landed in the dirt several feet from me. I could've ported it back to my hand if I'd had even a second between her attacks. Weaponless now, I gripped her sword hand with my prosthesis and continued firing energy balls. But even I could see them grow weaker by the moment.

With a growl of frustration, I released her, stepped away, and raised my arms in our agreed-upon signal for halting action.

She lowered her sword and I rested my hands on my knees while I tried to catch my breath. She, of course, wasn't winded at all.

I felt her eyes on me, studying me.

"Let's take a break," she finally said.

I nodded and dug the water bottles from the small backpack I'd brought. Handing one to her, I drank from the other and wiped my mouth on my arm.

Anu replenished my reserves, drawing energy from the earth and conveniently storing it for me.

"No offense," the Morrigan said. "But you need a lot of practice."

"Yeah, I know." I wasn't offended in the least. "And I can't tell you how much I appreciate this."

Damn Mike for withholding this type of training from me. Thank the gods I'd made the decision to go around him and do it on my own.

She shrugged. "I'm happy to help. You should've learned this months ago."

I sighed and tossed her empty bottle back in the pack with mine. "Sometimes I really wonder about Mike. If he really knows what he's doing, I mean."

She took a few practice swings with her sword. "For the most part, he does. For as long as I've known him, he's been very good at his work. But I just don't understand why he didn't want you to learn this."

It was almost as if... no, it couldn't be.

Could it?

"Maybe he wants me to fail." My voice was a bit unsteady.

Her eyes narrowed in thought. "It's possible, I suppose. But that doesn't make sense. If you fail, it reflects on *him*." She shook her head. "Regardless, we're correcting the situation now."

"True." I took a couple of practice swings. "By the way, I need to tell you something. I spoke up for myself at the post-mortem the other day, and now he's avoiding me." At her puzzled look, I explained. "I sort of got pissed off at him. I told him he wasn't getting his hands dirty on any of these missions."

She laughed. "Good for you. You're right, you know. He hasn't been. But then again, neither have I. Yet," she added with a wink.

"Well, your part is still to come. We all know that." I took a couple more swings, then let my sword droop. "He kept saying *we* this and *we* that, but there's no *we* when it comes to the killing. It's all on *me*. Except for the leadership team on the last mission, which the guys from the firm took care of. So I guess I just lost my temper." Just talking about it had riled me up again, and I had to take a couple of deep breaths to calm myself.

She lightly placed a hand on my arm. "Hey, if you want to call it a day, we can meet up again tomorrow morning."

"No, please." I shook off my emotions. "I'd like to keep at it. At least for another hour, if that's okay. I want—I *need*—to get really good at this."

"Fine by me." She got into position and raised her sword with a feral grin. "So enough talk, Keeper."

Indeed.

After my session with the Morrigan, I took a quick shower to wash off the sweat and headed into the main living area. It was just about time for lunch and I was hungry.

But I stopped in my tracks and stared at the stranger unloading groceries.

"Excuse me... who are you?" I asked.

He turned and smiled warmly. Blindingly white teeth almost glowed under a bushy black moustache and a shiny bald head. "I'm José, your personal chef, ma'am."

What? "But—"

"You must be Dee," he said with the slightest hint of an accent. He approached with an extended hand, and was only a couple of inches taller than me. So unusual, since I was normally surrounded by nothing but tall men.

"Yes, I am."

"I look forward to preparing healthy and delicious meals for you."

Shit. He sounded like an infomercial.

We shook hands and he went back to unloading the groceries.

"By the way, who hired you?"

"Michael Fleming." He glanced at me and added, "No need for concern, ma'am. I've been with the firm for quite some time."

Which meant he'd been thoroughly vetted and cleared for this job. I didn't need to worry about what he'd overhear. Or would happen to see.

"Um, do you happen to know where he is? Mike, I mean."

He shook his head. "No, I'm sorry."

"Oh. Well, welcome aboard."

He flashed another quick, blinding smile. "Would you like lunch now?"

On cue, my stomach growled. "Um... sure."

I had to admit I was impressed. He made an incredible sandwich with crusty bread, crispy bacon, sweet lettuce, and heirloom tomatoes.

"This is amazing," I said, and quickly wolfed it down.

He nodded his thanks. "I have a system. You will choose your meals in advance each day. I'll provide a form every morning. Simply make your selections for each meal and circle the times you'd like them ready. Leave the completed form where I can easily find it—next to the stove, or on the refrigerator, for example." He handed me a piece of paper. "These are your choices for dinner tonight."

He had to be kidding. I glanced at the paper.

He wasn't.

I stared at him for a moment, then nodded and left to find Mike. I had to know what the hell was going on.

After several unsuccessful minutes, I finally found him in the training room, covered in sweat, and chopping the shit out of a broken practice dummy with his sword.

"Hey there," I said from the doorway.

He whirled, sword raised threateningly and eyes glowing golden.

I didn't dare move, so we just stood facing each other.

Just when I thought I'd have to port my sword from my room to defend myself, he slowly lowered his blade. His eyes returned to their normal brown color, but they shifted away from mine.

"So. I just met José." Thank the gods my voice was even.

He nodded but didn't reply, and his jaw clenched and unclenched.

"What's up with that? I mean, if you didn't want to cook anymore, you could've just said so." I'd tried for a light tone, but still he didn't say anything.

"Mike, what's going on? *Talk* to me."

"There's nothing to say," he snapped.

Every time I took a step closer, he took a step away. We slowly circled the room.

"What's going on?" I asked again.

His jaw worked for a moment. "You are the Keeper. You ordered me to *get my hands dirty*, I believe were your exact words. I work for you, so I will comply. And now, if you'll excuse me, I have training to finish." Without waiting for me to reply, he turned and continued hacking at the practice dummy. The damn thing was in pieces already; I didn't know how much more it could take.

But obviously, I'd get nowhere with him like this, so I left.

José wasn't in the kitchen, but it was spotless.

Except for the slip of paper on the granite island. Tomorrow's choices for my meals.

I sat and rested my head in my hands.

A part of me felt the loss of a friend. After all, Mike and I had sort of grown close for a bit there. So much had changed in the past year, but even more had changed in the past two weeks.

Another part of me was confused at his behavior. His reaction to this whole thing seemed way out of proportion—and out of character. Even when we'd fought last year and I'd thrown him across the room, he hadn't been like this.

Then there were my upcoming obligations in Finn's Cove: Mabon was coming up in a week, and right now I didn't even want him to go with me. It's not like he really had to; as the autumn equinox, Mabon wasn't a ritual event. It was just a harvest festival.

But after Mabon came Samhain, at the end of October, and that *did* require a ritual. Mike was supposed to be the avatar of the Horned God for that, but what if he didn't get over this thing by then?

Maybe Kevin could be the avatar instead. That would make things a lot easier.

But this whole thing just didn't make sense.

There had to be more to this than just what I'd said at the post-mortem. Something else had to be going on.

Hmm. The security team had worked with Mike for years. Maybe they knew how I could fix this. I headed out to the guesthouse to find out.

Randy opened the door at my knock, and didn't hide his surprise. I'd only been out here a few times and hadn't made it a regular habit.

"Oh. Hi, Dee. I wasn't expecting company." He glanced at the untidy living room with a frown, but stepped aside to let me enter. "Please excuse the mess. I'm working on the kitchen now but I'll just get some of this stuff out of the way." He grabbed a pile of discarded clothing from a side chair, looked around, then dumped it on the floor a few feet away.

I closed the door behind me and sat in the newly-vacated chair. "Thanks. I won't stay long. I just need to ask you something."

He carried an old pizza box from the coffee table to the kitchen. "Can I get you something to drink?"

"No, thanks."

He returned and sat on the sofa. "What's up?"

"I... it's about Mike."

Immediately, he seemed wary.

"No, don't look at me like that," I said. "Anything we say will be held in the strictest confidence." I sighed. "I just don't know who else to talk to. You seem to know him better than just about anyone, and I don't know what to do."

Now he looked like he'd just swallowed something disgusting, but nodded. "Go on."

The words came out in a rush. "He's barely speaking to me, and now he's hired a personal chef to take over the cooking. I... this is impacting our relationship. I mean, we're supposed to go to Finn's Cove next week, but at this point, I don't even want him to go with me. It's obvious he doesn't want to be anywhere near me—he's been avoiding me—and I just don't know what to do."

He'd been staring at his hands while I'd spoken, and now he looked up and met my gaze. "Pinky swear you won't say a word?"

Huh? That was still a thing?

After only a slight hesitation, I pinky swore and tried not to feel like an idiot.

"Yeah, I've known him for a long time," he started. "And he's never acted like this before." At my startled look, he clarified. "Oh yeah, he's not talking to any of us either. I mean, not any more than is absolutely necessary. We're all confused. It seemed to start right after the last mission, which none of us were part of." He cocked his head. "Did something happen that we don't know about?"

Dammit.

"It wasn't the mission. It was the post-mortem. I sort of lost my temper. I told him he wasn't getting his hands dirty, like I've been. As soon as I said that, he pretty much lost it."

Randy blinked at me with wide eyes. "Holy shit."

"What?"

He raked a hand through his reddish hair. "There's no way you could've known."

"Known what?"

He took a deep breath. "He has a problem with killing. I think it has to do with his shifter blood. He loses control. It's why he was reassigned to security detail."

What?

"I don't understand. When was this? He told me he'd trained to be my Assistant ever since he could remember. And I know damn well other Assistants had to fight—and kill—with their Keepers. Does the firm know?"

"Well, yeah. They're who reassigned him."

"So why the hell did they make him my Assistant?"

He shook his head. "I don't know anything about that. All I know is, we all got to know each other when we went on missions together."

And the asshole had had the nerve to ask me if *I* had a problem with killing. This was so confusing. I rubbed my temple, trying to think.

When had he been a soldier? He'd never said anything about that. None of this jived with what he'd told me. But why would he lie?

"Wait a minute, back up. What do you mean *he loses control?*"

Randy hesitated slightly before answering. "There's only so much I can tell you. It's classified. There was a... a mission. He got the target just fine. A little more bloody than necessary, but we didn't care about that. But then it was like he couldn't stop. He took out everyone else, the target's whole family. And there was a lot of collateral damage—innocent folks in the wrong place at the wrong time. When we tried to stop him, he turned on us and almost took us out, too. The mission team, I mean. Went berserk, you could say."

Oh no.

So if he went on the next mission as planned and then went berserk again, all those deaths would be my fault.

What had I done?

"So basically I just put everyone at risk."

I put my head in my hands.

"There's no way you could've known."

"Maybe I *should've* known." I met his gaze again. "Maybe someone should've told me. How can I do my job, make the right decisions, without all the information I need?"

He didn't reply.

I sighed again. "So how do I fix this? He basically said I ordered him to kill. And apparently he's been training like a maniac ever since."

He thought for a moment. "He recognized your words as a command, so maybe it's as easy as giving him another command: to stand down. And I'll try talking to him too, now that I know what's going on."

"Do you think he'll go back to being his old self after that?"

He shook his head. "Probably not right away. You can't flip that switch, magick-like."

Goddammit.

That meant until further notice, he'd have to stay behind on missions and trips to Finn's Cove.

"Thanks, Randy. I really appreciate this." I stood on shaky legs. "And remember, I won't tell anyone what we talked about."

He nodded and walked me to the door. "I'm sorry it wasn't better news."

"We'll deal with it."

Just like we've dealt with everything else.

One step at a time.

CHAPTER FOURTEEN

O N THE MORNING of Mabon, I packed a small tote with some snacks and a change of clothing—jeans, long-sleeved top, and light jacket—because I expected Ireland to be much cooler when we got there, since it'd be night. I planned on changing out of my shorts at Ard na Mara before heading to Finn's Cove for the festival.

But when Kevin saw my bag, he frowned. "What's that for?"

"Warm clothes for tonight and some snacks."

"You don't need any of that."

Now it was my turn to frown. "Of course I do."

"Nope. I'm porting us from your room right to the village green. So just change into whatever you're planning on wearing."

Why did I keep forgetting he could teleport without a portal?

"Well, that's convenient." I unpacked and left my clothes on the bed.

"So when do we need to leave?"

I calculated the eight-hour time difference in my head. "Not for a few hours yet."

"Want to get some training in?"

"Sure."

After a couple of grueling hours in the training room with our swords, we stopped for lunch. I'd chosen the grilled chicken sandwich on José's menu for the day, and it was absolutely delicious. He'd made one for Kevin, too, and it made me wonder if everyone else had to fill out a form every day.

Well, except for Mike, who hadn't been around since last week.

I'd found him in the training room and told him my previous *order*, as he'd referred to it, was reversed. I'd made it clear he was not to participate in the execution missions in any way.

He'd simply nodded and left the room, and I'd thought the situation was handled. Later, I'd overheard that his vehicle wasn't in the garage and no one knew where he'd gone.

I had to leave that for Randy and the security team to deal with, though, because I had enough on my plate as it was. Between training with Kevin and the Morrigan, meeting with Arddhu, Reshep, and Athena to discuss mission details, and planning the Mabon trip, I was at my limit.

After lunch, I showered and dressed. Kevin met me in my suite wearing casual clothes like me, since Mabon wasn't a formal gathering. As the second of the three traditional harvest festivals that began with Lammas and ended with Samhain, Mabon was pretty much just a feast.

Kevin pulled me close to teleport and I placed my hand on his chest. "Wait. Instead of porting us to the green, could we go to my patio instead? It's sort of a custom to walk through the woods to Finn's Cove."

"Sure."

If I'd blinked I would've missed it. A quick, dizzying moment of foggy grayness and we were already there.

"That was way too easy," I said.

He grinned. "Right? Way better than your beginner-level portal shit."

"*Hey.*" I punched his arm lightly. "Remember, not all of us can do what you do."

His grin widened. "I know."

I rolled my eyes and turned toward the path through the woods.

The sun had just dipped below the trees, but there was still plenty of light to see our way. The air was a bit cool, making me thankful I'd worn my jeans and long-sleeved shirt. But the evening was simply gorgeous and perfect for the walk to the village.

I never got tired of it.

After a dozen or so yards on the path, Kevin's warm hand folded around mine. I couldn't remember the last time I'd held hands with someone like this, if ever. It was nice.

No, it was better than nice. It was fucking *awesome*.

"So what's going on with Mike?" His soft voice broke the silence.

Of course he'd noticed.

I cleared my throat. "Remember the post-mortem?"

He nodded.

"Well, he thought I'd commanded him—as the Keeper—to kill." I paused, thinking of what I could say without betraying Randy's confidence. "That's not what I'd intended, so I thought all I had to do was reverse the command, tell him I didn't want him involved in the killings, and he'd go back to normal. But instead he took off. Nobody knows where he went and he won't answer his cell. I finally called the firm, and they weren't very happy he disappeared and left me without an Assistant."

"Shit."

"Yeah."

We walked in silence for a while. An occasional bird called, but it was eerily quiet except for the crunch of twigs under our shoes. Not even the crickets were chirping.

"How are the battle magick lessons with the Morrigan coming along?"

"Really good, I think. And I feel so much better now, more confident. Like I can hold my own. I used to feel like I'd be taken out in the first five minutes of a real fight, like I didn't even have a chance."

"You have no idea how happy I am to hear that." He gave my hand a quick squeeze and flashed a smile at me.

I couldn't help but smile too, but it faded as we passed Mike's cottage.

Somehow I'd have to find a way to mend the break in our relationship. Otherwise, I'd have to fire him. What good was an Assistant who refused to communicate with me? Or who went berserk in battle? And I couldn't help but feel responsible in a way, since it'd been my thoughtless, angry words that'd started this whole mess.

Kevin squeezed my hand again, and it was a welcome break in my thoughts.

"It's so peaceful here," I murmured. "It's not like anything back home. I mean, sure, we have pine forests in the high country, but they're not like these woods."

"But it's so beautiful there," he countered. "It's nothing like I expected it to be. Somehow, I expected something like the Sahara: all lifeless sand dunes. But it's so *alive*. There are trees and flowers everywhere, and birds. Gods, I've never seen so many birds. And those—what'd you call them? Dust devils?" I nodded. "Those things are so fucking *cool*."

When I'd first moved to Arizona, I'd thought the dust devils were cool, too. Now, I had to admit, I barely even noticed them. They were just another part of the landscape. But seeing everything through the Morrigan's or Kevin's eyes made it all new again, in a way, and made me appreciate it more.

"Hey, when's your birthday?" he asked.

I frowned. "Why?"

"Just curious." He shrugged. "Usually, humans make a big deal out of their birthdays, but you've never even mentioned yours."

"It's in March. The tenth." I paused before continuing. "I'd actually completely forgotten about it this year, since I was still on Cromm's world."

"Tell you what: I'll make you a cake."

I laughed. "You cook? Since when?"

He placed his free hand over his heart. "You wound me." Then he flashed a grin. "I know how to make a few things. I figure I can learn how to make a cake."

Now we'd come to the bridge, but I didn't see Pete anywhere. I wondered how he and Petunia were doing, but I didn't want to bother them if they were in the middle of something, so we just continued over the bridge toward Finn's Cove.

At the village green, we were greeted warmly, which meant Garrett had done a fine job at spreading the word about Kevin.

Even so, I caught more than a few of them frowning and peering behind us, as if looking for Mike. Thankfully, no one asked about him. I had no idea what I would've answered. Maybe just that he wasn't feeling well.

It wasn't exactly a lie.

Garrett spotted us and brought two cups of his special harvest brew. The autumn flavors were exceptional: cool starlit nights, ripe apples and sweet berries, golden honey, and warm spice.

How did he *do* that?

"Oh, this is divine," I said.

He grinned and left.

None of the tables were unoccupied, so Kevin and I sat on a fragrant hay bale. I smiled and nodded to passersby and savored my ale.

"You hungry?" Kevin asked.

"Nah," I shook my head. "But I'll definitely want more of this." I indicated my cup.

"It is very tasty. Garrett is truly a master."

That he was. He never failed to impress me, whether it was with his food or drink.

The flames of the torches placed on the perimeter of the village green danced in the breeze and gave everything a warm glow. I was glad I'd worn my jacket, though, because the air was noticeably cooler now that it was full dark. Above us, the night sky was dense with bright stars, although the moon hadn't risen yet.

The musicians finished warming up and began playing a slow reel.

"May I have this dance?" Kevin asked.

It'd been ages since I'd danced. Why the hell not?

"Sure." I downed the rest of my ale and set my empty cup near his on the hay bale. He took my hand and pulled me close, right there by the bale.

I'd never danced with him before. He was a mighty fine dancer, and his body pressed against mine did all sorts of things to me.

After the song finished and the musicians began a lively jig, he kissed me. Softly. Deeply.

Hmm. Maybe it was a good thing Mike wasn't with us on this trip. Because for once, we had a promise of privacy—*real* privacy, like we'd never really had before. At Ard na Mara, there was no security. No cameras. No one but us.

So Kevin wouldn't have to put up any sound shields, either.

The thought almost made me giddy.

But first, I wanted another of Garrett's ales.

I turned away to get my cup, and immediately sobered.

Mike stood on the edge of the green, far from anyone else, with his arms crossed. The flickering torch light kept his face mostly in shadow. Although I couldn't see his eyes clearly and couldn't be sure, his head seemed to be turned toward us and I assumed he'd been watching us.

So this is where he'd come, when he disappeared from Scottsdale. None of us had thought to check the airport for his vehicle.

He might've even been there in his cottage when we passed by earlier.

"You okay?" Kevin asked quietly.

I glanced at him, but he wasn't looking at me. No, he stared at Mike with a carefully neutral expression.

"Yeah," I replied, just as quietly. "I just didn't expect to see him here."

As I watched, a guy I didn't recognize stepped close to Mike and they spoke.

"Maybe I should go talk to him. Maybe this is his way of saying he'll listen to me now."

Kevin's hand on my arm stopped me. "I'm right here. I'll be watching. If he tries anything—or if you need me—just say my name and I'll get us out of here."

"Thanks." With a little luck, that wouldn't be necessary.

As I headed toward Mike, the guy he'd been talking to glanced at me and left. Mike stayed where he was, waiting and watching me approach.

When I was close enough, I smiled. "Hey."

"Blessed Mabon." His voice was soft.

"Blessed Mabon to you." I indicated an empty hay bale nearby. "Got a minute?"

"Sure."

We sat, but now that I had my chance, I didn't know where to begin or what to say.

He spoke first, although he didn't look at me; instead, he watched the villagers and occasionally nodded to any who'd smiled his way. "I just wanted to apologize. I know I've been acting like an asshole. I overreacted, and I'm sorry."

Truth, my witchy-sense told me.

Wow. This was the old Mike, the one I'd known when I first became the Keeper.

"And I'm sorry, too." I needed to tread carefully here; I couldn't let him know what Randy had told me. "I was out of sorts at the post-mortem and didn't mean to take it out on you. I shouldn't have said what I said."

He nodded, but still wouldn't look at me. After a moment I realized now he was staring at Kevin, who stood where I'd left him and was watching us closely. The tension in Kevin's body was obvious, as if he was ready to spring into action.

Mike cleared his throat softly. "I also wanted to let you know I'll be staying here—at my cottage—for a while."

"For how long?"

"I don't know yet. I need to work through some things."

Shit. With him away for an indefinite period of time, I'd have to coordinate the missions myself.

But as if he'd read my mind, he added, "If you call Victor at the firm—the number's on the office desk—he'll get you all the info on the upcoming targets."

"Okay." That'd make it a bit easier.

He stood. "Well, that's all I wanted to say. I'm going down to the harbor for a bit, so it isn't awkward for you to have me hanging around. Have a good time at the festival."

"Wait—that's it?"

He hesitated. "I'm not ready to talk about anything else right now. Sorry."

"I thought we were friends, Mike."

One eyebrow lifted. "Maybe we were. Once." He shook his head. "Never mind. Like I said, I have some things to work through. And I really don't know how long that'll take." He turned to leave.

"Well, take care, then." What else was there to say at this point?

He nodded once and left, keeping a wide berth between himself and Kevin as he passed. I watched until I couldn't see the white of his shirt anymore.

Kevin sat next to me. "How'd it go?"

"Okay, I guess. We both apologized, and he seemed more like his old self, but I don't think anything will ever be the same as it was. He said he's staying here—at his cottage—for a while. That he needs to figure some things out." I shrugged.

"But he was the liaison with the firm."

"I know. I guess that's me now. He told me who to call."

"Fuck. Don't you think you've got enough on your plate as it is?"

I tried a smile. "At least I won't have to cook, too."

My weak attempt at a joke fell flat.

Kevin just shook his head. "We have to tell Arddhu."

"Yeah, I know. I'll schedule something with him when we get back. In the meantime, let's just enjoy the festival."

So we ate a little bit even though we weren't really hungry, and we drank, and we danced, and we drank some more.

Much later, under the bright half-moon and a thousand stars, we walked back to Ard na Mara with our arms around each other.

Once again, the bridge was quiet. Maybe Pete and Petunia had moved somewhere else?

When we reached the patio, Kevin pulled me against him and wrapped his arms around me. His mouth was hot on mine as he ported us to my bedroom, and we fell into bed without interrupting our kiss.

He undressed me ever so slowly, teasing me and making me want him desperately.

But when it was time for him to undress, of course he just waved a hand.

Someday, I vowed, I'd undress him slowly, like unwrapping a present.

For now, his soft raven hair brushed my skin as his lips moved across and down my body, and my brain stopped thinking.

It was going to be a glorious night.

The next morning, we didn't get dressed and leave until we'd worn ourselves out from yet more sex.

By then, it was just after midnight in Arizona, and Kevin ported us directly to my bedroom. But he didn't let me go, just kept his arms wrapped around me, holding me tight against him while his face nuzzled my neck.

"Don't get any ideas," I pushed at him. "I'm still sore. And hungry."

"Damn." He kissed my forehead. "I keep forgetting you're human."

"And I keep reminding you I'm not. Right now, I'm going to shower—alone—and get something to eat."

"I guess I'll see you later, then." After one last smoldering kiss, he reluctantly let me go and ported to his own room.

Even though we spent most nights together, I'd insisted on keeping our separate rooms for now. Sometimes I really needed some private time, especially without him distracting me, and he probably did, too. Good thing the house was big enough for that.

As I showered, I couldn't keep the dopey grin off my face.

If someone had told me a couple of years ago that I'd be the girlfriend of a gorgeous demi-god who was over a thousand years old, I would've told them they were insane. Or smoking some funny stuff. And then I probably would've laughed myself silly.

Sometimes, when I thought about how much my life had changed since that day Mike rang my doorbell...

Oh.

Mike.

My smile faded as I finished my shower.

Well, I'd done what I could as far as that whole thing went. Now I had to wait and see how—and if—he worked things out. In the meantime, I didn't have an Assistant. Maybe I didn't need one anymore? After all, my training with Kurt had ended several weeks ago. I was finally learning battle magick from the Morrigan. And it wasn't like I needed a minder anymore. So that part of his job was moot at this point.

But I really didn't want to be responsible for managing the security team and all the things that Mike usually did. Like Kevin said, I had enough on my plate already.

Maybe the firm could send a temporary Assistant. I'd ask Victor about it when I called.

First things first, though. I needed to update Arddhu on the situation with Mike.

But how was I supposed to get in touch with him? Mike had been able to contact him without porting to his world or summoning him to ours. As far as I knew, Arddhu still hadn't installed any technology on his world, so I couldn't exactly call him, text him, or send an email.

Besides, I was pretty sure there was no internet in space.

Well, maybe I'd find some clues in the home office.

After I dressed, I padded through the main living area to the office. As Mike had told me, I found a phone number on the notepad by the laptop docking station with *Victor* written underneath.

But after several minutes of searching, I didn't find anything on how to contact Arddhu. Which meant I had two choices: either ask the Goddess to relay a message, or go to the portal and summon him directly, like I'd done last year.

Neither was particularly appealing.

The Goddess probably wouldn't appreciate being Her Consort's answering service. And I didn't want to summon him—what if I were interrupting something important?

Nothing else for it, I supposed.

"*My lady,*" I mentally called to the Goddess. "*I have need of your assistance.*"

After a long moment—*too* long, actually—Her voice filled my mind. "*Yes, Deirdre. What is it?*"

She seemed cold, more aloof. Had I pissed Her off or something?

"*I need to speak to Arddhu but I don't want to formally summon him. Could you please ask him to attend a meeting? We have a—a situation.*"

"*When is the meeting?*"

"*As soon as possible.*"

A moment passed. Then: "*He will arrive within the hour.*"

"*Thank you, my Lady.*"

She was gone without another word.

Damn.

Maybe I *had* pissed Her off.

It was never a good idea to piss off the Goddess.

Well, I'd just have to worry about that later. Right now I had shit to do.

Like find something to eat.

As soon as I left the office I smelled the tantalizing aroma of grilled beef.

Apparently, in the short amount of time I'd spent in the office, José had prepared a meal for me. Almost as if he'd known I was hungry and wanted something to eat at this hour—which was odd.

Especially since it wasn't a time normally covered in his funky little menu system.

I sat at the granite island, where he'd set a napkin and condiments. "How'd you know I was starving?"

He smiled. "It's my special talent."

Oh. His *magick*, as Mike used to call it.

I stared at the plate he set in front of me.

A small but fully-loaded burger with a few thick-cut homemade potato chips on the side.

What the hell? How did he know that was just what I'd been craving?

"The carbs will restore your energy usage from... earlier... and the protein will build muscle for your practice session later this morning, after your meeting."

I lifted my eyes and stared at him.

He knew an awful lot about what I'd been doing. And what I planned to do.

"It's my special talent." He smiled, shrugged, and began cleaning up.

So casual. As if I shouldn't be concerned about him invading my privacy. As if it were nothing at all to be concerned about.

I wasn't sure I shared that viewpoint.

But after my stomach growled again, I set aside my unease—for now—and dug in.

The burger was delicious, and I even licked my fingers clean of the melted cheese and meat juices.

A gift such as this came with a cost, I supposed.

CHAPTER FIFTEEN

"**T**HIS IS INDEED a problem." Arddhu frowned. "Michael was responsible for coordinating the missions and communicating with his firm."

Arddhu, Kevin, and I had convened the meeting in the VIP tent to give it a sense of formality and to maintain some semblance of privacy.

When I'd told Kevin about the meeting—and complained about having to ask the Goddess to let Arddhu know—he shook his head at me. "You could've just asked me. I can contact him anytime."

Well, shit. I hadn't even thought of asking him. Sometimes I still felt like an idiot.

Now, I replied to Arddhu. "Mike told me to contact Victor at the firm. He's supposed to complete the briefing for the next mission, which is within the next week or so, I think. I'll call him as soon as we're done here. I just wanted to update you first."

The worry on Arddhu's face didn't fade. "You must focus on training and preparing for the missions, not performing Michael's duties. This is too much." He shook his head. "I am very disappointed in Michael for doing this."

He wasn't the only one.

"I thought I'd ask Victor if the firm has someone they can send to fill in. Just until Mike... resolves his issues." I'd almost said *gets his shit together* but I didn't want to have to explain it to Arddhu, who probably wouldn't know what it meant.

"That's actually a pretty good idea," Kevin said.

"I agree." Arddhu studied me, his frown gone. "You have done well, Keeper. I've watched you grow into your role over the past Wheel of the Year, and I am quite pleased with how you handle yourself." Now his eyes sparkled. "And you look quite lovely in your armor."

"What would the Goddess say about your shameless flirting?" I teased.

His smile faded immediately.

"She does not care." He turned to Kevin. "I believe you would say, *She does not give a shit.*"

Uh oh. This wasn't good. And it might have something to do with why She'd been so cold to me earlier.

"Would you care for some mead?" I offered.

He brightened. "Yes, please."

Before I could even think about porting it myself, Kevin teleported to the house to personally fetch it from the bar.

I lightly rested my hand on Arddhu's. "If you need to talk, I'm here. Maybe there's something I can do to help."

He gazed at my hand for a moment, then met my eyes. "I doubt there is anything you could do. She has... changed. I do not know why." He hesitated before continuing. "I am no longer Her Consort."

Oh no. This just kept getting worse.

Kevin reappeared with the mead and some glasses, and poured one for each of us.

Arddhu drank his in one swallow, took command of the bottle, and refilled his glass. But then he just stared at it morosely.

Kevin and I shared a glance, and his eyes held the same concern I felt.

"You two have been together for a very long time," I pointed out. Millennia, in fact. "Has anything like this ever happened before?"

He shook his head. "Not like this, no." He sipped his mead, then met my eyes. "You should know this will most likely affect the Samhain ritual. You may choose a replacement for Michael, and I will participate regardless of whom you choose. However, if I do so, She may not participate. So you may have to perform the ritual yourself."

179

Shit.

Last Samhain, the Goddess had basically taken control of my body and Arddhu had taken control of Mike's. This year, if I chose a replacement for Mike I could probably still do the ritual without the Goddess, since I knew the words to use and could probably complete it without Her.

But that wasn't what worried me.

What worried me was the Petitioning Ceremony after the ritual, where the villagers addressed the Goddess directly while She was in my body. I didn't think I could fake it well enough to be convincing; besides, She granted requests and answered questions during that Ceremony, and I sure as hell didn't have that kind of power.

So even if I chose a replacement for Mike, it wouldn't matter if the Goddess didn't show up to do Her thing.

I rubbed my forehead. "What a fucking mess."

"Indeed."

"It'll be the same for Beltaine, too," Kevin pointed out. "Unless Mike gets his shit together by then."

Surprisingly, Arddhu didn't ask for an explanation, as I'd expected.

"Don't remind me," I muttered.

But Beltaine was a completely different problem; occasionally, the Goddess and Her Consort used their avatars as mortal vessels to perform the Sacred Union, which promoted abundance and fertility on Earth.

Public sex, in other words.

The memories of prior Keepers showed me that sometimes, that Sacred Union resulted in a special child being born.

Since I'd missed Beltaine earlier in the year due to my extended recovery on Arddhu's world, this next one would be my first as the Keeper. And unless the Goddess participated, it'd just be me and whichever body Arddhu occupied performing the Sacred Union.

Which wasn't the point of it, and wouldn't really fulfill the requirements.

But if the rite were skipped, that'd be at least two Beltaines without it. A quick check of Maggie's memories told me she also hadn't performed the rite for the past several years, due to her advanced age. It was way overdue, and Earth clearly suffered from its loss. It was another part of healing the planet, and I couldn't help but feel it was something I had to do.

Part of my mission.

"For the record," Kevin said to Arddhu, "I wouldn't mind if you used me for either Samhain or Beltaine. Or both, even."

I almost snorted.

Of *course* he wouldn't mind. Especially not Beltaine, if the Sacred Union was performed.

"Let's not get ahead of ourselves," I said. "It's eight months away, and anything could happen by then."

Arddhu looked thoughtful. "There is another option for the rituals. No rule exists that I must use an avatar. I may also participate in corporeal form."

What?

I almost choked on my mead as I briefly pictured Arddhu and me having sex at Beltaine in front of everyone in Finn's Cove.

Then I glanced at Kevin, expecting to see jealousy on his face.

Instead, he winked at me. "You didn't know?"

"No, it's not that... I... uh..." I was at a complete loss for words.

"It is merely an option," Arddhu said mildly.

Knowing my cheeks were red, I cleared my throat. "Let's table that discussion for another time and get back to the other thing. Do you think it would help if I talked to Her?"

After all, maybe there was something I could do. The Goddess was still a woman, right? So maybe, woman to woman, I could help.

Arddhu took a deep breath and let it out slowly. "I do not know."

"That might actually make the situation worse," Kevin said. "She'd know you two talked about it. About *Her*."

Oh damn. Good point.

And since She seemed pissed at me already, I sure as hell didn't want to make it worse.

"Let us do nothing about that for now," Arddhu said. "And as far as Michael is concerned, continue with your plan to contact the firm. Inform me of what is decided. As we have done previously, we will schedule a meeting to discuss the next mission. And regardless of whom you choose to serve as my avatar, I will attend the Samhain ritual."

I nodded. "Can I contact you directly?"

His brows lifted. "Of course. I deeply apologize, I had completely forgotten." Gently, he pressed his cool fingertips to my temple, and I heard his voice in my head just like I did with the Goddess. "*You may now speak directly with me at any time.*"

"*Is this how you and Mike communicated?*"

"*Yes. Our link was established early on, before your rescue from Cromm's world. I do not establish these links without consent, however. I am glad you asked.*"

"*This'll be so much easier. And convenient.*"

"*Indeed.*"

"Okay, knock it off you two." Kevin said. "It's rude." Despite his words, his lips quirked.

"Thanks, Arddhu." I spoke aloud. "This link will be perfect to keep you updated in a timely manner." Dammit. There I was, talking like him again.

He nodded and took my hand, raised it to his lips, and brushed a warm kiss on my skin. The whole time his eyes never left mine, and I shifted uncomfortably under their intensity. "Until next time, Keeper."

Now his voice was lower, deeper. More seductive.

Ugh.

This was going to get a helluva lot messier if he and the Goddess didn't reconcile.

Soon.

CHAPTER SIXTEEN

"**I** STILL THINK I look ridiculous," I complained. Even though I'd worn my armor for the past few missions and I'd sort of gotten used to it, I couldn't help but think I was still trying to be an imposter superhero.

"And *I* still think you look hot," Kevin said.

"And I still agree with him," Arddhu chimed in.

"Oh, for fuck's sake," I muttered.

These two were almost more infuriating than Mike ever was.

Arddhu cocked his head. "Do all Americans use such language in general conversation?"

Oh, for fuck's sake.

Swearing. He meant my swearing.

Before I could reply, Anthony—my temporary Assistant the firm had sent a few weeks ago—cleared his throat and cut cleanly through the conversation. "Are we ready?" he asked.

He never engaged in any light-hearted banter, and actually seemed to avoid it at all costs.

In fact, I thought he was too stuffy and uptight, and I hoped Mike would get his shit together and come back soon. And on that subject, I absolutely refused to consider the possibility of him *not* coming back.

Truth be told, I missed our friendship—or what'd seemed like friendship. For a while, he'd been like the older brother I'd never had but always wanted.

But Anthony was here for now, and we were all dealing with it.

As far as his appearance was concerned, Anthony was almost the polar opposite of Mike: where Mike was tall, dark-haired, and lean with sinewy muscle, Anthony was shorter, sandy blonde, and brawny. And somehow, he seemed younger than Mike, but not in any way I could identify.

But he was highly organized, competent, and efficient; he'd taken charge of the security team immediately upon arrival. The team wasn't easy and friendly with him, though, like they'd been with Mike. They kept it completely professional.

And I'd noticed something odd pass between Nat and Anthony.

They'd stared at each other for an awkward few seconds. Then, once Nat had realized I'd witnessed the interaction, she'd quickly looked away and kept her face carefully blank. Anthony, too, had looked away and more or less ignored her for the rest of the moment. Since then, they only spoke to each other when absolutely necessary.

Sure, I was curious. But it wasn't my business to know what was going on with them. Not unless or until things changed and whatever it was had a negative impact on our security or operations.

And when Anthony and I had initially met, he'd been polite and respectful, and had made it quite clear I was the boss; he intended to perform only an advisory role and would defer to me in all decisions. Almost the opposite of the way Mike had been, and I was both impressed and apprehensive in equal measure.

After all, the responsibility of success—and failure—was all mine from this point forward, and that was both empowering and scary.

Now, I made a final adjustment to my baldric and answered Anthony's question.

"Yeah, let's do this."

Over the past few missions, we'd developed an efficient process, and this one was no different.

Kevin ported to the target site under cover of an invisibility spell, and returned seconds later with a thumb's up, which meant our target was alone. While he'd been there, he'd used a spell to deactivate all technology, communication, and security systems.

Then, Arddhu opened the portal, and the tactical team—no fewer than five highly-trained soldiers from the firm—went through and secured the site. They'd also provide backup if necessary.

Next, I went through, gave my little speech to the target, and performed the execution quickly and flawlessly.

We were back through the portal within five minutes of the mission start. In fact, the whole thing had taken less time than it'd taken for me put on the damn armored suit to begin with.

I hadn't even gotten any blood on me at all.

We'd become a well-oiled machine.

"Well done," Arddhu praised.

"Good job," Anthony said.

I nodded and headed to my suite to change.

Later, at the post-mortem, Reshep and Athena reported the asset destruction operation had been accomplished just as quickly and easily. It was our shortest post-mortem yet, at only seven minutes.

I almost felt guilty at how smooth everything was going without Mike.

But we needed everything to go smooth. When he'd been in charge, I hadn't seen the list of targets so I'd had no idea there were so many. That changed when Victor sent me the list.

Ninety-eight assholes were destroying the planet.

So far, we'd taken out ten, so eight-eight remained, which was a helluva lot of targets.

At our current average of one mission each week, we'd be at this for *years*.

Earth couldn't wait that long.

So when Anthony suggested we could increase the pace to three missions per week, we'd all quickly agreed.

After all, the missions were going so efficiently. So effortlessly.

And at that new rate, we'd be done before Beltaine. By the end of May, we could gather the necessary nature deities and convene another all-hands alliance meeting to plan the healing of Earth.

But a lingering doubt nagged at me: it shouldn't be this easy.

And I should've known better.

We all should've.

The mission had started out just like the last several: smooth and efficient. Flawless.

I'd just set myself in position for the sword strike when the door opened.

We'd never had anyone secure the doors because we'd always been so quick.

But this time, Malsumis strolled in.

He paused, took in the scene, then quietly closed the door behind him. He wore an expensive-looking charcoal gray suit, nicely tailored to his lean frame. His long black hair was bound at the back of his neck, which somehow made his angular, clean-shaven features even more pronounced.

"I see we have guests once again." His voice was melodious and pleasant. Almost seductive.

"Help me," the target begged. "They're going to kill me."

"Yes, I see that." Clearly amused, Malsumis glanced at the team members before his gaze rested on me. One side of his mouth curled almost imperceptibly as his bizarre red-gold eyes swept me from head to toe. "*You* again." He cocked his head but made no move toward me. "You've become quite the pest, Keeper."

Before I could say a word, Arddhu stepped in front of me. His horns had grown large and menacing.

"Do not threaten the Keeper." His voice was as I'd never heard it, low and deadly. He didn't just *look* intimidating; he sounded it, too. "If you do not leave immediately, I will have no choice but to dispatch you."

Malsumis just chuckled. "Come now, why don't we discuss this like civilized men?" A quick glance at me. "And women."

"You can't be serious," the target said. "*Get rid* of them."

Malsumis smiled, a cold and calculating stretch of his thin lips. "All in good time. Now, cease your blubbering. The adults in the room are trying to talk."

The target had opened his mouth to speak, but now his eyes widened and one hand went to his throat. It didn't take a genius to figure out

Malsumis had just cast a silencing spell, even though I hadn't seen a gesture or any evidence of a spell being cast. He hadn't even looked at the target.

Damn, this guy was *good.*

"Shall we sit comfortably and discuss this like civilized adults?" Malsumis sauntered to the leather sofa, unbuttoned his suit jacket, and sat gracefully. When none of us moved, his eyebrows lifted.

"We have nothing to discuss," Arddhu growled.

Malsumis studied my prosthesis with interest before lazily meeting my eyes. "And what does the Keeper say?"

I glanced at Arddhu, but he hadn't taken his eyes from Malsumis.

"Same. We have nothing to discuss." Thankfully, my voice was strong. But my sword had started to slip in my sweaty palm, so I adjusted my grip as inconspicuously as I could.

"Pity." Malsumis crossed his legs, rested his elbow on the sofa's armrest, and tented his fingers against his temple. His movements were slow and deliberate, almost lazy. And he appeared completely relaxed, not threatened in the least.

But at the first mission, we'd seen just how quickly he could throw fatal firebolts. None of us were relaxed.

"Regardless," he continued. "I must inform you of a few things."

For the most part he addressed Arddhu directly, but occasionally glanced at me as if to include me or gauge my reaction.

Fuck if he didn't remind me of Cromm. Arrogant yet refined. Well-spoken yet borderline maniacal. Handsome but terrifying.

Thank the gods he wasn't triggering any flashbacks. Yet.

"Know this," he continued. "Even if you remove every single one of my subordinates, you will not stop my efforts. And you most certainly will not stop me in my mission."

I remembered all too well what his mission was: to destroy humankind.

"I can stop you," Arddhu said. "I can *destroy* you."

Malsumis threw his head back and laughed. "You *think* you can. But you cannot. Don't you remember? You tried. And *failed.* You will fail. Every time. I am more powerful than you believe."

While he'd been speaking, from the corner of my eye, I'd noticed Kevin slowly shifting his position from behind Arddhu to between us. I assumed they were communicating mentally to coordinate a magickal attack.

Within seconds, I had confirmation of that.

"Deirdre, on my signal prepare to launch firebolts at Malsumis. Together with Kevin, we will destroy him once and for all."

I sent him a quick acknowledgement and shifted a bit, trying to make it look like I was just restless or tired of standing. But in fact I'd switched my sword to my prosthesis to free up my left hand to use magick. The Morrigan had trained me well in both fireballs and firebolts, so I felt confident and ready.

Malsumis grinned. As if he knew what we planned.

"By all means, try again," he said. "But how many of your friends—" he glanced at the security team before locking his eyes on mine "—will die *this* time?"

I stared at him. It was as if he knew I'd sworn no others would die on my missions.

He waved a long-fingered hand. "You may proceed with your execution, Keeper. I will not stop you."

"*What*? You're supposed to *protect me*." The target panicked, scrambling out of his desk chair and tipping it over with a crash. He stumbled over his own feet and slammed his hip into the side of his desk. He fell across it but was able to keep his head from hitting the expensive granite.

It'd obviously been a short-term silencing spell.

Smirking, Malsumis waved his hand again, and now the target was immobilized, awkwardly sprawled over his desk but conveniently presenting his neck for me. "There. I've even made it easier for you." He hadn't taken his eyes from me, and his intense gaze made my skin crawl.

Uncertain, I hesitated.

"*Do it*," Arddhu commanded through the communication link.

I'd already made my little speech before Malsumis had arrived, so without any further ado, I stepped close to the target and made my strike.

For just a few seconds, nothing happened.

The target didn't move. The head didn't separate from the neck.

Then the immobility spell must've released; now the head rolled off the desk and onto the floor, and the body slowly slid off the edge. Crimson blood spurted across the glossy granite and spread on the thick beige carpet.

Bending, I wiped my blade on the target's expensive suit then returned to Kevin's side with it still gripped in my prosthesis.

Malsumis applauded softly, mocking me. "Well done, Keeper. I see you've improved significantly since last we met."

"*Now.*" Arddhu's voice seemed loud in my mind.

Without hesitation, I raised my left hand and sent the strongest series of firebolts I could muster. At the same time, both Arddhu and Kevin did the same.

Flames engulfed Malsumis and spread quickly to the sofa.

I had a few seconds of feeling smug satisfaction.

Then, as if doused with an extinguisher, the flames sputtered and died.

Malsumis grinned through the smoky haze.

He was completely unhurt. Even his clothing was untouched by the fire. All around him, the sofa was charred, thin tendrils of smoke rising. The acrid smell of burnt plastic assaulted my nose.

Huh. So it hadn't been a leather sofa after all.

He sighed dramatically. "I see you didn't believe me. I'll forgive you. This time."

I swallowed but my throat was bone dry.

Why wasn't he a crispy pile of ashes right now?

Malsumis stood, buttoned his jacket, and straightened his cuffs. "Well, it's been entertaining, but I really must be going now." Again his eyes met and held mine. He snapped his fingers, and the sound was softer than it should've been in the quiet office. As if muffled. "Oh dear, I almost forgot. I have a message for you, Keeper. From an old friend of yours."

He stepped closer, and now I clearly saw the tiny flecks of red in his black irises. The golden hue from earlier had completely disappeared. I tried to lift my sword, but I seemed pinned in place, unable to step away or do anything other than stare into those disturbing eyes.

He was close now, too close. Close enough for his scent to fill my nostrils: cloves and cinnamon, charcoal and smoke.

"Cromm misses his plaything," he softly crooned. "But it won't be long now. He'll see you soon. *Very* soon." He winked at me and moved toward the door.

I could breathe again.

But my relief was short-lived when he turned back, his hand on the doorknob. "And he says this time, *I* can play, too."

The gods only knew what my face looked like. He grinned and left, closing the door quietly behind him.

No one moved, as if they'd had immobility spells put on them, too.

My mind raced.

Yes, we'd known Malsumis had become an ally of Cromm. But this... this put a completely different spin on the situation.

This time, I can play too...

I shuddered and fought the flashbacks that threatened to flood my vision.

Long strips of skin slowly cut from my body...

"We have to go." Anthony's voice seemed to come from far, far away.

A soft, warm tongue running along my raw flesh, licking the blood greedily...

"C'mon, Dee." Kevin's voice from even further away.

Then someone grabbed my arm and pulled me through the portal.

My legs gave out and I landed hard on the marble floor of The Hacienda's living room.

Both Kevin and Arddhu rushed to help me. Each slipped an arm around my waist and lifted me from the floor, then guided me to the sofa. They stood staring at me while Anthony took care of getting the tactical team out of the house.

"I'm fine." The words were automatic.

"Bullshit," Kevin replied.

"No, really. I'm fine. It... it just all came back at once."

Arddhu sat beside me and took my hands in his, not caring that one of them was my prosthesis. "We will protect you from Cromm. Do not worry."

Gently, I pulled my hands free and patted his. "Are we going to have the post-mortem?"

"Anthony suggested we convene later," Arddhu replied.

"Oh."

"I need a drink," Kevin said.

"Me too." I flashed a tiny smile at him.

So he fetched the bottle of Irish whiskey and three glasses from the wet bar.

Both of them threw theirs back in one gulp, so I decided to try that too, even though it seemed a bit disrespectful to the expensive whiskey. Maybe it was better than the long, slow burn of sipping it. Sort of like ripping off a bandage instead of peeling it off slowly.

After I stopped coughing and could breathe again, my face was wet with tears and my throat burned like I'd swallowed fire. But then the wonderful warmth started, and the discomfort faded.

I stood, both surprised and relieved that my legs supported me. "I'll be right back. I have to get this thing off me."

Huh. For once, I got no wisecrack from Kevin.

When I returned a few minutes later in my comfy pants and tee shirt, Arddhu and Kevin seemed to be lost in a private, silent conversation on the sofa.

So I poured myself another whiskey and sat in the chair, tucking my legs up under me. I sipped it slowly this time and watched them as covertly as I could. Occasionally, one of them nodded or shook his head, but it was eerily quiet.

Such a strange way to communicate. But I definitely understood its advantages.

My mind drifted; I was still feeling a bit strange from the flashbacks and the rush of emotions.

Why the hell hadn't Malsumis been burned to a crisp by our firebolts?

Did that mean he was, indeed, indestructible?

Finally, Kevin nodded one last time and they both turned toward me.

"Sorry. Didn't mean to interrupt you two."

Kevin smiled. "We needed to talk about a few things. We both think it'd be a good idea to hold off on any missions for the next couple of weeks."

"But—"

Arddhu spoke. "We must discuss Malsumis and how to destroy him. Before the next mission. We cannot continue to encounter him at the target sites. This must end."

Oh.

Well, he had a good point.

"We also discussed Samhain," Kevin said. "Since it's next week."

I nodded. I'd thought of that a few days ago, but now my mind was occupied with other thoughts.

"Have you decided who will attend the ritual with you?" Arddhu asked.

Now? He wanted to discuss this *now*? It couldn't wait a couple of days, at least?

Then again, it'd get my mind off Cromm, wouldn't it?

Besides, I'd already decided who'd be Mike's stand-in. I just didn't know if either of them would like it.

"Yeah, I have. I'd like both of you to attend."

They frowned and glanced at each other with perfect timing, and if things weren't so seriously fucked up right now it would've been funny.

They spoke at the same time. Arddhu said, "I do not understand," while Kevin said, "Huh?"

Arddhu said, "I do not understand."

At the same time Kevin said, "Huh?"

"I'll need you both there. Arddhu, I'd like you to attend in person. I think the villagers would really appreciate it. Especially if the Goddess doesn't show. It'll give them some confidence in the ritual and the Petitioning Ceremony. Because I'll have to fake it. And if both of you are there, maybe everyone will be so distracted they won't notice my shitty acting job."

"And what if Mike shows up again?" Kevin asked. "Will you be okay?"

"That's the other reason I want you both there. Kevin, you'll have to keep him on the sidelines while Arddhu and I complete the ritual and Petitioning Ceremony. Plus, if something goes seriously wrong you can port us out of there."

Arddhu nodded. "That is actually quite wise. You impress me yet again, Keeper."

Dammit. It was too much. I shuddered as his words provoked another round of flashbacks.

"I have need of your skin, Keeper." The sharp little blade—the scalpel—flashed in the lighting, and his immobility spell wrapped around me like a cement cocoon. I lay on my bed, helpless. Then he grabbed my ankles and pulled me toward him, pushing my legs apart to either side of him.

"No," I croaked.

"Oh yes," he crooned, and pushed my shift up around my hips, exposing me to him. His dark eyes drank me in. *"Hmm. Where shall I take my piece of skin?"*

His long fingers brushed over my thigh, inching close to... no. No, he couldn't mean to rape me.

"Here, I think," he said. His fingers on my thigh, then the pain of the cutting as he sliced into my skin...

"Dee? You okay?" With a jolt, Kevin's voice brought me back to the present.

Goddammit. Just when I thought I was long past being triggered by Arddhu calling me *Keeper*, I'd gotten lost in flashbacks again.

"Yeah." My hand shook as I drank the last of my whiskey, this time not caring at all about the burn. "*Fuck.* Y'know, I haven't thought about Cromm in months. Now it's all coming back again."

Arddhu leaned forward and refilled my glass.

"What was the trigger for this flashback?" Kevin's voice was soft.

I knew what he was up to, because he already knew the answer. I'd asked him months ago not to call me only by my title. But I'd never asked Arddhu. Somehow it'd seemed discourteous to do so, since he only meant it respectfully. Over time, I'd just learned to deal with it.

Until now.

"When... when Arddhu called me *Keeper*." I didn't look at him, just stared at the amber liquid in my glass. "That's what Cromm always called me. Right before he cut into my skin."

"*Fuck.*"

That made me look up; I'd never heard Arddhu swear before. Even though his voice had been soft, it'd somehow still conveyed his anger and disgust.

Maybe I was a bad influence on him.

"Please forgive me," he said. "I would not have... I would never... all this time, I never knew." Arddhu's eyes were liquid pools of sympathy and regret.

"I know." My fingers traced the design on my cut-crystal glass. "I'm sorry I never told you. I actually thought I'd gotten over it. Until—until today."

"I shall only call you Deidre from now on," he promised.

"You could just call me Dee, like everyone else does." I shrugged.

Kevin went to look for another bottle of whiskey, since this one was almost empty.

Arddhu met my gaze. "That seems somewhat disrespectful."

I shook my head. "It's actually what I prefer."

"Very well, I shall call you Dee." He inclined his head politely.

"Thank you."

"I guess we're out," Kevin said, returning empty-handed from the wet bar.

"No, there's another bottle or two in the tent," I said. "I think the mead's still out there, too."

"In that case, I'll be right back." He ported there and back quickly. He set four bottles on the coffee table, then refilled our glasses.

"There are a few things I wanted to talk to you two about before the post-mortem," I said. "The biggest one is: Malsumis."

"Y'know," Kevin cocked his head. "When he said he had *a message from an old friend*, I assume that meant he's been in contact with Cromm recently. And that really worries me. It means Malsumis knows where Cromm is."

"Remember how difficult it was for us to find Cromm's world to rescue you last year?" Arddhu asked. After I nodded, he continued. "It seems Malsumis has no such difficulty."

"And I wonder how long they've been working together," Kevin added.

I nodded again. "For me, it was when he said Cromm would be seeing me soon. To be honest, that scared the shit out of me."

"Like maybe he's found a way to come back," Kevin said.

"He could not have," Arddhu pointed out. "Not yet. His monument must be rebuilt for him to return to Earth."

I sipped my whiskey and remembered what I'd read about Cromm in that book Zara had brought me when I'd been Cromm's prisoner. "Wasn't his old monument located somewhere north of Dublin?"

"Magh Slécht." Kevin nodded. "In County Cavan."

"He is not bound to that location," Arddhu cautioned. "He may choose another."

I thought for a moment. "Can he build it anywhere? Even here in the US?"

"Yes," Arddhu confirmed. "He is free to build it anywhere. We should assume he will build where he knows it will cause the most chaos."

America was pretty much chaotic already, so it'd be the perfect place.

"He probably already has some people working on it by now," I said. "So we should be able to find out where. Maybe the firm can study some satellite photos."

"Ooh, that's a great idea," Kevin said.

"Let me tell Anthony about that before I forget." I set my glass on the coffee table and headed for the handheld radio base in the kitchen.

"What is a *satellite photos*?" Arddhu asked.

As I thumbed the talk button and hailed Anthony, Kevin began explaining. It was nice not being the one to define something for Arddhu, for a change.

Anthony sounded tense. "Has something happened?"

"No," I quickly replied, and explained what we needed. He repeated it back to me to confirm his understanding of the request and promised to keep me updated.

Returning the radio to the base, I just caught the tail end of something Kevin had said to Arddhu: "... she's not gonna go for that."

"Who's not gonna go for what?" I crossed the room and sat in the chair again.

Both of them looked at me but hesitated before replying.

"Dammit." I sighed. "You two have *got* to stop talking about me."

"We weren't... well, not like you think." Kevin shook his head. "We were talking about postponing the missions indefinitely. Until we know more about where Cromm is rebuilding and how far along the monument is."

"Oh no, you don't." I pointed a finger at him. "We can't stop now. We still have way too many targets on the list. We need to move *faster*, not stop and take a break."

"Told you so," Kevin muttered.

Arddhu cleared his throat. "However, it would be wise to wait. Malsumis has already taunted us and proven he is impervious to our combined magick. We must be cautious or all could be lost."

He had a point, but that didn't mean I had to like it.

But that brought up another point I'd wanted to talk about. "Speaking of that—just how the hell did he do it? Avoid burning, I mean. His clothes weren't even the tiniest bit scorched."

"He must've had some kind of shield in place," Kevin said. "But I sure couldn't detect one." He turned to Arddhu. "Whatever it was, it was new— he didn't have it the last time, or he wouldn't have taken any damage."

And he'd seemed fully recovered from those injuries, too.

"Indeed." Arddhu nodded, then grimaced. "I regret I did not finish him at that time."

He seemed so damn sure he could destroy Malsumis, but a tiny flicker of doubt had taken hold in me. What if he couldn't? What if *none* of us could? What would happen if we couldn't overcome Malsumis?

If he was invincible *and* working with Cromm... I didn't even want to think about that.

And what if he decided to attack us here, at The Hacienda? Could my wards hold against him? Would the security team's weapons do anything at all to him?

"Anyway," Kevin said, interrupting my thoughts. "Samhain is next week. Why don't we concentrate on that while we wait for more info from your firm?"

It sure as hell wasn't *my* firm, but I didn't bother to correct him.

"Where do you wish to meet for Samhain?" Arddhu asked.

It didn't make much sense to have him meet us here and then have Kevin port all three of us. "Can you just meet us at Ard na Mara? Last year, Mike arrived with the villagers and we walked to town. I'd like to keep doing that."

"Yes, I remember." He nodded. "I will continue to follow the custom."

Oh yeah. Of course he'd remember. Unbelievably, sometimes I forgot who I was talking to.

He stood. "Now, I wish to rest before the post-mortem. I will return later." He brushed his lips against my hand once again, then left for the portal.

Huh. It seemed like he had to rest more often lately. I wondered what was wrong, and hoped he was feeling okay.

We really needed him.

CHAPTER SEVENTEEN

K EVIN PORTED ME to Ard na Mara in the late morning on Samhain
Eve. With the eight hours difference, we arrived with plenty of time
for me to take my ritual bath, dress, and prepare.

Just like last year, the Samhain Oil in the bath allowed my consciousness
to recede in preparation for receiving the presence of the Goddess.

If She decided to attend, that was.

None of us were sure, and when I'd tried to contact Her directly to ask a
couple of days ago, She hadn't responded. It made me nervous and more
than a little frustrated. At some point, we'd all have to sit down and figure
out what to do, but I didn't think any of us were interested in starting that
discussion.

Also, just like last year, I wore Maggie's beautiful garnet silk and black
lace gown. I left the shawl in the dresser drawer, though, because the
weather was much warmer this year. In fact, it was supposed to set a
record high temperature.

Once again, I waited on the patio at sunset for Arddhu and the villagers
to arrive and escort me to the village green.

Except this year, Kevin was at my side.

He'd dressed in his embroidered dark green tunic and trousers, but left
his hair unbound except for the warrior braids at each temple.

The villagers arrived at sundown, singing their songs to honor the
ancestors.

Maura, the village elderwoman, stepped forward with the ritual potion, and my consciousness retreated further, preparing for the presence of the Goddess.

But She didn't come. I remained completely myself, although feeling somewhat disconnected and weird.

"*Lady?*" I tried to reach Her, but there was no response.

Then the group parted for Arddhu to come forward, and despite my dulled senses, I was awe-struck, and all thoughts of contacting the Goddess faded.

His face and broad chest were painted with ancient symbols, just as Mike's had been last year. But he certainly didn't need Mike's antler headdress. No, he'd allowed his natural horns to grow to their fullest, and they were impressive antlers. Magnificent and regal, they towered over all of us.

For the first time, I understood why he was the Consort to the Goddess. He exuded raw masculine sexuality and truly personified his aspect of Cernunnos, Lord of the Animals.

His sable brown hair hung down to his chest and flowed over his shoulders, and I didn't remember ever seeing it that long.

Just like Mike last year, Arddhu was mostly naked with only a scrap of soft leather covering his groin. He was more muscular than I'd thought, and I'd never see him the same way again after this.

But the one thing that was truly striking about his appearance were the blue-hued tattoos covering his bronze skin. Twining from his left shoulder across his chest and abdomen to his right hip, down his long leg, and ending on the instep of his right foot, the Celtic knotwork was adorned with intricate vines and leaves.

In the twilight, the vines seemed to shift and move, and I blinked at the tiny faces that seemed to peek out at me.

Unlike Mike, who'd been distant while filled with Arddhu's presence, Arddhu was completely aware and totally himself. I watched his eyes travel across my face, rest on my cleavage, sweep over the rest of my body, then return to meet my gaze. He took my hand in his and pressed his lips against it, dark eyes never leaving mine.

His desire was plain for anyone to see, and in the little corner of my mind where my consciousness watched, I shivered with pleasure. After all, he was the perfect manifestation of masculine deity, and he wanted *me*.

But I also frowned.

He belonged to the Goddess as Her Consort, not to a mere mortal woman like me.

By now, I felt the full effects of Maura's potion, and my consciousness had retreated to the furthest corner of my mind. I was more than ready for the presence of the Goddess.

Yet, I was still just myself.

"*Lady?*" I tried again to contact Her. "*Great Goddess?*"

No answer.

Gently, Arddhu tugged me into place beside him and we headed to the village on the path through the woods. The villagers once again sang their song to the ancestors, their voices harmonizing perfectly.

> This night the veil 'tween the worlds is thin.
> Hail! Blessed ancestors and kin.
> Honor to ancient ones who died long ago,
> Their bones buried deep below.
> Sorrow for those who passed this year,
> 'Tis for them we shed these tears.
>
> O, Dark Mother, attend us now,
> With sacrifice we keep our vow.
> O, Horned God, attend us now,
> With sacrifice we keep our vow.
> O, Wise Goddess, O, Horned God,
> Accept our sacrifice of sacred blood.

At the village green, the torches flared in the twilight's gentle breeze. The branches of the skeletal tree in the center of the green were covered in little scraps of paper tied with black ribbons. The villagers stood silent, respectfully observing the ritual.

Arddhu and I waited near the tree as Maura chanted her sacred blessings, then it was time for the ritual sacrifice. Just like last year, she provided the bone-handled golden blade and I slashed into the skin just above Arddhu's heart, then exchanged the blade for the ceremonial wooden bowl. I pressed the bowl against his chest and collected the blessed blood.

The cut healed itself in seconds and left behind only a smudge of dried crimson. Arddhu took the burning branch from Maura's hand and set the tree alight, and the aged dry wood burst into flame quickly. The heat engulfed me as I stepped close and offered the blood sacrifice to the flames.

Finally, I spoke the spell to release the words written on the paper scraps, and they were set free to travel to the ancestors.

Words of comfort, honor, and love.

The ritual was complete. Now it was time for the Petitioning Ceremony. The enormous carved chair was brought forward and the cushion set in place.

My senses were still dulled, my consciousness was still in the far corner of my mind, and all was as it should be.

But the Goddess still hadn't come. I was alone in my body.

I tried one last time to reach Her, pleading with Her again and again from the little corner of my mind.

But the silence continued. My fears had come true: I'd have to fake my way through the Petitioning Ceremony.

As I sat in the chair, I reminded myself not to speak, because Her voice and mine were as different as night and day. I did my best to keep my face serenely blank and hoped no one would notice anything amiss.

Each villager came forward to ask their question of the Goddess, and I either shook my head or nodded. Once or twice someone gave me a puzzled look, but nothing more than that.

Of course they wouldn't question the Goddess.

Something seemed wrong, though; the potion had started to wear off, which meant the Ceremony was taking way too long. My senses were rapidly returning and I caught myself concentrating too closely on a villager.

I unfocused my eyes, settled my face into detachment, and continued to either smile benevolently or give small nods and shakes of my head.

My fingers desperately wanted to fidget. Forcing myself into absolute stillness was driving me insane. A scream of frustration began to build inside me.

Then, finally, it was over. The last villager had come and gone.

But now I had to fake coming back to myself.

I shook my head as if to clear it, and sat for a moment with my eyes closed, as if waiting for dizziness to pass. Then Kevin and Arddhu each took an arm, and I leaned on them as we walked to our reserved table.

It was over, and I didn't think anyone had caught on to my ruse. I breathed a sigh of immense relief.

Arddhu's horns had returned to stubs and all but disappeared into his wild mane of hair. He didn't seem to care that he was mostly naked while everyone else was fully clothed. Many of the villagers openly stared at him in awe, and I wondered how long it'd been since he'd attended a ritual here in person.

Even I couldn't keep from sneaking looks at him.

And every time I did, his gaze was glued to me.

A bell rang, signifying the Dumb Supper had begun. Until the bell rang again in about an hour, no talking of any kind was allowed. This was to show respect for the ancestors who attended the feast at the nearby table, set just for them.

Then, servers arrived with full plates and mugs for each of us, and we ate.

At least no one was staring at *me*. Which hopefully meant I'd pulled it off.

I'd been starving, so I finished my food before either Arddhu or Kevin had. To keep myself from staring at Arddhu, I turned in my seat and watched the brightly burning tree as it sent sparks up into the night air.

"*You did well, Dee.*" Arddhu's voice was soft, almost a caress in my mind. I whipped my head around, but he hadn't paused in his eating.

Well, technically, it didn't break the rules of the Dumb Supper.

"*Do you think anyone noticed She wasn't here?*"

"*No. And I have made note of the requests. I will fulfill as many as I can.*"

That would be fantastic. I'd worried about the villagers not getting their answers or boons.

"*I didn't know you could do that.*"

"*It is one advantage of being a god.*" His voice held a smile, but he didn't look up from his plate.

Yeah, I'd say that was a helluva advantage.

"*Thank you. I was worried about that.*"

"*It was the one aspect of this ruse that we did not consider in greater detail.*"

Yeah, it could've used some additional thought, that was for sure.

Kevin finished his food just a bit before Arddhu, and within moments the servers had returned to whisk away our plates.

I glanced at Arddhu and caught him staring at my cleavage.

Fuck.

I was pretty sure I blushed. My face felt hot enough.

"*Please don't do that,*" I told him.

"*Why not?*" His eyes focused on mine.

"*It makes me uncomfortable.*"

"*Why?*"

Did I really have to spell it out? "*Because you're the Consort to the Goddess. Even if She said you weren't. You'll always be the Consort to the Goddess. To me, it feels like cheating.*"

His smile was tinged with sadness. "*For you, I will try to curb my impulses. However, I must tell you that such coupling is natural among our kind.*"

"*Our kind?*"

"*We are immortals.*"

Ridiculous. How could he lump me in with him and the others?

"*No, I'm just a human,*" I insisted.

He gave just the tiniest shake of his head. "*No, you are not. You are the Keeper. You are no longer completely human. You are more like us than not.*"

I frowned. "*I know I'll live longer than other humans now, and yeah, I have magick, but that doesn't make me immortal. Take the Sphere from me and I'd be just like I was before. I'm only the Keeper because of the Sphere.*"

Again, he shook his head. "*The longer you protect the Sphere, the less human you are.*"

What?

I searched the memories of the Keepers, but didn't find anything to back up what he'd just told me. Maggie had been the longest-lived of the Keepers, but even she'd still been human.

I decided to ask Anu. *"Anu, what is Arddhu talking about? I'm still human, aren't I?"*

Her reply was swift. *"No, Deirdre. You are no longer entirely human. However, you are not quite immortal, either. You are in metamorphosis."*

Impossible.

"But Arddhu, that doesn't make any sense. Maggie lived the longest of any of the Keepers, and she wasn't immortal."

He leaned forward and rested his folded arms on the table. My eyes dropped again to his tattoos, and I wondered if gods had a special tattoo shop they went to. Or did they just go to a human shop, wherever one was convenient?

"But you are not Maggie," Arddhu replied. *"And yes, after so many centuries wielding the power of the Sphere, even she became more than human."*

I wondered if Maggie had known that.

Then the bell rang again, which meant we were free to speak, although we needed to keep our voices low to maintain respect for the dead.

"Okay, you two. Cut it out. It's rude." Kevin's voice was soft, pitched only for our ears.

He was one to talk. Hadn't he had a long private conversation with Arddhu in my presence not too long ago?

I almost laughed, but it didn't seem right. It was Samhain, after all; a solemn occasion such as this shouldn't include laughter.

The servers came and refilled our mugs from a pitcher of ale, which made me look around for Garrett. I hadn't seen him. He usually made a point of asking my thoughts on his latest brew.

I hoped he wasn't sick or something.

Then I saw Mike.

Well, I *thought* it was him. In the near-darkness beyond the torchlight of the village green, I couldn't be sure. I only had a feeling it was him.

"Is that Mike?" I quietly asked, nodding toward the shadowy figure.

Both Arddhu and Kevin looked, and after a moment the figure melted into the darkness.

"Yes," Arddhu replied. "It was Michael. He wishes to speak with us, but not here. He will meet us at your cottage."

"Is there danger?" Kevin asked. "I can port us there."

"No. No danger. We can return on the forest path at our leisure."

I didn't know about the guys, but my curiosity was definitely in high gear. What could Mike possibly have to talk to us about that needed such privacy?

After a few moments, we finished our ales and left.

The night was simply gorgeous and not the least bit chilly. The warm breeze held notes of salt air and rich earth, and the nearly-full moon was bright enough to clearly light our way on the path. Fallen leaves crunched under our feet, breaking the stillness of the woods.

We didn't talk on the way.

Well, at least, I didn't. They might've been deep in a private conversation for all I knew.

When we reached the cottage, I didn't see Mike waiting on the patio, as I'd expected. But I'd never revoked his access through the wards either here or at The Hacienda, so he'd probably gone inside.

We'd just entered the kitchen when the living room light came on, and I saw Mike waiting in the chair beside it.

I don't know what made me glance at the clock on the mantle, but then I did a double-take because it showed the correct hour. When had it started working again?

Whatever. I'd worry about it some other time.

For a moment, Mike's gaze held mine, and I didn't know what to say to him.

But then he turned toward Arddhu. "Thank you for meeting me. I figured this was the safest place, with the wards and all."

Arddhu sat in the other chair, which left the sofa for Kevin and I.

Unfortunately, that meant Arddhu was directly in my line of sight, distracting me with only the scrap of leather between his legs.

"What is it, Michael?" Arddhu asked. "What has happened?"

"I have information. I'm sure you're aware Cromm has a crew rebuilding his monument." He paused for Arddhu's nod. "Well, I know where they are."

Arddhu leaned forward eagerly.

"They're in Arizona," Mike continued. He didn't take his eyes from Arddhu. "In the desert between Phoenix and Tucson."

What? Why the hell would Cromm build it there? Was it just a coincidence that it was only about an hour away from me?

"Isn't that mostly reservation land?" I asked.

Before he could reply, Arddhu asked, "Are you certain?"

"Yes. To both questions." Mike hadn't even glanced in my direction.

"But that doesn't make sense," Kevin said, frowning.

Mike shrugged. "It's true, all the same."

My witchy-sense agreed: Mike spoke *truth*.

"How?" I asked. "How do you know this?"

"I can't tell you that." He still wouldn't look at me.

Something was off about this. My witchy-sense couldn't tell exactly what, though. But he knew I could detect lies, so was that why he couldn't answer? Or *wouldn't* answer?

"What's really going on?" I asked.

"I don't know what you mean."

Lie.

"I know you're lying. And you know I know."

Now, finally, he met my gaze. But I almost wished he hadn't because there was absolutely no emotion in his eyes. It was as if he were looking at a stranger.

He shrugged again.. "Doesn't matter. I have to go." He stood and nodded at Arddhu. "Good luck."

"Wait." My shoe caught on the rug as I stumbled after him. "That's it?"

At the back door, he half-turned and spoke over his shoulder. "Take care, Dee."

Then he was out the door and gone. No use chasing after him.

Maybe Kevin should've put a compulsion spell on him. Made him tell us the truth.

Too late now.

With a sigh, I returned to the sofa. "None of this makes any sense." I met Arddhu's gaze. "If that's all he had to say, he could've told you weeks ago, using your communication link with him."

"No, he could not. The link was terminated some time ago."

"By him?"

"Yes."

"But you obviously reconnected with him back at the village green, when he told you he wanted to meet. Why didn't he just tell you then? Why go through all this... this... drama?"

"He said he wished to speak to all of us."

I could've growled with frustration.

Something didn't seem right, but I couldn't put my finger on it.

"I hate to say it," Kevin said, voice quiet. "But I really think he's working for him. Cromm, I mean."

My head swiveled toward him.

Expecting a verbal attack, he put his hands up defensively. "Hey, don't look at me like that." To Arddhu, he said, "Tell me this doesn't seem odd to you."

Arddhu leaned back in his chair, and the movement made the scrap of leather shift. I quickly looked away to avoid seeing something I shouldn't.

"It does seem strange, yes." Arddhu seemed deep in thought. "Tonight, Michael was not his usual self."

"He hasn't been his usual self for months," I pointed out.

Kevin grimaced and ran his fingers through his hair. "I need a fucking drink."

With little effort, I used my magick to port Maggie's bottle of Irish whiskey from the sideboard in the kitchen, along with the two glasses. One of us would either have to drink from the bottle or share a glass.

The bottle was half empty, but I poured a couple of fingers' worth in each glass anyway.

"You're not drinking?" Kevin asked.

"I've got the bottle."

He snorted. "Not very ladylike."

"I don't give a shit."

"Neither do I." He tossed his whiskey back in one swallow and held his glass out for a refill.

I poured him a double then took a swig from the bottle, not caring that it burned on the way down.

"So what do we do about Mike?" I asked.

Arddhu abruptly got up from his chair and sat beside me. Now I was sandwiched between him and Kevin. "That discussion will keep until the morning. Right now, you must relax."

I growled. "I can't relax. You guys are crowding me."

"It's a small sofa," Kevin pointed out.

"There are two empty chairs," I snapped.

Arddhu shifted, then his strong hand gently but firmly massaged the back of my neck, digging into the tense muscles there.

Oh. That felt *wonderful*.

"You've been way too tense lately," Kevin said, voice low and soothing. "Let us help you."

Lifting an eyebrow, I just looked at him. "Help me? How?"

"We think you need a massage."

I almost laughed, but that would've probably been rude.

"What? Now you guys are licensed massage therapists?"

He grinned. "Did you know you can learn anything on the internet?"

Now I did laugh.

Never in my life had I ever received a proper massage. I'd sometimes thought about using one of those half-price offers in the junk mail circulars, but I just never got around to it.

I had to admit I was intrigued.

And more than a little attracted to the idea of two gorgeous immortals giving me a massage.

"Okay. I'm willing to give it a try."

Kevin took the bottle from me and set it on the coffee table with their glasses. Both of them wrapped their arms around me, and a sudden sense of vertigo made my stomach flip.

Kevin had just ported the three of us to my bed.

CHAPTER EIGHTEEN

"**W**HAT—" KEVIN SILENCED me with a finger on my lips. "Shh. Just relax," he crooned. "You've been so tense for so long, it's not healthy. We're gonna fix that."

"But I thought you meant you'd massage me *there*, on the sofa."

"Not enough room." He shook his head. "And can't do it properly there. This is better. Trust us."

Arddhu had started a fire in the fireplace, and its crackle was comforting. And more than a little romantic.

Now he sat on the bed beside me. "Please trust us."

Thing was, I *did* trust them. Well, for the most part.

There was a part of me that still remembered all too well what Kevin had done to me before I'd been captured by Cromm, and that part didn't trust him completely. Not yet. Maybe never.

Even after all this time, and with absolutely no reason to *not* trust him.

But Arddhu I'd always trusted completely, ever since we'd become allies. I didn't think he'd betray that trust.

I sighed. "So I suppose now you want me to undress."

A corner of Kevin's lips quirked. "It's generally considered necessary."

I stood, and he gently pulled my dress off.

Thank the gods I'd worn clean underwear today.

While Kevin stowed the dress in the armoire, Arddhu eased me down to sit on the edge of the bed, then knelt and gently massaged my legs before gliding his hands down to remove my shoes. He handed them to Kevin, who put them away and returned.

"Lay on your stomach," Kevin instructed.

I complied.

Arddhu resumed working on my calves, and it was heavenly. I'd had no idea my muscles there were so tight. I could almost feel them relaxing under Arddhu's strong fingers.

Movement on the bed, then another pair of hands massaged my shoulders and neck, and I figured that was Kevin. And he found knots that must've been there so long they'd probably thought they'd found a permanent home.

Oh my gods. This was bliss.

Bit by bit, I relaxed and my muscles loosened.

Kevin kneaded my spine from my neck to my tailbone, radiating outward to my sides in long, sweeping motions. Once or twice his fingers caught on my bra straps, and at this point I saw no reason for that.

"You can undo it," I said.

"Are you sure?"

"Yes."

He unfastened it and continued to work on my spine.

Eyes closed, I sighed and drifted with the sensations.

Arddhu worked his way down to my feet, and now he dug his thumbs into my soles. I'd never had a foot massage either, and it felt fucking awesome. Damn good thing I wasn't ticklish or he might've gotten kicked in the teeth.

That almost made me laugh, but when he started pulling gently on each toe to stretch the muscles, all humor disappeared as I concentrated on not moaning.

Damn. If they kept this up much longer I'd just be a puddle of goo on the bed.

"It'd be even better if we had some proper oil," Kevin complained.

"Tell you what," I said, voice muffled from the comforter. "If you both promise to do this again, I'll buy whatever kind of oil you want."

Arddhu chuckled softly.

Kevin snorted. "Deal." Then he moved up to my scalp and began massaging that, too.

This time, I couldn't hold back the groan.

Never in my life had I ever felt anything like this.

Arddhu, meanwhile, had moved up to my thighs. I hadn't realized I'd had knots in those muscles too, but I sure as hell felt them being worked out.

"The buttocks also contain bundles of fibrous tissue," Arddhu said. "They are called the gluteal muscles. May I include them in my massage?"

Why the hell not?

"Yes." I didn't even have to think about it. "You can pull my panties down."

He eased them down, and I almost laughed again at the absurdity of the situation: me being rubbed down by two immortals.

One of whom was actually massaging my ass.

But his strong hands kneading the muscles there made me sigh again. Who'd have thought that a butt massage could feel so damn good?

I'd just started drifting off when Kevin spoke. "We'd like you to turn over now."

Oh. There was more?

"Okay."

Rolling over, I removed my undone bra and flung it away. But I pulled my panties back up.

For now, anyway. Because I had a pretty good idea where this was headed. And I'd have some time yet to decide whether or not to let that happen.

Kevin's hands smoothly moved down my left arm to my hand, and as he worked on my fingers, I almost gasped at how good it felt.

Damn. I sure could've used this during my sword training days. I didn't even know hand massages were a thing.

Arddhu, still working on the lower half of my body, now kneaded my thighs. I watched him, bent over my body, and the days of thinking of him as a father figure were long gone.

Shadows and light from the flickering fire played over his body, making his tattoos seem to writhe and shift. His wild mane hung free and hid his face from my view—until he suddenly raised his head and met my eyes with a piercing look that made me catch my breath.

He was magnificent.

Not taking his gaze from mine, his fingers slipped under the elastic waistband of my panties and stopped, as if waiting for my permission to continue.

"Yes." My voice was barely above a whisper, but he acknowledged me with a tiny nod and eased my panties down my legs, then tossed them aside. Slowly, he pushed my legs slightly apart and massaged my inner thighs.

Well. That didn't take long.

Now I was naked in bed with two glorious gods who were totally focused on giving me the most incredible full-body massage of my life.

I could've never imagined this scenario, not in a million years. My former coworkers would never believe me if I told them about this.

Not that I would, of course.

Kevin, meanwhile, had shifted position to sit behind my head, and now he worked on my shoulders and upper chest. I hadn't realized that even my chest muscles had been so tight. I couldn't help but groan again.

After a slight hesitation he moved down to my breasts, but this wasn't at all the same way he stroked them when we had sex. No, this was almost asexual, but felt absolutely wonderful. He even carefully avoided touching my now-hard nipples, even though they begged for attention. At this point, I didn't know how much more massaging they could do anyway; between the two of them, they'd worked almost every inch of my body. And I didn't feel like a languid puddle anymore; on the contrary, my heart was pounding and I was so fucking turned on, I felt like I'd go insane if my needs weren't met. *Now.*

I decided to take matters into my own hands.

Um, so-to-speak.

"So which one of you is going to fucking kiss me already?" My voice was thick and husky.

A quick glance passed between them, then Arddhu bent his head to my skin. "I will."

That's when things *really* heated up.

I woke sandwiched between two warm, firm bodies.

Kevin's arms were wrapped around me from behind while Arddhu faced me with his hand resting possessively on my hip. Long legs were hooked over mine, but without shifting my position—and probably waking one or both of them—I had no idea whose they were.

Their soft, even breathing was almost synchronized, and I wondered at these two who had somehow become so close as to share me. Especially Kevin. He'd seemed a bit possessive at times last year; now he'd willingly allowed Arddhu to have sex with me.

Speaking of... I studied Arddhu's handsome face with new eyes.

Long, dark lashes brushed his cheeks. His wild, tangled locks of dark brown hair made my fingers itch to smooth them. His full, swollen lips invited soft kisses.

The things we'd done... well, I'd simply never look at him quite the same way again.

It'd been a helluva night, and although it hadn't ended as I'd originally planned, I had no regrets.

For one thing, these two old gods sure knew how to give pleasure. Then again, they both had much more experience at pleasing women than the average guy with a normal lifespan. I knew Kevin had lived for about a thousand years, but I could only guess Arddhu's age was somewhere between ten and fifteen thousand.

Undeniably, he was an ancient creature.

His eyes blinked open and found mine.

"Morning," I whispered.

"Blessed morn," he whispered back.

"I'm awake," Kevin said, voice soft. "No need to whisper on my account." He pulled me closer against him and nuzzled my neck, raising goosebumps on my skin.

Of course he had morning wood. Arddhu probably did, too. But I was *not* going to look.

I assumed we'd probably have another round or two before we dressed and left for Arizona, but they surprised me.

Arddhu gave me a soft, sweet—and quick—kiss, then he disentangled himself and headed for the bathroom.

That I hadn't expected.

As if reading my mind, Kevin murmured in my ear. "We'll probably get back together again later. We both know you need time to recover."

Oh. How thoughtful.

With a soft kiss on my shoulder, Kevin got out of bed and went across the hall to the shower.

Stretching lazily, I couldn't help but grin.

Never in a million years had I ever thought my life would turn out like this.

Loved by two gorgeous immortals. Friends with the Goddess of Battlefield Death. Trained to defend and kill. And able to do some kick-ass magick.

Not bad for a thirty-something accountant. Well, *former* accountant.

Shaking my head, I got out of bed and padded to the bathroom. Arddhu hadn't closed the door, so I leaned against the doorway and watched him.

He stood at the sink and used a soapy washcloth to remove the smeared remnants of the ochre symbols on his chest and abdomen.

His body was just as gorgeous as Kevin's, but in a different way. While Kevin was slim with lean sinew and smooth lines, Arddhu was more muscular. His broad shoulders and narrow hips formed the classic triangular shape coveted by male models and actors.

In the bright light of day, his tattoos seemed much more stark.

"Are your tattoos new?" I asked.

In the mirror, he met my gaze with a tiny smile. "No. They are quite old, in fact." He fussed with the cloth in his hands and looked away, suddenly troubled. "I have kept them hidden for some time. Until now."

He'd missed a few spots. I stepped close and took the cloth from him, then rewet it and added more soap before rubbing at the smudges. "Why?"

"*She* did not like them."

I glanced up in surprise. "What? Why not?"

He shrugged. "I think they reminded Her of… our early days together."

Geez. When had the Goddess become such a *bitch*? Or had She always been one and just hidden it from everyone?

Or maybe... just from me.

He stood still as I lightly brushed my fingers across the inked designs and looked closer.

Finely drawn, with exquisite detail, they were beautifully done in shades of blue with bits of green and brown. Zoomorphic figures were cleverly hidden in the twisting Celtic knotwork: foxes danced among the trees on his shoulder, stags gracefully leapt over the foliage on his chest, ravens peeked from the vines along his abdomen, and wolves chased rabbits around the ivy trailing down his leg.

"I think they're beautiful," I murmured.

He captured my hand in his and brought it to his lips. "Thank you."

His eyes held hunger, but it wasn't exactly sexual. Or at least, not just that. He also seemed lonely and starved for the admiration and attention of a woman.

My anger spiked, and I clenched my jaw. The Goddess was really doing a number on him emotionally, and it pissed me off.

He stepped close and brushed his lips on mine, and I felt the evidence of his obvious arousal pressed against my torso.

Gently but firmly, I pulled away. "Let me finish these last two spots. Then I need to shower. We have to get going."

His state of arousal didn't lessen in the least.

"You may want to put that thing away before someone gets hurt," I teased.

He laughed then, a deep throaty sound full of warmth and pleasure.

I'd never heard that particular laugh from him before, but I liked it.

And I wanted to hear it again.

Finished with removing the last smudges, I tossed the cloth in the sink and returned to the bedroom just as Kevin arrived, fully dressed. He plopped into a chair near the fireplace with a grin.

"Your turn," he said.

Gathering my clothes, I headed across the hall and took a quick shower. I didn't bother to dry my hair; I just brushed it back into a ponytail and put my clothes on.

When I re-entered my bedroom, I stopped short. I wasn't exactly sure what my eyes were seeing, or if I was interrupting something I shouldn't.

Arddhu had dressed, and was locked in an embrace with Kevin. I couldn't tell if it was friendly or sexual in nature.

They pulled away but continued gripping each other's arms, then nodded and smiled before turning to face me. Neither seemed embarrassed that I'd caught them doing... whatever it was they'd been doing.

So I probably shouldn't be concerned, either.

Arddhu looked happier than I'd seen him in weeks, and my heart did a funny little flip.

I stepped close to them. "Before we go back, I just wanted to take a minute and thank you both for... such a wonderful night. I haven't been this relaxed in—well, I don't think I've *ever* been this relaxed." I pulled them into a three-way hug. "Thank you both so much."

"It was our pleasure," Kevin said, chin resting on my head.

"As he said, our pleasure," Arddhu added.

It felt so good to be surrounded by their solid warmth, I had to force myself to pull away. "Okay, time to go."

Kevin ported us to my bedroom at The Hacienda, and Arddhu prepared to leave for his own world.

"Until next time," he murmured. His lips once again brushed the back of my hand, and his eyes were soft and liquid on mine.

He looked, for all intents and purposes, like a man in love, and I couldn't help but worry.

Had I opened a huge can of worms by sleeping with him?

Technically, though, we hadn't done much sleeping. Which was now obvious by my persistent yawning. It'd been morning in Ireland, but it was late afternoon here at The Hacienda, and I was exhausted.

After Arddhu left for the portal, Kevin touched my arm. "You should probably get some sleep."

"I plan on it. Right after I have something to eat."

"Mmm. Food. I could go for something, myself."

"Let's go see if there's some leftovers in the fridge."

But the kitchen wasn't empty, as I'd expected it to be.

José was busy preparing something on the stove that smelled a lot like bacon. He barely glanced at us before turning back to the pan. "This'll be ready in just a minute."

Kevin and I shared a glance, then sat at the island.

Where two place settings waited.

I tried to remember what I'd picked for dinner for the day, but my mind drew a blank.

Shortly afterward, José placed a plate in front of each of us.

Bacon, lettuce, and tomato sandwiches on crusty homemade bread, with a bit of creamy coleslaw on the side.

I met José's gaze. "Wow. This looks great. Thank you."

He smiled, then quietly left us alone to devour our food.

"So," I said between bites. "Do I have to worry about getting pregnant?"

"I don't think so. I mean, you're still taking your potion, right?"

I'd been taking a weekly herbal concoction ever since he and I had resumed our sexual relationship. The time just wasn't right for a kid, and we both knew it.

"Yeah, but he's a fertility god. Isn't he extra potent or something? Is my potion enough?"

"It should be. Although, to be honest, I thought he might've let his magick loose once, last night."

"What does that mean?"

He finished his sandwich and wiped his mouth. "Remember that weird golden glow? When that happened, did you feel or smell anything odd?"

Oh yeah, there'd been that moment of weirdness during the night. At one point, the three of us had been enveloped in a bright golden light that'd emanated from Arddhu, then the rich smell of damp earth, as if from a recent rain, had filled the room. And there'd also been a delicious but strange warmth that'd spread through my body, nothing at all like the usual sensations of arousal or release. I'd thought I'd imagined it all, but apparently not. Not if Kevin had experienced it, too.

I nodded. "A strong earthy smell. And heat inside me."

"Then yeah." Kevin frowned. "He lost control of his magick."

"But what does that *mean*?"

"Nothing bad, I think. And no, I don't think you're pregnant. But we should probably ask him what it all means. Just to be sure."

"You seem to know an awful lot about this."

He shrugged. "We've become close. Especially with Mike gone. It's only the two of us now to protect and take care of you."

I remembered that went back to last year, after my rescue from Cromm. Arddhu had told me the three of them had sworn to protect me. Sort of like the Three Musketeers or something.

But now there were just the two of them.

I finished my coleslaw and couldn't hold back a yawn. "Fine. I'll ask him after I find Anthony and tell him what Mike told us."

"Go get some sleep. Tell him later."

"But—"

"Go."

"Okay, okay." I brushed his lips with mine and left.

I didn't bother to undress. I just laid down on my bed fully clothed, and was instantly asleep.

After I'd told Anthony what we'd learned from Mike—without giving specifics on *how* we'd found out—he contacted the firm to request satellite photos of the area between Phoenix and Tucson.

And, after Arddhu had given an update to Reshep and Athena, they'd insisted we needed a meeting as soon as possible to begin planning a sortie.

Now, two days later, we held an all-hands meeting in the VIP tent.

I couldn't help but notice that Tyr stayed as far away as possible from Ares, which meant they still hadn't resolved their issues.

Belatucadros, for some reason, was surlier than he'd ever been, and stayed mostly to himself.

In contrast, Begtse and Nayenezgani had become much closer, and now seemed almost inseparable.

Once again, Marisha-Ten was a no-show. I was beginning to wonder if she even existed.

But this time, Kali had come in person.

I'd really expected her to have blue skin, flaming hair, multiple arms, and carry a monster sword, like some depictions I'd seen.

Nothing could've prepared me for the truth.

She wore soft flowing blue robes, had deeply tanned skin that didn't have a single wrinkle or blemish, and sleek black hair that fell like a thick curtain to her knees. Her golden jewel-encrusted crown flashed in the tent's lighting, and it looked heavy. Her smile was genuine and warm as she enveloped me in a loving hug.

I'd expected a terrifying monster, not this sweet, kind, and gentle woman who seemed like a mother or grandmother.

"*Do not let her appearance fool you,*" Arddhu sent to me via communication link. "*She is quite fierce.*"

"*Of that, I have no doubt,*" I sent back.

With everyone settled, Anthony distributed handouts that were still warm from the printer. Due to the short notice, he hadn't briefed me beforehand, so I had no idea what was on the report.

Staring at the photos, I fought a rising sense of panic. In the shocked silence of the room, the others' sharp intakes of breath seemed abnormally loud.

Cromm's original monument in Ireland had consisted of a circle of twelve upright stone slabs with a single gold column in the center. We'd assumed the new monument would be the same specifications.

Unfortunately, one of the satellite photos clearly showed ten standing stones had been completed. Another one showed only three, and was obviously an older photo.

Shit.

How quickly were they building this thing?

"When was this photo taken?" Trying to keep my voice calm, I tapped the one with the ten completed stones.

Anthony calmly met my gaze. "Yesterday."

"And the other? The one with only three stones?"

"Last week."

Everyone spoke at once with some variation of "impossible" or "that can't be right."

Arddhu and I shared a worried glance.

When everyone had quieted down, I cleared my throat. "At this rate, it'll be finished before we can gather our forces and get to the site."

"We'll have to cut some corners," Anthony suggested.

Reshep and Athena spoke quietly for a moment, then he addressed the group. "I believe we can assemble a team within two days."

"It could be finished by then." I rubbed my forehead; a headache had come out of nowhere.

"Or we could be just in time," Athena countered.

I nodded. "That's true." Again, I turned to Anthony. "Do we know how many workers are out there?"

"We counted six one day and ten another day."

I blinked. "That's all?"

On the one hand, how only six to ten workers could get so much done so fast was disturbing and hinted at the use of magick. But on the other hand, it could be relatively easy to take out such a small crew, as opposed to fifty or a hundred workers.

Anthony leaned forward and rested his arms on the table. "We think they have a portal open, and maybe there are hundreds of workers moving through it at times. Just not when the satellite captures the images. And we're pretty sure they're prepared for our forces to show up. There could be thousands on the other side of that portal, ready to come through at a moment's notice and slaughter us."

Damn. That was a good point.

"Which means we'll have to do the same. We muster as many troops as we can," Kevin said, then looked at Arddhu. "Then open a portal to get them there."

Arddhu seemed deep in thought, but he nodded.

"Can't we just drop a small bomb on the area?" I asked. "That would destroy the stones with minimal loss of human life."

Anthony shook his head. "The firm has vast resources, but they're not infinite. And we don't have access to fighter jets with bomb or missile technology. Either of which would raise way too many questions with the local—and federal—authorities. And I'm sure the tribal elders wouldn't appreciate their land becoming a giant worthless crater."

Shit, shit, shit. He was right again.

"Do you think they—the tribal elders, I mean—know what's happening?" I asked. "Do you think they've agreed to this misuse of their land?"

Anthony smiled bitterly. "I'm sure Malsumis was very persuasive."

Ugh. Good point.

"So we go to battle," the Morrigan said. "Who here doesn't want to get our weapons bloody? It's been far too long."

That got everyone excited, and they all started talking at once.

Yes, it'd clearly been far too long since they'd all had a chance to participate in a good old-fashioned bloody battle.

Ugh. Were we *really* going to go all medieval in the desert in this day and age?

Swords, for fuck's sake. Swords and shields instead of tactical weapons.

"I'm pretty sure someone would notice two massive armies going at each other with swords," I pointed out. "What would we tell the cops? 'Cause you just *know* somebody'd call them."

That shut them up for a minute or two.

Until Kevin spoke up. "No. *We* call the cops." When everyone started talking at once again, he held up a hand. "Hold on a sec. What I mean is, we tell them we're having a practice battle re-enactment. Be proactive, maybe even request a permit for it."

There were a few thoughtful expressions around the table, but also a couple of puzzled ones, as everyone digested that idea.

I wasn't about to explain what a battle re-enactment was.

"That's... actually... brilliant," Anthony said, and stared at Kevin with something that looked a lot like awe. "And I think the tribal elders would welcome our efforts to clear their land of both Cromm and Malsumis."

Kevin grinned.

Anthony blinked, then wrote a note on his pad. "I'll take that action item."

One obstacle down, a million to go.

I cleared my throat, cutting through the chatter that had started up again. "But there's another problem: if everyone's busy fighting, who's left to destroy the stones?"

"We three—" Arddhu indicated Kevin, me, and himself "—can accomplish that. We will combine our magick as we did against Malsumis."

I almost made a snarky remark about how ineffective *that'd* been. Instead, I said, "We can use a boulder out on the property for testing. There are a bunch of really huge ones out there, close to the foothills."

Anthony made a note. "Okay, that's an action item for the three of you."

Reshep and Athena said they'd brief the asset destruction teams, and Tyr offered to hunt down some extra weapons. Begtse and Nayenezgani agreed to supply additional warriors, which would definitely come in handy.

Kali tapped her long pointed fingernails on the table. "I will contribute a thousand of my best warriors."

I smiled at her and nodded my thanks.

But Belatucadros sat fuming silently and wouldn't meet anyone's eyes.

Just what the hell was his problem?

Lastly, Anthony added another action item for himself: contacting Victor at the firm to request as many specialized troops as they could spare on such short notice. With a little luck, we'd end up with a few thousand or so to put up against our opponent's unknown numbers.

We adjourned the meeting, but everyone continued sitting and talking quietly among themselves.

Then I overheard Arddhu and Kevin planning a quick look-see to the monument site. Kevin would cast an invisibility spell on both of them, port them to the site for an in-person observation, then port them back.

"Wait a sec," I interrupted them. "If we take that idea a step further, why can't you just do that with a few guys to take out the workers? Easy peasy."

The room immediately fell silent and everyone's eyes were on me.

I had to force myself to sit still and not fidget under their scrutiny.

Kevin smiled kindly. "Even if it were only ten soldiers, I can't port that many people at one time. And even if I could, that'd still leave the monument mostly finished. He'd just send more workers."

Oh. Duh.

I felt like an idiot.

My cheeks heated and I hung my head to avoid the scorn I expected to see in everyone's eyes.

"But don't feel bad," he continued. "It was a good idea. You just didn't know my limitations."

I nodded, not trusting myself to speak.

Arddhu rested his hand on my arm. "*Do not be discouraged*," he sent via communication link. "*You are too hard on yourself. No one here thinks any less of you.*"

I glanced around, and realized he was right. I didn't see anything other than respect in anyone's eyes.

Except for Belatucadros, who still wouldn't look at anyone.

Taking a deep breath, I let my frustration go and held my head high instead.

CHAPTER NINETEEN

T WO DAYS LATER, we were ready. This time, *everyone* was dressed for battle—although in a wild assortment of getups—and I didn't feel quite so conspicuous in my armored suit.

Arddhu and Kevin wore odd, complicated armor constructed of leather and metal. It looked heavy, uncomfortable, and ancient. The armor was covered in scratches, stains, and scuffs that testified to its age and frequent use.

Did they have any idea how hot the Arizona sun could be this time of year? They sure as hell were about to find out. Although it was mid-November and cold and snowy in some parts of the country, here we had gorgeous blue sky without a single cloud in sight, and high temperatures in the upper seventies.

Under the relentless sun, they'd roast in all that leather.

Unlike me. As I'd discovered throughout the summer, my armored suit was quite comfortable in heat.

Arddhu didn't seem to have any weapons on him—maybe he planned to rely solely on his magick—but Kevin had his sword in a baldric. I, on the other hand, was fully armed once again: Ire was in her baldric, my pistol was holstered on my left, and my knife was sheathed on my right. Extra magazines for the pistol were in a small canvas bag attached to the belt at my waist, but I really didn't expect to need them. I expected to use my magick and sword. The pistol was a last resort.

In the past two days, the experiments of using our magick to destroy boulders had been flawless; the combined power of the three of us had completely disintegrated the massive rocks and reduced them into fine powder that floated in the air before drifting away to join the desert soil.

Those successful tests made us confident we'd be able to destroy the monument stones while Cromm's workers and allies were preoccupied with fighting for their lives.

Even so, it all made me even more curious why we hadn't been able to injure Malsumis. He must've had a helluva shield in place.

And once we were on the battlefield, the risk of injury or death was real. Despite Kevin's invisibility spell on the three of us, we'd be in the middle of the action. A stray bullet, sword thrust, or firebolt could still damage any of us.

Not to mention I could be killed fairly easily.

Earlier, Anu had hailed me with good news. "*Deirdre, I have placed a shield upon your person. It will protect you against most small human projectiles.*"

Small human projectiles ... oh. Bullets. She meant bullets

"*Thank you, Anu. That was very thoughtful.*"

"*Go forth a conqueror and win a great victory.*"

From the memories of prior Keepers, I knew she'd just quoted the ancient poet Virgil.

"*With your help, I'm sure I will.*"

Arddhu had insisted I continue wearing the ring he'd enchanted for me before the first alliance meeting. It protected me against spells or mind-magick, but even with Anu's shield, the ring, and my armored suit, I'd still be vulnerable to a certain level of firepower. After all, I wouldn't survive a direct hit of a mortar round, if those were used. And I certainly wouldn't survive a beheading. I'd just have to do my best to stay out of the line of fire as much as possible.

Despite the intelligence gathered by the firm, there was still so much we didn't know, such as how many fighters Cromm had assembled or what kind of weaponry they had. Going blind into battle was never a good idea, but we didn't have much choice.

And then there was the alarming news that Arddhu's and Kevin's look-see had given us: eleven completed stones now stood at the site.

Apparently, the workers had split up into two teams to simultaneously work on the single remaining stone and the gold column.

It was almost as if Cromm knew what we planned to do, and it made me wonder if we had a spy among us. He couldn't just be that damn good at guessing.

It'd be a photo finish if we got there before the entire monument was completed.

To make things worse, this portal would be the most complex Arddhu had ever created: it had to combine six different origin points into a single destination point. Our troops waited at four portal sites worldwide, and the asset destruction team was gathered at another site. The sixth location was here in Scottsdale, with the three of us.

The plan was relatively simple. Arddhu would open the destination portal just outside the monument site and we'd all arrive at more or less the same time. With a little luck, we wouldn't trample each other.

He and Kevin had worked out how to manage all that. I'd stayed out of it, for the most part. At first I'd tried to follow their discussion, but honestly, the terminology had bored me. Same old shit about realms, pocket universes, dimensions, space and time, and other stuff that made my brain ache.

Sometimes, like this, I wished I was still just an accountant. Things had been so much easier back then.

This battle, though... I'd be lying if I said I wasn't apprehensive. So much could go wrong.

After all, this wasn't like the missions, where I'd had a backup team and felt somewhat protected. No, this was much more dangerous.

We were heading into a *battlefield*. With an unknown number of enemy combatants. And unknown weaponry.

What if Kevin and Arddhu were killed? Would the portal collapse, stranding me there with the battle raging around me?

What if *I* were killed? What would happen to Anu? Would Cromm command the Sphere after all?

"It's go time," Anthony said, interrupting my thoughts, and my heart leapt into my throat. He was staying behind to monitor the situation remotely and contact the firm for reinforcements, if necessary. At least until he got the all-clear from Reshep or Athena.

After checking my weapons one last time, I gripped my prosthesis firmly so no one would see my hand shaking from nerves.

Kevin cast the invisibility spell on us, and a serious flaw in the plan became immediately obvious to me: I couldn't see either of them.

Goddammit.

But wait—there. Two vaguely shimmery forms moved just ahead of me.

"This flicker is all you'll see of us," Kevin explained, his disembodied voice seeming strangely hollow to my ears. "No one else will even see that."

Just how the hell did he always seem to know what I was thinking?

Arddhu went through the portal first, then me, then Kevin.

We quickly stepped aside so we weren't in the way of our troops, who'd be coming through any minute, and I took in the scene.

Cromm's workers stepped away from the completed gold column and seemed to look straight at me with almost comical expressions of surprise.

Fuck.

We were too late.

Then all hell broke loose.

As our troops streamed from the portal, a much greater number of fighters swarmed from another portal on the far side of the monument. The two groups immediately rushed toward each other and clashed in a cacophony of gunfire, screams, firebolts, and metal on metal.

In the distance, Kali roared and transformed into her battle aspect, and I stared in disbelief.

Impossibly tall, with indigo skin and ten slashing arms her voice rose in a vicious ululating war cry that made the hair on the back of my neck stand up and goosebumps rise on my skin. She tore into Cromm's army as if it were just toy soldiers, and body parts flew as her deadly swords flashed in the bright sun. All the while, her tongue poked grotesquely from her red grinning mouth.

I shuddered. She was, indeed, fearsome and formidable.

A hundred yards away, the Morrigan's own battle cry pierced the commotion as she engaged her opponents, again making goosebumps break out on my skin. She was relentless and efficient, whirling and stabbing and chopping and slicing. Blood spewed, and it only took a moment until she was covered.

And from the grin on her face, she reveled in it.

Not far from her, Ares charged his chariot into the thick of Cromm's fighters. The four massive horses mowed many of them down while Ares used his famous battle spear to skewer more fighters with alarming speed—and accuracy. He was deadly with that thing, even in such close quarters. I hissed when it looked like he'd take out one of our own guys, but no, he'd taken out an enemy combatant less than a foot away.

I admit it: I was impressed.

The whine of stray bullets came way too close for comfort, and I instinctively ducked for cover. That's when I saw something from a nightmare.

Or at least a scary movie.

A hideous beast with bright red skin, three eyes, a headdress of skulls, and long, nasty-looking fangs dripping with spit—or venom, I couldn't tell which—snarled as it slaughtered Cromm's fighters with a massive sword.

"Who's that—that *monster*?"

"That is Begtse in his warrior form," Arddhu calmly replied.

Holy fucking shit.

If I never saw him like this again, it'd be too soon.

A dozen or so yards to the right, I got a glimpse of Nayenezgani—mostly naked, with white zigzags painted on his face and body—before he became a flash of lightning, leaving charred and blackened bodies in his wake.

He was formidable and frightening, yet somehow graceful and beautiful at the same time.

Navajo Slayer of Alien Gods, indeed.

Then my attention was quickly captured by a slim, elegant warrior dressed all in black, nimbly balanced on the back of an enormous snarling boar, whirling and slicing through opponents with eight swords gleaming in a deadly and efficient dance.

Eight. Fucking. Swords.

Before I could ask, Arddhu said, "And that is Marisha-Ten."

Ah, the elusive Japanese Goddess of War and Victory, who'd never bothered to show up for any of our alliance meetings.

Instantly, I forgave her that slight because she was simply *awesome* to behold.

Glancing around, I didn't see the others, though; where were Reshep and Athena? Belatucadros and Tyr? The battlefield was crowded and chaotic, sure, but shouldn't I have seen them by now?

Then my breath caught and my heart skipped a beat.

Tall and nasty and clearly visible among the chaos strode Cromm, in the same leather armor he'd worn the first time I'd seen him.

Arrogant as ever and seemingly invincible, with one side of his mouth quirked in his typical sneer, he moved through the battlefield as if it were just a harmless training exercise.

Straight toward me.

I almost lost my balance as I was roughly tugged back toward the portal.

"What are you doing?" I protested, resisting. "We have to stick to the plan."

"No," Arddhu snarled. "We must get you out of here."

"We have a job to do." I continued to fight until Kevin grabbed my other arm to help Arddhu physically remove me from the battlefield.

I couldn't fight them both, but maybe I could convince them. I just needed a minute.

Maybe less.

I sure as hell wouldn't have much more than that.

"*No.*" I dug my heels into the soft ground. "We *have* to destroy the stones. We may never get another chance. It's the only way to stop him now."

"Shit," Kevin said. "She's right." He released me, but Arddhu doggedly held on.

"I know she is," Arddhu growled. "But if he captures her again..."

He didn't have to finish. We all knew what would happen then.

The thought of Cromm slicing my skin and licking my blood made my stomach roll, but I straightened my back and stood my ground. I couldn't let him have control of Anu and the power of the Sphere.

"He won't." I'd said it with way more confidence than I felt. "Let's just do this and get the hell out of here."

Arddhu finally agreed and released me.

Without delay, we headed to the nearest stone, dodging firebolts, stray bullets, and lots of pointy weapons on the way.

After we arrived, Kevin said, "On three," and counted it down.

Each of us blasted a powerful stream of destructive energy, focused on the center of the tall column.

At first it glowed red-hot, then it pulsed white just before it exploded and sprayed everyone within a five-foot radius with lethal needles of sharp stone fragments. I ducked and covered my face, but I still felt the shards. They hit Anu's shield and pinged off my armored suit, but the fighters around us screamed in agony. I hoped we hadn't accidentally taken out any of our own guys.

It was called *friendly fire*, but there was nothing friendly about any of this.

This was madness.

When we'd tested our magick on the boulders, they hadn't exploded into shards like this; something must be different about these stone columns. But there was nothing we could do at this point except proceed with the plan.

A piercing cry on my left made my ears ring, and someone jerked me away just as a gigantic sword hacked where I'd been standing only seconds earlier. Furious, I whirled and prepared to blast my attacker.

The wielder of the sword stood only an arm's length away, helmet askew, Roman-era armor covered in blood and disgusting bits, and grinning manically as he looked at me.

Despite his filth-splattered face, I immediately recognized him.

Belatucadros.

But I'd been mistaken. He wasn't looking at me, and he hadn't tried to kill me; somehow, he'd actually defended me against an enemy attack.

The fallen fighter lay on the ground at my feet, body cleaved almost in two. As I stared, the pieces twitched, spilling more blood and guts onto the already-soaked ground, and I quickly looked away.

Belatucadros was already off, hacking his way through more members of Cromm's army with another of those bizarre battle cries.

"We must get to the next stone," Arddhu urgently said.

Ducking and weaving around combatants, slipping on disgusting stuff covering the bloody earth, we headed toward the next stone. I was only a few feet away when a hacked-up body fell in front of me and I almost tripped over it. Somehow keeping my balance, I stumbled around it and rejoined Arddhu and Kevin.

I knew it wouldn't be long before Cromm found us, regardless of Kevin's invisibility spell. So we didn't hesitate. We quickly destroyed the second stone, and again caused damage to the nearby fighters.

Then I glanced over my shoulder and gasped.

Only two hundred yards or so away, Malsumis stood calmly impervious to the battle raging around him, studying the battlefield. Surprisingly, he wore no armor, just his familiar black designer suit.

Maybe that *was* his armor? No weapons even came anywhere close to him, as if he had some kind of force field in place. As I watched him, he turned his head and seemed to stare right at me with those strange red eyes.

No. Impossible. There's no way he could see me. I'd be in deep shit if he could.

A wide grin spread over his face, and I remembered his words the last time I'd seen him: that Cromm missed his plaything and would let him play, too.

Fuck no. Over my dead body.

But that made me wonder... where was Cromm? After seeing him earlier, he'd disappeared from the battlefield. He should be somewhere nearby, but I didn't see him. And that worried me. Because even though I sure as hell didn't want to see his face, at least I'd know where he was.

He could be anywhere right now. Maybe even at the next stone, waiting for us.

As Arddhu tugged me toward the next monolith, I returned my gaze to Malsumis. That was when I saw him look ahead of us to the stone, then start heading there himself.

"Wait," I said. "Malsumis is expecting us at that one."

"Shit," Kevin said.

So we backtracked to one of the other stones, as far away from Malsumis as we could get.

But just as we got there, Cromm came around from the back side of it. Almost as if he'd been lurking there, waiting for us.

Goddammit.

We froze in our tracks, hoping he couldn't track movement despite our invisibility.

Only a dozen feet or so separated us. I held my breath as I watched Cromm glance around expectantly, eyes narrowed as if looking for us.

But his gaze skipped past me, and I breathed again. Softly, just in case he could hear it over the battlefield din.

Huh. Maybe it'd just been luck earlier, when it'd seemed he could see us and headed in our direction. Or maybe he only could track us when we were moving.

Even so, we couldn't destroy the stone with him there. We'd never even finish the job before he'd be on us.

In unspoken agreement, we stayed still—although it was becoming increasingly difficult, since a group of fighters were getting closer to us by the second. In a matter of moments, we'd be forced to either move or defend ourselves.

Movement on my right: only a few feet away, Malsumis passed me and stood beside Cromm.

Sweat broke out on my skin, and the urge to draw my sword was almost unbearable.

Malsumis lifted his head slightly and his nostrils flared, as if scenting prey, and my heart almost stopped.

Fuck.

If he could smell us, even above all the nastiness of battlefield odors surrounding us, it was all over.

Someone grabbed my arm, and in that instant Cromm and Malsumis locked on to us. Then vertigo and fog obscured my vision, and it was a moment before I realized Kevin had ported us away.

Ported us.

Shit.

Goddamn fucking shit.

Why the hell hadn't we been teleporting to the stones instead of running around the battlefield like idiots, wasting valuable time and risking injury or death?

Bloody fucking hell. None of us had thought of it. Not during the alliance meeting, and not at any of the planning sessions.

Not until now.

When my vision cleared, we'd arrived at another stone. I looked around wildly, but didn't see either Cromm or Malsumis.

It'd just be a matter of time, though.

"Quickly now, we must destroy the stone," Arddhu said

The shards and dust hadn't even settled yet when Malsumis appeared, right in front of us.

He'd somehow tracked us and teleported to our location, but at least we'd had enough time to destroy the stone first.

And then, just as Kevin prepared to port us away again, Malsumis's hand shot out and seized my ponytail in a vice-like grip. He yanked me closer, pulling on my hair painfully, and I bit my lip to keep from crying out.

"Gotcha," he crowed.

I desperately looked for the slight shimmery forms of Arddhu and Kevin, but I didn't see them, and my heart sank. Somehow Malsumis had stopped me from porting with them, and who knew where they were now. Probably far away.

"Now, let's get a good look at you," Malsumis said. As he snapped his fingers, I became visible.

Shit.

Laughing, he lifted me off the ground with his iron grip on my hair, and shook me like a rag doll. The pain brought tears to my eyes.

"Oh, what fun," he taunted. "I snagged the Keeper. Lucky me."

I tried to lift my arms, but they were frozen at my sides, and that could only mean he'd cast an immobility spell. But why hadn't Arddhu's ring protected me? Or was Malsumis more powerful than Arddhu's magick?

Maybe there was another option.

"*Anu, can you break his spell?*" I begged.

Malsumis pulled me hard against him, finally letting go of my hair and choosing instead to hold my body in one strong arm. "Let's go somewhere quiet. Just the two of us. Hmm?"

"No," I snarled, and shook my head. Interesting; he'd left my head free. I became feral and tried to bite his throat. Or anything within reach, really.

"Anu?"

"Patience, Deirdre. I am working on it."

He just laughed again. "Oh, he told me you were fun. He wasn't lying."

Then, Anu's blessed voice. *"The spell has been lifted. You are free."*

Since I was too close to use a firebolt effectively, I grabbed his throat with my prosthesis and squeezed with every bit of its superhuman strength.

His eyes widened in surprise, but he recovered quickly. He grabbed my arm and pulled it away as if I were weak and helpless.

How the hell could he be that strong?

"Come now, don't be like that," he chided, and we were gone.

Vertigo blurred my vision, but only for a few seconds. It seemed he'd ported us only a short distance away. But before I could catch my breath, another bout of vertigo hit as he ported us again.

Hmm. So he could only port both of us a little bit at a time? That was good to know.

Twice more he did this, and then I turned my head and saw where we were headed: the portal on the far side of the battlefield.

Cromm's portal.

"No," I said again, and began to struggle harder. I didn't make much headway, though; with one arm around my waist and his free hand holding my prosthesis tightly, there wasn't much I could do. Once, I tried kicking him, but missed completely. I ended up losing my balance and falling hard against him.

He chuckled and rubbed himself against me. "Mmm. I like that."

Ugh.

And then I caught a break; I'd twisted my torso just enough that he lost his grip on my waist. As his hand slipped on my smooth armored suit, the other loosened on my right arm. Taking advantage of the opportunity, I boosted my strength and shoved him away from me.

He stumbled, but didn't fall. His eyes widened again in surprise, then narrowed as his mouth formed a cruel smile. "Go ahead and run, Keeper. You won't get far. And you'll just make the hunt that much sweeter."

I raised my left hand and began blasting him with firebolts.

"*Deirdre, where are you?*" Arddhu's concerned voice was loud in my head, and startled me enough to break my concentration. The firebolt sputtered out, but it didn't matter. Just like the last time, when we'd all tried it, Malsumis was completely unhurt.

He laughed and took a step toward me. I turned and ran, back toward our portal.

"*Near their portal,*" I sent back to Arddhu. "*Malsumis tried to take me through. I'm headed back toward you now.*"

Evading skirmishes while trying to put some decent distance away from Malsumis was a challenge. Too many blades and bullets came way too close to me.

And then Malsumis appeared, blocking my way.

Goddamn teleporting. Why hadn't *I* been doing it? I would've been back with the guys by now.

He reached for me again, but I quickly ported away, back to our side.

Using a standing stone for cover, I searched the battlefield for two shimmery forms, but it was no use. Only then did I realize how impossible—and stupid—it was to look for two invisible immortals among the chaos of two armies fighting.

"*I can't see you guys. Where are you?*" I asked Arddhu.

Just then, another standing stone exploded off to my right, and I figured it had to be them. Who else would be destroying the stones?

Now there were only five left.

"*We will find you. Remain where you are,*" Arddhu replied.

One of Cromm's fighters came at me with a wild swing of his metal-gloved fist. Instinctively, I ducked and blasted him with a firebolt, and got covered in blood and disgusting bits as a reward.

Shit. I'd forgotten I wasn't invisible anymore. No, now I was quite the visible target.

And of course it got worse. Cromm headed straight toward me with his mouth stretched wide in the grin from my nightmares.

I shuddered and glanced around wildly, but saw no friendlies I could call on for help.

But why didn't he just port to me? He could've been here with little to no notice. He probably knew he could instill more fear in me this way, making me watch him close the distance between us across the battlefield.

"*Hurry, please,*" I sent to Arddhu. "*Cromm is headed my way.*"

Taking a deep breath, I prepared for a fight, although I wasn't sure how much chance of success I had.

Drawing my sword, I gripped it in my prosthesis to keep my left hand free for battle magick.

And then from behind, two strong arms wrapped around my torso like iron bands, and crushed me against a rock-hard body. Both of my arms were pinned at my sides, and a quick downward glance told me it wasn't an ally; the sleeves belonged to an expensive black suit jacket.

Goddammit.

Malsumis.

"Hello again, Keeper." His voice was low in my ear and gave me chills. "That was fun. I do enjoy a good hunt."

Yes, I could tell just how much he enjoyed it, based on the long, hard length pressing against my backside. It made me want to vomit.

He chuckled and tightened his arms around me even more, constricting my chest painfully and forcing me to gasp for breath.

Fuck, Malsumis was strong. My arms tingled from the restricted blood flow.

Of course, then Cromm arrived, dramatically twirling a lethal black staff.

He held my gaze with his, and the triumph I saw there was infuriating.

"Well met, Keeper," Cromm said. His gaze flicked to my prosthesis before returning to my eyes. "I see you have a new toy since last we met."

His voice made my skin crawl. To my dismay, I started shaking and couldn't stop.

His grin widened, as if he knew what he did to me. Knew how I feared him.

No. I wouldn't give him that satisfaction.

My chin rose with determination. "Fuck you, asshole." If my mouth hadn't been so dry, I would've spit at him for good measure.

He laughed, and for once, the flashbacks didn't threaten me. The real threat was right here and now.

"She's shaking like a leaf, you know," Malsumis said conversationally, and rubbed against me again.

This time, I can play too, he'd said.

No. No fucking way.

My mind frantically considered ways to get out of this mess, but then Cromm stepped closer and I stopped being able to think at all.

"Good," he said. "That means she remembers how much fun we had together."

Oh gods. My stomach rolled, and I sort of hoped I'd puke on Cromm's dusty black boots.

But then, from the corner of my eye, I noticed a shimmery blob approaching us. It could only mean one thing: Arddhu and Kevin had arrived. It took almost all my willpower to maintain eye contact with Cromm and not give away their presence.

But he turned so fast he was just a blur as he whirled his staff, striking his target with a dull and brutal thud.

Instantly, Kevin became visible and fell to the ground, where he lay unmoving. Blood gushed from the nasty-looking gash near his temple, which meant his head had taken a direct hit. My heart sank.

Unfortunately, he'd been maintaining the invisibility spell. And now, with Kevin out of commission, Arddhu also became visible. He was only a couple of feet away from Cromm and had just drawn his sword to attack when Cromm must've sensed him. He spun toward Arddhu and cruelly shoved the sharpened tip of his staff into his chest. Blood spurted from the gaping hole in the worn leather armor and Arddhu flailed on the end of the staff like a speared salmon. Cromm continued to press the lethal tip further into the wound, and Arddhu's face contorted in a rictus of pain. He didn't seem able to fight back in any way; maybe Cromm's staff was poisoned or enchanted?

My anger spiked, but it wasn't Cromm I was pissed at. Irrationally, I was furious at Arddhu. Just what the hell had made him think leather would be adequate protection against swords, spears, and bullets, let alone magick? If we all made it through this alive, I was going to strangle him.

Behind Cromm, a small group of our elite soldiers slowly advanced with their weapons drawn and ready. "Release them and step away," one commanded.

"You can't possibly be serious." Cromm rolled his eyes and turned his head slightly to speak over his shoulder. "You are in no position to make demands. I hold the advantage here." As if to prove it, he thrust his weapon further into Arddhu's chest.

Arddhu's eyes closed as he moaned pitifully. His face was now a sickly gray, and his hand relaxed, making his sword fall into the muck at his feet.

Not to be outdone, Malsumis dipped his head to my neck and nuzzled behind my ear—then savagely bit into my flesh.

I gasped and convulsed at the sudden burst of pain, and Malsumis chuckled. As he licked and sucked at the wound, he made disgusting smacking noises and rubbed himself against me.

Gross.

So he was another blood-loving asshole. I clenched my jaw and tried to stay calm. I wouldn't give him the fear and revulsion he wanted.

But the message was loud and clear: no one could make a move on Cromm without risking injury—or even death—to Arddhu and me.

The soldiers glanced at each other, and it was obvious they weren't sure how to proceed. Disappointment flooded me as I realized I wouldn't get any help from them. And I wasn't impressed: this wasn't exactly the response I'd expected from elite soldiers.

By now I couldn't feel the fingers of my left hand because it'd gone completely numb. Malsumis's hold on me was way too tight, and if he didn't let up soon I wouldn't be able to do much of anything with that arm until the circulation returned.

Maybe if I stomped on his foot with my boot heel...

Then, unexpectedly, I got a lucky break. The second of the day so far.

Apparently bored with my lack of response, Malsumis decided to take out the soldiers himself.

Keeping his left arm wrapped tight around me, he used his right to shoot fireballs at the group. They screamed as they went down and desperately rolled on the ground to put out the flames, but that method didn't work on this type of fire. As they slowly burned to death, I took advantage of the chaotic distraction.

I dropped my sword, curled my prosthesis into a tight fist, boosted my strength magickally, and punched Malsumis over my shoulder.

The side of my face and neck was instantly sprayed with warm sticky wetness, and he gasped. I'd taken a wild guess, but I must've hit his nose. Maybe even broken it.

Apparently, his shield didn't protect against that kind of attack.

Now I needed to finish this before he recovered and retaliated.

I broke free and pivoted, wincing from the pins and needles in my left arm and hand as circulation returned. But Malsumis wasn't even paying attention to me; his bloody hands covered his face, and his eyes were wide and unfocused.

Must've been the first time he'd ever been punched in the nose. And it'd also be the last.

I ported my sword to my prosthesis, boosted my strength again, and made my well-practiced sword strike. The momentum carried me around to face Cromm at the same time as I heard two dull thuds behind me, only seconds apart.

Malsumis' severed head and body, hitting the ground.

One down, one to go.

CHAPTER TWENTY

I STOOD FACING Cromm with my bloody sword raised between us, but he didn't even flinch.

Never taking his gaze from mine, he grinned obscenely then deliberately pushed his weapon even deeper into Arddhu's chest. Arddhu slumped forward and his head lolled as if he'd lost consciousness.

Cromm and I stood only a few feet apart in an awkward tableau, and it was one I hadn't expected. Or prepared for.

If I made a move on him, he'd kill Arddhu. Kevin still lay unmoving, so I could only assume he was already dead.

All around us, the fighting continued, and it sure seemed like our guys were getting their asses kicked. I couldn't see any of the allies in a quick glance around, but I didn't dare take my eyes off Cromm any longer than that for a more thorough search.

This was up to me.

Swallowing my fear, I raised my sword and pressed the sharp tip against the patch of soft white flesh just above Cromm's armor.

"Let him go." Unbelievably, my voice—and my sword—was mostly steady. Thank the gods I'd stopped shaking.

He laughed. "You truly believe you can harm me with that puny thing?"

"I *know* I can." Now, I sounded confident and strong.

"So what's stopping you?" His eyes remained locked on mine and his lips stretched in a wide grin as he drove his staff all the way through Arddhu's chest, until the end protruded several inches from Arddhu's back.

Arddhu's agonized groan almost made me drop my sword in the hope Cromm would let him go if I gave up.

But I doubted it.

No, Cromm would simply finish off Arddhu before he took me through his portal. And I couldn't let any of that happen.

Oh Arddhu, I prayed silently. *Please don't die before I can save you.*

Since Cromm had clearly dared me to retaliate, I stepped forward and pushed my sword tip farther into his soft throat, to a depth of about two inches. Blood flowed from the wound. "I said, *let him go.*"

"You surprise me, Keeper." His voice sounded normal; maybe I hadn't hit his larynx. But I thought something flickered in his eyes. Wariness, maybe, with a tinge of respect. Or maybe it was just disbelief that I'd actually done it, stood up to him. "You've changed since we last met."

"You have no idea," I replied. Then, movement at ground level distracted me.

Kevin.

Thank the gods he wasn't dead.

After a moment, he disappeared, and Cromm's eyes shifted to focus on something—or *someone*—behind me.

A cold blade pressed into my neck. The sharp edge bit my skin, letting me know it'd drawn blood.

Goddammit.

Was it Kevin? Had he betrayed me?

No. I refused to believe he'd take Cromm's side against me, after all we'd said and done.

"Checkmate, Keeper." Cromm was too fucking smug, and I clenched my jaw in frustration.

"Not quite." Kevin's voice came from somewhere behind me, and Cromm's grin slipped a bit.

I knew it. He *hadn't* betrayed me, after all.

But if it wasn't Kevin holding the knife at my throat, who was it?

I'd find out soon enough. My left arm had fully recovered, but it was getting tired from holding my sword at such an odd angle. I needed to wrap this up. "I'll tell you one last time: let him go."

Surprisingly, Cromm's eyes narrowed and his grin completely disappeared. For just one tense moment, I thought he'd make me do it: lunge forward to kill him and slit my own throat in the process.

Instead, he slowly pulled his weapon from Arddhu's chest, and it made a horrible sucking sound. Arddhu tumbled to the ground and didn't move.

A tiny thrill of triumph ran through me. Cromm had probably expected me to back down. Give up.

He'll never know that the thought had crossed my mind.

"Now drop your weapon and tell your friend here to step away."

His mouth lifted in a sneer, but he let the staff fall from his fingers and waved off his accomplice. After a slight hesitation, the knife was gone from my throat.

Slowly, carefully, I shifted position to keep Cromm in view while at the same time seeing just who the hell his crony was.

And then I faltered, staring dumfounded.

Why was Mike standing there with a dagger in his hand?

His gaze steadily met mine, but there was absolutely no expression on his face. Behind him, Kevin held his own blade at Mike's throat, where blood welled from a small cut. Kevin seemed more than eager to finish Mike off.

But I had questions.

"Such a pleasant little reunion." Cromm's voice was smooth satin despite the biting sarcasm of his words and my sword tip buried in his throat.

Fuck, I really hated this asshole.

Dealing with Mike would have to wait. Cromm had to come first.

"Kevin, please make sure Mike doesn't move."

I hoped he knew I wanted him to use an immobilization spell.

"Done."

In my peripheral vision, Arddhu stirred soundlessly. Not taking my eyes off Cromm, I sent via communication link, "*Are you okay?*"

"*Yes. I have begun to heal and will be able to assist in several moments.*"

We didn't have several moments. Cromm would make his move any second now. In fact, I couldn't believe my luck had held this long, unless he was just playing along or stalling for some more time.

"What's the best way to get rid of Cromm for good?"

"Take his head. Destroy his remains."

Then, everything happened so fast.

Cromm took a step backward to free himself from my sword, and the wound immediately healed. His staff was once again in his hand, although I hadn't seen him bend to pick it up. I was forced to step back, too, to remove myself from its reach.

I'd seen just how much of a menace he was with that thing.

"Still think you're not in checkmate, Keeper?" he smirked.

He obviously thought he had the advantage. Or maybe he knew something I didn't. But I drew as much energy from Earth as I could, boosted my strength magickally, and drew even more. I prayed it'd be enough.

At first, we circled each other warily, he with his lethal staff poised to strike, and me with my trusted sword in a firm two-handed grip. I wouldn't bother to aim any strikes at his body; it was covered in leather armor and I'd have to work too hard to penetrate it. Instead, I'd go for his unprotected throat.

Or maybe, if the opportunity presented itself, I'd cut off one of his hands. That'd be poetic justice.

But I'd try to save my battle magick as a nasty little surprise.

Cromm feinted, and I almost fell for it. Only a second late, I stabbed at his neck but hit air. I swerved to avoid the expected blow from his staff, but there hadn't been one.

He stood smirking. "Ah, I've missed your liveliness, Keeper. Your *passion*. It's intoxicating."

Asshole. He was playing with me.

Part of me wanted to scream and charge at him, but I resisted. That was probably just what he wanted. Instead, I growled, "Fuck you."

He grinned. "I think... I would like that. Very much."

My stomach rolled. "Over my dead body."

His grin widened. "That wouldn't stop me."

Ugh.

I shot a quick firebolt at his head, but as I expected, it disintegrated on contact with his shields.

Too bad. I'd really wanted to see his head explode.

Now he laughed.

If I couldn't get past his shields, how the hell could I take him out? I thought quickly; maybe his shields only protected against magick. Maybe mundane weapons would still work. After all, I'd been able to get my sword tip into his throat.

Which meant I'd have to get inside the reach of that damn staff.

Unless... there was one other mundane weapon I could try.

I drew my pistol and thumbed off the safety, and he laughed again as he realized what I meant to do.

Even though I rapidly fired off three shots to his face, they never touched him. Each bullet had curved wildly around his body and left him completely unscathed.

He was still laughing as he moved so quickly, he was again just a blur. My legs went out from underneath me, and my ass hit the dirt. *Hard.*

My calves ached from the blow, and I wasn't sure I'd be able to stand. Then Cromm stepped closer and loomed over me, and I fought a surge of panic.

No. It couldn't end this way.

I stared in disbelief at the hand he offered.

"Allow me to help you rise."

Oh, hell no. He'd probably port me away as soon as I took it.

"I assure you, Keeper. No tricks. I'm having too much fun for this to end just yet."

"No thanks." I sent healing to my legs and quickly got to my feet, sword raised and ready once again.

He just grinned. "That's the spirit. Such a fighter."

This time, I somehow sensed his attack seconds before he made it, and was able to block it with my blade. The impact, though, sent painful vibrations through my arms to my shoulders.

Fuck, he was strong.

Slowly, never taking his eyes from mine, he pressed his staff forward against my blade. I was forced to maintain my boosted strength to keep my distance, and I could almost feel the drain on my energy reserves.

Goddammit. What chance did I possibly have against someone so much stronger than me?

Stop it. I couldn't let my own head help him beat me. I could do this.

Even so, he was still just toying with me. Wearing me down. The only way I could win would be to go on the offensive.

Alright then. Time for something I'd pulled from the memories of Siobhan, the warrior Keeper from another age. But to do it, I'd need to use Anu's energy management system like I've never had to before.

Flooding my arms with boosted strength, I shoved him away from me. While he stumbled two steps backward, I drew energy from Earth and topped off my tank, so-to-speak. Then I spoke to Anu.

"Anu, I'll need to use a lot of energy, and I'll need it indefinitely."

"I will maintain your reserves. Do not be concerned."

"Thank you."

Unsheathing my knife, I gripped it firmly in my left hand and continued to use my prosthesis for my short sword. Then I advanced on him, whirling and slashing and stabbing, relentlessly driving him back and keeping too short a distance for him to use his staff effectively. As I expected, he blocked most of my strikes, and others fell ineffectually on his armor.

But some hit home and opened wounds on his hands, face, and throat. Yes, they healed almost immediately, but I planned to maintain this flurry of attacks as long as it took.

I was betting that sooner or later, unlike me, he'd need to rest and heal.

As he backed into the battle raging around us, we were both at risk for secondary injuries. Again, I was gambling; since he was a much bigger target, he should get most of the injuries. Steadily, I pressed on, hacking and slashing.

I knew the moment our battle had turned in my favor: Cromm's eyes lost their smugness and his wounds weren't healing as quickly. Blood began to trickle, then stream from his open cuts. His movements began to slow, and more of my attacks struck home. My knife opened a deep slash on his throat, and suddenly his staff was gone. He'd lost his grip on it.

I continued to press my advantage, as relentless as a machine.

At one point, his right hand got in the way of my knife and I sliced it off at the wrist. His howl of pain flooded me with a warm glow of perverse satisfaction.

A moment later, he tripped and landed on his back. Without hesitation, I shoved my sword tip into his neck with everything I had.

His eyes bulged in disbelief and horror as the sharp blade slid deep, moving smoothly and easily until it met the resistance of his spine. He choked and emitted a strangled gurgle. Blood gushed from the ugly wound.

Another push and the blade severed vertebrae messily, leaving his head to fall to one side. At this point it was only attached to his body by tendons.

I kept my eyes focused intently on his. He stared but didn't see me. There was no recognition there. His remaining hand twitched violently but it was no longer under his control. The movement was all autonomic.

It was finally, blessedly, over.

But I had to move quickly now to finish, before his body could automatically heal itself. His head had to be completely separated so he couldn't be resurrected.

Bending over his body, I hacked at the tendons and didn't care about the blood and nasty bits spraying everywhere.

Finally, the deed was done, although I'd truly made a gruesome mess of it.

It was even worse than my first mission had been.

But it was done.

Cromm's head was successfully separated from his body.

I straightened and blasted destructive energy at his remains. Unfortunately, they didn't burn up neatly, as I'd expected.

Instead, they exploded, sending more blood and bits of disgusting brain, bone, and tissue in all directions. My armor, especially, was coated.

For just a moment, I closed my eyes and savored the knowledge that I'd never have to fear Cromm again.

Then I remembered: Malsumis.

I had to destroy him, too.

Turning, I headed back toward his remains. More than once I defended myself against Cromm's minions who'd stumbled into my path. My firebolts turned them into gory rain.

Finally, I arrived at my destination.

Kevin was battling one of Cromm's soldiers, successfully keeping him from Arddhu, who was still down in the muck. At least he was sitting up instead of crumpled on his side, as I'd last seen him.

I took a moment to study Kevin, evaluating whether I needed to help or not.

He was glorious in battle, slicing and dodging and lunging with the same gracefulness I'd seen in practice sessions. Then he blasted the enemy with a fireball, and it was over.

Turning away, I destroyed Malsumis's remains and made another gory mess.

Now I was just as disgustingly filthy as the battlefield itself.

But surprisingly, I hadn't vomited, despite being surrounded—and covered—by the nastiest shit I'd ever seen.

Instead of feeling victorious, I was uneasy.

A nagging suspicion had been building for a while now. As if I'd missed something. Something important.

Part of it was: it shouldn't have been that easy to take out Cromm and Malsumis. Especially without any help from Arddhu or Kevin. Which didn't make sense at all, since the three of us hadn't even made a mark on Malsumis the last time we'd seen him.

But I'd have to figure that out later. My job wasn't done yet.

While Anu replenished my energy and I mentally prepared myself for what I'd have to do next, I took in the battle around me.

Cromm's army was shattered.

Some of his fighters—the ones in the immediate vicinity—had seen what'd happened and now stood motionless with their weapons down, staring in shock at me. I could only assume they were trying to cope with the brutal loss of their leader.

But our troops showed no mercy, and cut them down where they stood.

Everywhere I looked, I saw death.

Many of Cromm's fighters were still alive but badly wounded, moaning and crying out. And now I saw Reshep and Athena: they, with some of our soldiers, roamed the battlefield and finished off the enemy, whether armed or not.

High above the mess, the vultures soared like solo dancers in an azure ballroom, waiting to feast.

The smell of it all was horrible, the stuff of nightmares.

Blood. Guts. Piss. Shit. And under it all, something I couldn't quite identify. Something acidic that seared my nostrils and throat and made me want something strong like whiskey to burn it all away and leave me clean and raw.

That would have to wait.

And now I was ready to deal with Mike, the fucking traitor.

While I'd been assessing the battlefield, Arddhu had gotten to his feet. He still looked weak and in pain, but at least he was alive. We shared a glance and a nod, then Kevin joined us.

We stood together as I turned to face Mike.

His eyes held no fear as they met mine. Just resignation.

"Why?" My voice seemed too quiet, especially with the noise of the battlefield, but somehow he heard me.

"Why not?" I imagined he probably would've shrugged if he could've.

"Played both sides, did you?"

He held my gaze unflinchingly, and didn't reply at first. I watched his eyes flick to Arddhu, then to Kevin, before returning to me. "It doesn't matter now."

"It does to me." Instead of screaming the words and giving him the satisfaction of knowing how furious I was, I'd barely whispered them. Only his shifter ears would hear.

He closed his eyes and breathed deeply. His Adam's apple bobbed as he swallowed. Then he opened them again. "It's not what you think. I wasn't working with him. Cromm."

Truth. My witchy-sense was quite clear on that.

I frowned. That made absolutely no sense. "Malsumis, then."

"No, not him either."

Truth.

What the fuck?

"Then who?"

"I... I can't tell you that."

"Oh yes, you can. And you will." My voice was iron. I stepped forward and raised my sword, still crusted with blood and disgusting bits.

"Go ahead." He barked a brittle laugh. "Kill me. I welcome it."

I faltered at the truth in his words.

So maybe a different tactic was required in this situation.

I lowered my blade. "I thought we were friends." I forced my voice to be softer. Cajoling.

His eyes skittered away and he blinked rapidly. Was that the shimmer of tears I saw? Nah. Probably just an optical illusion.

"We were. Once." His voice was just as soft as mine. Then he seemed to gather himself, and his expression hardened with his voice. "But that doesn't matter anymore. If you're going to kill me, get it over with. I'm tired of being forced to stand here like a trussed goat."

"You know we'll eventually find out who you're working with. And I'm not above torturing you to get answers."

Once again his gaze met mine. He'd probably intended to make some sarcastic remark, but whatever he'd seen in my eyes and face had stopped him.

Later, I'd think about the coldness that had spread through me. Right now it was useful.

We stood facing each other in silence for a moment, and it hit me with enough force to make me stagger a step: this was the scene of the vision I'd had last year, after I'd read Maggie's letter to Stuart. The same scene that Anu had cut short and refused to explain.

Now I knew why she'd done that.

And I'd sure as hell have some words with her about it.

Later.

"I can't tell you," Mike said, bringing me back to the present.

"Can't, or won't?"

"Does it really matter?"

I growled in frustration. He was still infuriating. Maybe even more so now.

"Yes, it fucking matters. *Can't* means you don't know. *Won't* means you're just being an asshole."

Another bark of wild laughter. "Always so black and white with you. You need to grow up and see there are only ever shades of gray. *Thousands* of shades of gray."

My anger spiked again, and I flung my sword in irritation. Then, I raised the knife that was still in my left hand—the first gift he'd ever given me—and moved in close, the tip of the blade near his temple.

"I think I'll start with an eye." My voice was steady. And ice-cold. "Do you have a preference? Right or left?"

"Dee," Kevin said, with a tone of warning.

Mike's Adam apple bobbed again, and I could almost smell his fear. "You... you wouldn't."

I got right in his face, only inches away. "Try me."

"B-but if I tell you, She'll kill me." His eyes widened as he realized he'd let his secret slip after all, and I hadn't even touched him. Yet.

A thrill of triumph ran through me, then his words registered.

She?

Oh fuck.

Now I knew *exactly* who he'd been working with.

So many things made sense now.

"How could you?"

He wouldn't look at me. "I had no choice."

"Since when? Since you ran away to Ireland?"

"No. Long before that." He hesitated, then must've realized it didn't really matter anymore. Despite the immobility spell, his shoulders slumped noticeably. "After your rescue."

My knife started to slip from my fingers, and I gripped it tighter.

No. Couldn't show weakness. Not now.

"She—what? Forced you? Made you an offer you couldn't refuse?"

Resignation flickered again in his eyes, but he still wouldn't look at me. "She promised me the power of the Sphere." Now he glared at me with venom and contempt. "And why not? You've never had the proper respect for it. Not like I do. You aren't worthy of it." Abruptly, the hatred eased. "That's pretty much it," he finished.

I shook my head in disbelief, but my jaw clenched as I thought it all through.

Back on Arddhu's world, when we'd all had the discussion after my rescue, Mike had stated anyone could command the Sphere, not just a Keeper. And not just a female, as I'd thought at the time. That discussion took on a completely different meaning now.

And then there was how much he'd changed since then, sometimes making me think he wanted me to fail in my mission. Now I knew it was so he could have Anu for himself.

There'd been clues all along, I'd just been too blind—too trusting—to see them.

But why hadn't he just killed me after my rescue, when Anu was still on my severed arm? He would've easily been able to claim the Sphere. Unless he'd known Arddhu and Kevin would've stopped him, by any means necessary.

Unless he'd waited until now for some other reason, some other piece of the puzzle that I hadn't figured out yet.

Then my thoughts turned to the Goddess.

Had She ever truly been a friend, as I'd first thought? Or had She played me from the start, all to further Her own plans and ambitions?

Was that why She'd dumped Arddhu, terminated him as Consort? Because he'd become my close ally?

She obviously didn't care who She hurt to make Her own agenda happen.

She wasn't kind and benevolent, as She'd made me believe.

And that made me think of something else.

"*Anu, did you know about any of this?*" I asked.

She hesitated before replying. "*I suspected, but did not know for certain.*"

"*And you didn't think it was important enough to tell me?*"

"*Not until I was certain, Deirdre. Please understand.*"

Ugh. What a mess.

"*We'll discuss it later,*" I said in dismissal.

Without taking my eyes from Mike, I turned my head slightly. "Arddhu, did you know about all this?"

"No, I did not." His voice was harsh. "But it explains much."

"Better watch your back," Mike said to Arddhu. "She'll be coming for you." Next his eyes moved to Kevin. "You, too." To me, he said, "Then—and only then—will She come for you. When you're grieving and distracted. When you're alone and vulnerable."

Not if I could help it.

But I'd worry about that later. Right now I had a job to finish.

"Out of respect for being Maggie's son, I'll give you a choice. You can do it yourself or I'll do it for you. But you know I can't let you live. Not now."

"I'd rather die with honor." His chin lifted and there was defiance in his eyes. "Release me from this fucking spell and *fight me*."

"And what? Winner gets the Sphere?" I shook my head. "I don't think so."

"What's wrong?" He sneered. "Afraid I'll win?"

It was true, he *was* excellent in combat—I'd seen it many times during our training sessions—and I'd definitely be taking a risk if I granted his request.

But then again, he couldn't really hurt me now. He didn't have magick, and I had Anu's shield to protect me from dagger wounds.

"*No, Deirdre,*" she said. "*I will not shield you in this battle.*"

What? "*Why not?*"

"*It would be an unfair advantage.*"

Oh for fuck's sake.

Fine. I'd just have to deal with cuts. Because I'd decided to do it, but not for him and his so-called honor.

For me. For *my* honor.

I nodded at Kevin and stepped back.

"Are you sure?" he asked, clearly worried.

"Yes."

Mike stumbled a bit as the spell lifted, but he quickly straightened and stood tall, bringing his dagger up in a defensive position.

We'd sparred with swords during our many practice sessions, but we'd never fought with knives. I didn't care; I had magick and he didn't. I knew who'd win this fight.

We circled as we each took measure of the other and probed for an opening. He made a quick slash to test me, which I easily dodged. The next one, though, hit its mark: a long slice opened on my bare right bicep.

Shit. He'd drawn first blood.

No matter. I'd just have something to heal later.

But he'd focused on my exposed arm, and it made me wonder if he'd incorporated any other vulnerabilities when he'd had my suit designed. Ones that he'd obviously neglected to tell me about.

His next move was easily deflected by my own. Then another slash, but this time when I moved aside he followed through with his fist, catching me on the right side of my jaw.

My head jerked sharply left and I hissed at the burst of pain. Before I could retaliate, he'd seen his advantage and pressed it: he got his blade past mine and opened another cut, this time on my throat just under the jawline and above my armor.

Without hesitation, he lunged forward and forced me to pivot to avoid the blade. But then he punched me again, this time right on the chin. My head snapped back and I staggered off balance, seeing stars as the pain blossomed and brought tears to my eyes.

Good thing my tongue hadn't been between my teeth. I could've bit it in two from the force of that hit.

I shook my head and pulled energy from the earth to do a quick healing so I could concentrate again. When my vision cleared, he'd shifted to his wolf form and was tensed to spring at me. Shredded clothing lay scattered in the bloody mud.

Shit. I should've known he'd use every advantage he had.

Just like I would.

But he didn't know I'd learned battle magick. I still had that secret weapon.

Then I was out of time, because he was on me.

I hit the ground hard. I had to drop my knife to use both my hand and my prosthesis—and all my strength—to keep his jaws from ripping my throat out. His sharp claws skidded against my armor, unable to break through.

Thank the gods for that.

Those deadly fangs were inches from my face as his powerful jaws repeatedly snapped shut. His fetid breath filled my nostrils, and saliva dripped from his fangs as a constant low growl came from deep in his throat.

There was *no fucking way* I was going to die like this.

Pulling more energy from Anu's reserves, I flooded it into my arms and shoved Mike away from me. He flew through the air and landed several feet away with a yelp, but was back on his feet even before I'd risen from my knees.

Goddammit. Not exactly an advantageous position.

His once-gorgeous black fur was now covered in bloody mud and disgusting bits from the battlefield. Snarling, lips curled back to expose his deadly fangs and golden eyes glowing with rage, once again he launched himself at me.

It was time to use my battle magick.

I raised my hand and sent a red bolt of destructive energy at his chest. He took a direct hit. Unfortunately, his momentum continued to carry him forward. He crashed into me, and I went sprawling. My breath was forced from my lungs as his heavy, furred body lay unmoving on my chest.

Somehow his claws had caught and ripped open my cheek, and the pain made spots explode in my vision. My blood ran down into my ear while his drenched my suit. The smell of burned hair was nauseating.

His eyes were closed and he whined pitifully.

How the hell could he still be alive with his chest blasted open?

But then I remembered he, too, could heal himself. He'd be fully recovered soon if I didn't finish this now, while I still could.

Once again boosting my strength magickally, I pushed him off me and got to my feet. He lay motionless in the mud, but the gaping hole in his chest had already started to close.

And even while I stood gawking, his eyes snapped open and focused on me, and he snarled again.

Goddammit.

Enough of this. Time to finish it.

I blasted him again to buy myself time, then ported my sword from where I'd dropped it. I quickly readied myself with the double grip I'd learned from the Morrigan.

For just a second, I saw something flicker in his eyes; was it sadness? Acceptance?

Maybe it was just good old-fashioned hate.

Despite the gaping wound, he rose and sprang at me one final time, but my killing strike was powerful, swift, and accurate.

I'd done it without hesitation, before I could make excuses.

Before I could change my mind.

His head flew in one direction and his body the other. For a moment, blood continued to spew from both. One paw twitched twice, then his remains shifted back to human.

Unexpectedly, I flashed back to the first time I'd seen him shift, when I'd admired his nude body and thought it beautiful. And when I'd thought the wolf simply gorgeous with his lustrous black fur so soft and thick.

Now he just looked sad and broken.

I raised my left hand and blasted his remains. More gore splashed my suit, but I was beyond caring. Beyond feeling.

The cold, hard knot inside had loosened to spread its numbness through me.

I'd expected Anu to say something, like she had last year when I'd accidentally thrown Mike across my room at Ard na Mara and she'd scolded me to not hurt friends.

But now she was silent.

Oh. Of course. Because he hadn't been a friend anymore and she knew it.

How long had she known? And why hadn't she told me? Maybe I could've somehow stopped it. Or at least *tried* to stop it.

Oh yeah, she and I were definitely going to have a little chat later.

For now, the battle was finally over.

Nearby, several of Cromm's fighters lay dead in the blood-soaked dirt. I wiped my blades on the closest one, sheathed them, and glanced around.

The last stragglers of Cromm's army were chased down and executed. Our troops still covered the battlefield, so I assumed our losses were few. I recognized Anthony in the distance; he must've gotten the all-clear from Reshep or Athena. Now he walked to where Tyr, Reshep, and Athena were gathered, and looked completely out of place since he was the only one not covered in gore.

At first, expecting to see her human aspect, I couldn't find the Morrigan. Then the piercing caw of a raven made me look up into the cloudless blue sky.

There she was, soaring on the air currents and observing the battlefield from above.

"We should destroy the last standing stones and the gold monument," Kevin said.

Oh. Yeah. Good idea. Gotta be thorough.

It only took a few minutes, now that we didn't have to dodge weapons or enemies. And it gave me immense satisfaction to destroy the gold monument—although I was careful to place a shield around it as it exploded. The shield successfully contained the golden shards and prevented injury to our soldiers in the immediate area.

Afterward, Arddhu and Kevin led me back to the portal. There was nothing more for me to do here.

My job was done.

"I will assist in cleaning up," Arddhu said to Kevin. "Take her home."

I sure as hell didn't want to know how they planned to clean up this nasty mess.

Kevin gently took my arm and guided me through the portal.

The exhaustion hit me almost immediately, and I stumbled on the cool marble tile of the living room. Shaking off Kevin's assistance, I drew more energy from Anu's reserves and headed to my room.

All I wanted right now was to be alone.

CHAPTER TWENTY-ONE

IN MY SUITE, I peeled off the disgusting armored suit and ported it directly to the laundry room. I left my filthy prosthesis on the bathroom floor, for now. Since Mike had never shown me how to clean them, I really had no idea how to properly remove all the gore without causing any damage—especially to the intricate and delicate inner workings of the prosthesis.

I'd worry about them later. I needed to get myself clean first.

Tapping into my energy reserves, I sent healing to my cuts. The knife wounds mended without leaving a trace, as usual. But for some reason, wherever Mike had clawed me I now had a scar. My cheek was marred with three long pinkish lines, and there were a few more on my right bicep. I didn't really care, though; I wouldn't be entering any beauty contests.

My mind was blank as I stood under the hot shower and let the water rinse as much dried gore from my hair as it could before I added shampoo.

It took half the damn bottle to get my hair clean.

Letting the water run, I sat on the ledge with a nail brush between my knees and removed the crusted blood and dirt from my fingers.

After I felt clean enough and the water ran clear, I stood with my head down and let the flow cascade over me until it turned cool.

I knew I needed time to process everything that'd happened, especially before I hung out with other people. I didn't plan on leaving my suite for a while, so I didn't bother to get dressed. Besides, my sword needed cleaning and sharpening and that gave me the perfect excuse. I grabbed a few washcloths from my linen closet, got one wet and soapy, then plopped down on the carpet near the foot of my bed and got to work.

It took a lot of scrubbing to get the blade clean, and then I stared at the filthy washcloths for a moment before I realized they were goners.

In the quiet room, the characteristic scrape of stone on metal followed by a distinctive ringing tone seemed a bit loud. But the rhythm of it was somehow soothing.

I was dry-eyed. I hadn't cried for Mike, not even a single tear. Maybe they'd surprise me and come at some inopportune moment, like at the next mission.

Or maybe they'd never come.

Mostly, I was numb. It was almost as if part of me was dead, killed by his betrayal.

The woman I'd been when I'd first become the Keeper didn't exist anymore. I was someone else now. A murderer, definitely.

According to the news media, I was a terrorist.

More accurately, I was a fool.

I'd taken so much at face value and hadn't bothered to question anything or think for myself. I'd never once doubted the Goddess, believing Her to be pure and good. I'd agreed to do Her bidding without much of a second thought.

Even the killing I'd done for Her fucking mission hadn't given me pause.

What did that say about me? Nothing good.

And the more I thought about it, the less numb and the more angry I became.

"*Deirdre, we must speak.*" Anu's voice was soft and clear in my mind.

"*Yes.*"

"*I am sorry.*"

I didn't reply, just continued slowly stroking the whetstone along my blade.

Scrape. Ring.

"*You had much to learn from Michael. If you had seen the vision in full, you would not be who you are now.*"

That was an understatement. "*Whatever.*"

"*I do not understand.*"

I almost snorted a laugh. She was almost as bad as Arddhu. "*It's just an expression that means I don't care.*"

"*I am sorry.*"

"*You already said that.*" I couldn't resist the snarky remark. "*It's almost unforgiveable, you know. Last year, you could've told me this was what was going to happen. Maybe I could've done something to prevent it.*"

"*You could not have prevented it.*"

"*Oh you know that, do you? Are you so sure?*"

"*Yes.*"

"*How? How do you know that?*" I challenged.

Silence for a moment. Then, "*Deirdre, you must rest.*"

"*Later.*" After I finished taking care of Ire, my beautiful sword. Such a thing was important. Especially after the heavy use she'd seen today.

And that was the end of my conversation with Anu.

For now.

There was still quite a bit I needed to discuss with her.

Scrape. Ring.

At least Cromm was no longer a threat. Ditto with Malsumis. It should've made me feel relief, but I still felt that nagging sense of missing something.

Something important.

It shouldn't have been that easy for me to defeat them. Hell, the fight with Mike had actually been more of a challenge.

And that bothered me. What was I missing?

Unexpectedly, Zara's face came to mind. She'd been kind to me during my captivity on Cromm's world, but what would happen to her now? With Cromm gone, would his whole world cease to exist? Did that mean Zara was gone, too? Maybe I'd effectively killed her when I'd killed him.

Shit.

Now the sting of tears came.

I blinked them away.

Scrape. Ring.

A soft knock.

"Dee? May I come in?" Kevin's voice was muffled on the other side of my bedroom door.

"Sure," I called out.

Scrape. Ring.

He entered and closed the door quietly behind him. After a moment he sat cross-legged near me.

But not too close.

Wise decision. I wouldn't want to accidentally nick him with my blade.

From under my lashes, I noticed he'd cleaned up and changed into jeans and a tee shirt. His hair was still damp from the shower, and fell in loose waves over his shoulders. He smelled like spicy vanilla.

"You okay?" His voice was low and hesitant.

"Yeah." Another stroke. "I'm actually surprised at how okay I am."

"Good." He nodded. "That's really good."

Scrape. Ring.

"You know, if you keep that up much longer, you won't have a blade left."

I hadn't been paying attention, lost in the rhythm and motion. And lost in thought. Now I looked closer, and saw what he meant. My blade was plenty sharp enough. I wiped it with the dry cloth, sheathed it, and set it aside, then neatly folded the cloth and set it nearby.

After a few seconds, I placed the whetstone on top of the cloth.

A few more seconds passed and I straightened the whetstone.

Shit.

Now I had nothing to keep my hand busy.

Kevin cleared his throat. "There's something I need to tell you."

I met his gaze but didn't reply.

A corner of his mouth lifted in a wry smile. "I figured I'd better tell you now, before you find out some other way."

Uh oh. Here it comes. Another betrayal.

I remained silent, and his smile slipped.

He cleared his throat again, a sure sign he was nervous. "Remember when you asked me where I got all my new powers? The time-bending and stuff?"

I nodded once.

"Well." He looked like he'd swallowed something nasty. "From Her. I got them from Her."

At my continued silence, he alternated between studying me, running his fingers through his hair, and picking at a nail.

"I used to think She did it without any strings attached, but now I've got a bad feeling. I'm worried She'll expect me to do Her bidding."

Oh. Was that all? Well, that wasn't as bad as I'd thought. No betrayal. Yet.

I took a deep breath and let it out slowly. "You're right. It'll just be a matter of time before She asks you to do something for Her And by *asks*, I mean *orders*."

He scooted closer and took my hand. "I'm telling you right now: I'll never do anything to hurt you. That's what I vowed back when we rescued you, and I'm promising it again, here and now. I'd rather *die* than hurt you."

Truth.

How strange: the one person I'd trusted had betrayed me, and the one I'd been so sure would betray me actually hadn't.

I turned my hand over and wove my fingers into his. "Thank you."

"And when you're ready, Arddhu wants to talk to you, too."

I just bet he did. There was a lot to talk about.

He'd been Her Consort; he *had* to have known about Her schemes. Maybe he'd even taken part in them. Possibly unknowingly, or possibly just a tiny bit knowingly.

As if reading my mind, Kevin said, "He didn't know. And you can trust him. I've never seen him so angry. I think he wants to strangle Her."

"He'll have to get in line."

He snorted, then turned serious. "One more thing I wanted to mention: I noticed something at the battle."

Again, I didn't reply, and he continued. "You destroyed all three of them without any help from us. Cromm, Malsumis, and Mike."

"Yeah. So?" I shrugged, not understanding his point.

"Don't you get it?" He cocked his head. "You're more powerful than you were even a couple of days ago."

Oh.

My mind sharpened as I thought back through the sequence of events.

Yes, I'd needed both of them to destroy the first monuments, but neither of them had been around when I'd taken out Malsumis. And I'd also been alone when I'd finished off Cromm. And the battle with Mike had pretty much been single combat, so neither of them had been involved. And it all had seemed so easy—*too* easy, as I'd thought earlier.

But after that, when the three of us had destroyed the remaining standing stones, I hadn't stopped to think when I'd turned toward the golden column and blasted it inside a protective shield.

Alone. Without anyone's help.

That, too, had seemed easy.

"Okay. And?"

He shrugged. "I just thought it was interesting. You're growing. Changing. Evolving."

I nodded, and studied our linked hands. "Getting back to Her... you know, I'm pretty sure She set the whole thing up. She wanted us—or maybe just *me*—to take out Cromm and Malsumis. I have absolutely no proof of it. Just a feeling."

"Sure, to get them out of Her way." Then he frowned. "I remember when you told me Her mission for you was removing the targets and healing Earth. Now I'm thinking She probably has some ulterior motive for that. Something that isn't from the goodness of Her heart. Something bad."

"Doesn't matter. We can't stop now. And it doesn't matter that it was Her plan to begin with, it's *mine* now. *I* want to heal Earth. And I can't do that until we remove the targets."

"*Dee?*" Arddhu's sudden voice in my head startled me. "*Where are you? Is Kevin with you?*"

"*Yes. We're in my bedroom. Talking,*" I quickly added. "*Give us a minute. We'll meet you in the living room.*"

"Arddhu's waiting for us," I said to Kevin. "I need to get dressed."

It seemed like such a long time ago that I'd ever cared about him seeing me naked. Right now, it sure as hell didn't bother me that he watched as I moved around the room and pulled lounge pants and a tee shirt from the dresser.

I silently thanked him for not offering to help me put them on, even though it wasn't as easy to do without my prosthesis.

Arddhu waited on the sofa. He'd also cleaned up and changed into comfy clothes, but he looked exhausted and his expression was anything but relaxed. He reminded me of a storm cloud during the monsoon: ready to unleash an angry and dangerous outburst.

Thank the gods it wasn't directed at me.

While Kevin poured three glasses of whiskey, I sat in one of the chairs.

Kevin sat at the other end of the sofa, leaving obvious room for me. But I needed some space right now, especially for this discussion. So I stayed put.

We sipped our whiskies in silence for a moment, almost as if none of us wanted to start.

Fuck that.

"So," I said. "How much time do we have before She comes for us?"

"Not enough," Arddhu replied. "We must prepare."

"But wouldn't She want us to take out the rest of the targets first?" Kevin asked. "She doesn't seem interested in doing the dirty work Herself."

For just a second, I had a flashback to my argument with Mike. The one about him getting his hands dirty. Looking back on it, that's when things really went off the rails. But I didn't feel any guilt over it now.

I actually didn't feel anything.

"She cannot do the *dirty work*, as you call it." Arddhu's voice was stiff with anger. "She cannot exist on Earth until the atmosphere is once again in balance."

"What?" I was sure the confusion was plain on my face.

Kevin's eyes widened. "Wait—*that's* why She left?"

Arddhu nodded at Kevin and answered me. "She cannot breathe this composition of air for longer than a few moments. Not as we can. She requires the mixture as it was thousands of years ago, before mankind's progress altered it."

I was dumbfounded. "Why can't She just fix it Herself? She's the Goddess, for fuck's sake. What good is all that power if She can't use it?"

Arddhu shook his head. "There are limits to Her power."

Something clicked then. "So that's why She needs someone else to do it all. Someone here, on Earth."

"You." Kevin pointed at me.

I snorted. "She could've picked anyone. For starters, why not Maggie? Or one of the other Keepers?"

Arddhu shook his head again. "I do not know. Perhaps She was not ready to implement Her plan then."

"Lucky me." My mind raced. "So that's Her *real* plan: with Earth healed, She'd come back here to stay."

"No. Not just to stay." Arddhu hesitated, then a corner of his lip curled in disgust. "To *rule*."

"And then what?" Kevin asked. "Or don't you know?"

"I know of Her plans. Some of them, at least." He drank some of his whiskey before he continued. "She will begin by destroying anyone who has opposed Her in the past, and anyone who does not worship or believe in Her."

"But that—that's *insane*," I blurted. "That's like, millions of people. Possibly even billions. Hardly anyone believes in Her anymore, and hasn't for... well, I don't know. Maybe centuries at this point. It's all Christians, Jews, Muslims, and assorted other faiths now. And none of them worship the Goddess."

Kevin's face was pale. "At one time or another, I think every deity who's ever existed has opposed Her or at least gotten on Her bad side. She'd wipe them all out? There'd be *no one* left."

That meant... Reshep and the other Egyptian deities.

Ares and Athena, and whatever other Olympians were still around.

Tyr and the Norse.

All the allies. Countless others.

The Morrigan, too.

She'd destroy them all. It was beyond belief.

I couldn't let that happen.

"Okay." My voice was firm with determination. "So then we destroy Her first. Before we heal Earth or do anything else."

Again Arddhu shook his head. "We cannot. She is bound to Earth, even though She cannot exist on it. If She is destroyed, so is Earth."

"*What?*" How could this possibly get any more fucked up?

Arddhu's eyes met and held mine. "You did not know this? She is this planet's Goddess. It would no longer exist without Her. Likewise, if Earth is destroyed, so is She."

"I actually think She's the Goddess for the whole dimension," Kevin corrected. "We should assume so, anyway. Just to be on the safe side."

"Wait a minute. How did this happen?" I poured more whiskey into our glasses, starting with my own and filling it almost to the brim, instead of just the customary one or two fingers' worth. Maybe I was getting used to it.

"I am not certain. It was long before my time began. But you should know that the realms which lie outside of Earth and connect to it, such as my own world or the Morrigan's, are separate and not affected."

"Mine too," Kevin added.

"So they're not part of this dimension," I ventured.

"Right," Kevin confirmed. "They're other dimensions."

"So if She is destroyed, Earth is destroyed, but not all the other dimensions or worlds that only connect to Earth and aren't part of it," I concluded.

Arddhu nodded. "That is correct."

"And Her own world, where She lives now, is it part of this dimension?"

"Yes."

"Okay. So what if, instead of destroying Her, we only banish Her to one of those other dimensions?"

Arddhu shook his head. "Earth would still be destroyed. She must remain within this dimension."

"Shit." I rubbed my forehead. "What if we banish Her to Her own world? Or somehow make Her stay there?"

"That is a possibility," Arddhu said.

Anthony entered the room and paused. "I don't mean to interrupt... but may I join you?"

I glanced at Kevin and Arddhu then nodded. "Sure."

He continued to the chair opposite me and more or less collapsed into it. He looked like shit. He'd cleaned up but hadn't shaved his five-o'clock shadow, and his eyes held a haunted look.

"Is this our post-mortem?" I asked.

He shook his head. "No, I don't think we need one this time."

He had a point. Truthfully, the last thing I wanted to talk about right now was Mike's betrayal and execution.

"I just wanted to apologize," he continued. "We had no idea Mr. Fleming had been compromised. The firm takes these things quite seriously, and they're rechecking every employee, contractor, and affiliate to make sure we have no other compromised parties."

Arddhu must've filled him in on all we'd learned at the end of the battle. But Anthony's words raised a question in my mind, and I decided to go ahead and ask it.

"But don't you guys—the firm, I mean—work for the Goddess?"

"Yes and no," he replied. "We primarily work for you. The Keepers, I mean. And since the Keepers usually work with the Goddess, so do we. But we're not beholden to Her. And we rarely get direct orders from Her."

"Oh. I think I understand." I paused. "By the way, Mike fooled all of us. So don't feel too bad."

Actually, that wasn't exactly true. He hadn't fooled Kevin. At Samhain, Kevin had said he thought Mike was working for Cromm. Although he'd gotten the *who* wrong, he hadn't gotten the *what* wrong. I just hadn't wanted to believe it.

"The allies have asked when the next meeting will take place," Anthony continued.

"That is a good question," Arddhu said. "We should have one as soon as possible. We must discuss the latest developments, as they affect us all."

I nodded. "Good point." I met Anthony's gaze again. "Can you schedule it and get the word out, please?"

He hesitated. "Am I to assume you wish me to stay on as your Assistant? Permanently?"

"If you'd like to, absolutely."

"Yes, I would. Thank you." A tiny smile. "I'll get right on scheduling the meeting." Another hesitation. "There is another matter. A... a legal one. Mr. Fleming had a will on file at the Phoenix office, and they've requested you attend a reading. The firm is a bit old-fashioned about that sort of thing."

So he wasn't *Mike* or *Michael* anymore, but *Mr. Fleming.* It seemed odd, somehow. So formal.

I frowned. "I'd rather not."

"I will relay the message, but they may insist."

"I don't understand. What's the big deal?"

"I thought you knew." His brow furrowed. "He named you his sole and primary beneficiary."

Goddammit.

What kind of asshole betrays someone then puts them in their fucking will?

"Fine. I'll go, but only if they insist. In the meantime, can you pack up all his stuff? Clear out his room? I don't care what you do with it—maybe the security team would want some of it. For mementos or something. They used to be close, I think."

And then I realized I hadn't spoken to the team since coming back from the battle. They were probably grieving the loss of their long-time teammate and I hadn't even apologized for murdering him.

I made a mental note to visit and give my condolences. And maybe beg their forgiveness.

"Will do," Anthony said, but continued sitting.

"Was there something else?"

"Yes. I wasn't sure if you knew that José quit. His official last day was Monday. He said he found a better position, for a local baseball player and family."

So that's why I hadn't seen him around the past few days. I'd thought maybe he'd taken time off that I'd forgotten about. I'd been grabbing a quick bite from the fridge or a snack from the pantry, which wasn't exactly healthy for the long-term.

"Well, shit." I really didn't want to cook again. I'd been spoiled rotten this past year, not having to worry about grocery shopping, meal planning, doing the dishes, or any of it. Truth be told, I wasn't sure I even remembered how to cook pasta correctly.

"If you wish, I'll ask the firm for a replacement," he said.

"Oh yes, I definitely wish." As he started to get up, I smiled ruefully. "Oh, one more thing, since you're officially my Assistant now. Do you know how to clean my prosthesis? Mike always did it and I don't know what he used. I don't want to ruin it."

"I'll take care of it. And I noticed your armor in the laundry room. I will return both to you spotless."

"Thank you." I ported my prosthesis from my bathroom and gingerly handed the gore-crusted thing over.

He barely spared it a glance, just nodded and left.

I sipped my whiskey. "Where were we?"

"I do not recall," Arddhu said. "But for the foreseeable future, I do not wish to return to my world. I would be vulnerable."

She's coming for you next, Mike had said to Arddhu. It would make sense for him to stay here on Earth, where She couldn't get to him.

But it said something that he seemed afraid of Her, and it wasn't good.

"you're welcome to stay here. I think we still have a couple of empty rooms."

"I am grateful." His relief was obvious. "I will take Michael's room after his things are removed."

I nodded. "Okay. So. When we meet with the alliance members, how much are we going to tell them?"

Both Kevin and I looked at Arddhu expectantly.

"At this point, I believe we can trust the allies," Arddhu replied. "They were all present and accounted for at the battle. We will tell them everything."

Kevin nodded. "And hopefully we can come up with a plan."

I sighed and cracked my stiff neck. I knew just what I needed to help soothe my tired and aching muscles.

"Since you're going to be staying here..." I stood and offered my hand to Arddhu. "Allow me to introduce you to one of the finest amenities The Hacienda has to offer: the spa."

He frowned, but set his glass on the table and accepted my hand.

Next I nodded to Kevin. "C'mon. You too."

He grinned and quickly joined us.

It was a bit chilly out, but we'd be warm enough in just a few minutes.

Arddhu awkwardly waited while I stripped. Kevin, of course, simply waved his hand and was naked. So although Kevin was first into the spa, I wasn't far behind.

We settled in and glanced up through the steam at Arddhu, who stood frowning.

"Well?" I asked. "Aren't you going to join us?"

He undressed, leaving his clothing in a neat pile beside mine, and cautiously stepped down into the spa.

The shifting expressions on his face as he experienced the hot water, constant bubbles, and jets for the first time were highly entertaining to watch. He went from curious to apprehensive to fascinated within the first five seconds alone.

After a few minutes, at my urging, he finally stopped trying to figure out how the jets worked and just relaxed.

Kevin and I smiled knowingly at each other when Arddhu groaned loudly.

"*Now* do you believe me?" he asked Arddhu. "How many times have I told you Earth has the best shit?"

The moon was two days from full and had just peeked over the foothills, shining brightly on us and turning everything to hues of blue-gray. The heated water was perfect: not hot enough to make me feel like a boiled lobster, but not lukewarm, either. Just right.

And I spent a mighty fine evening with the two remaining members of my protection squad.

The next morning, I knocked on the door of the guesthouse.

When Randy answered, he seemed surprised to see me. So surprised, he was actually speechless.

"Hi. May I come in?"

He nodded and stepped aside.

Nat and Joe were on the couch immersed in a video game, which meant Sam and Steve must be out on patrol. I hadn't heard if Anthony had hired someone to replace Jason or not.

"Hey guys." I sat in the one empty chair.

They paused their game and greeted me with a polite nod while Randy tossed a pile of crap onto the floor and sat in the other chair.

"I, uh, just wanted to say I'm sorry." At their blank looks, I tried to explain. "About Mike. I had no choice. I just wanted you to know that."

Randy hunched forward, arms resting on his knees. "We know, Dee." His voice was kind.

Joe tossed his game controller on the coffee table and shook his head. "What—did you think we blamed you, or something? Look: he didn't just betray you. He betrayed *all of us*. If you hadn't taken him out, I would've. Hell, any one of us would've."

I hadn't realized I'd been tense, not knowing the kind of reaction I'd get. Now my shoulders slumped as the tension released. "Okay. Yeah, I did wonder about that."

"Besides," Randy said. "It's not like we were all best buddies with him. It was just a professional relationship." He hesitated then added, "You seemed closer to him than we were."

I swallowed. "At one time I thought he and I were friends."

Nat snorted. "He was too much of a bossy dickhead to be a friend."

We all laughed, and it broke the hint of tension that I hadn't realized was there.

"We haven't seen you around much," Nat chided. "Not for months."

Last year, she and I had sort of become close for a while, when she'd had to shadow me for my last two weeks at my old accounting job. Now, I felt a stab of guilt. I'd been so busy I hadn't spent any time with her at all.

But she also didn't know I'd visited with Randy not too long ago.

"Shit," I said. "I'm sorry. Things have been so crazy."

She smiled wryly. "Yeah, I know. Just thought maybe we could have lunch sometime. Or maybe target practice. Or work out."

An idea formed then: a way to reconnect with the team, maybe bond with them a bit. With Mike gone, I felt more personally responsible for them. After all, they put their lives on the line every day to protect me. And to protect Kevin too, come to think of it.

And soon, they'd also be protecting Arddhu.

"You know, that's a great idea. I think we should have a little get together every week. Not a big deal, just maybe a lunch or dinner." I included Joe and Randy in my glance. "I know we can't all be together at the same time since some of you have to be on duty, but maybe we can figure something out. Even if it's only pizza and beer."

Randy nodded. "Yeah, that'd be cool."

"Great. I'll work on a schedule and get back with you."

And as I walked back to the main house, I had a little spring in my step again.

CHAPTER TWENTY-TWO

ONCE AGAIN, THE alliance members were gathered in the VIP tent—except for Marisha-Ten, Begtse, and Belatucadros, who were on the casualty list. Out of almost three thousand, our total lives lost were only one hundred and three.

Although Marisha-Ten's gigantic battle boar had also been slain, it hadn't been technically counted as a casualty.

Cromm's fighters, on the other hand, had been completely eliminated. We'd intentionally planned it that way, so they couldn't regroup under someone else.

It'd only been a week since the battle, but it seemed much longer. Almost a lifetime.

Anthony had returned my prothesis promptly, and it gleamed under the tent's lighting. But it completely slipped my mind to ask him how he'd gotten it so clean.

For maybe the first time, as I mingled among the allies, I felt like I really and truly belonged here with them.

And, just as Arddhu had said some time ago, Kali was indeed in attendance at this meeting. In her sweet motherly form, thank the gods.

It'd take some time to forget her battle form.

Despite our losses, everyone seemed in high spirits. Apparently, the bloody battle had been good for these immortals who'd become bored over the centuries. Even Tyr and Ares got along better now: they smiled, joked, and slapped each other on the back as they headed toward their seats—which were actually next to each other.

It all seemed a bit surreal.

As I started for my seat, the Morrigan drew me aside.

"Kevin told me about Mike," she said. "I wish I'd known sooner. I would've taken care of him myself. Drawn out his suffering. Nice and slow." Her dark eyes glittered with bloodlust and her full red lips curved into a vicious smile.

I almost spit out my drink.

"Remind me never to piss you off," I replied.

She threw her head back and laughed so loud, it drew everyone's attention.

At the head of the table, I stood and addressed the group. "Okay, everyone, please take your seats so we can get this thing started." Arddhu sat on my right, Kevin on my left, and Anthony on Kevin's left.

Within seconds, they were seated and the room was quiet.

What a difference from the first alliance meeting. Maybe I'd finally gained their respect.

"Thank you all for coming. First, a recap: as you're aware, we've successfully removed several targets, although not recently. We've also removed Malsumis and Cromm, and completely eliminated Cromm's army."

A loud cheer erupted, started by Tyr of course. Ares banged his fists on the table—cracking his section—and several others followed suit.

I raised my hand for silence, and they quieted.

"Unfortunately, we lost three among us in the battle, along with one hundred fighters."

"Glorious deaths," the Morrigan said.

Another round of cheering and pounding on the table, followed by toasting and drinking.

And more cracks in the table's surface.

Great. We'd probably have to get a new one after this.

"We will always be grateful for the assistance of Marisha-Ten, Begtse, and Belatucadros. They are heroes, and we honor them as they travel beyond the veil." Arddhu had suggested those words to me, and I'd gratefully used them.

Solemn nods now.

The next part would be harder. I took a drink to stall.

"Not counted among the casualties is my Assistant, Michael Fleming. I wish I could say he also died a hero, but I can't. He betrayed us, and received the consequences."

"Who did it?" Tyr asked.

"Did what?" I frowned.

"The execution."

"I did."

He nodded his approval. "Despite his betrayal, it couldn't have been an easy task for you. Well done, Keeper." Several murmurs and nods of assent from the others followed.

It sure as hell didn't feel well done.

I took another drink, hoping it would clear the bitter taste in my mouth.

I shook it off and continued. "Before he died, he gave us information that may surprise some—if not most—of you." I briefly met the eyes of each of the allies around the table as I said my next words. "He was working directly for the Goddess, who plans to eliminate us all."

Everyone reacted at once.

"The hell you say," Tyr shouted. He rose so quickly he knocked his chair over with a loud crash.

Athena cursed and smacked the table hard enough to break it into three pieces.

Ares roared with laughter.

The Morrigan didn't seem at all surprised, just disgusted.

Nayenezgani spat out a long string of what I assumed were Navajo curse words.

But Reshep only looked quietly thoughtful, a tiny line between his brows.

Once again, I held my hand up for silence, and they complied. I waited while Tyr reseated himself and Athena moved to an open seat where the table wasn't broken, then leaned forward and braced myself on the table.

"As you can imagine, this presents a problem. We have credible information that if we complete the original plan—eliminate the targets and heal Earth—the Goddess will then be able to return here and rule. She also plans to remove any humans who don't worship Her. Which is most of the planet's population, by the way."

Ares laughed. "How is that *our* problem? The humans are an infestation, like cockroaches. It'll be good for them to be gone."

Thankfully, no one else agreed with his opinion. Not openly, anyway.

"It's not just the humans," I pointed out. "She's going to eliminate all of us. All of *you*. As well as any other deities who've ever opposed Her."

That sobered him up.

"Because She's connected to Earth, if we destroy Her, we also destroy Earth." Ares opened his mouth, but shut it when I glared at him. "But before you say *so what*, I'd like to point out there are many reasons we can't let Earth be destroyed." I took a deep breath. "This is home to a great number of lifeforms that don't exist anywhere else. We can't just let them all die. And what about all the other deities who still call this planet home? You'd let them all die, too?" I shook my head. "No, we can't let Earth be destroyed."

"There's another reason," the Morrigan quietly added. She looked directly at me when she continued. "The Tuatha dé Danann—the Aes Sídhe—still live here."

I sank into my chair and just blinked at her.

The fae really existed.

They weren't just legends and mythology.

Someday, I wouldn't be surprised to hear this sort of stuff anymore. But today wasn't that day.

"Wait," Kevin frowned. "I thought they all left millennia ago?"

"I heard they went to another realm," Athena said.

"Tír na nÓg *is* another realm," the Morrigan replied. "But it exists within Earth's dimension. Actually, so does the entire Otherworld."

I remembered reading something about the fae leaving the realm of humankind and going underground after they lost the battle for Ireland. They were called the People of the Mound in some places, for the supposed faery mounds they lived in.

"So... if Earth is destroyed, the Otherworld is, too. Including the Aes Sídhe," Kevin said.

The Morrigan nodded. "And I'm sorry, but I can't let that happen." She raised her chin, daring anyone to oppose her.

"Could they relocate?" I asked.

She shook her head. "No. They're actually trapped there, in Tír na nÓg. The Goddess felt threatened and banished them."

Back to Her again.

"Did you know about this?" I asked Arddhu.

He shook his head. "Like Kevin, I thought they had simply fled Eire."

I rubbed my forehead as another headache began. "So how many of them are we talking about here? Fifty? A hundred?"

The Morrigan snorted. "They've probably been bored and breeding like rabbits, so I'd say closer to several thousand."

Shit.

"So what I think you're saying is, we need to free them."

She nodded. "And I think that when you do, you'll find they can help you defeat the Goddess without destroying Earth."

More help would be welcome. The more the merrier, right?

"I object," Athena said.

"Why?" I couldn't imagine what her problem was with this.

"They were always belligerent, arrogant, elitist assholes who constantly fought with Olympians," she sneered. "Earth has been peaceful without them. I say we can take care of our problems without them. Leave them exiled."

Was it hot in here? Had the heat come on?

The Morrigan stared daggers at Athena. "They deserve their freedom just as much as you do."

Arddhu spoke with a firm voice. "We will free the Aes Sídhe. It is the right thing to do."

Athena fell silent when no one else agreed with her. But her jaw clenched and she visibly fumed.

She might be a problem, but I couldn't deal with that now.

"Okay," I nodded at the Morrigan. "So how do we free them?"

"I have no idea," she shrugged. "If I knew, I would've done it myself, centuries ago."

Shit. Why was everything always so complicated?

Arddhu turned to me. "I will search my library." Then, to the Morrigan he said, "I once saw a spell that mentioned rescuing someone from a realm of banishment. Perhaps such a spell could be modified for an entire population."

She nodded. "I can help with that."

"So can I," Kevin said.

Arddhu shook his head at Kevin. "No, you must stay with the Keeper. Ensure she remains safe at all times."

Reshep cleared his throat. "In the meantime, should we continue to plan and execute missions?"

I shared a glance with Kevin and Arddhu, but it was Arddhu who spoke. "No. We should pause the missions for now. As long as Earth is not healed, the Goddess cannot step foot here for longer than a few moments. We must take advantage of that to plan our offensive against Her."

"What would you have the rest of us do, then?" Reshep asked.

Arddhu hesitated.

My mind worked, but came up blank. The three of us hadn't really discussed any of this. We were winging it.

"Perhaps you and Athena can oversee the combat practice of our fighters?" he said. "We will require them to be ready to resume the missions at a moment's notice."

Reshep nodded and seemed satisfied. Athena remained sullenly silent.

Arddhu glanced around the table. "My friends. Allies. It has been an honor fighting at your side. I look forward to our next victory. We will meet again in a week's time, and continue this discussion with further information."

The allies converged on the food and drink like a swarm of locusts, boisterous and ready to go, fight, and win.

It seemed I was the only one filled with doubt.

True to his word, Anthony had the firm send a new chef to replace José. Her name was Brianna, and she was only a tiny bit taller than me. She was a welcome change from all these tall men I'd been surrounded by for so long.

He'd just introduced her to Kevin and I when Arddhu and the Morrigan arrived for an impromptu meeting. I hadn't had lunch yet, and my stomach growled noticeably. They assured me the meeting wouldn't take long, so I asked Brianna to make lunch for all of us to enjoy afterward.

Her cool blue gaze flicked to the others before returning to me. "Got a hankering for anything in particular?"

I shook my head. "Nope. Surprise me with whatever you can make out of what we've got on hand."

Someone had recently done the grocery shopping because I'd seen fresh milk in the fridge earlier, so I assumed she had some stuff to work with, at least.

"Challenge accepted." She grinned and got to it while the rest of us headed to the VIP tent.

We seemed to hold all our meetings there these days.

It was an unusually warm day for early December: low eighties without a single cloud in the deep blue sky. The tent was quite comfortable without either air conditioning or heat.

For this type of informal meeting, we used the plush seating in the lounge area instead of sitting at the conference table. More intimate and comfortable.

"We have good news," Arddhu began. "We believe we have found the correct combination of spells to free the Tuatha."

Wow. I was impressed. It'd only taken a couple of days instead of the week or so we'd expected.

"It'll take a lot of energy, though," the Morrigan cautioned. "We'll probably need everyone to contribute."

"Okay, so we'll let everyone know at next week's meeting," I said, nodding at Anthony, since he took care of the meeting agendas and such.

"Hold on," Kevin said. "It's the solstice in only a couple of weeks. Do we want to do this before or after that?"

The winter solstice was also known as Yule, when Finn's Cove would have a feast and celebration. I'd missed last year's and didn't want to miss this year's too.

"I have plans for Yule." I addressed Arddhu. "Can't we do it after?"

Arddhu deferred to the Morrigan.

She shrugged. "I don't see why not. They've waited this long, what's another couple of weeks or so? But if we do it *on* the solstice, we could tap into some of that universal energy."

Suddenly Arddhu stilled and his face turned chalk white. He stared off into the distance with unfocused eyes, and I realized someone must be communicating with him via mental link.

His hands gripped the chair arms and he shuddered, then blinked.

"What is it?" I asked, not at all wanting to hear the answer.

His eyes were haunted, his voice a harsh whisper. "Tyr has been found dead."

Oh no.

"Who did it?" My first thought had been Ares, but I should've known better.

"*She* did. The Goddess."

Of course it was Her.

"Shit," Kevin hissed.

I opened my mouth to speak, but Arddhu cocked his head and held up a hand. After a moment he continued. "Reshep is on his way. He will explain further."

Without a word, I retrieved two bottles of Irish whiskey and several tumblers from the wet bar. I wasn't sure about the others, but I sure as hell needed it.

As I poured one for each of us, the liquid sloshed a bit, proof I was shaken by the news.

If She was going to take us out one by one even before Earth was healed, we'd have to completely rethink our approach.

When Reshep showed up a few minutes later, he almost collapsed onto a sofa. I'd never seen him in such a state. He'd always been so calm and composed. Wordlessly, I handed him a drink and he downed it in one swallow, then grimaced. His hand shook as he placed the empty glass on the nearby table. "Thank you," he murmured to me.

He addressed our group in a normal but unsteady voice. "Tyr was planning the combat exercises for our troops. He and I had a meeting scheduled for this morning, and when I arrived he was—he—" He shook his head, then continued in a subdued voice. "He'd been torn apart. If it hadn't been for his personal effects—his jewelry and other items—I wouldn't have even known it was him."

My hand went to my mouth. "Oh gods."

"*Fuck.*" That was Kevin.

"Where was he?" Anthony asked in a strained voice.

"At his home."

"Asgard," Arddhu helpfully clarified for those of us who didn't know where Tyr's home was.

For once, hearing that another piece of mythology was real—that Asgard actually existed, and was truly a physical place—didn't even surprise me.

But I had to ask the question. "Are you absolutely positive it was Her?"

Reshep turned his haunted eyes on me. "Yes. She left a message."

A message? She left a *fucking message?*

"What kind of message?" Kevin asked.

Without a word, Reshep retrieved his cellphone. As he scrolled, I raised my brows. I hadn't realized he was tech savvy. Then Reshep handed the phone to Kevin, who blanched and passed it to Arddhu.

A moment later I stared at a photo of what looked like bloody rope arranged in a messy symbol on the floor next to what I assumed were Tyr's unrecognizable remains. Blood was everywhere.

"What am I looking at?" I asked.

"It's a triskele—triple spiral—inside of a triangle," Kevin said. "It's Her symbol. Like a calling card."

"She used Tyr's intestines to form the symbol," Arddhu added with a grimace.

Fuck. That was disgusting.

I quickly handed the phone to Anthony, who gave it only a cursory glance before passing it on to the Morrigan.

The Morrigan studied the photo for a moment. "Asgard isn't in the same dimension as Earth. So those of us who have our own worlds apart from it are not safe from Her," she said as she returned the phone to Reshep.

Arddhu turned bleak eyes on me. "Do you still wish to wait until after Yule?"

I shook my head. "No. That's off the table now." The people of Finn's Cove would understand, I was sure of it.

He nodded. "Good. We must work quickly. Our lives depend upon it. And we should stay together from now on. I strongly suggest everyone come here. To Earth."

"Safety in numbers," I murmured. "There's plenty of room, between the house and this tent."

"I'll beef up security," Anthony added. "And we've received some new weapons from the firm. If She comes here, they won't knock Her down permanently, but maybe just long enough for us to get away. And maybe live for a while longer."

Live to fight another day, as the saying went.

There wasn't much more to say. Arddhu and Reshep left to gather the allies, Anthony to brief the security team, and the rest of us headed back to the house.

Although the mesquite smoked turkey sandwiches Brianna had prepared looked and smelled delicious, my appetite had completely disappeared. The Morrigan chowed down with no trouble, even smacking her lips, but I could only stare at mine before I pushed the plate away.

"I'm so sorry, Brianna. This looks amazing, but... I have an upset stomach."

Before she could reply, Kevin pushed the plate close again and insisted I eat. "You have to keep up your strength. Especially with so much going on."

I knew he was right.

So I forced most of the sandwich down, but just couldn't make myself finish it.

Within the hour, the rest of the allies—some with attendants and assistants in tow—descended on The Hacienda in a clamor of voices raised in alarm and excitement. My mostly-empty house was a bit crowded now.

Brianna took one long look at the newcomers and immediately began preparing more food.

Smart woman.

Then Anthony left for the store, to purchase more booze.

Smart guy.

Of all of them, Athena seemed to be the most shaken—although Ares was uncharacteristically quiet, bordering on morose. He and Tyr had just started to get along, after all. Seemed a shame they couldn't have had more time to work out their differences.

Soon after Anthony returned with the booze, Brianna asked him for the credit card and left to buy more food.

Unfortunately, the guest rooms filled up fast. We had to double and triple the allies up. I'd thought we'd have more than enough for everyone, but I hadn't expected they'd bring so many others with them.

I refused to think of the servants as slaves, although that's how some were treated—especially those that Ares had brought. The two pretty young females wore skimpy outfits that didn't hide the multiple bruises on their slim bodies. They both hung their heads and didn't speak to anyone, not even each other. I clenched my jaw when I saw the thick metal collars around their necks.

We wanted to lump them all together in a single room, but that caused a ruckus. The females didn't want to share their space with the males, and the attendants—who apparently were *not* servants—didn't want to be in the same room as the servants.

So we had to get creative.

We put the female attendants in the training room, where they'd have to sleep on the floor. At least it was covered in padded exercise mats. But since they wouldn't share with the female servants, we moved those to the home office, since it had carpeting.

The male attendants and assistants went in the library, which was also carpeted. Unfortunately, the only room left for the male servants was the laundry room, but at least there were only three of them.

Most of the male allies seemed to prefer female servants.

And there were other issues, of course.

Athena and Kali didn't want the Morrigan with them, so in a fit of pique I gave her Mike's old room, with its nice private entrance, which Arddhu had only recently taken over. She had it all to herself.

Which, of course, made the others extremely jealous.

And since Kevin gave his room up to Reshep, Nayenezgani, and Ares, he was displaced along with Arddhu.

Which meant they had to bunk with me.

Good thing I had a king-sized bed.

None of my former coworkers would ever believe I'd soon be sharing a bed every night with both the Consort of the Goddess and an Irish trickster demi-god.

Anthony had been staying in the guesthouse with the security team, and Brianna volunteered to stay there too, sharing Nat's room.

Finally, we had everything sorted out.

Until Anthony's extra security showed up.

The only place to put them was the VIP tent. As they claimed their spots and unrolled their sleeping bags on the carpeting, one snorted at my embarrassed apology. "Ma'am, we've stayed in way worse places, believe me," he said.

For some of the allies, this was their first time staying on Earth for longer than a few hours. Some of their entourages had never been to Earth, the servants in particular. Kevin offered to show everyone how to use the technology in the house as well as its amenities, and was kept fairly busy with that.

After everyone settled in, I called them together to lay down some basic house rules.

"No relieving yourselves or vomiting in the pool or spa." I waited until the boos and groans stopped before I continued. "Absolutely no fighting. Be courteous to the other guests here. No loud noise after ten at night." At a few blank looks, I clarified. "If you don't know how to read a clock, Kevin or I would be happy to show you. There are no servants except for those you've brought with you, so there's nobody to clean up any messes. You'll have to clean them up yourselves. Brianna—" I nodded to her, busy preparing dinner in the kitchen— "is our chef. She will prepare your meals. If you have any special dietary restrictions, please let her know. But remember we only have Earth food and drink available here. No requests for meat or drink from other worlds, please.

"Lastly, we'll be having another alliance meeting in the next couple of days, so please try to hold off asking a lot of questions until then."

One of the attendants—I wasn't sure which ally he worked for—raised a hand. "Do you have any of that refreshing citrus flavored water injected with carbon dioxide?"

Refreshing citrus flavored... it took me a moment to realize he was asking for soda.

Brianna answered that one. "Yes, we have several varieties. Just ask me and I'll be happy to help you."

I smiled my thanks and she grinned.

"And by the way, dinner is ready," she added.

Everyone clamored to dig in, and I overheard an attendant praising Earth food. "Oh, I hope it's the large hooved bovine. I hear it's divine, when prepared properly." I covered my mouth to hide my smile.

But when some began pushing and shoving the servants aside, I was forced to step in. "No shoving. Wait your turn. Everyone here will get food and drink."

Goddammit. This was more like a college house party than an emergency shelter for deities and their entourages.

With a little luck, it wouldn't be for long.

After dinner, Anthony pulled me aside to let me know the firm's reading of Mike's will had been postponed indefinitely, under the circumstances. Priorities had definitely shifted, and it'd have to wait.

I sure as hell had no problem with that.

Weary and tense, I grabbed my towel and headed out to the spa.

But after only a few steps beyond the patio, I stopped short.

Kevin was busy showing several of the guests how the spa worked; I had no idea if any of them were going to get naked or not, but I wasn't about to find out.

Quietly, before anyone noticed my presence, I slipped back into the house and filled my bathtub instead. It didn't have as many jets as the spa did, but it had something the spa didn't have right now: privacy. I dimmed the lights, closed my eyes, and laid back, letting the heat and bubble action soothe and relax me.

I had a feeling these private moments would soon be a thing of the past.

Especially since I'd be sharing my bedroom—and bathroom—with Arddhu and Kevin.

Although we'd occasionally had sex or slept together since that first time at Samhain, this was the first time we'd share a bed every night. I knew they were decent sleeping partners; they didn't kick my shin or jab me with a sharp elbow during the night, and neither snored. And when I woke, it was to a pleasant tangle of limbs and bodies, sort of like a puppy pile. It never failed to make me smile, because it just felt good to be held and snuggled through the night.

But later on that first night with a full house, the three of us didn't do anything but drag ourselves to bed and wake up in the same position we fell asleep in.

And in the morning, my normal tai chi session in the backyard with Kevin became crowded as first Ares, then Athena, then the others joined in—even Reshep.

It was peaceful and quiet, with the birdsong and soothing harp music playing in the background.

Until Ares lost his balance and bumped into Kali, who immediately began transforming into her scary battle aspect.

Luckily, I was able to calm them down before a nasty fight broke out, but the sooner this was all over and things were back to normal, the better.

Two days later, we held the alliance meeting. The allies had invited some of their assistants to attend, so the table was full again. Everyone listened intently to Arddhu and the Morrigan as they explained the spell they'd developed to free the Tuatha.

Then Arddhu walked us through the plan.

"We will travel to Eire and gather at Brú na Bóinne at sundown on the solstice. The Morrigan and I will speak the spell. I will open the portal to Tír na nÓg. Each of you will draw energy from Earth, for I will require as much as possible to hold the portal open long enough for all the Tuatha to come through." He nodded at me. "The Keeper will be the conduit. Each of you will feed your energy to her, and she will amplify it before sending it to me."

"Wait—I'll do what?" This was the first I'd heard of my part in this. I'd assumed I'd just be pulling energy like everyone else. "And where's this *broona* place?"

"Brú na Bóinne is the ancient name for Newgrange," Kevin explained.

Arddhu spoke next. "You are the conduit. Since you have an unlimited reservoir, you alone are able to collect and hold the energy from everyone else."

I stared at him. Unlimited reservoir? Where'd he get such nonsense?

"First of all, Newgrange is massively popular," I pointed out. "Especially at the solstice. And it's probably heavily guarded. There's no way we'll be able to just waltz right in. Second, no, my reservoir is *not* unlimited. Third, I don't know what you mean by *amplify*."

He frowned. "We will not be dancing." He turned to Kevin. "Have you not told her?"

I ignored his misnomer and nearly growled as my anger spiked. "Told me what?" Dammit, this was just like last year, before I became the Keeper. Mike had kept secrets, such as what it'd truly meant to inherit Maggie's estate.

Kevin had the good sense to look uncomfortable. "Not yet, no."

Arddhu sighed and turned to me again. "You have several unique talents that none of us have. Yes, your reservoir *is* unlimited. Apparently you are not aware of that, and do not have the knowledge of managing it. We will help you. And yes, we will also show you how to amplify it, as is required of you. As for Brú na Bóinne—*Newgrange* as you call it—being inaccessible, Kevin will provide spells to disable technology and for invisibility."

"I can't cast invisibility on huge crowds," Kevin pointed out. "So it'll only be useful until the Tuatha start pouring out of the portal. But hopefully they'll be able to use their own magick from that point."

"This is all news to me. But sure, I'm game," I shrugged. When Arddhu frowned at my words, I added sweetly, "It means I look forward to learning how to use these new talents you say I have."

Kevin snorted and hid a smile behind his hand.

Arddhu nodded and continued as if I'd never interrupted, and he certainly didn't get my snark. "After all the Tuatha are free, I will close that portal and open another to... to..." He paused and glanced around. "Where are we bringing them? Here?"

I hated to be *that* person, but I spoke up again. "Nuh-uh. We just don't have the room here. Especially not for thousands of them. Can we take them to someone else's world?"

Everyone looked at each other and shook their heads.

Reshep spoke first. "I, like many others, do not wish the Tuatha on my world. It would upset the delicate balance of power I maintain there. And if they are angry—as I assume they will be—I do not wish my people to be harmed in any way."

The others murmured in agreement.

My head began throbbing, making my anger spike.

"Oh for fuck's sake," I muttered. But when my gaze fell on Kevin, inspiration hit. "What about your place?" I asked him. "You haven't been there in months. Your big palace is still empty, right?"

His eyes widened but before he said a word, the Morrigan barked a laugh. "Oh, that'd be *hilarious*."

I must've missed something. "Why?"

She smirked. "They didn't care much for Bricriu, back in the day. They'd dismember him before they'd ever consider staying on his world."

I sighed.

My patience was quickly wearing thin with this group.

"Well they'll just have to get over it," I snapped. "Beggars can't be choosers."

The Morrigan lifted one eyebrow. "Careful, Keeper. You don't want to get on their bad side." Then her look softened. "Look, I understand. And when the time comes, I'll do what I can to explain how much things have changed while they've been gone. But don't be surprised if I'm not successful. You need to have a contingency plan."

"Fine." I rubbed my forehead. "Anyone else have any ideas? 'Cuz I'm all out."

While the allies murmured amongst themselves, Arddhu leaned close. "Are you feeling well? You rub yourself often."

I almost snorted at his unintended innuendo.

"I've been having a lot of headaches lately, that's all." His worried reaction was immediate, and I tried to set him at ease. "They're just headaches, Arddhu. I'll take an aspirin when we're done here."

He nodded, but the concern didn't leave his eyes.

"I have a suggestion," Reshep said. When everyone quieted down, he continued. "We let *them* decide where they want to go after they are free."

"But there may not be enough time for that," I pointed out. "We'll need to get them away from Newgrange as fast as possible. So at the very least, they'll need to go somewhere temporarily while they take their time deciding where to go permanently."

The Morrigan tapped a finger against her chin. "Actually, that's not a bad idea. They'll most likely create a place of their own, and it'll be quick. At least as quick as sending them through another portal to here, or another dimension."

"Oh." Well, that solved that problem.

I thought we were done, but Arddhu spoke next. "Reshep, have you reassigned Tyr's duties?"

"Athena and I will complete his work, with assistance from Kali." He nodded at her, and she smiled in return—her kindly-mom smile.

"Excellent," Arddhu nodded. "So to recap: the Morrigan, Kevin, and I will work with the Keeper to help her understand and prepare for her role in the solstice operation. On solstice eve, we will all meet again for a final pre-operation discussion."

I stood. "Once again, thank you all for attending. Please help yourself to the refreshments."

As everyone swarmed the bar and food tables, I slipped away and ported to the house.

I needed that aspirin badly.

For the next couple of days, I spent most of my time in the desert away from the house, beyond the lush backyard, with Arddhu, the Morrigan, and Kevin.

First, using his mind-link connection with me, Arddhu showed me how vast my energy reservoir was, diving deep within my core as if my body were an undiscovered realm. It was like an entire universe within me, and I was shocked. He sure as hell hadn't exaggerated when he'd said my reservoir was unlimited.

But where had it come from? I couldn't have had it all this time. I would've known. Wouldn't I?

While Arddhu spoke briefly with Kevin and the Morrigan, I asked Anu.

"Why didn't you tell me about this earlier? I could've used this so many times, instead of constantly needing to replenish my energy."

"You did not have this reservoir last year. It is a recent development."

Oh really? That was interesting. *"How recent?"*

"It occurred after Samhain."

When I'd been forced to fake being the Goddess? That made no sense.

Then she clarified: *"When you coupled with Arddhu. The first time."*

Oh. *That.*

But why would having sex with him change me?

Wait—hadn't Kevin mentioned something about Arddhu's wild forest magick being released? That must have something to do with it.

And come to think of it, that was when I'd started getting these frequent headaches, too. I wondered if that was another symptom of this— whatever *this* was.

"Dee," Arddhu's voice interrupted my thoughts. "We are ready to begin showing you the amplification process."

It was astonishingly simple: Kevin and the Morrigan pulled energy from the earth and transferred it to me, but instead of storing it in the reservoir inside me, I quickly boosted it, similar to how I boosted my strength using my magick, then transferred it to Arddhu. For these practice sessions, he returned the energy to Earth, but at the solstice he'd channel it to the portal.

If I looked closely and sort of squinted, I could almost see it: a flow of pale iridescence that shimmered in the warm sunlight.

At first, Kevin and the Morrigan passed the energy to me in small, short bursts, to give me time to practice the amplification and get used to the whole process. Once I had that down, they fed it to me in a steady stream that gradually increased.

To my surprise, I had absolutely no trouble handling the energy surging into and through me. I'd been skeptical at first, but it was almost too easy to manipulate the streams.

In fact, it was almost fun.

"That is enough for now," Arddhu said.

Kevin and the Morrigan stopped feeding energy to me, and I passed the last of it to Arddhu. He sent it back into the earth and smiled.

"Well done. *Very* well done. Do you still doubt your powers?"

I shook my head. "No. But really, I had no idea I had this new reservoir. So thanks for letting me know about it."

He frowned. "New? You had it from the beginning. When you became the Keeper."

"No, I didn't. Anu told me I started changing after Samhain—that's when this happened."

"Samhain," Kevin murmured, and we all turned to him. He shot a quick glance at the Morrigan before he continued. "We talked about your wild forest magick, Arddhu, and what it can do in... uh, certain circumstances."

The Morrigan studied each of us before returning her gaze to Kevin. "Are you guys talking about what I think you're talking about? Look, we're all adults here. I think I can handle you discussing fucking." She laughed. "It's not like I didn't know, anyway."

"What?" My cheeks heated. "You *knew?*"

I thought we'd always tried to stay low-key. And Kevin always put a sound shield on the bedroom when the three of us had sex. *Always.*

Her eyes sparkled. "Of course I knew. I can smell it on all three of you. You're bonded. I think it's great."

Kevin wouldn't meet my eyes, but Arddhu continued to frown as he stared at the Morrigan.

"Does anyone else know?" I asked.

She shrugged. "Probably every single one of the allies and their attendants. But hey, it's no big deal. And it's good for them to see you're evolving into something more than just a typical Keeper. Gives them more confidence in you as our leader. Especially since we'll be going up against Her."

At Samhain, Arddhu had said I wasn't exactly human anymore, and the Morrigan had just said pretty much the same thing.

I didn't know how to feel about any of this.

In my stunned silence, she put her arm around my shoulders. "Oh, don't be so freaked out. It'll be fine. *You're* fine. You'll see." Gently, she steered me toward the house and spoke over her shoulder. "Now, how about we all go for a dip in that nice hot tub I've heard so much about?"

CHAPTER TWENTY-THREE

O N SOLSTICE MORNING, I could only pick at the delicious breakfast
Brianna had prepared for me. The plate of scrambled eggs with
gooey melted sharp cheddar cheese, chives, and bacon bits, with a
side of rye toast spread with creamy butter, looked like something out of
an expensive foodie magazine.

But I was too nervous to eat, despite my confidence in my relatively new
abilities.

In just a few short hours I'd actually be meeting the Tuatha. The fae.

Popular culture portrayed them as impossibly tall and beautiful,
brilliantly intelligent and cultured, with delicately pointed ears.

But in mythology, they had a reputation for being fierce fighters,
powerful, intimidating, scary, and completely untrustworthy.

The Morrigan thought they'd be surly from their long banishment in Tír
na nÓg, despite it supposedly being pretty much a tropical paradise where
no one aged or got sick.

I hoped they didn't lash out as soon as they were freed; I sure as hell
didn't want to be a target of all that anger.

"Not to your liking?" Brianna interrupted my thoughts, nodding at my
plate.

"Oh, no, it's not that. I just... my stomach is tied in knots."
Apologetically, I lifted a forkful to my mouth.

She nodded and continued cleaning the frypan she'd used. "I heard about the mission. I'm sure it'll go off without a hitch. Everyone seems very qualified. Experienced."

"Thanks." After a couple more bites, I set my fork down. "I'm sorry, that's all I can handle right now." My stomach was full of frantic butterflies.

Her eyes dropped to my plate then back to mine but she didn't allow any disappointment to show. "If you get hungry later, just grab a couple of protein bars from the drawer."

I nodded and headed to the training room, thinking maybe some tai chi would help me calm down. Since a cold front had come through during the night, it was too chilly outside for my normal session.

But I found the room occupied by the Morrigan and Kevin, practicing swordplay.

Quietly, I entered the room, closed the door, and leaned against it.

They were graceful yet savage, both covered in bloody gashes and glistening sweat. The Morrigan's ferocious grin was disturbing; it was quite obvious she was enjoying herself immensely.

Kevin whirled and slashed, and I admired his technique. We'd practiced a few times, but now I realized he'd held back during those sessions with me. Maybe he'd been afraid to hurt me.

He sure as hell didn't hold back with the Morrigan.

Now he lunged forward with a particularly vicious stroke, and I sucked in a breath. But the Morrigan blocked it effortlessly with her own blade, and after a moment of holding his sword in place with hers, she was only a blur as she easily pivoted away. He'd had his blade pressed so hard against hers, he lost his balance and almost fell. He quickly corrected himself, but not before her blade flashed and blood stained his shirt from another slice on his torso. She laughed tauntingly from well beyond his reach.

Then she noticed me.

"Care to join us?" Her voice held a musical quality that clearly reflected how much fun she was having.

I shook my head. "Nah. I came here to do some tai chi to calm down. I didn't mean to interrupt, but I just had to watch you two for a while. You're both amazing. I'll just go somewhere else."

"Good," Kevin said, slightly out of breath. "I can only handle one of you at a time."

"Why do you need to calm down?" The Morrigan asked, bright eyes narrowed.

No harm in being honest.

"I'm nervous about tonight. The—the mission."

Smiling, she sheathed her sword and leaned it against the wall. "Don't be. It should go well." She drank some water from her bottle, then nodded at Kevin. "Thanks for the workout."

"Anytime." He sheathed his own sword and it disappeared. Probably back to its pocket dimension.

"I find this tai chi intriguing," she said to me. "Let's do it together."

So an hour or so later, that's what Arddhu found us doing when he abruptly entered the room. He closed the door behind him, and his face was strained, paler than usual.

"We have lost Nayenezgani," he said.

Oh no. Not another one.

"What? How?" I asked.

"He went for a walk and never came back."

"So he's missing," I clarified. Not the same as dead. There was still a chance.

He nodded.

The Morrigan frowned. "That doesn't sound like him. He must've been taken."

"It is what I believe as well," he replied.

Closing my eyes, I probed the wards I'd placed over the property, searching for any weakness or breach. But there were none. The wards were secure.

How had She gotten through them?

"Shit." My headache came roaring back, and I rubbed my forehead. "That means no one's safe here, after all."

"Until we know for certain, I do not wish to alarm the rest of the group. It is why I have only told you three." His gaze was sharp on me. "Another headache?"

"Yeah. They're getting more frequent. I'll take an aspirin when we're done here." He and Kevin shared a pointed look. "What?"

Kevin responded. "We're not sure. We've talked, and we think maybe your headaches are part of your body changing. Evolving."

"Much like the caterpillar in its chrysalis will become the butterfly." Arddhu opened the door and gestured for me to leave. "Now show me this *aspirin*."

Conveniently, I kept a bottle in the kitchen now, so that's where we headed. Brianna sat at the island, flipping through a cookbook. She glanced up at us but didn't say anything.

Arddhu didn't read the aspirin bottle; he shook out a tablet and sniffed it, then placed it on his tongue. After a moment, he chewed it and grimaced at the bitter taste.

"It's just a modern form of willow bark," I explained, trying not to smile at his obvious discomfort.

"Yes, I see."

He gave the bottle back to me and I took two with some water, then we sat in the living room to continue our discussion. Except Arddhu didn't sit; he moved behind me and massaged my neck and shoulders with his strong hands.

I bit back the groan. Gods, it felt so *good*.

"We need you at your best for this mission," he chided.

"I know. I will be."

Now Brianna spoke up. "Maybe it would help if you ate something more substantial than the three bites of your breakfast."

Shit. *Thanks for ratting me out.*

"What is this?" Arddhu's voice was sharp. "You must eat."

Kevin added, "That's not good, Dee."

"Sorry." I sighed. "My stomach was upset. I figured I'd grab a protein bar or two before we left, if I can keep that down."

I hated feeling so defensive. I wasn't a child, for fuck's sake.

Arddhu's voice held unquestioning command. "Brianna, please prepare another nutritious meal for Deirdre. We will ensure she eats every bite of it."

Goddammit.

"Yes, sir." Pots and pans immediately clanged on the stove.

"You guys drive me crazy, you know that?" But his hands on my tense muscles were simply amazing, and now my headache was completely gone. Even my stomach had settled.

"Trust us, love, it's mutual," Kevin smirked.

Arddhu abruptly broke off his impromptu massage and sat on the sofa with a sigh. He looked exhausted.

"Are you okay?" I asked. "You don't seem your normal self."

He smiled, a tiny little thing. "I have been feeling more drained than usual. I may need to ask you to cease wearing the ring of protection I gave you. But just for a short period of time. Just long enough for me to recover."

I stared at him. "What does that have to do with—oh." He must be powering the ring himself. "Why didn't you tell me you maintain the ring? I don't have to wear it all the time."

"Yes, you do. You must be protected at all times," he stubbornly replied.

I shook my head. "You just said you need me at my best. Well, what about *you*? We need *you* at your best, too." I immediately took off the ring. "Now, stop powering it. I insist."

He opened his mouth to argue, but Kevin interrupted. "She's right, you know."

"Now, will you have enough time to recover before the mission?" I asked.

"Yes. I'll go and rest for a while, and that should do it." He turned to Kevin. "Please make sure she eats every bite of whatever Brianna prepares for her."

"You got it." Kevin grinned.

They made me wear the damned armored suit again.

I'd given up trying to argue about it, though. It just wasn't worth it. Just as he'd done with my prosthesis, Anthony had cleaned the suit exceptionally well; it was spotless.

Since County Meath was further north than Ard na Mara—and County Cork was known for its mild climate, even in late December—I expected Newgrange to be much colder. And with the time difference, it'd be just after sundown when we arrived.

This would be my first time wearing the suit in cold temperatures, and I was curious if it'd keep me as comfortably warm as it had kept me nicely cool in the heat of the Arizona summer.

I left my long hair loose and flowing. Not just as a change from my typical ponytail, but also because it'd help keep my ears warm.

Ire was in her baldric and my knife was on my thigh; I left my pistol home for this operation.

Arddhu's leather armor had been repaired and modified since the battle in the desert. Now, his chest was covered in a golden metal plate engraved with intricate Celtic knotwork. His hair was bound at the nape of his neck, and the stubs of his horns were barely visible.

Kevin also wore his leather armor, but it was the same as the last time I'd seen it, with its tooled leather breastplate. He wore his warrior braids, and looked devastatingly handsome.

The Morrigan, too, wore armor. She was covered from neck to ankle in sleek black leather accented with silver and gold metal that flashed in the bright Arizona sun. Like me, she was armed; she wore twin daggers on her hips.

The four of us joined the rest of the allies at Arddhu's portal site just beyond the VIP tent. For just a moment, I felt intimidated being among these immortals, but the feeling passed relatively quickly. After all, if the Morrigan and Arddhu were right, I was well on my way to becoming immortal, too. Even so, we were a pitiful group of only eight now.

Since Anthony had no ability to work with Earth energy, he'd stay here and keep an eye on all the attendants and assistants to make sure there was no trouble.

The day before, he'd handed out the special firearms the firm had provided, and the security team had immediately started working with them to become familiar with their use. I hoped it'd be enough, just in case the Goddess—that *bitch*—showed up here while we were busy in Ireland freeing the Tuatha. And I really hoped the eight of us would be able to give Arddhu the energy he needed to keep the portal open long enough.

I'd been struggling with thinking of Her as the Goddess ever since I'd learned of Her treachery. That title implied a level of honor, respect, and deference that I just didn't think She deserved anymore.

So maybe I'd just call Her the Bitch from now on.

Yeah. I liked that idea. It had a nice sound to it.

Anthony had come to see us off. "Best of luck on the mission," he said, and stood back from the portal.

It was go time.

Kevin cast his invisibility spell over us, and Arddhu opened the portal as close to Newgrange as we dared. We stepped through, from bright sunlight to pale moonlight, and my heart dropped.

Shit. I hadn't expected full dark. I'd only been to Ireland in late summer and autumn, not midwinter, so I'd expected twilight. I should've realized it'd be dark this time of year. Had we missed an important detail in our planning?

But as my eyes adjusted, I realized it wasn't complete darkness; the entrance to the chamber was well lit, and cast enough light that I actually could see the faint shimmer of everyone's forms around me as we advanced toward the structure.

My face and bare right arm felt the chill, but my armor did indeed keep me comfortably warm.

Earlier in the day, the place had probably been packed with visitors eager to watch the famous solstice alignment at sunrise through the monument, but now it was eerily quiet and had an abandoned feel. I didn't see any guards posted, but I'd bet there were lots of security cameras. Which Kevin had already taken out with his anti-technology spell.

Even with that spell, we still ran a high risk of discovery by human security if someone made occasional rounds. We also could be attacked by someone sent by the Bitch.

But the Morrigan made quick work of the lock on the gate, and we were in with no alarms raised.

The interior of Newgrange was dimly lit, with deep shadows and almost a spooky atmosphere that'd be more suited for Samhain than Yule.

To conserve energy that'd be needed for channeling to Arddhu, Kevin dropped the invisibility spell as soon as we were all inside. We traveled the narrow passageway single-file, and this was one time that being short was definitely an advantage, since I didn't have to crouch under the low ceilings like Arddhu and the others did.

I'd never visited Newgrange before, although I'd seen pictures of it. But they didn't do the place justice. Spirals, circles, lines, dots, and other markings of some long-forgotten language seemed to leap from the shadows. I could probably spend a lifetime studying this ancient and sacred site.

We entered the central chamber, and without a word—almost as if we'd rehearsed it—the allies formed a three-quarter circle along the walls and immediately began drawing energy from Earth. I took my place in the center and took a deep breath, grounding myself, before accepting the flows from each. A few feet away, Arddhu faced a small, dark chamber with his back toward me. From our briefing the night before, that chamber contained the portal to Tír na nÓg, and apparently only he could see it. I sure as hell couldn't see anything in the shadows beyond him.

Just as I'd practiced, I amplified the energy and passed it to Arddhu, and he focused it on the banishment seal of the portal. During that practice session, the energy flow had been faintly iridescent and barely noticeable in the Arizona sun, but here in the darkened chamber it glowed a pale, eerie green.

Dammit. Would a passing security patrol see it? Maybe we should've posted a guard at the entrance, like Anthony. He would've been a valuable member of this team after all.

But it was too late now. I just had to stay hopeful that everything would go according to plan.

I shook off the distracting thoughts and concentrated on my task.

The energy flowed easily through me. Almost *too* easily. I'd expected to have a bit of trouble with six powerful immortals sending that much juice to me, but it seemed just as effortless as when I'd practiced with just the Morrigan and Kevin.

How strange.

And it was a weird feeling, all that energy. Not hot, but not cool either, it entered and exited my body like a wave of water that flows over a swimmer—except internally instead of externally. And it was invigorating, which made me wonder if my system was siphoning off a tiny bit of that energy for itself.

Now, Arddhu and the Morrigan chanted the spell in a low voice. The hairs on the back of my neck rose and goosebumps broke out on my skin. I didn't recognize the language—it wasn't Old Irish Gaelic or anything the prior Keepers knew—but probably something else that was much older. Every syllable seemed to contain power and magick.

The air became heavy, as if pressurized. The energy stream glowed brighter and cast the chamber in deep green hue.

The Morrigan broke off, and I assumed she'd finished her part of the spell. Arddhu's voice continued but shook a bit, and my heart skipped a beat. He couldn't be tiring already. Gods, I hoped this was going to work. We hadn't exactly come up with a backup plan.

He paused his chanting to take a long, deep breath, and when he continued his voice was steady and firm again.

Then... *there*, in the darkness, I saw a tiny point of light.

It was working.

The point expanded, but ever so slowly. Much too slowly. At this rate, we'd be here for hours.

Unless...

What if I joined in the effort of pulling energy from Earth? Could I do that at the same time as maintaining the continuous flow from the others, without any detrimental effect?

There was only one way to find out, and hope nothing went wrong in the process.

Drawing energy from the hard-packed dirt floor at my feet, I amplified it and added it to the stream I fed to Arddhu. Now, the flow turned bright green and lit up the entire chamber like a neon sign.

Shit. We'd be even more noticeable to anyone who happened to pass by outside.

But at least it was helping: the portal to Tír na nÓg opened twice as fast now, and the chamber was almost as bright as day with its white light—although with an otherworldly green tinge from the energy stream.

And the best news of all: I felt no adverse reaction.

This was way too easy, and I didn't want to think about what that actually meant.

After several more minutes of chanting and channeling energy, the portal widened to the physical limits of the chamber.

With a loud pop that made my ears buzz, the seal finally ruptured. A super-bright flash of light blinded me, and it seemed as if someone had sucked all the air out of the chamber. Blinking rapidly to clear my vision, I gasped for breath and struggled to maintain the energy flows while hoping this wouldn't kill me.

A moment later, I could breathe again, and I took huge gulping breaths to ease the pain in my lungs. The pressurized feeling from earlier was gone now, and I realized I could also see Arddhu against the white light emanating from the portal. According to the plan, now he'd use the energy I sent him to keep the portal open for as long as possible.

I blinked and squinted, trying to see more clearly, as a figure appeared in all that whiteness. It stepped through, hesitated, then moved aside.

Now I had a good view: a tall man, slender, and dressed in a strange shimmery fabric that seemed to be all the colors of the rainbow at the same time. He seemed noble and majestic. His unbound hair fell past his shoulders in a soft curtain that shone like pale gold, and his intense blue eyes met mine briefly before moving on.

No pointy ears, though, so that part of mythology was a lie.

"Welcome home, Brother." The Morrigan spoke softly in Old Irish Gaelic, which of course I understood because of that weird magick thing.

"'Tis true, then?" The man's voice was deep and rich, with a musical quality that was simply ethereal. "We are free of the banishment?"

"Yes," Arddhu replied. "But you must bring everyone through quickly. I do not know how much time we have until we are discovered."

He didn't mention we also didn't know how long we could keep the portal open.

The man nodded once and quickly disappeared back into the light.

"That was Midir," Kevin murmured helpfully to me. "The son of Dagda."

Huh. So why did the Morrigan call him *brother*? Were they related? I glanced at her, but the sheen in her eyes made me decide not to ask right now. I'd never seen her cry, and it made me a bit uncomfortable, although it shouldn't have.

After all, strong people cried, too.

Then I got distracted.

The portal flickered—that was the only way to describe it. A quick blink of dimness that was there and gone.

But there was another. And a third.

"I need more." Arddhu spoke over his shoulder, and the glisten of sweat on his face was reflected in the light. He seemed to be struggling, and this wasn't good. Not one bit.

"I'm giving all I can," Athena said. Her voice sounded strained from effort.

Others murmured the same.

Dammit. We couldn't fail now. Not when we were so close.

Maybe there was one more entity to ask.

"*Anu, can you help?*"

"*Yes, Deirdre. I will also draw energy from Earth.*"

"*Oh thank you.*"

"*Much love, Deirdre.*"

Immediately, I felt her energy flow join the others. I amplified it and sent it to Arddhu.

A moment later, he said, "Good. Now, just a bit more, please."

There was only one thing left to do. Gritting my teeth, I focused on pulling even more energy from Earth. I felt a sharp twinge inside, not quite painful but almost as if something had cracked open.

The energy flow turned from bright green to pure, brilliant white.

Arddhu gasped as it reached him, but the portal visibly strengthened.

What was that blob of deep blue I saw in all that whiteness? Was that sky? Was I seeing Tír na nÓg?

"Excellent," Arddhu said.

Then: movement from the portal. A particularly large male emerged. His clothing also shimmered strangely, as if all colors the colors of the ocean— and yet no color at all—had been woven into the fabric.

"Manannán," Arddhu said with urgency in his voice. "You must cast the *féth fíada* immediately. We risk discovery at any moment."

After a slight hesitation, the man nodded and brushed past me to exit the chamber.

"What's that feth thing?" I asked Kevin.

"The Cloak of Concealment."

That didn't tell me much. Maybe it was like a big invisibility spell over the whole monument.

But now a steady stream of magnificent and proud people emerged from the portal, all clothed in that strange shimmery fabric that defied description.

The Tuatha were coming through.

They came slowly at first, gazing around in wonder, then faster as they hurried past us, down the passage, and outside into the cool night.

The men were beautiful, the women stunning. Many had skin so pale it was almost translucent, hair so pale it was almost white, and light-hued eyes of blue, lavender, gray, or the faintest green. They were so graceful they seemed to float across the chamber instead of mere walking. Many wore circlets of gold or silver on their brows and bracelets on their arms; some were plain while others were richly adorned with glittering jewels. Some had elaborate belts around their waists or hips, but I didn't notice any weapons.

I stopped trying to count them after a while, and still they poured from the portal. Then I realized something strange. Maybe hundreds had come through, but I hadn't seen a single child. At least, not any beings who were significantly shorter than the rest. Maybe they were freakishly tall even as children.

And, thank the gods, they didn't seem to be filled with rage, as I'd feared.

A grunt from somewhere behind me, then a dull thud, and the energy flowing to me dropped.

"It's Ares, he's collapsed." That was Athena, her voice ragged and weak.

Shit.

"We will take over." That was a different voice, rich and smooth with that odd underlying musical quality. For some strange reason it made me think of a gorgeous summer day, lying on lush emerald grass under a brilliant azure sky with birds singing in the trees.

The energy flow increased tenfold. After my initial surprise, I recovered quickly and it was easy to continue to amplify it and send it to Arddhu.

But then he staggered, and my heart leapt into my throat. We couldn't lose him now.

Immediately, another Tuatha was there, impossibly tall with a broad chest and wide shoulders yet slim waist and hips. Again, the cloth of his tunic and trousers shimmered in a kaleidoscope of color. The wide belt around his waist looked like it was made of solid gold. His hair was silvery-white and fell down his back, and his full beard was neatly trimmed. I shivered when he turned his ice-blue eyes to me. His gaze dropped to study my prosthesis for a moment before returning to mine. "Send it to me instead."

It was a seamless transition of power. I caught a flicker of surprise and respect in his gaze before he curtly nodded and turned toward the portal. I swallowed as my nerves jangled; what could make a Tuatha react like that?

Arddhu nearly collapsed onto the low flat stone near the wall. His head dropped to his chest as he rested and began to heal.

Why hadn't *I* collapsed? Why wasn't *I* feeling any negative effects from the massive flow of energy moving through me?

This wasn't normal. Why should Arddhu—and Ares and the others—be exhausted but not me?

What was happening to me?

I forced myself to breathe slowly and evenly to calm down.

As still more Tuatha poured from the portal, the energy flow to me increased again and again. I could only assume some of them took over for our exhausted allies. The stream of energy was now so intense it was hard to see, and it hurt my eyes.

Yet somehow, I still wasn't the least bit tired.

Kevin stepped close, and his look of concern confused me. "Uh, are you okay?"

"Never better." It wasn't an exaggeration. I actually *did* feel fantastic. "I could do this for days."

At that, Arddhu's head came up and he and Kevin shared a glance.

"Why? What's wrong?" I asked.

"Nothing." His eyes said otherwise.

"Bullshit." I put iron in my voice. "Tell me."

But it was Arddhu who replied, with a note of wonder in his voice. "You have become lit from within."

Huh?

I glanced down and blinked in amazement.

The armored suit did nothing to diminish the bright glow of my body underneath. The white light, almost as bright as the energy flow itself, burst through the fabric's millions of tiny holes and illuminated everything around me like sunlight.

What the...

But no, I couldn't worry about this now. It'd just have to wait.

"Later," I said. "I've got a job to finish."

Kevin's frown remained as he sat down next to Arddhu. They both watched me, but I did my best to ignore them.

Time passed.

The stream of Tuatha continued.

And continued.

And continued.

Finally, Midir came through. "That is everyone," he said, with an unmistakable note of triumph in his voice.

The Tuatha who'd taken over for Arddhu nodded. As he turned away from the portal, he altered the direction of the energy flow down into the earth. With no more energy to keep it open, the portal closed with a soft pop.

To me, he said, "Continue sending energy to me for now." To the others, he said, "Everyone, cease drawing energy." A moment later, after the streams to me stopped, he directed me to send the excess into the earth, and I complied.

With the flow of energy gone, I'd expected the chamber to dim, but it was still bright as day.

Glancing around, I couldn't find the source for the light. But I did see everyone staring at me with their odd pale-hued eyes. The allies, sitting along the wall, also stared.

Then I remembered, and I looked down.

I still glowed. The light came from me.

Awe-struck, I studied my left hand, at how the light made my veins and bones clearly visible beneath the skin.

"*An Dagda*, where do you wish to go from here?" That was Arddhu. He sounded like he'd recovered and was almost like his normal self again.

But then his words sank in.

In Irish, *An Dagda* meant *The Dagda*.

Which meant... the Tuatha male who'd taken over for Arddhu was Dagda? The head of the entire Tuatha?

Forgetting about my fascinating luminescence for the moment, I stared at him in wonder and remembered the respect I'd seen in his eyes when he'd taken over for Arddhu.

Thankfully, he didn't notice my scrutiny; he'd turned toward Arddhu. "Where is She? The one who betrayed us?"

"She has Her own realm and cannot abide this one for longer than a moment or two. She is not here."

"Then we will stay here."

Arddhu shook his head. "You have been away for too long, my friend. Much has changed. This world is no longer suitable for your kind."

Dagda sighed. "What do you propose, then?"

The glow from my body had slowly faded as they spoke. As my eyes adjusted to the normal dim chamber lighting, their faces became shadowy and vague.

"Can you create a safe haven?" Arddhu asked.

"Yes." Dagda hesitated. "But we have much to discuss."

"We will convene a council as soon as your people are safe," Arddhu assured him.

"Very well."

Dagda left the chamber, and Arddhu took my elbow with Kevin on his heels.

"We must leave this place. Now."

The allies had already filed out. The three of us exited, walking single-file down the long passageway to the fresh yet frosty air.

Under the brilliant star-filled night sky, thousands of fae covered the grounds as far as I could see. They seemed subdued; for such a large crowd, there was barely a murmur from them. Maybe the Cloak of Concealment muted the crowd noise?

In contrast, the crickets chirped loud and clear from the nearby fields.

The Morrigan drifted among the Tuatha, greeting many with warm affection. Dagda and a chosen few stood together some distance away, deep in discussion.

"I'm glad to see you're back to normal," Kevin murmured.

I laughed softly. "As normal as I can be, I guess."

"My people." Dagda's voice carried easily without seeming loud or even raised. "We are free, but we are not safe here. I have made a new home for us, and it is waiting." He turned to the male who'd been first—and last—to emerge from the portal. The one who Kevin had told me was Dagda's son. "Midir, open a portal and lead our people through while I council with Arddhu and his allies." Midir nodded, and Dagda gathered two others to him.

The Morrigan took her leave of the Tuatha and joined us.

As Dagda and his companions approached our group, Midir opened a portal and the Tuatha began moving through to their new home.

Arddhu nodded at Dagda. "I will open a portal to our meeting place. It is safe there."

For once, I kept my mouth shut. This was definitely *not* the time to point out maybe it wasn't so safe after all.

CHAPTER TWENTY-FOUR

I NSIDE THE VIP tent, I watched as Dagda's highly intelligent eyes took in the plush furnishings, and wondered what he thought of it all. In this lighting and up close, I could see details of his appearance better, and his eyes were definitely not normal.

For one thing, instead of a single pupil, each eye had a cluster of dozens of tiny black dots. And the ice-blue irises were surrounded by a dark blue outer ring. The power in their depths was amazing.

When he met my gaze with those strange eyes, it was unnerving. It took all my willpower to maintain eye contact, especially after a shiver of unease crept up my spine.

Our allies, although they'd come back to Arizona with us, went directly to the main house to rest and recover from the mission.

Except for the Morrigan, who was attending this council with drooping eyelids and barely-suppressed yawns.

I remembered only a little of what I'd read in the book Zara had brought me from Cromm's library last year. The Dagda, known as the Irish All-Father, was loosely compared to Odin, the All-Father of the Norse pantheon. His name was roughly translated from Old Irish into modern English as *The Good God*. He was said to have great magick and was the personification of strength, wisdom, and masculinity.

Curious, though: he didn't wear a crown or any other symbol of being the ruler of his people. Although I'd seen other Tuatha wearing various jeweled and plain headpieces, I had no idea if they were just fashion accessories or meant something more.

Before we sat in the comfortable lounge area, he introduced his two companions.

Ogma was unique among the Tuatha I'd seen so far; unlike the others, who were extraordinarily tall and slender, he was slightly shorter with wide shoulders and a broad chest. He was darker than the others, too. His complexion was slightly swarthy, and his brown eyes were normal-looking. His hair was dark and close-cropped, and his beard was well-trimmed. And instead of the color-changing shimmering cloth, he wore finely tooled leather armor, which clearly distinguished him as a warrior.

Somehow, he reminded me of Tyr.

Lugh, of course, was widely known in Irish mythology, and I remembered he'd been the one to banish Cromm from Ireland centuries ago. He looked young—too young to be one of the most powerful Tuatha in existence and supposedly the master of all arts. His long hair was the shade of ripe wheat in the late summer sun, his eyes were warm honey, and his smile was sincere and friendly. His tunic was shimmering yellow gold.

With all that, I couldn't help but think of him as a golden boy, which wasn't exactly flattering.

When Arddhu introduced me to the three Tuatha, I tried not to fidget under their intense scrutiny.

Finally, Dagda spoke. "You wield more power than any Keeper I have ever known. How is this possible?"

I had no idea how to reply to that.

"There are a number of reasons for this," Arddhu smoothly replied. "Which we will discuss at a later time."

Lugh eyed my prothesis with interest. "What is wrong with your hand?"

I glanced at Arddhu before responding, because I really didn't want to get into the whole story of Cromm and my captivity last year. Not yet, anyway.

But he had no such reservations. "For a time, Deirdre was held prisoner by Cromm Crúaich. He attempted to claim the Sphere by removing her limb but was not successful. She regained the Sphere and acquired a specialized replacement for her amputated limb."

Wow. What a brilliantly succinct explanation. I couldn't have said it better.

Ogma and Lugh shared a look.

"Just like Nuada," Lugh said.

"Except hers is not silver," Ogma countered.

I remembered reading about Nuada of the Silver Hand, who'd been a famous Tuatha king centuries ago. His silver hand was eventually replaced by a flesh-and-blood one.

"Exactly," Arddhu smiled. "It is made of a modern material unlike anything we old ones understand."

"Cromm, you say?" Lugh frowned. "I got rid of him a long time ago."

"You did," I said. "But he found a way to come back, so we just got rid of him again. For good this time."

Lugh's eyes bored into mine, and he seemed about to ask for more information but Dagda interrupted.

"And what of *him*?" Dagda's lip curled as he glowered at Kevin. "Bricriu has always betrayed all that is good and right. Why is he here?"

"He is no longer the trickster you once knew," Arddhu calmly replied. "He is known as Kevin now, and has done naught but good works. He aided our mission to rescue Deirdre from Cromm and has been at our side ever since, fighting against Cromm and our enemies, and protecting Deirdre."

"*Kevin*, eh?" Ogma's eyes narrowed with disdain. "A leopard may change its name but it cannot change its spots."

Poor Kevin. His cheeks reddened and his jaw clenched, but he remained silent amid the rising animosity.

Ugh. Enough of this shit. I was losing my patience with immortals, in general.

"It's true," I said, with only a bit of annoyance. "I wouldn't even be here right now if it hadn't been for him." Three sets of eyes scrutinized me, and I glared at each of them in turn. "And frankly, neither would you," I said to Lugh. To Ogma, I said, "Or you." I held my gaze with Dagda for a bit longer and added, "None of you or your people would be here if it hadn't been for Kevin."

The Morrigan cleared her throat delicately. "Brother, trust us. Trust *me*. Kevin is an ally."

"Regardless," Arddhu said with mild irritation. "We must now discuss other important matters."

"But first, may I offer some refreshment?" I'd fetched the last two bottles of the Polish mead from the bar when we'd first arrived, and now I poured a small glass for everyone.

Arddhu smiled, and I knew he was pleased. This mead was his favorite, and he appreciated it even more than Irish whiskey.

"This is a very special mead," he said. "I do believe you will enjoy it as much as I do."

That stuff always helped to break the ice. I'd need to get a few more bottles soon. Hell, maybe I should clean out the liquor store of their entire stock, since it was so popular among immortals.

After a cautious sip, Dagda and Lugh emptied their glasses and politely asked for more. Their attitudes were noticeably more pleasant.

Ogma, however, had merely sniffed at his glass and set it untasted on the table. "Would you happen to have any fermented mare's milk?" he asked, hopefully.

I blinked at him. "Um, no, I'm sorry."

"Ogma, don't be such a pain in the ass," the Morrigan teased. "Just try it. If you don't like it, I'm sure the Keeper has something else you might like. Irish whiskey, for example."

He made a face at her but picked up the glass again and took a tiny sip. Then another. "It does taste better than it smells," he admitted, but didn't toss it back in one swallow like the others had.

"Now," Dagda began, settling back in his seat more comfortably. "You must tell us all that has happened during our banishment."

Yikes. That would take *days*. Maybe even weeks.

Arddhu smiled faintly. "There is far too much to tell and too little time to tell it."

"How much can possibly happen in only a hundred years," Lugh scoffed.

Trust immortals to use the word *only* together with the words *a hundred years*.

Arddhu shook his head. "My friends, it has been much longer. Over two thousand years."

According to legend, time passed differently in the Otherworld realms; they must've thought their banishment was much more recent.

But that also meant Kevin was much older than I'd thought, since they knew of him before their banishment. I glanced at him, but he was watching Dagda.

"Impossible," said Ogma.

"*What?*" said Lugh.

But Dagda was silent, thinking. Finally, he nodded. "I see. Yes, that is a substantial amount of time. We agree to wait for a later opportunity to catch up. For now, let us discuss only what is relevant." He sipped his mead before continuing. "Where is the foul usurper who banished us? I would take my vengeance for what has been done to my people."

I frowned at his use of the word *usurper*. What exactly had the Bitch usurped? Or maybe he'd chosen that expression because She'd removed the Tuatha from power and basically taken over. But the conversation continued before I could ask for clarification.

Arddhu raised a hand in caution. "We have a problem. She is connected to Earth. If we harm Her, we harm Earth. There are billions of humans here now, plus other immortals and life forms who would also be harmed. We cannot terminate Her." He paused before continuing. "However, we had hoped that perhaps we, with your knowledge, could devise a plan together. Something that would stop Her from harming any of us, but not harm Earth or its inhabitants."

Dagda's grin was feral. "Then we will banish Her to Tír na nÓg."

"So She'd still be a part of Earth, but unable to do any harm to Earth," Kevin mused. "Brilliant."

Dagda nodded once, exquisitely regal for such a simple gesture. "Just so."

"But wouldn't She still have Her power?" I asked. "Couldn't She eventually find a way out?"

"Technically, yes," Lugh replied, then turned to Dagda. "We must strip Her power prior to the banishment."

Dagda nodded again, and his features brightened, as if inspired. "Of course." His gaze met mine. "You hold the power of Anu, our Elder Mother. Anu can certainly take the power from the foul usurper."

What? I glanced at Arddhu and Kevin, but they seemed just as confused as I was.

There was someone else I could ask.

"Anu? Is this true? You can take the Bit—uh, Goddess' power?"

She hesitated before replying. *"I am incorporeal and unable to act independently as long as you and I are together. However, with your assistance, yes. We can remove Her power."*

At Arddhu's questioning look, I explained. "Anu just confirmed that she—*we*—can remove the Goddess's power."

All three of the Tuatha gasped.

"What? What is it?" I stared at each of them.

The Dagda's wide eyes shifted from my bracelet to my gaze with new respect. "If Elder Mother has spoken to you thus, you are blessed indeed."

Why were they so surprised? Maybe they just didn't know much about Keepers. Maybe they didn't know Anu and I spoke often.

Whatever.

We had the beginnings of a plan, and that's all that mattered for now.

Curled up in my bed, I alternated between staring at nothing and rubbing my temples with my eyes closed.

I'd begged off from the rest of the discussion with the Tuatha because of another nasty headache. I'd taken aspirin, changed into comfy clothes, and now I snuggled my pillow. Even though it was long past midnight, I wasn't at all sleepy, just in a lot of pain.

I didn't understand why I kept getting these headaches.

They were the only thing marring my perfect health.

Some time ago, I'd realized that after I became the Keeper, I didn't get sick anymore. Just a couple of months ago, Anthony had caught a bad cold, and the bug had spread through the security team like wildfire. Nat had been down for almost a whole week.

Even a couple of the allies' servants had been sick lately.

But not me. Not even a sniffle.

I'd stopped getting colds, the flu, or stomach bugs. Hell, I hadn't even had headaches anymore until lately.

But now they'd become something else. Not quite migraine-level, but close. And the aspirin didn't seem to work anymore. I'd tried using my healing energy, but that didn't help either.

Maybe it was time to try something else. Or maybe I should get it checked out by a doctor. There was a well-known medical center not far from The Hacienda. They'd probably love to diagnose my problem. Then again, they'd probably order an MRI or other imaging, which would probably show something I wouldn't be able to explain logically. Like something magick-related.

So maybe that wasn't such a good idea.

"Dee? May I come in?" Kevin's voice was muffled.

"Yeah."

The door opened and closed. He sat on the edge of my bed. "How's the headache?"

"Bad. The aspirin's not working this time."

"We—Arddhu and I—are concerned."

"Yeah. Me too," I admitted.

"You've told us before they started around Samhain."

"Yeah."

"So we think Arddhu's wild forest magick is causing them. It's probably running through your system and altering it. First it was the bottomless reservoir. Now these headaches. So I have to ask: have you noticed anything else?"

I rubbed my forehead. Trying to think made the pain even worse.

Gently, Kevin brushed aside my fingers and laid his palm on my forehead. Within seconds, the pain was bearable. Still there, but not nearly as bad.

"Oh, thank you," I breathed.

But I didn't understand; why did his healing work, but not mine?

"You're welcome. I hate seeing you in pain."

I sat up and leaned against the headboard.

"The only thing I can think of that's new was how I glowed at Newgrange."

"That just could've been the after effects of so much energy passing through your body, though." He shook his head. "We all need to keep a closer eye on this. And *you* need to let us know if you notice anything different, no matter how small or insignificant you think it is."

I could do that. "Okay."

He hesitated. "There's other news. Nayenezgani has been found. I should say: his *body* has been found."

"Shit." I'd really been hoping it'd been something simple, like he'd gone back to his realm or world for an item he'd forgotten to bring with him and got delayed coming back.

"Yeah. Thing is, he wasn't torn apart like Tyr, but I heard it was still pretty bad."

"Same calling card?"

"Yeah."

"Where? Where was he found?"

He gestured vaguely *out there*. "At the far corner of the property. He was covered in dirt and branches. And it looked like... uh, part of him was eaten."

How strange. I hadn't seen any coyotes or other wildlife since I'd moved here, and I'd thought my wards were keeping them out.

Obviously not.

My jaw clenched as my anger spiked. That fucking *Bitch* had some nerve. Taking out *my* allies. On *my* turf.

Then my head throbbed again, and I forced myself to calm down and release my anger.

"There's one more thing," Kevin continued. "Ogma left to bring some of the Tuatha back here. Arddhu's called a meeting to plan our next steps. And yes, you're required to attend."

"Okay."

"But you should have something to eat before then."

Naturally, my stomach chose that particular moment to grumble loudly. "Fine."

I threw the covers back and got out of bed, and he pulled me close.

"I just wanted to let you know, before everything gets crazy and I don't get the chance, that I think you're gorgeous." He kissed my forehead. "And fucking sexy." Another kiss, this time on my nose. "And brilliant." Now a kiss on my left cheek. "And brave." Right cheek. "And strong." Chin. "I've never known anyone like you, and you've made me a better man." Only now did he kiss my lips, soft and gentle and sweet.

Afterward, he leaned his forehead against mine, eyes closed, and I could've sworn my headache eased up even more.

"Thank you," I whispered.

But just as he turned toward the door, I caught a flicker of sadness in his eyes.

"Hey, wait." I pulled him back.

That flicker I'd seen was gone now. Or maybe, it was just carefully hidden.

"Is there anything about this whole thing you're not telling me? Anything I should know about the Tuatha, for example?"

His eyes studied me for a moment, then he shook his head. "Not that I can think of. Maybe the Morrigan will have more info. She's one of them, you know."

"*What?*"

"Truth."

Yeah, I *knew* it was the truth, my witchy-sense had told me that.

"But she doesn't even look like them." Then again, neither did Ogma.

He smiled. "Not all of them are blonde and blue-eyed. It just seems that way."

I cocked my head. "Are you ever going to tell me about the two of you?"

"What do you mean?" He seemed suddenly guarded.

"I mean, were you two together once? As a couple?"

He hesitated, then nodded. "Yeah. We were almost handfasted at one point. But that was centuries ago."

Huh. "Any chance of getting back together?"

No hesitation this time. "Nope. We've both moved on."

Truth.

He lifted my hand to his lips. "Besides. As far as I'm concerned, there's no one who could hold a candle to you."

316

"Aww. How sweet."

One eyebrow shot up and his arm curled around my waist, crushing me against him so I could feel every inch of his body.

"Oh, it's not *sweet*, love. You're fucking hot. And you drive me insane with it."

Now, his mouth was demanding. Insistent. And definitely anything but sweet.

My body filled with need, but we just didn't have time for this right now, even though he could turn an hour into only a few minutes. I didn't need the distraction, especially before an important meeting.

His voice was breathless as he released me. "I know we don't have time for more. I just wanted to make sure you know how much you're wanted."

There he went again, reading my mind.

"I've never doubted that. Not once." And it'd been quite obvious, too, when I'd been pressed against him.

"Good." His eyes glittered like fire. "Now let's get out of here before I lose control and make us forget the meeting."

CHAPTER TWENTY–FIVE

OUR CONFERENCE TABLE had been repaired and would be fully occupied again with the addition of the Tuatha. The security team was posted outside, and Anthony had enlisted a full staff of servers for the food tables and bar. Somehow, Brianna had managed to prepare a mountain of exquisite culinary delights in almost no time at all.

Maybe that was her magick. Or maybe she had a pocket universe, too, where she kept food ready to go at any time. At this point, I wouldn't be at all surprised.

Ogma had brought back three additional Tuatha, and there were a few moments of formal introductions before we were all seated.

Angus Og, the God of Love in mythology, was youthful, handsome, and charming, and was another of the Dagda's sons. His reddish-gold hair reminded me a bit of a fox, and his baby blue eyes with their ring of indigo twinkled as he pressed his soft lips against my hand in greeting.

I'd glimpsed the other two at Newgrange: Dagda's son Midir, and Manannán, Lord of the Sea. With the introductions, however, I got a better look at each.

Midir didn't much resemble Dagda, except for his seeming agelessness—but that could be said about any of the Tuatha. His hair was brilliant yellow gold, his eyes were deep blue, and he would've been considered quite handsome if not for the hawkish nose that somehow seemed out of place on such an otherwise human-looking face. He was the only one here who wore a modest gold circlet, and his deep purple tunic was also different from the others. I figured Dagda must've told him about me because Midir openly studied me with intense interest, although at least he was respectful about it and didn't leer.

The full name of the Lord of the Sea, Manannán mac Lir, meant *Son of the Sea* in Irish. And even if I hadn't known that, I would've guessed he had a strong connection to water. His silvery blue hair waved gently as if it were seaweed under water, which was incredibly distracting, and his eyes seemed at first green, then blue, as if they couldn't decide which to be. His tunic was the myriad and changing shades of the ocean itself: stormy gray, aqua, turquoise, and deep green, as iridescent and shimmery as sunlight reflecting on water.

It was still unsettling to see the Tuatha's cluster of tiny black points instead of normal pupils, but at least it was getting easier for me to maintain eye contact.

With the Dagda and Lugh, that made six Tuatha in attendance.

Actually, seven, counting the Morrigan.

I still struggled thinking of her as one of them, though. Sure, she was pale-skinned, but with her dark eyes and raven-black hair, I'd never in a million years guessed she was Tuatha.

After the introductions, I took a moment to note where everyone chose to sit. Of course, I was flanked by Arddhu and Kevin, as usual. But Athena, Ares, and the rest of the allies took over the right half of the table while the Tuatha sat together on the left.

The Morrigan sat across from me.

Interesting choice. Did she see herself as a mediator, separating the two groups? Or was it simply because she belonged in both groups and didn't want to appear as if choosing one side over the other?

Another thing I noticed: the allies were subdued, and I wasn't sure if it was due to the presence of the Tuatha or something else. They'd rested after coming back from Newgrange, but maybe it'd take a couple more days to fully recover.

Arddhu stood, interrupting my thoughts.

"Be welcome allies, and please join me in welcoming the Aes Sídhe in their triumphant return to Earth." Most of the allies nodded to the Tuatha respectfully. "We now must recognize the sacrifice of Nayenezgani, whose remains were discovered earlier today."

Anger from Ares. Athena and Kali leaned close and murmured. Reshep, always calm and thoughtful, simply frowned.

The Morrigan clenched her jaw but remained silent.

"Now," Arddhu continued. "Of course, we must plan our next mission. It is a vital one, to be sure. Put simply, we must strip the Goddess of Her power and confine Her. This will prevent Her from harming any of us, other deities, and all the inhabitants of Earth."

A low murmur then, which broke off as he sat and nodded to me.

Taking my cue, I stood. "During a preliminary discussion earlier, we learned that Dagda believes Anu can take the Goddess's power." I raised my left arm, and the VIP tent lighting reflected on my shiny bracelet for a moment. I lowered my arm again and continued. "I consulted with Anu and she confirmed she can indeed remove the Goddess's power, with my help. Afterward, Dagda will cast a spell to banish the Goddess from Earth."

The muttering started as soon as I sat down.

Ares asked the first question. "Where will She be banished to?"

Dagda chose to answer. "She will spend eternity where She trapped my people: Tír na nÓg."

The Morrigan delicately cleared her throat, drawing everyone's attention. "So how do we get close enough to Her to do this? She can't come here for any real length of time, so if we go to Her... well. We could all die. It's a risk."

"That is why we are gathered here, in this meeting," Arddhu patiently replied. "We need ideas."

As my thoughts wandered, turning over a germ of an idea, my ears tuned out everyone else.

If we could get the Bitch here—even for only the few minutes She could tolerate—we could spring a trap. Manannán could cast his Cloak of Concealment on everyone, Anu and I could do... whatever it was we had to do to strip Her of Her power, then Dagda could banish Her to Tír na nÓg.

But what would bring Her here? The last few times I'd tried to call Her, She hadn't responded.

Then again, I'd asked nicely. What if I *wasn't* nice? What if I poked the bear, so-to-speak?

What if I told Her I'd fucked Her Consort—and not just once, but many times? Sure, She'd dumped him, but She was still a woman. She was bound to be jealous.

"Dee?" Kevin interrupted my thoughts. "You okay?"

"Hmm?" I met his eyes. "Oh. Yeah, I'm okay. It's just... I think I might have an idea."

The room immediately hushed as all attendees turned to me.

Shit.

I'd thought I'd just be telling Kevin, not everyone.

"Tell us," Arddhu prompted.

Oh no. What if they all laughed? What if it was a stupid idea?

Swallowing that fear, I focused only on Arddhu. "What do you think would happen if I told Her about you and me? In the crudest, *cruelest* way possible?"

His brows rose, but then his eyes narrowed in thought.

"Doesn't She already know?" Athena asked.

Arddhu shook his head. "She is not omniscient. She most likely does not."

"Holy shit," Kevin breathed. "She'd go berserk."

I grinned at him. "That's what I was thinking."

The Morrigan leaned forward, her arms resting on the table and her eyes bright with excitement. "She'd have to confront you."

I nodded. "Yes. She'd come here, to Earth. And then—"

"Then," Dagda interrupted, "we raise the *Claíomh Solais* to hold Her here while the Keeper and Anu strip Her power, and I perform the banishing spell."

"What's that?" I asked. "That cloh something."

"The Sword of Light," Lugh replied. "No one can escape from its magick when it is drawn. Not even the Goddess."

"There's just one problem with that," the Morrigan said. "No one knows where the *Claíomh Solais* is. And I don't think we'll have enough time to look for it."

Manannán spoke. "That is true. However, we have other tools at our disposal. Fand—" he glanced at me and quickly explained "—my wife, can craft a special net that will ensnare anyone, even the Goddess. She learned the technique from Indra, an old friend from the Ancient East."

"How much time would she need to create such a net?" Arddhu asked.

"I will ask, but perhaps only a few days."

"That'd work," I said. "We'd really only need a few days to finalize a plan."

Manannán nodded. "Then I will return home as soon as we are finished here, and conscript whatever assistance and materials she requires."

"I have a question for the Keeper." Athena's eyes were fixed on me. "How *exactly* do you plan on stripping Her power?"

Shit. I'd been afraid someone would ask that.

"I, uh, don't know that yet. We—Anu and I—didn't get into specifics."

"Perhaps you should," she snapped.

My cheeks heated. Maybe she wasn't intentionally being bitchy, but it sure as hell felt that way.

Or maybe I was just being overly defensive again.

"That is the very next thing on my to-do list," I assured her.

She nodded, somewhat calmer. "Then we should have a final meeting before the mission. Just to make sure we're all clear on what needs to happen, by who, and when."

No wonder she was our expert on strategy.

"We most certainly will," Arddhu assured her.

Reshep cleared his throat. "I, too, may have a few tools that may help. I will check my inventory and report my findings."

Kevin nodded. "The more we can throw at Her, the better."

With no further questions, we adjourned, and everyone helped themselves to the food and drink. Except, of course, for Manannán; he immediately left to talk to Fand about the magickal net.

Arddhu put a plate in front of me, but I stared at it in dismay. I wasn't really hungry. Come to think of it, I didn't feel hungry most of the time now, and I wondered if that was one of the changes I was supposed to be tracking and informing Kevin and Arddhu about. I picked at my food and got a stern look from both Brianna and Arddhu.

Ugh. Sometimes these two were worse than Mike ever was.

And then, I felt guilty for even thinking that. Which only added to my frustration.

"Fine," I snapped. "I'm eating, see?" I quickly shoveled three heaping forkfuls of potatoes into my mouth. Frowning, Arddhu and Brianna got up and left.

Kevin's hand rested on my leg. "Easy, love."

After I swallowed my food, I pushed my plate away. "Sorry. I'm just not hungry."

"You haven't been hungry a lot lately," he pointed out. "When did that start? Samhain?"

"Yeah."

"Hmm." He finished his food and took our plates back to the table, stopping to talk to Arddhu on his way back.

The Morrigan sat next to me. "How are you holding up?"

"So-so."

She smiled sympathetically. "If you want, I can help you work on the power stripping thing."

"Huh? How?"

She shrugged. "You can practice on me."

I stared at her. "You can't be serious. I don't even know what I'm doing. What if I can't restore it afterward?"

She laughed. "I'm not worried. Just ask Anu."

Oh.

But before I could, Anu replied.

"*Yes, Deirdre, I can restore the Morrigan's power.*"

I relayed her response to the Morrigan, who smiled.

"We'll start in the morning, then. After breakfast." She stood, but waited for my nod of acknowledgement before turning to leave.

"*Raise your left hand with your palm facing the Morrigan,*" Anu instructed.

We were in the training room. Kevin stood guard outside the door to prevent any unnecessary interruptions or distractions. He'd also placed a shielding spell around the room to keep any power or magick from leaking past us, since we weren't exactly sure of this whole thing.

Well, *I* wasn't, anyway.

Belatedly, I wondered if maybe we should've gone outside for this instead.

But I followed Anu's directions and tried to keep my hand from shaking.

Hell yes, I was nervous. But the Morrigan stood facing me with a little smile, and didn't seem at all concerned, so I did my best to hide my fears.

"Now, maintain that position while I send a tendril of magick to the Morrigan. It will pull her power away. Tell her to prepare herself now."

"Anu says, get ready."

She nodded, but the little smile stayed in place.

Anu's magick flowed through me and exited my hand in a visible wisp of gray smoke. When it hit the Morrigan, she gasped and her eyes widened. Her normally pale skin turned paper white, and she grimaced.

Anu drew the Morrigan's power from her—it was so strong, I actually felt the pull—and it drifted in the air between us in a luminous purple cloud.

The Morrigan crumpled to the padded floor with her eyes closed.

Without thinking, I reached for her with my prosthesis.

"Deirdre, stop." Anu's voice was a strong command. *"She will be fine."*

I obeyed, but my stomach lurched seeing the Morrigan so helpless.

"Now I will send it back to her."

"She's sending it back," I relayed.

The Morrigan nodded, but her eyes remained closed and her face was still pinched.

The purple vapor flowed toward the Morrigan and disappeared into her body. She gasped again, but seemed to recover immediately.

"Wow." She rose to her feet. "That was... interesting."

"Are you okay?"

"Oh yeah, I'm fine." Her eyes sparkled. "But let me grab that chair over there before we do it again."

"Again?"

"Of course." Her gaze was stern. "You need a lot of practice. So you need to do it at least a few more times. We can't afford to make any mistakes."

I sighed, knowing she spoke the truth but not liking it, not one bit.

"I just don't like hurting you."

She smiled. "You're not hurting me."

"Right." I didn't hold back the sarcasm. "You always make that face when you're having fun."

Now she laughed. "It's not pain, exactly. It's just a weird sensation. Like someone's pulling a part of you out of your body, right through your skin."

Not sure I would classify that as just a *weird sensation*. More like creepy. Or horrible, maybe.

She'd moved the chair from the corner—where Mike always used to sit during my training sessions with Kurt so long ago—and now sat with a raised brow.

"Okay, fine," I huffed.

After a few more times, the whole process became smooth and easy. And the Morrigan didn't seem to be suffering any adverse effects, thankfully.

"*Very good, Deirdre,*" Anu said. "*We are ready.*"

But I sure as hell didn't feel ready.

We were gathered in the VIP tent, again, for our final meeting before the mission.

Anthony had informally named it the Santa Sortie. Privately, I called it OGIF: Operation Goddess is Fucked.

Fand had come through with making the magickal net, and had actually brought it in person, although she wasn't going on the mission with us.

She was beautiful and ethereal, tall and slender and graceful like the other Tuatha. Her aquamarine eyes were huge and wide-set, giving her a youthful and innocent appearance. Her unbound golden hair fell almost to the floor in a thick curtain, capped with a gold circlet of gems in every color of the ocean, from the deep blue of calm waters to the aqua of the Caribbean to the dark gray of stormy seas. Her gown, too, shimmered in a thousand colors of iridescent blue and green. In that respect, she and her husband were well-matched.

She'd handed Manannán a tiny square, and with a shake of his hand the net opened to roughly the size of a standard king blanket. It glittered like a thousand black diamonds had been sewn to an incredibly fine mesh fabric.

The net was passed around for everyone to admire, then they took their seats. Fand refolded it and placed it on the table in front of her.

I remained standing to call the meeting to order and review the plan. "We have assigned two crews: the banishment crew, which is Dagda and Arddhu, and is responsible for banishing the Bit—er, the Goddess—and the net crew, consisting of Reshep, Athena, Ares, and Kali. Their job is to throw the net on Her at the right time and make sure it stays on so She can't get away. Kevin will be there to port me to safety in case something goes wrong, and Lugh and the Morrigan will be there as backup.

"So first, I'll head to the site tomorrow morning—"

"Wait," Kevin interrupted. "Where's the site?"

"Not too far from here. There's a nice empty spot of land that'll give us enough room to maneuver."

"And doing it outside will maximize the effects of the atmosphere on Her," Arddhu added.

I nodded and continued. "Next, Manannán will cast the Cloak of Concealment on everyone but me. The banishment crew and the net crew will wait nearby for their cues. When She shows up, Anu and I will pull Her power. You should be able to see it in the sunlight; it'll look like smoke. As soon as it's out of Her, the net crew will throw the net to hold Her. Arddhu will open a portal to Newgrange and transport Her and the Dagda. In the central chamber, Arddhu will open the portal to Tír na nÓg, Dagda will remove the net and speak his banishment spell. After She's gone, Dagda will seal the portal, and they'll return here. And then, um, we'll celebrate."

There were a few chuckles around the table at my improvised ending, but Athena frowned.

"What is it?" I asked her. "Did I forget something?"

"Yes. What happens to Her power?"

I blinked. "Anu gets it."

Her gaze flicked around the table before settling on Dagda. "I suppose that was *your* idea." She barely contained her hostility.

"No," Arddhu calmly replied. "It was mine."

"Why?"

"Anu is not a threat. She is an ally." He was way more patient than I'd be.

"But she'd have the *power of the Goddess*." Her sharp eyes returned to me. "And the Keeper just happens to have sole possession of her."

I'd been about to object at her choice of words—no one *possessed* Anu—but Dagda had his own objection.

"What are you insinuating about our Elder Mother?" His voice was jagged ice.

"Wait a minute," Kevin interrupted again. "Why didn't you bring this up the other day, when we were coming up with all this? It's a little late to change plans now."

Athena pressed her point doggedly. "I'm just saying we should think very carefully about this. Maybe Anu should relinquish the power to someone else. Someone *corporeal*."

"Like who?" Kali countered. "You?"

Now Athena's cheeks reddened. "Well, why not? I have as much risk in this as any of you. Why shouldn't I have a reward?"

Kali snorted. "If the power of the Goddess is up for grabs, I'll add my name to the list. The *top* of the list."

Instant chaos ensued as multiple nasty arguments broke out over who was more worthy of the power of the Goddess.

But not everyone participated: the Morrigan frowned and studied those around her with alarm, Reshep sat in stunned silence, and Kevin and Arddhu shifted closer to me, as if to protect me.

What a fucking shitshow.

I'd just raised my arms to call for order when Anu flashed red, bright enough for me to see it reflected on everyone's faces, and her voice in my head was loud enough to make me wince.

"*Enough!*"

Unbelievably, there was immediate, complete silence. Almost as if they'd heard her.

Maybe they had.

They all stared at my bracelet, at Anu's angry red glow.

"*Tell them I will not keep the power. I will send it into Earth instead.*"

In a quiet voice, I relayed her words.

327

"And we're supposed to believe her?" Ares sneered.

Dagda reddened in rage and opened his mouth to speak, but I beat him to it.

"What is *wrong* with you? With *all of you*?" I glared at everyone who'd jumped into the fray.

"I suppose you want it for yourself." Kali raised her chin in defiance.

My anger spiked. "I can't believe you just said that. *Of course* I don't want it. No one in their *right mind* would want it. Do you have any idea what kind of responsibility comes with that power? *Do you?*"

My outburst had apparently shocked them into silence, because no one said a word.

But I wasn't done.

"You'd have to protect the entire planet and everyone and everything that lives on it. *Forever.* Do you have any idea how hard that is, when humans are constantly trying to kill each other? And everyone and everything else? Make no mistake: *that would be your job.* And if you failed, one of two things would happen: either everything would be destroyed—which means every single one of us, including you—or you, too, will end up being stripped of your power and banished. Because if this current situation has told us anything, it's that *we cannot tolerate anyone who won't do their job.*"

That last bit had come out too loud, but my fury was finally spent.

I took a couple of deep breaths while the room remained quiet.

"For fuck's sake, you guys." My voice cracked but was closer to a normal tone now. "Haven't you learned *anything* in your very long lives? I've only been a Keeper for a year and a half, but honestly sometimes I think I'm already light-years ahead of you in understanding this shit."

None of the troublemakers—not Athena, nor Ares, nor Kali—would meet my eyes. They kept their heads down in what I assumed was shame.

Arddhu gazed at me with warmth and something that looked a lot like pride.

Kevin looked like he wanted to kiss me—and probably more than that.

The Morrigan smiled at me, a lazy cat's smile that I couldn't quite interpret but didn't seem at all malicious.

Reshep sat immobile but his gaze held deep respect and a hint of something I couldn't identify.

Dagda, Lugh, Ogma, and Fand seemed mostly aloof, but cautiously watched me with their uncanny eyes, as if they weren't sure what I'd do next.

I sighed. "I don't know about anyone else, but I need a fucking drink now."

The early January sun was hot on my shoulders, but the morning air was chilly, and I was actually glad for the warmth of my armored suit. A cold front had come through during the night, and the expected high temperature was only in the mid-fifties—which was well below normal for the time of year. And it was partly cloudy for a change, with thin wisps of soft white brushed against the deep blue sky.

As I walked to the spot chosen for OGIF, I took a deep breath of the fresh air and tried to steady my nerves. I'd been too nervous to eat breakfast but had forced it down after a glare from Brianna. For this critical mission, I couldn't take the chance of needing that extra bit of energy and not having it. I had Arddhu, Kevin, Lugh, Dagda, and the Morrigan with me, but Manannán and the net crew planned to meet us there.

Arddhu and Kevin had insisted I wear my armored suit as a precaution, and they'd also recommended that I be armed. So I wore Ire in her baldric at my side and my knife sheathed on my thigh, but I'd stored my firearm and holster some time ago. I never really used it except for the occasional target practice. Looking back on it all now, it'd been a stupid idea anyway, since bullets were pretty much useless against immortals and I'd never really been threatened by humans like Mike had thought I'd be.

If that was even what he'd really thought. After all, so much of what he'd told me had been lies, it wouldn't surprise me if that'd been one, too.

And Arddhu had insisted I wear his enchanted ring. "She may attempt to use a spell or other working," he'd said. "This will prevent such from harming you."

I'd frowned. "But can you spare the energy to power it?"

He'd smiled. "For this, of course."

If all went well, I wouldn't be wearing it for long.

As we reached the site, I overheard Lugh murmur to Dagda, "The Keeper's lands are quite beautiful, in a stark and desolate way."

I bit my lip to keep from laughing.

My *lands*, indeed.

The mood among the allies was cautiously optimistic; the squabbles that'd broken out at the meeting the day before seemed to be forgotten— for now, at least. It'd probably be a good idea to keep an eye on Athena, Ares, and Kali, though, since they'd openly shown their ambition and lust for power.

Everyone got into position several yards from me, and Manannán cast his Cloak of Concealment. Now they were only a faint shimmer.

I took another deep breath and willed myself to be calm. If this went wrong... well. No sense thinking of that now. But the Bitch might sense my nerves and get suspicious, so I took the extra moment now to steady myself.

"*Ready, Anu?*"

"*Yes, Deirdre. I am ready.*"

I pitched my summons in the rudest tone possible. "*Hey, Goddess, You there?*"

No response. As I'd expected.

I let my anger build. I'd need it.

"*You know, I'm getting real tired of this shit. You never even showed up at Samhain. Left me hanging and didn't do Your job.*"

Still nothing.

"*Not that I care about myself that much. No, what really pisses me off is how You treat my friends like shit. Especially Arddhu.*"

There it was: a slight stirring in my mind. My heart rate sped up.

"*By the way, You should probably know he's much more than just my friend now. I guess I could say Your Consort likes me better.*"

Ooh—I definitely felt *that*: a sharp spike of shock and anger.

Time to poke the bear.

"*And You know what? He told me I'm a much better fuck than You ever were.*"

Her rage filled my mind, and I winced at the intense pain. She replied, "*You dare speak to Me thus!*"

330

Thankfully, Anu and I had figured this would happen. She surrounded my mind with a shield, and the pain abruptly stopped. As we'd discussed, that shield would protect me from any type of mental harm the Bitch tried to inflict on me.

"*Yeah, I dare. What're You gonna do about it?*"

"*I can destroy you, Keeper. Is that what you want?*" Her voice was so cold, my mouth went dry with dread. This was such a dangerous game, even with the protections I had in place.

"*If You want to destroy me, You're gonna have to do it to my face. Because I've got a shield and You can't hurt me like this.*"

She howled in fury, but I felt absolutely nothing.

"*Like I said, You can't hurt me,*" I taunted.

Now, the air in front of me rippled, and there She was.

In all Her bitter glory.

Her pale blue gown swirled angrily around Her body as if it were alive, and Her long dark hair lifted and whipped around Her head as if in a strong wind. Her normally blue eyes were almost white with fury, and Her normally pleasant face was now a mask of hatred.

If looks could kill, I'd just be a greasy spot in the dirt of the desert.

"How dare you," She spat. "After all I've done for you. You ungrateful *bitch*."

A flashback threatened, but I shook it off. I narrowed my eyes and cocked my head in an extremely disrespectful attitude. "That's funny. Mike said almost those exact words to me once. What a coincidence. *Not*."

She stared at me calculatingly, then Her gaze dropped to my bracelet. "So the little twit just had to get involved. Couldn't leave well enough alone. She's the one shielding you, isn't she?"

"Yep." I smirked. "Guess she likes me better, too."

She began chanting what I assumed was a spell, but I had no idea what it was supposed to do because Arddhu's enchanted ring activated and pulsed bright red, and I didn't feel a thing.

She broke off chanting, and the confused shock on Her face was almost comical. Her gaze swept over me then locked on to the ring with frightening intensity.

"What is that?" Her voice was almost a whisper as She stared at it. "Why does it have Arddhu's energy?"

"Why do you think?" I retorted. "I already told You: he likes me better."

"*Arddhu!*" She screamed in rage, and it was a terrible sound, like a banshee's screech at point-blank range. "Show yourself and answer to this betrayal. I demand it." She glanced around wildly, and I realized this moment of distraction was a perfect opportunity.

I raised my left hand and Anu's magick rushed toward Her. The Goddess's power flowed from Her and coalesced into a pale blue cloud that hung suspended between us.

"What—" Her eyes widened and she gasped, but it was too late. She collapsed to the ground, where her now-lifeless gown trailed in the dirt and her hair hung limp.

Now, she was just an ordinary woman. A sad, pathetic, jealous one, but totally normal.

Immediately, Fand's net descended and covered her completely.

"What is this?" she asked in a tiny, shaking voice. The power and terror of it was gone, and now she sounded like a pitiful old crone. She struggled to free herself, but the net caught on her fingers and tightened. She seemed to realize her folly and stopped fighting to stare at me with hatred.

The Cloak of Concealment lifted. The group who'd acted against her approached and stood over her. She glared at each of the net crew, attempting to intimidate, but she couldn't pull it off. She just looked pathetic.

Things happened quickly then.

Arddhu opened the portal to Newgrange, and Manannán and Dagda lifted her easily. She shrieked and sobbed as they carried her through the portal. Her loud cries abruptly cut off, and the quiet, peaceful morning returned.

Kevin was immediately at my side with a grin. "Great job. It went off without a hitch."

I had just enough time to notice Athena and Kali staring at the blue cloud of power with undisguised lust, then it suddenly rushed toward me.

"No—" was all I got out.

Oh shit.

Searing pain tore through me and stopped all thought. It felt as if every cell in my body exploded.

I fell to my knees in the dirt and clenched my jaw to keep from screaming.

Anu's voice then, soft and soothing. *"Deirdre, I am sorry I cannot shield you from this pain. It will be over soon."*

Fuck, this hurt. Way more than when Cromm had cut off half my arm.

More than the excruciating pain of when I'd first become the Keeper, too.

Raised voices. Arguing. It could've been Ares and Athena but with the roaring in my ears, I couldn't be sure or hear what was said.

"Breathe, Dee." That was the Morrigan, close by, but at the same time sounding distant. "Tell us what to do."

"I... can't," I ground out. "I... don't... know."

Someone's hand on my back, then quickly gone. "Gods, she's burning up." That was Kevin's voice.

Behind my tightly closed eyelids, bright spots formed and burst, like fireworks. Or a hundred suns.

"What is happening?" Arddhu's voice, loud and frantic with near panic.

Had they come back already? Or had this gone on for that long? I had no sense of time.

"We're not sure," Kevin said. "This started right after you left."

Now the roaring in my ears became a high-pitched whine that drowned out all other sound, and the pain stopped as quickly as it'd started.

I could breathe again.

Anu's voice: *"Deirdre, watch closely."*

A vision unfolded in my mind, just like when I'd first become the Keeper.

... a volatile yet beautiful young planet with water and atmosphere but not much else. The World Seed hurtled through space, crashed onto the planet's surface, and sparked life. As millennia passed, the atmosphere stabilized, oceans formed, plants abounded, and lifeforms of all types developed.

Including humanoid.

The remnants of the World Seed evolved into a Sphere of pure power, and waited.

Time passed.

One day, a certain woman discovered the Sphere and understood its vulnerability. She became its first Keeper. In return for her protection, the Sphere bestowed upon her long life, healing, and other gifts.

After thousands of years, the Sphere bestowed another special gift on the Keeper: she was transformed into the Goddess and charged with protecting Earth and its life.

All *its* life.

She blessed the flora and fauna, and they flourished.

She blessed humans, watched over them, and kept them safe. She gave them many gifts, such as health, peace, and prosperity. She was loved in return; loved and honored, worshiped and revered.

She chose Consorts and had many sons, who also helped humans to evolve and grow. Some of those sons still live: Dagda. Manannán. Lugh. Ogma.

Her name was Danu, and She was the first Goddess.

Danu also had many daughters.

One of them was Ida, who was highly intelligent and beautiful beyond compare. Many of the gods as well as humans lusted after her.

Unlike her mother, Ida was greedy and self-centered. Not content with her own power and magick, she wanted Danu's power, and more. She wanted it **all**.

One day she cast a spell, a spell no one had ever thought of before or had reason to use.

The spell transferred Danu's power to Ida, leaving Danu helpless and easy to depose. However, unwilling to take the final step and murder her own mother, Ida banished Danu from this universe.

And so Ida became the Goddess.

At first, She continued doing many of the good works that Danu had done: helping humans, blessing Earth, and saving lives. But as time passed, She became increasingly stingy with her power and magick, and She no longer blessed humans or Earth.

Humans turned away from worshiping Her. Other gods took advantage of the imbalance and rose in popularity. Those gods taught humans to worship greed, power, and wealth; to subjugate women and others whom they deemed less than men. Those same gods later helped humans to build machines that poisoned the air, spoiled the waters, and required the fuel of entire forests.

Earth suffered. Flora and fauna suffered. Humans suffered.

But Ida didn't care. She was too concerned with Herself and Her own power.

Over time, the Tuatha had also risen in power on Earth, and Ida believed they plotted and schemed against Her. They wielded too much power for Her comfort, and could harm Her like no others could.

When the Dagda named one of his daughters Danu in honor of the Elder Mother, Ida became enraged and banished the Tuatha to Tír na nÓg. She sealed the portal with a special spell so they could never return to Earth

Eventually, humans' unchecked behavior forced the planet out of ecological balance. As a consequence, Ida could no longer tolerate the poisons in the atmosphere for longer than a few moments. She became weak and vulnerable on Earth, so She retreated to Her own world: a place apart yet still of Earth.

She pulled away from Earth's concerns even further, choosing instead to focus on Her own world. She established its lush gardens, lavishly furnished a beautiful palace, and enjoyed the pleasures of mating with Her Consort. Her visits to Earth dwindled to an occasional event in small villages such as Finn's Cove, where She bestowed Her presence on a human avatar during rituals attended by the tiny groups of Her remaining faithful worshipers.

Unbeknownst to Ida, during those long centuries outside of this universe, Danu evolved into something else and became Anu.

She never stopped searching for a way to return.

And then one day, she found it: a tiny crack in space and time that led back to this universe. Eagerly, she traveled through it, but came to Earth in a far different form than when she'd left it.

Anu was now a Sphere.

The same Sphere that had guided many Keepers over the centuries.

The same Sphere that another woman, Deirdre Connor, first held in her hands just over a year ago...

The vision abruptly ended.

My eyes snapped open and focused on my hands spread on the dirt in front of me.

And I stared in wonder.

My prosthesis was gone. In its place was flesh. Skin and bone and muscle.

I'd been made whole, just like Nuada of the Silver Hand.

And my body glowed with a soft white light, reflected in the thousands of specks of mica in the desert dust.

Raising my head, I took in my surroundings.

Colors were brighter in my new, enhanced vision, and my sense of smell was overpowered by the creosote, mesquite, and other scents of the desert I'd only had a whiff of previously. I blinked and squinted in the blinding sunlight, then something shifted and my vision was somewhat normal—except for how everything was exquisitely clear and sharp. Even the foothills hundreds of yards away were in astounding detail.

My gaze zoomed in on sudden movement and easily tracked a desert pocket mouse as it scurried under the scrub vegetation on the mountainside.

"Dee?" Kevin's voice brought me back, but it sounded different, somehow; more complex than just the average human voice. Now, I could hear deep tones, mid tones, and high tones.

My enhanced ears processed other sounds differently, too. Birdsong was a cacophony that overwhelmed me, and the buzz of insects was deafening. Again, something shifted, and the noise returned to a normal level.

I glanced up.

Arddhu, Kevin, and the Morrigan stood a few feet away, cautiously studying me. A bit further away, the Tuatha and Reshep watched with wide eyes.

Athena, Ares, and Kali were nowhere in sight.

Before I talked to anyone, I had a question for someone else.

"*Anu, what happened?*"

"*I gave You a gift.*"

"*No. You were supposed to send the power into Earth. I didn't want this.*"

"*That is exactly why I gave it to You. Deirdre, You alone are deserving of the power of the Goddess.*"

For only the second time in my life, I fainted.

CHAPTER TWENTY-SIX

I WOKE IN my bed with the covers snugly tucked around me. My armored suit was gone, replaced with comfy clothes. I didn't remember changing them—hell, I didn't even remember going to bed—but I did recall snippets of some really wild dreams.

Dreams of Spheres—yes, more than one—and Goddesses and Earth.

I shook my head and stretched languidly, then sat up.

And caught sight of my hand and stared.

My flesh-and-blood right hand.

It glowed with a soft white light.

I wiggled my fingers and the room tilted crazily.

And then I noticed my whole body glowed with that strange light.

Now everything came back in a rush: Anu had given me the power of the Goddess. And a vision of the past, which explained how Ida had become the Goddess.

And who Anu really was.

"Anu, you owe me an explanation," I said, not exactly nicely. *"You could've told me the truth about Ida a long time ago. And about what she did to you."*

"For what purpose?" She replied. *"There was nothing You could have done to change it."*

"If I'd known Ida wasn't the benevolent Goddess I'd been led to believe, I..." What? What exactly would I have done?

Dammit. Anu had a point.

"*Deirdre, You would not be here now if You had known. She would have removed You and found another to execute her plan.*"

Yeah. I had no doubt she was right about that.

"*Okay,*" I conceded. "*I know you're right. It just feels... a bit like I was betrayed. By almost everyone.*"

"*I am truly sorry.*" She sent a warm sensation through me, and it was like being hugged internally. "*I meant only to spare You any distress.*"

Closing my eyes, I relaxed into an almost blissful state, filled with her gift of comfort. Eventually it dissipated, but the feeling of contentment and love remained with me.

And then every cell in my body tingled, and I felt alive like I'd never felt before.

My sense of touch was so acute it was almost painful for the soft sheets to lay against my skin. And the smells... the open bottle of shampoo in my shower could've been right under my nose, its scent was so strong.

My sensitive ears picked up snatches of a conversation from somewhere in the house.

"... when She wakes up ..." I recognized Arddhu's voice.

"... wait, She's awake now ..." And that was Kevin. But how did he know I was awake? For that matter, how did he always seem to know what I was thinking?

Within seconds, there was a soft knock on my bedroom door. "Deirdre?" Arddhu's voice was muffled. "May we come in?"

"Sure." I threw aside the covers and sat on the edge of my bed.

Arddhu entered with Kevin only a step behind. While Kevin quietly closed the door, Arddhu approached and dropped to one knee with his head bowed.

"My Lady," he said.

This was awkward and made me incredibly uncomfortable.

"No." I shook my head. "Please don't."

The confusion was plain on his face. "But—"

"*No.*" I winced; it'd come out sharper than I'd intended. "Look, this is all just a big mistake."

Kevin, though, had no problems approaching me informally, as if nothing had changed. He sat next to me. "Dee, it can't be undone."

I patted the bed on my other side. "Arddhu, please sit. You're making me feel weird kneeling like that."

He rose and after a slight hesitation, he sat.

I turned to Kevin. "What do you mean, it can't be undone? Of course it can. I'll just ask Anu to remove the power and send it into Earth, like we originally planned."

"*No, Deirdre, I will not.*" Anu's voice was firm.

Goddammit.

"Great," I muttered. "She says she won't, and I don't think I can make her."

"It's probably too late, anyway." Kevin gently took my hand in his. "It's already changed You, altered every cell of Your body. That's permanent."

I clearly heard the reverence and emphasis he'd put on the capital Y, and it irritated me. I pulled my hand away, got up, and paced. "I can't accept that. After all, the Goddess—um, *Ida*—had the power removed and she's just fine."

"We don't know that," Kevin said. "Not for sure. And even though she's in Tír na nÓg, where she'll never age or get sick, we just don't know what'll happen to her with her power and magick gone."

Shit. He had a point.

"My Lady," Arddhu interjected. "Simply accept that You are our Goddess now. You will be exceptional. Anu chose well."

My irritation spiked. I stopped pacing and faced them. "Stop doing that. Both of you. You're using a capital Y when you address me, and I don't like it."

They shared a look.

"But it's proper," Kevin said. "It's protocol for deity."

Deity? *I was not deity.*

"I don't care what it is. Fuck that shit. I'm just Dee. No special treatment. No *My Lady* bullshit. *Please.*" Ugh. I'd practically begged, and that irritated me even more.

They shared another look, and Arddhu's frown deepened.

Then I realized this had to be all new for Arddhu, and felt ashamed. After all, he'd been Ida's Consort for thousands of years, and I couldn't expect him to adopt such drastic changes in mere seconds. He'd need some time to adjust, and I'd have to be patient.

Kevin's mouth quirked as he jerked his head sideways to indicate Arddhu. "You're giving him conniptions, y'know."

"I know. And I'm sorry about that." I stepped closer to Arddhu and placed my hands on his shoulders. "Look, I understand this informality is all probably very different from what you're used to. But please understand. I'm having a hard enough time adjusting to all the changes happening in my body. I've got enhanced senses that are overwhelming me, and I'll have to get used to having a right hand again. I just don't need any more stress right now. I really need both of you to just... treat me the same way you did yesterday."

"Yesterday?" Arddhu echoed. "You have slept for three days."

My jaw dropped. *Three days?* "That's impossible."

"Well, you've been through a lot," Kevin explained. "You needed time to recover."

"Three days." Irritation completely gone now, I sat on the bed again. "So what've I missed?"

"Not much," Kevin replied. "Ares, Athena, and Kali are gone. They took off right after they saw what happened."

A scrap of a memory returned. "I think I heard them arguing."

"Yeah, we—Reshep, the Morrigan, and me—we had to grab them and hold them back from trying to get to you. We didn't think they wanted to help."

"They're probably not our allies anymore." For some reason, the thought made me a bit sad. Not so much about Ares and Athena, honestly, but I'd really liked and respected Kali.

"No, they are surely enemies now," Arddhu confirmed. "Most likely, they are already gathering others to oppose us."

Shit.

It seemed there was just one thing after another.

Sometimes, I really regretted the day Mike rang my doorbell and I answered.

But that was a lifetime ago.

"The shit just never ends, does it?" I sighed. "It's always something."

"That is life," Arddhu said.

Great. Now he was Mr. Philosopher.

Then I felt bad for even thinking snarky.

I sighed again. "So what do we do first? Go after them, or get back on track with the original plan? If we wait, they'll gather an army and then we'll have to fight three thousand instead of only three."

"True," Kevin replied. "But do you really want to be known as the Goddess who, as Her first action, eliminated three other deities who'd been known allies?"

Ouch. That was basically what despots did: as soon as they rose to power, they took out their rivals. And anyone who didn't bend the knee.

"Good point," I conceded. "Maybe if we let them go—for now—I can win them over. Prove to them that Anu's trust in me isn't misplaced."

"Wise decision, My La—uh, *Dee*," Arddhu said.

"We should probably have a meeting," Kevin suggested.

I nodded. "Reassure the rest of the allies, and get us back on track."

"Okay," Kevin said. "I'll let Anthony know." He paused, then looked away and continued with noticeably less confidence. "Unless you'd rather have someone else do it."

"No, I absolutely want you to. Thank you."

He smiled and seemed relieved, but it'd made me think. I was in unknown territory here and didn't want to offend anyone. Kevin had mentioned something about protocol, but I was clueless. I didn't have a flood of memories from prior Goddesses to help me understand what I was supposed to do. Not like when I'd become the Keeper.

"I have a big question," I said. "Since I'm apparently stuck being the Goddess, what are my duties? Am I like a president now? Do I need a cabinet of advisers? Or do I do everything myself?"

Arddhu chuckled. "It is up to You. You may do as much or as little as You wish. You may choose a council, or not. But if I may be so bold, I would strongly recommend You appoint council members."

I nodded. "In that case, I think I need to take stock of who's still with me. Er, *us*. I mean, is Anthony going to stay? Since I don't think I'm technically the Keeper anymore, I probably don't need an Assistant. But he's been really good at the logistics of the meetings and managing the security team, and I'd rather keep him around. Oh—that's another question: do I still need the security team? I'm thinking yes."

Arddhu nodded. "We must discuss these matters. That is, if You wish us—Kevin and I—to be Your advisers."

"Of course I want you to be my advisers. I'd be lost without you two." I put my arms around them. "Seriously, guys. You've always been there for me. Stood by me. I treasure your friendship, your counsel, and your wisdom. Nothing will change that." Then I turned to Arddhu and filled my voice with command. "But I mean it. Stop with the capital Y thing. That's an order."

I'd never seen Arddhu's face flush as red as it did now. But when he replied, his voice was strong and firm, and unhesitant. "Yes, Dee."

My stomach rumbled loudly, and for once, I was actually hungry. Apparently, becoming a Goddess had brought my appetite back.

"Okay. We'll figure out the rest soon enough. Right now, I'm starving. Who's up for lunch? Or dinner? Or whatever meal it's time for?"

"So, in other words, you're telling me someday I won't have to eat anymore?" I eyed the food on my plate before meeting Arddhu's gaze. "But *you* do." Then Kevin's. "*Both* of you."

We sat at the kitchen island, where Brianna had whipped up a fantastic meal for us. I'd automatically picked up my fork with my left hand, then stared at my restored right hand for a moment before placing the fork in it.

And strangely enough, it was as if I'd never lost it or had a prosthesis; I had absolutely no trouble using my restored hand.

Thank the gods I wouldn't have to go through training yet again.

"Yes, I still consume food." Arddhu replied. "But it is because I enjoy the flavors and textures, not because I require it for nourishment. It does not affect me either way. You, however, have not completed your transformation and are still somewhat human. Therefore, you will require nourishment for the foreseeable future."

Kevin added, "I'm young enough that I still need to eat, more often than not."

It was bizarre to think of being two thousand years old as *young*.

"And water? Will I still need to drink water, too?"

Arddhu shook his head. "No, when the time comes that you no longer require sustenance, you will also not require hydration. Your physical form will be beyond such things."

While I mulled this over, I ate a few more bites. The depth of flavors and textures now were incredible, all due to my newly-enhanced taste buds.

Someday, when I was fully non-human, if I became like Arddhu and consuming food didn't hurt me, I'd probably continue doing it. As long as I still had an appetite, that was. And I'd probably still drink booze, even if it didn't affect me; I truly loved the taste of a good beer or wine.

Or my special Polish mead.

But probably not whiskey. Unless it didn't burn my throat anymore, now that I was the Goddess. Maybe I'd enjoy it more than I used to.

Between bites, I resumed my questions. "So how long will it take? Until I'm fully transformed, I mean."

"It is difficult to say. You are unlike me. Or the Morrigan or Kevin." Arddhu looked thoughtful. "Perhaps a hundred sun cycles, perhaps a thousand."

My fork slipped from my fingers and clattered on my plate.

Oh yeah. I'd forgotten about that part. The part where I would live forever. It'd been one thing to know I'd live for hundreds of years, like Maggie had, as the Keeper; it was a whole different thing to expect to live for *thousands*—maybe even *millions*—of years as the Goddess.

"The thing is," Kevin started, "we really don't know for sure. Remember Arddhu's wild forest magick?" After I nodded, he continued. "It started changing you even *before* you got the power of the Goddess. So this is completely different."

He had a point.

"Can I still die? I mean, if someone cuts off my head, I'll die, right?"

"No one survives a beheading," Kevin confirmed. "Not even a deity. So yeah, you can still die. But so would Earth and everything on it."

Back to that being tethered to this planet thing.

343

But according to the vision I'd had, Danu hadn't been tethered. If she had, wouldn't Earth have crumbled to dust when Ida had banished Danu? What had changed?

Maybe Arddhu knew. "Danu was Earth's Goddess when Ida stole her power and banished her to another universe. So why wasn't Earth and this universe—or dimension—destroyed?"

Arddhu frowned and shared a look with Kevin before shaking his head. "I do not know."

Kevin said, "That's a damn good question."

"*Deirdre, it was I.*" Anu chose to answer. "*When Ida performed her spell, I had only a moment before it took effect. I used that moment to create the tether, then sent a message to the Dagda informing him. He, in turn, surely informed others such as Arddhu.*"

Oh. That's right, Dagda was one of her sons.

I relayed her answer to the guys, and we sat lost in our own thoughts for a few moments.

So I'd need to make sure I was never hurt or killed. To protect Earth.

At least I could still live here, though. Unlike Ida.

Hmm. Maybe I'd better ask about that to be sure.

I pushed my empty plate away. "I can still live here, right? Or do I have to move somewhere else?"

Arddhu replied. "You may live anywhere you wish. Ida's world, including her palace and gardens, are now yours. You may choose to live there if you wish. Or, you may choose to build a new palace somewhere else. Perhaps even Eire."

A palace, huh?

I glanced around at my beautiful home, then gazed through the window-wall to my backyard paradise. "Okay, I'll check her old place out, but I think I'd rather stay here for now. Or maybe I'll split my time between Ard na Mara and here."

Arddhu nodded, but Kevin frowned.

"What?"

"You might think about getting another place. Somewhere remote, like an island in the Mediterranean, for peace and quiet. And safety. Especially as word gets out, people see you, and you become popular."

He had a point. I could just imagine the chaos if, for example, Zeus lived down the street and everyone knew about it.

But I didn't think that was a decision I needed to make immediately. I planned on staying out of the public eye as much as possible.

"I'll worry about that later. There's too much other stuff to think about right now."

Brianna swept in and whisked our empty plates away. I thanked her for the delicious meal and we moved to the living room to continue our discussion.

"You're gonna have a lot of decisions to make," Kevin said. Suddenly he seemed nervous; he ran a hand through his hair, just like Mike used to do.

Mike.

I hadn't thought about him in a while. What would he have thought about this turn of events? Would he even have guessed it possible?

Maybe I could've saved him…

No. I shook off that line of thought and brought myself back to the here and now.

"What's first on the list?" I asked, brightly.

"Well, who do you want on your council?"

"You two, for starters. The Morrigan. Maybe Anthony, if he's interested. And Reshep, for sure." I paused, thinking. "Does everyone get a title? I mean, do I have to create a position for each of you?"

Arddhu shook his head. "Not necessarily, but it is customary. Traditional. For example, perhaps Reshep would be your Chief of Military Operations. Anthony might be Chief Administrator. And so on."

"Okay." As soon as I'd thought of a notepad and pen, they appeared in my hands. It hadn't been teleportation, though; more like materialization, since it was a brand-new notepad and unfamiliar pen. I stared at the items for a moment, shrugged, and began taking notes. "Then Brianna would be Executive Chef, and Randy would be Chief of Security." I met Kevin's gaze. "What do you want to be?"

He shared a meaningful glance with Arddhu and immediately, the tension in the room became thick. "That's up to you," he smoothly replied.

Arddhu refused to meet my gaze, and I wondered what the hell was going on.

A whisper in my mind then: *oh please pick me for Consort.*

It'd been Kevin's voice, but I'd never had a mental communication link with him. At least not that I knew of.

Maybe this was another physical change due to being the Goddess?

Then another voice, this time Arddhu's: *perhaps She will choose me.*

Oh. Now I understood.

Neither of them was actively communicating with me. These were their internal thoughts, which I could now hear.

Well, this was awkward.

Did they know?

Kevin seemed calm and cool as his steady gaze remained on me, but Arddhu continued to stare at the wall behind me, unable to meet my eyes.

No, I didn't think either of them knew I could hear them.

But it needed to stop. I didn't want to know their innermost thoughts. It just wasn't right.

Using knowledge I didn't know I had, I visualized a shield between me and each of them, and slid it down over my mind. Their voices cut off in mid-sentence.

First problem solved.

As to which of them would be my Consort... shit. I couldn't make that decision right now. It was too soon. And there were other priorities. *Many* other priorities.

In frustration, I rubbed my forehead, and immediately Arddhu's concern spiked enough that it cascaded over me like a wave.

"What's wrong?" I asked.

"Are you still having your headaches?"

Oh. *That.*

"No. I guess it's just a habit now."

His relief was just as obvious, as another wave cascaded over me.

I sighed. "Guys, I know you're probably expecting me to name a Consort, but I'm just not ready yet. I need more time."

Thankfully, the tension eased instantly.

"Understood," Arddhu said. With a quick glance at Kevin, he added, "We shall await your decision when you are ready."

"Thanks." I flashed a quick smile. "So what's next on the to-do list?"

"As we've already discussed, we'll need to schedule the alliance—uh, make that *council*—meeting," Kevin said. "It should be as soon as possible."

Arddhu nodded. "Yes, to reassure the others they are valued and no changes are planned."

"But I *do* have changes planned," I argued. "Like naming the council members. And replacing the ones we lost." Not just the ones who'd been murdered by Ida or lost in the battle with Cromm, but also the three who were now our—or *my*—enemies.

"Well, we have the Tuatha now," Kevin said. "They'll probably jump at the chance to help restore order here on Earth."

"Indeed they would," Arddhu nodded. "However, before we ask that of them, I suggest we inform them of all that has occurred in their long absence."

That'd be a helluva job.

"Maybe it'd just be easier to show them how to use a computer," I mused.

Kevin's eyes lit up. "I was just thinking the same thing. We could get a few laptops, set them up in the VIP tent, and I could show them how to access and search the internet."

I couldn't help but smile at his enthusiasm. "I guess that means you're Chief Technology Adviser. Just don't show them where to find all the porn," I teased. Kevin winked and grinned.

Next, I met Arddhu's gaze. "Could you help get them up to date on everything they should know?" He nodded. "Then you're Chief Information Advisor, for now. When you two think they're ready, we'll ask some of them to join the council. Maybe Dagda, Lugh, and Ogma for starters. Oh, and probably Manannán, too."

"That's a good list," Kevin said.

"How long do you think you'll need to get them all up to speed? Just your best guess is fine."

Kevin thought for a moment. "Maybe a month. I'll have a better idea once they're actually in the room and I see how fast they catch on."

"Okay, so that would put the council meeting just after Imbolc." Oh shit. *Imbolc.* "Which reminds me: I have to go to Finn's Cove this year for the festival."

Arddhu's somber gaze caught and held mine. "As the Goddess, you must do more than simply attend festivals from now on. At Imbolc, you must bless the fields and the livestock, and the fisher-folk. For *everyone*, not just the people of Finn's Cove."

Shocked into silence, I stared at him. He was absolutely correct. My responsibility now was to the *entire* Earth, not just whoever still honored the Goddess.

The weight of that responsibility began to feel massive.

In the silence, the whispers that had tickled the edges of my consciousness for the last half-hour or so had grown persistent and impossible to ignore.

Then I realized: they were the voices of faithful followers.

They were *prayers.*

"Guys, you'll have to excuse me." Distracted, I stood. "I have some prayers to answer."

Arddhu's smile was warm and full of pride. "Of course. We will talk again later."

Oh Goddess, hear my plea. My need is great, send money to me...

Dear Goddess, please help. My son is so sick and I'm afraid...

My Lady, please give me strength. I just lost my job and I don't know what to do...

Is there anyone out there? Can anyone hear me? Please help me...

The warmth of the sun was on my shoulders and the desert air was cool and fresh as I sat on a patio chair with my eyes closed and listened to the prayers, one by one.

It was an interesting process. As I attuned to each, the person appeared in my vision—no matter where in the world they were—almost as if I were in their presence. Except I didn't think they saw me.

It was strange. And a bit scary.

And having the actual power to *answer* those prayers?

Overwhelming.

I almost broke down at the mix of strong emotions that swelled within me for these people who begged for help.

For the broke college student in Ann Arbor, Michigan, I made some cash appear instantly on the sidewalk in front of him. Not too much, just enough so he could buy some food to tide him over until his next paycheck. I watched as he stopped and stared for a moment in disbelief, then tears came to his eyes after he picked up the money. His gratitude and sense of relief was so strong, I felt my own sting of tears.

The worried immigrant single mother sat on her son's bed in a darkened room in a small town outside Knoxville, Tennessee. He was only four years old, and his fever was burning him up from the inside. The medicine from the pediatrician wasn't working for some reason, and she had no money for an emergency room visit. She was panicking because the boy had lost consciousness, so I had to work quickly, before he slipped away. I sent my strongest healing energy to the boy, and only a moment later, when he blinked and sat up with a tired smile, his mother hugged him tight against her with tears of joy streaming down her face and whispered prayers of gratitude.

With a shaky breath, I wiped my own tears and continued to the next prayer.

The older man on the island of Sicily was a talented traditional baker and had just been fired by the new owner, who planned on turning the old bakery into an American-style coffee bar. To him, I sent more than the strength he asked for. First, I sent a bit of money to get by, then a vision of how and where to get enough funds to start his own bakery business and make his long-time customers happy. His smile lit up his whole face, and made me grin in response.

Then there was the young woman in rural Texas who sat on her bathroom floor, hugging her knees and sobbing. She'd been through a lot in her thirteen years, and it wasn't going to get any better soon. She'd been beaten and raped by her stepfather several weeks earlier—just after her junior high school graduation party—and now she'd just learned she was pregnant. The home pregnancy test kit lay on the floor next to her, with an obvious positive result.

349

Her prayer? She wanted to die.

Even though she hadn't specifically prayed to the Goddess—to *me*—somehow I'd heard her prayer anyway. And then a strange thing happened: I had a flash of who she would become in the future—if she lived—and I just knew I had to do something.

For her, a drastic and immediate response was needed.

Without much conscious thought, somehow I found myself physically there with her, and she made an involuntary squeak as I appeared out of nowhere.

"No, Sarah." I closed the lid to the toilet and sat. "I can't answer your prayer. I can't let you die."

She stared at me, taking in my casual clothing with wide eyes.

I didn't blame her. Except for the soft glow coming from my body, I probably didn't look much like a Goddess.

"I have a better idea. Call the help line in Houston. They'll know just what to do."

Somehow I knew Houston was the big city that was only about an hour away, and they had people who would help her.

"What help line?" Her voice was just above a whisper.

Again, without consciously knowing what I was doing, I pulled a piece of paper from my pocket and handed it to her. "This one."

She took it, but her eyes never left mine.

"Promise me you'll call," I said.

Her head cocked. "But who are You?"

I heard the reverence in her voice, and smiled. "Just call me Dee."

Now she frowned. "Okay, but *what* are You?"

My smile slipped a bit. "Um... I'm..." This was awkward. Then inspiration hit. "My job is to take care of Earth and everyone on it. Today's my first day, actually."

"So you're an angel?" Her eyes lit up with hope.

"Sort of." Hell, she could think of me as an angel if she wanted to. "Sure."

Now she glanced at the slip of paper. "And these people will help me?"

"Yes." I didn't know how I knew, I just *knew*.

"Okay." She met my eyes again. "I'll call them right now. Before my mom gets home from work." She sniffled and wiped her nose with the back of her hand.

I smiled again. "Thank you, Sarah." I got up and turned toward the door, then realized I didn't know how to leave, since I didn't really know how I got here.

It was a long way to Scottsdale.

Without warning, a pulling sensation began inside me and I knew I had only a few seconds. I turned back to Sarah. "One more thing: take the intern job." The last thing I saw was her puzzled look, then I was back on my patio at The Hacienda.

I took a moment to settle myself, took a deep breath, then answered more prayers.

There were many more, from the smallest village in remote Africa to the trendy studio apartment in New York City and everywhere in between.

And I answered each and every one, until at last the voices were silent.

The flood of strong emotions hit suddenly and almost overwhelmed me. I let the tears run free as I stared at the foothills and tried to make sense of it all.

For most of my adult life, I'd donated often to the local homeless shelters, animal rescue organizations, and veteran groups. But somehow I'd always felt like it wasn't enough, that I could've—and should've—done more to help others.

But now, this prayer thing was something else completely, and it went way beyond simply helping an impersonal organization with an annual monetary donation or canned food drive.

This was direct, immediate, and personal.

Especially in the case of Sarah, which had been all three.

And it filled me with an exquisite sense of love. Plus something else I couldn't exactly identify. A sense of purpose, maybe. A feeling of *rightness* to it all.

Oh, I knew better than to think they were worshiping *me*. They had no clue who I was, or that I was a real, flesh-and-blood person.

Well, except for Sarah, who thought I was an angel.

No, they probably worshiped the generalized *idea* of the Goddess: a vague, formless female deity who existed somewhere *out there.* Just like I had, back before all this started. Back then, even though I'd known there were thousands of named goddesses in multiple pantheons, whenever I'd thought of the Goddess, I'd imagined a nameless, faceless and amorphous deity.

Ida had changed all that. But so had the Morrigan, Athena, and Kali.

It was all so surreal.

My gaze dropped, and I studied my new right hand. I still glowed, and just as in the chamber at Newgrange, I could see my veins, tendons, and bones through the skin. It was truly a wonder.

I'd spent so much time learning to use my left hand, then I'd spent an equal amount of time learning to use the prosthesis. And now I had a real right hand again, and for some strange reason I didn't need to learn how to use it. It was as if it'd never been severed at all. All because I'd absorbed the power of the Goddess.

This transformation thing was crazy shit. If it weren't actually happening to me, I'd never have believed it possible.

But this weird glowing thing was a bit embarrassing, and I wished it would stop. I felt like I belonged in an old science fiction movie. I was the normal woman who'd been bitten by a radioactive ant or something and had superpowers and glowed.

Or maybe here in the desert it'd be a radioactive scorpion.

Then again, I hadn't exactly been normal even before this Goddess thing, as Arddhu had pointed out at Samhain. Even when I'd only been the Keeper, I'd been something *more* than a normal human.

At least I still looked—and felt—mostly human. But for how long? And what would I transform *into*? Ida had seemed mostly human the two times I'd seen her in person, so would I stay basically the same as I was, or would I grow multiple arms like Kali?

One good thing: unlike Ida, at least I'd have no problem existing full-time here on Earth. The composition of the atmosphere was just fine for my survival, in fact it was all I knew.

I sure as hell didn't want to move to another realm permanently; that would totally suck.

Another thought occurred: unlike her, I wouldn't need an avatar to interact with humans. So when the time came to perform the rituals at Finn's Cove—or any place else that still followed the Old Ways—I could be myself.

Which made me wonder... how the hell was I supposed to be in two or more places at once? Arddhu had said I'd have to bless *all* the livestock on Imbolc. All over the world. How the hell was I supposed to do that?

If Santa Claus were real, I could sure use some of his advice right now.

"Ah, there you are." The Morrigan sauntered toward me. "Am I disturbing you?"

"Nope. I just finished answering prayers a little bit ago. For now, anyway. I'm sure there'll be more."

"Especially as the word gets out." She sat on the other patio chair and grinned. "So what do you think?"

"About what?"

"Prayers."

"Honestly?"

She nodded.

"It's pretty cool to help people."

One side of her mouth quirked. "Well, I'm sure your prayers are a whole lot different than the ones I get."

"Hmm. I bet." I could just imagine. Or maybe not. "Mine pretty much ask for money, healing, and good parking spots at shopping malls and grocery stores." For some reason, I didn't want to mention Sarah and her death wish.

She laughed. "Sounds about right. I don't have as many followers as I used to, but their numbers have actually started to rise in the past few years. More people are returning to the Old Ways." She paused to eye me thoughtfully for a moment. "And I suspect you'll help bring even more back to the fold when the word spreads that someone's actually answering prayers these days."

I snorted. "So cynical."

"When you've lived as long as I have and seen as much as I have, you can't be anything but cynical. Besides, it's not like the other gods are answering any. People have felt abandoned for a long, long time. It's not a recent thing."

I frowned. "Wait—you mean Zeus and the others aren't around anymore?"

She shook her head. "As far as I know, only Ares and Athena represent the Olympians now. There's one weird group that follows and worships them, so that's why they're still relevant. They're actually called The Siblings now." She snorted. "Everyone else seems to have faded into obscurity. Oh sure, they're still in the mythology books and in popular movies once in a while, but there haven't been any true believers in the Olympians for a very long time."

That was depressing. So gods just faded away into nonexistence when humans stopped believing in them? How sad. Would that happen to me?

"What about the Norse pantheon? Any of them still around?"

"That would've been a question for Tyr. But we can send a delegation to Asgard to find out for sure. We should probably send our condolences anyway."

Shit.

"I'd forgotten about that." My notepad and pen materialized in my hands and I made my notes. "And to the others, too. The Navajo, Japanese, Tibetans, and... uh, whichever people claimed Belatucadros."

"I see you're getting the hang of some things pretty quickly."

"Yeah. I got the idea of a pocket dimension from Kevin. It's so much easier than carrying or porting my stuff around."

She smiled. "He gave me the idea, too. A long time ago. It's where I keep my stuff." After a pause, she continued. "As far as other gods go, with the Tuatha back, maybe word will spread and they'll get back into the believer game. So-to-speak."

"So they had worshipers too?"

She nodded. "Oh yeah. These days though, humans think the Tuatha are *elves*." She shook her head in disgust.

Not too long ago, I'd thought the Tuatha had pointed ears, so I kept my mouth shut on that subject. "I'm hoping to add them to the council. Not all of them, of course. At least Dagda, Manannán, Lugh, and Ogma."

"Council?" She frowned.

Oh that's right, I hadn't told her yet. "It's basically still the same old alliance, but I like the idea of a council better. It's more of a decision-making body now than just a group of allies. What do you think?"

"So instead of allies, we're council members? Sure," she shrugged. "Sounds good."

"I'm going for a team vibe. Less of a loosely-associated group. If that makes sense." I waited for her nod, then continued. "So which position would you like?"

She looked at me sidelong. "Well, you're the boss, so whatever you want me to be."

"Uh, no. That's not how this is gonna work. I'm not a dictator here, just the team leader. None of this bowing and scraping shit."

She laughed again. "Oh, I heard. Arddhu's exact words were: *do not speak to her as you spoke to Ida.*" She'd even deepened her voice to try and imitate him, and I couldn't hold back my grin.

I really did like her. A lot.

"And before I came out here, he made sure I understood not to use a capital Y when I talked to you."

Yeah, I'd noticed she hadn't put that reverent emphasis. "Well, I'm still just Dee. I mean, I guess I'm not the Keeper anymore, but I sure as hell don't think of myself as *the Goddess*. Know what I mean?"

"I do." She nodded. "But for the record, I think you're still the Keeper as well as the Goddess." She glanced at my bracelet. "After all, Anu is still on your wrist."

Good point. Maybe she was right, and I could be both.

"Now, as far as your council goes," she added. "I'll give it some thought and let you know what I decide I want to be."

"Great."

We fell silent for a moment, and I sent my notepad and pen back into my pocket dimension.

Damn handy, that.

In the bright sunlight, the glow coming from my body was barely visible—but it was still there. "I wish I could stop glowing." I murmured.

She raised a brow. "Why can't you?"

"Uh..." Now I frowned. She had a damn good point. Why couldn't I? With a thought, the glowing stopped and I looked like a normal human again.

"See?" She smiled. "You put limits on yourself when you don't need to."

"You're absolutely right. I need to remember that." After a moment, I continued. "You know, I'd rather not repeat any of Ida's mistakes. For one thing, I'm staying here, where I can be close to everyone and everything I'm supposed to take care of. I won't be running off to some other world to hide. Especially since I don't need to. I've got this beautiful home and Ard na Mara. Besides, we still have so much to do: we need to finish the missions and heal Earth, then we need to start working on making this a better world for everyone. Including other deities, like the ones who weren't our allies before this whole thing started."

She eyed me curiously. "Even the bad ones?"

Oh. I hadn't thought of that. She had another point. What if there were hundreds more like Malsumis and Cromm out there?

"Well, maybe not them," I conceded. "But then again, they sort of balance things, don't they? I mean, some of them probably serve a purpose. Like Loki in the Norse pantheon, for example. He's not exactly evil. He's basically the court jester for the other gods, right?"

She laughed. "Don't let *him* hear you say that."

Dammit. I'd read that about Loki somewhere and thought it'd made sense.

I sighed. "I see I have a lot more to learn about deities."

Now she smiled. "It'll come. In a way, you were born yesterday. No one expects you to be at a higher level so soon."

So I was back to being a newbie again. Except this time I was a newbie Goddess instead of a newbie Keeper.

She studied me for a moment. "So we're moving ahead with Ida's plan?"

"Why the hell not? It was a good idea, even if it was for the wrong reasons."

"True. And I do agree with you. We should finish it. Earth by herself can't recover from the toxins that humans are poisoning her with. Unless the healing is done, it'll be too late. We're probably past the point where the damage can be reversed completely." She paused, as if not sure

356

whether to continue, then she appeared to make her decision. "By the way, you'll be able to heal Earth yourself, after the transformation is complete. You won't need anyone else's healing magick."

I opened my mouth to argue, but Anu stopped me.

"The Morrigan is correct. You have the power to heal. And the power to create. But You also have the power to destroy."

A shiver of fear traveled up my spine, and I took a deep breath.

With a little luck, I wouldn't have to worry about any of that last part for quite some time yet.

As I thought about it, the knowledge came to me: I could clean the air of its toxins, purify the soil and water, and heal Earth with about as much effort as I'd used when I'd teleported to Ard na Mara as the Keeper.

And, although right now I had to focus to answer prayers, I realized that wouldn't always be the case. As I continued to transform, it'd get easier. Eventually, I'd be able to do other things while I answered prayers.

"I see you understand," the Morrigan murmured.

"Yeah," I nodded. "But Arddhu said it could take a thousand years—or even longer—to fully transform. We can't wait that long. I'll still need the others to heal Earth *now*."

"Possibly." She shrugged. "None of us—not even Arddhu—really knows for sure how long it'll take for you. Yes, it could take a thousand years. But maybe it'll only take fifty. None of us have seen a human-to-Goddess transformation in our lifetimes. In a way, we only know as much as you do about all this."

Great.

Just what I didn't want to hear. I thought they'd be the experts, but it seemed we were all winging it.

CHAPTER TWENTY-SEVEN

ONE MORNING AFTER my tai chi session with Kevin, I entered the kitchen and immediately halted.

Three Tuatha—Dagda, Lugh, and Ogma—were crowded around the cooktop, towering over the diminutive Brianna.

"... these knobs control the different burners," she said. "You can think of each burner as a miniature cook-fire that has an adjustable level of heat. For example, this one can be low while that one can be high." She glanced up and noticed me. "Did you need something, Dee?"

I shook my head. "Just passing through. Keep doing... whatever it is you're doing."

She grinned. "I'm giving home-ec lessons. Today it's how to use common household appliances."

I smiled at Dagda, who'd turned his strange eyes on me. "Well, sorry I interrupted. I'll just be on my way—"

"We must discuss some things, You and I," Dagda interrupted.

Yes, I heard the reverence in his voice but decided to ignore it. For now. "Okay. We'll meet when you're done with your... uh, lesson... for today."

He nodded, and I continued on my way.

A bit later, after a quick meeting with Anthony, Dagda found me. I indicated for him to sit and poured a small glass of mead for each of us.

He savored a sip with obvious pleasure, then didn't waste any time getting down to business.

"My people wish to return to Eire, our home, as soon as possible. The realm I created was only meant to be temporary, You see."

I nodded; yes, I remembered.

"But it seems there is much for us to learn before we may return." He pointedly glanced at the flat-screen television on the wall. "Our goal is to become self-sufficient in this modern age, but I fear it will not be for some time yet."

"I can't even imagine how overwhelmed you and your people must feel right now. Humans invented a great many things while you all were... away."

He nodded. "There is a greater emphasis on payment for goods and services than in our own time, and we will need methods to earn such modern currency. But we are learning necessary skills such as using Your technology and appliances, and for that I am deeply indebted to You."

"Please," I shook my head. "There is no debt. I—we—are honored to help in any way we can."

"Even so, I wish to repay You for this kindness."

"I'm sorry, but I won't accept any repayment."

I swore the lightshow in his eyes just intensified, making it hard for me to stay focused. Was he working magick on me?

"There must be something You desire." His voice had lowered an octave. "Jewels, perhaps. Or favors."

I shook my head again and put some iron into my words. "I said *no*. No fucking repayment."

Now his brows lifted. "Do all Americans use such... profane speech?"

I almost laughed, but since he was serious I didn't think he'd appreciate that.

"Don't tell me the Irish never spoke vulgar words back in your day."

A tiny quirk in the corner of his mouth belied his amusement. "Yes, they did. But generally no one of high station spoke them so freely."

I'd better warn him, then.

"As a matter of fact, yes, it's fairly common these days. But not just Americans; almost everyone all over the world does this. When you're out among humans, you'll hear just about every nasty word ever invented.

Right now, I think everyone's favorite is *fuck* but *shit* is probably a close second."

"I see." His mouth quirked again. "I will certainly mention it to my people."

"Glad to help." I smiled.

His eyes were sharp as they held mine and he became serious once again. "Unfortunately, I have realized there is much more for us yet to learn, and I would ask for You to continue providing masters of the various arts we require, such as acquiring goods and operating conveyances."

Operating conveyances?

Oh.

Vehicles. He wanted his people to learn to drive.

When I didn't reply, he continued. "In return, despite Your wish for no repayment, I will offer as much in-kind knowledge as we are able to provide. For example, in return for Brianna's instruction on the proper operation of modern cooking devices, we will provide her with the procedure for preparing some of our most treasured dishes." He paused with an apologetic half-smile. "I must confess we find most food here to be bland and tasteless."

Our food was *bland and tasteless?* I hadn't found that to be true, but Brianna could boost the Southwestern heat a bit. Maybe some serrano or habanero peppers would liven things up.

"I'll talk to Brianna about introducing you to some of our local spices. They might be a bit more... exciting... for your palates."

He shifted then, gracefully crossing one long leg over the other, and I eyed his clothing. He wore the same shimmery iridescent tunic and trousers he'd had on when we'd first released him and his people from the banishment. Out among humans, they'd attract way too much attention. People would think the Tuatha were crackpots.

Or worse, aliens.

Especially with those strange eyes they had. Sunglasses or contact lenses would help them to appear normal and keep the humans from freaking out.

So not only would we have to replace their clothing, but change their general appearance too.

My to-do list was growing quickly.

"I need to make some notes," I explained as I pulled my notepad and pen from my pocket dimension, and he watched me quietly while I wrote.

Anthony: driving lessons, investments and banking, and basic money management.

The Morrigan: updating their appearance.

Kevin: assigning and usage of mobile phones, how to shop online, and the pitfalls of social media.

And maybe Randy should show them some modern methods of self-defense, because we couldn't have the Tuatha running around in public with swords or whatever, and openly using their magick.

Which reminded me...

I cleared my throat. "Here's what we'll do: we'll schedule additional classes on all the things you and your people will need to meet your goal of being self-sufficient. And I'll pay for any initial supplies you need, such as some new clothes so that you all blend in better with humans. But—" I lifted my index finger "—I want your solemn promise that none of you will use any magick when you're out among the humans."

A deep line formed between his perfect silvery brows. "Is it truly that important?"

I leveled my gaze on him. "Do you remember learning about the witch trials?" Arddhu had told me they'd recently covered the subject in their history lessons.

"Yes, I remember. It seemed to be a mass hysteria of some sort several centuries ago. Thousands of men and women were needlessly murdered. But my understanding is they were not actual witches."

I nodded. "They weren't. Mostly it was fear: back then, things happened that science couldn't explain yet, like freak weather or sickness, and humans blamed other humans. Usually the ones they already had a grudge against. But politics, power, and greed were a big part of it, too. The so-called witch finders made their living finding people to accuse, torture, and murder. In some cases, they even confiscated the property of the accused." I leaned forward. "A lot has changed since then, but a lot hasn't. People still fear what they don't understand, and fear breeds hate and violence. Magick is not exactly understood or widely accepted right now.

So if you openly use it among the humans, you and your people—and me, too—will be targets for attack. So yes, it *is* that important."

"I see," he murmured, eyes wide. "No, we do not wish any attacks on ourselves or our friends. I vow to You: my people will understand and will not use their magick while among humans on Earth."

"Thank you." I smiled and relaxed in my chair, then glanced down at my notes. "So let's see: I have driving lessons, modern clothing, money management and our systems of banking and investment, mobile phones and social media, and online shopping. I'll meet with the necessary people to set all that up, and if I think of any more categories, I'll add them to the list. I'll get back with you on scheduling the classes."

He smiled broadly, the first I'd seen for him, and seemed much happier now. But his ethereal beauty combined with the strangeness of his dazzling eyes made me realize we'd never get any of them to be less than conspicuous among humans without major modifications.

"I do have one more item," he added hesitantly. "I have heard of a delightful object called *the spa*. I would like for it to be added to Your list."

Goddammit.

Everybody loved the spa. So much so, I hardly ever got to use it anymore—at least not in peace and quiet.

I drained the rest of my mead and for the first time wished it was whiskey. Smiling as graciously as I could, I said, "It would be my pleasure to show you the spa. We'll have our first lesson after the sun sets. You and whomever else you'd like to attend will learn how to operate the spa's controls and enjoy its many... um... benefits."

His brilliant smile almost made me feel ungracious for my selfishness. Almost.

"Deirdre." Arddhu was outside my suite door, and he sounded impatient. "It is time to go."

"Okay. Just one more minute."

It was Imbolc Eve, and I was nervous. Almost as nervous as I'd been at my first Lammas Festival as the Keeper, seemingly so long ago.

I'd wanted to wear my jeans, a sweater, and my usual ponytail, but I'd been overruled by the Trusty Trio—my private pet name for Arddhu, Kevin, and the Morrigan.

"You are the Goddess," Arddhu had argued. "For this first appearance, you must look the part."

"People will expect you to look a certain way," the Morrigan had agreed.

"As time goes on, you'll be able to just be yourself, like you are with us," Kevin had said.

"They'll never get used to me being myself if I don't *look* like myself," I'd argued.

"Dee," Kevin had said. "Trust us."

"Remember that chat we had a couple of weeks ago?" the Morrigan had asked. "About how we've all lived long enough to be excellent advisers?"

Yeah, I'd remembered.

"Fine," I'd huffed.

But when Arddhu had produced a floaty blue gown that instantly reminded me of Ida, I'd balked.

"Ugh, no. Can't I wear this instead?" With just a thought, I'd changed my jeans and sweater into a pale yellow chiffon gown with pretty blue and purple flowers embroidered on the neckline and hem.

Yep, I could now change my clothes as easily as Kevin did, and it was *awesome*.

"Blue is traditional for the Goddess," Arddhu had insisted.

But when the Morrigan—and Kevin—had agreed with me, he'd backed down.

"It is Imbolc, after all," she'd argued. "Yellow's a better choice."

The win hadn't felt like one. After all, it was still a flimsy gown. And the way it seemed to float on the air by itself was incredibly annoying. I had no idea how I was supposed to *walk* with that shit going on. Must've been a Goddess thing.

Now, I was still holed up in my bedroom because I couldn't stop fussing with my appearance. By accident, I'd discovered I could curl my hair with just a thought, so I'd given myself bouncy curls—which looked ridiculous—straightened it again, and finally decided on soft waves. All of that was stuff I rarely ever did because it was usually too much work.

But doing my hair with just a thought made it way more easy.

And more fun.

I could even change the color, from my usual chestnut brown to anything I wanted. I'd tried out a lavender shade, laughed, then made it normal again.

"Deirdre." Arddhu's muffled voice was stern.

"Okay, okay," I called, and with a final huff, I opened the door.

Arddhu smiled in approval and escorted me to the living room.

Kevin and the Morrigan turned at my approach.

"Don't forget to glow," the Morrigan said. "You *have* to glow."

I rolled my eyes. "Fine." Dropping the shield I'd put in place to control the glowing thing, the room immediately brightened.

"How's this?" I asked.

Kevin squinted. "Maybe tone it down a bit. We don't need a sunburn."

I sighed and slipped the shield back in place, but with partial opacity instead of clear. "Better?"

"Perfect." He grinned.

Over the past couple of weeks I'd learned quite a bit, and most of it by accident. For example, I didn't need a portal anymore to travel from one place to another. It was a quicker and long-distance version of how I used to port around the property. I thought of it as *zipping*, since it was so much faster and easier.

So now, while Kevin ported Arddhu and the Morrigan to Ard na Mara, I just *zipped* myself there and we all met on the patio, since that was sort of the tradition.

Leaves had just started to bud on the trees, but small patches of snow were still in the shadows of the undergrowth in the woods. My breath puffed in the air as we followed the path, but for some reason I didn't feel the chill, not even in my flimsy gown.

The sky overhead flared brilliant blue in the moment before the sun dipped below the horizon, then it became the gorgeous purple hues of twilight. The colors were even more beautiful with my enhanced vision.

The three of them headed to the village green in Finn's Cove to give me time to bless the livestock and fields, and I'd meet them there after I was done.

If the farmers were surprised to see me in person, they hid it well.

"Imbolc blessings, My Lady," each greeted me. They gifted me with offerings: an oat cake, a cup of mead, or a bit of whiskey. Every front door had a Brigid's cross, and candles flickered in the windows.

And each had a dish of cream on the stoop, a traditional offering for the fae.

What would happen when the Tuatha returned to Earth? Would they give blessings to these folk who still remembered and honored them?

I discovered the Imbolc blessing itself was easy. It was nothing more complicated than sending a strong feeling of love and light into the object of the blessing, whether it was a field ready for crops, a flock of sheep, or the ocean.

Just before I started, I remembered that spring was only in the Northern Hemisphere right now, so I'd have to perform the Imbolc blessing for the Southern Hemisphere later in the year, at Lammas.

Eyes closed, I concentrated on a farmer's field and pushed the blessing down into the Earth, extending it into both rich and poor soil everywhere. Earth responded under my feet with a faint vibration and a deep sense of contentment.

Next was the livestock. But I worried I might miss some unfamiliar animals, so I decided to just go ahead and include *all* the animals, even the wild creatures of forest, field, and desert. And I didn't forget pets. It was all as easy as forming a thought.

Lastly, I sent my blessing to all the fisherman, and all the oceans, lakes, streams, and waterways.

Best of all, I was able to move effortlessly from field to paddock to harbor in less than the blink of an eye.

Earth vibrated much stronger now, and radiated deep contentment and peace.

It made me grin with such joy, I almost felt I could burst.

Then I *zipped* to the village green, expecting the festival to be well underway by then.

But just as I arrived, so did Arddhu, Kevin, and the Morrigan.

Impossible.

How could that be? The blessing couldn't have taken only a few minutes.

Maybe they'd just taken their time getting there, or they'd stopped to talk to Pete and Petunia along the way.

As I approached, the Morrigan grinned from ear to ear. "Well done," she praised.

But the village green had become silent. The villagers stared at me, and I felt overly self-conscious.

Especially with the way my gown was billowing around me, all by itself.

Nearby, a woman gasped. "You're here. You're well and truly here."

Huh. Was she referring to me or to the Goddess?

I supposed it didn't matter. I smiled at her and raised my voice for all to hear. "Imbolc blessings, everyone. Please begin the festivities. Enjoy yourselves."

As I walked with Arddhu, Kevin, and the Morrigan, I dropped my shield into place and stopped the glowing act.

Hmm. Was it too soon to change into more comfortable clothing?

I felt Arddhu's intense dark eyes on me, and turned to him with an eyebrow raised. He studied me closely with an inscrutable expression.

"What?" I asked, almost afraid of his answer.

"I can feel the blessing," he murmured.

"So Earth is vibrating for you, too?" I grinned, still feeling her contentment.

"No." Now his eyes held wonder. "Earth is *singing*."

As soon as he'd said it, I heard it too, and the hairs on the back of my neck stood up. It wasn't actual singing, like a human did; it was more like an odd mix of whisper-soft musical tones that drifted on the light breeze.

"I can't believe it." The Morrigan stood with her head cocked. "I haven't heard Earthsong in... centuries." When she met my gaze, I swore I saw tears in her eyes. "Do you know what this means?"

I shook my head, at a loss for words.

"The dryads will come back."

Dryads? The tree spirits?

"They've been gone almost as long as the Tuatha," she added, then pulled me into an embrace. "Thank you."

"Shit, Dee," Kevin said with awe. "You've already started healing Earth with just your blessings tonight."

Oh.

Oh.

The Morrigan pulled away, wiping her eyes. "Sorry. Didn't expect to get so emotional."

"No problem." My brows knit. "So, this Earthsong... can everyone hear it?"

"Not yet," Arddhu replied. "Only immortals, for now. But when Earth is fully healed, all living creatures will hear it."

I thought about that for a moment. "So that means others—like Ares and Athena—can probably hear it, too?"

He nodded.

What would they think? Would they know it was me? And would it make them hate me even more? Or hate me less?

The villagers still stared at me in wonder and awe, and it made me uncomfortable.

"Hey, can I change into my comfy clothes now?"

Arddhu smiled. "Yes."

With just a thought, I exchanged the billowy yellow gown for my jeans, a light sweater, and my favorite boots. I made the pins holding my hair disappear so it fell in soft waves over my shoulders, and extinguished the glowing thing.

"That's better," I sighed in pleasure. Now maybe I wouldn't stand out so much among the villagers.

In the center of the green, the ubiquitous bonfire raged. Tables of food and drink ringed the perimeter, as they always had at every festival I'd ever attended.

But I wasn't hungry tonight, so I didn't plan on eating. But one of the attendants at the meat table caught my eye and beckoned me, so I walked over.

"My Lady, will You bless our feast tonight?"

"Of course." I smiled and extended my hands over the table, although that was just for show, since I didn't need to do more than speak the blessing. "Bless this Imbolc feast, and all who are gathered here tonight."

The attendant beamed. "Thank you, My Lady."

I nodded and met the Trusty Trio at the drink station. The young guy I remembered from my first Lammas festival had poured cups for Arddhu, Kevin, and the Morrigan.

"My Lady," he nodded and handed me a cup. I knew better than to ask what it was; his magick was serving us exactly what we wanted.

I thanked him and the four of us sat at a table.

One sip of the ale and I knew it was one of Garrett's special brews, though I'd never had his spring offering before. It tasted of longer days, tender green shoots pushing up through fertile soil, the crispness of an early spring evening, and snowmelt.

And then I saw him: Garrett made his way through the villagers, never taking his eyes from mine. A new reverence clearly showed there and told me he knew exactly who I'd become. He immediately went to one knee and bowed his head.

"My Lady." He raised his head and smiled. "It is good to see You."

"Garrett, please, get up." Gods, I hated this part of the whole thing, when people made such a fuss.

Arddhu smiled warmly at Garrett's obvious confusion. "Our Goddess dislikes ceremony, old friend."

Garrett stood, but didn't appear any less confused. "I don't understand."

"I'm just Dee," I explained. "Mostly the same as I was before. So that's how I want to be treated. No bowing or special treatment, please. But I'm glad you stopped by—this ale is *wonderful*. You've outdone yourself once again."

He smiled. "Ah, thank You, My Lady. Er... Dee," he quickly corrected at my scowl. Then he added apologetically, "This informality will take some getting used to. For all of us."

I still heard the reverence in his voice, but decided to let it go for now. "If you could spread the word, I'd be very grateful."

"Of course." He hesitated before continuing. "Are You staying for a while? I... I'd like to discuss some things with You tomorrow. Some things of importance." Again a pause. "Privately."

I glanced at the others. "I wasn't planning on it, but sure. Let's meet in the morning. I'll come to the pub for breakfast."

"Excellent, My—*Dee*. Thank You." He nodded to the others and left.

"I guess I'll go back home with you guys, then pop back in the morning." I sipped my ale.

"Alone? Absolutely not." Arddhu's voice was stern.

"Look, I don't need a minder anymore," I snapped. And then instantly regretted it. But I didn't even need any of my weapons if anyone threatened me. I could just use my power to defend myself. What would a bodyguard do for me now?

"It's not a good idea," the Morrigan added. "At least not until we know where the others are."

Ah yes. The traitors. Athena, Ares, and Kali.

She had a point.

"And you're not invincible," Kevin pointed out. "As much as you'd like to be, you're not."

I sighed. "Okay, fine. We'll figure it out. But I do want to meet with Garrett and see what he wants."

"Promise?" Kevin asked. He knew they couldn't really stop me if I wanted to come alone. Not unless I promised not to, because I kept my promises.

I sighed again. "Yes, I promise." I refrained from rolling my eyes, but only barely.

We sat and drank for a moment, and the small group of musicians in the corner of the green began tuning up their instruments.

When they finished and launched into a rousing jig, my feet tapped on the soft grass and I remembered the dance circle of my first Lammas festival. It felt like years since I'd had any fun.

Well, why not have fun now?

I stood. "Who wants to dance with me?"

"Shit. I haven't danced in ages," the Morrigan said. But she grinned and was on her feet in seconds.

Not wanting to be left out, Kevin stood next, then finally Arddhu.

That's how a trio of Irish immortals—and one American sort-of-immortal—ended up dancing the night away on Imbolc Eve in Finn's Cove.

And became the talk of the whole village, I was sure.

CHAPTER TWENTY-EIGHT

SINCE I WAS still mostly human, I needed sleep. But not nearly as much as I used to; maybe only half as much now. When I woke I was wrapped in Kevin's arms, and it was so pleasing and comforting, I just lay quietly and enjoyed his closeness for a while.

The four of us had raced each other from the village green in the wee hours. Of course I'd won, because I'd cheated and *zipped* myself to the cottage. Kevin had ported a split-second after me. Laughing ourselves silly, we'd crashed through the back door and almost took it off its hinges. When Arddhu and the Morrigan had arrived, breathless because they'd run the whole way, they found us collapsed on the floor in near hysterics.

"Kids." The Morrigan had shook her head, but I caught the gleam of delight in her eyes.

"Hey, just because you two are old farts, that doesn't make us *kids*," I'd mock-protested.

"Holy shit," Kevin had said with wide eyes. "I can't believe you just called Arddhu and the Morrigan *old farts*."

Then we broke out in uncontrollable laughter again.

Arddhu and the Morrigan stepped carefully around us with their heads held high and continued into the cottage without another word.

When we'd finally stopped laughing, Kevin had helped me up and we'd dusted ourselves off. I'd had some trouble closing the door, but with a bit of magick I'd fixed it and got it back in place.

Arddhu and the Morrigan had made themselves comfortable in the living room, so I'd wished them goodnight and headed up to my room. It was only when I'd turned to shut my door that I'd realized Kevin was right behind me.

"Let me hold you while you sleep," he'd asked, and after only a second or two, I consented. And I'd drifted off into the most peaceful dreams.

Now, I smiled at the memories and stirred. Kevin's arms tightened before releasing me. "Morning," he said.

I leaned over and kissed him since I didn't have morning breath anymore. Maybe that was strictly a human problem.

"Mmm." His arms wrapped around me. "Y'know, it's been a while. Do we have time for... ?"

Sure, he could bend time, but I shook my head. "Sorry. I want to get to Garrett's and see what he needs to talk to me about, and I want to stay focused since he said it's important. How about after we get home?"

His grin was sly. "I'll hold you to that."

I shivered with anticipation. "You do that."

It didn't take long for me to get myself presentable and we went downstairs. Arddhu and the Morrigan had found a board game somewhere and were engrossed at the coffee table.

"Who's winning?" I asked.

"He is," the Morrigan grumbled. "I haven't won a single game all night."

Arddhu smiled sheepishly. "My apologies, Morrigan. If it is any consolation, you always win at fidchell."

She grinned. "You know, that's true. Hey, do either of you have a fidchell board we can use?"

I laughed. "I have no idea if there's one around here, but you're welcome to look. I need to get to Garrett's."

Immediately, they both stood. "We're coming with you," the Morrigan said.

Ah yes. Couldn't leave without my minders.

Then I shook off the snark. They were only doing their best to protect me, after all. I needed to be less of a bitch.

So instead of *zipping* to the pub, I headed toward the trail through the woods, trailed by the Trusty Trio. After only a few steps it hit me: I hadn't wanted coffee this morning. In fact, I couldn't remember the last time I'd had any—and I hadn't experienced caffeine withdrawals, either.

I guess Goddesses didn't have caffeine dependence.

My body was still changing. Transforming. Evolving. Just like that caterpillar in its chrysalis Arddhu had mentioned some time ago.

The morning was gorgeous, and the birdsong was sweet. My eyes followed the erratic path of a yellow butterfly over the long grass of the meadow, but the poor thing didn't have anything to feed on just yet. In another month or so the meadow would be filled with wildflowers.

My breath puffed in the chilly air, but I sensed the warmer temperatures of spring were due to arrive any day now.

"The Morrigan told me how much she enjoyed dancing last night," Arddhu said. "We should do it more often."

I pictured the four of us piling into my SUV and heading to a dance club in Scottsdale, and had to bite my lip to keep from laughing inappropriately.

Probably not a good idea.

Maybe we could just put on some music at the house and have a little party there. Away from prying eyes. Maybe the allies and the Tuatha would join in, too.

"Sure, sounds like fun," I responded.

As we passed Mike's cottage, I felt a tiny pang of something, but wasn't sure what it was. Regret? Sorrow?

Then a certain knowledge came to me: if I really wanted to I could reach beyond the veil and communicate with him. It was one of the powers of the Goddess.

But no, not yet. The wounds were still too fresh.

As we approached the bridge over the creek, Pete the Troll scrambled up the bank and hurried toward me.

"Oh, My Lady! Wait, please wait."

"Good morning, Pete." I'd already stopped. "Imbolc blessings to you and Petunia."

Sweeping off his wide-brimmed hat, he squinted up at me. Was he— yes, he was. He was trembling.

He couldn't be afraid of me now, could he?

"My Lady, I just wanted to give my condolences. And I swear I didna know Michael would betray us."

"Oh hey, none of us knew," I reassured him. "But thank you."

He fidgeted with his hat and blinked at me, as if he were reluctant to say more.

"How's Petunia? Everything good?"

"Oh yes, My Lady. She's expecting a little one. We're both thrilled." Now he grinned, and seemed more like his normal self. He'd stopped trembling, too.

"That's wonderful, I'm so happy to hear it." I squatted down to his level. "Listen, Pete, please just call me Dee. I'm not as formal as... well, as everyone used to be. Okay? Just Dee."

His face wrinkled in a frown, but he nodded. "If You say so, I'll abide."

Guess I could let him keep that little bit of reverence for now.

"Thanks. Hey, I hadn't seen you in a long time. Is everything okay?"

"Oh, yes, My—er, *Dee*. Petunia took me to meet her folk and we stayed there in her father's lands for a bit."

"Ah, I see." I straightened. "Well, it was great seeing you. Say hi to Petunia from me. And be sure and let me know if you need anything."

But as I started to walk past him, he didn't move. He just stood there awkwardly fiddling with his hat.

"Was there something else?"

"Aye, My La—uh, Dee. But..." He glanced behind me, and I knew he'd looked at my companions.

Hmm. He wanted to talk to me privately.

There was another way we could do that, since I'd discovered I could open mental communication links, just like Arddhu.

"*You can talk to me this way, Pete.*"

"*Oh thank You. It's just that... I've heard some disturbing things.*"

"*Go on.*"

"*I've heard the Tuatha have been freed.*"

"*Yes, they have.*"

His eyes widened and he began shaking again. "*Oh no. That's not good. Not good at all.*"

I frowned. "*Why not? What's wrong?*"

"*It was they who killed most of my kind. The few who survived were scattered to the winds and only I stayed here. At Finn's Cove, I mean.*"

What?

"*When was this?*"

"*Before the Goddess—Ida, I mean—banished them.*"

Well, of course it would've been before they were banished. But it was the first I'd heard of it. And why didn't he want to talk about it openly? What could Arddhu, Kevin, or the Morrigan possibly have to do with it?

"*Thank you for telling me. I didn't know. I'll make sure they don't hurt anyone. Especially your folk.*"

"*But how will You stop them? They're awful powerful.*"

I squared my shoulders. "*So am I.*"

"*I beg Your pardon.*" He bowed his head. "*I didn't mean to imply You weren't.*"

"*No worries, Pete. Trust me.*"

Now he looked up and met my gaze again, but the worry was still plain in his eyes. And the fear. "*Y-yes, but... she used to say that, too. The other one.*"

I knelt on one knee. "*Pete, I'm not her. I know you don't know me very well, but I'd never let anyone hurt you or your folk. And I've already started healing Earth, too.*"

His eyes widened again. "*Oh, I just knew that was You! I felt it. And I couldn't believe my ears when I heard the Earthsong last night.*" He bowed his head again. "*You've given me hope.*"

I took his rough hand in mine. "*Good. Keep that hope alive. Now, I have to get going, but I won't forget what we talked about, and we'll talk again soon. I promise.*"

He squeezed my hands gently before releasing them, and as I stood he put his hat on and scrambled back under the bridge.

"What was that all about?" Kevin asked as we continued on our way.

I hesitated before replying. I didn't want to discuss what Pete had told me—not just yet. It seemed no one had told me the whole truth about the Tuatha, and I didn't know exactly what that meant, but I'd have to find out. And it'd be better if I did before the Tuatha returned to Earth permanently.

So maybe I could get away with a partial truth.

"He and Petunia heard the Earthsong last night."

His eyes on me were sharp, and I knew he wasn't completely fooled, but thankfully he didn't question me. I probably wasn't off the hook, though; he might bring it up again later, when we were alone.

"Wait until Earth is healed," the Morrigan said. "The Earthsong will be so loud, we probably won't be able to talk like this anymore."

I stared at her. "Really?"

She laughed. "Nah, I'm kidding."

I just shook my head. "So, after I talk to Garrett, what do you guys want to do?"

"We should probably just go home," the Morrigan said.

Interesting. She called my house her *home*, which gave me a weird feeling. Not exactly bad, but not exactly good, either. Just weird.

"Sounds good to me," Kevin said.

"I agree as well," Arddhu added.

When we stepped inside Garrett's Pub, the few patrons stopped talking and watched us as we chose and sat at a table. It reminded me of the first time I'd walked in with Mike, a lifetime ago.

I nodded to the older gentlemen at the bar, and they nodded back before turning away on their barstools to resume talking and eating—although quieter, as if they didn't want to disturb us.

Just then Garrett emerged from the kitchen with plates of food for another table. He caught my eye and nodded, then served the table and chatted with the patrons for a moment. One of the men laughed a bit too loudly, then Garrett came over.

"What can I get for you?" He wiped his hands on a towel as he spoke.

"Just a pint for me," Kevin said.

"A glass of mead, please," Arddhu smiled.

"I'll take a pint too," the Morrigan said.

But before I could tell him what I wanted, he turned and left.

What the hell? He'd never been rude to me before. I glanced at the others, but they didn't seem to notice anything strange.

He brought the drinks on a tray, including a third pint, which he set in front of me.

Huh.

"Come, Dee," he said, gesturing for me to follow him beyond the kitchen door. "We'll talk in the office."

I'd never seen an Irish pub's kitchen. Garrett's was incredibly small and cramped, with every available surface in use. There weren't any high-end professional-grade appliances here, just an old-fashioned combo stove and oven, and an ancient fridge.

One modern touch: a microwave.

On the other side of the room, Garrett patiently held open another door. I hurried past the scarred butcher-block island then stopped suddenly in the doorway.

This was no office.

Instead of the cluttered desk and old chair I'd expected to see, a lush but small oak grove beckoned me.

It was as if I'd suddenly stepped into balmy summertime.

The tall, mature oaks were covered in the glorious dark green leaves of June or July, instead of the lighter shade of springtime. Planted in a circle, the wide canopies had grown into a roof that sheltered the glade and filtered the sunlight into bright but indirect light. Below, the lush grass was soft and thick, and begged for me to kick off my shoes and dig my toes into. A scattering of pastel wildflowers sweetened the air and made me think of warm honey. Unseen birds chirped and sang a beautiful background tune.

This *had* to be another dimension.

"Where—"

"This is my office." He guided me to a wide bench placed on one side of the glade. "I call it *áit na darach.*"

Place of oaks in Irish Gaelic.

"Oh." We sat and I turned toward him. "So, what's going on?"

"First, I wanted to apologize. If I'd known that Michael... well, let's just say I would've done something about it."

"None of us knew. Not even the guys who worked with him for years."

He stared up at the green canopy for a moment. "Tell me more about Bricriu and why You trust him."

I heard the reverence in his voice, but something told me not to press him on it just now.

"First of all, I've already told you. He goes by Kevin now. He's been consistently loyal and has proven himself many times. If you'll remember, I told you at Lammas how he helped rescue me from Cromm last year. And he fought at my side in the battle against Cromm and Malsumis." Almost as an afterthought, I added, "And Arddhu trusts him completely."

"Ah, well." He nodded. "If he trusts him, then 'tis good. You need trustworthy folk around You. Now more than ever." He paused before wryly adding, "However, it does seem to be somewhat hazardous to be counted as Your ally."

I'd just opened my mouth for a smart-ass reply when I noticed his teasing grin and the twinkle in his eyes.

We shared a laugh, then he sobered. "And the Morrigan? She is *aes sídhe*, you know."

"Yes, I know. And yes, I trust her." I paused, thinking. "To a point."

He nodded again. "I've heard the *aes sídhe* have been freed. I must caution You; they were warlike and untrustworthy for many centuries and may not be who You think they are."

"Yeah, I just found out they killed most of the troll-kind before they were banished. I plan on discussing that with the Dagda and making sure they understand they can never do anything like that again. After all, everyone on Earth is under my protection now."

"I truly hope they will cooperate. Too many folk lived in fear when they ruled this realm." He paused before continuing. "I've also heard there are some others who had been allies but are now stirring up troubles."

Well, he sure heard quite a bit, didn't he?

I nodded. "Ares, Athena, and Kali. Did you happen to hear where they are now?"

He shook his head. "No, but I've heard they are hiding. And plotting. They say You stole the power of the Goddess and are unworthy of it. They will try to sway others to their cause. You'd do well to keep Yourself surrounded by Your... council... at all times."

Wow. He already knew about the council, too?

"I plan on it. You know, this whole thing wasn't even my idea. It was Anu. Instead of sending the power into Earth like she was supposed to, she gave it to me instead. As a gift." I sighed and rubbed my forehead. "This shit just never ends."

Unexpectedly, his arm went around my shoulders. "Take heart. You have more allies than You know. And as You continue to heal Earth and do good deeds, Your faithful will swell in number. Just keep doing what You're doing."

A sarcastic laugh escaped me. "*Good deeds?* You know I've been murdering people, right? One could argue those aren't exactly *good deeds.* I've even been called a terrorist by the American media."

He studied me for a moment before he replied. "Humans like the concept of the lesser of two evils, which gives us the age-old question: is it better to allow a monster to live and fulfill its destiny of heinous deeds, or to remove the monster when it is young, so that others will not die or suffer?"

I was familiar with that argument. "But that whole thing falls apart if you consider the possibility of the monster not fulfilling its destiny. Maybe it would've just been another normal... um, person. In that case, an unjustifiable murder was committed."

He nodded. "That is true. However, You are removing the enemies of Earth, those who have harmed her and caused untold suffering among humans as well as the flora and fauna. This has already happened. It is not a future possibility. If allowed to continue their course, millions of humans—and other life here—will continue to suffer and die as Earth is slowly destroyed." He paused before continuing. "By removing them, they are paying the price for their evil. Is that not justifiable?"

Of course, he was right. And I'd already worked through the reasoning for removing Earth's enemies, months ago.

"Well, yeah, but it's still murder. Still terrorism. And if I get caught, I'll either spend the rest of my life in prison or be given the death sentence, depending on what the judge and jury decide."

"They would not dare. You are the Goddess. You are a higher authority. The *highest* authority."

I laughed. "They wouldn't see it that way."

He shook his head. "Why does it matter? You know what You are doing is the right thing."

That was just it, though: if I truly knew it was the right thing, why did I feel like such a bad person for doing it?

"Ah, I think I understand." He squeezed my shoulder. "Because You have grown up human, their laws and customs have become a part of You. And You think You must still adhere to those laws and customs, even though You are no longer human."

Well, since he put it *that* way...

"Deity makes its own laws and customs," he continued. "It does not abide by those of mortals. And make no mistake: You are deity."

Mythology was full of stories of gods—even the popular ones—destroying entire populations just because they did something the gods didn't like. I wasn't doing that; I was removing specific and proven threats to the entire planet in order to prevent massive loss of life and the destruction of Earth.

It was like comparing apples to bananas.

"Thanks, Garrett." I rested my head on his shoulder. "I really appreciate your wisdom. Sometimes I doubt myself and I guess I overthink things."

"That is normal."

"I've been busy answering prayers, too."

"That is very good to hear." He squeezed my shoulder again. "Anu did well, choosing You. You have great compassion and love in Your heart, and You are exactly who we needed at this time. And... You are everything Ida was not."

"But she wasn't always bad. Anu showed me the past," I explained. When he didn't say anything, I looked up at him and continued. "What if the same thing happens to me? What if I get... corrupted? Influenced, somehow?"

He smiled warmly. "The fact that You are concerned about it tells me it will not happen."

We sat in companionable silence for a moment and I listened to the soft breeze rustle through the leaves.

"By the way," I said. "I didn't see you around for a while. I was a little worried."

He took so long to respond, I thought maybe I'd overstepped a boundary of some kind and should apologize.

"Unfortunately, I was viciously attacked and required a lengthy recovery."

"*What?*" I sat up. "Are you okay? Is there anything I can do?"

"I am healed. I am fine. And no, there is nothing You can do." He met my gaze. "I believe it was a warning from Cromm. And since You have already dispatched him and his minions, it has been taken care of."

"I'm pretty sure he's gone for good this time."

His mouth quirked. "That is exactly what Lugh said to me once, long ago."

"Wait—you know Lugh?"

He studied me for a moment. "Yes. All of the *aes sídhe* are known to me, and I am known to them. I am Goibhniu."

I stared at him as if seeing him for the first time. "Wasn't Goibhniu— weren't you—a metalsmith for the Tuatha?"

He nodded. "Once, I worked metal for my people, and brewed a special ale. But I gave up the smithing long ago and now I only brew and cook for my pub customers."

I remembered Arddhu had called him *old friend* last night.

Pieces were clicking into place.

"Why weren't you banished with the others?"

He hesitated and looked up at the oak canopy. "I... was away at the time. As were a few others. When we learned of the banishment, we scattered and hid among the humans of Earth."

"And Ida never knew?"

"No." He shook his head. "I have used a spell to conceal my true nature at every festival and ritual. But some were not so lucky. Ida found them and eliminated them."

Oh gods. He'd been hiding alone here for *centuries,* knowing his people had been banished and there wasn't a damn thing he could do about it. I couldn't imagine.

"Are there others here? In Finn's Cove?"

"Not Tuatha, no. But over the years there have been an interesting assortment of refugees—for lack of a better word."

"Refugees? How do you mean?"

"A group of selkies were hunted almost to extinction and fled Scotland some time ago to settle here. They are our fishermen. And there are also unusual humans: hedge witches and cunning men. The rest are shifters—most are canine, but there are a few felines and others. Long ago, we all agreed to live together in peace, and follow the Old Ways."

Well, shit. That explained the strangeness of the place, I supposed. Witches, selkies, and shifters. And Mike had once mentioned the people of Finn's Cove were formidable but refused to explain; now I understood. "And everyone here worships the Goddess?"

He shook his head again. "No, not everyone. Only some. Most of the hedge witches—such as Maura—and the cunning men do, but everyone else simply enjoys the festivities and the sense of community."

Garrett fell silent and I studied him for a moment. There were fine lines around his eyes and mouth, and his thick hair was more gray than dark, but he seemed no older than forty or fifty. And he didn't have the otherworldly paleness that most of the Tuatha had.

But then again, neither did the Morrigan or Ogma.

"How old are you?" I asked.

"You Americans." He scowled. "Such a rude question to ask immortals." But when he saw my cheeks redden, his expression softened. "I will allow it this time. I was born six thousand three hundred and forty-five years ago."

"Well, I think you don't look a day over fifty."

His laugh was full-throated, the throw-your-head-back sort, and I had to laugh with him. "Ah, for that sweet and kind flattery, I shall create a special brew in Your honor." Then he sobered. "I have one last item to discuss: what will You do with Michael's property?"

I'd forgotten about meeting with the firm for the reading of Mike's will, but how did Garrett know about me being sole beneficiary? I decided to play dumb.

"You must know something I don't."

He lifted one eyebrow. "Apparently I do. In fact, he made sure we *all* knew the property was Yours upon his death."

"*We*? Who's *we*?"

"The council of Finn's Cove."

Ah, so he was on the village council. I hadn't known that.

I cocked my head. "I'm curious. When did he let you know that?"

"Last summer. July, I think it was."

Interesting. It'd been as if Mike had known his days were numbered.

"To answer your question: I don't know what I'll do with it, to be honest."

"If I may make a suggestion, it would make a fine home for a young couple."

Yes, it would. And it deserved someone to take care of it, rather than just letting it sit abandoned and crumbling. "I agree. How should I proceed?"

"You could make the property a gift to the village. The council will take it from there."

I nodded. "Of course. I'll talk to the firm as soon as I get back to Arizona, and get that ball rolling. I'll also make sure his things get cleared out as soon as possible."

"We are grateful for Your generosity." He stood and offered his hand. "I will also watch for any who would do You harm, and I will let You know if I hear any news regarding Your former allies."

"Thank you, Garrett." I accepted his hand and got to my feet. "Um, do I still call you Garrett, or—?"

"Yes, please do. I have used my alias for so long, I will not change it now." As we walked through the doorway and back into the pub's kitchen, he added, "I almost forgot to mention that we heard the Earthsong. You have done well in such a short period of time."

I smiled. "There's still a lot of work to do, but it's a start."

He held the door open for me and followed me into the pub. "Shall I bring some food?"

"Yes, please." My stomach rumbled for the first time in days. "I've been told that someday I won't need food or drink anymore, but today's not that day. I'd love some of your stew, or whatever's the special for today."

He smiled, but it held a tinge of sadness. "Aye, that day will come but I won't be pleased when it does. I find great joy in Your appreciation of my simple fare."

He returned to the kitchen, and I took my seat at our table. Arddhu, the Morrigan, and Kevin were expectantly silent.

I drank some of my ale, then updated them on my discussion with Garrett—most of it, at least.

"So, he's going to keep an eye and ear out for any news on our former allies," I finished.

Arddhu frowned. "I do not recommend he remove his sensory organs. They are quite necessary."

Oh, Arddhu. We couldn't help but laugh.

After we returned to The Hacienda, Kevin and I quietly snuck into my suite and made love—just as I'd promised him.

As always, he was a skilled and satisfying lover and never minded cuddling afterward. But as I lay drowsing in his arms, a curious wave of disappointment washed over me.

It hadn't come from me; I was far from disappointed. Ditto for Kevin. After a moment, I located its source: Arddhu.

Oh no. He probably thought I'd already made up my mind and chosen Kevin as my consort. But actually, I hadn't made my decision yet. I needed to fix this. I didn't want Arddhu sad. We'd all been through enough.

I rolled out of bed with a sigh.

"What's wrong?" Kevin murmured.

"I have to go talk to Arddhu."

With just a thought, I dressed. Kevin was on my heels when I left the suite.

I found Arddhu outside on the patio, staring morosely at the foothills with a small glass of mead cradled in his hands.

"Hey there." I sat in the chair next to him.

He nodded and sipped his mead.

"Just to let you know: I haven't made a decision yet on Consort."

He lifted an eyebrow. "I think you are quite clear on who you have chosen, even if not officially announced."

Oh, for fuck's sake.

"Arddhu, you know damn well Kevin and I were together long before Samhain. Before this whole Goddess and Consort thing. Just because we still have sex without you doesn't mean I've chosen him over you as Consort."

Arddhu's gaze held mine and the sadness there almost broke my heart. "You and I have coupled, yes, but not for quite some time. It is obvious whom you have chosen."

"So, if we go and have sex right now, you'll believe me if I say I haven't chosen?"

"I do not understand." He frowned. "You are not sated?"

I glanced at Kevin, who'd sat in another chair and now tried desperately to hide his smirk.

These immortals were so infuriating.

"I didn't say that." I sighed. "I just want you to believe me when I say I haven't made my decision yet." I stood and held out my hand. "You want to go have sex or not?"

After a moment's hesitation, he quickly finished his mead and set the glass on the table, then clasped my hand and stood.

I loved having sex with Arddhu. His techniques were somewhat similar to Kevin's in that they each made me feel beautiful, loved, and adored. But Arddhu, being significantly older, had learned some things that almost drove me out of my mind with pleasure, and it involved his wild forest magick.

Normally, he kept it tightly controlled. Especially since Samhain.

But for some reason, this time was different.

A *lot* different.

We glowed as bright as the sun, and I had to squeeze my eyes tightly closed. Irrationally, I thought if I didn't hold on to him, I'd be swallowed up in that light and there'd be nothing left of me except atoms.

Of course, that didn't happen, and I felt ridiculous afterward when everything went back to normal and the glowing stopped.

Well, normal except for how my nerve endings still vibrated—which was an incredibly strange sensation.

Arddhu lay on his back staring at the ceiling with wide eyes and breathing heavily, and I propped myself on one arm next to him.

"So. What the hell was that?" I asked.

"I apologize." He turned his head toward me. "I... lost control."

Lost control? Of his magick? What did that even mean?

"Are you okay?" I scanned his naked body, unsure exactly of what I was looking for.

"I am unhurt. It is *you* I am concerned about."

"I'm fine," I said automatically.

He narrowed his eyes. "Are you quite certain? That was... an excess of power."

"Yeah, I figured that's why we glowed like the sun."

Still he studied me, making me uncomfortable.

"Arddhu, please. Stop worrying."

His hand found mine. "I will never stop worrying." His voice was quiet, and he gently lifted my hand to his warm, soft lips.

He was truly so sweet and caring, and as I watched him press the back of my hand to his cheek, I suddenly realized I loved him.

Not the same way I loved Kevin—with passion and heat and kinky lust—but with warmth and comfort and deep devotion. Regardless, love was love.

"Well, I worry about you too, you know." My voice was soft. "You've been more tired lately."

"I am fine." His warm brown eyes met mine and he smiled, transforming his face. "Especially now."

He did seem younger somehow. Almost rejuvenated.

"I wish to have dinner with you," he said, then raised a brow. "That is, if you are hungry?"

I wasn't exactly hungry, but I definitely wanted to dine with him. "Yes. Let's do it." I tugged my hand free of his and gave him a quick kiss.

In the kitchen, Brianna was already preparing dinner, as if she'd known. She glanced up at our footsteps.

"Will you eat tonight, Dee?" she asked.

"Yep." I smiled. "In fact, that's exactly why I'm here."

Pleased, she returned the smile. "Great. It'll be ready in about thirty minutes."

I nodded and sat at the kitchen island with Arddhu. A shadow passed by the pool outside: Nat, doing her rounds.

A pang of guilt hit me. I hadn't talked to her in weeks. Those weekly dinner plans I'd made with the security team had fizzled out after the whole Goddess thing had happened..

Shit. They all probably hated me by now.

"Oh, by the way," Brianna said. "Kevin said to tell you he's in the VIP tent with a class and won't be joining you for dinner."

Good. It'd be a nice quiet dinner alone with Arddhu, then. "Thanks."

Anthony entered and glanced at Arddhu and Brianna. "Dee, if you have a moment, I'd like to go over a few things."

"Sure. You've got me for about a half hour."

I followed him to the living room, with Arddhu only a couple of steps behind.

Anthony tapped his tablet and began. "Kevin delegated the council meeting to me, so I've tentatively scheduled it for next week. All invitations have been accepted. I've worked out a menu with Brianna for the refreshments. Would you like to approve it?"

"Nope. I trust you both completely."

He nodded and made a note. "I've drafted an agenda for the meeting based on prior discussions we've had. Resuming the missions is a discussion item, since you mentioned it's a priority. Was there anything else you specifically wanted to include?"

I thought out loud for a moment. "Well, I want to let everyone know that even though I have the power of the Goddess now, I'm not really any different than I was before, when I was the Keeper. I want them to feel confident in me. To know I valued them as allies, and I value them now as council members." I smiled apologetically. "So I guess I'll just draft an opening statement that says all that. The real purpose of the meeting is to discuss resuming the missions, so you've already got that covered. We'll just see what comes out of that discussion."

He nodded again. "So, on to other business then: a representative from the firm will be here tomorrow morning at nine to review Mr. Fleming's will with you. He got tired of waiting and I couldn't delay it anymore."

Well at least it was more convenient than heading down to the Phoenix office with an entire entourage in tow. Somehow I didn't think my security team would appreciate it if I just *zipped* there by myself.

"Sorry about that. With everything that's happened, I sort of forgot all about it. I'll explain it to him tomorrow and beg his forgiveness."

"The Goddess *does not beg.*" Arddhu's voice was sharp and ugly, and I stared at him in surprise. He'd never spoken to me like that before.

To diffuse the situation, I kept myself extremely calm. "It's just a figure of speech, Arddhu. Trust me, I won't be doing any *actual* begging."

"Oh." Chagrined, he glanced from Anthony to me. "That is good then."

Looked like I'd have to teach him the phrase *never mind.*

Returning my attention to Anthony, I nodded for him to continue.

"I should mention that a will reading is not customary. It's Hollywood fiction. Usually a copy is just mailed to any and all beneficiaries. But in this case, the firm has been quite insistent."

I frowned. "Do you have any idea why they want this formality?"

He shook his head. "No, but I'll attend with you, so we'll find out tomorrow."

"Okay. Anything else?"

He skimmed his notes. "No, that's it." He stood. "Thank you."

"Wait, I have something for you." He sat again, and I continued. "Mike's cottage in Ireland... I'd like to gift it to the village of Finn's Cove. Can you make that happen?"

"Certainly." He made a note on his tablet, then met my gaze. "What would you like done with the personal items inside?"

Good question.

"Um... maybe have them boxed up and sent to my cottage? I'll go through them when I get a chance."

He made another note. "Anything else?"

"No, that's it."

"Then, enjoy your evening." He smiled and left.

I turned to Arddhu and found him staring thoughtfully at my bracelet. "Something wrong?"

"I am uncertain." His gaze met mine. "I had assumed the Sphere—Anu—would separate from you after you became the Goddess, but she has not."

Now I glanced down; Anu glowed a soft sky blue, her normal shade for a calm, peaceful state.

"Yeah, I've wondered about that too. Do you think it means I'm still the Keeper?"

"I do not know."

"Has there ever been a Keeper who was also the Goddess?"

"Not in my time."

Given that his *time* was thousands of years, it was interesting.

"Well, I'm not going to worry about that right now. We've got bigger—uh, other priorities." I'd been about to say *bigger fish to fry*, but figured he'd be just as lost on that idiom as he was with most others.

He nodded. "That is true."

We still had a few minutes until dinner was ready and he seemed much calmer now, so I decided to ask him something I'd been thinking about.

"So, about this Consort thing. Is there any reason I can't have more than one?"

His brows shot up. "You wish an entire *harem* of Consorts?"

I had to laugh. "No, no, no. Just two."

"You mean to choose *both* of us? Kevin and myself?" He was incredulous.

"Sure. Why not? I mean, I don't really want to have to choose between the two of you. I love you both, you know."

Now he was completely gobsmacked. "You... *love* me? Us?"

"Yes."

Why was that really so hard to understand? The human heart could expand to hold many individuals close: family members, lovers, friends, and pets. Why shouldn't mine allow for two Consorts?

He was silent for a moment, lost in thought. When he spoke again, it was with deep affection and a hint of amusement. "There is no precedent for more than one Consort concurrently, but you *are* the Goddess. What this means is: you are not constrained by rules, only tradition."

I quirked a brow. "To me, tradition is more of a guideline. Not a rulebook."

"That is a relatively modern viewpoint, but completely understandable, as you are a modern Goddess. So, in summary, you may create as many of your own traditions as you wish."

"Excellent." I flashed a grin. "That's settled then. I'll make the announcement at the council meeting next week."

Kevin entered from the panel in the window-wall, but Arddhu hadn't noticed as he said, "You should advise Kevin before then."

"Of course."

"Advise me of what?" Kevin plopped down in the chair opposite mine.

"Oh, no big deal," I teased. "I've only made my decision on Consort."

He stiffened, and his face became a mask.

Immediately, I regretted being playful, as this was obviously a serious subject. I didn't delay any longer. "I'd like you both to be my Consort. Er... *Consorts*."

"Whoa." His eyes widened, and his posture eased. "That's... wow. Unheard of. But hey, you're the Goddess. You can do just about whatever you want."

Not exactly the joyous reaction I'd expected. "Is anyone going to give me—or us—any shit about it?"

He shook his head. "I don't think so. I mean, like the Morrigan said, it's not like they don't know we're already bonded." He glanced at Arddhu to include him. "The three of us."

"Okay, great." I frowned. "But you don't seem very happy about it."

Now he grinned. "Oh, I am. Trust me. You just took me by surprise."

"Dinner's ready," Brianna called from the kitchen.

Well, now that Kevin was here, it seemed rude to exclude him from dinner. I stood. "Will you join us?"

He accepted, and Arddhu didn't seem at all disappointed we wouldn't be dining alone, after all. When we got to the kitchen island, I stared for a moment at the three place settings already set on the counter.

Her magick? Or she'd just assumed?

Shrugging, I took my seat between the two guys. Brianna had prepared a wonderful steak dinner complete with baked potato and a small side salad, and paired it with a delicious cabernet sauvignon from a local vineyard in the Verde Valley, the high country north of Phoenix. She'd quietly left as we began to eat.

"How are the classes coming along?" I asked Kevin between bites.

"Surprisingly well. Dagda and his people are catching on quick. They're already searching the internet and reading about history on their own. This is the second group, and so far they're all pretty tech-savvy too. I think I'll be done with classes in about a week."

"Just in time for the council meeting," I said.

From checking with the others, I knew that their classes were also going well. The Morrigan mentioned she'd had a hard time convincing the Tuatha to update their clothing at first, but after they saw the variety of styles, fabrics, and colors available, they'd become quite enamored.

"You know," I added, "We should probably reserve some time at the meeting for them to ask questions or bring up any topics from their research for discussion." I turned to Arddhu. "And I was thinking that maybe you should attend one of Kevin's classes, too."

He tensed, but it was Kevin who replied. "We've, uh, been having private lessons." He continued via mental communication link. "*He doesn't want the Tuatha to know he's technically challenged. For some reason it's really hard for him to learn this stuff.*"

"*Oh. Thanks for letting me know.*"

Aloud, I quickly said to Arddhu, "That's great then. I just didn't want you to feel left out."

He relaxed. "Thank you. You are thoughtful."

I tried to imagine being ancient and incredibly powerful with unparalleled wisdom yet struggling with technology and modern slang. But because I'd been raised differently and was a modern human, I just couldn't. And although he'd had a shower in the guest bathroom I'd used on his world, he hadn't had electricity or other modern conveniences. Instead, he'd preferred to use magick for the basics like lighting and cooking.

It was almost as if he'd purposely shut himself off from most human advancements over the centuries. There was probably a reason for that, and maybe someday I'd find out what it was.

But in the meantime, I probably should try to be more understanding. And it was probably a good thing I hadn't made a wisecrack about old dogs and new tricks.

CHAPTER TWENTY-NINE

A NTHONY INSISTED ON holding the reading of the will in the VIP tent instead of the main house, to give it more of a formal setting. We were using the tent increasingly more often for meetings and gatherings, and I had to admit it'd been one of Mike's best ideas.

I'd never met anyone from the firm's Phoenix office except for Mike. So I didn't know what to expect, but William Woolston certainly wasn't it.

William was late middle-aged and about the same height as me. Tufts of white hair ringed his otherwise bald pate, and his matching white mustache had been groomed into curly handlebars for a distinctive appearance. He was impeccably dressed in a beautifully tailored navy suit, and his black shoes were polished to a high gloss.

For this reading, none of my other councilors were present. They didn't need to be, really, as it didn't concern them.

After William politely declined refreshments, the three of us settled in the plush seating area. He opened his briefcase, produced three copies of the will, and handed one to Anthony and me. He immediately began reading aloud and I quietly followed along.

The will wasn't much different in format than a typical will here in the States—I'd had one drawn up just a few weeks ago—but some of the terminology was unmistakably Irish.

Periodically, William paused and asked if either of us had any questions. When we didn't, he resumed.

Finally we got to the meat of it.

"To Deirdre Ann Connor, I bequeath my entire estate, including my property and dwelling in the village of Finn's Cove, County Cork, Ireland, as well as my personal property currently located within Ms. Connor's dwelling in Scottsdale, Arizona, United States."

William continued reading through the rest, but I tuned him out as I stared at the date under Mike's signature.

He'd had this will written two years ago. In late November, just before I'd been captured by Cromm.

Somehow, I'd expected it to be more recent, like last summer. When things had gone to shit.

"Dee?" Anthony interrupted my thoughts.

"Hmm?"

"Any questions, Ms. Connor?" William asked.

"Oh. Yes. I've already mentioned to Anthony that I intend to gift the cottage and property in County Cork to the village of Finn's Cove. Can you two handle that for me?"

"Of course." If he was surprised, he didn't show it. "I must advise, however, that the payment of proper inheritance taxes will still be required. Both in Ireland and the US."

"I understand." I turned to Anthony. "Can you take care of that, too? I think Mike set up some kind of LLC for me or something, but I'm not sure. I've never had much to do with any of that." In fact, I'd never even seen a bill or bank statement. Everything had always been taken care of for me, first by Mike and now by Anthony.

"Yes," Anthony replied. "I'll have the paperwork ready for you to review and sign as soon as possible, and I'll work with William to transfer everything quickly and smoothly."

"Thanks." I turned back to William. "And thank you for your patience. I'm so sorry I kept you waiting—things have been crazy around here for quite a while."

One corner of his mouth quirked. "I've heard. But not to worry, we're done now."

I studied him as he gathered his things and prepared to leave. "Can I ask you a question?"

"Of course."

"Why did you have to do this in person? I mean, there wasn't anything earth-shattering in the will. It just seems... sort of strange."

"No, You are quite correct. It wasn't about the will at all." Now he smiled. "It was a requirement of our branch manager. He insisted I meet the Keeper of the Sphere. And now I can also say I've met the Goddess."

Fuck me. That's what this was all about? If he asked for a selfie, I was going to scream.

As I handed Anthony my copy of the will, he and I shared a glance. I rolled my eyes, and he ducked his head to hide the grin that twitched on his lips.

But thankfully, no selfie request. William and I simply shook hands and Anthony left with him. I went back to the house, shaking my head.

Kevin and Brianna were in the living room watching television, and it caught my attention. Some guy was talking with a morning news anchor about the eco-terrorists, pointing out there hadn't been any attacks in quite some time.

And he tried to take credit for it.

He appeared to be in his late sixties, but well taken care of in the way rich guys always seemed to be. His dark hair was perfectly coiffed but probably dyed to cover the gray. His face was tanned and almost unnaturally smooth, as if he'd had too much anti-aging work done.

But somehow he seemed slimy, like a mobster. His attitude toward the female anchor was condescending, arrogant, and rude. As I watched in disbelief, his eyes boldly dropped to the anchor's cleavage before lazily returning to her face, not caring in the least that he was on camera the whole time. His smug grin was infuriating.

Asshole.

The guy's name flashed across the bottom of the screen and I immediately recognized it. I must've memorized the list of targets at some point, because I could clearly see it in my mind.

And yeah, this asshole was on the list.

Angelo Marinelli, primarily the Chief Executive Officer of a multinational oil and gas firm, but he was involved in lots of other industries that reeked of the international crime syndicate. He routinely bragged about his lobbyists successfully convincing influential members of Congress to remove regulations on air-quality emissions and water standards.

And I remembered he'd recently completed the acquisition of a huge corporation best known for bottling spring water in drought-stricken states.

Like California. And Arizona.

He was still boasting to the pretty blonde anchor. "Some people say Homeland Security must've taken them out," he said, then looked directly into the camera. "But I'm certain I've scared the bunch of little cowards off."

He seemed to stare right at me with a wicked grin that reminded me way too much of Cromm. My stomach rolled and I shuddered even as my anger spiked higher than it'd ever been.

The anchor smiled flirtatiously at the camera. "Mr. Marinelli has been very vocal on this issue. Not just here in our studio, but on social media as well." Now she faced him directly and leaned forward as she continued speaking.

Her blouse must've fallen open, from how he shamelessly ogled her cleavage.

"This guy is such an asshole," I growled.

"He's trying to draw us out," Kevin said. "Make us come after him."

Now he was bragging about his company's stock price.

The longer I watched—the more he talked—the more it fueled my rage.

"Is this live or recorded?" I asked.

"Live broadcast," Brianna murmured, frowning at the screen.

Not taking my eyes from Marinelli, I clenched my fist.

He stopped his prattle in mid-sentence. His grin faded and his eyes widened. His face turned from tan to pink to red to sickly gray, and his mouth opened and shut like a fish gasping for water. The mic clipped to his collar clearly picked up the strangled gurgle just before he pitched forward onto the news desk and lay motionless.

The news anchor stared in mute horror for a moment, then pandemonium broke out in the studio. Someone off-camera yelled for an ambulance to be called. The anchor finally shook herself and reached forward to delicately feel for a pulse.

She raised her head and looked at someone out of the camera's view. "He's—he's dead." Her voice shook, and she looked like she was about to cry.

Abruptly, the camera cut away to another desk, where a man kept his eyes firmly on the camera and began running through the day's headlines in a steady, controlled voice.

"Dee?"

Calmly, I met Kevin's wide eyes.

He pointed at the screen without looking at it. "Did you just do that?"

I slowly nodded.

Brianna quickly stood and left for the kitchen, mumbling something about starting lunch even though it was way too early for that.

"Why?"

"Why not?" I countered.

But the concern—and was that fear?—in his eyes hurt me.

"What's wrong?" I asked.

He clicked the remote and the screen went dark. He ran his fingers through his hair, then shook his head. "I can't believe you just did that."

"What's wrong?" I said again.

He met my gaze somewhat reluctantly. "I have a really bad feeling about this. You should've waited for the missions to start again."

"Why? I don't see what the big deal is."

He hesitated before continuing, and I hated the measured caution I heard in his voice. "What did you do to him?"

"I executed him."

"No, I mean, what *exactly* did you do?"

"I... I strangled him."

"So, when they perform the autopsy on him, they'll find what, exactly?"

I frowned. What the hell was he getting at?

"I don't know," I shrugged. "I'm not a doctor."

He shook his head. "Oh, Dee." Now his voice held something I'd never heard in it before: disappointment.

Disappointment in *me*.

That hurt even more. I couldn't bear it. Tears came to my eyes.

"Kevin?" I murmured. "What is it? Talk to me."

His eyes lifted and held mine, but the sadness there tore my heart into pieces. "It'll raise questions when they open him up and find everything normal except a crushed esophagus. It'll draw unwanted attention. To us immortals. To *you*."

"Only if they can link it to me. Or us. But they won't be able to."

"Are you sure?"

"Well, yeah. Why aren't *you*?"

"Because I've seen mortals turn against immortals before. It gets ugly, real fast. And for a lot less of a reason than a spontaneous, live, on-camera execution."

He'd know.

At roughly two thousand years old, he'd probably witnessed much of the witch trials. Most likely he knew first-hand how horrible they'd been. And back then, they didn't have the internet and social media. What would that be like now?

I sank into a chair and tried to think through the consequences of my act, but no matter how hard I tried, I couldn't see any reason to worry. I couldn't tell him that, though. I didn't think he'd believe me.

"And there's another reason I'm concerned," he said in a quiet voice. When I met his gaze, he continued. "What's the point of having a council—having us as advisers—if you just do whatever you want anyway? Without talking it over with any of us first?"

To that, I had nothing to say. Because he had an excellent point.

"How does what you just did make you any different from Ida?" His voice was measured, but his eyes were tortured.

And with those words, he'd stuck a knife in my gut and twisted it.

"How can you say that? I'm *nothing* like her."

"Right now, yes, you are." He shook his head in frustration. "Can't you see it, Dee?"

Standing, I snapped, "*No, I'm not.*"

And I *zipped* myself to Ard na Mara, where I hoped to calm down before I said or did anything else I'd regret.

Kicking at a piece of driftwood on the beach in frustration, I let my rage boil over.

How *dare* he say that to me?

All I'd done was take out a target—one who'd already been on the list, for fuck's sake. It wasn't like I'd killed another immortal. Or an innocent human or something. Why did it matter so goddamn much? Just what was the big fucking deal?

The late afternoon sun sparkled on the deep blue ocean. I dug my toes into the warm sand, something that I'd always enjoyed, but even that didn't ease my anger as I paced a groove into the beach and muttered to myself.

The sudden dimming of the sun made me look up with a frown. What now?

Above my head, dark storm clouds swirled in what had been a cloudless blue sky only a moment before.

Shit.

A shiver of apprehension tickled my spine.

I'd done that.

No, my *anger* had done that.

"*Deirdre, you must calm yourself,*" Anu urged.

The storm could grow out of control if I let it. And I knew the fishermen were still out in their boats.

Shit. The absolute last thing I ever wanted to do was hurt innocents.

Quickly, I closed my eyes and converted my anger into neutral—yet powerful—energy, then sent it into Earth. Under my feet, the ground rumbled then was still.

The black clouds slowly dissipated. A moment later, the cloudless blue sky had returned.

Taking a deep breath, I sent gratitude to Anu. "*Sorry, I forgot myself.*"

In reply, she pulsed sapphire blue but remained silent.

From now on, I had to be more careful; such strong emotions could become unpredictable actions with possibly devastating consequences.

This had been a somewhat harmless lesson for me. I had to maintain better control, now that I had the power of the Goddess.

I continued walking along the shore, calmer now but still a bit unsettled from the disagreement with Kevin.

Not an argument. I refused to call it that.

Regardless of the semantics, though, it'd been our first. And I was a bit embarrassed that I'd run away rather than face him and state my case with better logic. I'd let my emotions get the better of me and hadn't been thinking clearly.

Then again, I'd also been afraid I'd lash out and hurt him.

Dangerous state of affairs.

And if I had lashed out, would he have retaliated? I sure as hell didn't want to get into a knock-down, drag-out magickal fight with him.

I *loved* him, for fuck's sake.

My eye caught a sparkle of blue on the sand, and I bent to pick it up.

It was one of the elusive cobalt blue glass beads Mike had told me about, so long ago.

Well, it was only a year and a half ago, but it felt like a lifetime.

I gently brushed the sand off the bead and as I stared into its blue depths, the tears came.

Collapsing onto the soft sand with my fist curled protectively around the bead, I wrapped my arms around my knees and buried my head in them. I let the tears flow as they'd never done before, and didn't hold back. After all, no one was around to see or hear me, and the crash of the waves drowned out my wails.

Eyes tightly closed, I sobbed even harder than I had after my first mission as I berated myself, hated myself, and felt sorry for myself.

I thought of all I'd lost since that day Mike rang my doorbell.

My old self, innocent of the cruelty of immortals.

My boring life, so steady and predictable.

The pain of the loss of my parents, made fresh by the recent knowledge of how and why they'd died.

The lives of other people I'd cared about, like Jason.

The friendship I'd had with Mike.

The career I'd worked so hard for.

All the sorrows of the past year and a half washed over me in waves: all the pain and frustration and loss.

And, most recently, the disappointment, the fear, and the sadness in Kevin's eyes. All caused by *me*. It made my heart ache so badly I thought it would burst.

The tears fell relentlessly; for everyone, for everything, but most of all for myself.

I'd never asked for any of this.

I hadn't asked to be Keeper. And I sure as hell hadn't asked to be the Goddess.

But I'd been so proud of how well I'd dealt with all the changes.

I thought I'd been so strong.

And I'd wanted to make others proud of me.

Arddhu. Kevin. The Morrigan. The people of Finn's Cove. Even the Tuatha.

But especially Kevin.

It dawned on me then, how much I loved him—that the disappointment I'd seen in his eyes had more than just hurt. It'd cut me to the core.

What would happen when he told Arddhu—and the Morrigan—what I'd done? How I'd acted unilaterally and without thought of consequence? How I'd put them all in danger?

Would I see the same disappointment, fear, and sadness in their eyes?

My tears fell even harder at the thought, and I rocked and trembled, lost in my pain.

How could I face them, knowing I'd failed them all so soon?

Oh, to have someone dry my tears, hold me, and tell me everything would be okay... but no. That was impossible. I'd run away from everyone.

I was alone on my beach at Ard na Mara.

A moment later, an arm circled my shoulders, startling me. I raised my head and blinked through my tears, but I couldn't see who it was because it was dark.

Wait—when had the sun set?

"Hush now, dear girl." The voice was soft and lilting, and I recognized it immediately.

Maggie?

My breath hitched in my throat and I burrowed into her warmth and softness. Both arms around me now, she held me close. "All will be well, you'll see," she murmured.

"Oh Maggie," I croaked, my voice hoarse from all my wailing. "I'm a fucking mess right now."

She chuckled. "As are we all, from time to time. It's part of living, dear one."

She stroked my hair, smoothing it from its wind-blown mess and calming me at the same time. She even sang softly, a sweet Irish lullaby, which somehow carried over the sound of the waves as if they were silent.

After a while, my eyes had finally run out of tears and felt like I'd rubbed sand in them. I gulped air in deep, shuddering breaths with my mouth, since my nose was completely clogged with snot.

As if she knew, she pressed a handkerchief into my right hand—the one without the precious blue glass bead still clutched inside. "Here now, dry your tears and blow your nose," she said.

I could've used two, but after I was done, I stared at the soggy mess in my hand, unsure what to do with it.

"Go on and keep it," she said with a laugh.

I stuffed it in my pocket then opened my fist to show her my prize, suddenly feeling as if I were five years old again.

"Look. I found one." Which was completely irrational, since it was full dark now and she couldn't possibly see it.

"Oh, that's wonderful." I heard rather than saw her smile. "String it onto a cord and wear it around your neck, and you'll always have the comfort of this moment with you."

Sniffling, I tucked it away in another pocket.

"Come with me, now." She stood and helped me up, holding my hand in hers. "We have much to talk about, you and I."

When had the moon risen? It'd been dark just a moment ago.

Now the half-moon illuminated our way just enough to make sure I wouldn't trip over a piece of driftwood. She didn't lead me to the stairs and up to the cottage, though; instead, she guided me toward the cliffs.

And then I knew.

She was taking me to the cave.

The Sanctuary.

Once we stepped inside, a small fire flared to life in the firepit; was that Maggie's magick at work? I remembered her being an Earth witch, but maybe she had a bit of Fire witch in her, too.

Or maybe, things like that changed after someone traveled beyond the veil.

In the firelight, Maggie didn't look any different than the last time I'd seen her, back when I'd become the Keeper. I was surprised she was dressed in jeans and a sweater because somehow I'd expected her to wear something more old-fashioned.

We sat on one of the large rocks surrounding the firepit and she opened a flask. She took a long drink and handed it to me with a grin and a sparkle in her eye.

Not sure what it was, I took a small, cautious sip. Sweet berries burst on my tongue, with an underlying hint of a fragrant spice like cinnamon. It was one of Garrett's unique meads; I'd recognize it anywhere. I took a longer swallow, and it spread delicious warmth and comfort throughout me.

But when I tried to return the flask, Maggie waved me off. "Keep that, too. You've more need of it than I."

I recapped it and set it on the rock between us.

"So," I started. "You know what's happened, right? That I'm the Goddess now?"

"Aye," she nodded. "But I think you'd like to just be Deirdre right now. So, I left my reverence at the beach."

I blinked at her. How astute. Was this part of her magick, too?

As if she'd read my mind, she smiled. "It's not hard to guess that's what you want or need. No magick is required to see that."

"Thank you. I appreciate it."

We sat in silence for a few moments while I stared into the flames and collected my thoughts. Then I asked, "Am I still the Keeper?"

She pursed her lips before answering. "Aye, I suppose. If you want to be. We've never had a Keeper who became the Goddess until now, so it's a bit of unchartered territory." She cocked her head. "Have you asked Anu what she thinks?"

I could've smacked myself; it hadn't occurred to me. "No."

She smiled but didn't say anything, and seemed to be waiting.

Oh. She wanted me to ask Anu *now.*

Okay then.

"*Am I still the Keeper?*" I sent to Anu.

"*Of course.*" Her reply was almost immediate. "*Until You no longer have need of me, You are still the Keeper.*"

Wait—what? That didn't make sense. "*But I'll always need you, Anu.*"

She didn't exactly laugh, but I clearly heard the amusement in her voice. "*No, Deirdre. Someday, You will indeed no longer need me. And we will separate. But worry not, it will be a happy occasion. You will see.*"

When I met Maggie's eyes, there was amusement there, too. "She says yes, I'm still the Keeper."

"There you go, then," she said, and nodded at the flask. "Have another drink."

That seemed a bit strange, but I complied.

"So why are you here, all by yourself?" she asked.

"I'm not by myself. I'm with you." I grinned at my cleverness.

"Cheeky girl." She laughed, a pleasant tinkling sound that echoed in the stone chamber. "Now, I'll ask again: why are you here?"

"I... I needed some space."

She nodded. "Someone told you something you didn't like, eh?"

I stared at her.

How the hell—?

She smiled again. "I see I'm right."

I sighed and watched the flames dance in a small draft of air. "It was Kevin." Then I remembered she'd known him by his former name. "Uh, Bricriu."

Her elegant brows knit. "What's this? He changed his name?"

"Yeah. He did it when *he* changed, became a better person, I mean. He's vowed to only do good deeds now. And he has—he even helped rescue me from Cromm last year, and he's been one of my most loyal allies."

She nodded absently, then her gaze turned sharp. "He's also your Consort, isn't that right?"

Again, I stared at her. She seemed to know an awful lot for a dead person.

"How do you know all this?"

"One of my many gifts is the sight. But it's not consistent—especially now that I'm dead—and I can't see as much as I could when I still lived. No, I only see bits and pieces, never the entire picture. It's like when you buy a jigsaw puzzle. There are always some pieces already fitted together, but most are loose."

What a charming way of describing it. Gods, she was a fascinating woman.

So that's how she knew that Kevin was my Consort, but not that he'd changed his name from Bricriu.

"Yes," I finally confirmed. "He's one of my Consorts."

"Ah, defying tradition already? Spunky girl. I like it." She smiled again, then one eyebrow lifted. "I've seen Cernunnos with you often. Is he another of your Consorts?"

Cernunnos... that was one of Arddhu's other names.

"Yes. I actually only have the two."

"Well, you made good choices." She nodded at the flask again. "Drink."

Okay, enough of *that*.

"Why's it so important that I drink this mead, Maggie?" My voice had come out a bit more sharp than I'd intended, but I let the question stand.

She seemed surprised at my mistrust, though. "Because it will help you. That's all."

Eyes narrowed, I drank.

Well, she wasn't wrong. It must be helping me, because I did feel better. Emotionally and mentally. And I was calm and relaxed now. The earlier emotional storm was completely gone, although I truly didn't know if it was because it'd worn itself out or was due to the mead's influence.

Whatever. Maybe there really wasn't any harm in it.

Besides, it wasn't like I was driving anywhere. And it wasn't like drinking mead would hurt me in any way; my evolving physical form now metabolized alcohol differently than it had when I'd been fully human. I wouldn't be able to drink myself to death.

"So why did you run away from your Consort?" she asked.

No way was I going to admit to her what I'd already admitted to myself: that I had, indeed, run away. Not just from Kevin, but from everyone.

"I *didn't* run away." I hated how defensive I sounded, but she just calmly met my eyes as if to say, *oh really?* "Look, I know that's what it seems like, but I really just wanted some peace and quiet."

"To cry your eyes out where no one could see or hear."

"What's the big deal?" I snapped. "So what if I did?"

She leaned forward, her elbows on her knees. "Dear girl, there is nothing wrong. You don't need to be so defensive. I'm only trying to help you."

"Help me? I'm glad you comforted me out there—" I jabbed my thumb over my shoulder to indicate the beach "—but I didn't ask to be psychoanalyzed."

Belatedly, I wondered if she even knew what the word meant, but I needn't have worried. She knew.

And she was insulted. It showed in every line of her stiff posture.

Straightening, she lifted her chin. "I apologize for offending You, My Lady. I'll leave if You wish."

Shit. I hated that she'd gone all formal on me. But it was my own damn fault.

Why did I get so damn defensive, anyway?

"No, please. You didn't offend me." I sighed and rubbed my forehead. "I'm sorry I snapped at you. I guess I'm just... out of sorts. This whole thing—becoming the Goddess but even before that, becoming the Keeper—has been nothing but a massive roller coaster. Something good would happen, then nothing but horrible things." And then, as if a dam had broken, the words tumbled out almost faster than my mouth could keep up with. "I mean, I thought I had my life all planned out, with a good career and promotions to look forward to. I figured I'd eventually get married, have a house and kids. Probably a dog, too. Grow old with a great guy and die of old age with a bunch of grandkids. And no regrets."

Abruptly I stopped, a bit stunned at what I'd just said. I hadn't even realized any of that had been bothering me that much. Especially the loss of a normal existence.

"And then I came into your life," she said quietly. "And turned it upside down."

"Yeah." My voice was just as quiet. "So now I'm going to live forever, and I'm responsible for the entire *fucking planet*, and nothing is simple anymore. Not even something that I thought was the right thing to do but found out it was for the wrong reasons." At her puzzled look, I remembered she only saw bits and pieces, not the whole picture, so I explained. "We—the allies and me—we were removing the threats to Earth before we could heal it when I became the Goddess. But earlier today, I... I lost my temper and removed a threat all by myself. With just a thought. On live, nationwide television."

To her credit, she didn't seem surprised or shocked. Or disappointed. She just nodded for me to continue.

"So when Kevin got upset and told me I wasn't any different from Ida, I..." How should I put this? Oh the hell with it. "... I came here before I said or did something I'd regret. Like maybe hurt him. Just like I hurt Mike once, when I lost my temper. But now, with the power of the Goddess, I'd do more than just hurt him. I'm afraid I'd kill him." I paused to take a breath. "And so, yeah, fine. I ran away. I came here."

When I'd mentioned Mike, she'd frowned and watched me closely. And I remembered that Mike was her son.

I took a deep breath. "Oh. I have some bad news for you. It's about Mike."

She met my gaze but didn't seem upset, so she probably hadn't seen this part with her gift of sight.

"He... he's dead."

She squeezed her eyes shut with a small moan, then only a few seconds later they flashed open. "Once, I was granted a vision of him fighting at your side. Was he killed in battle?"

I stalled by taking another drink from the flask. I'd never had to tell someone their son was dead, and it was harder than I'd thought. It'd be even harder if I had to admit I'd been the one to kill Mike. I hoped I didn't. Maybe I could just skirt around that bit.

"No," I murmured. "I'm sorry. He... he betrayed us, me and the allies. He conspired with the enemy." At the question in her eyes, I was more specific. "He joined with Cromm against us."

"I see." Now her face fell and she looked older, somehow. "My goodness, you've certainly been given more than your share of challenges."

I snorted. "Oh come on. I have your memories, remember? I saw what you went through. Especially with that Prince what's-his-name—how could you tolerate his touch after the atrocities he did?"

She raised a brow. "Because I didn't question what the Goddess—Ida—asked of me. She needed me to complete a mission. And if I hadn't, where would we be now? The world would be a much darker place."

Well, there was that. By her actions, Maggie had probably prevented a third world war.

"I know Ida wasn't always bad," I argued. "But in the end, we had to banish her. She'd been planning some terrible things. Horrific things."

I didn't miss the heartbreak in Maggie's eyes, but as if to hide it, she quickly closed them. A single tear leaked from one corner and glistened in the fire's glow.

Her voice was barely above a whisper. "Tell me."

"Are you sure you want to know?"

She nodded. "I must."

So, I told her about Ida's plans. I told her what Ida had done to Tyr and Nayenezgani. I didn't hold anything back. I even told her that Ida had promised Mike the power of the Sphere for himself.

When I finished, Maggie grimaced and shook her head. But when she opened her eyes, the grief I'd seen earlier had been replaced with anger.

"Now I feel foolish for never questioning her," she said, and reached for the flask. She took two long swallows.

"You couldn't have known. We only just found out before... before we freed the Tuatha."

"Ah, yes, I saw something of that. I never knew them, they were gone from here before my time. But I'd heard the stories, of course."

She handed the flask back to me, and before she could say it, I drank. Then I shook it, expecting it to be almost empty by now, but the damn thing was still full. What the hell? A magick flask?

"It can't have been easy, having all this thrust on you with little to no choice," she said.

"Yeah, I think that's probably the one thing that really bothers me the most."

"So how do you think you could feel more in control?"

Staring into the fire, I frowned, thinking.

The lack of control I'd felt with Mike when he always bossed me around had somehow stuck with me even after he'd died. And even though Anthony had made sure I was in on every decision, I'd still felt like a subordinate.

The Morrigan had once asked me who was the boss, me or Mike. I'd thought I was, but then I'd never really taken control as I'd expected to, because that roller coaster had kept on running. There'd always been something going on that'd made me feel like I had to defer to the others.

And because I'd always felt like the newbie—first as the Keeper and now as the Goddess—I'd been deferring most of the heavy lifting of the decision-making to Arddhu, the Morrigan, and Kevin, since they were all so much older and more experienced immortals than I was.

It sure as hell didn't make sense to willingly delegate my authority then complain I didn't have any.

Then there was the part of me that felt a bit like an imposter Goddess, since I hadn't exactly been accepted by Ares, Athena, and Kali, and who knows who else I hadn't even met yet.

No, I could only blame others for so much. Most of this I'd put on *myself* and created all this stress for *myself*.

Fuck, I was a mess.

But all that was in the past. I needed to think about the future. How could I change it?

Maggie had asked how I could feel more in control.

To do that, I needed my council to advise me but leave the decision-making authority to me. Then, I needed to actually *make* those decisions instead of passing them off to others.

And I should probably take a more active role in the day-to-day operations, like spending more time with the security team I'd neglected so badly, and also with the Tuatha. Maybe a daily or weekly briefing with Anthony, too.

To be the boss, I needed to *act* like the boss.

"I think I need to be the boss," I finally said.

"Yes." She smiled. "Because, dear girl, you *are* the boss."

I took a deep breath and slowly released it.

Yes. I could do this. I know I could.

"So how do you feel now?" she asked.

How *did* I feel? Better, for sure. Calmer, absolutely. And I wasn't sure what Maggie had really done for me with this little talk, but at least I felt like I could go home to Scottsdale, rationally discuss what I'd done, and not lose my shit.

Most importantly, not hurt anyone.

"Good," I said. "I feel good."

I smiled at her, and she smiled back.

"Then my job here is done. Unless You have further need of me, My Lady?"

I'd only shaken my head but before I could say a word of thanks, she disappeared and the fire went out, leaving me in darkness.

No, not darkness.

As my eyes adjusted—much quicker than when I'd been fully human—the cave was clearly illuminated by the phosphorescent rock in the pool nearby, and by the moon shining through the smoke hole in the roof. It was now directly overhead, which meant hours must've passed while we'd talked and drank.

It hadn't seemed that long, but there was no other explanation.

The flask lay on the rock beside me; I tucked it into the back pocket of my jeans. After a thought, I checked my front pockets. The snotty handkerchief was still in one, and the blue bead was still in the other. I left the cave feeling lighter, and in better spirits than I'd felt in a long time.

The beach was beautiful in the moonlight. The waves on the shore seemed peaceful somehow, as they gently rolled on the sand with barely a sound.

How odd.

As I walked along the beach, I took stock of myself.

I felt refreshed, as if I'd slept for days.

I felt relieved, as if my worst fears had been put to rest.

I felt energized, confident I could tackle my new challenges.

My new *job*.

Oh sure, it was a helluva lot different from my old accountant job, and it wasn't one I'd originally signed up for.

But it was still my job, nonetheless.

And I was finally at peace with it—both of my jobs, actually. The Keeper and the Goddess.

I was ready for whatever came next.

EPILOGUE

A THENA DRUMS HER fingers on the beat-up bar table, impatient for her cheap glass of wine. The table wobbles annoyingly; it desperately needs to be balanced. "Where's that damn waitress?"

"Patience is a virtue, sister," Ares murmurs, completely distracted by the gorgeous woman laughing with her friends at the next table.

Kali remains silent. She hardly ever speaks, she mostly just glares at anyone and everyone. And occasionally, she growls. The sweet old motherly demeanor is gone.

They are in a dark corner of a run-down bar somewhere in Detroit. Bob Seger blares from the speakers mounted high on the walls. The floor is sticky, but the table is clean—at least the top is. No one dares explore the underside.

Not even a god. Or goddess.

Athena used her magick to alter their appearances and make them less noticeable among humans. They blend in with the background of the bar, and no one knows there are three immortals sitting amongst them.

Finally, the harried server appears with a tray full of drinks. She sets the thick glass mug of domestic lager in front of Ares, the chipped glass of house white in front of Athena, and the tall, frosted-red plastic cup of fake peach-flavored iced tea in front of Kali.

The server grabs the twenty-dollar bill from the center of the table. "I'll be right back with your change," she says and turns to go.

"Keep it," Athena says.

The server, startled, tries to make eye contact with Athena but Athena avoids it. "Thank you," she says, then dashes away to fetch the next order for her section.

"She's already started healing Earth." Athena's voice is low, but she needn't worry; the music is loud enough to cover their voices. "We have to do something before it's too late."

When Athena heard the Earthsong, she wanted to scream. Or kill something. Even better: scream *while* killing something.

Ares had calmed her down, but she still wants to scream.

All that power and the bitch uses it to heal Earth.

Ares doesn't say anything now, and she frowns at him.

He's still staring at the human woman, trying to catch her eye.

Athena jabs him in the ribs. "Stop that. You'll attract attention."

Reluctantly, he meets Athena's gaze with a glare of his own. "I can't help it. I'm fucking *horny*."

Athena rolls her eyes and sighs. "So what else is new? You're *always* horny. But right now, we need to talk about what we're going to do."

Ares downs half his beer in one swallow, then wipes his mouth with the back of his hand with a grimace. "Fuck, this tastes like piss."

Athena rolls her eyes again. "Focus, brother. What are we going to *do?*"

"Kill them. Kill them all. Destroy everything," Kali growls, just loud enough for them to hear.

The casual menace in Kali's voice gives Athena chills. There's no other way to put it: Kali creeps her out. She didn't really want Kali to join up with them, but she didn't have much choice. Kali just attached herself to them as they deserted the rest of the group. After that Keeper *bitch* became the Goddess.

She should've known better than to trust Anu. *That* bitch had been trouble from day one with her high-and-mighty, better-than-anyone-else attitude.

Athena rolls her eyes—making sure Kali doesn't see her do it—and runs her hand through her hair. "We *can't* kill them and destroy everything. This is our planet, too."

"We can go somewhere else," Ares points out. "There are lots of other worlds out there. Especially once we get the power of the Goddess."

We? Athena lets that slide and suppresses a smirk. Let them both think the power will be split between the three of them.

She knows better.

She's not going to share that power with *anyone*. She's waited long enough.

One might say she'd do anything to have it, but they'd be wrong.

She'd do *almost* anything. She wouldn't give up her own magick, for example.

She'd kill her brother, though, who's been an albatross around her neck for millennia.

And she'd kill Kali. In a heartbeat.

Athena raises her wine glass. "Here's to somewhere else."

The trio clink their glasses—well, Kali's plastic cup only makes a dull *clunk*—and now Athena allows a smile as she thinks about having all that power at her fingertips.

The woman at the next table rises and says goodbye to her friends, then heads for the exit. Ares quickly moves to follow her.

"Don't come back to the motel right away," he says over his shoulder with a grin. "I'll be busy."

As he pursues the woman, Athena sighs and sets her glass down. The wine is disgusting. It shouldn't even be called wine. It's hog swill, that's what it is. Or vinegar.

"Do you want me to stop him?" Kali asks, a malicious gleam in her eye.

"No, don't bother," Athena replies. Then she studies Kali. "Maybe we can work on our plans without him here distracting us."

Distracting *me*, she thinks.

Kali smiles, and again Athena shivers.

The smile is not a pretty one. It's a good thing none of the humans can see it. Athena can barely stand to look at it, and she's seen some horrifying shit in her long lifetime.

"Yes. Let us do that," Kali purrs.

ACKNOWLEDGEMENTS

Once again, I couldn't have done this writing thing without Darren, my alpha reader and muse. His love, support, and encouragement has been priceless. From countless hours spent throwing shit against the wall to see what would stick, to the often heated discussions while playing the evening Egyptian Senet game, he was incredibly patient. Love you so much, hon.

My beta readers Heidi and Tabi are da bomb. Their feedback was invaluable and helped me to make this a much better book. I truly hope they enjoy this finished version.

My favorite graphic artist, Farah Evers, has once again created an amazing cover. She even fast-tracked a late change to the sword, creating a custom digital painting of a Celtic short sword only a week before release. Her talent never ceases to amaze me, and I always look forward to what she'll come up with next.

Jen, an editing genius, has again worked her magic. Her wit, wisdom, and patience have been a lifesaver during the long process of fine-tuning this book. (And a side note to readers: any errors in this book are mine and mine alone.)

The unwavering love and support of my fam—Mom and Dad, Diana, Mark, and Natalie—has kept me motivated and confident. I love you all so, so much.

And finally, to each and every reader of my first book, I can't thank you enough for your feedback, support, and encouragement. I hope you enjoy this one as much as *Legacy*.

AUTHOR'S NOTE

Throughout this series, the spelling of "magick" is used instead of "magic" to distinguish between the use of power (magick) and illusion (magic).

I have tried my best to be respectful to the deities of numerous cultures, while still maintaining the story. If you feel something wasn't treated correctly, please drop me a note and let me know. I'll do my best to make it right.

Regarding sources used for this book: Wikipedia was my most-used research tool for the deities and cultures referenced in *Chrysalis*, followed by specific mythology and religion websites. If you'd like to know the exact sources I used, drop me a line and I'd be happy to share.

ABOUT THE AUTHOR

After a lifetime of reading just about anything she could get her hands on (especially science fiction, fantasy, and anything related to Ireland) and dreaming of becoming an author someday, D M Youngblood became inspired by someone who said, "write what you want to read," and a new chapter in her life began.

She lives in suburban Phoenix, is married, and has three rescued doggies who love to bark and disrupt the creative process. She also has an unhealthy obsession with the Marvel Cinematic Universe, especially Loki. (Don't judge.) Other interests include knitting and casual gaming.

Follow the author on:

Facebook: DMYoungblood

Twitter: D_M_Youngblood

Website: dmyoungblood.com